A World of Stories

Traditional Tales for Children

Edited by
Raymond E. Jones and Jon C. Stott

OXFORD
UNIVERSITY PRESS

OXFORD
UNIVERSITY PRESS

70 Wynford Drive, Don Mills, Ontario M3C 1J9
www.oup.com/ca

Oxford University Press is a department of the University of Oxford.
It furthers the University's objective of excellence in research, scholarship,
and education by publishing worldwide in

Oxford New York

Auckland   Cape Town   Dar es Salaam   Hong Kong   Karachi
Kuala Lumpur   Madrid   Melbourne   Mexico City   Nairobi
New Delhi   Shanghai   Taipei   Toronto

With offices in
Argentina   Austria   Brazil   Chile   Czech Republic   France   Greece
Guatemala   Hungary   Italy   Japan   Poland   Portugal   Singapore
South Korea   Switzerland   Thailand   Turkey   Ukraine   Vietnam

Oxford is a trade mark of Oxford University Press
in the UK and in certain other countries

Published in Canada
by Oxford University Press

Copyright © Oxford University Press Canada 2006

The moral rights of the author have been asserted

Database right Oxford University Press (maker)

First published 2006

Library and Archives Canada Cataloguing in Publication

A world of stories : traditional tales for children/edited by Raymond E. Jones and Jon C. Stott

Includes index.

ISBN-13: 978–0–19–541988–7.   ISBN-10: 0–19–541988–X.

1. Children's stories.   2. Tales.   3. Folklore.
I. Jones, Raymond E.   II. Stott, Jon C., 1939–.
PZ5.W68 2005   808.8'99282   C2005–904752–6

Cover and Text Design: Vivian Martinho
Cover Image: Jerzy Kolacz/Getty Images

1 2 3 4 – 09 08 07 06

This book is printed on permanent (acid-free) paper ♾.
Printed in Canada

Table of Contents

Preface

The editors could not have completed this ambitious project without the help of a number of people. First of all, we wish to thank Jane Tilley, Marta Tomins, and Laura Macleod, of Oxford University Press, Toronto, who saw the merit in our proposal and provided us with unwavering support throughout the development of the project. We also wish to thank Jessica Coffey of Oxford University Press, Toronto, for her keen eye and attention to detail during the editing of the manuscript. Finally, we wish to thank the anonymous reviewers who provided valuable suggestions for revision and improvement throughout the development of the project.

Introduction

'I wonder which came first,' a self-styled humourist once remarked in paraphrasing the old conundrum, 'the campfire or the campfire story?' As mildly amusing as the question was, underlying it was an interest in the origin of stories. An old Yiddish saying provides a humourous answer: 'God created human beings because he liked listening to stories.' Whether stories have been around since the beginning of the world or not, people have been telling them for a very long time. Storying—the creating and receiving of stories—seems to be a basic human activity. British critic Barbara Hardy views storying as innate, saying that 'Nature, not art, makes us all storytellers' (7). American children's author Jane Yolen expresses a similar view, finding it a defining trait of humans: 'Stories distinguish us from animals more than any opposable thumb' (1). Robert Bly, a popular poet and motivational speaker, compares the instinctual knowledge of birds to the story-making abilities of humans, stating that people

> desired to store . . . knowledge outside the instinctual system: they stored it in stories. Stories, then—fairy stories, legends, myths, hearth stories—amount to a reservoir where we keep new ways of responding that we can adapt when the conventional and current ways wear out. (xi)

Long before the invention of writing systems, human beings created and shared stories. Anthropologists have discovered that most pre-literate cultures had a rich heritage of tales. These narratives formed part of their orature, a term applied to jokes, songs, stories, poems, dramas, and other forms that are transmitted orally rather than in written form. These oral narratives were sometimes accompanied with dance and music; sometimes they became parts of dramas and ceremonial rituals. The tales covered a range of topics: the lives of supernatural beings and their interactions with human beings; the deeds of heroes of the past; ordinary people's encounters with magic; the adventures of animals who spoke and acted like human beings. The characters in the tales were young and old, male and female, brave and cowardly, wise and foolish. In tones that ranged from serious to comical, the stories presented religious beliefs, cultural values, and moral lessons. They instructed and entertained audiences, and they kept alive, from one generation to the next, the ideas, facts, and emotions that each culture held important.

Even after the development of literacy, the unlettered people continued to transmit and treasure these stories as they had done for centuries. The existence of literate classes, however, had a profound effect on the transmission of many of the traditional tales. Whereas such tales had once existed only during the moment of telling and in the memory of those who heard them, and, therefore, were subject to alteration with each retelling, they now could be fixed in print and given definite form and finite details. This fixing was especially important for stories embodying religious and cultural beliefs and values; it made them seem permanent and immutable. Still, the existence of writing also affected more humble tales, those told primarily for entertainment. Scholars examining the European tradition of storytelling, for example, have clearly established that oral narratives influenced the composition of written fiction and that, in turn, written fiction affected traditional storytelling. For example, servants who would hear printed tales read aloud, a common custom, would repeat orally what they had heard to others, who, in turn, would repeat these tales, adding and modifying them as memory and circumstances dictated. The result was a constant interchange between the oral and literary traditions in many cultures, one that kept traditional stories alive and meaningful.

Traditional stories are frequently divided into four major categories, or genres, according to their specific foci and purposes:

- Myths are a culture's narratives about gods, demi-gods, or the conditions of the world before the current natural or social order became fixed. Myths have three major functions, although these may overlap in any given narrative. First, myths may embody sacred histories through their accounts of divine beings and their influence on the world. Second, myths may be charter narratives, stories that validate or endorse a culture's social, legal, and political institutions. Third, myths may be didactic narratives, stories whose plots teach lessons about acceptable and unacceptable behaviour by offering models and, in many cases, by issuing warnings about the consequences of unacceptable actions.
- Hero tales, including legends, sagas, romances, and epics, focus on the stories of human beings who are usually believed to have lived in the past, who often possess superhuman abilities, and whose deeds and personalities reveal the values of a culture.
- Folktales are short, imaginative stories about people, animals, and magical beings whose adventures frequently reflect the culture's attitudes about magic, the natural environment, and positive or negative human behaviours. Many folktales are rather arbitrarily labeled as fairy tales, but people most commonly use the term 'fairy tale' for those fictional narratives that contain magic, especially when they also include a love interest, whether these tales come from oral sources or from authors who employ the conventions of those sources.
- Fables are brief narratives specifically developed to exemplify, in a concrete form, simple, basic morals and rules of conduct.

In their stories, many known authors have consciously imitated the conventions, character types, plots, and themes found in traditional tales. The terms literary myths, literary hero tales, literary folktales, or literary fables have been applied to these works.

Wide reading of traditional stories reveals that similar plots, incidents, and character types appear in narratives from different cultures. To account for these similarities, scholars had previously advanced two major theories. Monogenesis is the belief that all stories originated in one area and, over centuries, spread to other areas and cultures. The theory of polygenesis states that similar stories developed independently, in different locations, and that the similarities in these stories result from physical, emotional, intellectual, and social characteristics that all human beings possess. Most contemporary scholars admit, however, that it is virtually impossible to establish the origin of many tales found in widely separated areas of the world. They tend to believe that tales did not all develop in single geographical area, but they do not accept the theory of polygenesis. Rather, contemporary scholars advance a diffusionist theory that claims various individual tales originated in different areas and were carried into other locales by military conquerors, traders, and other travellers, but in a modified form designed to make the tales comprehensible to a new audience. In other instances, they suggest, conquering forces may have overlaid the tales of subject peoples with elements of their own culture, transforming these tales and making them resemble those originating elsewhere.

In any case, the recognition of similarities in stories from different cultures, however such similarities have arisen, should not lead us to minimize the importance of the differences in these tales. Even if a tale has migrated from one culture to another, the receiving culture gives details and provides emphases that reflect its own beliefs. The story thus becomes a part of the shared cultural heritage of the group telling it. Native American novelist Leslie Silko explains the connection between stories and cultural identity: 'It's stories that make us into a community. There have to be stories. That's how you know; that's how you belong; that's how you know you belong' (190). To focus only on the similarities found throughout the stories, therefore, is to underemphasize how much a specific culture defines a people's sense of self and its relationship to its human, natural, and supernatural environments. The confusion many readers experience upon encountering a narrative from a culture whose physical, social, and spiritual lives are unfamiliar to them illustrates just how important cultural specificity can be to the meaning of a traditional tale.

Although traditional stories were transmitted orally, from generation to generation, and from culture to culture, at some point, as we noted above, many of the most common and frequently told ones were written down. Homer's epics, the *Iliad* and the *Odyssey*, for example, are believed to have been recorded in the eighth century BC, and the Bible has existed in its present form since approximately the fourth century AD. With the arrival of printing technology in the late fifteenth century, these and other works began to be copied and distributed to larger audiences. William Caxton, England's first printer, published Aesop's *Fables* in 1484 and, a year later, Sir Thomas Malory's *Le Morte d'Arthur*, the legends of the Round Table. Many popular tales, such as those about Reynard the Fox and Robin Hood later circulated in chapbooks—small, cheap, often crudely illustrated books or pamphlets that were sold by peddlars—from the fifteenth century until as late as the middle of the nineteenth century.

In the European tradition, the collections of several authors have been especially important in providing versions of traditional stories that have become staples of children's literature. Charles Perrault's *Histoires ou Contes du temps passé* (1697), published during the vogue period for fairy tales in the French court, is the source for two of the Western world's favourite tales, 'Cinderella' and 'The Sleeping Beauty in the Woods'. Jacob and Wilhelm Grimm's *Kinder -und Hausmärchen* (*Children's and Household Tales*) (1812, 1815), a collection of German traditional stories including 'Hansel and Grethel', not only became internationally popular, but also established a pattern for collectors and retellers in other countries. Among the most notable of these are Hans Christian Andersen, who, beginning in 1835, published fairy tales based on traditional Danish stories; Peter Christen Asjørnsen and Jørgen Moe, whose *Nowegian Folktales* (1843–4) Sir George Webbe Dasent translated into English in 1858; the Scottish folklorist Andrew Lang, who, beginning with *The Blue Fairy Book* (1889), published a series of volumes that gathered tales from all over the world; and Joseph Jacobs, who published *English Fairy Tales* (1890) and *Celtic Fairy Tales* (1891). In North America, Richard Chase's collection, *Jack Tales* (1943), demonstrated how European tales changed in new cultural settings.

Other stories came from sources outside of the dominant culture. During the nineteenth century, for instance, traditional stories of Native American and African-American groups appeared in print. Among the earliest and most notable of these are Henry Wadsworth Longfellow's *Song of Hiawatha* (1859), a collection of retellings of Ojibway legends of the upper Great Lakes, and Joel Chandler Harris' *Uncle Remus: His Songs and Sayings* (1880), based on tales he had been told by African-American plantation slaves. As the science of anthropology developed in the late nineteenth and early twentieth centuries, collections of the tales of pre-literate groups appeared and provided the basis for later children's adaptations. More recently, members of a variety of so-called minority cultures have published collections, and many of these are based on tales they heard as children or collected, as adults, from other adults.

Although most traditional stories were not created specifically for children, young listeners no doubt paid attention to those that interested them and were within their range of understanding. As the listeners grew older, these, as well as more complex tales, became part of their cultural and spiritual heritage. Over the past two-and-one-half centuries, many stories have been adapted for children. During the nineteenth century, the majority were European stories: the tales of Perrault and the Grimms, myths and legends of ancient Greece, the sagas of the Norsemen, and narratives from the Bible. A careful process of selection and adaptation took place. Adults chose to distribute only those stories that reflected the values that they believed appropriate for children, and they either excised or modified any details that they deemed to be inappropriate or too complex.

A similar process occurred with tales from non-European cultures. In the latter nineteenth and earlier twentieth centuries, these stories were generally edited so that they did not conflict with the values or tastes of the mainstream culture. For example, supernatural beings were labeled with such familiar European terms as 'fairies', 'elves', 'magicians', and 'witches'. Unfamiliar beliefs and practices were sometimes presented as being strange or curious. During the last half of the twentieth century, more and more adaptors from non-European cultures have attempted to retell traditional tales in ways that explain the significance of details from the originating point-of-view. Even retellers from outside a story's originating culture have treated the material with respect and have striven to be accurate in interpreting details. Respect for cultural difference has now become one of the hallmarks of publishing traditional tales aimed at children.

A World of Stories: Traditional Tales for Children contains 130 traditional stories that have been adopted by or adapted for children. In making their selections, the editors have included
- Familiar and lesser known stories
- Works that feature both males and females as central characters
- A selection of myths, hero tales, folktales, fairy tales, and fables, along with a few stories by known authors who have consciously used characteristics or conventions found in traditional stories
- Retellings and adaptations from the eighteenth century to the end of the twentieth century, many of which have become classics in their own right and have become the basis for later retellings and adaptations. As the number of excellent adaptations and retellings is continually increasing, the editors have selected what they feel is the best representation; however, all readers are encouraged to seek out additional resources in order to expand their knowledge of and exposure to this constantly evolving genre.
- Stories that are accessible to children of a range of ages

These stories are grouped into ten topics. By reading several tales on a given topic from a variety of cultures, readers will be able to see how different cultures and different retellers, writing in different periods, have treated similar themes, conflicts, plots, and character types. Readers can consider such questions as, 'Do the similarities reflect aspects of human nature that cross cultures?' 'What do details reveal about the beliefs and attitudes of the culture that originally told a specific tale?' 'How have retellers from other cultures, living in different periods, altered the narratives?' 'What do their alterations reveal about their attitudes toward the originating cultures and about what is suitable for young, new audiences of another culture?'

The selections in Part One, 'Cinderella and Her Cousins: A Tale and Its Variants', provide illustrations of two essential features of traditional literature. First, different cultures tell versions of the same tale-type, containing very similar plot patterns, incidents, and conflicts, as well as similar motifs, small elements such as symbolic objects, specific actions, and types of minor characters. Second, each culture uses and interprets these patterns and details in ways that reveal and reflect its beliefs and values. The Cinderella tale-type is one of the best examples of these features: one of the most widely-distributed folktale types and one of the earliest to be recorded, it is certainly one of the most frequently retold for children. Each year there are more retellings, not only of the well-known versions by Charles Perrault and the Brothers Grimm, but also of similar narratives from non-European cultures. Interestingly, some of these retellings contain the word 'Cinderella' in the title, along with the country or culture of origin. In this way, the retellers make the unfamiliar tale more saleable by linking it to one that is very well-known and popular. This section begins with 'The Golden Carp', a version of a Chinese narrative that is the oldest known variant of the tale. There follow Perrault's and the Grimms' versions and then versions from seven other cultures including Native North America, Japan, and Russia. Readers can notice which of such familiar motifs as the father's remarriage, the evil stepmother, the mistreatment of the main character, the helper figure or helper object, and the identity test are included in specific versions, and how they are presented, and how the omission of some motifs and the addition of others give each tale a unique meaning.

'Creating and Shaping the World: The Mythic Vision', Part Two, contains a type of story found in all cultures: the account of the creation of the world and its creatures, along with the origins of constellations and of the distinctive features of living beings and the landscape. In most cultures, the early stages of creation are attributed to the actions of supernatural beings. However, the motivations and attitudes of these beings often reveal the specific values of the culture that tells the story. If, to paraphrase the Bible, 'the creator made the world in his image and likeness,' it could be said that the creators of these stories created their supreme beings in their own cultural images and likenesses. This section also includes two literary myths, stories by known authors who imitate themes and topics found in traditional myths: Rudyard Kipling's 'The Elephant's Child', a humourous *pourquoi* tale about the origin of the elephant's trunk, and *Little Badger and the Fire Spirit*, by Métis author Maria Campbell. In this story, a grandfather, in order to instruct a little girl about her people's traditional values, tells a story about the human acquisition of fire.

Part Three, 'Larger than Life: Tales of Heroes', and Part Four, 'Unlikely Heroes: Triumphs of the Underdog', present two types of traditional heroes that have been very popular with young readers. In the former, the central figures often possess superhuman abilities and their actions frequently reflect the qualities for which their cultures express approval. Certainly, in their abilities they are superior to child readers, who can look up to and admire them. The heroes of the latter section are initially more like average people, particularly children, limited by size, age, experience, and/or social and economic status. The popularity of stories of unlikely heroes is a result, in part, of the reader's ability to identify with the central characters in their struggles against controlling, more powerful individuals.

While many of the tales of great heroes are set in a distant, pre-historical, almost mythic past, others, such as the Mali epic about Sundiata and the saint's legend about Joan of Arc, are set within the previous millennium. Tales of John Henry and Paul Bunyan, both Americans, are set in the later nineteenth century. In the twentieth century, the process continues. Superman, a literary hero created in the 1930s, possesses many of the qualities of earlier heroes. Luke Skywalker was an unlikely hero in *Star Wars*, the 1977 motion picture that used many of the conventions of traditional stories.

Part Five, 'Purposeful Journeys: Errands and Quests', presents stories that contain one of the most frequently used plot structures—the journey to a specific location in order to fulfill a specific objective or to acquire a specific object. Whether the journeys are undertaken to rescue a maiden, to prove worthiness to a loved one, or to find food necessary to survive, incidents in these stories are generally tests of the characters' intentions and their inner moral and psychological strengths and weaknesses. The settings through which they pass as they progress to their destinations, along with their encounters with other characters and the actions that take place, provide young readers with vivid and exciting details. More importantly, they provide concrete symbols that reveal the inner conflicts of the adventurers. The stopping points along the way are, in a sense, 'milestones of the mind, heart, and soul'.

The narratives found in Part Six, 'Loves Won and Lost: Tales of Courtship and Marriage', are what most child and adult readers of traditional tales think of when they hear the term 'fairy tales'. Indeed, some of the tales in the section, including 'The Sleeping Beauty in the Woods' and 'Rumpelstiltskin', are among the most popular and widely-known traditional stories among modern audiences. These tales generally conclude with a marriage and the lovers living happily ever after. That this ending frequently does not reflect the realities of the modern world may help to explain their popularity. They represent wish fulfillment, what readers hope will be the result of courtship. They promise that, in spite of hardship and struggles, married bliss can be achieved.

As several of these selections reveal, however, courtship does not always lead to a happy marriage. Although she is able to keep her child, the heroine of 'Rumpelstiltskin' still lives with a king who married her only because he thought she possessed a wealth-increasing magical talent, and nothing in the tale suggests that he will not again demand that she exercise this supposed talent. The husbands of 'The Crane Wife' and 'The Goodman of Wastness and His Selkie Wife' both lose their mysterious spouses through faults of their own. In the case of 'The Moon', the ineptitude of the suitor results only in his receiving mockery and rejection from those he courts.

As the creation of families frequently follows marriage, so we have followed 'Loves Won and Lost' with 'It's All Relative: The Trials and Triumphs of Family Life', Part Seven. For children, security within the home and the presence of a stable family are basic needs; cruel treatment, abandonment, or the breakup of the family unit are great fears. Nine of the stories in this section deal with these conflicts. Taken from eight cultural groups, they examine, in part, the vulnerability of children and the heroic measures they often take to save themselves. Many of these children are unlikely heroes. In two stories, 'The Woman Who Flummoxed the Fairies' and 'The Smith and the Fairies', parents are the heroes, reconstituting the broken family unit. Two other stories focus on relationships between spouses: in

'Jacques the Woodcutter', the title hero uses deception to drive away his wife's male visitor, and, in 'The Barber's Clever Wife', the wife is able to defeat thieves.

'Living by Wit: Trickster Tales' and 'Wise and Foolish: Tales of Cleverness and Stupidity', Parts Eight and Nine respectively, form companion sections dealing with characters who succeed or fail because of their mental abilities or lack of them. The former section focuses on a character type recognizable in widely separated cultural areas. Anansi, the Ashanti trickster from West Africa, and Coyote, whose adventures are related by many North American tribes, share many personality traits and are frequently involved in similar types of adventures. One could argue that, more than any of the other character types included in this anthology, the trickster presents evidence that stories reflect universal aspects of human nature. Audiences everywhere, such an argument could continue, enjoy the actions of a character who defeats apparently superior adversaries and who often displays, with impunity, self-centeredness and audacity, qualities that readers cannot generally display in real life without negative consequences. Moreover, until recent times, during which women have acquired more social and political power, female readers may have taken vicarious pleasure in the victories of female tricksters over males.

All audiences respond to wise persons who emerge victorious because their cleverness is not recognized by people who feel themselves superior. The case is different in reading stories about fools; virtually all who read or listen to their stories can feel superior to them. The inability of these characters to deal successfully with the most basic, simple situations makes them inferior to even the children, who laugh at their ridiculous situations and actions. Perhaps these fools are popular because they operate as scapegoat figures: audiences laugh at them in order to exorcise from themselves any sense of personal inadequacy or stupidity.

Whereas the opening section focused on the best known, most widely distributed type of tale, the Cinderella tale, Part Ten deals with the most widely distributed general type of story, one that is highly popular with younger children: the animal story. As the title, 'Nature Humanized: Animal Tales', suggests, the central characters in these tales act and speak like human beings; thus, audiences can readily recognize the motivations and conflicts. In such traditional societies as those of pre-contact North America, where animals were considered to possess souls and to be equal to human beings, the stories were often set in early times when people and animals could communicate. When, in real life, they saw the various animals portrayed in stories, audiences would remember the tales and the cultural values these communicated. Other creators of animal stories, such as Aesop and Hans Christian Andersen, created purely fictional stories that emphasized the human personalities of the characters so that audiences would be aware of the lessons that were being presented for their edification.

In order to assist readers in their understanding and enjoyment of the selections in *A World of Stories*, the editors have included a range of editorial apparatus:

- **Part introductions**. Brief essays outline the characteristics of the types of stories included and discuss how the stories both reflect some or all of these characteristics and reveal specific cultural treatments.
- **Headnotes**. Each tale is preceded by a headnote that points out aspects of cultural backgrounds, characteristics of its adaptation, and the importance of key elements in the tale.

- **Links to Other Stories**. Recognizing that many, if not all, of the stories in a section could have been placed in one or more of the other sections, the editors have listed some of the other stories in the anthology that might have been included in each particular chapter.
- **Illustrations**. For a limited number of selections, the editors have provided illustrations from either the editions from which the tales were taken or other notable illustrated retellings. By looking at these illustrations readers will gain an idea of the approaches taken by illustrators from different periods and cultures.
- **Glossary**. In the glossary, readers will find definitions of terms important to the study and understanding of traditional stories.
- **Topical Index**. To show some more of the links between various tales and to facilitate further exploration of the tales, the editors have listed a number of the selections under such topics as specific character types, significant details, actions, and conflicts.
- **Further Reading**. 'Selected Critical Studies' lists works that will enable students to learn about theories and critical approaches to traditional tales. 'Selected Folktale Collections' offers an opportunity to examine other works from the cultures whose tales are represented in the anthology. Finally, a list of 'Selected Illustrated Editions of Single Tales' will allow readers to delve more deeply into variant versions, adaptations, modernizations, and parodies of many of the stories included in the anthology.

Works Cited

Bly, Robert. *Iron John: A Book about Men*. Reading, Mass: Addison-Wesley, 1990.

Hardy, Barbara. *Tellers and Listeners: The Narrative Imagination*. London: Athlone Press, 1975.

Silko, Leslie. 'Interview', *This Song Remembers: Self Portraits of Native Americans in the Arts*. Ed. Jane B. Katz. Boston: Houghton Mifflin, 1980.

Yolen, Jane. 'Introduction', *Favorite Folktales from Around the World*. New York: Pantheon, 1986. 1–16.

Part One

Cinderella and Her Cousins
A Tale and Its Variants

Cinderella is undoubtedly the most popular and well-known of fairy tale characters. For many literate people in the Western world, Cinderella embodies the very essence of romance: as a girl, she endures neglect, abuse, and obscurity; as a woman, she gains recognition, power, and love. Because it traces her rise through tribulations to triumph, her story exerts a strong appeal for all children and adults who have felt that their true identities are unappreciated. Cinderella—a character whose maturation holds out the promise that one can overcome one's environment and develop a meaningful and satisfying identity—is, in other words, a potent symbol of wish fulfillment.

Although Cinderella is a popular figure in many cultures, her story is not identical in each, nor is it necessarily the same in all retellings within any culture. Cinderella thus provides a strong introduction into the diversity exhibited by tales classified as belonging to the same tale type, that is, by tales containing such significant similarities in plot patterns, conflicts, central incidents, character types, and motifs that folklorists have grouped them as variations of a basic story. Furthermore, because Cinderella's story is one of the most widely distributed traditional tales, it offers an opportunity for readers to examine the way in which various cultures and various historical periods modify, add, or omit basic elements of the tale type to produce unique meanings.

In the Western world, Cinderella's story is best known in the version told by the French author Charles Perrault, who published 'Cendrillon, ou la petit pantoufle de verre' ('Cinderella, or the Little Glass Slipper') in *Histoires ou Contes du temps passé* (1697). Perrault's story had its genesis in oral tales, but he did not attempt to replicate the manner of an oral tale teller. A member of the court of Louis XIV at a time when fairy tales were in vogue, Perrault created an urbane and witty narrator who spoke to a sophisticated and literate audience that would appreciate details and comments about fashionable society. He also filled the tale with magic transformations that foreshadow and underscore Cinderella's ultimate transformation from scullery wench to princess when she puts on her lost slipper.

In fact, one of Perrault's most memorable inventions in the story was the use of the glass slipper as the device by which Cinderella is recognized and rewarded.[1] This slipper of glass, a rarity and wonder in both stories and real life, intensified the magical appeal of Cinderella's physical and social transformation. It also dictated a change in the plot devices from those used in the traditional versions of the tale that employ a slipper of gold or other rich materials. Obviously, because a foot is visible within a glass slipper, which cannot stretch,

Cinderella's rivals could not mutilate their feet by chopping off a heel or a toe, as they do in 'Aschenputtel', the version later collected in Germany by the Brothers Grimm, nor could they resort to other tricks, such as binding their feet to make them small, as does the step-sister in the Chilean 'Mary Cinderella'. As a consequence, the glass slipper's transparency became the ultimate analogue to Cinderella's honesty, or virtue, supplementing the slipper's traditional role as a test of the petite female's beauty.

Although Perrault's version of the tale was greatly responsible for establishing it in the popular imagination, the Cinderella tale was already old when he published his version. In fact, the oldest known version was recorded by a Chinese official about 850–60 AD, and R.D. Jameson has argued that, even then, it was not a new story (92). This version tells of a girl named Yeh-hsien,[2] who, following the death of her father, suffers abuse at the hands of his second wife. Several details of this brief tale are notable because they appear in later varia-tions found around the world. First, a helper animal, in this case a fish, provides company to the isolated girl and, after the stepmother kills it, its bones provide magical help. A help-ful fish appears in a number of other tales, especially in China, but the animal friend in ver-sions from other parts of the world may be a cow, a goat, or a bird. In many instances the bones or entrails of this animal helper are instrumental in the heroine's changing fortunes. Interestingly, Yeh-hsien learns how to make her wishes come true because of a second important detail, the appearance of a man who descends from the sky and tells Yeh-hsien where her stepmother hid the fish bones and how she can use them.[3] Obviously, this mys-terious informant is a precursor of the fairy godmother in Perrault's tale, and he may be one form of the supernatural aid that, in other tales, Cinderella receives from her deceased mother or a symbol connected to the deceased mother. The third notable detail is the use of a lost shoe as a marriage test. In this case, Yeh-hsien loses a gold shoe when she leaves a festival, a peasant finds and sells it, and the buyer gives it to the king, who immediately desires the woman whose foot can fit into such a small shoe.[4] Symbolically, shoes have con-nections to sexuality and fertility, a point made apparent by the fact that people still tie shoes to the bumper of a newlywed couple's vehicle. Finally, a minor detail first noted by Jameson (78), deserves mention. After the festival, Yeh-hsien's stepmother finds the girl, attired in rags, sleeping with her arm wrapped around a tree. (The version we include has Ye Syan sleeping beneath a fruit tree.) In later variants, trees are important: they may be the source of magical gifts and, as in the Grimms' version, they may grow out of the birth mother's grave, thereby becoming a symbol of continuing maternal aid.

Scholars generally credit the Italian author Giambattista Basile (c. 1575–1632) with producing what Allen Dundes says is 'probably the earliest full telling of the tale in Europe' (4). Although some variants of the Cinderella tale did appear earlier, 'The Cat Cinderella' ('La Gatta Cenerentola'), which appeared in the posthumously published Il Pentamerone (1634–36), has many of the plot elements found in the versions by Perrault and the Grimms: a stepmother pampers her own daughters but makes a kitchen servant of young Zezolla, who even loses her name, becoming known as the Cat Cinderella; Cat Cinderella uses a magic tree to obtain fancy clothing and a carriage so that she can attend a feast, where the king becomes enamoured of her; on three occasions, she flees the feast, but she loses a shoe during her last escape; the love-smitten King, who says that he will marry only the woman whose foot fits into the shoe, stages another feast, at which all the women are to try on the shoe; after all others fail, Zezolla puts on the slipper and later marries the king.[5]

The slipper test is the most notable detail in the versions mentioned so far, but folk-lorists do not regard it as essential to a Cinderella tale. In fact, folklorists see slipper test stories as only one line of a group of related stories forming the Cinderella cycle. They do not agree, however, on ways of classifying tales within the cycle. In the first scholarly treatment of the Cinderella tale, *Three Hundred and Forty-five Variants of Cinderella, Catskin, and Cap o' Rushes, Abstracted and Tabulated, with a Discussion of Medieval Analogues and Notes*, Marian Roalfe Cox linked the three well-known tales mentioned in her title and further went on to group Cinderella tales into five categories according to plot. In a later study, *The Cinderella Cycle*, Anna Birgitta Rooth also divided the tale into five groups, although her groupings were not identical to Cox's. In *The Folktale*, Stith Thompson discusses the cycle in terms of related tales classified according to the Aarne and Thompson system as type 510A (Cinderella), 510B (The Dress of Gold, of Silver, and of Stars), 511 (One-Eye, Two-Eyes, Three-Eyes), and 511A (The Little Red Ox).

In spite of the differences in these classification systems, however, scholars generally agree that the plots of Cinderella cycle tales flow from three basic situations:

1. A girl suffers persecution from her stepmother and stepsisters.
2. A girl suffers persecution from her father.
3. A boy suffers persecution from his stepmother or other family members.

The first plot pattern, which governs the best known variants, contains five basic incidents. First, the young girl suffers abuse from the stepmother and stepsisters. This abuse includes a loss of station and usually includes loss of identity that is signalled by a name change linking the girl to ashes (hence, the names Cenerentola, Cendrillon, Cinderella, and Aschenputtel). Second, the girl receives some form of magical aid during her time of suffering. This help may come from a fairy godmother (though that form of help is not the most common), a peculiar old woman, some kind of animal (cow, sheep, goat, or bird), or a tree (sometimes growing from her mother's grave). Third, the girl, dressed in finery, meets a prince at a ball, a feast, a festival, or a church service. Fourth, because the prince or king has fallen in love with her when she was in her finery, she must later, when she is without such finery, prove her identity as the beloved one by putting on a shoe, by admitting ownership of a ring she placed in the prince's soup or bread, or by performing some seemingly impossible task, such as picking golden fruit from a tree that has defied all previous attempts from harvesters. Finally, having successfully proved her identity, she marries the prince.

The second pattern begins with a young girl abused by her father, who either wishes to marry her or demands, as did the father in Shakespeare's *King Lear*, that she declare her whole-hearted love for him. In the first instance, after receiving finery in preparation for the wedding, she flees. Because the subject of incest is one adults often do not want to bring up with children, this version of the story seldom appears in collections for children, and when it does, it is usually presented in a significantly altered form. In *The Green Fairy Book*, for instance, Andrew Lang changed the initial situation of the girl in 'Allerleirauh', a tale from the Brothers Grimm: the girl flees from home, not because her father wants to marry her, but because he intends to wed her to a monster. In the other plot pattern, the Lear-like father drives his daughter out of his home when she tells him that she loves him as she loves salt. In both cases, she becomes a kitchen servant in the house of a prince. Later, at a feast, a ball, or a church service, she wears finery and meets the prince. Having fallen in love with her when she is dressed in finery, the prince learns that the servant is his beloved either through the shoe test or the identification of a ring placed in his soup or bread. She then marries the prince and, in tales that began with the Lear-like questioning of her love, serves her father unsalted food so that he can see the necessity of salt.

The most notable feature of the third major pattern is that its central character is a male. Maria Tatar claims that in nineteenth-century Germany female Cinderellas did not outnumber the male ones (47); now, however, male Cinderellas are a distinct minority. The plot of the male Cinderella tale begins with a boy being abused by members of his family. An animal helper, most often a bull, then provides the starving boy with food. After the boy's enemies kill the animal helper, the boy, by following the animal's last instructions and retaining some part of the animal's remains, is provided with magical aid in subsequent adventures. These adventures vary greatly from version to version, and the tale often becomes a giant-killer or dragon-slayer tale. Nevertheless, the tale usually concludes with some kind of identity test, with the heroic lad being identified as one worthy of a noble marriage because of a hair, a ring, or even a shoe that he left behind during an adventure.

Scholars have offered various ways of interpreting Cinderella tales. In the nineteenth century in particular, they tried to explain the elements of Cinderella, and many other fairy tales, as mythic remnants—parts of etiological myths accounting for either the rising and setting of the sun or the changes of the seasons. Such ingenious theories carry little conviction today, and interpretive scholars have generally approached the tale from sociological and psychological perspectives. For example Jack Zipes, who employs the principles of Marxist criticism to reveal ideological implications, examines this tale as a didactic story in which characterization and plot inculcate particular social values. Arguing that Perrault 'sought to portray ideal types to reinforce the standards of the civilizing process set by upper-class French society' (Zipes 1988, 26), he points out that 'Cinderella displays all the graces expected from a refined, aristocratic young lady' (27). He similarly notes that the Brothers Grimm included their version of the Cinderella tale in an 1825 selection of magic tales, 'All of which underline morals in keeping with the Protestant ethic and a patriarchal notion of sex roles' (Zipes 1999, 75).

Numerous feminist critics have also examined Cinderella as a role model, condemning in particular the way her tale offers female passivity as an ideal. Marcia K. Lieberman points to an association of beauty with a good temper and meekness, and of ugliness with bad temper, saying that 'The most famous example of this associational pattern occurs in "Cinderella". . .' (188). She further notes, 'In "Cinderella" the domineering stepmother and stepsisters contrast with the passive heroine. . . . Being powerful is mainly associated with being unwomanly' (197).

Other scholars have approached the stories from psychoanalytic perspectives. Bruno Bettelheim applies the psychological theories of Sigmund Freud to argue in *The Uses of Enchantment* that the story symbolically works out issues of sibling rivalry, that its plot has a strong emotional appeal to children who feel that their parents neglect them in favour of their older siblings, and that it also helps children to cope with oedipal conflict and guilt. In *Problems of the Feminine in Fairytales*, Marie-Louise von Franz offers a different perspective: she sees the tale as a symbolic representation of the operations of the psyche as described by Carl Jung. Focusing on a notable variant, the Russian story of Vasilisa, she claims that the tale is a symbolic exploration of female individuation. Its plot, she contends, dramatizes the development of the daughter, who moves away from the mother so that she can have her own identity as a woman (143–57).

Scholars are not alone in analyzing the meanings of the Cinderella tale. Some authors have critiqued what they see as the conservative and masculine social biases of the Cinderella cycle by offering parodies. Parody—which exaggerates, distorts, and makes ridiculous conventional elements in a tale—forces readers to look closely at conventions and, perhaps, to explore their implications. Restrictions of copyright and space do not permit us to include modern parodies, but readers wishing to explore some Cinderella tale parodies should look at *Cinder Edna*, by Ellen Jackson, illustrated by Devin O'Malley, in which Cinderella's next-door neighbour, instead of waiting for a fairy godmother, displays self-reliance and courage to secure her own happiness, or *Prince Cinders*, by Babette Cole, a role-reversal parody in which an incompetent fairy turns a skinny, pimply prince into a hairy ape, who, nevertheless, manages to win the hand of a princess. Readers may also wish to examine comic updatings of the tale such as *Cinder-Elly*, written by Frances Minters and illustrated by G. Brian Karas, a hip-hop version set in modern Manhattan.

This section presents a variety of Cinderella cycle tales from a variety of cultures. It opens with a Chinese tale, 'The Golden Carp', as a retelling of the oldest tale in the cycle. Next come the two best-known versions in the West, those by Perrault and the Brothers Grimm. The following tale, 'Cap o' Rushes', is an example of the second main form of tales in the Cinderella cycle, those in which the persecutor is the father, not the stepmother. Unlike in the 'Cat-skin' variation, in which a father is driven by incestuous desire rationalized by the fact that his dying wife told him to choose only someone like her for his next wife, the father in this tale is unnatural only in demanding that his daughters display excessive love for him. 'Billy Beg and the Bull', the next tale, is an example of the third major form of tales in the Cinderella cycle; the persecuted child is a boy.

The remaining tales demonstrate variations on the first pattern in which her family persecutes the girl. Both 'Mary Cinderella', from Chile, and 'Conkiajgharuna', from nineteenth-century Georgia, include the familiar shoe test, but they also are notable for incorporating parallel scenes in which two girls literally mark themselves with symbols of their moral natures. The last three tales do not include shoe tests or any variation of a test that depends upon the heroine's beauty. Rather, each presents a test of abilities or a culturally specific valued characteristic. In 'Vasilisa the Beautiful', a Russian tale, Vasilisa shows that she has the skill to make fine clothing, a skill that would have been prized among peasants in nineteenth-century Russia. In 'The Indian Cinderella', a Native tale from Canada's east coast, a girl demonstrates that she has the integrity to be a good wife. Finally, in the Japanese tale of 'Benizara and Kakezara', Benizara demonstrates a poetic talent that signals she is refined and cultured enough to marry an important man.

Notes

1. Although some writers have suggested that Perrault's creation arose from the fact that, in a French oral telling, *vair* (fur) sounds like *verre* (glass), folklorists insist that he did not make a mistake in creating a slipper of glass. See Alan Dundes, *Cinderella: A Folklore Casebook*, 110–12, for a brief account of the argument about Perrault's invention.

2. The authors of the version we have included call her Ye Syan because they follow the Princeton system of transliteration.

3. In our version, the man just appears suddenly.

4. It is tempting to see the shoe test as originating in China, where foot binding later became a cultural imperative, but the Chinese king was not the first to use a shoe as a test of worthiness for marriage. The historian Strabo, in the first century BC, claimed that an eagle carried away the shoe of Rhodopis, an Egyptian courtesan, while she was bathing in the Nile. The eagle dropped the shoe onto the lap of the king in Memphis. Intrigued by the small shoe, he ordered his servants to find the owner, whom he then married.

5. In spite of these seemingly conventional plot ingredients 'The Cat Cinderella' presents a heroine who is decidedly different in one major respect. Zezolla, urged on by her duplicitous governess, kills her first evil stepmother so that her father will marry the governess, who soon becomes as evil as the previous stepmother. Interestingly enough, the crime does not dampen the narrator's presentation of her as a sweet and loving girl who deserves happiness after unjust suffering.

Works Cited

Bettelheim, Bruno. 1976. 'Cinderella', *The Uses of Enchantment: The Meaning and Importance of Fairy Tales*. New York: Alfred A. Knopf.

Cole, Babette. 1987. *Prince Cinders*. New York: Putnam.

Cox, Marian Roalfe. [1893] 1967. *Three Hundred and Forty-five Variants of Cinderella, Catskin, and Cap o' Rushes, Abstracted and Tabulated, with a Discussion of Medieval Analogues and Notes*. London: David Nutt for The Folklore Society; rpt. Nendeln, Liechtenstein: Kraus Reprint.

Dundes, Alan, ed. 1982. *Cinderella: A Folklore Casebook*. New York and London: Garland.

Franz, Marie-Louise von. [1972] 1976. *Problems of the Feminine in Fairytales*. New York: Spring Publications.

Jackson, Ellen. 1994. *Cinder Edna*. Illus. Kevin O'Malley. New York: Lothrop, Lee & Shepard.

Jameson, R.D. 1982. 'Cinderella in China', *Cinderella: A Folklore Casebook*. Ed. Alan Dundes. New York and London: Garland.

Lang, Andrew. 1892. *The Green Fairy Book*. London: Longman's Green.

Lieberman, Marcia K. 1989. '"Some Day My Prince Will Come": Female Acculturation through the Fairy Tale'. *College English* 34 (1972): 383-94. Rpt. in *Don't Bet on the Prince: Contemporary Feminist Fairy Tales in North America and England*, edited by Jack Zipes [1987]; New York: Routledge.

Minters, Frances. 1994. *Cinder-Elly*. Illus. G. Brian Karas. New York: Viking.

Rooth, Anna Birgitta. 1951. *The Cinderella Cycle*. Lund: Gleerup.

Tatar, Maria. 1987. *The Hard Facts of the Grimms' Fairy Tales*. Princeton, NJ: Princeton UP.

Thompson, Stith. [1946] 1967. *The Folktale*. [New York: Holt, Rinehart and Winston] Berkley: University of California Press.

Zipes, Jack. [1983] 1988. *Fairy Tales and the Art of Subversion: The Classical Genre for Children and the Process of Civilization*. New York: Methuen.

———. 1999. *When Dreams Came True: Classical Fairy Tales and Their Tradition*. New York and London: Routledge.

The Golden Carp

'The Golden Carp', in which a magical fish is instrumental in changing the fortunes of a girl persecuted by her father's second wife, is a version of the oldest known Cinderella tale, one recorded in China by Tuan Ch'êng-shih in his *Miscellany of Forgotten Lore* (850–60 AD). Its richer detail and its omission of a series of concluding episodes that remove the focus from the protagonists make it a more coherent and dramatically interesting narrative than the version Arthur Whaley first presented to the English-speaking world in *Folklore* 58 (1947). One omission, however, may disappoint readers who demand an obvious distribution of rewards and punishments in fairy tales. 'The Golden Carp' makes no mention of the fate of the stepmother and stepsisters. In Whaley's translated version, however, these evildoers die when they are 'struck by flying stones' (229). (It seems that supernatural forces propel these stones, but one critic has suggested that they were hurled by a mob.) Readers conditioned by the romantic conventions of European fairy tales may also be surprised to see that this tale continues past Ye Syan's marriage to show that she, unlike the brides in European fairy tales, did not necessarily live 'happily ever after'.

At the foot of a soaring mountain, there once lived a tribe of people whose chieftain was known as Cave Lord Wu. He was called by this name for he had chosen to make a home for his two wives within the rocky vastness of a large, high-domed cave.

It was Wu's misfortune that his first wife died shortly after giving birth to a baby girl. From an early age it was evident that the girl, named Ye Syan, was endowed with grace and charm. Gentle of nature and kind of heart, she was dearly loved by her father who saw in her all the admirable qualities of his departed wife.

Destiny did not decree that Wu have a long life. Well before Ye Syan reached marriageable age, he sickened and lapsed into a lethargy from which he could not be roused. All the healing herbs gave him little relief, and all the sacrifices offered to bring about his recovery were useless. Within a week of the onset of his illness, he was dead, leaving Ye Syan in the care of his second wife.

Now that Wu was gone, Ye Syan was at the mercy of her stepmother, a mean, jealous woman. She had long resented Wu's favouritism toward Ye Syan while he ignored her own daughter, an unattractive, dull girl. Wu's death left the stepmother free to take out her bitterness by mistreating Ye Syan without fear of interference from anyone.

Her own daughter was given easy tasks to perform and kept close to home, while Ye Syan was assigned the most unpleasant, arduous chores. Daily, in fair weather or foul, the stepmother would send her out to gather firewood in the higher mountain forests or to lug back buckets of drinking water from distant streams.

On one such errand, Ye Syan happened upon a lake fed by underground springs. As she was about to dip her bucket into the mirror-clear water, she was attracted by a sudden flash of colour. It was a tiny fish, no longer than her pinky. Scooping it up, she watched with fascination as it swam round and round inside one of her wooden buckets. How she longed to take it home! The little fish would be a friend when she was lonely, and a comfort when she was abused. Her stepmother was sure to disapprove, but Ye Syan decided there and then to keep it as a pet. She hitched the two buckets full of water to her carrying pole. Unmindful of the heavy weight across her back, half walking, half running, she managed to arrive home without spilling a drop.

Before entering the cave, she transferred her precious fish to an old basin, and thereafter kept it hidden, tucked out of sight. Each day she secretly fed it a few grains of rice from her own bowl, and each day she saw it become longer and more beautiful.

With bright orange fins and a lacy fantail, it soon outgrew the basin, and Ye Syan realized that her fish needed more space. Taking care not to be seen by her stepmother, she was able to carry it, undetected, out of the cave. She took it to a nearby pond, where, within a short time, it reached full size.

Whenever Ye Syan came to the pond, her wonderful fish would surface and flash its fiery fins as if to greet her. Then it would twist sideways, jump straight up into the air, and splash back into the water. As long as she remained there, it entertained her with its playful antics.

The stepmother's curiosity was aroused when she noticed that Ye Syan was spending a great deal of time near the pond. 'That lazy wastrel of a girl, idling away hours better given to useful work,' she complained. 'I'll soon find out what she is up to.'

When Ye Syan left the cave that evening, her stepmother followed her. Hidden behind a scraggly bush, she witnessed a strange spectacle. As Ye Syan neared the edge of the pond, a brilliant orange fish with glassy, bulging eyes emerged from the water. It rested its scaly head on the gravel bank and permitted Ye Syan to stroke it. With a wave of its lacy tail, it turned and plopped back into the pool.

From Yin-lien Chin, Yetta S. Center, & Mildred Ross, trans., *Traditional Chinese Folktales*. (Armonk, NY: M.E. Sharpe, 1989), 50.

'So that is how she spends her time, in useless play with a fish!' the stepmother fumed. 'This I will not tolerate! Besides, that fish will make a delicious meal. I must have it.'

Several times thereafter the determined woman came to the pond and waited patiently, but in vain. The fish never showed itself. Disappointed, she would leave empty-handed to return again and again for naught. During the ensuing days she could think of nothing else but how to catch the fish.

Ye Syan came home later than usual one day, tired and footsore, having carried a heavy load of kindling from a far-off woodland. She steeled herself against the usual scolding she expected. Instead, her stepmother greeted her with disarming kindness.

'You dear girl, how hard you have been working,' she cooed. 'Because you are not lazy and do your chores without complaining, you deserve a reward. See, I have made you a new blouse. Do try it on and give me the old one you are wearing. I shall put it in the rag pile, for it is too shabby to be worth mending.'

Ye Syan did not comprehend the change in her stepmother's attitude. Nevertheless, she accepted her offer with a great sense of relief. 'Perhaps,' she dared to hope, 'my life will not be so hard from now on.'

The blouse, with its embroidered neck and narrow sleeves, was very becoming. Ye Syan was happier than she had been in all the time since her father's death.

The following morning she was sent off as usual to fetch the day's supply of drinking water.

'I have learned of a spring that has the sweetest and clearest water to be found anywhere,' explained her stepmother. 'To reach it you must follow the path that winds to the top of the mountain. It is a long distance to go, and you may need to rest along the way. Do not worry if you return later than usual. I shall keep your supper warm.'

Within moments after Ye Syan left the cave the scheming stepmother changed into Ye Syan's old clothes, concealing a knife in her waistband. So anxious was she to reach the pond, she almost tripped in her haste to get there. Out of breath, she sat down at the water's edge, when, to her amazement, the fish appeared at her feet. Quick as lightning she pulled it from the water, lopped off its head, and carried it back to her cave home. A pot of simmering fish broth soon filled the air with a delicious aroma. The stepmother and her daughter feasted on the tasty fish to the last savoury morsel.

'I shall bury the fish bones in the dunghill,' the stepmother said to her daughter. 'No one will ever find them there.'

Tired from her unusually long walk, Ye Syan returned to find only a bowl of cold rice for her evening meal. Her stepmother spoke not a word, and her stepsister sat fidgeting with her fingers. Ye Syan ate in silence, washed the rice bowl, and, as was her custom, rushed to the pond to visit with her pet. For the first time ever, the fish failed to greet her. Though she called to it repeatedly, the water's surface remained unruffled. She scanned every inch of the pond till her eyes ached. That evening and the next and the next, Ye Syan came to the pond, praying that her fish would return. Each time, she threw grains of rice into the water to tempt it with food, but her friend did not appear. At last, overwhelmed with a sense of loss, she burst into tears. For a long time, she sat near the pond, sick at heart and weeping.

By this time it had turned quite dark. Ye Syan stood up and brushed the soil from her clothes. She had not noticed the bent old stranger leaning on a cane, watching her from the shadows.

'Dry your tears, my child,' he said. 'The evil deed is done. The fish was killed by your stepmother. You will find its bones in the dunghill. Dig them out and keep them always. Wherever fortune may lead, they will serve you well.'

Before Ye Syan could open her lips to reply, the stranger was gone.

The day of a great festival was at hand. In cave homes tunnelled into the hillsides and in huts that dotted the valleys, people prepared for the celebration. They looked forward to seeing richly costumed dancers perform to the beat of drums and the clash of cymbals. They would watch acrobats and mummers entertain with acts of daring and pantomime. All manner of delicacies would be offered to please the eye and tempt the appetite. It was the one time in the entire year when people could cease their daily labours and lose themselves in the gaiety of the festivities.

'You will remain at home to guard the fruit orchard,' Ye Syan's stepmother declared while she and her daughter readied themselves for the grand occasion. On the way out the door, arrayed in their gaudiest dresses, the stepmother hurled a parting warning at Ye Syan. 'When we return, if a single piece of fruit is missing, you will pay dearly!'

Ye Syan often brooded over the unfair treatment she suffered at the hands of her stepmother. For the most part she accepted her lot with resignation. Now to be kept from attending the festival was a cruelty hard to bear. Recalling the stranger's talk about the fishbones, she decided to put them to the test, but so great was her gloom she doubted they would be of any help to her.

With great care, Ye Syan took the fishbones from their hiding place. Then, covering her face with her hands, she made a silent wish.

When she opened her eyes, all about her was a soft mist. Suddenly, a beam of intense light pierced the greyness and shone down on her bed. There, neatly laid out, was a skirt of patterned satin, a matching blouse, and a pair of exquisitely embroidered slippers. Reaching out, she touched them lightly. Yes, they were real! With hesitation, Ye Syan put on the skirt and blouse. The fabric was as soft as gossamer, the colours deep and rich. Then she pulled on the slippers. The transformation was almost miraculous. She looked like a goddess!

A bird released from its cage could not have been happier than Ye Syan as she set off to join the festival celebration. Mingling with the crowds, the extraordinarily beautiful girl became the object of much attention. Along with everyone else, her stepmother and stepsister wondered who she might be.

'Does she not resemble Ye Syan?' the stepsister asked her mother.

'Nonsense', replied the stepmother, dismissing the idea as preposterous. She had told Ye Syan to stay at home and she did not expect to be disobeyed.

Ye Syan joined a ring of spectators that had formed around a group of acrobats. Directly opposite her she spied her stepmother and stepsister. Terrified that they might recognize her, she fled. Frantically pushing her way through the dense crowd of merrymakers, she lost one of her slippers. In her panic, she did not stop to look for it but continued to run, swiftly as a deer, straight toward home.

Upon returning from the festival, the stepmother found Ye Syan asleep in the orchard under a pear tree.

'You see,' she said to her daughter, 'you were mistaken. The beautiful girl we saw at the festival could not have been Ye Syan.'

On the following day, the slipper was found by a poor peasant who sold it for a few coins to an official of the Tuo Huan kingdom.

The Tuo Huan king ruled over a vast territory that included twenty-four islands. Because of his legendary wealth and powerful army, he was envied and feared by all the other weaker tribes. Though he lacked for nothing, he was never content with the riches he had amassed. His craving for more gold, more jewels, even pretty trinkets that caught his fancy, could not be satisfied. The official, anxious to find favour at court, presented the slipper to his king as a gift.

The king was intrigued by the tiny embroidered slipper. 'Where is there a maiden,' he wondered, 'with a foot so dainty? Surely the slipper must belong to a high-born beauty.' He resolved to find its owner.

All the young women attached to the palace were required to try on the slipper. Not one of them did it fit. The king then issued a decree that every woman in his kingdom try on his treasured slipper. He sent couriers to every corner of his twenty-four islands, but they all returned without success. Finally, he decided to extend the search beyond his own lands.

The soldier who was dispatched to the area of the cave people never believed he would find the owner of the slipper among its poor inhabitants. When Ye Syan's stepmother led him into her cave dwelling, he was convinced that neither of the two young girls he saw there would be the one he sought. But the king's decree was plain. No one was to be overlooked. The soldier asked Ye Syan's stepsister to try on the slipper first. She tugged and pulled but could not squeeze more than her big toe into it. He handed the slipper to Ye Syan, fully expecting the same results. To the soldier's great surprise, it clung to her foot as though it had been made especially for her.

Still the soldier was unconvinced. It was so unlikely that this ragamuffin would own such a fine slipper. 'Give me that slipper', he demanded. 'I shall try it on your foot myself.' Again, the fit was perfect. Still beset by doubts, he asked Ye Syan if she could produce its mate.

From under her straw mattress Ye Syan drew out the other slipper and stepped into it before her open-mouthed stepmother and stepsister.

'You must come with me to the king's palace,' the soldier said. 'My orders are to bring back the maiden whose foot fits the slipper.'

Ye Syan asked for time to change her clothes. Quickly, she threw off her old worn rags. She returned wearing her lovely new outfit. The stepmother, astonished by the change in her appearance, recognized that the attractive girl she had seen at the festival was indeed Ye Syan. Her jealousy and wrath knew no bounds, but she could only look on helplessly. Escorted by the king's soldier, Ye Syan went to the palace carrying the magic fishbones with her.

At first sight, the Tuo Huan king was taken with her lovely face and the grace with which she moved in her dainty slippers. He listened courteously while she recounted the story of her golden fish and its cruel end at the hands of her stepmother. Spreading out her fishbones before him, she told of their magic power to grant her wishes.

Unbelieving, the king requested that she demonstrate their power by making a wish for a golden bracelet. In less than a breath, a band of purest gold lay on the table before him. Still unsure, the king asked Ye Syan to wish for a gold ring. In a twinkling, on his third finger appeared a ring encrusted with glittering rubies. The king was jubilant.

'I shall take Ye Syan for my wife, and she will be forever at my side,' he announced to his courtiers.

From the day of their marriage, the temptation of the magic fishbones gave the Tuo Huan king no peace. He demanded that Ye Syan ask them for more and more precious gifts to fill the coffers of his island kingdom. Although his wealth increased a hundredfold, his thirst for still greater riches was never slaked.

After a time the bones grew weary of satisfying the greedy ruler's incessant requests. They would give no more. Disgusted with their lack of response, the king ordered Ye Syan to discard them.

But Ye Syan remembered the golden carp that had befriended her in her loneliest and most desperate hours. She gently placed the bones in a silken pouch and carried them a great distance to a remote spot on the beach. With her own hands she dug a bowl-shaped hole. Wishing each bone a fond farewell, she lowered them into the cool earth. Reverently she marked their burying place with a circle of precious pearls.

The waves that lapped the shore flowed endlessly in and out. The tide rose and ebbed. The water scoured the beach and carried the bones out to sea.

From *Traditional Chinese Folktales*, by Yin-lien C. Chin, Yetta S. Center, and Mildred Ross (Armonk, NY and London, England: M.E. Sharpe, 1989).

Cinderella, or the Little Glass Slipper

Almost from the time it was first translated into English in 1729, Charles Perrault's 'Cinderella' has been popular, and because it is the basis of ballets and an animated Disney film (1950), it has come to be seen as the quintessential version of the tale. Perrault, who fashioned the tale for sophisticated adults, elaborated and refined oral ingredients, invented such things as the glass slipper and the magical transformation of the pumpkin into a coach, and introduced a fairy godmother in a role played by animals or the spirit of the girl's dead mother in other versions. When published in his collection *Histoires ou Contes du temps passé* (1697), a collection ascribed to his teenaged son, but generally acknowledged to be his own work, 'Cendrillon', as it is known in French, concluded with two verse morals. The first insisted that the tale illustrated that charm was the true gift of the fairies to women, whereas the second, a slightly more sardonic or cynical verse, suggested that shrewdness, wit, courage, and other virtues are useless unless one has a fairy godmother to help. Versions for children omit these morals, allowing events alone to suggest lessons about the aristocratic but relatively passive Cinderella.

Once upon a time there was a gentleman who married, for his second wife, the proudest and most haughty woman that ever was seen. She had two daughters of her own, who were, indeed, exactly like her in all things. The gentleman had also a young daughter, of rare goodness and sweetness of temper, which she took from her mother, who was the best creature in the world.

The wedding was scarcely over, when the stepmother's bad temper began to show itself. She could not bear the goodness of this young girl, because it made her own daughters appear the more odious. The stepmother gave her the meanest work in the house to do; she had to scour the dishes, tables, etc., and to scrub the floors and clean out the bedrooms. The poor girl had to sleep in the garret, upon a wretched straw bed, while her sisters lay in fine rooms with inlaid floors, upon beds of the very newest fashion, and where they had looking-glasses so large that they might see themselves at their full length. The poor girl bore all patiently, and dared not complain to her father, who would have scolded her if she had done so, for his wife governed him entirely.

When she had done her work, she used to go into the chimney corner, and sit down among the cinders, hence she was called Cinderwench. The younger sister of the two, who was not so rude and uncivil as the elder, called her Cinderella. However, Cinderella, in spite of her mean apparel, was a hundred times more handsome than her sisters, though they were always richly dressed.

It happened that the King's son gave a ball, and invited to it all persons of fashion. Our young misses were also invited, for they cut a very grand figure among the people of the countryside. They were highly delighted with the invitation, and wonderfully busy in choosing the gowns, petticoats, and headdresses which might best become them. This made Cinderella's lot still harder, for it was she who ironed her sisters' linen and plaited their ruffles. They talked all day long of nothing but how they should be dressed.

'For my part,' said the elder, 'I will wear my red velvet suit with French trimmings.'

'And I,' said the younger, 'shall wear my usual skirt; but then, to make amends for that I will put on my gold-flowered mantle, and my diamond stomacher, which is far from being the most ordinary one in the world.' They sent for the best hairdressers they could get to make up their hair in fashionable style, and bought patches for their cheeks. Cinderella was consulted in all these matters, for she had good taste. She advised them always for the best, and even offered her services to dress their hair, which they were very willing she should do.

As she was doing this, they said to her:—

'Cinderella, would you not be glad to go to the ball?'

'Young ladies,' she said, 'you only jeer at me; it is not for such as I am to go there.'

'You are right,' they replied; 'people would laugh to see a Cinderwench at a ball.'

Anyone but Cinderella would have dressed their hair awry, but she was good-natured, and arranged it perfectly well. They were almost two days without eating, so much were they transported with joy. They broke above a dozen laces in trying to lace themselves tight, that they might have a fine, slender shape, and they were continually at their looking-glass.

At last the happy day came; they went to Court, and Cinderella followed them with her eyes as long as she could, and when she had lost sight of them, she fell a-crying.

Her godmother, who saw her all in tears, asked her what was the matter.

'I wish I could—I wish I could—' but she could not finish for sobbing.

Her godmother, who was a fairy, said to her, 'You wish you could go to the ball; is it not so?'

'Alas, yes,' said Cinderella, sighing.

'Well,' said her godmother, 'be but a good girl, and I will see that you go.' Then she took her into her chamber, and said to her, 'Run into the garden, and bring me a pumpkin.'

Cinderella went at once to gather the finest she could get, and brought it to her godmother, not being able to imagine how this pumpkin could help her to go to the ball. Her godmother scooped out all the inside of it, leaving nothing but the rind. Then she struck it with her wand, and the pumpkin was instantly turned into a fine gilded coach.

She then went to look into the mousetrap, where she found six mice, all alive. She ordered Cinderella to lift the trap-door, when, giving each mouse, as it went out, a little tap with her wand, it was that moment turned into a fine horse, and the six mice made a fine set of six horses of a beautiful mouse-coloured, dapple gray.

Being at a loss for a coachman, Cinderella said, 'I will go and see if there is not a rat in the rat-trap—we may make a coachman of him.'

'You are right,' replied her godmother; 'go and look.'

From Arthur Rackham, *Cinderella*. Illustrated by C.S. Evans. 1919. (London: William Heinemann, 1972), 61.

Cinderella brought the rat-trap to her, and in it there were three huge rats. The fairy chose the one which had the largest beard, and, having touched him with her wand, he was turned into a fat coachman—with the finest moustache and whiskers ever seen.

After that, she said to her:—

'Go into the garden, and you will find six lizards behind the watering-pot; bring them to me.'

She had no sooner done so than her godmother turned them into six footmen, who skipped up immediately behind the coach, with their liveries all trimmed with gold and silver, and they held on as if they had done nothing else their whole lives.

The fairy then said to Cinderella, 'Well, you see here a carriage fit to go to the ball in; are you not pleased with it?'

'Oh, yes!' she cried; 'but must I go as I am in these rags?'

Her godmother simply touched her with her wand, and, at the same moment, her clothes were turned into cloth of gold and silver, all decked with jewels. This done, she gave her a pair of the prettiest glass slippers in the whole world. Being thus attired, she got into the carriage, her godmother commanding her, above all things, not to stay till after midnight, and telling her, at the same time, that if she stayed one moment longer, the coach would be a pumpkin again, her horses mice, her coachman a rat, her footmen lizards, and her clothes would become just as they were before.

She promised her godmother she would not fail to leave the ball before midnight. She drove away, scarce able to contain herself for joy. The King's son, who was told that a great princess, whom nobody knew, was come, ran out to receive her. He gave her his hand as she alighted from the coach, and led her into the hall where the company were assembled. There was at once a profound silence; everyone left off dancing, and the violins ceased to play, so attracted was everyone by the singular beauties of the unknown newcomer. Nothing was then heard but a confused sound of voices saying:—

'Ha! how beautiful she is! Ha! how beautiful she is!'

The King himself, old as he was, could not keep his eyes off her, and he told the Queen under his breath that it was a long time since he had seen so beautiful and lovely a creature.

All the ladies were busy studying her clothes and headdress, so that they might have theirs made next day after the same pattern, provided they could meet with such fine materials and able hands to make them.

The King's son conducted her to the seat of honour, and afterwards took her out to dance with him. She danced so very gracefully that they all admired her more and more. A fine collation was served, but the young Prince ate not a morsel, so intently was he occupied with her.

She went and sat down beside her sisters, showing them a thousand civilities, and giving them among other things part of the oranges and citrons with which the Prince had regaled her. This very much surprised them, for they had not been presented to her.

Cinderella heard the clock strike a quarter to twelve. She at once made her adieus to the company and hastened away as fast as she could.

As soon as she got home, she ran to find her godmother, and, after having thanked her, she said she much wished she might go to the ball the next day, because the King's son had asked her to do so. As she was eagerly telling her godmother all that happened at the ball, her two sisters knocked at the door; Cinderella opened it. 'How long you have stayed!' said she, yawning, rubbing her eyes, and stretching herself as if she had been just awakened. She had not, however, had any desire to sleep since they went from home.

'If you had been at the ball,' said one of her sisters, 'you would not have been tired with it. There came thither the finest princess, the most beautiful ever was seen with mortal eyes. She showed us a thousand civilities, and gave us oranges and citrons.'

Cinderella did not show any pleasure at this. Indeed, she asked them the name of the princess; but they told her they did not know it, and that the King's son was very much concerned, and would give all the world to know who she was. At this Cinderella, smiling, replied:—

'Was she then so very beautiful? How fortunate you have been! Could I not see her? Ah! dear Miss Charlotte, do lend me your yellow suit of clothes which you wear every day.'

'Ay, to be sure!' cried Miss Charlotte; 'lend my clothes to such a dirty Cinderwench as thou art! I should be out of my mind to do so.'

Cinderella, indeed, expected such an answer and was very glad of the refusal; for she would have been sadly troubled if her sister had lent her what she jestingly asked for. The next day the two sisters went to the ball, and so did Cinderella, but dressed more magnificently than before. The King's son was always by her side, and his pretty speeches to her never ceased. These by no means annoyed the young lady. Indeed, she quite forgot her godmother's orders to her, so that she heard the clock begin to strike twelve when she thought it could not be more than eleven. She then rose up and fled, as nimble as a deer. The Prince followed, but could not overtake her. She left behind one of her glass slippers, which the Prince took up most carefully. She got home, but quite out of breath, without her carriage, and in her old clothes, having nothing left her of all her finery but one of the little slippers, fellow to the one she had dropped. The guards at the palace gate were asked if they had not seen a princess go out, and they replied they had seen nobody go out but a young girl, very meanly dressed, and who had more the air of a poor country girl than of a young lady.

When the two sisters returned from the ball, Cinderella asked them if they had had a pleasant time, and if the fine lady had been there. They told her, yes; but that she hurried away the moment it struck twelve, and with so much haste that she dropped one of her little glass slippers, the prettiest in the world, which the King's son had taken up. They said, further, that he had done nothing but look at her all the time, and that most certainly he was very much in love with the beautiful owner of the glass slipper.

What they said was true; for a few days after the King's son caused it to be proclaimed, by sound of trumpet, that he would marry her whose foot this slipper would fit exactly. They began to try it on the princesses, then on the duchesses, and then on all the ladies of the Court; but in vain. It was brought to the two sisters, who did all they possibly could to thrust a foot into the slipper, but they could not succeed. Cinderella, who saw this, and knew her slipper, said to them, laughing:—

'Let me see if it will not fit me.'

Her sisters burst out a-laughing, and began to banter her. The gentleman who was sent to try the slipper looked earnestly at Cinderella, and, finding her very handsome, said it was but just that she should try, and that he had orders to let every lady try it on.

He obliged Cinderella to sit down, and, putting the slipper to her little foot, he found it went on very easily, and fitted her as if it had been made of wax. The astonishment of her two sisters was great, but it was still greater when Cinderella pulled out of her pocket the other slipper and put it on her foot. Thereupon, in came her godmother, who, having touched Cinderella's clothes with her wand, made them more magnificent than those she had worn before.

And now her two sisters found her to be that beautiful lady they had seen at the ball. They threw themselves at her feet to beg pardon for all their ill treatment of her. Cinderella took them up, and, as she embraced them, said that she forgave them with all her heart, and begged them to love her always.

She was conducted to the young Prince, dressed as she was. He thought her more charming than ever, and, a few days after, married her. Cinderella, who was as good as she was beautiful, gave her two sisters a home in the palace, and that very same day married them to two great lords of the Court.

From *The Tales of Mother Goose as First Collected by Charles Perrault in 1696*, translated by Charles Welsh (New York: D.C. Heath, 1901).

Aschenputtel

The German Cinderella tale collected by the Brothers Grimm is significantly different from Charles Perrault's version. Aschenputtel is a more active heroine; she must be because she faces greater tribulations, including rejection, not just neglect, by her father. The Grimms' version also makes a more pointed contrast between the duplicitous stepmother and the birth mother, who keeps watch on her child even after death by acting through the tree that grows from her grave. Although both versions include the shoe test and the heroine's marriage to the prince, the German version eschews the Christian charity evident when the French Cinderella arranges marriages for her stepsisters. Possibly because he wanted an instance of poetic justice to make the tale more didactic, Wilhelm Grimm altered the text published in 1812, adding the incident in which birds peck out the eyes of the stepsisters. Such editorial changes may have weakened its authenticity as an example of an oral folk tale, but other folkloric elements are still evident. Scholars continue to debate, for example, the significance of and connections between the hazel twig that touches the father's hat, the tree that grows from the mother's grave, and the pear tree in which the girl hides on the night of the second ball. In spite of what may be inexplicable remnants from earlier oral versions, 'Aschenputtel' is a literary work whose popularity has been exceeded only by that of Perrault's 'Cinderella'. (To avoid confusion with Perrault's tale, we have given this tale its German title, and we refer to the protagonist by her German name. The translator, however, uses her French name.)

The wife of a rich man fell sick, and as she felt that her end was drawing near, she called her only daughter to her bedside and said, 'Dear child, be good and pious, and then the good God will always protect thee, and I will look down on thee from heaven and be near thee.' Thereupon she closed her eyes and departed. Every day the maiden went out to her mother's grave and wept, and she remained pious and good. When winter came the snow spread a white sheet over the grave, and when the spring sun had drawn it off again, the man had taken another wife.

The woman had brought two daughters into the house with her, who were beautiful and fair of face, but vile and black of heart. Now began a bad time for the poor stepchild. 'Is the stupid goose to sit in the parlour with us?' said they. 'He who wants to eat bread must earn it; out with the kitchen-wench.' They took her pretty clothes away from her, put an old grey bedgown on her, and gave her wooden shoes. 'Just look at the proud princess, how decked out she is!' they cried, and laughed, and led her into the kitchen. There she had to do hard work from morning till night, get up before daybreak, carry water, light fires, cook, and wash. Besides this, the sisters did her every imaginable injury—they mocked her and emptied her peas and lentils into the ashes, so that she was forced to sit and pick them out again. In the evening when she had worked till she was weary she had no bed to go to, but had to sleep by the fireside in the ashes. And as on that account she always looked dusty and dirty, they called her Cinderella. It happened that the father was once going to the fair, and he asked his two step-daughters what he should bring back for them. 'Beautiful dresses,' said one. 'Pearls and jewels,' said the second. 'And thou, Cinderella,' said he, 'what wilt thou have?' 'Father, break off for me the first branch which knocks against your hat on your way home.' So he bought beautiful dresses, pearls, and jewels for his two step-daughters, and on his way home, as he was riding through a green thicket, a hazel twig brushed against him and knocked off his hat. Then he broke off the branch and took it with him. When he reached home he gave his step-daughters the things which they had wished for, and to Cinderella he gave the branch from the hazel-bush. Cinderella thanked him, went to her mother's grave and planted the branch on it, and wept so much that the tears fell down on it and watered it. It grew, however, and became a handsome tree. Thrice a day Cinderella went and sat beneath it, and wept and prayed, and a little white bird always came on the tree, and if Cinderella expressed a wish, the bird threw down to her what she had wished for.

It happened, however, that the King appointed a festival which was to last three days, and to which all the beautiful young girls in the country were invited, in order that his son might choose himself a bride. When the two stepsisters heard that they too were to appear among the number, they were delighted, called Cinderella and said, 'Comb our hair for us, brush our shoes and fasten our buckles for we are going to the festival at the King's palace.' Cinderella obeyed, but wept, because she too would have liked to go with them to the dance, and begged her stepmother to allow her to do so. 'Thou go, Cinderella!' said she; 'Thou art dusty and dirty, and wouldst go to the festival? Thou hast no clothes and shoes, and yet wouldst dance!' As, however, Cinderella went on asking, the stepmother at last said, 'I have emptied a dish of lentils into the ashes for thee, if thou hast picked them out again in two hours, thou shalt go with us.' The maiden went through the backdoor into the garden, and called, 'You tame pigeons, you turtle-doves, and all you birds beneath the sky, come and help me to pick

'The good into the pot,
The bad into the crop.'

Then two white pigeons came in by the kitchen window, and afterwards the turtle-doves, and at last all the birds beneath the sky, came whirring and crowding in, and alighted amongst the ashes. And the pigeons nodded with their heads and began pick, pick, pick, pick, and the rest began also pick, pick, pick, pick, and gathered all the good grains into the dish. Hardly had one hour passed before they had finished, and all flew out again. Then the girl took the dish to her stepmother, and was glad, and believed that now she would be allowed to go with them to the festival. But the stepmother said, 'No, Cinderella, thou hast no clothes and thou canst not dance; thou wouldst only be laughed at.' And as Cinderella wept at this, the stepmother said, 'If thou canst pick two dishes of lentils out of the ashes for me in one hour, thou shalt go with us.' And she thought to herself, 'That she most certainly cannot do.' When the stepmother had emptied the two dishes of lentils amongst the ashes, the maiden went through the back-door into the garden and cried, 'You tame pigeons, you turtle-doves, and all you birds under heaven, come and help me to pick

'The good into the pot,
The bad into the crop.'

Then two white pigeons came in by the kitchen-window, and afterwards the turtle-doves, and at length all the birds beneath the sky, came whirring and crowding in, and alighted amongst the ashes. And the doves nodded with their heads and began pick, pick, pick, pick, and the others began also pick, pick, pick, pick, and gathered all the good seeds into the dishes, and before half an hour was over they had already finished, and all flew out again. Then the maiden carried the dishes to the stepmother and was delighted, and believed that she might now go with them to the festival. But the stepmother said, 'All this will not help thee; thou goest not with us, for thou hast no clothes and canst not dance; we should be ashamed of thee!' On this she turned her back on Cinderella, and hurried away with her two proud daughters.

As no one was now at home, Cinderella went to her mother's grave beneath the hazel-tree, and cried,

> 'Shiver and quiver little tree,
> Silver and gold throw down over me.'

Then the bird threw a gold and silver dress down to her, and slippers embroidered with silk and silver. She put on the dress with all speed, and went to the festival. Her stepsisters and the stepmother however did not know her, and thought she must be a foreign princess, for she looked so beautiful in the golden dress. They never once thought of Cinderella, and believed that she was sitting at home in the dirt, picking lentils out of the ashes. The prince went to meet her, took her by the hand, and danced with her. He would dance with no other maiden, and never left loose of her hand, and if anyone else came to invite her, he said, 'This is my partner.'

She danced till it was evening, and then she wanted to go home. But the King's son said, 'I will go with thee and bear thee company,' for he wished to see to whom the beautiful maiden belonged. She escaped from him, however, and sprang into the pigeon-house. The King's son waited until her father came, and then he told him that the stranger maiden had leapt into the pigeon-house. The old man thought, 'Can it be Cinderella?' and they had to bring him an axe and a pickaxe that he might hew the pigeon-house to pieces, but no one was inside it. And when they got home Cinderella lay in her dirty clothes among the ashes, and a dim little oil-lamp was burning on the mantelpiece, for Cinderella had jumped quickly down from the back of the pigeon-house and had run to the little hazel-tree, and there she had taken off her beautiful clothes and laid them on the grave, and the bird had taken them away again, and then she had placed herself in the kitchen amongst the ashes in her grey gown.

Next day when the festival began afresh, and her parents and the stepsisters had gone once more, Cinderella went to the hazel-tree and said—

> 'Shiver and quiver, my little tree,
> Silver and gold throw down over me.'

Then the bird threw down a much more beautiful dress than on the preceding day. And when Cinderella appeared at the festival in this dress, everyone was astonished at her beauty. The King's son had waited until she came, and instantly took her by the hand and danced with no one but her. When others came and invited her, he said, 'She is my partner.' When evening came she wished to leave, and the King's son followed her and wanted to see into which house she went. But she sprang away from him, and into the garden behind the house. Therein stood a beautiful tall tree on which hung the most magnificent pears. She clambered so nimbly between the branches like a squirrel, that the King's son did not know where she was gone. He waited until her father came, and said to him, 'The stranger maiden has escaped from me, and I believe she has climbed up the pear-tree.' The father thought, 'Can it be Cinderella?' and had an axe brought and cut the tree down, but no one was on it. And when they got into the kitchen, Cinderella lay there amongst the ashes, as usual, for she had jumped down on the other side of the tree, had taken the beautiful dress to the bird on the little hazel-tree, and put on her grey gown.

On the third day, when the parents and sisters had gone away, Cinderella once more went to her mother's grave and said to the little tree—

> 'Shiver and quiver, my little tree,
> Silver and gold throw down over me.'

And now the bird threw down to her a dress which was more splendid and magnificent than any she had yet had, and the slippers were golden. And when she went to the festival in the dress, no one knew how to speak for astonishment. The King's son danced with her only, and if anyone invited her to dance, he said, 'She is my partner.'

When evening came, Cinderella wished to leave, and the King's son was anxious to go with her, but she escaped from him so quickly that he could not follow her. The King's son had, however, used a stratagem, and had caused the whole staircase to be smeared with pitch, and there, when she ran down, had the maiden's left slipper remained sticking. The King's son picked it up, and it was small and dainty, and all golden. Next morning, he went with it to the father, and said to him, 'No one shall be my wife but she whose foot this golden slipper fits.' Then were the two sisters glad, for they had pretty feet. The eldest went with the shoe into her room and wanted to try it on, and her mother stood by. But she could not get her big toe into it, and the shoe was too small for her. Then her mother gave her a knife and said, 'Cut the toe off; when thou art Queen thou wilt have no more need to go on foot.' The maiden cut the toe off, forced the foot into the shoe, swallowed the pain, and went out to the King's son. Then he took her on his horse as his bride and rode away with her. They were, however, obliged to pass the grave, and there, on the hazel-tree, sat the two pigeons and cried,

> 'Turn and peep, turn and peep,
> There's blood within the shoe,
> The shoe it is too small for her,
> The true bride waits for you.'

Then he looked at her foot and saw how the blood was streaming from it. He turned his horse round and took the false bride home again, and said she was not the true one, and that the other sister was to put the shoe on. Then this one went into her chamber and got her toes safely into the shoe, but her heel was too large. So her mother gave her a knife and said, 'Cut a bit off thy heel; when thou art Queen thou wilt have no more need to go on foot.' The maiden cut a bit off her heel, forced her foot into the shoe, swallowed the pain, and went out to the King's son. He took her on his horse as his bride, and rode away with her, but when they passed by the hazel-tree, two little pigeons sat on it and cried,

> 'Turn and peep, turn and peep,
> There's blood within the shoe,
> The shoe it is too small for her,
> The true bride waits for you.'

He looked down at her foot and saw how the blood was running out of her shoe, and how it had stained her white stocking. Then he turned his horse and took the false bride home again. 'This also is not the right one,' said he, 'have you no other daughter?' 'No,' said the man, 'There is still a little stunted kitchen-wench which my late wife left behind her, but she cannot possibly be the bride.' The King's son said he was to send her up to him; but the mother answered, 'Oh no, she is much too dirty, she cannot show herself!' He absolutely insisted on it, and Cinderella had to be called. She first washed her hands and face clean, and then went and bowed down before the King's son, who gave her the golden shoe. Then she seated herself on a stool, drew her foot out of the heavy wooden shoe, and put it into the slipper, which fitted like a glove. And when she rose up and the King's son looked at her face he recognized the beautiful maiden who had danced with him and cried, 'That is the true bride!' The stepmother and the two sisters were terrified and became pale with rage; he, however, took Cinderella on his horse, and rode away with her. As they passed by the hazel-tree, the two white doves cried,

> 'Turn and peep, turn and peep,
> No blood is in the shoe,
> The shoe is not too small for her,
> The true bride rides with you,'

and when they had cried that, the two came flying down and placed themselves on Cinderella's shoulders, one on the right, the other on the left, and remained sitting there.

When the wedding with the King's son had to be celebrated, the two false sisters came and wanted to get into favour with Cinderella and share her good fortune. When the betrothed couple went to church, the elder was at the right side and the younger at the left, and the pigeons pecked out one eye of each of them. Afterwards as they came back, the elder was at the left, and the younger at the right, and then the pigeons pecked out the other eye of each. And thus, for their wickedness and falsehood, they were punished with blindness as long as they lived.

From *Grimm's Household Tales*, Vol. 1, translated by Margaret Hunt (London: George Bell and Sons, 1884).

Cap o' Rushes

The English tale 'Cap o' Rushes' belongs to a group of Cinderella tales in which the father, not the stepmother, is the persecutor. In this particular tale, the father is not incestuous, but he is unnatural in his demands for displays of love. The basic elements of this tale, except for the 'as salt loves meat motif', appears in Geoffrey of Monmounth's *Historia Regum Britanniae* (completed c. 1136–8), which may have been the source of Shakespeare's use of a similar test of love in *King Lear*. Stories of the demanding father differ from those about the incestuous father in the way they employ the ring, used instead of a shoe, in the crucial test of identity. In incestuous father tales, the ring is a small one that belonged to the deceased mother; in tales in which the father demands unnatural testimonials of his daughters' love, the ring belongs to a future husband and, as a result, becomes a symbol of proper love. What is particularly notable about this latter form of the tale is that it requires two males, the father and the future husband, to discover the truth about the Cinderella figure.

Well, there was once a very rich gentleman, and he'd three daughters, and he thought he'd see how fond they were of him. So he says to the first, 'How much do you love me, my dear?'

'Why,' says she, 'as I love my life.'

'That's good,' says he.

So he says to the second, 'How much do *you* love me, my dear?'

'Why,' says she, 'better nor all the world.'

'That's good,' says he.

So he says to the third, 'How much do *you* love me, my dear?'

'Why, I love you as fresh meat loves salt,' says she.

Well, but he was angry. 'You don't love me at all,' says he, 'and in my house you stay no more.' So he drove her out there and then, and shut the door in her face.

Well, she went away on and on till she came to a fen, and there she gathered a lot of rushes and made them into a kind of a sort of a cloak with a hood, to cover her from head to foot, and to hide her fine clothes. And then she went on and on till she came to a great house.

'Do you want a maid?' says she.

'No, we don't,' said they.

'I haven't nowhere to go,' says she; 'and I ask no wages, and do any sort of work,' says she.

'Well,' said they, 'if you like to wash the pots and scrape the saucepans you may stay,' said they.

So she stayed there and washed the pots and scraped the saucepans and did all the dirty work. And because she gave no name they called her 'Cap o' Rushes'.

Well, one day there was to be a great dance a little way off, and the servants were allowed to go and look on at the grand people. Cap o' Rushes said she was too tired to go, so she stayed at home.

But when they were gone she offed with her cap o' rushes, and cleaned herself, and went to the dance. And no one there was so finely dressed as she.

Well, who should be there but her master's son, and what should he do but fall in love with her the minute he set eyes on her. He wouldn't dance with anyone else.

But before the dance was done Cap o' Rushes slipt off, and away she went home. And when the other maids came back she was pretending to be asleep with her cap o' rushes on.

Well, next morning they said to her, 'You did miss a sight, Cap o' Rushes!'

'What was that?' says she.

'Why, the beautifullest lady you ever see, dressed right gay and ga'. The young master, he never took his eyes off her.'

'Well, I should have liked to have seen her,' says Cap o' Rushes.

'Well, there's to be another dance this evening, and perhaps she'll be there.'

But, come the evening, Cap o' Rushes said she was too tired to go with them. Howsoever, when they were gone she offed with her cap o' rushes and cleaned herself, and away she went to the dance.

The master's son had been reckoning on seeing her, and he danced with no one else, and never took his eyes off her. But, before the dance was over, she slipt off, and home she went, and when the maids came back she pretended to be asleep with her cap o' rushes on.

Next day they said to her again, 'Well, Cap o' Rushes, you should ha' been there to see the lady. There she was again, gay and ga', and the young master he never took his eyes off her.'

'Well, there,' says she, 'I should ha' liked to ha' seen her.'

'Well,' says they, 'there's a dance again this evening, and you must go with us, for she's sure to be there.'

Well, come this evening, Cap o' Rushes said she was too tired to go, and do what they would she stayed at home. But when they were gone she offed with her cap o' rushes and cleaned herself, and away she went to the dance.

The master's son was rarely glad when he saw her. He danced with none but her and never took his eyes off her. When she wouldn't tell him her name, nor where she came from, he gave her a ring and told her if he didn't see her again he should die.

Well, before the dance was over, off she slipped, and home she went, and when the maids came home she was pretending to be asleep with her cap o' rushes on.

Well, next day they says to her, 'There, Cap o' Rushes, you didn't come last night, and now you won't see the lady, for there's no more dances.'

'Well I should have rarely liked to have seen her,' says she.

The master's son he tried every way to find out where the lady was gone, but go where he might, and ask whom he might, he never heard anything about her. And he got worse and worse for the love of her till he had to keep his bed.

'Make some gruel for the young master,' they said to the cook. 'He's dying for the love of the lady.' The cook she set about making it when Cap o' Rushes came in.

'What are you a-doing of?' says she.

'I'm going to make some gruel for the young master,' says the cook, 'for he's dying for love of the lady.'

'Let me make it,' says Cap o' Rushes.

Well, the cook wouldn't at first, but at last she said yes, and Cap o' Rushes made the gruel. And when she had made it she slipped the ring into it on the sly before the cook took it upstairs.

The young man he drank it and then he saw the ring at the bottom.

'Send for the cook,' says he.

So up she comes.

'Who made this gruel here?' says he.

'I did,' says the cook, for she was frightened.

And he looked at her.

'No, you didn't,' says he. 'Say who did it, and you shan't be harmed.'

'Well, then, 'twas Cap o' Rushes,' says she.

'Send Cap o' Rushes here,' says he.

So Cap o' Rushes came.

'Did you make my gruel?' says he.

'Yes, I did,' says she.

'Where did you get this ring?' says he.

'From him that gave it me,' says she.

'Who are you, then?' says the young man.

'I'll show you,' says she. And she offed with her cap o' rushes, and there she was in her beautiful clothes.

Well, the master's son he got well very soon, and they were to be married in a little time. It was to be a very grand wedding, and every one was asked far and near. And Cap o' Rushes' father was asked. But she never told anybody who she was.

But before the wedding she went to the cook, and says she:

'I want you to dress every dish without a mite o' salt.'

'That'll be rare nasty,' says the cook.

'That doesn't signify,' says she.

'Very well,' says the cook.

Well, the wedding day came, and they were married. And after they were married all the company sat down to the dinner. When they began to eat the meat, it was so tasteless they couldn't eat it. But Cap o' Rushes father tried first one dish and then another, and then he burst out crying.

'What is the matter?' said the master's son to him.

'Oh!' says he, 'I had a daughter. And I asked her how much she loved me. And she said "As much as fresh meat loves salt." And I turned her from my door, for I thought she didn't love me. And now I see she loved me best of all. And she may be dead for aught I know.'

'No, father, here she is!' says Cap o' Rushes. And she goes up to him and puts her arms round him.

And so they were all happy ever after.

From *English Fairy Tales*, 3rd ed., by Joseph Jacobs (London: David Nutt, 1898).

Billy Beg and the Bull

Its use of runs—long, repeated phrases that are often nonsensical—tends to make this Irish male Cinderella tale more comical than romantic. 'Billy Beg and the Bull' has obvious connections to conventional female Cinderella tales: it begins with abuse of the child by a stepmother, and Billy has an animal helper who provides food, advice, and magical implements. Once the bull is killed, however, the tale follows a pattern typical in the male Cinderella variants: the protagonist becomes a giant killer and a dragon slayer, albeit one who tends to resemble humble Jack more than Saint George. In most such variations, the protagonist, who has performed his deeds of valour while in disguise, offers the tongues of his victims as proof of his actions when an impostor tries to claim the glory for ridding the kingdom of its enemies and the reward of marriage to the king's daughter. In this case, the tale is unusual because it reconnects to the female Cinderella tradition by using the familiar shoe test to determine Billy's identity and his right to marry the princess.

Once on a time when pigs was swine, there was a King and a Queen, and they had one son, Billy, and the Queen gave Billy a bull that he was very fond of, and it was just as fond of him. After some time the Queen died, and she put it as her last request on the King that he would never part Billy and the bull, and the King promised that, come what might, come what may, he would not. After the Queen died the King married again, and the new Queen didn't take to Billy Beg, and no more did she like the bull, seeing himself and Billy so *thick*. But she couldn't get the King on no account to part Billy and the bull, so she consulted with a hen-wife what they could do as regards separating Billy and the bull. 'What will you give me,' says the hen-wife, 'and I'll very soon part them?' 'Whatever you ask,' says the Queen. 'Well and good then,' says the hen-wife, 'you are to take to your bed, making pretend that you are bad with a complaint, and I'll do the rest of it.' And, well and good, to her bed she took, and none of the doctors could do anything for her, or make out what was her complaint. So the Queen axed for the for the hen-wife to be sent for. And sent for she was, and when she came in and examined the Queen, she said there was one thing, and only one, could cure her. The King asked what was that, and the hen-wife said it was three mouthfuls of the blood of Billy Beg's bull. But the King wouldn't on no account hear of this, and the next day the Queen was worse, and the third day she was worse still, and told the King she was dying, and he'd have her death on his head. So, sooner nor this, the King had to consent to Billy Beg's bull being killed. When Billy heard this he got very down in the heart entirely, and he went doitherin' about, and the bull saw him, and asked him what was wrong with him that he was so mournful, so Billy told the bull what was wrong with him, and the bull told him to never mind, but keep up his heart, the Queen would never taste a drop of his blood. The next day then the bull was to be killed, and the Queen got up and went out to have the delight of seeing his death. When the bull was led up to be killed, says he to Billy, 'Jump up on my back till we see what kind of a horseman you are.' Up Billy jumped on his back, and with that the bull leapt nine mile high, nine mile deep, and nine mile broad, and came down with Billy sticking between his horns. Hundreds were looking on dazed at the sight, and through them the bull rushed, and over the top of the Queen, killing her dead, and away he galloped where you wouldn't know day by night, or night by day, over high hills, low hills, sheep-walks, and bullock-traces, the Cove of Cork, and old Tom Fox with his bugle horn. When at last they stopped, 'now then,' says the bull to Billy, 'you and I must undergo great scenery, Billy. Put your hand,' says the bull, 'in my left ear, and you'll get a napkin, that, when you spread it out, will be covered with eating and drinking of all sorts, fit for the King himself.' Billy did this, and then he spread out the napkin, and ate and drank to his heart's content, and he rolled up the napkin and put it back in the bull's ear again. 'Then,' says the bull, 'now put your hand into my right ear and you'll find a bit of a stick; if you wind it over your head three times, it will be turned into a sword and give you the strength of a thousand men besides your own, and when you have no more need of it as a sword, it will change back into a stick again.' Billy did all this. Then says the bull, 'At twelve o'clock the morrow I'll have to meet and fight a great bull.' Billy then got up again on the bull's back, and the bull started off and away where you wouldn't know day by night, or night by day, over high hills, low hills, sheep-walks and bullock-traces, the Cove of Cork, and old Tom Fox with his bugle horn. There he met the other bull, and both of them fought, and the like of their fight was never seen before or since. They knocked the soft ground into hard, and the hard into soft, the soft into spring wells, the spring wells into rocks, and the rocks into high hills. They fought long, and Billy Beg's bull killed the other, and drank his blood. Then Billy took the napkin out of his ear again and spread it out and ate a hearty good dinner. Then says the bull to Billy, says he, 'at twelve o'clock tomorrow, I'm to meet the bull's brother that I killed the day, and we'll have a hard fight.' Billy got on the bull's back again, and the bull started off and away where you wouldn't know day by night, or night by day, over high hills, low hills, sheep-walks and bullock-traces, the Cove of Cork, and old Tom Fox with his bugle horn. There he met the bull's brother that he killed the day before, and they set to, and they fought, and the like of the fight was never seen before or since. They knocked the soft ground into hard, the hard into soft, the soft into spring wells, the spring wells into rocks, and the rocks into high hills. They fought long, and at last Billy's bull killed the other and drank his blood. And then Billy took out the napkin out of the bull's ear again and spread it out and ate another hearty dinner. Then says the bull to Billy, says he—'The morrow at twelve o'clock I'm to fight the brother to the two bulls I killed—he's a mighty great bull entirely, the strongest of them all; he's called the Black Bull of the Forest, and he'll be too able for me. When I'm dead,' says the bull, 'you, Billy, will take with you the napkin, and you'll never be hungry; and the stick, and you'll be able to overcome everything that comes in your way; and take out your knife and cut a strip of the hide off my back and another strip off my belly and make a belt of them, and as long as you wear them you cannot be killed.' Billy was very sorry to hear this, but he got up on the bull's back again, and they started off and away where you wouldn't know day by night or night by day, over high hills, low hills, sheep-walks and bullock-traces, the Cove of Cork, and old Tom Fox with his bugle horn. And sure enough at twelve o'clock the next day they met the great Black Bull of the Forest, and both of the bulls to it, and commenced to fight, and the like of the fight was never seen before or since; they knocked the soft ground into hard ground, and the hard ground into soft, and the soft into spring wells, and spring wells into rocks, and the rocks into high hills. And they fought long, but at length the Black Bull of the Forest killed Billy Beg's bull, and drank his blood. Billy Beg was so vexed at this that for two days he sat over the bull neither eating or drinking, but crying salt tears all the time. Then he got up, and he spread out the napkin, and ate a hearty dinner for he was very hungry with his long fast; and after that he cut a strip of the hide off the bull's back, and another off the belly, and made a belt for himself, and taking it and the bit of stick, and the napkin, he set out to push his fortune, and he travelled for three days and three nights till at last he come to a great gentleman's place. Billy asked the gentleman if he could give him employment, and the gentleman said he wanted just such a boy as him for herding cattle. Billy asked what cattle would he have to herd, and what wages would he get. The gentleman said he had three goats, three cows, three horses, and three asses that he fed in an orchard, but that no boy who went with them ever came back alive, for there were three giants, brothers, that came to milk the cows and the goats every day, and killed the boy that was herding; so if Billy liked to try, they wouldn't fix the wages till they'd see if he would come back alive. 'Agreed, then,' said Billy. So the next morning he got up and drove out the three goats, the three cows, the three horses, and the three asses to the orchard and commenced to feed them. About the middle of the day Billy heard three terrible roars that shook the apples off the bushes, shook the horns on the cows, and made the hair stand up on Billy's head, and in comes a frightful big giant with three heads, and begun to threaten Billy. 'You're too big,' says the giant, 'for one bite, and too small for two. What will I do with you?' 'I'll fight you,' says Billy, says he stepping out to him and swinging the bit of stick three times over his head, when it changed into a sword and gave him the strength of a thousand men besides his own. The giant laughed at the size of him, and says he, 'Well, how will I kill you? Will it be by a swing by the back[1], a cut of the sword, or a square round of boxing?' 'With a swing by the back,' says Billy, 'if you can.' So they both laid holds, and Billy lifted the giant clean off the ground, and fetching him down again sunk him in the earth up to his arm pits. 'Oh have mercy,' says the giant. But Billy, taking his sword, killed the giant, and cut out his tongues. It was evening by this time, so Billy drove home the three goats, three cows, three horses, and three asses, and all the vessels in the house wasn't able to hold all the milk the cows give that night.

'Well,' says the gentleman, 'this beats me, for I never saw anyone coming back alive out of there before, nor the cows with a drop of milk. Did you see anything in the orchard?' says he. 'Nothing worse nor myself,' says Billy. 'What about my wages, now,' says Billy. 'Well,' says the gentleman, 'you'll hardly come alive out of the orchard the morrow. So we'll wait till after that.' Next morning his master told Billy that something must have happened one of the giants, for he used to hear the cries of three every night, but last night he only heard two

1. A wrestle.

crying. 'I don't know,' says Billy, 'anything about them.' That morning after he got his breakfast Billy drove the three goats, three cows, three horses, and three asses into the orchard
again, and began to feed them. About twelve o'clock he heard three terrible roars that shook
the apples off the bushes, the horns on the cows, and made the hair stand up on Billy's head,
and in comes a frightful big giant, with six heads, and he told Billy he had killed his brother
yesterday, but he would make him pay for it the day. 'Ye're too big,' says he, 'for one bite,
and too small for two, and what will I do with you?' 'I'll fight you,' says Billy, swinging his
stick three times over his head, and turning it into a sword, and giving him the strength of
a thousand men besides his own. The giant laughed at him, and says he, 'How will I kill
you—with a swing by the back, a cut of the sword, or a square round of boxing?' 'With a
swing by the back,' says Billy, 'if you can.' So the both of them laid holds, and Billy lifted the
giant clean off the ground, and fetching him down again, sunk him in it up to the arm pits.
'Oh, spare my life!' says the giant. But Billy taking up his sword, killed him and cut out his
tongues. It was evening by this time, and Billy drove home his three goats, three cows, three
horses, and three asses, and what milk the cows gave that night overflowed all the vessels
in the house, and running out, turned a rusty mill that hadn't been turned before for thirty
years. If the master was surprised seeing Billy coming back the night before, he was ten
times more surprised now.

'Did you see anything in the orchard the day!' says the gentleman. 'Nothing worse nor
myself,' says Billy. 'What about my wages now,' says Billy. 'Well, never mind about your
wages,' says the gentleman, 'till the morrow, for I think you'll hardly come back alive again,'
says he. Well and good, Billy went to his bed, and the gentleman went to his bed, and when
the gentleman rose in the morning says he to Billy, 'I don't know what's wrong with two of
the giants; I only heard one crying last night.' 'I don't know,' says Billy, 'They must be sick
or something.' Well, when Billy got his breakfast that day again, he set out to the orchard,
driving before him the three goats, three cows, three horses, and three asses and sure
enough about the middle of the day he hears three terrible roars again, and in comes another
giant, this one with twelve heads on him, and if the other two were frightful, surely this one
was ten times more so. 'You villain, you,' says he to Billy, 'you killed my two brothers, and
I'll have my revenge on you now. Prepare till I kill you,' says he; 'you're too big for one bite,
and too small for two; what will I do with you?' 'I'll fight you,' says Billy, shaping out and
winding the bit of stick three times over his head. The giant laughed heartily at the size of
him, and says he, 'What way do you prefer being killed? Is it with a swing by the back, a
cut of the sword, or a square round of boxing?' 'A swing by the back,' says Billy. So both of
them again laid holds, and my brave Billy lifts the giant clean off the ground, and fetching
him down again, sunk him down to his arm pits in it. 'Oh, have mercy; spare my life,' says
the giant. But Billy took his sword, and, killing him, cut out his tongues. That evening he
drove home his three goats, three cows, three horses, and three asses, and the milk of the
cows had to be turned into a valley where it made a lough three miles long, three miles
broad, and three miles deep, and that lough has been filled with salmon and white trout
ever since. The gentleman wondered now more than ever to see Billy back the third day
alive. 'Did you see nothing in the orchard the day, Billy?' says he. 'No, nothing worse nor
myself,' says Billy. 'Well, that beats me,' says the gentleman. 'What about my wages now?'
says Billy. 'Well, you're a good mindful boy that I couldn't easy do without,' says the gentleman, 'and I'll give you any wages you ask for the future.' The next morning, says the gentleman to Billy, 'I heard none of the giants crying last night, however it comes. I don't know
what has happened to them?' 'I don't know,' says Billy, 'they must be sick or something.'
'Now, Billy,' says the gentleman, 'you must look after the cattle the day again, while I go to

see the fight.' 'What fight?' says Billy. 'Why,' says the gentleman, 'it's the king's daughter is going to be devoured by a fiery dragon, if the greatest fighter in the land, that they have been feeding specially for the last three months, isn't able to kill the dragon first. And if he's able to kill the dragon the king is to give him the daughter in marriage.' 'That will be fine,' says Billy. Billy drove out his three goats, three cows, three horses, and three asses to the orchard that day again, and the like of all that passed that day to see the fight with the man and the fiery dragon, Billy never witnessed before. They went in coaches and carriages, on horses and jackasses, riding and walking, crawling and creeping. 'My tight little fellow,' says a man that was passing to Billy, 'why don't you come to see the great fight?' 'What would take the likes of me there?' says Billy. But when Billy found them all gone he saddled and bridled the best black horse his master had, and put on the best suit of clothes he could get in his master's house, and rode off to the fight after the rest. When Billy went there he saw the king's daughter with the whole court about her on a platform before the castle, and he thought he never saw anything half as beautiful, and the great warrior that was to fight the dragon was walking up and down on the lawn before her, with three men carrying his sword, and everyone in the whole country gathered there looking at him. But when the fiery dragon came up with twelve heads on him, and every mouth of him spitting fire, and let twelve roars out of him, the warrior ran away and hid himself up to the neck in a well of water, and all they could do they couldn't get him to come and face the dragon. Then the king's daughter asked if there was no one there to save her from the dragon, and get her in marriage. But not one stirred. When Billy saw this, he tied the belt of the bull's hide round him, swung his stick over his head, and went in, and after a terrible fight entirely, killed the dragon. Everyone then gathered about to find who the stranger was. Billy jumped on his horse and darted away sooner than let them know; but just as he was getting away the king's daughter pulled the shoe off his foot. When the dragon was killed the warrior that had hid in the well of water came out, and cutting the heads off the dragon he brought them to the king, and said that it was he who killed the dragon, in disguise; and he claimed the king's daughter. But she tried the shoe on him and found it didn't fit him; so she said it wasn't him, and that she would marry no one only the man the shoe fitted. When Billy got home he changed the clothes again, and had the horse in the stable, and the cattle all in before his master came. When the master came, he began telling Billy about the wonderful day they had entirely, and about the warrior hiding in the well of water, and about the grand stranger that came down out of the sky in a cloud on a black horse, and killed the fiery dragon, and then vanished in a cloud again. 'And now,' says he, 'Billy, wasn't that wonderful?' 'It was, indeed,' says Billy, 'very wonderful entirely.' After that it was given out over the country that all the people were to come to the king's castle on a certain day, till the king's daughter would try the shoe on them, and whoever it fitted she was to marry them. When the day arrived Billy was in the orchard with the three goats, three cows, three horses, and three asses, as usual, and the like of all the crowds that passed that day going to the king's castle to get the shoe tried on, he never saw before. They went in coaches and carriages, on horses and jackasses, riding and walking, and crawling and creeping. They all asked Billy was not he going to the king's castle, but Billy said, 'Arrah, what would be bringin' the likes of me there?' At last when all the others had gone there passed an old man with a very scarecrow suit of rags on him, and Billy stopped him and asked him what boot would he take and swap clothes with him. 'Just take care of yourself now,' says the old man, 'and don't be playing off your jokes on my clothes, or maybe I'd make you feel the weight of this stick.' But Billy soon let him see it was in earnest he was, and both of them swapped suits, Billy giving the old man boot. Then off to the castle started Billy, with the suit of rags on his back and an old stick in his hand, and when he came there he found all in great commotion trying on the shoe, and some of them cutting down their foot, trying to get it to fit. But it was all of no use, the shoe could not be got to fit none of them at all, and the king's daughter was going to give up in despair when the ragged looking boy, which was Billy, elbowed his way through them, and says he, 'Let me try it on; maybe it would fit me.' But the people when they saw him began to laugh at the sight of him, and 'Go along out of that, you example you,' says they shoving and pushing him back. But the king's daughter saw him, and called on them by all manner of means to let him come up and try on the shoe. So Billy went up, and all the people looked on, breaking their hearts laughing at the conceit of it. But what would you have of it, but to the dumbfounding of them all, the shoe fitted Billy as nice as if it was made on his foot for a last. So the king's daughter claimed Billy as her husband. He then confessed that it was he that killed the fiery dragon; and when the king had him dressed up in a silk and satin suit, with plenty of gold and silver ornaments everyone gave in that his like they never saw afore. He was then married to the king's daughter, and the wedding lasted nine days, nine hours, nine minutes, nine half minutes and nine quarter minutes, and they lived happy and well from that day to this. I got brogues of *brochan*[2] and breeches of glass, a bit of pie for telling a lie, and then I came slithering home.

From *In Chimney Corners: Merry Tales of Irish Folk Lore*, by Seumas MacManus (New York: McClure, Phillips & Co., 1904).

Mary Cinderella

This Cinderella version from Chile presents a heroine who is passive and deferential, very much like Perrault's Cendrillon, yet, once she receives a magic wand, she becomes somewhat more active, and more closely resembles the Grimms' Aschenputtel as she pursues her own desires. This tale also incorporates several common motifs. One of these is the glass slipper, but the most prominent motif is the marking of the sisters, the placement a star on Maria's fore- head and a turkey crest on Sofia's as an outward symbol of each girl's inward qualities. 'Mary Cinderella' also presents two animal helpers, the familiar cow and a dog, whose role is reminiscent of that of the birds at the end of 'Aschenputtel'. Additionally, 'Mary Cinderella' includes a mysterious old female helper whose sudden appearance suggests her connection to the fairy godmother in Perrault's version.

Once upon a time there was a widower who had a daughter by the name of María. Every morning the girl used to go to her next door neighbour for embers with which to start her fire. The neighbour, a widow, would give her morsels of bread dipped in honey, saying: 'Tell your father to marry me and you will have honey-dipped bread the rest of your life.' The girl would go back to her father and say to him: 'Father, you should marry our neigh- bour; she is very kind and always gives me bread dipped in honey.'

2. Porridge

Her father would reply: 'No, María. Now she dips it in honey, but later she would dip it in gall.'

'I don't believe it, father,' the girl would insist. 'Our neighbour is so very kind.'

At last her father agreed to marry the woman, but he warned María not to complain if her stepmother should prove to be wicked.

The neighbour had a daughter of her own, whose name was Sofía. She was María's age. No sooner did the marriage take place than the woman began to beat and maltreat María, who was so much prettier than Sofía; she nicknamed her la Cenicienta, Cinderella, and put her to work in the kitchen dressed in old rags.

María Cenicienta owned a heifer calf with which she loved to play every free moment of the day. The envious woman persuaded her husband to buy a calf for her own daughter to play with, too, and eventually she demanded that he should have María's calf slaughtered because la Cenicienta wasted too much time playing with it. The father thought it best to give in for fear of further irritating his wife against the girl.

When María heard about this, she burst into tears and ran to her calf. While she petted it and fondled it, the calf said to her: 'Do not cry, María; the moment I am killed, you ask to wash my insides in the brook; next to my heart you will find a small magic wand which has the power to make all your wishes come true. Take it and keep it securely attached to your waist, so that no one may see it.'

The following day the calf was slaughtered and María went to the brook to wash the insides. Sure enough, she found the magic wand and hid it in her sash. When she had finished rinsing the insides and had placed them, nice and clean, in her washbasin, they slipped away and drifted down the stream. Terrified at the thought of the punishment that awaited her at the hand of her stepmother, she began to cry.

'Why are you crying, María,' said a kind voice in back of her. The girl turned about and saw a little old lady dressed in blue. 'Why should I not cry, my good lady?' answered María. 'My washbasin and the insides of a calf I just finished washing drifted down the stream; when my stepmother sees me come home without them, she is going to beat me to death.'

'Do not cry,' said the little old lady. 'Go to that cottage by the brook, lie down and sleep a while; in the meantime I shall look for what you have lost.'

María went to the cottage; she swept it, made a fire, and prepared supper for the little old lady and then she lay down and fell asleep. After some time there was a knocking at the door. She got up and went to open it: the washbasin and the insides were on the doorstep. She picked them up and went home.

'What took you so long?' asked the stepmother. María told her just what had happened, how the insides had slipped down the stream, how the little old lady had told her to go to the cottage and lie down while she would look for them, and how on waking up she had found them at the door.

'What is that on your forehead?' asked the stepmother.

'I don't know,' said María.

A mirror was brought to her and in it she saw a star shining on her forehead. The stepmother tried to rub it out, but the harder she rubbed the more the star would sparkle. Finally, she bandaged the girl's head with an old rag so that no one should see the shining star which made Cinderella stand out even more brightly next to her step-sister.

Sofía then said to her mother: 'Mother, I want to have my calf killed and I will do just as Cinderella did so that I, too, will have a star on my forehead.'

The woman had Sofía's calf killed; the girl went to the brook, began to wash the calf's insides, sent the washbasin down the stream, and then she pretended to cry. Immediately the little old woman in blue appeared and said: 'Why are you crying, little girl?' 'Should I not cry when my washbasin went down the stream?' said Sofía. 'Go and take a nap in that cottage by the brook,' said the little old lady, 'and when you wake up you will find your washbasin.'

The girl went to the cottage and said to herself, peevishly: 'Am I supposed to sleep in this dirty house, on that hard bed?' She sat down on a chair and waited. After some time, she went to the door and, finding her washbasin there, she took it and went home. When the mother saw her, she said: 'What is that on your forehead, Sofía?' A mirror was brought and the girl saw she had the crest of a turkey in the middle of her forehead. The mother tried to remove it but the harder she pulled, the larger and uglier the crest would grow. Finally, seeing that all her efforts were in vain, she bandaged her daughter's head in a silk kerchief.

One day there was to be a ball at the palace and María Cinderella, who wanted to go, took out her magic wand and wished for fine clothes, carriages, and servants, so that she might appear in grand style. Instantly her wish was granted and with those fine clothes she appeared even prettier than she had been before. When everyone in her house was fast asleep, she stepped into her carriage and soon arrived at the palace in such grand style that even the prince came out to see who was coming. The ballroom became suffused with the light of the star on María's forehead and the prince was so taken with her that all night long he danced with no one but her. When the time came for María to leave, she fled from the ballroom and ran to her carriage. The prince tried to follow her, but she was so quick that he could not catch up with her and was left holding one of the girl's glass slippers which she had lost in her flight.

The next morning the prince gave orders to all his servants to search the city for the girl who had worn the glass slipper, announcing that he wanted her, and no one else, for his wife. The servants went from house to house, but in vain: the slipper would fit no one.

When Cinderella's stepmother heard that the prince's servants were to stop at her house, she told her daughter to bandage her feet very tightly so that the slipper would fit her and that the prince would marry her. Fearing that they might see María with the star on her forehead, she hid her under the kneading trough.

Sofía had a little dog and when the prince's servants arrived and were trying the slipper on the girl's foot, the dog began calling out: 'Bow-wow-wow! A turkey crest upon the bench; a star beneath the kneading trough!' And as the dog kept repeating the same thing again and again, one of the servants became suspicious; he went to the kneading trough and lifted it, finding Cinderella. The servant tried the glass slipper on her: it fitted perfectly. Then Cinderella took out of her pocket the other slipper and put it on her other foot; she uncovered her forehead, showing her shining star, and everyone knew that she was the one who had danced with the prince the night before.

In spite of the stepmother's opposition, Cinderella was taken to the prince, who recognized her immediately. A royal wedding was arranged then and there and Cinderella and the prince lived happily ever after.

From *Folklore of Other Lands*, by Arthur M. Selvi, Lothar Kahn, and Robert C. Soule (New York: S.F. Vanni, 1956).

Conkiajgharuna

'Conkiajgharuna' (Little Rag Girl), a tale from Georgia, is built upon a series of tests. Most obviously, it concludes with the bridal shoe test that is prominent in many tales of the Cinderella cycle. Furthermore, the stepmother, eager to humiliate Conkiajgharuna, sets for her a series of seemingly impossible tests, such as gathering scattered millet, a test reminiscent of the lentil sorting in the Grimms' 'Aschenputtlel'. In addition to these formal, or announced, tests, there are also unwitting tests in which the participant is unaware that she is being tested. The unwitting tests occur when the *devi* woman (a human-like creature sometimes classified as a devil) asks the two girls to look at her head. 'Conkiajgharuna' is also notable for employing a series of female helpers—the cow, the *devi*, and the neighbour woman— yet the final scene of the tale shows the protagonist as an independent and active agent in determining her own fate.

*T*here was and there was not, there was a miserable peasant. He had a wife and a little daughter. So poor was this peasant that his daughter was called Conkiajgharuna[1] (the little girl in rags).

Some time passed, and his wife died. He was unhappy before, but now a greater misfortune had befallen him. He grieved and grieved, and at last he said to himself: 'I will go and take another wife; she will mind the house, and tend my orphan child.' So he arose and took a second wife, but this wife brought with her a daughter of her own. When this woman came into her husband's house and saw his child, she was angry in heart.

She treated Conkiajgharuna badly. She petted her own daughter, but scolded her stepdaughter, and tried to get rid of her. Every day she gave her a piece of badly cooked bread, and sent her out to watch the cow, saying: 'Here is a loaf; eat of it, give to every wayfarer, and bring the loaf home whole.' The girl went, and felt very miserable.

Once she was sitting sadly in the field, and began to weep bitterly. The cow listened, and then opened its mouth, and said: 'Why art thou weeping? what troubles thee?' The girl told her sad tale. The cow said: 'In one of my horns is honey, and in the other is butter, which thou canst take if thou wilt, so why be unhappy?' The girl took the butter and the honey, and in a short time she grew plump. When the stepmother noticed this she did not know what to do for rage. She rose, and after that every day she gave her a basket of wool with her; this wool was to be spun and brought home in the evening finished. The stepmother wished to tire the girl out with toil, so that she should grow thin and ugly.

Once when Conkiajgharuna was tending the cow, it ran away on to a roof.[2] The girl pursued it, and wished to drive it back to the road, but she dropped her spindle on the roof. Looking inside she saw an old woman seated, and said to her: 'Good mother, wilt thou give me my spindle?' The old dame replied: 'I am not able, my child, come and take it thyself.' This old woman was a *devi*.

---

1. The Georgian Cinderella or Tattercoats. Cf. Miss Roalfe Cox's *Story-Variants of Cinderella* for parallels.
2. In some parts of the Caucasus the houses of the peasantry are built in the ground, and it is quite possible to walk on to a roof unwittingly.

The girl went in and was lifting up her spindle, when the old dame called out: 'Daughter, daughter, come and look at my head a moment, I am almost eaten up.'

The girl came and looked at her head. She was filled with horror; all the worms in the earth seemed to be crawling there. The little girl stroked her head and removed some, and then said: 'Thou hast a clean head, why should I look at it?' This conduct pleased the old woman very much, and she said: 'When thou goest hence, go along such and such a road, and in a certain place thou wilt see three springs—one white, one black, and one yellow. Pass by the white and black, and put thy head in the yellow and lave it with thy hands.'

The girl did this. She went on her way, and came to the three springs. She passed by the white and black, and bathed her head with her hands in the yellow fountain. When she looked up she saw that her hair was quite golden, and her hands, too, shone like gold. In the evening, when she went home, her stepmother was filled with fury. After this she sent her own daughter with the cow. Perhaps the same good fortune would visit her!

So Conkiajgharuna stayed at home while her stepsister drove out the cow. Once more the cow ran on to the roof. The girl pursued it, and her spindle fell down. She looked in, and, seeing the *devi* woman, called out: 'Dog of an old woman! here! come and give me my spindle!' The old woman replied: 'I am not able, child, come and take it thyself.' When the girl came near, the old woman said: 'Come, child, and look at my head.' The girl came and looked at her head, and cried out: 'Ugh! what a horrid head thou hast! Thou art a disgusting old woman!' The old woman said: 'I thank thee, my child; when thou goest on thy way thou wilt see a yellow, a white, and a black spring. Pass by the yellow and the white springs, and lave thy head with thy hands in the black one.'

The girl did this. She passed by the yellow and white springs, and bathed her head in the black one. When she looked at herself she was black as a negro, and on her head there was a horn. She cut it off again and again, but it grew larger and larger.

She went home and complained to her mother, who was almost frenzied, but there was no help for it. Her mother said to herself: 'This is all the cow's fault, so it shall be killed.'

This cow knew the future. When it learned that it was to be killed, it went to Conkiajgharuna and said: 'When I am dead, gather my bones together and bury them in the earth. When thou art in trouble come to my grave, and cry aloud: "Bring my steed and my royal robes!"' Conkiajgharuna did exactly as the cow had told her. When it was dead she took its bones and buried them in the earth.

After this, some time passed. One holiday the stepmother took her daughter, and they went to church. She placed a trough in front of Conkiajgharuna, spread a *codi* (80 lbs) of millet in the courtyard, and said: 'Before we come home from church fill this trough with tears, and gather up this millet, so that not one grain is left.' Then they went to church.

Conkiajgharuna sat down and began to weep. While she was crying a neighbour came in and said: 'Why art thou in tears? what is the matter?' The little girl told her tale. The woman brought all the brood-hens and chickens, and they picked up every grain of millet, then she put a lump of salt in the trough and poured water over it. 'There, child,' said she, 'these are thy tears! Now go and enjoy thyself.'

Conkiajgharuna then thought of the cow. She went to its grave and called out: 'Bring me my steed and my royal robes!' There appeared at once a horse and beautiful clothes. Conkiajgharuna put on the garments, mounted the horse, and went to the church.

There all the folk began to stare at her. They were amazed at her grandeur. Her stepsister whispered to her mother when she saw her: 'This girl is very much like our Conkiajgharuna!' Her mother smiled scornfully and said: 'Who would give that sun-darkener such robes?'

Conkiajgharuna left the church before anyone else; she changed her clothes in time to appear before her stepmother in rags. On the way home, as she was leaping over a stream, in her haste she let her slipper fall in.

A long time passed. Once when the king's horses were drinking water in this stream, they saw the shining slipper, and were so afraid that they would drink no more water. The king was told that there was something shining in the stream, and that the horses were afraid.

The king commanded his divers to find out what it was. They found the golden slipper, and presented it to the king. When he saw it he commanded his viziers, saying: 'Go and seek the owner of this slipper, for I will wed none but her.' His viziers sought the maiden, but they could find no one whom the slipper would fit.

Conkiajgharuna's stepmother heard this, adorned her daughter, and placed her on a throne. Then she went and told the king that she had a daughter whose foot he might look at, it was exactly the model for the shoe. She put Conkiajgharuna in a corner, with a big basket over her. When the king came into the house he sat down on the basket, in order to try on the slipper.

Conkiajgharuna took a needle and pricked the king from under the basket. He jumped up, stinging with pain, and asked the stepmother what she had under the basket. The stepmother replied: "Tis only a turkey I have there.' The king sat down on the basket again, and Conkiajgharuna again stuck the needle into him. The king jumped up, and cried out: 'Lift the basket, I will see underneath!' The stepmother entreated him, saying: 'Do not blame me, your majesty, it is only a turkey, and it will run away.'

But the king would not listen to her entreaties. He lifted the basket up, and Conkiajgharuna came forth, and said: 'This slipper is mine, and fits me well.' She sat down, and the king found that it was indeed a perfect fit. Conkiajgharuna became the king's wife, and her shameless stepmother was left with a dry throat.

From *Georgian Folk Tales*, translated by Marjory Wardrop (London: David Nutt, 1894).

Vasilisa the Beautiful

The cruelty of the stepmother and stepsisters and the magical help provided by the dying birth mother are the two motifs that immediately mark this Russian tale as part of the Cinderella cycle. This tale also includes, however, a variation on another motif found in some Cinderella variants, the encounter with a strange old woman. In this case, Vasilisa does not encounter a benign helper. Instead, she undertakes a journey into the dark forest to confront a witch. Because Baba Yaga—a cannibalistic witch who appears in many Russian tales—lives in a house surrounded by human bones, Vasilisa's journey takes on the overtones of the mythic hero's journey to the underworld, a mythic connection further underscored by the riders symbolizing day and night. Vasilisa successfully completes her quest for fire because of magical help and her own developing wit. In the concluding stages of the story, Vasilisa, who has matured into a self-reliant woman, successfully passes an informal bridal test by sewing a fine shirt.

$\mathcal{L}$ong, long ago, in a certain tsardom there lived an old man and an old woman and their daughter Vasilisa. They had only a small hut for a home, but their life was a peaceful and happy one.

However, even the brightest of skies may become overcast, and misfortune stepped over their threshold at last. The old woman fell gravely ill and, feeling that her end was near, she called Vasilisa to her bedside, gave her a little doll, and said:

'Do as I tell you, my child. Take good care of this little doll and never show it to anyone. If ever anything bad happens to you, give the doll something to eat and ask its advice. It will help you out in all your troubles.'

And, giving Vasilisa a last, parting kiss, the old woman died.

The old man sorrowed and grieved for a time, and then he married again. He had thought to give Vasilisa a second mother, but he gave her a cruel stepmother instead.

The stepmother had two daughters of her own, two of the most spiteful, mean, and hard-to-please young women that ever lived. The stepmother loved them dearly and was always kissing and coddling them, but she nagged at Vasilisa and never let her have a moment's peace. Vasilisa felt very unhappy, for her stepmother and stepsisters kept chiding and scolding her and making her work beyond her strength. They hoped that she would grow thin and haggard with too much work and that her face would turn dark and ugly in the wind and sun. All day long they were at her, one or the other of them, shouting:

'Come, Vasilisa! Where are you, Vasilisa? Fetch the wood, don't be slow! Start a fire, mix the dough! Wash the plates, milk the cow! Scrub the floor, hurry now! Work away and don't take all day!'

Vasilisa did all she was told to do, she waited on everyone and always got her chores done on time. And with every day that passed she grew more and more beautiful. Such was her beauty as could not be pictured and could not be told, but was a true wonder and joy to behold. And it was her little doll that helped Vasilisa in everything.

Early in the morning Vasilisa would milk the cow and then, locking herself in the pantry, she would give some milk to the doll and say:

'Come, little doll, drink your milk, my dear, and I'll pour out all my troubles in your ear, your ear!'

And the doll would drink the milk and comfort Vasilisa and do all her work for her. Vasilisa would sit in the shade twining flowers into her braid and, before she knew it, the vegetable beds were weeded, the water brought in, the fire lighted, and the cabbage watered. The doll showed her a herb to be used against sunburn, and Vasilisa used it and became more beautiful than ever.

One day, late in the fall, the old man set out from home and was not expected back for some time.

The stepmother and the three sisters were left alone. They sat in the hut and it was dark outside and raining and the wind was howling. The hut stood at the edge of a dense forest and in the forest there lived Baba-Yaga, a cunning witch and sly, who gobbled people up in the wink of an eye.

Now to each of the three sisters the stepmother gave some work to do: the first she set to weaving lace, the second to knitting stockings, and Vasilisa to spinning yarn. Then, putting out all the lights in the house except for a single splinter of birch that burnt in the corner where the three sisters were working, she went to bed.

The splinter crackled and snapped for a time, and then went out.

'What are we to do?' cried the stepmother's two daughters. 'It is dark in the hut, and we must work. One of us will have to go to Baba-Yaga's house to ask for a light.'

'I'm not going,' said the elder of the two. 'I am making lace, and my needle is bright enough for *me* to see by.'

'I'm not going, either,' said the second. 'I am knitting stockings, and my two needles are bright enough for *me* to see by.'

Then, both of them shouting: 'Vasilisa is the one, she must go for the light! Go to Baba-Yaga's house this minute, Vasilisa!' they pushed Vasilisa out of the hut.

The blackness of night was about her, and the dense forest, and the wild wind. Vasilisa was frightened, she burst into tears and she took out her little doll from her pocket.

'O my dear little doll,' she said between sobs, 'they are sending me to Baba-Yaga's house for a light, and Baba-Yaga gobbles people up, bones and all.'

'Never you mind,' the doll replied, 'you'll be all right. Nothing bad can happen to you while I'm with you.'

'Thank you for comforting me, little doll,' said Vasilisa, and she set off on her way.

About her the forest rose like a wall and, in the sky above, there was no sign of the bright crescent moon and not a star shone.

Vasilisa walked along trembling and holding the little doll close.

All of a sudden whom should she see but a man on horseback, galloping past. He was clad all in white, his horse was white, and the horse's harness was of silver and gleamed white in the darkness.

It was dawning now, and Vasilisa trudged on, stumbling and stubbing her toes against tree roots and stumps. Drops of dew glistened on her long plait of hair and her hands were cold and numb.

Suddenly another horseman came galloping by. He was dressed in red, his horse was red, and the horse's harness was red too.

The sun rose, it kissed Vasilisa and warmed her and dried the dew on her hair.

Vasilisa never stopped but walked on for a whole day, and it was getting on toward evening when she came out on to a small glade.

She looked, and she saw a hut standing there. The fence round the hut was made of human bones and crowned with human skulls. The gate was no gate but the bones of men's legs, the bolts were no bolts but the bones of men's arms, and the lock was no lock but a set of sharp teeth.

Vasilisa was horrified and stood stock-still. Suddenly a horseman came riding up. He was dressed in black, his horse was black, and the horse's harness was black too. The horseman galloped up to the gate and vanished as if into thin air.

Night descended, and lo! the eyes of the skulls crowning the fence began to glow, and it became as light as if it was day.

Vasilisa shook with fear. She could not move her feet which seemed to have frozen to the spot and refused to carry her away from this terrible place.

All of a sudden, she felt the earth trembling and rocking beneath her, and there was Baba-Yaga flying up in a mortar, swinging her pestle like a whip and sweeping the tracks away with a broom. She flew up to the gate and, sniffing the air, cried:

'I smell Russian flesh! Who is here?'

Vasilisa came up to Baba-Yaga, bowed low to her and said very humbly:

'It is I, Vasilisa, Grandma. My stepsisters sent me to you to ask for a light.'

'Oh, it's you, is it?' Baba-Yaga replied. 'Your stepmother is a kinswoman of mine. Very well, then, stay with me for a while and work, and then we'll see what is to be seen.'

And she shouted at the top of her voice:

'Come unlocked, my bolts so strong! Open up, my gate so wide!'

Irina Zheleznova, trans., 'Vasilisa the Beautiful', *Vasilisa the Beautiful: Russian Fairy Tales*. (Moscow: Progress Publishers, 1966), 11.

The gate swung open, Baba-Yaga rode in in her mortar and Vasilisa walked in behind her. Now at the gate there grew a birch-tree and it made as if to lash Vasilisa with its branches. 'Do not touch the maid, birch-tree, it was I who brought her,' said Baba-Yaga. They came to the house, and at the door there lay a dog and it made as if to bite Vasilisa.

'Do not touch the maid, it was I who brought her,' said Baba-Yaga.

They came inside and in the passage an old grumbler-rumbler of a cat met them and made as if to scratch Vasilisa.

'Do not touch the maid, you old grumbler-rumbler of a cat, it was I who brought her,' said Baba-Yaga.

'You see, Vasilisa,' she added, turning to her, 'it is not easy to run away from me. My cat will scratch you, my dog will bite you, my birch-tree will lash you, and put out your eyes, and my gate will not open to let you out.'

Baba-Yaga came into her room, and she stretched out on a bench. 'Come, black-browed maid, give us something to eat,' she cried. And the black-browed maid ran in and began to feed Baba-Yaga. She brought her a pot of *borshch* and half a cow, ten jugs of milk and a roasted sow, twenty chickens and forty geese, two whole pies and an extra piece, cider and mead and home-brewed ale, beer by the barrel and *kvass* by the pail.

Baba-Yaga ate and drank up everything, but she only gave Vasilisa a chunk of bread.

'And now, Vasilisa,' said she, 'take this sack of millet and pick it over seed by seed. And mind that you take out all the black bits, for if you don't I shall eat you up.'

And Baba-Yaga closed her eyes and began to snore.

Vasilisa took the piece of bread, put it before her little doll and said:

'Come, little doll, eat this bread, my dear, and I'll pour out all my troubles in your ear, your ear! Baba-Yaga has given me a hard task to do, and she threatens to eat me up if I do not do it.'

Said the doll in reply:

'Do not grieve and do not weep, but close your eyes and go to sleep. For morning is wiser than evening.'

And the moment Vasilisa was asleep, the doll called out in a loud voice:

> 'Tomtits, pigeons, sparrows, hear me,
> There is work to do, I fear me.
> On your help, my feathered friends,
> Vasilia's life depends.
> Come in answer to my call,
> You are needed, one and all.'

And the birds came flying from all sides, flocks and flocks of them, more than eye could see or tongue could tell. They began to chirp and to coo, to set up a great to-do, and to pick over the millet seed by seed very quickly indeed. Into the sack the good seeds went, and the black went into the crop, and before they knew it the night was spent, and the sack was filled to the top.

They had only just finished when the white horseman galloped past the gate on his white horse. Day was dawning.

Baba-Yaga woke up and asked:

'Have you done what I told you to do, Vasilisa?'

'Yes, it's all done, Grandma.'

Baba-Yaga was very angry, but there was nothing more to be said.

'Humph,' she snorted, 'I am off to hunt and you take that sack yonder, it's filled with peas and poppy seeds, pick out the peas from the seeds and put them in two separate heaps. And mind, now, if you do not do it, I shall eat you up.'

Baba-Yaga went out into the yard and whistled, and the mortar and pestle swept up to her.

The red horseman galloped past, and the sun rose.

Baba-Yaga got into the mortar and rode out of the yard, swinging her pestle like a whip and whisking the tracks away with a broom.

Vasilisa took a crust of bread, fed her little doll and said:

'Do take pity on me, little doll, my dear, and help me out.'

And the doll called out in ringing tones:

'Come to me, o mice of the house, the barn and the field, for there is work to be done!'

And the mice came running, swarms and swarms of them, more than eye could see or tongue could tell, and before the hour was up the work was all done.

It was getting on toward evening, and the black-browed maid set the table and began to wait for Baba-Yaga's return.

The black horseman galloped past the gate, night fell, and the eyes of the skulls crowning the fence began to glow. And now the trees groaned and crackled, the leaves rustled, and Baba-Yaga, the cunning witch and sly, who gobbled people up in the wink of an eye, came riding home.

'Have you done what I told you to do, Vasilisa?' she asked.

'Yes, it's all done, Grandma.'

Baba-Yaga was very angry, but what could she say!

'Well, then, go to bed. I am going to turn in myself in a minute.'

Vasilisa went behind the stove, and she heard Baba-Yaga say:

'Light the stove, black-browed maid, and make the fire hot. When I wake up, I shall roast Vasilisa.'

And Baba-Yaga lay down on a bench, placed her chin on a shelf, covered herself with her foot, and began to snore so loudly that the whole forest trembled and shook.

Vasilisa burst into tears and, taking out her doll, put a crust of bread before it.

'Come, little doll, have some bread, my dear, and I'll pour out all my troubles in your ear, your ear. For Baba-Yaga wants to roast me and to eat me up,' said she.

And the doll told her what she must do to get out of trouble without more ado.

Vasilisa rushed to the black-browed maid and bowed low to her.

'Please, black-browed maid, help me!' she cried. 'When you are lighting the stove, pour water over the wood so it does not burn the way it should. Here is my silken kerchief for you to reward you for your trouble.'

Said the black-browed maid in reply:

'Very well, my dear, I shall help you. I shall take a long time heating the stove, and I shall tickle Baba-Yaga's heels and scratch them too so she may sleep very soundly the whole night through. And you run away, Vasilisa!'

'But won't the three horsemen catch me and bring me back?'

'Oh, no,' replied the black-browed maid. 'The white horseman is the bright day, the red horseman is the golden sun, and the black horseman is the black night, and they will not touch you.'

Vasilisa ran out into the passage, and Grumbler-Rumbler the Cat rushed at her and was about to scratch her. But she threw him a pie, and he did not touch her.

Vasilisa ran down from the porch, and the dog darted out and was about to bite her. But she threw him a piece of bread, and the dog let her go.

Vasilisa started running out of the yard, and the birch-tree tried to lash her and to put out her eyes. But she tied it with a ribbon, and the birch-tree let her pass.

The gate was about to shut before her, but Vasilisa greased its hinges, and it swung open.

Vasilisa ran into the dark forest, and just then the black horseman galloped by and it became pitch black all around. How was she to go back home without a light? What would she say? Why, her stepmother would do her to death.

So she asked her little doll to help her and did what the doll told her to do.

She took one of the skulls from the fence and, mounting it on a stick, set off across the forest. Its eyes glowed, and by their light the dark night was as bright as day.

As for Baba-Yaga, she woke up and stretched and, seeing that Vasilisa was gone, rushed out into the passage.

'Did you scratch Vasilisa as she ran past, Grumbler-Rumbler?' she demanded.

And the cat replied:

'No, I let her pass, for she gave me a pie. I served you for ten years, Baba-Yaga, but you never gave me so much as a crust of bread.'

Baba-Yaga rushed out into the yard.

'Did you bite Vasilisa, my faithful dog?' she demanded.

Said the dog in reply:

'No, I let her pass, for she gave me some bread. I served you for ever so many years, but you never gave me so much as a bone."

'Birch-tree, birch-tree!' Baba-Yaga roared. 'Did you put out Vasilisa's eyes for her?'

Said the birch-tree in reply:

'No, I let her pass, for she bound my branches with a ribbon. I have been growing here for ten years, and you never even tied them with a string.'

Baba-Yaga ran to the gate.

'Gate, gate!' she cried. 'Did you shut before her that Vasilisa might not pass?'

Said the gate in reply:

'No, I let her pass, for she greased my hinges. I served you for ever so long, but you never even put water on them.'

Baba-Yaga flew into a temper. She began to beat the dog and thrash the cat, to break down the gate and to chop down the birch-tree, and she was so tired by then that she forgot all about Vasilisa.

Vasilisa ran home, and she saw that there was no light on in the house. Her stepsisters rushed out and began to chide and scold here.

'What took you so long fetching the light?" they demanded. 'We cannot seem to keep one on in the house at all. We have tried to strike a light again and again but to no avail, and the one we got from the neighbours went out the moment it was brought in. Perhaps yours will keep burning.'

They brought the skull into the hut, and its eyes fixed themselves on the stepmother and her two daughters and burnt them like fire. The stepmother and her daughters tried to hide but, run where they would, the eyes followed them and never let them out of their sight.

By morning they were burnt to a cinder, all three, and only Vasilisa remained unharmed.

She buried the skull outside the hut, and a bush of red roses grew up on the spot.

After that, not liking to stay in the hut any longer, Vasilisa went into the town and made her home in the house of an old woman.

One day she said to the old woman:

'I am bored sitting around doing nothing, Grandma. Buy me some flax, the best you can find.'

The old woman bought her some flax, and Vasilisa set to spinning yarn. She worked quickly and well, the spinning-wheel humming and the golden thread coming out as even and thin as a hair. She began to weave cloth, and it turned out so fine that it could be passed through the eye of a needle, like a thread. She bleached the cloth, and it came out whiter than snow.

'Here, Grandma,' said she, 'go and sell the cloth and take the money for yourself.'

The old woman looked at the cloth and gasped.

'No, my child, such cloth is only fit for a Tsarevich to wear. I had better take it to the palace.'

She took the cloth to the palace, and when the Tsarevich saw it, he was filled with wonder.

'How much do you want for it?' he asked.

'This cloth is too fine to be sold, I have brought it to you for a present.'

The Tsarevich thanked the old woman, showered her with gifts, and sent her home.

But he could not find anyone to make him a shirt out of the cloth, for the workmanship had to be as fine as the fabric. So he sent for the old woman again and said:

'You wove this fine cloth, so you must know how to make a shirt out of it.'

'It was not I that spun the yarn or wove the cloth, Tsarevich, but a maid named Vasilisa.'

'Well, then, let her make me a shirt.'

The old woman went home, and she told Vasilisa all about it.

Vasilisa made two shirts, embroidered them with silken threads, studded them with large, round pearls and, giving them to the old woman to take to the palace, sat down at the window with a piece of embroidery.

By and by whom should she see but one of the Tsar's servants come running toward her.

'The Tsarevich bids you come to the palace,' said the servant.

Vasilisa went to the palace and, seeing her, the Tsarevich was smith with her beauty.

'I cannot bear to let you go away again, you shall be my wife,' said he.

He took both her milk-white hands in his and he placed her in the seat beside his own.

And so Vasilisa and the Tsarevich were married, and, when Vasilisa's father returned soon afterwards, he made his home in the palace with them.

Vasilisa took the old woman to live with her too, and as for her little doll, she always carried it about with her in her pocket.

And thus are they living to this very day, waiting for us to come for a stay.

From *Vasilisa the Beautiful: Russian Fairy Tales*, edited by Irina Zheleznova (Moscow: Progress Publishers, 1966).

The Indian Cinderella

This Native tale from the Canadian East Coast may, as Charles Leland, Stith Thompson, and others have argued, show the influence of European stories told in North America during the eighteenth and early nineteenth centuries. The connection to European tales is certainly evident in the abuse the girl suffers from her two sisters, her connection to the fire and ashes, and her birch bark clothing, which is reminiscent of that in 'Cap o' Rushes'. The bridal test, however, depends on qualities other than beauty. It thus reflects the values of Native peoples, for whom marriage defined roles necessary for survival: males hunted for materials necessary to sustain life, while females prepared the products of the hunt, cooking them or making them into clothing. As a result, marriage required the man and the woman to be able to trust each other to perform their respective duties. Another possible Native element may be found in the punishment of the wicked sisters, whose transformation into trees that shiver in the wind turns the conclusion into that of a *pourquoi* tale.

On the shores of a wide bay on the Atlantic coast there dwelt in old times a great Indian warrior. It was said that he had been one of Glooskap's best helpers and friends, and that he had done for him many wonderful deeds. But that, no man knows. He had, however, a very wonderful and strange power; he could make himself invisible; he could thus mingle unseen with his enemies and listen to their plots. He was known among the people as Strong Wind, the Invisible. He dwelt with his sister in a tent near the sea, and his sister helped him greatly in his work. Many maidens would have been glad to marry him, and he was much sought after because of his mighty deeds; and it was known that Strong Wind would marry the first maiden who could see him as he came home at night. Many made the trial, but it was a long time before one succeeded.

Strong Wind used a clever trick to test the truthfulness of all who sought to win him. Each evening as the day went down, his sister walked on the beach with any girl who wished to make the trial. His sister could always see him, but no one else could see him. And as he came home from work in the twilight, his sister as she saw him drawing near would ask the girl who sought him, 'Do you see him?' And each girl would falsely answer 'Yes.' And his sister would ask, 'With what does he draw his sled?' And each girl would answer, 'With the hide of a moose', or, 'With a pole', or 'With a great cord'. And then his sister would know that they all had lied, for their answers were mere guesses. And many tried and lied and failed, for Strong Wind would not marry any who were untruthful.

There lived in the village a great chief who had three daughters. Their mother had long been dead. One of these was much younger than the others. She was very beautiful and gentle and well beloved by all, and for that reason her older sisters were very jealous of her charms and treated her very cruelly. They clothed her in rags that she might be ugly; and they cut off her long black hair; and they burned her face with coals from the fire that she might be scarred and disfigured. And they lied to their father, telling him that she had done these things herself. But the young girl was patient and kept her gentle heart and went gladly about her work.

Like other girls, the chief's two eldest daughters tried to win Strong Wind. One evening, as the day went down, they walked on the shore with Strong Wind's sister and waited for his coming. Soon he came home from his day's work, drawing his sled. And his sister asked as usual, 'Do you see him?' And each one, lying, answered 'Yes.' And she asked, 'Of what is his shoulder strap made?' And each, guessing, said 'Of rawhide'. Then they entered the tent where they hoped to see Strong Wind eating his supper; and when he took off his coat and his moccasins they could see them, but more than these they saw nothing. And Strong Wind knew that they had lied, and he kept himself from their sight, and they went home dismayed.

One day the chief's youngest daughter with her rags and her burnt face resolved to seek Strong Wind. She patched her clothes with bits of birch bark from the trees, and put on the few little ornaments she possessed, and went forth to try to see the Invisible One as all the other girls of the village had done before. And her sisters laughed at her and called her 'fool';

Cyrus Macmillan, 'The Indian Cinderella', *Canadian Wonder Tales*. Illustrated by George Sheringham. (London: John Lane, 1918), facing 118.

and as she passed along the road all the people laughed at her because of her tattered frock and her burnt face, but silently she went her way.

Strong Wind's sister received the little girl kindly, and at twilight she took her to the beach. Soon Strong Wind came home drawing his sled. And his sister asked, 'Do you see him?' And the girl answered 'No,' and his sister wondered greatly because she spoke the truth. And again she asked, 'Do you see him now?' And the girl answered, 'Yes, and he is very wonderful.' And she asked, 'With what does he draw his sled?' And the girl answered, 'With the Rainbow', and she was much afraid. And she asked further, 'Of what is his bowstring?' And the girl answered, 'His bowstring is the Milky Way.'

Then Strong Wind's sister knew that because the girl had spoken the truth at first her brother had made himself visible to her. And she said, 'Truly, you have seen him.' And she took her home and bathed her, and all the scars disappeared from her face and body; and her hair grew long and black again like the raven's wing; and she gave her fine clothes to wear and many rich ornaments. Then she bade her take the wife's seat in the tent. Soon Strong Wind entered and sat beside her, and called her his bride. The very next, day she became his wife, and ever afterwards she helped him to do great deeds. The girl's two elder sisters were very cross and they wondered greatly at what had taken place. But Strong Wind, who knew of their cruelty, resolved to punish them. Using his great power, he changed them both into aspen trees and rooted them in the earth. And since that day the leaves of the aspen have always trembled, and they shiver in fear at the approach of Strong Wind, it matters not how softly he comes, for they are still mindful of his great power and anger because of their lies and their cruelty to their sister long ago.

From *Canadian Wonder Tales*, by Cyrus Macmillan (London: John Lane, 1918).

Benizara and Kakezara

Although they did not become known in the West until the second half of the twentieth century, numerous versions of the Cinderella tale exist throughout Japan. 'Benizara and Kakezara', a version relatively well-known in Japan, falls into two distinct but related parts. The first establishes Benizara as a victim of her stepmother's cruelty and provides her with a magical means of escape, the box that the mother of the *oni* gives her. (*Oni* are malicious ogres who are basically human in shape, but they have both tusks and horns, and their skin is brightly hued, usually red or blue.) The second part shows Benizara using her magic aid and undergoing the requisite identity test. The test in this tale is unusual within the Cinderella cycle because it does not turn on a proof of physical beauty, as in shoe tests, but on a contest of talent. In this contest, Kakezara, whose name means Broken Dish, sings a bland and unmetrical song that reveals her lack of imagination. In contrast, Benizara, whose name means Crimson Dish, a name that suggests good fortune because it includes the colour red, sings a song that translates the banal subject into a meaningful metaphor. Furthermore, she employs the correct 5–7–5–7–7 syllable arrangement of the Japanese poetic form known as *tanka*.

ong ago in a certain place there were two sisters. One was named Benizara, 'Crimson Dish' and the other Kakezara, 'Broken Dish'. Benizara was a former wife's child, while Kakezara was the stepmother's child. Benizara was a very honest and gentle girl, but her stepmother was very cruel to her.

One day she sent the two girls out to gather chestnuts. She gave Benizara a bag with a hole in the bottom, but she gave Kakezara a good one. 'You must not come back until you have each filled your bag,' she said.

The two set off for the mountains and began to pick up chestnuts. Before long Kakezara's bag was full, and she returned home, leaving Benizara alone. Benizara was an honest girl, and so she worked as hard as she could picking up chestnuts until it began to get dark. It got darker and darker, and she thought she heard a rustling sound, *gasa gasa*, as though a wolf were coming toward her. She suddenly realized how dangerous it was and ran off without even looking where she was going. In the meantime it had become very dark, and she was completely lost. She was filled with despair, but she knew that it would do no good to cry; so she kept on walking, thinking that perhaps she might find a house. Suddenly just ahead she saw a light. She went to where it was and found an old woman alone spinning thread. Benizara explained that she had gone to gather chestnuts but that it was late and she couldn't return home; then she asked if she might please stay overnight there.

The old woman said: 'I would like to let you stay here, but both my sons are *oni*. They will soon be coming home and would eat up anyone they found here. Instead, I will tell you how to find your way home.' And she carefully explained which road to take. Then she filled her bag with chestnuts and gave her a little box and a handful of rice. 'Take the chestnuts to your mother. This little box is a magic box; if there is ever anything that you need, just say what you would like, then tap on the box three times and what you want will appear. Now if you meet my *oni* sons on your way home, chew some of the rice and spread it around your mouth; then lie down and pretend that you are dead.'

Benizara thanked her for everything and started for home on the road she had been told to take. After a while she heard the sound of a flute coming toward her. She chewed some of the rice and spread it around her mouth, then lay down by the side of the road and pretended that she was dead. Soon a red *oni* and a blue *oni* came along. 'Hey, older brother, I smell human beings,' said one and went over to the side of the road to look. 'It's no good, older brother, she's already rotten. Her mouth is full of worms,' he said. And they went on down the road blowing their flutes.

Benizara listened to the sound of the flutes growing fainter and fainter in the distance; then she continued on down the road that she had been told to take.

Soon morning came. At home her stepmother was thinking to herself that during the night the wolves would have surely eaten Benizara, when just then the girl arrived home. Far from being dead, she had a whole bag full of chestnuts; so the stepmother had nothing to scold her about.

One day some time after this a play was to be given in the village. The stepmother took Kakezara and went to see it, giving Benizara a great deal of work which had to be done before they returned home. Benizara was working as hard as she could, when some of her friends came and asked her to go with them to see the play. Benizara said that her stepmother had given her so much work to do that she could not go, but her friends said, 'We will help you and then you can go,' and so, all working together, they soon finished a whole day's work.

Her friends were all wearing beautiful kimonos, but Benizara had nothing but rags to wear. She wondered what she should do; then she thought about the little box she had received from the old woman in the mountains. She took it out and said that she would like to have a kimono. She was given a beautiful kimono. She put it on and went to see the play. When she got there, Kakezara was begging her mother for some candies and Benizara threw her some. When she did this, a nobleman who had come to see the performance of the play saw what happened.

The next day the nobleman's colourful procession came to the village. The lord's palanquin stopped in front of Benizara's house. Kakezara's mother was overjoyed and dressed Kakezara in her very best to meet him. The lord got out of the palanquin and said, 'There should be two girls here; bring out the other one too.'

The stepmother had put Benizara in the bath tub to hide her, but there was nothing she could do but obey the lord's command, and so she brought her out. In comparison to Kakezara, Benizara looked very shabby, but the lord said, 'Which one of these two came to see the performance of the play yesterday?'

'It was this one, Kakezara.'

'No, it wasn't that one,' said the lord, but the mother kept insisting that it was. Finally it was decided to ask each of them to compose a song. The lord took a plate and put it on a tray; then he piled some salt in the plate and stuck a pine needle in it. He commanded that they each compose a poem, using that as a subject.

In a loud voice Kakezara sang,

> 'Put a plate on a tray,
> Put some salt on the plate,
> Stick a pine needle in the salt;
> It'll soon fall over.'

Then she hit the lord on the head and ran off. Next Benizara sang,

> 'A tray and plate, oh!
> A mountain rises from the plate,
> On it, snow has fallen.
> Rooted deep into the snow,
> A lonely pine tree grows.'

When he heard this song, the lord praised it very highly. Preparations were soon made, and Benizara was put into a beautiful palanquin; then she rode off to the lord's palace.

Kakezara's mother watched in silence; then she put Kakezara in a huge empty basket, saying, 'Now, Kakezara, you too may go to the lord's palace.' She dragged her along, but she did it so violently that Kakezara tumbled over the edge of a deep ditch and fell to her death.

From *Folktales of Japan*, by Keigo Seki, translated by Robert J. Adams (Chicago: University of Chicago Press, 1963).

LINKS TO OTHER STORIES
The Frog Maiden, 331

Part Two

Creating and Shaping the World
The Mythic Vision

Although it may be incorrect to speak of universal psychological traits, behaviours, and needs of human beings, it is a fact that cultures from around the world have asked similar questions about the physical and spiritual environments in which they have found themselves. 'How was the world created?' 'Who created it and when?' 'How did it acquire its present characteristics?' 'How did the geography, the plants, and the animals acquire their present natures?' 'What are the sun, moon, planets, and stars?' 'Why do people die?' 'What relationship do human beings have with supernatural powers or beings, and how is that relationship connected to one with the natural environment?'

Fairly frequently various cultures have formulated their answers as narratives, or rather, as stories involving characters in conflict. Some modern people view these narratives as a kind of pre-science. They argue that, lacking a scientific methodology and the tools for empirical investigation, these apparently simple and often superstitious people discovered in these types of stories—particularly in the motivations of characters and the consequences of their actions—profoundly convincing and sometimes comforting answers to questions about life.

To people with this attitude, the explanatory narratives of many early cultures are myths in the pejorative and demeaning sense of the word. That is, these narratives are viewed as obviously untrue, made up of characters and events to which no intelligent person should give credence. They are considered to be amusing narrative artifacts of benighted peoples who didn't know any better. This type of attitude was not only held by so-called civilized individuals about cultures that they deemed to be inferior, but was also applied to the religious stories of other cultures. Their own stories were part of a true religion; the others were 'myths', and so not true.

However, a study of stories from a variety of cultures reveals that for the originating cultures mythic narratives contain an intensity of belief concerning not only the events recounted but also the existence and great power of the supernatural beings involved in them. In this sense, any story embodying a culture's religious credos and depicting episodes of the supernatural beings who, it believes, once lived on earth or who are still present in some way can also be called myths. It is, to use Alan Dundes' term, a 'sacred narrative'. It is part of the religious history of a culture, which, joined with other sacred narratives of that culture, forms a mythology. In other words, a mythology is a connected series of narratives that contain the culture's spiritual values.

A study of some of the creation myths indicates why they have been considered so important for their cultures. Not only do they provide answers to questions of the type noted above, but they also provide these answers in ways that create emotionally, spiritually, psychologically, morally, and imaginatively satisfying frameworks with which to give shape and meaning to people's lives as members of a specific group.

Since the ancient Greeks, philosophers and theorists have advanced many explanations on the nature and origin of the creation myths in a variety of cultures. As early as the third century BC Euhemeris suggested that myths were based on historical events and individuals and that, over generations of retelling, the characters acquired divine status. For other Greeks, the myths embodied moral qualities allegorically presented through characters and actions. Asserting that human nature is the same everywhere, more recent thinkers have suggested that the narratives are the results of people projecting basic emotions and inner concerns onto larger than life beings. Still others see many myths as attempts to explain the beginnings of religious rituals (Bidney 3–24).

Certainly, myths do not explain the world so much as they embody a culture's way of looking at its natural and supernatural environments. In a sense, myths are comforting. Even if the supernatural beings are terrifying, they seem to behave in ways familiar to the culture portraying them. Moreover, as philosopher Ernst Cassirer has suggested, myths contain a vitality not always found in abstract scientific explanations of the world: 'The world of myth is a dramatic world—a world of action, of forces, of conflicting power. In every phenomenon of nature it sees the collision of these powers. Mythical perception is always impregnated with these emotional qualities' (84). The French anthropologist Claude Levi-Strauss stated that myths provided reconciliations between strong, conflicting emotions; in myths, opposing forces achieve harmony (Bidney 81–106).

Because a mythology explains the creation and shaping of the world; the interrelationship between supernatural and human beings; the causes of sin, disease, and death; and the eventual end of the world as it currently exists, it is a kind of sacred world history, an almost encyclopedic account of life from the beginning to the end of time, at least according to the culture that creates and perpetuates the mythology.

The most widely found subject presented in mythology explains the creation of the world. Raymond Van Over, in the introduction to his anthology *Sun Songs: Creation Myths from Around the World*, lists six categories of these narratives: 'The idea of a primeval abyss (which is sometimes simply space but often is an infinite watery deep. . . . (2) The originating god (or gods) is frequently awakened or eternally existing in this abyss. . . . (3) The original god broods over the water. (4) Another common theme is the cosmic egg or embryo. . . . (5) Life was created through sound, or a sacred word spoken by the original god. . . . (6) A peculiar theme, but quite common, is the creation of life from the corpse or parts of the primeval god's body' (10). Of the creation myths included in this section, 'How Light and Life Came into the World' and 'Heaven and Earth' are of the second type, whereas 'The Creation and the First Sin' is from the fifth category. Each of these stories also examines the creation of the heavenly bodies and the origins of the various creatures of earth.

In addition, many cultures possessed narratives that explained the seasonal cycles on which the production of food depended and the relationships between the hunters and their prey. The myth of Sedna is an Inuit embodiment of narratives that hunting cultures tell to reinforce the importance of establishing and maintaining grateful and respectful relationships with the spirit powers; a successful hunt depends on their good will. For the ancient Greeks and several North American Native cultures, the alternation of the warmer and colder periods that affected plant growth was determined by the actions of powerful spirit beings. An extended winter could bring death to the people. In Egypt, the annual flooding of the Nile that, for centuries, provided the water necessary for the growth of plants is linked to the tears shed by the grieving goddess Isis as she searched for her mate, Osiris.

From early oral narratives to such recent motion pictures as *Quest for Fire* (1981) and *Cast Away* (2000), the acquisition of fire has been a frequent subject matter of myths. Depending on climactic conditions, people have needed the element to provide warmth, light, and a way of cooking food. As both of these films and the Greek myth of Prometheus make clear, however, the successful quest for fire does more than fulfill physical needs; it marks a stage in human development. It is an achievement that emphasizes human dignity and sense of well being.

In the included fire myth selections a general narrative pattern is evident. For a variety of reasons, the people need fire but do not have it. Sometimes they fear fire; at other times it is in the possession of a powerful, often feared individual, who guards it jealously and will not share. The fire is acquired by an individual, not infrequently a culture hero, who exhibits both bravery and cleverness in making a dangerous journey to the possessor's home. There he uses trickery and, on some occasions, magical powers to achieve success.

Three of the myths included in this section deal with fundamental questions of human life: the presence of disease and sin and the inevitability of death. For the ancient Greeks, it was Pandora, a woman created by the gods, who, motivated by curiosity, opened a jar that contained 'madness, vice, old age, and crippling sickness'—forces that would beset the human beings who had recently been created by the titan Prometheus. In the Bible, the actions of Eve, succumbing to the temptations of the cunning serpent, brought about the sorrows that plague her descendents and make death inevitable. Among the Kiowa people of North America, Saynday, the trickster-hero, accepting the advice of a female red ant, agrees that death should be permanent. In each of these stories, the troubles originate because of the actions and personalities of specific individuals: Zeus' anger, Prometheus' sense of responsibility, Pandora's curiosity, Eve's 'foolish and wicked' actions, and the red ant's lack of foresight about the effects that the death of a loved one would have on her.

Although there are similarities in the plot structures and subject matters of these creation myths it should be remembered that each is an outgrowth of a specific culture and that, as such, it reflects the values and beliefs of that culture. For example, the Biblical narrative about the fall and the Greek myth about Pandora both portray the disastrous consequences of a woman's actions. However, in the former, the emphasis is on the blame attached to a woman's actions. The story of Pandora, which is linked to that of Prometheus, makes her a pawn in the intense psychological conflicts between powerful male deities. Considering the differences in the relationships between the women and the males (mortal and immortal) in the two stories, it would be a mistake to call Pandora the Greek 'Eve'. The Greek woman is a pawn in Zeus' plans to punish Prometheus; Eve is part of the grand design in Biblical history; her actions lead to the fall of human beings and make necessary the sacrificial death of Christ.

An awareness of cultural differences is an important requirement for the retellers of traditional myths. Adaptors must treat the narratives and the originating cultures with both knowledge and respect. The stories must not be viewed as being slightly different versions of tales from the adaptor's culture, differing only in superficial details such as costume and geographical features. Only by understanding what the narrative details meant to the originating cultures can writers transmit the meanings of the stories and, in doing so, broaden their audiences' understanding of other people. For example, Sedna, in Inuit culture, is not only a powerful sea goddess. Before her transformation, she was also a woman who went against her culture's norms and refused to marry. Her actions are not just personal foolishness; they represent the rejection of a relationship that was essential to the successful functioning of the family unit.

It is not sufficient merely to present cultural details accurately; the narratives must also be treated with respect. Early in the twentieth century, some retellers used the words 'odd' and 'superstitious' when describing other peoples and their beliefs, implying that the intended, usually European, audience was superior to the people whose story it was hearing or reading. It should be remembered that although some myths, such as those of the ancient Greeks, no longer form the basis of cultural and spiritual beliefs, others still do. As such, they should not be treated lightly or disrespectfully. The myths from within a young reader's culture forms part of his or her socialization process; those from other cultures provide opportunities for learning about different peoples.

It has been said jokingly that many children's favourite words are interrogative: who, why, what, when, how, and where. One of the satisfactions of creation and shaping myths arises from the fact that they provide answers to questions in an entertaining narrative form. Although the answers frequently deal with spiritual conflicts and supernatural beings, the answers are presented in terms of human motivations recognizable to young readers. When the characters are well-developed, the dynamic forces convincingly communicated, and the beliefs embodied portrayed accurately and respectfully, adapted versions of the great myths entertain and enlighten young readers about themselves and about the other people with whom they share the world.

Works Cited

Bidney, David. 1958. 'Myth, Symbolism, and Truth', in *Myth: a Symposium*, edited by Thomas A. Sebeok. Bloomington, IN: Indiana University Press.

Cassirer, Ernst. 1970. *An Essay on Man: an Introduction to a Philosophy of Human Culture*. New York: Bantam Books.

Dundas, Alan, ed. 1984. *Sacred Narrative: Readings in the Theory of Myth*. Berkeley: University of California Press.

Levi-Strauss, Claude. 1958. 'The Structural Study of Myth', in *Myth: a Symposium*, edited by Thomas A. Sebeok. Bloomington, IN: Indiana University Press.

Van Over, Raymond, ed. 1980. *Sun Songs: Creation Myths from Around the World*. New York: New American Library.

How Life and Light Came Into the World

In this creation myth of the Chibcha, the main pre-contact eastern Andean culture group of what is now Columbia, the movement is from dark to light. Nemequene, the father of a divine nuclear family that is living in desolation, fails in his first attempt to create living creatures out of mud. The warmth and light of the sun, combined with vegetation and water, are necessary for the various forms of animal life to survive. It is interesting to note the human motivations attributed to the creator in this simple narrative. Nemequene wishes not only to create life, but also to provide the necessary light and warmth. He is willing to assume a helping role, and, when people complain about lack of illumination at night, he transforms himself into the moon. In addition to explaining the origin of living beings, the narrative is also a *pourquoi* tale about the origins of the sun and moon and an account of how, through festivals, the story has been perpetuated.

*I*n the beginning there was no light. Everything was in darkness. The earth was soft and cold, and nothing grew. There was neither vegetation, nor animal life, nor beauty. Everything was desolate. There were no people. The only living creatures on earth were the god Nemequene, his wife, and his son.

Nemequene sought to create life and beauty on the earth. Out of the soft, cold mud, he fashioned the figures of people and animals. Day after day he worked at the task. But the figures he made were lifeless. They neither moved nor breathed. The years went by, and still there were only Nemequene and his family.

At last Nemequene called his son, and he sent him up into the sky to give light. Nemequene's son went into the sky and became Súa, the sun. Suddenly the dark world was illuminated. Súa's brilliant rays flooded the land. The cold mud became warm. Grass, trees, and plants began to grow. Where there had been only dark desolation, the world turned lush and green. Water began to flow and rivers and lakes began to form; the warm sunlight brought life into the mud figures which Nemequene had made. Some of them became birds, which flew up and nested in the trees of the forests; some became fish, which went into the water; some became animals; and some became humans.

Yet the people created by Nemequene were not altogether happy, for the light and warmth which Súa shed on them came only part of the time. Each night, while Súa rested, there was darkness. The people went to Nemequene and asked him to help them.

Nemequene loved the people whom he had created, and he wanted to help them. So he too went up into the sky and became Chía, the moon. He shared the task of giving light to the world with his son Súa. Súa cast his rays on the earth in the daytime, and Chía at night. From that time on, the people created by Nemequene were contented. They never forgot to give thanks.

They held feasts in honour of Súa and Chía, and sometimes they dedicated their children to the sun and the moon. Such children were known as Suachias long before they had names of their own.

Thus it was that life came into the world, and that the Chibchas—the people of Nemequene—remembered how it happened.

From *Ride with the Sun II: An Anthology of Folktales and Stories from the United Nations*, compiled by the United Nations Women's Guild (New York: UNWG, 2004).

Heaven and Earth

Like 'How Life and Light Came Into the World', this Maori creation myth from New Zealand deals with the actions of a family living in darkness. However, it is not a simple account of the actions of a father and son, but instead it is a complex presentation of events and the complicated relationships among a large number of sons. The opening actions, in which the sky father and earth mother are separated, is the result of the boys wishing for freedom and acquiring it by literally liberating themselves from confining parental bonds. By the end of the narrative, the earth and heavens have acquired their present state and the various living beings, including human beings, have been created. However, much of this process is accompanied by intense feuding among the brothers. Not only does each have a specific role in the acts of creation, but each also has a distinct personality that impels his actions.

In the far-off time before there was night or day, sun or moon, green fields or golden sand, Rangi the Sky-father lay in the arms of Papa the Earth-mother. For long ages they clung together and their children groped their way blindly between them. There was no light in the world where the children of Rangi and Papa lived, and they longed for freedom, for winds that would blow over the hill-tops and light that would warm their pale bodies.

The closeness of this narrow world at last became unbearable, and the sons of Earth and Sky met together, crawling through the narrow tunnels and caves of their land. They sat down where a few trees sprawled against the sky, twisting their branches into strange shapes.

'What shall we do?' asked the Children of the Gods. 'Shall we kill our Father and Mother and let in the light? Or shall we force them apart? We must do something, for we are no longer babies clinging to our mother's body.'

'Let us kill them,' said Tu-matauenga.

Tane stood up and straightened himself until his head pressed against the hanging sky. 'No,' he cried, 'we cannot kill them. They are Father and Mother to us. Let us force them apart. Let us throw the Sky away and live close to the heart of our Mother.' This he said because he was the god of trees that are nourished in the soil.

His brothers murmured their approval—all except Tawhiri-matea, the father of the winds. His voice whistled shrilly as he faced his brother.

'This is an idle thought,' he said fiercely. 'We are hidden here in safety where nothing can harm us. Out of your own mouth came the words: "They are our Father and Mother." Be careful, Tane, for this is a deed of shame.'

His words were drowned by the other gods crying aloud in the confined space. 'We need light,' they said. 'We need more room to stretch our cramped limbs. We need the freedom of space.'

They brushed past Tawhiri, while Rongo-ma-tane, the father of cultivated food, pressed his shoulders against the Sky-father and tried to straighten himself. In the darkness they could hear his breath, fast and heavy, but there was no movement in the body of Rangi, and the darkness hung heavily round the gods. Then Tangaroa, the father of the sea, of fish and reptiles, put out his strength. Then followed Haumia-tiketike, father of the wild berries and the fern-root, and after him Tu-matauenga, the god of war and father of man. Their efforts were all in vain.

Last of all, Tane-mahuta, the mighty father of the forest, of birds and insects and all living things that love light and freedom, rose to his feet. For as long as a man could hold his breath Tane stood silent and unmoving, gathering his strength. He stood on his head with feet planted firmly against the Sky-father, and his hands pressed against the Earth. Then Tane straightened his back and thrust strongly against the Sky. A low moaning filled the air. It crept through the gods as they lay on the earth, for the sound trembled through the body of the Earth-mother when she felt Rangi's arms loosing their hold upon her. The moaning

From A.W. Reed, *Myths and Legends of Maoriland*. Illustrated by Dennis Turner. (Wellington and Auckland: A.H. & A.W. Reed, 1961), 3.

grew louder until it became a roar. Rangi was hurled far away from Papa, and the angry winds screamed through the space that had opened between earth and sky.

Tane and his brothers looked round on the soft curves of their mother. For the first time they saw her in all her beauty, for the light had crept across the land. A silver veil of mist hung over Papa's naked shoulders and the tears that dropped fast from the eyes of Rangi were the sign that he grieved for her.

The gods breathed the free air and planned their new world. Although he had separated his parents, Tane loved them both, and he set to work to clothe his mother in beauty that had not been dreamed of in the dark world. He brought the trees, which were his own children, and set them in the earth; but because the world was still in the making and Tane was like a child learning by himself the wisdom that had not been born, he made mistakes, and planted the trees with their heads in the soil with the bare white roots stiff and unmoving in the breeze.

He rested against the bole of a tree and frowned at his strange forest. It was no place for the birds and the insects, who are the merry children of Tane. He pushed over a giant kauri and set the roots firmly in the soil. Then he looked with pride at its lovely crown of leaves set above the clean, straight trunk. The rustling of the leaves was music in his ears.

The earth looked beautiful in her mantle of green. The brown-skinned men and women had come from their hiding places to frolic under the leaves of the garden of Tane. They lived in peace with Rongo-ma-tane and Haumia-tiketike. Tane-mahuta raised his eyes to where Rangi lay, cold and grey and unlovely in the vast spaces above the earth. He wept as he looked on the desolation of his father. Then he took the red sun and placed it at the back of Rangi, with the silver moon at the front. Up and down the ten heavens went Tane, till at length he found a wonderful garment of glowing red, which he took with him. He rested seven days after his mighty labours, and then he spread the red cloak over the heaven, from north to south, from east to west, so that Rangi glowed brightly. But he was not satisfied. The garment was not worthy of his father. He stripped it off, leaving only a little at the end of heaven, where you may see it at the time of the setting sun.

By day Rangi was good to look upon, and Papa watched her husband with pride, but at night Rangi lay dark and shapeless until Marama, the moon, shone upon him.

'Great father,' cried Tane, 'in the long, dark nights, before Marama shines on your breast, all things sorrow. I will journey to the end of space, my father, that I may find adornment for you.' Somewhere in the silence far above Tane heard an answering sigh.

Tane remembered the Shining Ones who play in the Great Mountain at the very end of all things. He passed swiftly to the end of the world, out into the unknown where the smiling face of earth could be seen no more; out into the darkness until he reached Maunganui, the Great Mountain, where the Shining Ones, the children of his brother Uru, lived. Tane greeted his brother and together they watched the Shining Ones playing on the sand far below at the foot of the mountain.

Uru listened as Tane told him how Rangi and Papa had been separated, and how he had come to beg from his brother some of the Shining Lights to fasten to the mantle of the sky. Uru rose to his feet and shouted so that the sound of his voice rolled like thunder down the mountain slopes. The Shining Ones heard. They stopped their game and came romping up the mountain to Uru. As they came nearer, Tane could see them rolling over and over, for every Shining One was shaped like an eye—an eye that glowed and twinkled, lighting up the whole mountain.

Uru placed a basket before Tane, and they plunged their arms into the glowing mass of lights and piled the Shining Ones into the basket. Tane picked it up and went swiftly towards his father. He placed four sacred lights in the four corners of the sky; five glowing lights he arranged in a cross on the breast of Rangi; the tiny Children of Light he fastened on to his father's robe.

The basket hangs in the wide heavens where we can see its soft light—the light which we call the Milky Way. It is this light that shelters the Shining Ones and protects the Children of Light. When the sun sank to rest, the stars twinkled brightly and Tane lay on his back and watched his father shake out his robe till the heavens were filled with the beauty of Rangi and the glory of the Shining Ones.

While Tane and those of his brothers who had clung to Mother Earth were happy in their new-found freedom, black-browed Tawhiri-matea held the winds in the hollow of his hand and bided his time. He saw Tane wandering idly in the forest. Far out at sea he saw his brother, Tangaroa, who lived at peace with his grandchildren, Ika-tere, the father of fish, and Tu-te-wehiwehi, the father of reptiles. He rose and towered like a heavy black cloud over the distant sea and land. He opened his hand and hurled the winds across the empty spaces, and swept down from beneath his father's robes, wrapped in dark storm clouds and flashing lightning. He rushed over the land. The trees bent as the first winds reached them. Then came Tawhiri-matea and the tempest. The trees were uprooted, and when the wind died down the forest lay in tangled desolation.

The storm-god swept on to the brink of the ocean. The water boiled and surged in sudden fright. The waves rose until the sea seemed to empty itself and dissolve in the storm of flying spray and tempest-wrack. The empty sea-bottom appeared in the gaping valleys between the waves, and Tangaroa and his grandchildren fled down the valleys of their undersea kingdom.

Tu-te-wehiwehi cried: 'Let us fly to the shelter of the forest,' but Ika-tere replied: 'The sea is our only hope amidst the anger of the gods.' So were the children of the children's children of Tangaroa divided. Tu-te-wehiwehi fled with the reptiles to the land, while Ika-tere hid his children in the sea. As they parted their voices rose above the screaming of Tawhiri-matea.

'Fly inland,' shouted Ika-tere. 'Fly inland then; but when you are caught, before you are cooked for food, they will singe off your scales with burning bracken.'

'And as for you,' cried Tu-te-wehiwehi, 'who run away to the sea, your turn will come. When the little baskets of vegetables are given to the hungry ones, you will be laid on top to give relish to the food.'

And so unending strife was caused by Tawhiri-matea, for Tangaroa never forgave his children who fled to Tane of the dry land. When the winds roar, Tangaroa hurls his waves against the land and tries to break down the beautiful realm of Tane and cover it with the cruel waves of the sea; but when the wind has blown itself out and the waters are calm, the sons and daughters of Tane creep out in their boats and snare the children of Tangaroa, that they may be used as relish in the vegetable baskets of the children of men.

Tawhiri's anger had not died down. He rushed upon Tu-matauenga, leaving a trail of destruction behind him. The sea roared sullenly and the forest giants lay broken amongst the tangled undergrowth, but Tu-matauenga held himself erect and did not bend before the fierce blasts. Tawhiri called all his winds to help him, but Tu defied him until at last Tawhiri went back to the Sky-father, defeated by the father of man.

Tu looked at the broken forests and the beaten sea. 'I am the conqueror of all,' he said proudly. 'My children shall never fear the children of the wind; the sons of Tane shall be their subjects; the sea will obey them as they ride the waves in the canoes that Tane will give them; fish and bird and root and berry shall be their food. I am Tu!'

And for this reason the sons of Tu-matauenga are lords of the forest and sea.

The swift days passed by at the bidding of the sun while Tane fashioned the birds and sent them gliding down the wind, until the air was filled with the song of the feathered ones. This was the manner of their creation, but as yet they did not know where to find food. Tane called them to him and told them to fly to Tutu and Karaka, and many others, to feed among their hair. The birds flew off and there they found rich berries, for Tutu and Karaka were trees, and amongst the forest foliage the birds still find insects and berries and honey which Tane has appointed for their food.

The world grew older and the little feathered children of Tane grew in number. Some went down to the sea and played in the great waters, or on the wet shining sands where land and water meet; but most of them went inland among the bright lights and cool shadows of the trees, where their voices made the forest ring with music. Some came out only at night and crept through the gloom while the others slept. Each bird knew its home and its time for going out and coming in, its song to sing and its food to eat—everyone, until boasting Kawau, the river cormorant, visited his cousin the sea cormorant. Kawau of the river was given a fish to eat, but as it slipped down, the spines caught in his gullet.

'Ah!' said Kawau, 'you must come to my hunting place and I will show you eels that have no spines. In my kingdom I have fish a thousand times better than yours.' He took his cousin with him, and when the sea cormorant caught an eel and found that Kawau's words were true, he begged that he might share the river kingdom with him. When Kawau of the river saw how quickly the eel slipped down his cousin's throat, he was sorry that he had boasted so loudly, and drove him away. The sea cormorant went quickly, but he spread the news of the wonderful spineless fish that swam in the fresh water of the rivers. The sea birds gathered themselves into a mighty array and flew inland to attack the hosts of the land birds. On the morning of the battle, Pitoitoi the robin called out his warning and the land birds gathered together.

'Who'll be the scout,' asked Kawau. 'Who'll see when they are coming.'

'I'll be the scout,' said Koekoea the cuckoo, 'I'll see when they are coming.' Presently Koekoea saw a cloud of birds flying in from the sea.

'Koo-o-o-e!' The birds heard his cry, and a distant 'A-ha!' as Karore the gull called back his challenge.

'Who'll answer their battle-cry?' asked Kawau.

'I,' said the fantail. 'With my fluttering tail I'll flaunt a challenge.'

'Who'll lead the battle song?' asked Kawau.

'I,' said the tui. 'Let Hongi the crow and Tirauke the saddleback, and Wharauroa the short-tailed cuckoo, and Kuku the pigeon help me, and I'll lead the battle-song.'

When their song was ended, Kawau faced the angry birds.

'Who'll begin the fight?' he cried.

'I'll begin the fight,' shouted Ruru the owl. 'With my beak and claws I'll begin the fight.' He rose from his perch and swooped down on the sea birds, with the land birds flying in a great cloud behind him. Fierce was the battle, when feathers fell like snow-flakes as the sun rose high in the heavens.

At last the sea birds grew fearful. The land birds attacked yet more fiercely until the ranks of the sea birds wavered and broke, and they turned tail and flew to their homes. The mocking laughter of the grey duck rang in their ears as they flew. 'Ke-ke-ke-ke!' laughed Parera the duck as the gulls streamed out like a cloud unravelling in the wind.

No longer does the sea bird eat the land bird's food and there is peace between them in the world that great Tane-mahuta made with his hands when Rangi and Papa were separated and the light came in.

Tane had seen the beauty of earth and sky, but he was still dissatisfied. He felt that his work would be ended only when Papa was peopled with men and women. Children had been born to Tane and his brothers but they were celestial, never-dying gods who were not suited to earth and its ways.

The gods came down to earth and out of the warm red soil they made the image of a woman. She was lovely to look at, with soft skin and rounded form and long dark hair, but she was cold and lifeless. Then Tane bent down and breathed into her nostrils. Her eyelids fluttered and opened, and she looked round at the gods who were staring at her so intently. Then she sneezed. The breath of Tane had entered into her and she was a living woman.

The gods purified her and named her Hine-ahu-one, woman-created-from-earth. Tane became her husband and they had several girls as their children.

Tiki, the first man, was made by Tu-matauenga, god of war. He became the father of men and women who peopled the earth and inherited all the wonder and glory that Tane had made for them.

———

From *Myths and Legends of Maoriland*, by A.W. Reed. (Wellington and Auckland: A.H. & A.W. Reed, 1961).

The Creation and the First Sin

This very short adaptation of the first three chapters of the Book of Genesis provides a good example of how an extremely important cultural narrative was presented to children in the late nineteenth century. The basic events are included, however they are rendered in very simple terms and they are interspersed with what is extremely derogatory commentary. Eden is filled with 'sweet smelling flowers', and 'animals of every kind sported and played together'. The adaptors refer to 'the wicked Jews' and classify Eve as 'foolish and wicked'.

1. **The Creation of the World.**—At one time dear children, the world in which we live did not exist. There was no land nor sea nor bright blue sky. There were no trees nor plants nor flowers. There was no person nor thing but God. He always was and always will be.

Then God made the world, the land, and the water; the sun, the moon, and the stars; the birds and the fishes and all the creatures of the earth.

Last of all, God made a man and a woman, whom He named Adam and Eve.

And God is so great and powerful that He made all these in six days, and out of nothing, by His word alone.

On the seventh day God rested from His work, and blessed that day. For this reason the Jews kept it holy, and called it the *Sabbath*, which means to *rest from labour*. But after our blessed Lord was crucified by the wicked Jews the apostles chose Sunday, the first day of the week, as their day of rest, because on that day Our Saviour arose from the dead.

2. The Garden of Paradise.—The home of Adam and Eve was a lovely garden, in which sweet-smelling flowers and ripe, juicy fruits grew. Pretty birds sang in the branches of the trees, and animals of every kind sported and played together. Everything was peaceful and beautiful.

God told Adam that he and Eve might eat of the fruit of every tree in the garden, except of one, and that one they must not touch.

3. The First Sin.—This was a very little thing to require; and, had our first parents obeyed God, they would have lived forever and would have been happy in this beautiful garden. But one day the devil tempted Eve to eat the forbidden fruit and told her that if she ate it she would become as great as God Himself.

Eve was foolish and wicked enough to believe this, and in spite of God's command she ate the forbidden fruit. Then, not satisfied with sinning herself, she coaxed Adam to eat of the fruit also, and in this way sin was brought upon the earth.

Almighty God was angry with Adam and Eve for disobeying Him. To punish them He drove them from the garden, and condemned them to spend the rest of their lives in labour and suffering, until they returned to the dust out of which they were made.

This terrible curse was to fall not only on them, but on all who came after them. But so great is the love of God for His creatures that, even in spite of their sin, He promised that He would send a Redeemer to save mankind.

From *Bible Stories for Little Children* (New York: Benziger Brothers, 1894).

Sedna

The story of Sedna is one of the best-known and widely distributed Inuit (Eskimo) myths; it has been told in various forms across most of the Arctic. The narrative of a hunting culture, it embodies the necessity of showing respect for the animals on which the people traditionally depended for food, fuel, and clothing. It also reflects, in an ironic manner, the nature of relationships between spouses and between parents and children: both her father and her husband betray Sedna. The Inuit believed that if they violated one of the sea-goddess's many taboos she would not allow her children, the sea mammals, to give themselves to the harpoons of the hunters. The following narrative, in recounting the journey of the heroine from young woman to goddess, retains the violence found in the original, along with the sense of spirituality that is essential to the myth. The frame story explains the role of elders in passing down to children the essential myths and values that once guided and, in many ways, still guide Inuit life.

'You must remember, children,' the wise old man said to the boys and girls sitting around him, 'to honor the laws of Sedna. She is the mother of the sea creatures and it is she who allows them to give themselves to our hunters. When we offend her by breaking her laws, she keeps the sea creatures in her home beneath the sea. Then our people starve and many of them die.'

'But why would she do this to the people?' asked one of the children.

'It is because she knows that the lives of all beings are valuable and should be respected. And when people do not treat her children well, she is very angry, for she remembers that her own people were cruel to her when she was a person like you and I.'

'Please tell us about her,' another child asked. This little girl knew the story well and so did the other children. But she wanted to hear it again so that she could feel the power of Sedna and not forget the laws by which the people lived.

'When she lived as you and I do, Sedna was very beautiful,' began the old man. 'But she was also very proud. The other girls of her village had all married. They had husbands to catch the animals whose bodies gave people food, clothing, and oil for the lamps, and they worked in their igloos sewing and taking care of their children. But Sedna still lived with her father. She refused to marry any of the men who came to her; she had no one to sew for and no children. And she didn't care.

'One day, as she walked at the edge of the great sea, she saw a kayak in the distance, a tiny speck on the cold, shimmering waters. As it came closer, she could not recognize the man who paddled. But he was handsome, finer than any man she had ever seen before. Her heart stirred. This would be the husband she had hoped for.

'"Come with me," he said to her. "I will give you wonderful furs to make parkas with. My home is a fine one, the best in my village. I am a great hunter. We will have the best meat to eat, and our lamps will always burn brightly. We will have beautiful children."

'Sedna did not speak, but stepped quietly into his kayak. Surely this man is better than the men of my village, she thought to herself. I will always be happy. And so they traveled across the sea to the distant island where his village was.

'At first Sedna was happy. In fact, she had never been so happy in her life. Her husband was a good provider; and he loved her well.

'But one day, Sedna made a frightening discovery. She had been tricked. Her husband was not a man. He was a petrel, a sea bird; and he had great spirit powers. He had made himself look like a man so that she would live with him. He lived on a rocky island. His home was on a windswept ledge. It only looked like a warm, cozy home.

'Sedna did not know what to do. It was nearly winter; the winds were churning the sea into a dangerous chop; soon the ice would form and the blizzards would come. She was trapped.

'All that winter Sedna lived with her bird husband. She felt frightened and lonely and she knew that she was being punished for her pride. If only she were at home and safe, she would be happy to live with one of the men in her village. Even if he were not handsome, he would be good and kind.

'When the spring arrived, Sedna thought constantly of her village, and in her soul she prayed that her father would come to rescue her.

'So strong were the prayers in her soul that her father heard them. So he travelled over the sea in his umiak to find his daughter. When he arrived at the windswept, rocky island, the petrel was not home. Quickly he took Sedna to the boat and they began the long journey home.

'When the petrel returned from his hunting, he discovered that his wife was gone. He knew in his heart that she was leaving him to return to her village. He flew high above the seas searching for the boat. The anger grew and grew within him and he was filled with a terrible rage.

'Finally, he saw the umiak with his wife and her father. His body grew and grew until he was of gigantic size. He swooped down, beating his tremendous wings furiously, turning the ocean waters into mountainous waves.

'Sedna's father looked up. The bird seemed to fill the sky, and anger shone from his eyes. The man felt panic seize him and he thought only about saving himself. He grabbed his daughter and, made strong by his fear, he shoved her into the churning, icy waters.

'Sedna struggled, but his strength was too great, and she felt the chill of the sea as she fell beneath the waves. The water made her furs heavy and she felt herself being pulled toward the bottom of the sea. She struggled and came to the surface. Her father had grabbed a paddle and was trying to escape. Her hands were numb, but she reached up and clutched at the edge of the boat.

'When he felt her weight pulling against the boat; her father turned. His terror had transformed him into a madman. If he did not get away, the petrel would capsize the boat and he would drown. He lifted his paddle over his head and swung it down on his daughter's hands.

'So strong was the blow that it chopped her fingers off at the first knuckles and they dropped into the churning, grey water and sank from sight. Desperately, Sedna kept clinging to the boat and her father again struck down with his paddle. Now her fingers were completely severed from her hands and sank into the sea. She began to feel herself slipping, but she hooked her thumbs over the edge of the boat. With a final chop, her father took these off.

'Sedna could no longer grip the boat and she slowly sank into the sea. The pain in her hands was great; the pain in her heart was greater.

'In a few moments, the waters grew dark; but soon, a strange green light seemed to shine everywhere, and before her eyes she saw a wonderful thing.

'The parts of her fingers and hands which were floating down around her began to grow and change in shape. The smaller pieces became seals, the large ones, sea lions, and the thumbs, whales. And as she kept sinking, the new animals swam about, rubbing gently against her.

'Her feet touched the floor of the sea and she walked about. The animals stayed with her, as tame as sled dogs around an igloo and much friendlier. She discovered that she could breathe and she moved around, the seals, walruses, and whales following her.

'Suddenly Sedna understood. These animals were her children; they had been created from her body. At last she had a family, even if it was very different from the one she had hoped for when she was a girl.

'Sedna was a mother, and like all mothers she had to protect her children. As she looked at them, she knew that the people would want to hunt them. Their meat would give food; their fat, oil for the lamps; and their skins, fur for clothing and coverings for boats. Their bones could be made into harpoon heads.

'Sedna had lived on the land and she knew that the people would need her children to survive. She would give her children as gifts to them. But she also knew that people could be cruel and that sometimes they did not respect life. She remembered what her father had done to her.

'"My children have souls just as all living creatures do. The people must respect the souls of my children. If they do not show respect, I will not give them the gift of my children's bodies. I will let them starve."'

The old man looked at the children sitting around him. They sat very quietly. He knew that they were thinking about Sedna and about how they must obey their laws. If they did not respect the souls of her children, there would be great hardship for everyone. Many of the people would die.

The old man did not speak for a long time. He remembered the time he had first learned about Sedna. He had been frightened because he had learned how dangerous it was to anger Sedna.

Finally he broke the silence. 'Children,' he said, 'if you are good to Sedna's children, you will not have to fear. But if you are not good to them, she will know. In her home at the bottom of the sea, she knows all that happens to her creatures. She is very powerful. She can bring life or death to us. It all depends on how we think and what we do.'

From *The Family of Stories*, edited by Anita Moss and Jon C. Stott (Toronto: Holt, Rinehart, and Winston, 1986).

How Summer Came to Canada

Glooskap, the culture-hero of the Algonkian peoples of the Canadian maritimes and northeastern United States, is a semi-divine figure who, in addition to helping the people and giving many animals and parts of the landscape their distinctive characteristics, frequently indulged his love of playing tricks. Both his desire to help the people and his self-centeredness and mischievousness are reflected in this *pourquoi* myth explaining the origin of the seasonal cycles. Although he is powerless against the Giant Winter, he acts as an agent, bringing Summer to the north, where, although she defeats her adversary, she shares with him her right to rule over the land. Canadian Cyrus Macmillan, a professor at McGill University in the early twentieth century, stated about the collection of tales of which this is a part that 'the dress in which they now appear may be new, but the skeleton of each story has been left behind.' In this respect, the reteller is not unlike many of the earlier adaptors of Native folktales; he makes elements of a narrative of an unfamiliar culture similar to those of stories with which his intended audience would be familiar. The 'new dress' of which he spoke seems to be that of European fairy tales as they had been adapted for children. For example, Glooskap is said to be the possessor of magic, rather than spirit power, and Summer is referred to as a 'Fairy Queen', with her subjects holding 'chains of blossoms, like children in a Maypole game'. The narrator's reference to the Southern Cross is to a constellation that the original Native audience would not have known.

Once during Glooskap's lifetime and reign in Canada it grew very cold. Everywhere there was snow and ice, and in all the land there was not a flower nor a leaf left alive. The fires that the Indians built could not bring warmth. The food supply was slowly eaten up, and the people were unable to grow more corn because of the hard frozen ground. Great numbers of men and women and children died daily from cold and hunger, and it seemed as if the whole land must soon perish.

Over this extreme cold Glooskap had no power. He tried all his magic, but it was of no avail. For the cold was caused by a powerful giant who came into the land from the far North, bringing Famine and Death as his helpers. Even with his breath he could blight and wither the trees, so that they brought forth no leaves nor fruit; and he could destroy the corn and kill man and beast. The giant's name was Winter. He was very old and very strong, and he had ruled in the far North long before the coming of man. Glooskap, being brave and wishing to help his people in their need, went alone to the giant's tent to try to coax or bribe or force him to go away. But even he, with all his magic power at once fell in love with the

From William Toye, *How Summer Came to Canada*. Illustrated by Elizabeth Cleaver. (Toronto: Oxford University Press, 1969).

giant's home; for in the sunlight it sparkled like crystal and was of many wonderful colours, but in the night under the moonlight it was spotlessly white. From the tent, when Glooskap looked out, the face of the earth was beautiful. The trees had a covering of snow that gave them strange fantastic shapes. The sky was filled by night with flashing quivering lights, and even the stars had a new brightness. The forest, too, was full of mysterious noises. Glooskap soon forgot his people amid his new surroundings. The giant told him tales of olden times when all the land was silent and white and beautiful like his sparkling tent. After a time the giant used his charm of slumber and inaction, until Glooskap fell asleep, for the charm was the charm of the Frost. For six months he slept like a bear. Then he awoke, for he was very strong and Winter could not kill him even in his sleep. But when he arose he was hungry and very tired.

One day soon after he awoke, his tale-bearer, Tatler the Loon, brought him good news. He told of a wonderful Southland, far away, where it was always warm, and where lived a Queen who could easily overcome the giant; indeed, she was the only one on earth whose power the giant feared. Loon described carefully the road to the new country. Glooskap, to save his people from Winter and Famine and Death, decided to go to the Southland and find the Queen. So he went to the sea, miles away, and sang the magic song that the whales obeyed. His old friend Blob the Whale came quickly to his call, and getting on her back he sailed away. Now, the whale always had a strange law for travellers. She said to Glooskap: 'You must shut your eyes tight while I carry you; to open them is dangerous, for, if you do, I will surely go aground on a reef or a sand bar and cannot get off, and you may then be drowned.' And Glooskap promised to keep his eyes shut. Many days the whale swam, and each day the water grew warmer, and the air grew gentler and sweeter, for it came from spicy shores; and the smells were no longer those of the salt sea, but of fruits and flowers and pines. Soon they saw in the sky by night the Southern Cross. They found, too, that they were no longer in the deep sea, but in shallow water flowing warm over yellow sands, and that land lay not far ahead. Blob the Whale now swam more cautiously. Down in the sand the clams were singing a song of warning, telling travellers in these strange waters of the treacherous sand bar beneath. 'Oh, big whale,' they sang, 'keep out to sea, for the water here is shallow and you shall come to grief if you keep on to shore.' But the whale did not understand the language of the little clams. And he said to Glooskap, who understood, 'What do they sing?' But Glooskap, wishing to land at once, answered, 'They tell you to hurry for a storm is coming,—to hurry along as fast as you can.' Then the whale hurried until she was soon close to the land. Glooskap, wishing the whale to go aground so that he could more easily walk ashore, opened his left eye and peeped, which was contrary to the whale's laws. And at once the whale stuck hard and fast on the beach, so that Glooskap, springing from her head, walked ashore on dry land. The whale, thinking that she could never get off, was very angry, and sang a song of lament and blame. But Glooskap put one end of his strong bow against the whale's jaw, and taking the other end in his hands, he placed his feet against the high bank, and, with a mighty push, he sent old Blob again into the deep water. Then, to keep the whale's friendship, he threw her an old pipe and a bag of Indian tobacco leaves—for Glooskap was a great smoker—and the whale, greatly pleased with the gift, lighted the pipe and smoking it swam far out to sea. Glooskap watched her disappear from view until he could see only clouds of her smoke against the sky. And to this day the whale has Glooskap's old pipe, and sailors often see her rise to the surface to smoke it in peace and to blow rings of tobacco smoke into the air.

When the whale had gone, Glooskap walked with great strides far inland. Soon he found the way of which Loon had told him. It was the Rainbow Road that led to the Wilderness of Flowers. It lay through the land of the Sunrise, beautiful and fresh in the morning light. On each side were sweet magnolias and palms, and all kinds of trees and flowers. The grass was soft and velvety, for by night the dew was always on it; and snow and hail were unknown, and winds never blew coldly, for here the charm of the Frost had no power.

Glooskap went quickly along the flower-lined Rainbow Road, until he came to an orange grove where the air was sweet with the scent of blossoms. Soon he heard sounds of music. He peered through the trees, and saw that the sounds came from an open space not far ahead, where the grass was soft and where tiny streams were flowing and making melody. It was lilac-time in the land, and around the open space all kinds of flowers in the world were blooming. On the trees numberless birds were singing—birds of wonderfully coloured feathers such as Glooskap had never heard or seen before. He knew that he had reached at last the Wilderness of Flowers, of which old Tatler the Loon had spoken. He drew deep breaths of honeysuckle and heliotrope and countless other flowers, until he soon grew strong again after his long voyage.

Then he crept close to the edge of the open space and looked in from behind the trees. On the flower-covered grass within, many fair maidens were singing and dancing, holding in their hands chains of blossoms, like children in a Maypole game. In the centre of the group was one fairer than all the others—the most beautiful creature he had ever seen,—her long brown hair crowned with flowers and her arms filled with blossoms. For some time Glooskap gazed in silence, for he was too surprised to move or to utter speech. Then he saw at his side an old woman,—wrinkled and faded, but still beautiful,—like himself watching the dance. He found his voice and asked, 'Who are those maidens in the Wilderness of Flowers?' And the old woman answered, 'The maiden in the centre of the group is the Fairy Queen; her name is Summer; she is the daughter of the rosy Dawn,—the most beautiful ever born; the maidens dancing with her are her children, the Fairies of Light and Sunshine and Flowers.'

Glooskap knew that here at last was the Queen who by her charms could melt old Winter's heart and force him to go away, for she was very beautiful and good. With his magic song he lured her from her children into the dark forest; there he seized her and held her fast by a crafty trick. Then, with her as a companion, he began his long return journey north by land. That he might know the way back to the Wilderness of Flowers, he cut a large moose hide, which he always carried, into a long slender cord, and as he ran north with Summer, he let the cord unwind behind him, for he had no time to mark the trail in the usual way. When they had gone, Summer's children mourned greatly for their Queen. For weeks the tears ran down their cheeks like rain on all the land, and for a long time, old Dawn, the Queen's mother, covered herself with dark mourning clouds and refused to be bright.

After many days, still holding Summer in his bosom—for she loved him because of his magic power—Glooskap reached the Northland. He found none of his people, for they were all asleep under the giant's power, and the whole country was cold and lonely. At last he came to the home of old Winter. The giant welcomed him and the beautiful girl, for he hoped to freeze them both and keep them with him always. For some time they talked together in the tent, but, although he tried hard, the giant was unable to put them to sleep. Soon old Winter felt that his power had vanished and that the charm of the Frost was broken. Large drops of sweat ran down his face; then his tent slowly disappeared, and he was left homeless. Summer used her strange power until everything that Winter had put to sleep awoke again. Buds came again upon the trees; the snow ran down the rivers, carrying away the dead leaves; and the grass and the corn sprang up with new life. And old Winter, being sorrowful, wept, for he knew that his reign was ended, and his tears were like cold rain. Summer, the Queen, seeing him mourn and wishing to stop his tears, said: 'I have proved that I am more powerful than you; I give you now all the country to the far north for your own, and there I shall never disturb you; you may come back to Glooskap's country six months of every year and reign as of old, but you will be less severe; during the other six months, I myself will come from the south and rule the land.' Old Winter could do nothing but accept this offer gracefully, for he feared that if he did not he would melt entirely away. So he built a new home farther north, and there he reigns without interruption. In the late autumn he comes back to Glooskap's country and reigns for six months, but his rule is softer than in olden times. And when he comes, Summer, following Glooskap's moose-hide cord, runs home with her birds to the Wilderness of Flowers. But at the end of six months she always comes back to drive old Winter away to his own land, to awaken the northern world, and to bring it the joys that only she, the Queen, can give. And so, in Glooskap's old country Winter and Summer, the hoary old giant and the beautiful Fairy Queen, divide the rule of the land between them.

From *Canadian Wonder Tales*, by Cyrus Macmillan (London: John Lane, The Bodley Head, 1918).

Demeter and Persephone

The most important myth concerning Demeter, the Greek corn goddess, explains the origin of the seasonal cycles. Winter is caused by the grieving of the goddess because of the annual four-month return of her daughter, Persephone, to the underworld to live with her husband Hades. Proddow captures the poetic qualities of the ancient Greek Homeric Hymn on which her adaptation is based. She also communicates the emotional intensity of the angry and distraught mother and the conflicts that can arise between a mother and a son-in-law as they struggle for the affections of the daughter, who must, in the end, search for her own identity. In many ways, she must 'die' as a child and spend time underground before she returns as a mature woman, balancing her life between the old (her mother) and the new (her husband).

Now I will sing
of golden-haired Demeter,
the awe-inspiring goddess,
and of her trim-ankled daughter,
Persephone,
who was frolicking in a grassy meadow.

She was far away
from her mother.

With the deep-girdled daughters of Ocean,
the maiden was gathering flowers—
crocuses, roses, and violets,
irises and lovely hyacinths
growing profusely together,
with *one* narcissus. . .

This was the snare
for the innocent maiden.

She knelt in delight
to pluck the astonishing bloom

when, all of a sudden, the wide-wayed earth
split open
down the Nysian meadow.

Out sprang a lord
with his deathless horses.
It was He Who Receives Many Guests,
He Who Has Many Names.

Seizing Persephone,
he caught her up in his golden chariot
despite her laments.

Her screams were shrill
as she shrieked for her father, Zeus,
but no one heard
except kind-hearted Hecate
from her cave
and Helios, the sun.

Still glimpsing the earth,
the brilliant sky,
the billowing, fish-filled sea
and the rays of the sun,
Persephone vainly hoped to see her beloved mother
again.

The peaks of the mountains
and the ocean depths
resounded
with her immortal voice.

And her stately mother heard.
A sudden pang
went through Demeter's heart.

She set off like a bird
wildly
over the bodies of water
and the dry stretches of land,
but no one would tell her the truth—
not a god,
not a mortal,
not even a long-winged bird of omen.

She circled the earth
for nine days
steadily,
brandishing shining torches.

At the dawning
of the tenth,
Hecate approached,
holding a pine torch in her hands.

'Demeter!' she said.
'Bringer of the Seasons!
Giver of Rich Gifts!
What god in heaven,
what mortal,
has caused your heart such torment
and taken your daughter?
I heard her cries
but I did not see
who he was!'

They both hurried on
to the sun,
the watchman of gods and of men.

'Helios!' cried Demeter.
'Have pity on me—goddess that I am.
I bore a child
whose frantic voice I heard
through the barren air
as if she had been overpowered,
but I saw nothing.
Tell me,
was it a god or a mortal
who stole away my daughter
against her will—and mine?'

'Fair-tressed Demeter!' Helios replied.
'No one is guilty
among the immortals
but Zeus,
who gave her to Hades
to be his youthful bride.

'Now, Goddess,
you must stop this violent weeping!

'The Ruler of Many is not undesirable
as a son-in-law.
He wields great power,
for he is king over the dead,
with whom he lives
in the underworld.'

Anguish
rent the goddess' heart—
savage and terrible.

Embittered with black-clouded Zeus,
she departed broad Olympus
and the gatherings of the gods.
From that time forth,
she sought the villages and fields of mortal men
with her face disguised.

No one knew her
until she reached the palace of prudent Celeus,
lord over fragrant Eleusis.

There by the roadside,
she sank down
at the Well of the Maiden
in sorrow—
seemingly some poor old woman,
fit only for nursing a wise king's children
or keeping his shadowy halls.

The King's four daughters
saw her
when they came up with their golden pitchers
to draw sparkling water.

'Where have you come from,
elderly mortal?'
they cried

'Lovely maiden!' Demeter replied.
'Pirates seized me
and bore me over the broad sea's back
by force—but I escaped
and came hither.'

'On me, young girls, have pity!
Where can I go
to take up the tasks
allotted to elderly women—like myself
such as nursing a newborn child in my arms?'

'Gentle woman!' said Callidice,
the fairest of Celeus' children.

'Wait
while we go to our mother,
for she has a newborn child.'

Swiftly the four
sped to their mother
and she bade them bring the woman
at once
and promise a generous reward.

Back they bounded,
holding their full skirts high,
barely touching
the shady paths,
and their hair streamed over their shoulders—
the colour of yellow crocuses.

Her heart aching for Persephone,
Demeter covered her head with a veil
and followed
behind the maidens.

When they came to
the palace of god-favoured Celeus,
the goddess stepped on the portal
and her head came up to the rafters.
The splendour of an immortal
shone
in the doorway.

Awe seized their mother, Metaneira.

'Good Lady,
your birth cannot be lowly,'
she exclaimed.

'Here is my only son—
Damophon—
whom the gods bestowed upon me
as a companion for my old age.
If you nurse him
and he grows up handsomely,
then women throughout the land will envy you,
so great will be your reward.'

'Great lady,' replied Demeter.
'May the gods grant you riches!
I will bring up your son wisely.'

His mother rejoiced.

The boy then grew like a god.
He never ate food
nor drank any milk—
Demeter was feeding him ambrosia
by day,
as if he were the child of a goddess.

And, without the knowledge of his doting parents,
she put him to sleep
by night,
in the embers of the fire.

The goddess would have made him
deathless and immortal,
in this fashion,
had not Metaneira,
foolishly peeping out from her chamber,
spied her one night.

'My son!' she shrieked.
'This stranger is putting you in the fire!'

The bright goddess turned about.
Furious at the mother,
Demeter took the child
from the fire
and thrust him from her
with immortal hands.

'Senseless mortals!' she raged.
'You cannot see whether your fate
is good or bad,
even when it comes upon you!
I would have made your boy
deathless and immortal
all his days.
For I am dread Demeter!
Now, let this land build me a temple
and a broad altar
to win back my favor.'

Then the great goddess flung off her disguise
and her beauty appeared.
The light in her eyes
filled up the strong halls
like a flash of lightning.

She departed from the chamber.

Quickly, the Eleusinians
built the temple.
When they had finished,
they all returned to their homes.

But golden-haired Demeter
remained
enthroned within,
far from all of the festive gods,
wasting away with longing
for her graceful daughter.

She made that year
most shocking and frightening
for mortals
who lived on the nourishing earth.

The soil did not yield a single seed—
Demeter kept them all
underground.

In vain,
oxen hauled many curved ploughs
over the meadows.

Now, she was about to cause
the race of chattering men
to die out
altogether
from frightful hunger,
depriving those who lived on Olympus
of their lavish gifts and sacrifices.

Then *Zeus* noticed. . .

He sent golden-winged Iris first
to summon her.
On swift feet,
Iris spanned the distance
to Eleusis—now laden with incense—
and found Demeter
within her temple,
clad in a dark gown.

'Demeter!' she announced.
'Father Zeus

in his infinite wisdom
calls you back to the family
of the undying gods.'

Demeter's heart was unmoved.

Thereupon Zeus
sent forth all the gods—
the joyous beings who live forever.

Demeter scorned their speeches.
She vowed
she would not set foot on Olympus
nor let a fruit spring up on the earth
until she had seen
with her own eyes
the lovely face of her daughter.

Then Zeus dispatched Hermes
with his staff of gold.

Setting off from the Olympian seat,
Hermes dashed down
at once
into the depths of the earth.

He found Hades
in his halls
on a couch with his tender bride—
who was listless
out of longing for her mother.

'Dark-haired Hades!' said Hermes
'Zeus commands me
to bring back fair Persephone.
Her mother is planning a horrible deed—
to starve the tribes
of earth-dwelling mortals
and so, to deprive the gods
of their offerings!'

The king of the dead
raised his eyebrows,
but he did not disobey Zeus' order.

'Go, Persephone,' he said,
'back to your dark-robed mother!'

Persephone smiled,
as joyfully she sprang up from the couch,
but stealthily the lord of the dead
spread out about her
delicious pomegranate seeds
to make sure she would not remain
forever
at the side of her noble mother.

Soon after, Hades
harnessed up his deathless horses
to the golden chariot.

Persephone leapt into the car.
Hermes seized the whip and the reins
in his skillful hands
and they drove off together
away from the land of the dead.

Hermes guided the horses
to Eleusis where Demeter sat
waiting,
and they drew to a halt
in front of her incense-filled temple.
Demeter,
catching sight of Persephone,
flew forward
like a maenad on a mountain.

But, as she clasped her daughter,
she suspected treachery.

'My child!' she cried in fear.
'Could you have eaten anything
in the land of the dead?'

'Truthfully, Mother!'
exclaimed Persephone.
'When Hermes arrived from Zeus,
I arose with joy.
Then Hades brought out delicious pomegranate seeds
and urged me to eat them.'

'In that case,
you must return
to the land of the dead' said Demeter,
'for one third of the rolling seasons.

'But when you come back
to me
for the other two,
the earth will burst into bloom
with flocks of sweet-smelling, spring flowers—
a great marvel to all men.'

At that moment,
Wide-ruling Zeus
sent a messenger—
Rhea
with a golden band in her hair.

'Demeter, my daughter,' said Rhea,
'Zeus wishes you
to return to the company of the gods.
Yield to him,
lest you carry your anger
toward dark-clouded Zeus
too far.

'And now
bestow some nourishing fruit
on mortal men!'

Bright-garlanded Demeter
did not disobey.

Immediately, she caused the fruit
to grow in the fertile fields
and soon the wide earth
was weighted down
with buds and blossoms.

Hail to you, Demeter,
Lady of Fragrant Eleusis,
Leader of the Seasons and Giver of Shining Gifts,
you and your most beautiful daughter Persephone,
look kindly on me
and in return for my song,
grant abundant life to follow.

From *Demeter and Persephone: Homeric Hymn Number Two*, translated and adapted by Penelope Proddow (Garden City, NY: Doubleday, 1972).

The Myth of Osiris and Isis

For the ancient Egyptians, the myth of Isis and Osiris explained how Osiris, the culture bringer, gave both agricultural wealth and culture to his people. It also tells the story of a vegetation god whose death and resurrection parallels the yearly rebirth of the crops. The flooding of the Nile, upon which the agricultural cycle depended, was equated with the tears of Isis lamenting the death of her husband. While the myth celebrates Osiris, it also accounts for the cult of Isis, the perfect wife and mother who plays an active role throughout the narrative. As a goddess of earth, she makes Osiris aware of seeds; as a wife, she keeps her devotion to her husband and is responsible for his restoration to life. Even when the tasks seem insurmountable, she courageously and loyally continues her quest. The frame story introduces the concept of the corruption of true stories over generations of retelling. The garrulous old narrator, no longer able to go on pilgrimages, eases his loneliness by telling travelers what he considers to be the authentic version of the myth.

Welcome, pilgrims! Are you going to Abydos? Well, you have yet a long journey ahead. Won't you stop and rest awhile? You know, if I were not so old, I would join you. It has been too many years since I have been to Abydos for the eight days that re-enact the life of Osiris. When I was younger I went several times. I also went to other cities where priests claim that their temple is built over the burial place of some piece of Osiris. I have been to Athribis, where they say they have his heart; to Busiris, where they have his backbone; to Letopolis, where they have his neck; and to Memphis, where priests claim that they built the temple over the sacred head of Osiris. Yet at Abydos the great festival ends with a ceremonial restoration of the head of Osiris, which the priests keep in a box within the temple. Do you think, perhaps, that Osiris had two heads?

Stop! Do not leave. I did not mean to offend you. It is just that, if you are to worship Osiris properly, you must forget the tales you have heard. Sit. Rest. Listen well. I will tell you the true story of Osiris, the Drowned One.

To know anyone truly, you must know his origins. As you have heard, Osiris is a child of Nut, goddess of the sky, and Geb, god of the earth. Osiris came into this world in spite of the curse of Ra, the sun god. In anger, Ra said that Nut could not bear a child in any month of any year. But with the help of wise Thoth, Nut had five days added to our calendar of 360 days. These days were not in any month, so during the first of these, Nut gave birth to Osiris. In each of the other added days, she gave birth to his brothers and sisters.

When Osiris came to manhood, he replaced Ra as king of Egypt. The land he ruled was not as it is today. It was a violent land, a savage land. Men fought against each other, each thinking only of himself and trying to drive the other from good hunting grounds. Some say that the people were so wild that they even ate their enemies, but I do not believe that. In any case, everything changed when Osiris ascended the throne. His sister Isis, who had become his wife, gave him grain seeds, and he taught men how to plow fields, to plant those seeds, and to harvest the crops. He taught them how to grind wheat for flour and to use barley for beer. He also taught them how to grow vines and trees bending with fruit. Osiris made Egypt into a land of plenty.

Now that the people did not have to wander all over the land in search of food, Osiris ensured that they could live together in harmony by giving wise decisions to end disputes and by making just laws that would prevent later disputes. The people, happy to live in a peaceful land where food was plentiful, gave their king the title by which we most often honor him, the Good Being.

But Osiris the Good was not content. He wanted all peoples to be happy, so he decided to share his gifts with other nations. Leaving Isis to rule in his absence, Osiris traveled to other nations, bringing them knowledge so that they, too, could plant and harvest and live in peace. When he finally returned, in the twenty-eighth year of his rule, the people knew that he was a god, and they celebrated and gave him proper worship.

There were some, however, who did not add their voices to the rejoicing. His younger brother, Seth, who claimed rule of the dry desert lands, was jealous of Osiris. While Osiris had been absent, he had tried to take away the throne, but Isis had thwarted him each time. Now he saw an opportunity to rid himself of Osiris and become Egypt's ruler. He gathered seventy-two followers, and they devised a trick. At a lavish banquet, where Osiris made merry with his people, Seth brought forth a richly decorated chest shaped like the body of a man. When everyone present expressed admiration at this splendid chest, Seth declared that he would give it to the man who perfectly fitted inside it. Guests eagerly lined up to get inside the box, but it did not properly fit any of them.

At last, Seth persuaded Osiris that he, too, should try. Osiris set down his wine and allowed the conspirators to lower him into the chest. He fit it perfectly, his head just touching one end, his feet just resting on the other, and his shoulders, his hips, and his legs just brushing against the sides of the tapered chest. As he lay there, Osiris laughingly said that it fit him as if it had been made for him. Indeed it did, for Seth had ordered the chest made to fit Osiris exactly.

Now, just when Osiris thought that he had won a prize, Seth gave a signal to his fellow conspirators. They quickly shut the box, drove nails into the lid and sealed it shut with hot lead so that Osiris could no longer breathe the air of life. Through the midnight streets they then carried the box, now the coffin of Osiris the Good, and when they came to the river bank, they threw it into the Nile. The casket bobbed upon the water and floated along the river out to sea. Because he was thus thrown into the water, we also call Osiris the Drowned One.

When Isis heard of the evil trick that Seth had played on her husband, she wailed in sorrow, cut off a lock of her hair, and donned mourning robes. In spite of her great pain, Isis did not remain in her chamber. She vowed that she would find the body of her husband and give to it the honor it deserved. She thus began journeying along the Nile, questioning everyone she met about the coffin. None of those she asked helped her. One day, however, she came across a group of children playing by the river's edge. They told her that they had seen a richly decorated coffin floating from the Nile into the sea. Isis then boarded a ship to resume her search. Stopping at every port to ask for news of the coffin, she was able to follow it to Byblos, a great port in the land of the Phoenicians.

When she got off the ship at Byblos, people told Isis about a magnificent sycamore tree that had recently grown overnight near the shore. The king, marveling at its size and beauty, had cut it down and used it as a pillar in his palace. Isis knew immediately that this tree had grown around her husband's coffin to protect it. She therefore devised a plan to get near the pillar. She donned the clothes of a serving maid and sat silently by a spring.

Soon, the handmaidens of the queen approached to do their washing. They admired her elaborately plaited hair, so Isis offered to plait theirs, breathing her beautiful perfume over them as she did so. When the servants returned to the palace, the queen saw the beauty of their hair and smelled the intoxicating perfume that wafted from each head. Eager to see

From Gerald McDermott, *The Voyage of Osiris*. (New York: E.P. Dutton, 1977).

one who could bestow beauty upon any woman she met, the queen summoned the disguised Isis to the palace. Gentle Isis so pleased her that the queen appointed her the nurse of the infant prince.

Over the next days, Isis tended to the little prince. Each night she placed the infant over a fire, intending to reward the queen by burning off the young prince's mortality. While the infant lay in the fire, she herself assumed the shape of a swallow and flew in mournful circles around the pillar enclosing her husband's coffin. Unfortunately, the queen saw her babe in the fire and shrieked in fear and misery. Isis immediately resumed her own form and handed her the unharmed child, who, removed prematurely from the fire, lost the chance of becoming immortal. Seeing this transformation from a bird to a woman, the queen realized that Isis was a goddess. When Isis then told her sad story, the queen gave her the large pillar. Isis at once had it split open to reveal the rich coffin encasing her beloved husband. Taking the coffin onto a ship, Isis then sailed home to Egypt.

But the Egypt to which she returned was not the one from which she had departed. Seth had usurped the throne, and his ways were cruel and bloody. He did not follow the laws that Osiris the Good had decreed. Instead, he and his followers seized whatever they desired and put to the sword all who opposed them. It was not safe for Isis to go back to the palace; so she hid her husband's coffin into the reeds.

One night when the moon was full, Seth was out hunting, for he liked the night better than the day. Chasing a boar through the reeds, he came upon the coffin, near which Isis was sleeping. Filled with uncontrollable rage as soon as he saw it, he opened the coffin, cut the body into fourteen parts, and threw them into the Nile so that the crocodiles could devour them.

When Isis awakened and discovered the empty coffin, she was again smitten with grief. She wailed so loudly that her sister, Nephthys, rushed to her aid. While Isis paddled a papyrus boat along the river and through the reeds, Nephthys went along the shore searching for pieces of the body. Their long and arduous search was successful because the crocodiles, who feared Isis, had refused to eat any of the pieces, which then had floated among the reeds and onto the shore all along the great river. Isis was able to recover thirteen of pieces of her husband's body. One piece she did not find, for the Oxyrhynchus, or Sharp-Nosed Fish, the detestable fighting pike, had devoured it. That is why, to this day, the Sharp-Nosed Fish is an abomination and we do not eat it. Yes, I know that some worship the Sharp-Nosed Fish and say that they thus honour Isis, but I tell you that that fish is an abomination, and so is worship of it.

Isis was determined that Seth would never again be able to abuse the body of Osiris. Therefore, at each place where she and Nephthys found a part of the Good One's body, they buried an image of it. She then caused the priests to build in each of these places a temple for the worship of Osiris. In this way, she protected the real body of Osiris and also encouraged worship of him.

Having gathered the thirteen severed parts of Osiris, Isis fashioned from clay the missing part and then bound all the pieces together with linen. By wrapping the body tightly in the clean white cloth, she made it whole again. Isis and Nephthys then performed a secret rite, during which Isis assumed the form of a hawk and, beating her mighty wings, fanned life back through the nostrils of Osiris. Lovingly, she embraced her risen husband, and from that union came Horus, who was later to avenge himself upon Seth. After he had embraced his wife, Osiris went to the Western Region, the home of departed spirits. One day, we will all meet him, for he rules there and judges every spirit that leaves the land of the living. One day we will live again and become Osiris.

I know that you must resume your journey. Farewell. But on your way back, please stop and rest again. I will tell you how Horus defeated Seth and brought about the union of Upper and Lower Egypt.

───────

From Raymond E. Jones [previously unpublished]

How Fire Was Stolen from Rabbit

Set in a time 'when people were animals', this tale of the Toba people of the Argentina-Paraguay region focuses on Fox, the major trickster in their stories. Often an extremely selfish individual, in this particular instance he uses his ability to transform himself into a hummingbird in order to steal fire for the people. His concern for others is contrasted with the selfishness of Rabbit, who does not wish to share the fire. The importance of the acquisition of fire is that the people no longer have to eat their fish raw. An interesting aspect of this tale is the people's desire that fire should have a name and their search for a correct one, which Fox is able to supply.

*O*nce there was no fire. Nobody could produce it but Rabbit. When people caught fish, they had to eat it raw because Rabbit would not share his fire. When Fox heard that, he changed himself into a hummingbird and crept to Rabbit's home. Rabbit was asleep and so Hummingbird stole the fire from him, turned himself back into Fox and hurried home as fast as he could. When he arrived, Fox shouted, 'I've got it.' The people gathered and built a big fire.

Then Rabbit woke up and looked around him. There wasn't an ember left. He looked around, but couldn't find anything. He couldn't understand where it had gone.

Suddenly rain began to pour down and the fire started to hiss and sizzle. Before it could be extinguished Fox grabbed a fire-brand and hid it.

Later, the fishermen came home from the river with many baskets of fish. They again built a big fire and placed their catch directly on the ashes. Fox tasted the broiled fish and said, 'It is good.' The others tasted in turn, and then said, 'Let us all eat; raw food tastes unsavory, but the cooked meat is very juicy and good.' Then they decided to roast the fish by placing it on spits.

After they had finished eating, they asked each other, 'What shall we call this thing that cooks our food?' Someone suggested it be named 'the smoking thing'. Another felt that it should be called 'the thing that roasts for us'. A third person called it 'the thing that makes our food'. But none of them could agree on a name.

So they decided to visit Rabbit, who used to own the fire. They flattered him by calling him Master of the Burning One. But he was still annoyed that the fire had been stolen, so he said, 'I am not the master; someone stole it from me.' He asked who had stolen it and, when the people told him Fox had taken it, he told them to ask the new master what the name of the burning thing was.

So the people went to Fox's house. 'Rabbit is still angry,' they said. 'He will not tell us the name of the burning one. He told us to ask you.' And Fox replied, 'You can call this thing "fire".' And that is why people call the burning one 'fire' and why they eat cooked food.

Adapted from *Myths of the Toba and Pilaga Indians of the Gran Chaco*, by Alfred Metraux (Philadelphia: American Folklore Society, 1946).

How Nanabozho Brought Fire to His People

Nanabozho, the culture hero of the Ojibway people of the upper Great Lakes region, was the son of a mortal woman and the immortal spirit of the west wind. Although his actions were frequently beneficial to his people, he was often a selfish trickster who used his wits to fulfill his own wants and impulses. Many of the tales about him are *pourquoi* stories, recounting the origins of distinctive characteristics of the landscape and of plant and animal life. In this Native North American version of the widely distributed quest for fire tale-type, the central figure reveals both his concern for others and his selfishness, along with his creative problem-solving abilities and his power to transform himself. Dorothy Reid, a Thunder Bay, Ontario librarian who selected many of the character's better-known adventures and arranged them in the form of a biography, retells this version. Although she drew from many sources, she noted in the introduction that she tried to make her 'own versions true to the spirit of the original material, and above all to the qualities of humour, adventure, and fantasy in which it is so rich'. However, she does Europeanize her retelling somewhat. For instance, the original possessor of the fire is referred to as a 'magician', rather than a 'manitou', the Ojibway term for a person possessing great spirit power.

*O*n the early days of the world the people had no fire to warm them and to cook their food. Because they saw its destructive power when lightning set the forest ablaze, they were afraid of it.

Once the Coyote went to the underworld and brought back a brand of fire for the tribes. But the people forbade its use and appointed an old warrior-magician to watch over it. Some fearless braves tried to steal it for themselves, but it was always well guarded by the magician and his two fierce daughters.

As Nanabozho himself was young and strong, the lack of fire for heat did not trouble him particularly. His grandmother, however, was growing old and felt the cold severely. In the winter she spent much of the time huddled in her fur robe complaining bitterly.

Nanabozho entered the wigwam one day and, finding her thus, sought to cheer her. 'Come, Noko, come!' he cried. 'Get up and go with me into the forest. We will follow the hunting trail of the wolf, and the blood will flow warmly once more through your veins.'

Nokomis huddled deeper into her robe and turned her face away from him. 'It is well for you to talk,' she muttered wearily, 'but I am old and slow. Hunting trails are not for me and the bitter wind bites to the marrow of my bones.'

The thoughtless Nanabozho was touched with pity. With his own hand he brought her a piece of venison, hoping that food would put new spirit into her. But the raw deer-meat was frozen hard, and Nokomis had great difficulty gnawing it with her poor old teeth. As he watched her, Nanabozho resolved that he would steal some fire for her comfort before another winter came.

The next year, in the moon of wild rice[1], he set out for the region where the old warrior-magician lived. Arriving some distance from the lodge where the fire was jealously guarded, he hid his dug-out canoe in the willows. Then, changing himself into a small white hare, he jumped into the water in order to appear wet and bedraggled, for he was sure that this would arouse the pity of the magician's daughters.

As soon as he approached the lodge one of the girls' saw him, picked him up, and carried him inside, placing him near the burning brand to warm and dry him. Then she returned to her work.

Watching his opportunity, Nanabozho hopped a little closer to the fire. He had forgotten that when he moved he made the earth tremble, and this violent tremor wakened the old magician who had been sleeping on a heap of furs in a corner of the lodge.

'What was that noise?' the old man growled. 'What have you foolish women been doing while I slept?'

The girls protested that they had done nothing wrong, that they did not know what had caused the sound. They never thought of blaming the poor little half-drowned hare.

---

1. September.

From William Toye, *The Fire Stealer*. Illustrated by Elizabeth Cleaver. (Toronto: Oxford University Press, 1979).

Then the old magician caught sight of the hare. His suspicions were aroused and he got up to have a better look at him. But the small trembling animal seemed so powerless that the old man went back to sleep, muttering about the foolishness of women.

Huddling close to the fire, Nanabozho waited until he heard the old man snoring and until the girls were busy at the side of the lodge farthest from the door. Then, at exactly the right moment, he changed himself back into a fleet-footed Indian brave, seized the brand, dashed from the lodge, and ran towards the place in the willows where he had left his canoe.

But he had wakened the old magician who instantly saw what had happened and sent the girls in pursuit. Their father's shouts spurred them on, for they knew they would be cruelly punished if they lost the sacred fire.

Nanabozho sped swiftly down the trail quite confident that he could easily out-run two girls. But when he glanced over his shoulder, he was dismayed to see that they were gaining on him. He doubled his speed, but the girls, by means of magic, ran faster still.

'Come back, you trickster!' one of them yelled. 'Give us back our fire!'

By this time Nanabozho had reached his canoe. Behind him was a large meadow of dried grass. 'Here is your fire!' he yelled, and plunged the burning stick into the grass. It ignited and the wind carried the flames and dense smoke back towards the girls and halted their pursuit. They could do nothing but return to the fierce upbraiding of their father.

As Nanabozho watched the blaze he had made, he saw how the broad-leafed trees reflected the colours of the fire in brilliant shades of red and gold and bronze. This so pleased him that he decided to make them look this way every year in the autumn.

Nanabozho fixed the burning brand in one end of his canoe and set out, paddling swiftly and singing:

> 'Great is Nanabozho, mighty he
> Who captured fire and set it free.'

He finally reached home, and Nokomis received the gift of fire joyfully, basking in the heat it gave.

The people soon lost their fear and never tired of telling how Nanabozho brought them fire.

From *Tales of Nanabozho*, by Dorothy M. Reid (Toronto: Oxford University Press, 1963).

Maui the Half-God

Tales of the Polynesian trickster and culture-hero Maui are found from New Zealand to Hawaii. Son of a god and a mortal woman, he is the smallest and youngest of five brothers, who sometimes mock him and at other times are awed by his powers. The origins of many distinctive landscape features of specific areas and characteristic features of different creatures are attributed to his actions. He is motivated sometimes by curiosity, sometimes by a love of mischief, and sometimes by a desire to help others. However, the beneficial results of his actions are often an accidental result of his indulgence in trickery. Two of the most widely distributed tales recount his establishing the present course and speed of the sun's daily progress across the sky and his learning the secret of fire. Told by the Maori people of New Zealand, these versions of the events reveal his brothers' ambiguous attitude toward Maui and the essentially selfish motivations behind deeds that benefited others.

Maui grew up and became a man. He married a woman of the upper world and went to live in the village with his brothers. Each day the sun god rose with a bound and travelled quickly across the sky. While light remained, the morning meal was hastily prepared and eaten, and then in a little while it was dark again. The people grumbled because the hours of sunlight were so short, but no one ever thought of trying to alter them. Only Maui watched the sun hurrying across the sky, and thought about it, until at last he knew what could be done.

'The days are too short,' he said to his brothers.

'Yes, they are not long enough for us to do our work. That is why our games are always played in the dark,' they said.

'We must make them longer,' Maui declared.

His brothers laughed. 'Is the sun a bird, to be caught while it perches on a branch?' they asked.

'Yes,' Maui replied seriously. 'I will snare it like a sitting bird.'

His brothers laughed louder. 'Are you a god to think that you can face the sun god in his strength?'

Maui's eyes blazed. 'You forget my power too soon, my brothers. Can I not change myself into a bird? Am I not the strongest of all men? Whose is the magic jawbone of Muri our grandfather? Tomorrow we will journey towards the rising of the sun, and there we will make a snare of strong rope and catch him and tame him.'

'But the ropes will burn. He will break them like single threads, and we shall shrivel up in the heat of his anger,' they objected.

'Get your wives to bring flax and we will make the rope now,' Maui said firmly, and because of the fire in his eyes, and because they were afraid of him, Maui's brothers sat down and plaited a strong rope. Then Maui took the magic jawbone and, followed by his brothers carrying the rope, he set out towards the place of the rising sun. They hid in the daytime, but at night they travelled fast, until at last they reached the edge of the world. There they built a long clay wall behind which they could hide and shelter themselves from the heat of the sun. They built houses made of branches at each end of the wall, and hid themselves in them, Maui in one and his brothers in the other. Above the place where the sun rose they set a great rope noose and covered it with branches and green leaves.

Presently the sun rose in his strength. The brothers had the end of the rope in their hands. 'Steady,' whispered Maui. 'Wait till his head and shoulders are through. A-a-h! Now!' The brothers pulled on the rope. Aha, they pulled the rope which had settled round the body of Tama the sun, till it quivered and sang the song of strong ropes that are stretched to breaking point. Tama felt the pain like a circle of fire round his body. He saw the wall and the huts made of branches, and the rope that stretched from his body to the door of the hut. In his anger he threw himself from side to side. He caught the woven flax in his hands to snap it, but it was too strongly made. He pushed with his feet against the earth and the singing of the rope swelled like insects in the bush in summer. It slipped through the hands of the brothers, and the sound of their heavy breathing could be heard above the roaring of the sun.

Maui left his hut with his weapon in his hand, and ran along behind the shelter of the wall. He rose to his full height and brought Muri's bone down with all his strength on Tama's head. Again and again he struck, while the air rang with the cries of the sun god. His head fell forward, and Maui's brothers gathered up the slack of the rope. Maui's blows still felt like the noise of forest trees crashing to the ground when they are felled by fire. At length the sun god was beaten to his knees and cried for mercy.

Then they let him go, for he was badly wounded, and his strength had left him. Instead of leaping swiftly along the path from morning to night, he travelled slowly, as he does to this very day.

From A.W. Reed, *Myths and Legends of Maoriland*. Illustrated by Dennis Turner. (Wellington and Auckland: A.H. & A.W. Reed, 1961), 33.

Maui's restless mind was never satisfied with the answers he received to his questions.

'Where does fire come from?' he wanted to know.

'It is here,' they replied impatiently. 'Why do you want to know where it comes from? If it is ours, do we need to know how it comes to us?'

'But what happens if the fires go out?'

'We do not let them go out. If that should happen, our mother knows where to obtain the fire, but she will not tell us.'

That night, when everyone was asleep, Maui left his whare and crept to the cooking fires that were smouldering in the darkness. Quietly he poured water on them until the last spark was quenched.

As soon as the sky flushed with the first rays of dawn, Maui called to his servants, 'I am hungry. Cook some food quickly.' They ran to the fires, only to find heaps of grey ash. There was an outcry in the village as the servants rushed to and fro with the news. Maui stayed in his whare and smiled to himself as he listened to the noise. Presently he heard the sound of voices on the marae, the village meeting-place. His mother was telling the slaves to go to the underworld to get more fire.

Maui threw his kiwi feather cloak round him and strode on to the marae. The slaves were huddled together in terror, for they dreaded the underworld. 'I will go, my mother. Where shall I find the land of darkness? Who is keeper of the fire?'

Taranga looked at her son suspiciously. 'If no one will go, then my youngest son must make the journey. If you keep to the path that I will show you, you will come to the house of Mahuika, your ancestress. She is the guardian of the fire. If she asks your name, tell her who you are. You must be careful. Be respectful, my son. We know the ways of Maui-tiki-tiki-a-Taranga, but your ancestress is powerful, and if you try to deceive her, she will punish you.'

Maui grinned mischievously and set off at once with a long, steady pace that covered the ground quickly, and soon took him to the shadowy land where the fire goddess lived. Presently he came to a beautiful whare with splendid carvings, with paua-shell eyes that shone like flame in the darkness. A woman's voice, old and broken, like the crackling of branches in the fire, came to his ears.

'Who is the bold mortal that stares at the whare of Mahuika of the Fire?'

'It is Maui.'

'I have five grandchildren called Maui. Is it Maui-tikitiki-a-Taranga?'

'Yes, it is I.'

The old woman chuckled. 'What do you want from your grandmother, Maui-the-last-one?'

'I want fire to take back to my mother and my brothers.'

'I can give you fire, Maui.'

Mahuika pulled out one of her finger-nails, and it burst into flame. 'Carry it carefully, Maui, and light your fires with it.'

Maui took it away, but when he had gone a little distance, he threw it on the ground and stamped on it until the fire was beaten out. He went back to the whare.

'Aha, it is Maui again,' the old woman called. 'What do you want this time, Maui?'

'Fire. I have lost it. The flame went out.'

Mahuika scowled. 'Then you have been careless, my grandchild. I will give you another finger-nail, but you must shield the flame with your hand.'

Maui took the burning finger-nail. When he was out of sight, he beat out the flame and returned to Mahuika. The fire god scowled at him, and grumbled as she gave him another.

Five times Maui went away with the flame, and five times he returned empty-handed. Ten times he went away, and ten times he returned empty-handed. Mahuika's finger-nails had all been given away. Grudgingly she gave him one of her toe-nails, but in a little while the crafty Maui came back for another. Five times he went away, and five times he returned empty-handed. Nine times he went away and nine times he returned empty-handed.

Then at last Mahuika's patience was exhausted. The subterranean fires shook the house, and Maui had to force his way through the heat and the smoke that poured from the door and window. Mahuika's eyes glared through the darkness like flashes of lightning. She took her toe-nail and threw it at Maui. It fell short, and as it touched the ground there was a noise like thunder, and a sheet of flame travelled with the speed of wind towards Maui. He ran as quickly as he could, but the flames were like a taniwha roaring after him. He changed to the form of a hawk and flew onwards with great strokes of his wings, but still the flames gained on him. He could feel the heat singeing his feathers, and to this day you will see that the plumage of the hawk remains brown where the fire touched it.

A pool of water lay before him, and folding his wings he plunged into it. Presently the water grew warm. Maui stirred uneasily at the bottom of the pool. It was beginning to get hot now. A few moments later it started to boil and Maui flew upward. The air was full of flame. The forest was on fire and the flames were spreading up into the sky.

It seemed as though the whole world was in danger of being destroyed by fire. Then Maui remembered the gods he had known in Tama's house. He called to them and they saw that the earth was in peril. They sent down rain, heavy driving rain that hurled itself against the flames, and flattened their crests, and broke through the walls of fire. A harsh voice was heard crying in terror. Mahuika was in the midst of the fire, and as she turned and fled to her home, her strength began to fail her. The flames subsided into fitful little tongues, and died suddenly in a puff of steam. Mahuika threw the last of her fire into the trees, and they gave it shelter and saved it for the children of men. These trees were the kaikomako, the mahoe, and the totara.

At the last, then, there came goodness from the mischief of Maui, for men learnt to rub the wood of these trees together so that fire came from them, and they could at any time summon the fire children of Mahuika to their aid.

From *Myths and Legends of Maoriland*, by A. W. Reid (Wellington and Auckland, New Zealand: A.H. and A.W. Reed, 1961).

Fire and *An Ordinary Woman*

One of the best-known classical Greek myths—the story of Prometheus, who had helped Zeus become ruler of the gods and who created man—explains how human beings first acquired fire and how trouble came into the world. Prometheus defies the authority of the gods in order to give humanity the gift it needs to rise above the level of animals. For his punishment, he becomes a sacrificial hero who, like Odin and Christ, suffers for the good of those he leads. The myth embodies the Greek emphasis on the dignity of human struggle in the face of fate. Prometheus, whose name means forethought, is a contrast to his brother, Epimetheus, afterthought. The latter ignores his brother's warnings about his indulgent treatment of Pandora, a creation of the gods designed to be Zeus's revenge against his one-time benefactor. In their adaptation, Garfield and Blishen, British writers of children's and young adults' fiction, use such novelistic techniques as detailed characterization and extended description to communicate the intense emotional and psychological conflicts that mark the interrelationships between the main characters.

Fire

'*M*y father bids me tell you to destroy them, great Prometheus; or he will do so himself.'

Thus Hermes, messenger of the gods, as he stood, piercing bright, in the Titan's garden, washed by the morning sun.

'Why? Why? How have they offended? What is their crime?'

'Who knows what is in the mind of Zeus? Perhaps he is offended, Lord Prometheus? Perhaps he finds what you have made too close in aspect to the gods? Perhaps he sees them as a mockery? Gods who are subject to the Fates. . . . Destroy them, Prometheus. So my father says.'

'And you, good Hermes? Is it your wish, too?'

The god looked sideways, avoiding the Titan's despairing eyes; shifted from foot to winged foot and smiled as his shadow seemed to dance off into the trees.

'Between you and me, Prometheus. . . no. Not particularly, that is. I think they have a certain charm. Personally, I like them. I assure you, Prometheus, that such messages as, from time to time, I bring from this great god or that, do not necessarily reflect my own opinions.'

Hermes, ever politic, ever unwilling to offend, watched the mighty Titan curiously; he continued, 'Believe me, my friend—I understand your affection and your sorrow. When I summoned the shade of the one that died, I was troubled, Prometheus. As we entered the grove of black poplars, this shade and I, it asked me: Why, why? And I could not answer. Then, when I led it to the dark river and dragged it aboard the evil, rotting boat, and it saw there was no one else there but bony Charon, again it begged me: Why, why?'

'We came to the further bank, and still there was no one else by. And so to the Field of Asphondel: empty, empty. . . .'

'It clung to me, Prometheus, as I left it, still begging me to tell it why.'

'It knew nothing; had not lived more than the winking of an eye—yet it sensed the vastness of its loss. I looked back, and never in all the universe have I seen anything so lonely as that single, frightened shade wandering over the ashy ground and crying: Why, why?'

The Titan listened and groaned in anguish; then Hermes added softly: 'They are so frail, Prometheus. Your creatures are so pitifully frail. Are they worth their labour?'

Eagerly the Titan laid his hand on Hermes' ribboned staff—as if to deflect or soften the god's terrible message.

'But I will strengthen them! I will refine the substance, purify it and pluck out the seeds that menace. I—'

'It is too late, Prometheus. They are doomed.'

'By Zeus?'

'If not by my father, then by every wind that blows. How could they endure, never knowing when Atropos might take it into her blind head to slit the thread of their lives?'

How indeed? And the more Hermes argued, the more intolerable seemed the burden Prometheus' fragile creatures would have to bear.

Yet their very frailty stung the Titan's heart and strengthened his great will. He begged bright Hermes to plead with his father for a little respite. If the creatures were destined to flicker out—then let them perish of their own accord. But spare them the dreadful thunderbolt. Let them see and love the gods, however briefly, and, maybe, find some favour in their sight—

Here, subtle Hermes pursed his lips and tapped his staff against his head.

'Between you and me, my friend, I fancy you've hit on something. I don't promise—I never promise—but if your creatures were to find favour in great Zeus's eyes. . . that is to say, if they were to go out of their way to please, then who knows? Think on that, Lord Prometheus; and I will undertake to delay my father's hand.'

Between Arcadia and Attica, there was a place called Sicyon where the creatures of Prometheus had begun to make a home. It was here, in a myrtle grove—once dear to Hermes—that Prometheus put it into men's minds to honour the gods. A rich, red bull, sleek and portly, was sacrificed and the Titan cupped his hands to his vast mouth and shouted up to Olympus for almighty Zeus to descend and be mankind's first guest.

'See, great god! My creatures honour you and worship you! Come down so they may behold you and give you the best of the earth!'

He shaded his eyes and stared desperately up towards the curtains of cloud that veiled the mountain's divine summit.

Even as he watched, a finger of lightning crooked round them and drew them briefly apart. Then came a roll of thunder. The god had heard. The god would come.

Eagerly Prometheus stripped the blood-dappled skin from the bull and divided the carcass, laying the bones and fat beneath one part of the hide, and the steaming flesh beneath the other; but in his haste he had not detached the stomach. . . . Two portions: one for the god—and one for mankind.

Wide-eyed and innocent that they were, poised on the edge of extinction, the Titan's creatures watched as their great creator toiled and struggled to save them.

Suddenly they shrank back. A fearful radiance seared their naked eyes and scorched their skin. They cried out and fled into the shadows of the myrtles, hiding their faces in their hands. The blaze had been unendurable. It lingered on the inner eye where it burned its vision. Within the scalding radiance had been a shape. A shimmering fluent shape, part man-like, part immeasurably greater. Eyes had seen them—eyes like merciless suns.

It had been the god. . . .

'Welcome, mighty Zeus. Welcome father of the gods, lord of the sky! Your feast is ready. Mankind awaits.'

The Titan stood back as the fiery god stared round the grove. Then, seeing that Prometheus' poor creatures were blasted by his light, Zeus veiled his lustre and smiled.

He saw the covered portions of the slaughtered bull. He nodded. They had not skimped their offering. The beast had been of the finest.

He touched one portion, lifted a corner of the hide. The stomach, it reeked of offal. He turned to the other. He glimpsed rich fat. Prometheus trembled; all-seeing Zeus nodded.

He pointed to the second portion.

'I have chosen,' the mighty god decreed. 'From now through all eternity, in feast and holy sacrifice, this portion is for the immortal gods, and that for mankind.'

He flung back the skin he had chosen. Beneath the rich layer of fat lay nothing but the animal's wretched, meatless bones. The divine portion. . . .

Prometheus bowed his head to hide a helpless smile. He awaited the enraged god's thunderbolt. But Zeus' anger took a subtler form.

'Let them eat their flesh raw,' he said. 'I forbid them the use of fire.'

Without fire, they would die. Their slender limbs would freeze, their blood congeal and their bright eyes glaze and film like scum on a quiet pond. The angry god had doomed them as surely as if he'd hurled his thunderbolt and scorched them in an instant.

Prometheus' wept slow, bitter tears. It had been his own smile that had brought it about: mighty Zeus had taken this way of punishing him. The smile of the father was to be the death's-head grin of his children.

For a while, fury took hold of him—and his gentle brother watched with terror and awe as great Prometheus paced their garden, bursting asunder the well-tended trees as if they'd been straw. Then the Titan passed into despair. War and violence had ever been hateful to him. The mighty struggles his nature demanded had all been in the mind.

He knew he could not storm Olympus and drag down the father of the gods. He lacked both Zeus' strength and Zeus' instant passion. Thinking had ever held him back.

For long it had preserved him—and saved him from the fearful fate of all his race. But now that power had reached its end—the limits of his mind. Thought stared into soul; and soul stared back at thought. They were the same; and the tragic Titan knew he must destroy himself to save his children: men.

Some time during the night, mankind saw him shining among the thick trees that cloaked the northern slopes of Mount Olympus. His light pierced the branches so that it seemed as if some star had fallen and been caught in a vast black net.

Then his light was snuffed in a deep cleft in the rock, and the Titan mounted unseen.

An owl flew out of the trees, screeched several times, then fluttered uncertainly, hovering as if seeking its moment to pounce. It screeched again, and began to pursue a devious path in the night air, leading higher and higher up the mountain.

It was the owl of the goddess Athene.

The hidden Titan saw it and knew that the goddess had not turned against him. She had sent her owl to lead him secretly into the fortress of the gods. This was the most she could do for him. Mighty though she was, even she feared her blazing father's wrath.

Now came another bird out of the night. A crane perched in the Titan's twisting path. It stared at him with bright, inquisitive eyes.

'Though I will not help you, Prometheus,' whispered the voice of cunning Hermes, 'I will not stand in your path.' The crane flew off and its soft cry came back to the mounting Titan. 'There is what you seek in my brother Hephaestus' forge.'

Flames gleamed and danced on the twenty golden bellows as they rose and fell like twenty gigantic beating hearts. They breathed on the forge, increasing its fire till the lip of its rocky prison shivered and ran.

Shadows loomed and lumbered against the huge smithy's walls. Rods and crucibles made the shapes of nodding beasts; and in their midst crouched the shadow of a misshapen monster on bird-thin legs that were broken sharply by the angle of the floor and walls. Hephaestus was at work. He was making a wedding gift for Aphrodite, his wife. He scowled tempestuously as he beat out the gold on the black anvil with a loud, regular clang. He was fashioning the clasp of a girdle. . . .

Suddenly the god's heat-inflamed eyes quickened. A strange shadow had crossed his on the wall. It moved secretly among the beast-like shadows of the rods and crucibles which seemed to nod and swear at it, then crowd it under their own dangerous night.

Hephaestus turned. He saw a hand, holding an unkindled torch. He saw it reach forward, plunge in and out of the fire. The torch flared. It was alight.

The god looked up. Prometheus stood before him.

'For my children,' whispered the despairing Titan. 'For mankind.'

The two great outcasts stared at one another.

'Take it and be gone,' muttered the god.

For long after the Titan had departed, Hephaestus brooded over his anvil. His mighty hammer leaned against his knee. . . and the beaten gold grew cool. Then the god began again. His hammer rose and fell till fountains of sparks leaped up and seemed to engulf him in robes of broken fire.

At last he rested. The smithy grew quiet and the ugly god examined the clasp he had made. It was a golden hand holding a torch. It seemed to be caressing it, and the torch was spurting its vital fire. So delicately wrought was this hand that it seemed to tremble—to move, even with tenderness. . . .

The god nodded. Here in this eternal clasp was his own fierce love for Aphrodite—and Prometheus' aching love for mankind.

He fastened it to the girdle with rivets as fine as hair and hobbled off to the laughing goddess of his dreams.

An Ordinary Woman

Still Zeus did not strike the defiant Titan down. Prometheus had opposed him, set his command aside. Fire flickered below and strengthened the new, aspiring life.

Time and again Prometheus turned his eyes to heaven so that he might see his destruction blazing forth. But the lord of the sky seemed to have turned his back. Had grave Athene pleaded with her father? Had subtle Hermes put a case?

The Titan's uncertainty grew agonized as his time ran out. Nonetheless, he still laboured for his creatures, teaching them what he could to widen their narrow foothold between the Fates and the gods. At night he brooded in the mysterious room where man had been born. Already he had begun to refine the precious substance of chaos. Strange spots and scales he'd discovered on the bright seeds. These he scraped away and confined in a small jar which he sealed and hid. He suspected them to be some malignant rot. . . .

'Can you fashion a woman, my clever, ugly son? Can you make her as skilfully as Prometheus made his creatures below?'

The father of the gods stared down from his gold and ivory throne in the great council chamber. 'Not of gold, nor silver, nor imperishable bronze; but of the self-same clay the Titan used—the soft wet clay of Attica?'

Hephaestus shuffled and blinked his reddened eyes away from Zeus' radiance. The fire of his forge was as night beside the blazing noon of Zeus.

'Fetch me the clay and I will make such a woman.'

Zeus nodded; and swift as thought Hermes sped down, twisting through the cloudy swarms of bees that sang above the lower slopes of Mount Hymettus.

Hephaestus waited; and presently, the thieving god returned with Prometheus' clay.

Hephaestus set about his task and Hermes, leaning against the lintel post of the smithy door, watched the great artificer at his work.

Unlike Prometheus, the god worked slowly. He seemed to seek the form within the dull shapeless clay. Even as Hermes watched, his burnt and twisted fingers probed and dragged at hair, cheeks, lips, breasts, and limbs as if he was freeing rather than creating them. He tore the clay away from her eyes as if it had been a blindfold; and suddenly a woman stared at Hermes in the doorway. Even though he knew his ill-tempered brother's marvellous skill, Hermes was startled by this strange new evidence of it.

Her height was perhaps a finger's breadth below Aphrodite's; but otherwise her beauty was not of Olympus. It had the darker, richer colours of the earth. Hephaestus had fashioned a woman far beyond the Titan's skill.

She stood beside the mighty anvil and as the twenty golden bellows breathed on the fire, the heat drew tears of moisture out of the clay so that she seemed to be weeping before she had life. Then Zeus bade Aeolus, warder of the four winds, breathe life into her nostrils and mouth.

She stirred; she moved; she stared about her with a sweet vacancy, understanding nothing—feeling nothing.

Being formed from unseeded clay, she had neither passions nor qualities.

So life-giving Zeus commanded the immortal gods to enrich her with their gifts.

First Hestia, gentlest of the children of Cronus, gave this woman a gentleness and generosity not unlike her own; and the vacant eyes took on a soft and tender gleam. But Ares, roughly elbowing forward, forced on her a touch of himself, so that behind the tender gleam there glinted the flicker of a savage fire.

Next great Apollo gave her sweet and tempting grace of movement—such as he himself delighted in; but straightway his moon-sister Artemis gave her defensive quickness, modesty, and virginity.

Glorious Demeter shook her head. Never quite in sympathy with Artemis, she blessed the woman with a richly fertile womb—and the knowledge of it. This knowledge now glinted mysteriously from under the downcast lashes that the mighty huntress's gift had imposed.

'And I will give her wisdom,' said Athene suddenly. She had divined the danger there lurked in this woman, compounded as she was of so many opposing passions. 'I will give her wisdom so that her gifts may be well-used.'

Zeus frowned; but he could not deny the powerful goddess her right. So he bade Hermes give Athene's gift a double edge, with curiosity and deceit.

Now the woman turned and smiled gratefully at each of the gods in turn; her eyes seemed to linger so that her last look was always sideways. . . till imperious Hera hastened to cover her nakedness with fine, cloudy robes. This woman was curiously disturbing. Beside her, the hot numphs were but children—their amorous leapings and twinings as children's games. . . . Then Zeus gave her a name: Pandora—all giving.

She bowed her head. 'Great goddess,' she murmured, raising her face now to lovely Aphrodite while her eyes lingered timidly on smiling Zeus. 'Is there no gift from you? Are you displeased with me? Have I unknowingly offended you? If so I beg forgiveness. . . and plead for your gift. For without it, I think, all would wither away unused.'

So Aphrodite laughed—and lent Pandora the girdle that Hephaestus had made for her—the girdle that kindled desire.

'With such a piece of work,' murmured the king of the gods as he brooded down on Pandora, 'what need have I of thunderbolts?'

It was Hermes who led her down the slopes of Mount Olympus; and as the gods watched, none was sorry to see her go.

'What harsh message do you bring from Olympus now, Hermes?'

Prometheus and his brother were in their orchard, securing the well-filled branches with stout props, when the great herald rippled through the trees.

'No message, Lord Prometheus,' answered the god courteously. He had plucked an apple in passing and now speared it idly on his ribboned staff. He stared at it as if surprised. 'I bring a gift. Indeed, Prometheus, there is no need to look at me so angrily, as if you would refuse. The gift does not concern you. It is for your brother, Epimetheus.'

He pointed his staff, with the red apple on its head, at the second Titan, the ever-gentle, not over-wise Epimetheus.

'The gift of the gods is for you.'

Epimetheus came forward with a pleased smile. His heart was open; his nature unsuspecting. Such happy beings as he are always the last of their race.

'Beware the gods bearing gifts,' muttered his great brother whom he never understood.

Epimetheus looked uncertain. Hermes stretched out his staff. 'Come,' he called. 'Pandora!'

She came from behind the trees in the cloudy gown of Hera. She walked with graceful yet uncertain steps. Her eyes were downcast—though from time to time they glimmered with a curious sideways glance that lingered in Epimetheus' heart.

'Here is your new gift, Epimetheus. Pandora—gift of the Olympian gods.'

Epimetheus was entranced. Never had their orchard seen a richer fruit.

'Beware, brother—'

'Lord Prometheus, this is no concern of yours.' Hermes spoke calmly, but there was an edge to his voice. Then he laughed disarmingly. 'Epimetheus—our deep brother is too anxious. He mistrusts good fortune. Between you and me, I suspect a little envy. And who could blame him? See—'

He touched the trembling Pandora with his staff, laying its appled tip on her breast. She smiled timidly. 'She bears the gifts of us all.'

'She is the gift of Zeus, brother. Old Cronus once had such a gift. Do you remember a cup of honied drink—?'

Epimetheus hesitated; gazed uneasily from brother to the god. He avoided Pandora's eyes. He thanked Olympus, but begged time to consider. . . .

Prometheus smiled triumphantly.

'Do you refuse me, Epimetheus?' Pandora's voice was low. . . even pleading. The gentle Titan glanced at her. Modestly she cast her eyes down to Aphrodite's kindling girdle. Epimetheus felt desire rise like the all-covering sea.

Then briefly Pandora lifted her eyes and stared at Prometheus. Her look was still gentle and partly timid. She seemed to be bewildered and curious as to why this mighty being should bid his brother send her away. What had she done? Why did he stare at her as if to pierce her through and through? Why did his great brows furrow till his eyes were no more than pools of troubled shadow? Was it only because she had come between brother and brother? Was it as the bright god had said—that this vast soul was stabbed with envy for his brother's blessing?

If so, then it was not of her doing. . . .

See—he was drawing Epimetheus aside, talking with him—while the god who had brought her looked on with the strangest smile. What was to become of her, with all her beauty and gifts?

Why had the gods made her so?

'Do not refuse me, Epimetheus,' she pleaded; and such was her power that Epimetheus' heart faltered within him. She promised him such joy and fierce delight that even the gods would envy him. Epimetheus' eyes began to gleam. Whereupon the blessing of Hestia, momentarily conquering the passions of Aphrodite and Ares, prompted Pandora to speak of ease and sweet companionship, and the speaking silences of harmonious kinds. . . .

'Can there be danger in such a gift?' asked simple Epimetheus of his brother.

'Nor will their lives be fruitless, Lord Prometheus,' murmured Hermes, drifting close and leaning towards the Titan's ear. 'Glorious Demeter has blessed her, too. Even as your well-tended trees bear fine fruit, so will Pandora bear children to your home. Mark my words, Prometheus, her children will inherit our immortal gifts—for the gods' gifts do not die—and these children will mingle with mankind. Thus does my father mean well, Prometheus. He seeks to improve on your charming but fragile creation with some more durable qualities of the gods. Believe me, my friend—'

Suddenly the Titan turned with terror on the murmuring god of lies. His eyes were wild—his vast comprehension tilted so that all ran down into the pit of dismay. He had divined dread Zeus' purpose—and foreseen his own defeat. The creatures that he loved—the creatures who might have inherited the earth as neither gods nor Titans were permitted to do—were to be crippled before they had begun.

Even as in Pandora the passions of the gods opposed each other, so they would in men. All aspiration would be lamed, all achievement warped as man eternally fought within himself a battle that could be neither lost nor won.

The great Titan raised his eyes to Mount Olympus and cursed immortal Zeus.

He lifted up his voice and hurled his curses till they echoed in the far corners of the universe. Even in hateful Tartarus they were heard, like thin, high whispers over the ceaseless weeping and groaning of the Titans who were chained there.

Close by the dreary Fields of Asphodel, there is a pool beside which grows a bone-white poplar tree. It is the pool of memory. Here strayed the solitary shade of the man who had died. Vainly it drank of the pool; but what memories could it recapture of a life so fleeting, save an aching glimpse of a garden by night?

It heard Prometheus' curses and shook its thin head. 'Why? Why?' it wailed—and flittered away into the lonely gloom.

Grim Hades in his palace heard them—and nodded in expectation of his vast brother's revenge.

As in a dream, Prometheus saw Hermes flicker away; and with a last stab of anguish he saw his brother and Pandora retreat with frightened faces, and run from the orchard. Their hands had been clasped—and there was no undoing them now.

Prometheus bowed his mighty head. He heard a rushing in the air. It was coming; and he was almost glad of it—the thunderbolt of Zeus!

The trees blazed and, for an instant, their blackened branches reached up like imploring arms with fingers charred and flaming.

A radiance that seared even the Titan's ancient eyes stood in the ruined orchard like a fiery sword. Zeus in all his unendurable glory was come for his revenge.

Far, far to the north, amid the freezing mountains of the Caucasus, there stood a tall, cold pillar. Chains of unburstable iron hung from its base and capital. Here the naked Titan was manacled by wrists and ankles, stretched so that he could scarcely twist his body or avert his head.

He waited—then a shadow fell across his face. He rolled his eyes to see what had come between him and the pale, bitter, sun.

A vulture with hooked talons and greedy beak hung in the air. Its stony eyes met his. Then it swooped and the Titan writhed and screamed till the mountains cracked. His agony had begun. Again and again the hungry bird flew at him and tore at his undefended liver. When night came with biting frosts and whirling snow, the Titan's wounds healed and he grew whole again. But when the cold sun rose, the self-same shadow fell across his face and the Titan waited far his agony to begin once more. Such was the punishment of Prometheus, maker of men.

Epimetheus, the last of the Titans, wept for his mighty brother—whom he had never understood. In his great sadness Pandora comforted him, and little by little, Epimetheus began to think his brother had misjudged her. She was so quick to understand and minister to his every need. She never crossed nor questioned him; nor did she plead to enter his lost brother's mysterious room. For Prometheus, in his last moments of liberty, had charged his brother most urgently never to enter it or disturb what was hidden there.

Pandora nodded. Though she had not liked Prometheus, she was sensible of her husband's affection and was anxious for him to feel that she was of a like mind. For a while it seemed that the gifts of Hestia and Athene were uppermost.

Then, thanks to the rich soil of Attica, the black scars in the orchard healed over, and the reason for the great Titan's fall faded from Pandora's mind. More and more she came round to the view that the whole unlucky affair had blown up out of jealousy. Why else had her husband's brother so taken against her?

She gazed at her reflection in a pool. Certainly she was beautiful enough to stir envy in any one. After all, the gods had made her. She sighed. It had been tragic, but jealousy was an evil passion and Prometheus had paid for it. She only hoped it would serve as a lesson.

She stood up and thoughts of Prometheus slid into thoughts of the forbidden room. What was so particular about it? She suspected jealousy was at the root of it again. A jealous spirit is jealous in everything. Most likely the room was very handsome and Prometheus had forbidden it to her out of spite. The more she thought of it, the more she was convinced. It irritated her like a crumb in her bed. Wherever she turned for comfort, there it was, scratching away. Agitatedly she left the garden and entered the house. She paced the hall, pausing each time before the closed door. It was ridiculous. She felt she couldn't call her home her own. She laid her hand on the engraved bolt. Epimetheus would get over it. Naturally he'd be hurt at first and grieve for his brother again. But it would pass and then there'd be nothing to come between them. A shadow would have been removed. . . .

Pandora nodded. All in all, it would be for the best. She opened the door.

As she'd suspected, the room was the best in the house. A little dark, perhaps, and certainly dusty. . . but the fig-tree and its polished branches gave it great character and atmosphere.

She ran her finger along the wide bench that stretched from wall to wall. Idly she drew the shape of a baby in the dust. She smiled. The room would make a fine nursery. . . .

No sooner had she thought of it than she set to work. She swept and polished and transformed the shadowy room into a shining joy. She cleared out the cupboards of all old stone jars—but did not open them.

Here she respected her husband's wishes; besides—the jars seemed quite useless.

Then, quite by chance, she came upon a smaller one, tucked underneath the bench. She held it up. It was a pretty jar. Cleaned out, it would hold jewels or perfume. . . . She shook her head. No. She would defer to her husband's wish, foolish as it was.

Then she thought of Prometheus. How like him to keep such a jar for himself! What could he possibly want with it now? After all, it wasn't as though she intended to open all the jars.

She had her principles and would not have abandoned them for anything. She was perfectly certain that her husband would come to see it her way. He would admire her for leaving the other jars and so honouring his selfish brother's memory.

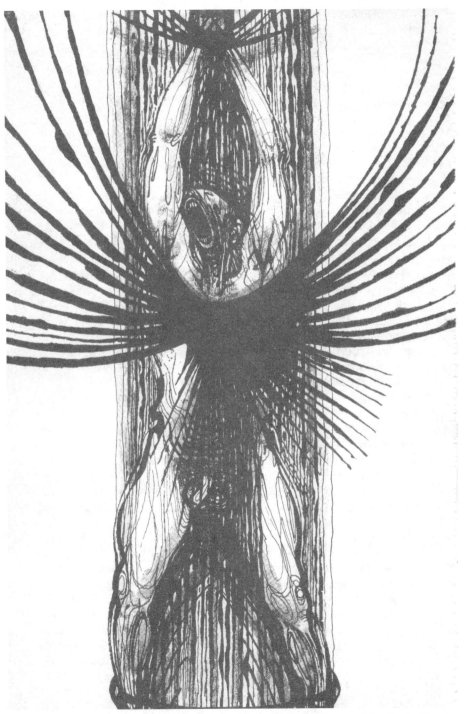

From Leon Garfield and Edward Blishen, *The God Beneath the Sea*. Illustrated by Charles Keeping (London: Longmans, 1970), 86.

She shook the pretty little jar gently. There was something inside. She listened. It gave a dry rattling sound. She shrugged her shoulders. She'd put up with the sacred memory of Prometheus for long enough. She opened the jar.

She screamed; she shrieked; she dropped the jar. Gentle Epimetheus came running to her cries.

There seemed to be a cloud, about Pandora: a whirling, malignant veil that glittered with ten thousand furious wings. They seemed to be insects of extraordinary venom and ferocity.

They bit and stung and beat against his crouching wife; then they turned on him and he felt their wicked little spears in every part of his body. He cried out:

'Prometheus, Prometheus! What have we done?'

Far in the north a fiercer pain than the vulture's beak stabbed at the chained Titan. From his icy place of punishment he saw what had befallen his children. His deep eyes filled with tears as a more terrible vulture tore at his heart.

Nor did this phantom bird depart with its bloody brother when healing night came. High in the freezing mountains, striped with the purple glaciers of his blood, Prometheus wept. His labours and his fall had been in vain.

The strange spots and scales he had imprisoned in the jar had been malignant indeed. Unhindered by the divine substance from which they'd been scraped, they had grown into hideous little furies. He had seen them fly out of his house in a wicked cloud to sting his helpless children. Madness, vice, old age, and crippling sickness had been let out upon the world as a birthright for man.

Prometheus raised his eyes and stared across the world's night. His eyes met those of bitter Atlas; and these two giants who had opposed the gods looked long and deep at each other from their separate high prisons of pain.

'Mankind,' whispered great Prometheus, 'forgive me; I have failed. Better that I never made you. . . for what is there left to you now?'

Pandora gazed down at the shattered jar. It was past repairing. She felt awkward. Her husband, inflamed from the strange insects' attacks, had looked at her reproachfully.

So, as mildly as she was able, she remarked that Prometheus was to blame. He should never have kept such things in a jar. She bent down and began to gather the broken pieces. Suddenly she came upon a curious stone. She picked it up. It was not a stone. She looked at it carefully. It seemed to be a chrysalis. . . .

She shivered as she tried to throw it away before it hatched. But it stuck to her fingers.

At last she scraped it off on a fragment of the jar. She rubbed her hands to rid herself of the gum-like substance the chrysalis had left. Her eyes brightened in surprise. The pain of the bites and stings seemed soothed. Eagerly she told Epimetheus. The chrysalis was a balm—a wondrous healing balm.

Pandora was delighted. She smiled at her husband. Was it not a good thing after all that she'd opened the jar? As she'd always told him, everything turned out for the best.

A sudden movement aloft distracted her. She looked up. A bird had been perched in the polished rafters, looking down with bright, inquisitive eyes. It flapped its wings and flew away. It had been a crane. She watched it through the casement as it flew with amazing speed towards the north. It pierced the colder air and crossed the mountains till at last it saw below it the pillar of Prometheus.

'What is there left to mankind now?' cried the despairing Titan as he saw the sideways-dropping god.

'Hope,' answered great Hermes. 'For better or worse—for who knows what may unfold from a chrysalis?—hope was left behind.'

From *The God Beneath the Sea*, by Leon Garfield and Edward Blishen (London: Corgi/Carousel, 1973).

How Death Came to the World

Narratives about the origin of death are essential elements of mythologies from around the world. Among the Kiowa people of the central plains, the trickster-hero Saynday is responsible for the arrival of death. In this version of a story found among many native cultures, anthropologists Marriott and Racklin portray Saynday's good intentions, which are criticized by the red ant mother as lacking foresight. While her argument is sensible and convincing, she rejects it shortly after, when death affects her personally. In addition to explaining the origin of death, the tale also explains how the red ant acquired its present state and how certain mourning customs of Kiowa women originated. The somewhat satiric tone toward woman could be explained by the fact that the retellers collected the story from a Kiowa man.

Saynday was coming along, and as he came he met the red ant. In those days the red ant was as round as a ball, like a lot of Kiowa women. It was a hot day. Saynday made himself small, no bigger than the ant, and they sat down in the shade of the prickly pear to talk.

'I've been thinking,' Saynday said.

'What about?' asked the ant. Like most other people, she wanted to make sure what Saynday had on his mind before she said anything herself.

'Well, I've been thinking that some of the old people and animals in my world are beginning to die,' answered Saynday. 'It's too bad. Nobody should have to die. I believe I could work out a way so that they could come back to life after four days.'

'Are you sure that's a good idea?' Ant asked.

'Why not?' inquired Saynday.

'Well, I think that if you keep bringing people back to life that way, over and over, the world will get too full. If you keep on bringing people and animals back to life, there won't be a place for anyone to go. I say that when people die, they should stay dead.'

'I think you are wrong,' Saynday argued.

'I think I am right,' Ant insisted. 'The old people have lived their lives. They're tired. I don't believe they even want to go on living.'

'But what about the young ones?' Saynday demanded. 'If a boy gets killed in a hunting accident or on a war raid, or if a young woman dies in childbirth, shouldn't they have the right to come back and take up their lives? They've just begun to live.'

Ant set her jaw stubbornly. 'Saynday,' she said, 'you always want your own way. Now this time I think you're wrong. When people die, let them stay dead. Don't try to bring them back.'

'If that's the way you want it, that's the way it shall be,' Saynday replied. 'If some day you regret your decision, remember that it was yours. If you make your decision, you have to keep it. From now on, you will have to mourn like all other people.'

'That's the way I want it,' Ant insisted, and Saynday got up and went away and left her, sitting under the prickly pear.

Four days later, Saynday was coming back along the same track. Suddenly the air was filled with sorrow, with tiny sobs and wails. He made himself small again, and found himself sitting beside Ant, under the same prickly pear.

'What in the world is the matter?' Saynday asked.

'He's all dead,' Ant sobbed. 'A buffalo stepped on him and he's all dead. There wasn't enough left of him to scrape up. Oh, my poor boy!'

'I warned you,' Saynday scolded her. 'If you had let me have my way, I could have brought him back to life in four days. But no. You women are all the same. You know the best and you're bound to have your own way. If you hadn't been so stubborn yourself, you son wouldn't have had to die.'

'Oh, my poor boy!' Ant wailed again, and she drew her butchering knife from its sheath at her belt. Before Saynday could move to stop her, she began cutting herself in two, just below the head.

'Now look here,' Saynday scolded, grabbing the knife before she could cut her head completely off. 'We've had enough dying around here for one day. Cutting yourself to pieces won't bring your son back; it will just make other people feel worse.'

'Now listen to what I say: From now on, when Kiowa women mourn, they should cut themselves—their arms, their legs, their hair—even cut off a finger joint, because a woman brought death forever into the world. But no woman shall ever kill herself for sorrow.'

And that's the way it was and that's the way it is, to this good day.

From *American Indian Mythology*, by Alice Marriott and Carol K. Racklin (New York: New American Library, 1972).

LINKS TO OTHER STORIES

Part Three

Larger Than Life
Tales of Heroes

In *The Hero with a Thousand Faces*, Joseph Campbell, a well-known scholar of myths and legends, wrote that no matter where a story originates 'it will always be the one, shape-shifting yet marvelously constant story that we find' (3). He believed that the pattern underlying stories of the great culture heroes was universal. The basic life story concerned an individual's search to discover his or her identity and role in society. Campbell, who had been influenced by the works of psychologist Carl Jung, believed that this basic story, or monomyth, was widely popular because it reflected a quest or search taken by every individual. Thus, the audience could identify with the aspirations and struggles of heroic figures, even if their conflicts occurred on grander scales.

In the great traditional tales, the hero's life was frequently presented as a biography, beginning with the hero's birth, which was often mysterious and indicated special status. Frequently, the heroes were products of unions between gods and mortals. Such was the case of Perseus, the Greek hero, who was the son of Zeus, king of the gods, and Danae, the daughter of the king of Argos. Krishna was a reincarnation of the Hindu god Vishnu. At the time of the birth of African-American hero John Henry, the moon was reported to have stopped and moved backward. Many of the heroes were markedly different as children. Krishna, Paul Bunyan, and Sundiata, hero of the Mali people, showed amazing strength as children. Often they were either rejected or abandoned: Sundiata and his mother were outcasts, Perseus and his mother were set adrift at sea, and Ned Kelly was a member of Australia's lowest social class.

Before they achieved status as leaders, the heroes frequently performed deeds that indicated their difference from other people. For example, when he was only seven-years-old, Sundiata uprooted an enormous baobab tree and carried it to his mother. This act significantly changed his status in his society. Once ridiculed, the future king was now regarded with awe by the villagers and with fear by his father's favourite wife because he was now a threat to her own son's ascension to the throne. While other warriors lived in terror, the Anglo Saxon hero Beowulf, when he was a young man, destroyed the evil, man-eating monster Grendel, and then Grendel's mother. Perseus killed the Gorgon Medusa and a vicious sea monster.

Although their deeds brought them fame and glory, the heroes generally faced great dangers and employed their abilities, courage, and strength for the benefit of others. Sundiata helped his mother; Beowulf made Hrothgar's kingdom once again safe; Perseus rescued the maiden Andromeda. Later, when they became leaders, they again served their people. Beowulf killed a dragon that threatened his land and Sundiata successfully battled against a tyrant. They do not, however, always use physical strength. Robin Hood and Ulysses, for example, often achieved success through their wits. The former played on the Sheriff of Nottingham's greed to lure the corrupt official into Sherwood Forest. Ulysses was able to save himself and many of his men from seemingly certain death by tricking the slow thinking but physically superior cyclops.

As their deeds indicate, heroes were generally superior to those around them and represented a higher level of human potential and achievement than their followers or those who heard the stories of their exploits. Generally, however, they were not perfect. For example, Ulysses and Robin Hood seemed to have an inordinate love of adventure and trickery; as a result, they often created unnecessary dangers for themselves and their followers. Like their followers and the audiences of stories about them, the heroes were mortal and accounts of their deaths frequently formed the dramatic conclusions of their biographies. Beowulf selflessly gave his life fighting the dragon; John Henry's heart burst after his prodigious feat of stream-drilling affirmed the superiority of humans over machines. Gilgamesh's last heroic quest was a failed search for immortality that ended with his acceptance of the inevitability of death. Superior though they were, heroes were not above the common human doom.

Reading the selections that follow, as well as some of the selections in 'Unlikely Heroes', 'Living by Wit', and 'Purposeful Journeys', readers will easily recognize many of the characteristics noted above and will notice similarities in the personalities and events in the lives of two or more specific heroes. These similarities have long intrigued readers, who have speculated about their causes. Perhaps, some have advanced, various hero tales are all descended from a very old, unknown original, and the significant patterns have been applied to local narratives, adapted by story tellers to meet expectations of their audiences. Certainly, parallels between stories from geographically proximate locations strongly suggest that one tale may have been influenced by another. Students influenced by Campbell and Jung explain the similarities by asserting that the stories reflect universal psychological patterns or archetypes. We tell similar stories, the argument states, because as human beings we are similar, no matter what culture we have come from.

Many people have objected to this 'universalist' approach. First, they argue, the presence of worldwide psychological archetypes cannot be proven. Culture, they say, determines the form and content of art more than any general psychological tendencies. Although there are similarities among stories, these similarities are less significant than the cultural differences. The major hero tales are thus important because they reflect the values of the people who tell them and meet their needs as members of a group. Moreover, the argument continues, the universalist interpretations are, in themselves, culturally influenced. Aspects that are advanced as reflecting worldwide psychological patterns are really male-centered, European-based ideas of heroism. That is why, it could be implied, European writers and critics have been attracted to non-European hero tales that most resemble European ones and have paid much less attention to those that do not.

While these discussions are part of a 'nature versus nurture' debate that is ongoing in many of the social sciences and humanities, the fact remains that each hero tale is the product of a distinct cultural group and, as such, must be approached in terms of that culture's beliefs, customs, and values if it is to be understood more fully. People have perpetuated the stories of their heroes because the characters and events embody many of their deepest, often most sacred, spiritual and cultural beliefs.

For example, Ulysses affirms the Greek belief in the value and dignity of humanity in an often hostile universe. Beowulf embodies the physical and mental courage so admired by the fierce warriors of northern Europe. Robin Hood possesses the qualities of the ideal English yeoman; John Henry, a member of a down-trodden race, is a symbol of his people's struggle for dignity. Sundiata, whose parents represented both the Islamic and indigenous African strains of his culture, is able to unify his country, making it a symbol of African greatness in the fourteenth and fifteenth centuries.

It is important to note that only three selections present women as the central heroes. This limitation arises from the fact that in most of the traditional epics, romances, and sagas that have provided the basis for modern adaptations, female characters have generally played minor roles. Moreover, until recently, sex-role stereotyping usually relegated girls and women to non-physical, 'lady-like' roles. People like Joan of Arc, who acted in aggressive, masculine ways, generally endured disapproval. Paradoxically, Joan, Atalanta, and Sally Ann Thunder Ann Whirlwind, the three dominant females in these selections, were deemed heroic precisely because they rose above their confining and limiting roles as women and acted like strong, brave men—as soldiers, athletes, and bear wrestlers. While there is no arguing that many women can succeed in physical male activities, these women almost seem to have been celebrated as heroic because they achieved their victories in a masculine way, in a man's world.

Although hero tales were not intended specifically for children, young audiences undoubtedly listened to them and the tales became a part of their socialization process. Not only did they acquire their culture's traditional narratives, but they also assimilated the social and religious beliefs that would guide them through their own lives. During the past two hundred years, however, many traditional hero tales have been specifically adapted for younger readers. Narratives of high adventure and of daring deeds appeal to children's enjoyment of almost bigger-than-life story characters confronting, and generally over-coming, formidable obstacles and adversaries.

The adapted versions, often separated from their sources by centuries, achieve varying degrees of accuracy in depicting the cultural elements of the originals. However, they do reveal the cultural values of the adaptors and their times. The ways they present the stories—what they add and delete, what they emphasize, what they comment on—reflect both what they and their publishers consider appropriate for younger readers and what they feel would make the tales more marketable to the adults who buy books for children.

During the middle of the nineteenth century adapted tales of heroes focused on biblical, classical, and mediaeval characters. At a time when many people accepted English thinker Thomas Carlyle's belief that study of world history should focus on the biographies of great men, noble Perseus, brave Ulysses, and freedom-loving Robin Hood represented ideal subjects for young people to read about. Their stories, appropriately modified, could inculcate young male readers with the character traits valued in the nineteenth century. Charles Kingsley, a clergyman, removed sexual incidents and character flaws from his adaptation of Greek hero tales. Except for his clothing and the specific settings and content of his adventures, Perseus would not have been out of place at a prestigious English school such as Rugby or Eton. Howard Pyle, an American, admired the egalitarianism of Robin Hood, who, like an American, resisted tyrants and enjoyed a kind of rugged frontier life in Sherwood Forest. Interestingly, Andrew Lang's surprisingly modern biography of Joan of Arc, although written for English children, has a decidedly anti-English tone, often emphasizing the villainy of the invaders of France. Perhaps, the author, who was from Scotland, is indulging in his countrymen's distrust of the English. It is also worth noting that his story of the French heroine is one of the lesser-known of his works for children. Perhaps this obscurity is because the story is fairly long. However, it is more probable that in presenting a woman hero who acts like a man, he was dealing with material unfashionable among those who purchased children's books a century ago.

Early 1950s adaptations of the stories of two North American heroes, Paul Bunyan and John Henry, offer insights into mid-twentieth century attitudes about hero tales. John D. Robins, a Canadian professor of English who had worked in logging camps and had originally presented the tales of the legendary logger on CBC radio, employs an interestingly restrained tongue-in-cheek, mildly ironic approach. It is possible to see in his tone a reflection of the Canadian self-deprecatory, understated view of larger-than-life figures, a view that contrasts the only partially ironic tone of bragaccio often found in American adaptations.

By the time Irwin Shapiro adapted the story of John Henry, legends of the steel-drivin' man were well-known. Shapiro emphasizes the hero's strength and sense of pride and dignity. The focus of the climactic event is humanistic, because John Henry sets out to prove man's superiority over machines. In this way, the episode belongs to a theme found frequently in literature since the beginning of the industrial age and is a major component of Virginia Lee Burton's award-winning picture books *Mike Mulligan and his Steam Shovel* (1939) and *The Little House* (1942). Shapiro makes little of the fact that the hero is African-American, an underemphasis that is not surprising because the inclusion of African-American legends and folktales in children's literature became substantial only after the Civil Rights movement gained momentum during the 1960s.

Although the story of John Henry was familiar to most North American readers during the first six decades of the twentieth century, the story of the legendary-historical African leader Sundiata was not. During the 1960s, as an integral part of the American Black Pride movement, scholars and teachers rediscovered and began to emphasize the rich historical, artistic, and literary heritage of Africa. In Africa, the legend of the great king of Mali had been kept alive over the centuries by the *griots*, traditional oral storytellers. Soon print versions appeared and, as the demand for African and African-American traditional literature increased, the deeds of Sundiata became more widely available in book form.

During the last half of the twentieth century, an increasing number of children's books presenting the deeds of minority cultures have appeared. In North America, these have included not only stories about African and Native Americans, but also tales from other cultures around the world. Significantly, all of these stories are frequently retold by members of the creating cultures. For example, Julius Lester, a notable African-American author, created the text for a picture book about John Henry, and, in *Seasons of Splendor*, Mahdur Jaffrey, Indian-born actress and author, recorded episodes in the life of Krishna, the Blue God.

These books and others reveal the great difference between the mid-nineteenth century children's versions of hero tales and those of recent decades. Charles Kingsley, as noted above, made his Greek characters act like morally upright, young British men. In 1855, Henry Wadsworth Longfellow, the American poet, published *Song of Hiawatha*, a poem about Nanabozho, the Ojibway culture hero of the upper Great Lakes. However, the poet gave the central character the name of an Iroquois leader from what is now upstate New York and made him a noble child of nature whose influence paved the way for the coming of Christianity. In contrast, Edward Benton-Benai, an Ojibway educator, wrote *The Mishomis Book* in 1988, in which he discussed the events of Nanabozho's life to indicate their continuing moral, social, and spiritual significance for his own people.

Whether hero tales adapted for children accurately reflect the beliefs of the originating culture, or whether they are modified to embody those of the adapting authors and their intended audiences, they share two characteristics. They are generally stories about adults and they are created specifically for young audiences. As such, the central characters are superior to the readers—in age, size and physical ability, experience, and, usually, intelligence. In their words and thoughts, motivations and deeds, the heroes embody qualities deemed admirable in adults. Be they characters from ancient or more recent cultures, from the reader's culture, or other cultures, they are presented by adapters as role models, people whom children should strive to be like as they progress toward adulthood.

Works Cited

Benton-Benai, Edward. 1979. *The Mishomis Book: The Voice of the Ojibway*. St. Paul, MN: Indian Country Press.
Campbell, Joseph. 1949. *The Hero With a Thousand Faces*. Princeton, NJ: Princeton University Press.
Lester, Julius, reteller. 1994. *John Henry*. New York: Dial.

Sundiata's Childhood

Based on the life of a thirteenth-century king, this epic from Mali has been retold over the centuries by *griots*—storytellers, teachers, and wise men whose role was to transmit the deeds, lessons, and cultural values of the past. The story of a man whose abilities as a warrior and leader enabled Mali to achieve cultural, political, and economic dominance that lasted for two centuries after his death, it reflects the mixing of traditional African and newer Islamic cultural ideas. Such local beliefs as the baobab tree being the 'tree of life' and a symbol of community unity are set beside references to the power of Allah and the 'fact' that Sundiata's father was a direct descendent of Mohammed. In addition to its account of the Battle of Kirina, in which the hero created the confederacy that defeated the evil devil-worshiping King Sumanguru and laid the foundations for the empire that followed, the epic presents elements of Sundiata's life that are similar to those found in other hero tales: the unusual childhood, a period of long exile, and his triumphant return to his home as an acclaimed leader. In the following selection, details of the hero's childhood are presented: a prophecy of his great destiny, his cruel treatment at the hands of adults and children, his seemingly miraculous first steps and first words, and his prodigious strength as he brings the baobab tree to his mother.

Childhood

God has his mysteries which none can fathom. You, perhaps, will be a king. You can do nothing about it. You, on the other hand, will be unlucky, but you can do nothing about that either. Each man finds his way already marked out for him and he can change nothing of it.

Sogolon's son had a slow and difficult childhood. At the age of three he still crawled along on all-fours while children of the same age were already walking. He had nothing of the great beauty of his father Naré Maghan. He had a head so big that he seemed unable to support it; he also had large eyes which would open wide whenever anyone entered his mother's house. He was taciturn and used to spend the whole day just sitting in the middle of the house. Whenever his mother went out he would crawl on all fours to rummage about in the calabashes in search of food, for he was very greedy.

Malicious tongues began to blab. What three-year-old has not yet taken his first steps? What three-year-old is not the despair of his parents through his whims and shifts of mood? What three-year-old is not the joy of his circle through his backwardness in talking? Sogolon Djata (for it was thus that they called him, prefixing his mother's name to his), Sogolon Djata, then, was very different from others of his own age. He spoke little and his severe face never relaxed into a smile. You would have thought that he was already thinking, and what amused children of his age bored him. Often Sogolon would make some of them come to him to keep him company. These children were already walking and she hoped that Djata, seeing his companions walking, would be tempted to do likewise. But nothing came of it. Besides, Sogolon Djata would brain the poor little things with his already strong arms and none of them would come near him any more.

The king's first wife was the first to rejoice at Sogolon Djata's infirmity. Her own son, Dankaran Touman, was already eleven. He was a fine and lively boy, who spent the day running about the village with those of his own age. He had even begun his initiation in the bush. The king had had a bow made for him and he used to go behind the town to practise archery with his companions. Sassouma was quite happy and snapped her fingers at Sogolon, whose child was still crawling on the ground. Whenever the latter happened to pass by her house; she would say, 'Come, my son, walk, jump, leap about. The jinn didn't promise you anything out of the ordinary, but I prefer a son who walks on his two legs to a lion that crawls on the ground.' She spoke thus whenever Sogolon went by her door. The innuendo would go straight home and then she would burst into laughter, that diabolical laughter which a jealous woman knows how to use so well.

Her son's infirmity weighed heavily upon Sogolon Kedjou; she had resorted to all her talent as a sorceress to give strength to her son's legs, but the rarest herbs had been useless. The king himself lost hope.

How impatient man is! Naré Maghan became imperceptibly estranged but Gnankouman Doua never ceased reminding him of the hunter's words. Sogolon became pregnant again. The king hoped for a son, but it was a daughter called Kolonkan. She resembled her mother and had nothing of her father's beauty. The disheartened king debarred Sogolon from his house and she lived in semi-disgrace for a while. Naré Maghan married the daughter of one of his allies, the king of the Kamaras. She was called Namandjé and her beauty was legendary. A year later she brought a boy into the world. When the king consulted soothsayers on the destiny of this son he received the reply that Namandjé's child would be the right hand of some mighty king. The king gave the newly-born the name of Boukari. He was to be called Manding Boukari or Manding Bory later on.

Naré Maghan was very perplexed. Could it be that the stiff-jointed son of Sogolon was the one the hunter soothsayer had foretold?

'The Almighty has his mysteries,' Gnankouman Doua would say and, taking up the hunter's words, added, 'The silk-cotton tree emerges from a tiny seed.'

One day Naré Maghan came along to the house of Nounfaïri, the blacksmith seer of Niani. He was an old, blind man. He received the king in the anteroom which served as his workshop. To the king's question he replied, 'When the seed germinates growth is not always easy; great trees grow slowly but they plunge their roots deep into the ground.'

'But has the seed really germinated?' said the king.

'Of course', replied the blind seer. 'Only the growth is not as quick as you would like it; how impatient man is.'

This interview and Doua's confidence gave the king some assurance. To the great displeasure of Sassouma Bérété the king restored Sogolon to favour and soon another daughter was born to her. She was given the name of Djamarou.

However, all Niani talked of nothing else but the stiff-legged son of Sogolon. He was now seven and he still crawled to get about. In spite of all the king's affection, Sogolon was in despair. Naré Maghan aged and he felt his time coming to an end. Dankaran Touman, the son of Sassouma Bérété, was now a fine youth.

One day Naré Maghan made Mari Djata come to him and he spoke to the child as one speaks to an adult. 'Mari Djata, I am growing old and soon I shall be no more among you, but before death takes me off I am going to give you the present each king gives his successor. In Mali every prince has his own griot. Doua's father was my father's griot, Doua is mine and the son of Doua, Balla Fasséké here, will be your griot. Be inseparable friends from this day forward. From his mouth you will hear the history of your ancestors, you will learn the art of governing Mali according to the principles which our ancestors have bequeathed to us. I have served my term and done my duty too. I have done everything which a king of Mali ought to do. I am handing an enlarged kingdom over to you and I leave you sure allies. May your destiny be accomplished, but never forget that Niani is your capital and Mali the cradle of your ancestors.

The child, as if he had understood the whole meaning of the king's words, beckoned Balla Fasséké to approach. He made room for him on the hide he was sitting on and then said, 'Balla, you will be my griot.'

'Yes, son of Sogolon, if it pleases God', replied Balla Fasséké.

The king and Doua exchanged glances that radiated confidence.

The Lion's Awakening

@ short while after this interview between Naré Maghan and his son the king died. Sogolon's son was no more than seven years old. The council of elders met in the king's palace. It was no use Doua's defending the king's will which reserved the throne for Mari Djata, for the council took no account of Naré Maghan's wish. With the help of Sassouma Bérété's intrigues, Dankaran Touman was proclaimed king and a regency council was formed in which the queen mother was all-powerful. A short time after, Doua died.

As men have short memories, Sogolon's son was spoken of with nothing but irony and scorn. People had seen one-eyed kings, one-armed kings, and lame kings, but a stiff-legged king had never been heard tell of. No matter how great the destiny promised for Mari Djata might be, the throne could not be given to someone who had no power in his legs; if the jinn loved him, let them begin by giving him the use of his legs. Such were the remarks that Sogolon heard every day. The queen mother, Sassouma Bérété, was the source of all this gossip.

Having become all-powerful, Sassouma Bérété persecuted Sogolon because the late Naré Maghan had preferred her. She banished Sogolon and her son to a back yard of the palace. Mari Djata's mother now occupied an old hut which had served as a lumber-room of Sassouma's.

The wicked queen mother allowed free passage to all those inquisitive people who wanted to see the child that still crawled at the age of seven. Nearly all the inhabitants of Niani filed into the palace and the poor Sogolon wept to see herself thus given over to public ridicule. Mari Djata took on a ferocious look in front of the crowd of sightseers. Sogolon found a little consolation only in the love of her eldest daughter, Kolonkan. She was four and she could walk. She seemed to understand all her mother's miseries and already she helped her with the housework. Sometimes, when Sogolon was attending to the chores, it was she who stayed beside her sister Djamarou, quite small as yet.

Sogolon Kedjou and her children lived on the queen mother's leftovers, but she kept a little garden in the open ground behind the village. It was there that she passed her brightest moments looking after her onions and gnougous. One day she happened to be short of condiments and went to the queen mother to beg a little baobab leaf.

'Look you,' said the malicious Sassouma, 'I have a calabash full. Help yourself, you poor woman. As for me, my son knew how to walk at seven and it was he who went and picked these baobab leaves. Take them then, since your son is unequal to mine.' Then she laughed derisively with that fierce laughter which cuts through your flesh and penetrates right to the bone.

Sogolon Kedjou was dumbfounded. She had never imagined that hate could be so strong in a human being. With a lump in her throat she left Sassouma's. Outside her hut Mari Djata, sitting on his useless legs, was blandly eating out of a calabash. Unable to contain herself any longer, Sogolon burst into sobs and seizing a piece of wood, hit her son.

'Oh son of misfortune, will you never walk? Through your fault I have just suffered the greatest affront of my life! What have I done, God, for you to punish me in this way?'

Mari Djata seized the piece of wood and, looking at his mother, said, 'Mother, what's the matter?'

'Shut up, nothing can ever wash me clean of this insult.'

'But what then?'

'Sassouma has just humiliated me over a matter of a baobab leaf. At your age her own son could walk and used to bring his mother baobab leaves.'

'Cheer up, Mother, cheer up.'

'No. It's too much. I can't.'

'Very well then, I am going to walk today', said Mari Djata. 'Go and tell my father's smiths to make me the heaviest possible iron rod. Mother, do you want just the leaves of the baobab or would you rather I brought you the whole tree?'

'Ah, my son, to wipe out this insult I want the tree and its roots at my feet outside my hut.'

Balla Fasséké, who was present, ran to the master smith, Farakourou, to order an iron rod.

Sogolon had sat down in front of her hut. She was weeping softly and holding her head between her two hands. Mari Djata went calmly back to his calabash of rice and began eating again as if nothing had happened. From time to time he looked up discreetly at his mother who was murmuring in a low voice, 'I want the whole tree, in front of my hut, the whole tree.'

All of a sudden a voice burst into laughter behind the hut. It was the wicked Sassouma telling one of her serving women about the scene of humiliation and she was laughing loudly so that Sogolon could hear. Sogolon fled into the hut and hid her face under the blankets so as not to have before her eyes this heedless boy, who was more preoccupied with eating than with anything else. With her head buried in the bed-clothes Sogolon wept and her body shook violently. Her daughter, Sogolon Djamarou, had come and sat down beside her and she said, 'Mother, Mother, don't cry. Why are you crying?'

Mari Djata had finished eating and, dragging himself along on his legs, he came and sat under the wall of the hut for the sun was scorching. What was he thinking about? He alone knew.

The royal forges were situated outside the walls and over a hundred smiths worked there. The bows, spears, arrows, and shields of Niani's warriors came from there. When Balla Fasséké came to order the iron rod, Farakourou said to him, 'The great day has arrived then?'

'Yes. Today is a day like any other, but it will see what no other day has seen.'

The master of the forges, Farakourou, was the son of the old Nounfaïri, and he was a soothsayer like his father. In his workshops there was an enormous iron bar wrought by his father Nounfaïri. Everybody wondered what this bar was destined to be used for. Farakourou called six of his apprentices and told them to carry the iron bar to Sogolon's house.

When the smiths put the gigantic iron bar down in front of the hut the noise was so frightening that Sogolon, who was lying down, jumped up with a start. Then Balla Fasséké, son of Gnankouman Doua, spoke.

'Here is the great day, Mari Djata. I am speaking to you, Maghan, son of Sogolon. The waters of the Niger can efface the stain from the body, but they cannot wipe out an insult. Arise, young lion, roar, and may the bush know that from henceforth it has a master.'

The apprentice smiths were still there, Sogolon had come out and everyone was watching Mari Djata. He crept on all fours and came to the iron bar. Supporting himself on his knees and one hand, with the other hand he picked up the iron bar without any effort and stood it up vertically. Now he was resting on nothing but his knees and held the bar with both his hands. A deathly silence had gripped all those present. Sogolon Djata closed his eyes, held tight, the muscles in his arms tensed. With a violent jerk he threw his weight on to it and his knees left the ground. Sogolon Kedjou was all eyes and watched her son's legs which were trembling as though from an electric shock. Djata was sweating and the sweat ran from his brow. In a great effort he straightened up and was on his feet at one go—but the great bar of iron was twisted and had taken the form of a bow!

Then Balla Fasséké sang out the 'Hymn to the Bow', striking up with his powerful voice:

> 'Take your bow, Simbon,
> Take your bow and let us go.
> Take your bow, Sogolon Djata.'

When Sogolon saw her son standing she stood dumb for a moment, then suddenly she sang these words of thanks to God who had given her son the use of his legs:

> 'Oh day, what a beautiful day,
> Oh day, day of joy;
> Allah Almighty, you never created a finer day.
> So my son is going to walk!'

Standing in the position of a soldier at ease, Sogolon Djata, supported by his enormous rod, was sweating great beads of sweat. Balla Fasséké's song had alerted the whole palace and people came running from all over to see what had happened, and each stood bewildered before Sogolon's son. The queen mother had rushed there and when she saw Mari Djata standing up she trembled from head to foot. After recovering his breath Sogolon's son dropped the bar and the crowd stood to one side. His first steps were those of a giant. Balla Fasséké fell into step and pointing his finger at Djata, he cried:

From David Wisniewski, *Sundiata: The Lion King of Mali*. (New York: Clarion Books, 1992).

'Room, room, make room!
The lion has walked;
Hide antelopes,
Get out of his way.'

Behind Niani there was a young baobab tree and it was there that the children of the town came to pick leaves for their mothers. With all his might the son of Sogolon tore up the tree and put it on his shoulders and went back to his mother. He threw the tree in front of the hut and said, 'Mother, here are some baobab leaves for you. From henceforth it will be outside your hut that the women of Nani will come to stock up.'

From *Sundiata, an Epic of Old Mali*, by D.T. Niane, translated by G.D. Pickett (London: Longman, Green, and Company, 1965).

Perseus Rescues Andromeda

Son of the god Zeus and a mortal, the Greek hero Perseus is noted for two heroic deeds: the killing of the Gorgon Medusa, a monster who could turn to stone those who looked on her face, and the rescue of the maiden Andromeda from a devouring sea monster. His semi-divine nature, his relatively obscure childhood, and his brave actions which lead to his marriage and his becoming a king, link him to other heroic figures. In this episode, Perseus has completed a seemingly impossible task assigned by an evil king who lusted after his mother and wanted him out of the way. In his quest, the youth was assisted by the goddess Athena, who provided him with a hat giving the power of invisibility and winged sandals, both of which he had to learn to use appropriately in order to be successful. Now on the long and difficult road home, he saves Andromeda. The episode is not unlike the knight and dragon stories popular among young readers of the nineteenth century, when this version of the Greek myth was written. The author, Charles Kingsley, a clergyman, reflects his belief in the religious movement of 'Muscular Christianity', which sought to inculcate in young men the virtues of courage, courtesy, purity of heart, and moral righteousness. Perseus thinks and behaves in an exemplary way. At one point, for instance, the author has the hero explain 'It is better to die like a hero than to live like an ox in a stall.' Furthermore, on seeing the trapped Andromeda, he is indignant: 'Where are those sea-gods, cruel and unjust, who doom fair maids to death?'

So Perseus flitted onward to the north-east, over many a league of sea, till he came to the rolling sand-hills and the dreary Libyan shore.

And he flitted on across the desert: over rock-ledges, and banks of shingle, and level wastes of sand, and shell-drifts bleaching in the sunshine, and the skeletons of great sea-monsters, and dead bones of ancient giants, strewn up and down upon the old sea-floor. And as he went the blood-drops fell to the earth from the Gorgon's head, and became poisonous asps and adders, which breed in the desert to this day.

Over the sands he went,—he never knew how far or how long, feeding on the fruit which the Nymphs had given him, till he saw the hills of the Psylli, and the Dwarfs who fought with cranes. Their spears were of reeds and rushes, and their houses of the egg-shells of the cranes; and Perseus laughed, and went his way to the north-east, hoping all day long to see the blue Mediterranean sparkling, that he might fly across it to his home.

But now came down a mighty wind, and swept him back southward toward the desert. All day long he strove against it; but even the winged sandals could not prevail. So he was forced to float down the wind all night; and when the morning dawned there was nothing to be seen, save the same old hateful waste of sand.

And out of the north the sandstorms rushed upon him, blood-red pillars and wreaths, blotting out the noonday sun; and Perseus fled before them, lest he should be choked by the burning dust. At last the gale fell calm, and he tried to go northward again; but again came down the sandstorms, and swept him back into the waste, and then all was calm and cloudless as before. Seven days he strove against the storms, and seven days he was driven back, till he was spent with thirst and hunger, and his tongue clove to the roof of his mouth. Here and there he fancied that he saw a fair lake, and the sunbeams shining on the water; but when he came to it it vanished at his feet, and there was nought but burning sand. And if he had not been of the race of the Immortals, he would have perished in the waste; but his life was strong within him, because it was more than man's.

Then he cried to Athené, and said—

'Oh, fair and pure, if thou hearest me, wilt thou leave me here to die of drought? I have brought thee the Gorgon's head at thy bidding, and hitherto thou hast prospered my journey; dost thou desert me at the last? Else why will not these immortal sandals prevail, even against the desert storms? Shall I never see my mother more, and the blue ripple round Seriphos, and the sunny hills of Hellas?'

So he prayed; and after he had prayed there was a great silence.

The heaven was still above his head, and the sand was still beneath his feet; and Perseus looked up, but there was nothing but the blinding sun in the blinding blue; and round him, but there was nothing but the blinding sand.

And Perseus stood still a while, and waited, and said, 'Surely I am not here without the will of the Immortals, for Athené will not lie. Were not these sandals to lead me in the right road? Then the road in which I have tried to go must be a wrong road.'

Then suddenly his ears were opened, and he heard the sound of running water.

And at that his heart was lifted up, though he scarcely dare believe his ears; and weary as he was, he hurried forward, though he could scarcely stand upright; and within a bow-shot of him was a glen in the sand, and marble rocks, and date-trees, and a lawn of gay green grass. And through the lawn a streamlet sparkled and wandered out beyond the trees, and vanished in the sand.

The water trickled among the rocks, and a pleasant breeze rustled in the dry date-branches; and Perseus laughed for joy, and leapt down the cliff, and drank of the cool water, and ate of the dates, and slept upon the turf, and leapt up and went forward again: but not toward the north this time; for he said, 'Surely Athené hath sent me hither, and will not have me go homeward yet. What if there be another noble deed to be done, before I see the sunny hills of Hellas?'

So he went east, and east for ever, by fresh oases and fountains, date-palms, and lawns of grass, till he saw before him a mighty mountain-wall, all rose-red in the setting sun.

Then he towered in the air like an eagle, for his limbs were strong again; and he flew all night across the mountain till the day began to dawn, and rosy-fingered Eos came blushing up the sky. And then, behold, beneath him was the long green garden of Egypt and the shining stream of the Nile.

And he saw cities walled up to heaven, and temples, and obelisks, and pyramids, and giant Gods of stone. And he came down amid fields of barley, and flax, and millet, and clambering gourds; and saw the people coming out of the gates of a great city, and setting to work, each in his place, among the water-courses, parting the streams among the plants cunningly with their feet, according to the wisdom of the Egyptians. But when they saw him they all stopped their work, and gathered round him, and cried—

'Who art thou, fair youth? and what bearest thou beneath thy goat-skin there? Surely thou art one of the Immortals; for thy skin is white like ivory, and ours is red like clay. Thy hair is like threads of gold, and ours is black and curled. Surely thou art one of the Immortals'; and they would have worshipped him then and there; but Perseus said—

'I am not one of the Immortals; but I am a hero of the Hellens. And I have slain the Gorgon in the wilderness, and bear her head with me. Give me food, therefore, that I may go forward and finish my work.'

Then they gave him food, and fruit, and wine; but they would not let him go. And when the news came into the city that the Gorgon was slain, the priests came out to meet him, and the maidens, with songs and dances, and timbrels and harps; and they would have brought him to their temple and to their king; but Perseus put on the hat of darkness, and vanished away out of their sight.

Therefore the Egyptians looked long for his return, but in vain, and worshipped him as a hero, and made a statue of him in Chemmis, which stood for many a hundred years; and they said that he appeared to them at times, with sandals a cubit long; and that whenever he appeared the season was fruitful, and the Nile rose high that year.

Then Perseus went to the eastward, along the Red Sea shore; and then, because he was afraid to go into the Arabian deserts, he turned northward once more, and this time no storm hindered him.

He went past the Isthmus, and Mount Casius, and the vast Sirbonian bog, and up the shore of Palestine, where the dark-faced Æthiops dwelt.

He flew on past pleasant hills and valleys, like Argos itself, or Lacedæmon, or the fair Vale of Tempe. But the lowlands were all drowned by floods, and the highlands blasted by fire, and the hills heaved like a bubbling cauldron, before the wrath of King Poseidon, the shaker of the earth.

And Perseus feared to go inland, but flew along the shore above the sea; and he went on all the day, and the sky was black with smoke; and he went on all the night, and the sky was red with flame.

And at the dawn of day he looked toward the cliffs; and at the water's edge, under a black rock, he saw a white image stand.

'This,' thought he, 'must surely be the statue of some sea-god; I will go near and see what kind of gods these barbarians worship.'

So he came near; but when he came, it was no statue, but a maiden of flesh and blood; for he could see her tresses streaming in the breeze; and as he came closer still, he could see how she shrank and shivered when the waves sprinkled her with cold salt spray. Her arms were spread above her head, and fastened to the rock with chains of brass; and her head drooped on her bosom, either with sleep, or weariness, or grief. But now and then she looked up and wailed, and called her mother; yet she did not see Perseus, for the cap of darkness was on his head.

Full of pity and indignation, Perseus drew near and looked upon the maid. Her cheeks were darker than his were, and her hair was blue-black like a hyacinth; but Perseus thought, 'I have never seen so beautiful a maiden; no, not in all our isles. Surely she is a king's daughter. Do barbarians treat their king's daughters thus? She is too fair, at least, to have done any wrong. I will speak to her.'

And, lifting the hat from his head, he flashed into her sight. She shrieked with terror, and tried to hide her face with her hair, for she could not with her hands; but Perseus cried—

'Do not fear me, fair one; I am a Hellen, and no barbarian. What cruel men have bound you? But first I will set you free.'

And he tore at the fetters, but they were too strong for him; while the maiden cried—

'Touch me not; I am accursed, devoted as a victim to the sea-Gods. They will slay you, if you dare to set me free.'

'Let them try,' said Perseus; and drawing Harpé from his thigh, he cut through the brass as if it had been flax.

'Now,' he said, 'you belong to me, and not to these sea-Gods, whosoever they may be!' But she only called the more on her mother.

'Why call on your mother? She can be no mother to have left you here. If a bird is dropped out of the nest, it belongs to the man who picks it up. If a jewel is cast by the wayside, it is his who dare win it and wear it, as I will win you and will wear you. I know now why Pallas Athené sent me hither. She sent me to gain a prize worth all my toil and more.'

And he clasped her in his arms, and cried, 'Where are these sea-Gods, cruel and unjust, who doom fair maids to death? I carry the weapons of Immortals. Let them measure their strength against mine! But tell me, maiden, who you are, and what dark fate brought you here.' And she answered, weeping—

'I am the daughter of Cepheus, King of Iopa, and my mother is Cassiopeia of the beautiful tresses, and they called me Andromeda, as long as life was mine. And I stand bound here, hapless that I am, for the sea-monster's food, to atone for my mother's sin. For she boasted of me once that I was fairer than Atergatis, Queen of the Fishes; so she in her wrath sent the sea-floods, and her brother the Fire King sent the earthquakes, and wasted all the land, and after the floods a monster bred of the slime, who devours all living things. And now he must devour me, guiltless though I am—me who never harmed a living thing, nor saw a fish upon the shore but I gave it life, and threw it back into the sea; for in our land we eat no fish, for fear of Atergatis their queen. Yet the priests say that nothing but my blood can atone for a sin which I never committed.'

But Perseus laughed, and said, 'A sea-monster? I have fought with worse than him: I would have faced Immortals for your sake; how much more a beast of the sea?'

Then Andromeda looked up at him, and new hope was kindled in her breast, so proud and fair did he stand, with one hand round her, and in the other the glittering sword. But she only sighed, and wept the more, and cried—

'Why will you die, young as you are? Is there not death and sorrow enough in the world already? It is noble for me to die, that I may save the lives of a whole people; but you, better than them all, why should I slay you too? Go you your way; I must go mine.'

But Perseus cried, 'Not so; for the Lords of Olympus, whom I serve, are the friends of the heroes, and help them on to noble deeds. Led by them, I slew the Gorgon, the beautiful horror; and not without them do I come hither, to slay this monster with that same Gorgon's head. Yet hide your eyes when I leave you, lest the sight of it freeze you too to stone.'

But the maiden answered nothing, for she could not believe his words. And then, suddenly looking up, she pointed to the sea, and shrieked—

'There he comes, with the sunrise, as they promised. I must die now. How shall I endure it? Oh, go! Is it not dreadful enough to be torn piecemeal, without having you to look on?' And she tried to thrust him away.

But he said, 'I go; yet promise me one thing ere I go: that if I slay this beast you will be my wife, and come back with me to my kingdom in fruitful Argos, for I am a king's heir. Promise me, and seal it with a kiss.'

Then she lifted up her face, and kissed him; and Perseus laughed for joy, and flew upward, while Andromeda crouched trembling on the rock, waiting for what might befall.

On came the great sea-monster, coasting along like a huge black galley, lazily breasting the ripple, and stopping at times by creek or headland to watch for the laughter of girls at their bleaching, or cattle pawing on the sand-hills, or boys bathing on the beach. His great sides were fringed with clustering shells and sea-weeds, and the water gurgled in and out of his wide jaws, as he rolled along, dripping and glistening in the beams of the morning sun.

At last he saw Andromeda, and shot forward to take his prey, while the waves foamed white behind him, and before him the fish fled leaping.

Then down from the height of the air fell Perseus like a shooting star; down to the crests of the waves, while Andromeda hid her face as he shouted; and then there was silence for a while.

At last she looked up trembling, and saw Perseus springing toward her; and instead of the monster a long black rock, with the sea rippling quietly round it.

Who then so proud as Perseus, as he leapt back to the rock, and lifted his fair Andromeda in his arms, and flew with her to the cliff-top, as a falcon carries a dove?

Who so proud as Perseus, and who so joyful as all the Æthiop people? For they had stood watching the monster from the cliffs, wailing for the maiden's fate. And already a messenger had gone to Cepheus and Cassiopeia, where they sat in sackcloth and ashes on the ground, in the innermost palace chambers, awaiting their daughter's end. And they came, and all the city with them, to see the wonder, with songs and with dances, with cymbals and harps, and received their daughter back again, as one alive from the dead.

Then Cepheus said, 'Hero of the Hellens, stay here with me and be my son-in-law, and I will give you the half of my kingdom.'

'I will be your son-in-law,' said Perseus, 'but of your kingdom I will have none, for I long after the pleasant land of Greece, and my mother who waits for me at home.'

Then Cepheus said, 'You must not take my daughter away at once, for she is to us like one alive from the dead. Stay with us here a year, and after that you shall return with honour.' And Perseus consented; but before he went to the palace he bade the people bring stones and wood, and built three altars, one to Athené, and one to Hermes, and one to Father Zeus, and offered bullocks and rams.

And some said, 'This is a pious man'; yet the priests said, 'The Sea Queen will be yet more fierce against us, because her monster is slain.' But they were afraid to speak aloud, for they feared the Gorgon's head. So they went up to the palace; and when they came in, there stood in the hall Phineus, the brother of Cepheus, chafing like a bear robbed of her whelps, and with him his sons, and his servants, and many an armed man; and he cried to Cepheus—

'You shall not marry your daughter to this stranger, of whom no one knows even the name. Was not Andromeda betrothed to my son? And now she is safe again, has he not a right to claim her?'

But Perseus laughed, and answered, 'If your son is in want of a bride, let him save a maiden for himself. As yet he seems but a helpless bridegroom. He left this one to die, and dead she is to him. I saved her alive, and alive she is to me, but to no one else. Ungrateful man! have I not saved your land, and the lives of your sons and daughters, and will you requite me thus? Go, or it will be worse for you.' But all the men-at-arms drew their swords, and rushed on him like wild beasts.

Then he unveiled the Gorgon's head, and said, 'This has delivered my bride from one wild beast: it shall deliver her from many.' And as he spoke Phineus and all his men-at-arms stopped short, and stiffened each man as he stood; and before Perseus had drawn the goat-skin over the face again, they were all turned into stone.

Then Perseus bade the people bring levers and roll them out; and what was done with them after that I cannot tell.

So they made a great wedding-feast, which lasted seven whole days, and who so happy as Perseus and Andromeda?

But on the eighth night Perseus dreamed a dream; and he saw standing beside him Pallas Athené, as he had seen her in Seriphos, seven long years before; and she stood and called him by name, and said—

'Perseus, you have played the man, and see, you have your reward. Know now that the gods are just, and help him who helps himself. Now give me here Harpé the sword, and the sandals, and the hat of darkness, that I may give them back to their owners; but the Gorgon's head you shall keep a while, for you will need it in your land of Greece. Then you shall lay it up in my temple at Seriphos, that I may wear it on my shield for ever, a terror to the Titans and the monsters, and the foes of gods and men. And as for this land, I have appeased the sea and the fire, and there shall be no more floods nor earthquakes. But let the people build altars to Father Zeus, and to me, and worship the Immortals, the Lords of heaven and earth.'

And Perseus rose to give her the sword, and the cap, and the sandals; but he woke, and his dream vanished away. And yet it was not altogether a dream; for the goat-skin with the head was in its place; but the sword, and the cap, and the sandals were gone, and Perseus never saw them more.

Then a great awe fell on Perseus; and he went out in the morning to the people, and told his dream, and bade them build altars to Zeus, the Father of Gods and men, and to Athené, who gives wisdom to heroes; and fear no more the earthquakes and the floods, but sow and build in peace. And they did so for a while, and prospered; but after Perseus was gone they forgot Zeus and Athené, and worshipped again Atergatis the queen, and the undying fish of the sacred lake, where Deucalion's deluge was swallowed up, and they burnt their children before the Fire King, till Zeus was angry with that foolish people, and brought a strange nation against them out of Egypt, who fought against them and wasted them utterly, and dwelt in their cities for many a hundred years.

From *The Heroes or Greek Fairy Tales for My Children*, by Charles Kingsley (London: Macmillan, 1951).

How Krishna Killed the Wicked King Kans

Krishna, the eighth avatar, or incarnation, of the Hindu god Vishnu, has characteristics similar to culture heroes from around the world. Born to mortals, he was hidden with the family of a cowherd to avoid being killed by his evil uncle, King Kans, who had usurped the throne. He revealed his amazing strength as a baby by destroying an evil demon sent to kill him and as a boy by winning a battle to the death with Kaliya, the enormous five headed serpent king. Many tales about Krishna deal with his love of playing tricks and his extremely amorous nature—both qualities he shares with other trickster-heroes. In this episode the young hero overcomes his arch enemy while the king employs strategies similar to those used by the Sheriff of Nottingham in the Robin Hood tales, including staging a contest to lure the hero out of hiding. Unlike the English hero, who relied on cunning and his skill as an archer, Krishna relies on his great strength. As a result of his killing the King, Krishna paved the way for just rule to return to the kingdom and proved his worthiness to become a leader later in his life.

'Let us begin a week of festivities,' the wicked King Kans proclaimed from his throne. 'All our enemies are dead or locked up. This winter's crop has been blessedly plentiful. Our granaries are full of wheat and dried beans, and our treasure houses are filled with gold and jewels. We have decided to celebrate with elephant races, wrestling matches, musical plays, and banquets. See that all is arranged.'

'Not a bad idea. Not bad at all,' said one of his informers. 'The granaries and treasure houses are full and *most* of your enemies are disposed of.'

King Kans turned sharply towards him, 'What do you mean by that remark?'

'Which remark, your highness?'

Kans snarled. 'That *most* of my enemies are disposed of.'

'Well, your highness, that is just what I meant. Your father is in a dungeon and your sister and her husband are in jail. *Most* of them are taken care of.'

'But not all?'

'Well, there is the small matter of Krishna, the cowherd, your sister's son. He is a youth now and very highly regarded across the river. Not everyone realizes that he is your heir. If he decides to spread this information around, your people could . . . could possibly . . . there is a chance . . . that they could reject you . . . in favour . . . of your nephew.'

'Nephew?' thundered Kans. 'I have no nephew.' The words of the wise Sage uttered almost eighteen years ago at his sister's wedding clutched at his heart and gave it a deadly squeeze. The Sage had said, 'Do not let this couple go. Do you not know that you are doomed to die at the hands of their child ?'

Kans' heart beat so hard he thought it would burst out of his chest.

'If you are talking about Krishna, then the matter was taken care of years ago by the demon, Pootana. Pootana never fails.'

'She must have failed this time. Krishna not only lives but he is reputed to be both popular and strong.'

'How do you know this?' Kans asked.

'All you have to do is to cross the Yamuna River . . . and you will hear of no one else. The people say Krishna is a god . . . that he killed Kaliya the dreaded Serpent King, that he sucked away the life of a nurse who tried to poison him . . . that . . . .'

'Ahhhhh,' cried Kans. He had begun to understand.

'As for his strength,' went on the informer, 'I understand Krishna and his foster-brother Balram are champion wrestlers. Even on this side of the river people are beginning to turn to him for help.'

Another evil scheme had started to form in Kans's mind. 'I know what we must do. Next week, for our festivities, let us put extra emphasis on the wrestling matches. Let us send out a challenge to all the young wrestlers within a thousand miles to come and try to beat our court champions, Chanur and Mustik.' Kans grinned with satisfaction. Chanur and Mustik were giants, stronger than bull buffaloes. They would take care of Krishna, once and for all.

Kans called his drummers and heralds and asked them to travel everywhere within a thousand miles of the palace with an announcement of the King's festivities, most especially the wrestling match.

'Come here', Kans said, calling his chief herald towards him. 'There is a cowherd by the name of Krishna. I want you to make sure that he not only hears the announcement, but that he and his brother accept the challenge. How you do this, I leave up to you. Here is a ruby for your extra trouble.'

The chief herald pocketed the ruby. He had of course heard of Krishna. Had not everyone? The herald had also seen Chanur and Mustik in action and no wrestlers on earth had been able to defeat them. Poor Krishna did not stand a chance.

The entire kingdom now heard about the festivities.

'Hear ye, hear ye,' the chief herald shouted above the drum rolls. 'Hear ye, hear ye. The almighty, all knowing, all seeing, father of the universe, King of Mathura, King Kans hereby offers a challenge to any youth within a thousand miles of his palace. If he can defeat the wrestlers Chanur and Mustik in a fair match, he will be rewarded with a treasure chest.'

Seeing Krishna and Balram standing with a group of friends, the herald went on, 'The court has heard of these two brothers by reputation. Will they agree to fight like champions or will they sneak away like cowards?'

The taunt had its desired effect.

'I will fight. I will accept the challenge,' Krishna said.

'So will I,' Balram followed.

'Well, then, it is all settled,' the herald said, his lips curling up in triumph. 'We will let the public know. It will be the match of the century.'

Wrestling matches are supposed to be played according to fair rules, but King Kans had no intention of letting Krishna survive.

On the day of the match, he called his Prime Minister aside and told him the plan. 'As soon as Krishna and Balram come into the wrestling ring, let loose the mad, wild elephant we have chained in the barn. Say that the elephant broke away by accident, but make sure that it charges straight at those two young men. They cannot possibly survive. We will all mourn the accident of course, and offer the family gold in compensation. Krishna will be dead and the world will consider us generous beyond measure.'

'What a perfect plan, your highness,' said the Prime Minister.

'There is a back-up plan too, if the first one fails. Chanur and Mustik will be waiting. If the mad elephant does not succeed, our wrestlers will go in and finish the brothers.'

'Perfect. Perfect. Your highness thinks of everything.'

All the spectators were now collected around the wrestling ring, with King Kans seated higher up on a dais.

Krishna and Balram walked into the ring.

The crowd got up on its feet and cheered.

King Kans did not like that too much. 'You won't be cheering for long,' he muttered between his teeth.

Just then a gate flew open and a trumpeting elephant came charging towards the brothers.

Without a second's hesitation, Krishna leapt upon the elephant's back and with his long, strong arms, squeezed its neck until the creature crumpled under him.

Dead. The elephant was dead.

The crowd got up and cheered.

Kans stared in disbelief. 'Hurry, hurry, send in Chanur and Mustik.'

The two giant wrestlers strutted into the ring, their well-oiled muscles rippling in the sun. They looked more like mammoths than men. Their shoulders were massive.

'I will take Chanur,' said Krishna.

'And I will handle Mustik,' said Balram.

Krishna took a flying leap at Chanur and wrestled him to the ground. Then he twisted his neck and broke it.

Balram picked Mustik up by his right leg and threw him to the ground. Then he squeezed his chest in a bear hug and burst his heart.

Both wrestlers were dead.

The crowd got up on its feet and cheered.

Kans called out to his soldiers, 'Get your swords. Kill those scoundrels. Rush in and kill them.'

But before the soldiers could move, Krishna jumped upon the dais and pulled Kans off the throne.

'You evil man, your time has come. You killed all my sisters and now you will die a terrible death.' Krishna picked Kans up with both his arms and hurled him against a wall.

That was the end of Kans.

Krishna freed his parents who were still in jail and his grandfather, who was still locked up in a dungeon.

'Grandfather,' he said, 'the throne is yours. We know you will rule justly.'

'As you will after me', the grandfather replied, tears rolling down his cheeks. 'The people have, at last, been freed from tyranny.'

From *Seasons of Splendour: Tales, Myths, and Legends from India*, by Madhur Jaffrey (New York: Atheneum, 1985).

Sally Ann Thunder Ann Whirlwind

During the first half of the nineteenth century, many tall-tale cycles loosely based on historical American figures were created. The improbable deeds of characters such as Davy Crocket and Pecos Bill presented exaggerated examples of the courage, strength, and cunning needed to survive on the dangerous frontier. In addition, the humour of the narratives provided a kind of comic relief for listeners. Wives and daughters were usually secondary characters in the stories and possessed, in lesser degrees, the characteristics of the male heroes. In the later twentieth century, however, writers have reexamined the lives of these women and retold many of their adventures making them the central characters. Mary Pope Osborne, who has retold traditional stories from many cultures, has here combined several female characters and tall-tale narratives about them to create a fictional character: Davy Crockett's wife. In this story, Sally Ann is as strong and resourceful as men. In a sense, she is a female version of the male hero rather than a different kind of hero.

(O)ne early spring day, when the leaves of the white oaks were about as big as a mouse's ear, Davy Crockett set out alone through the forest to do some bear hunting. Suddenly it started raining real hard, and he felt obliged to stop for shelter under a tree. As he shook the rain out of his coonskin cap, he got sleepy, so he laid back into the crotch of the tree, and pretty soon he was snoring.

Davy slept so hard, he didn't wake up until nearly sundown. And when he did, he discovered that somehow or another in all that sleeping his head had gotten stuck in the crotch of the tree, and he couldn't get it out.

Well, Davy roared loud enough to make the tree lose all its little mouse-ear leaves. He twisted and turned and carried on for over an hour, but still that tree wouldn't let go. Just as he was about to give himself up for a goner, he heard a girl say, 'What's the matter, stranger?'

Even from his awkward position, he could see that she was extraordinary—tall as a hickory sapling, with arms as big as a keelboat tiller's.

'My head's stuck, sweetie,' he said. 'And if you help me get it free, I'll give you a pretty little comb.'

'Don't call me sweetie,' she said. 'And don't worry about giving me no pretty little comb, neither. I'll free your old coconut, but just because I want to.'

Then this extraordinary girl did something that made Davy's hair stand on end. She reached in a bag and took out a bunch of rattlesnakes. She tied all the wriggly critters together to make a long rope, and as she tied, she kept talking. 'I'm not a shy little colt,' she said. 'And I'm not a little singing nightingale, neither. I can tote a steamboat on my back, outscream a panther, and jump over my own shadow. I can double up crocodiles any day, and I like to wear a hornets' nest for my Sunday bonnet.'

As the girl looped the ends of her snake rope to the top of the branch that was trapping Davy, she kept bragging: 'I'm a streak of lightning set up edgeways and buttered with quicksilver. I can outgrin, outsnort, outrun, outlift, outsneeze, outsleep, outlie any varmint from Maine to Louisiana. Furthermore, *sweetie*, I can blow out the moonlight and sing a wolf to sleep.' Then she pulled on the other end of the snake rope so hard, it seemed as if she might tear the world apart.

The right-hand fork of that big tree bent just about double. Then Davy slid his head out as easy as you please. For a minute he was so dizzy, he couldn't tell up from down. But when he got everything going straight again, he took a good look at that girl. 'What's your name, ma'am?'

'Sally Ann Thunder Ann Whirlwind,' she said. 'But if you mind your manners, you can call me Sally.'

From then on Davy Crockett was crazy in love with Sally Ann Thunder Ann Whirlwind. He asked everyone he knew about her, and everything he heard caused another one of Cupid's arrows to jab him in the gizzard.

'Oh, I know Sally!' the preacher said. 'She can dance a rock to pieces and ride a panther bareback!'

'Sally's a good ole friend of mine,' the blacksmith said. 'Once I seen her crack a walnut with her front teeth.'

'Sally's so very special,' said the schoolmarm. 'She likes to whip across the Salt River, using her apron for a sail and her left leg for a rudder!'

Sally Ann Thunder Ann Whirlwind had a reputation for being funny, too. Her best friend, Lucy, told Davy, 'Sally can laugh the bark off a pine tree. She likes to whistle out one side of her mouth while she eats with the other side and grins with the middle!'

According to her friends, Sally could tame about anything in the world, too. They all told Davy about the time she was churning butter and heard something scratching outside. Suddenly the door swung open, and in walked the Great King Bear of the Mud Forest. He'd come to steal one of her smoked hams. Well, before the King Bear could say boo, Sally grabbed a warm dumpling from the pot and stuffed it in his mouth.

The dumpling tasted so good, the King Bear's eyes winked with tears. But then he started to think that Sally might taste pretty good, too. So opening and closing his big old mouth, he backed her right into a corner.

Sally was plenty scared, with her knees a-knocking and her heart a-hammering. But just as the King Bear blew his hot breath in her face, she gathered the courage to say, 'Would you like to dance?'

As everybody knows, no bear can resist an invitation to a square dance, so of course the old fellow forgot all about eating Sally and said, 'Love to.'

Then he bowed real pretty, and the two got to kicking and whooping and swinging each other through the air, as Sally sang:

'We are on our way to Baltimore,
With two behind, and two before:
Around, around, around we go,
Where oats, peas, beans, and barley grow!'

And while she was singing, Sally tied a string from the bear's ankle to her butter churn, so that all the time the old feller was kicking up his legs and dancing around the room, he was also churning her butter!

And folks loved to tell the story about Sally's encounter with another stinky varmint— only this one was a *human* varmint. It seems that Mike Fink, the riverboat man, decided to scare the toenails of Sally because he was sick and tired of hearing Davy Crockett talk about how great she was.

One evening Mike crept into an old alligator skin and met Sally just as she was taking off to forage in the woods for berries. He spread open his gigantic mouth and made such a howl that he nearly scared himself to death. But Sally paid no more attention to that fool than she would have to a barking puppy dog.

However, when Mike put out his claws to embrace her, her anger rose higher than a Mississippi flood. She threw a flash of eye lightning at him, turning the dark to daylight. Then she pulled out a little toothpick and with a single swing sent the alligator head flying fifty feet! And then to finish him off good, she rolled up her sleeves and knocked Mike Fink clear across the woods and into a muddy swamp.

When the fool came to, Davy Crockett was standing over him. 'What in the world happened to you, Mikey?' he asked.

'Well, I—I think I must-a been hit by some kind of wild alligator!' Mike stammered, rubbing his sore head.

Davy smiled, knowing full well it was Sally Ann Thunder Ann Whirlwind just finished giving Mike Fink the only punishment he'd ever known.

That incident caused Cupid's final arrow to jab Davy's gizzard. 'Sally's the whole steamboat,' he said, meaning that she was something great. The next day he put on his best raccoon hat and sallied forth to see her.

When he got within three miles of her cabin, he began to holler her name. His voice was so loud, it whirled through the woods like a hurricane.

Sally looked out and saw the wind a-blowing and the trees a-bending. She heard her name a-thundering through the woods, and her heart began to thump. By now she'd begun to feel that Davy Crockett was the whole steamboat, too. So she put on her best hat—and eagle's nest with a wildcat's tail for a feather—and ran outside.

Just as she stepped out the door, Davy Crockett burst from the woods and jumped onto her porch as fast as a frog. 'Sally, darlin'!' he cried. 'I think my heart is bustin'! Want to be my wife?'

'Oh, my stars and possum dogs, why not?' she said.

From that day on, Davy Crockett had a hard time acting tough around Sally Ann Thunder Ann Whirlwind. His fightin' and hollerin' had no more effect on her than dropping feathers on a barn floor. At least that's what *she'd* tell you. *He* might say something else.

From *American Tall Tales*, by Mary Pope Osborne (New York: Alfred A. Knopf, 1991).

Meleager and Atalanta

In this story, from what reteller Roger Lancelyn Green calls 'the bright, misty morning of legend and literature', a female hero is looked upon as an oddity, as one whose life is only fulfilled when she has completed a linear journey to marriage and motherhood. The scorn Atalanta receives because of her hunting prowess and her refusal to marry reflects the male-oriented focus of Greek society. Her refusal can be compared to that in the Inuit myth 'Sedna' and contrasted to female character's desires for happy marriages in many European folk-tales. In the account of Atalanta's early life are found many traditional motifs: the unwanted child, the unusual upbringing, and the animal helpers.

𝕸eleager the Argonaut bore a charmed life. For when he was but seven days old the Three Fates appeared to his mother, Queen Althaea of Calydon, as she lay in the big shadowy room of the palace lit only by the flickering firelight.

The Fates were the three daughters of Zeus and Themis who presided over the fate of man: and when Althaea saw them, they were busy with the life-thread of her son Meleager.

One Fate spun the thread of life, and that was Clotho, and she was spinning busily, while Lachesis stood by with her rod to measure it. The third Fate, Atropos, held the shears, and she said to her sisters:

'Why trouble you to spin and measure? As soon as that brand on the hearth yonder is consumed to ashes, I must cut the thread with my shears, and Meleager's life will be ended!'

When Althaea heard this, she leapt out of bed, snatched the burning brand from the hearth and put out the flames. Then she hid it away in a secret chest of which she alone possessed the key.

'Now I defy you, Fates!' she cried. 'I have but to preserve that brand, and my son will live for ever!'

Then the three sisters smiled at Althaea, and there was a secret knowledge in their eyes which made her afraid. After that, they vanished, and only the charred brand in her secret chest remained to prove that she had not dreamed it all.

Years passed and Meleager grew into a brave young prince and went with Jason and the other Argonauts in quest of the Golden Fleece. On his return to Calydon he found a savage wild boar ravaging the land, destroying all the crops and killing any who tried to withstand it.

This great boar, with its wonderful tusks and hide was not to be slain by one man, and Meleager sent for his friends among the Argonauts, Heracles and Theseus, Peleus and Telamon, Admetus and Nestor, Jason himself, and several others—but in particular he sent for the maiden huntress Atalanta. For Meleager had fallen in love with her during their voyage on the Argo, and still hoped to persuade her to be his wife, though she had sworn never to marry.

Atalanta was a princess of Arcadia, but when she was born her father, King Iasus of Tegea, disappointed that she was not a boy, had cast her out onto the wild mountain side. Here a she-bear found the baby and brought her up among her own cubs; and Artemis, the Immortal Huntress, trained her in all matters of the chase and allowed her to join with the nymphs who were her followers.

Now she came eagerly to Calydon, and was welcomed by Meleager and the other Argonauts. But Phexippus and Toxeus, Meleager's uncles, the beloved brothers of Queen Althaea, protested when they saw Atalanta.

'It is an insult,' they cried, 'to expect us to go hunting in company with a woman! She should be weaving at her loom, not mixing with men and pretending to skill in the chase!'

Meleager angrily bade them be silent, and the hunt began, with Atalanta walking at his side—a lovely maiden, simple and boyish with hair falling to her shoulders, a tunic of skins, and a long bow in her hand.

'How happy will the man be who can call himself your husband!' sighed Meleager.

Atalanta blushed and frowned, saying: 'Never by my free will shall any man do so. . . . But let us give all our thoughts to this fierce boar which we seek.'

They had not far to go, for in a wooded dell overhung by willows and dense with smooth sedge and marshy rushes, the boar was roused. Out he came in a fury, levelling the young trees and bushes as he went, and scattering the dogs to right and left.

Echion flung a spear, but in his eagerness pinned only the trunk of a maple tree. Jason hurled his weapon, but it too passed over the boar's back. Squealing with rage, while its eyes flashed fire, it rushed upon young Nestor—who would never have lived to fight at Troy if he had not swung himself quickly into a tree out of harm's way.

Then Telamon rushed at the boar with his spear ready, but he tripped over an unseen root, and was barely rescued by Peleus. As he staggered to his feet, the boar charged: and it would have gone hard with them both if Atalanta had not, with quiet skill and courage, drawn her bow-string and sent an arrow into the boar's head close to its ear. Yet even her skill could not send an arrow right to the brain, so hard was the creature's skin.

There was no one so delighted as Meleager. 'See!' he cried, 'the princess Atalanta has taught us men how to hunt boars, and has smitten the creature with a mortal wound!'

Ancaeus, who had also objected to a woman joining in the hunt, was furious at this. 'Watch!' he cried, 'I'll show you how a man settles wild boars! No pin-pricks from a woman will do it. A battle axe is the weapon, and Artemis herself could not defend this boar against me!'

So saying, he rushed at the maddened creature and struck—but struck short. The next moment he was on his back, and the boar had killed him. In an effort to save him, Peleus flung his spear; but Eurytion sprang forward at the same moment with his weapon raised, and the spear meant for the boar passed through his body.

Theseus also launched a spear, but aimed high in his excitement and transfixed only the bough of an oak tree. But Meleager's aim was true, and the boar fell to the ground, and he dispatched it with a blow of his second spear.

Then the hunters shouted with joy, and stood around gazing in awe at the great creature covering so large a patch of ground. Meleager knelt down and set to work skinning the Boar, and when he had done so, he turned to Atalanta and presented her with the head and hide.

'Lady,' he said, 'take the spoils and share my glory with me. You were the first to wound the boar and more honour belongs to you than to me or any other one of us.'

Then the rest envied Atalanta her prize, and Phexippus, Meleager's uncle, could not contain his fury:

'This is the worst insult of all!' he shouted. 'My nephew won the skin, and if he did not want it, he should have given it to me, as the most noble person present! As for you, you shameless girl, do not think that we will suffer this dishonour. You may have bewitched Meleager with your beauty, but it has no power on us!'

At that he and his brother Toxeus seized hold of Atalanta and tore the spoils from her as roughly and insultingly as they could.

Then Meleager lost his temper completely. With a yell of rage he drew his sword and stabbed Phexippus to the heart. Next he turned upon Toxeus, who tried to defend himself, but soon lay dead beside his brother. Then the party set out sadly for the city, carrying the dead bodies with them, while Atalanta held the head and hide of the Calydonian boar.

When Queen Althaea saw that her two brothers were dead, her grief knew no bounds. But when she learnt that Meleager had killed them, her grief turned to a wild frenzy of fury and revenge.

Suddenly she remembered the charred brand which she had snatched from the hearth when Meleager was a baby. Rushing to her room, she drew it from the chest and cast it upon the fire, where it caught quickly, flamed up, and was soon reduced to ashes.

Now Meleager was feasting his friends in the hall and drinking the health of Atalanta. All at once the cup fell from his hand, and with a cry he sank to the ground, writhing there in agony. He cried out that he was burning from within, and that he wished the boar had killed him instead of Ancaeus; and in a few minutes he lay dead.

Then there was mourning throughout Calydon, and the great Boar Hunt which had begun so happily ended in sadness and tragedy. Queen Althaea, when she came to herself after her frenzy of grief and rage, was so horrified at what she had done that she hanged herself.

But one happy result came of the Calydonian Boar Hunt, for Heracles fell in love with Meleager's sister, the Princess Deianira. Now King Oeneus had promised her, against her will, to the River Achelous, who came to him in the shape of a fierce man and threatened to destroy his land if he refused his suit.

When Heracles heard this, he went to the river bank and cried: 'Noble River Achelous, we both love the same maiden! Come forth, then, in whatever form you choose, and fight with me for her!'

Achelous accepted this daring challenge, took the form of a great, savage bull, and charged at Heracles. But that mighty hero was experienced by now in such contests, and seizing Achelous by one horn he snapped it off at the root. Then Achelous submitted, and Deianira became the wife of Heracles, and they lived happily for a while at Calydon, helping Oeneus until his young son Tydeus should be old enough to rule.

The other hunters had, meanwhile, returned to their homes; but the beautiful Atalanta, famous now for her part in the battle with the boar, was claimed by her father, King Iasus.

She settled at his home, at Tegea in Arcadia, but still refused to marry.

From Heather Copley and Christopher Chamberlain, *Heroes of Greece and Troy*. Illustrated by Roger Lancelyn Green. (London: Bodley Head, 1960), 171.

'But I have no son to succeed me!' lamented Iasus. 'Choose whom you will as husband, and you shall rule here jointly, and your children after you.'

'I will obey you, as a daughter should,' said Atalanta at length. 'But on one condition. Every prince who comes as my suitor must race with me. Only he that is swifter of foot than I shall be my husband. But, those whom I beat in the race shall forfeit their lives.'

Iasus was forced to agree, and sent heralds throughout Greece proclaiming that whoever could outrun his daughter Atalanta, should marry her and be king of Tegea; but that those who lost the race would lose their heads also.

Several princes felt confident that they could run faster than any girl, and came to try their fortune. But each of them in turn left his head to decorate the finishing-post on King Iasus's racecourse.

Soon no one else dared to try, and Atalanta smiled happily, for she was determined never to marry.

At length her cousin Prince Melanion fell in love with her and knowing that he could not surpass her in running, he prayed to Aphrodite, the Immortal Queen of Love and Beauty, to assist him.

Aphrodite was angry with Atalanta for scorning love and refusing to marry, and she granted Melanion her help. She lent him the three golden apples which Heracles had brought from the Garden of the Hesperides, and which Athena had passed on to her for this very purpose.

Then Melanion presented himself in Tegea, and in spite of all King Iasus's warnings, insisted on racing for Atalanta.

The course was set, and the race began. At first Atalanta let Melanion gain on her, for she knew that she was twice as fast a runner as he was. When he saw her shadow drawing close to him, he dropped a golden apple which rolled in front of her.

Atalanta saw the apple, and was filled with the desire to possess this wonderful thing. So she stopped quickly, picked it up, and then sped after Melanion, certain of overtaking him easily. And so she did, but as she drew level, he dropped a second apple, and again she could not resist the temptation, but stopped and picked it up.

Once more she sped after Melanion, and once more she overtook him. But a third apple rolled across in front of her, and at the sight of its beauty and wonder, Atalanta forgot all else, and stopped to gather it.

'I can still overtake him!' she thought, and sped on like the wind. But Melanion touched the winning-post a moment before she reached him, and so he won her for his wife. And in a little while they were living happily together as king and queen of Tegea, with a small son to be king after them.

From *Heroes of Greece and Troy*, by Roger Lancelyn Green (London: The Bodley Head, 1960).

The Wanderings of Ulysses

After the Trojan War, Ulysses (the Roman name of Odysseus), hero of the Greek epic the *Odyssey*, spent many years attempting to return to his home on the island of Ithaca. Scholars believe that his many adventures along the way are based on earlier folktales that were adapted to reflect the character of the hero. The sequence of the events called forth his courage, cleverness, and, sometimes, vanity on the homeward voyage. Perhaps the most famous of these adventures is his confrontation with the one-eyed cyclops, Polythemus. The giant is part of a savage, lawless group and is markedly different from the clever hero. Ulysses, who is a trickster, nearly causes his own death and, indeed, is indirectly responsible for the deaths of many of his followers. Even though he devises a very crafty escape plan, he cannot resist revealing his own identity, calling out his name proudly. The story reveals the vengeful quality of the Greek gods. Poseidon, God of the Sea, will later avenge the death of the cyclops by causing many disasters to befall Ulysses and his men.

When Ulysses left Troy the wind carried him to the coast of Thrace, where the people were allies of the Trojans. It was a king of the Thracians that Diomede killed when he and Ulysses stole into the camp of the Trojans in the night, and drove away the white horses of the king, as swift as the winds. Ismarus was the name of the Thracian town where Ulysses landed, and his men took it and plundered it, yet Ulysses allowed no one to harm the priest of Apollo, Maron, but protected him and his wife and child, in their house within the holy grove of the God. Maron was grateful, and gave Ulysses twelve talents, or little wedges, of gold, and a great bowl of silver, and twelve large clay jars, as big as barrels, full of the best and strongest wine. It was so strong that men put into the mixing bowl but one measure of wine to twenty measures of water. These presents Ulysses stored up in his ship, and lucky for him it was that he was kind to Maron.

Meanwhile his men, instead of leaving the town with their plunder, sat eating and drinking till dawn. By that time the people of the town had warned their neighbours in the country farms, who all came down in full armour, and attacked the men of Ulysses. In this fight he lost seventy-two men, six from each of his twelve ships, and it was only by hard fighting that the others were able to get on board their ships and sail away.

A great storm arose and beat upon the ships, and it seems that Ulysses and his men were driven into Fairyland, where they remained for ten years. We have heard that King Arthur and Thomas the Rhymer were carried into Fairyland, but what adventures they met with there we do not know. About Ulysses we have the stories which are now to be told. For ten days his ships ran due south, and, on the tenth, they reached the land of the Lotus Eaters, who eat food of flowers. They went on shore and drew water, and three men were sent to try to find the people of that country, who were a quiet, friendly people, and gave the fruit of the lotus to the strange sailors. Now whoever tastes of that fruit has no mind ever to go home, but to sit between the setting sun and the rising moon, dreaming happy dreams, and forgetting the world. The three men ate the lotus, and sat down to dream, but Ulysses went after them, and drove them to the ships, and bound their hands and feet, and threw them on board, and sailed away. Then he with his ships reached the coast of the land of the Cyclopes, which means the round-eyed men, men with only one eye apiece, set in the middle of their foreheads. They lived not in houses, but in caves among the hills, and they had no king and no laws, and did not plough or sow, but wheat and vines grew wild, and they kept great flocks of sheep.

There was a beautiful wild desert island lying across the opening of a bay; the isle was full of wild goats, and made a bar against the waves, so that ships could lie behind it safely, run up on the beach, for there was no tide in that sea. There Ulysses ran up his ships, and the men passed the time in hunting wild goats, and feasting on fresh meat and the wine of Maron, the priest of Apollo. Next day Ulysses left all the ships and men there, except his own ship, and his own crew, and went to see what kind of people lived on the mainland, for as yet none had been seen. He found a large cave close to the sea, with laurels growing on the rocky roof, and a wall of rough stones built round a court in front. Ulysses left all his men but twelve with the ship; filled a goat skin with the strong wine of Maron, put some corn flour in a sack, and went up to the cave. Nobody was there, but there were all the things that are usually in a dairy, baskets full of cheese, pails and bowls full of milk and whey, and kids and lambs were playing in their folds.

All seemed very quiet and pleasant. The men wanted to take as much cheese as they could carry back to the ship, but Ulysses wished to see the owner of the cave. His men, making themselves at home, lit a fire, and toasted and ate the cheeses, far within the cave. Then a shadow thrown by the setting sun fell across the opening of the cave, and a monstrous man entered, and threw down a dry trunk of a tree that he carried for firewood. Next he drove in the ewes of his flock, leaving the rams in the yard, and he picked up a huge flat stone, and set it so as to make a shut door to the cave, for twenty-four yoke of horses could not have dragged away that stone. Lastly the man milked his ewes, and put the milk in pails to drink at supper. All this while Ulysses and his men sat quiet and in great fear, for they were shut up in a cave with a one-eyed giant, whose cheese they had been eating.

Then the giant, when he had lit the fire, happened to see the men, and asked them who they were. Ulysses said that they were Greeks, who had taken Troy, and were wandering lost on the seas, and he asked the man to be kind to them in the name of their chief God, Zeus.

'We Cyclopes,' said the giant, 'do not care for Zeus or the Gods, for we think that we are better men than they. Where is your ship?' Ulysses answered that it had been wrecked on the coast, to which the man made no answer, but snatched up two of the twelve, knocked out their brains on the floor, tore the bodies limb from limb, roasted them at his fire, ate them, and, after drinking many pailfuls of milk, lay down and fell asleep. Now Ulysses had a mind to drive his sword-point into the giant's liver, and he felt for the place with his hand. But he remembered that, even if he killed the giant, he could not move the huge stone that was the door of the cave, so he and his men would die of hunger, when they had eaten all the cheeses.

In the morning the giant ate two more men for breakfast, drove out his ewes, and set the great stone in the doorway again, as lightly as a man would put a quiverlid on a quiver of arrows. Then away he went, driving his flock to graze on the green hills.

Ulysses did not give way to despair. The giant had left his stick in the cave: it was as large as the mast of a great ship. From this Ulysses cut a portion six feet long, and his men cut and rubbed as if they were making a spear shaft: Ulysses then sharpened it to a point, and hardened the point in the fire. It was a thick rounded bar of wood, and the men cast lots to choose four, who should twist the bar in the giant's eye when he fell asleep at night. Back he came at sunset, and drove his flocks into the cave, rams and all. Then he put up his stone door, milked his ewes, and killed two men and cooked them.

Ulysses meanwhile had filled one of the wooden ivy bowls full of the strong wine of Maron, without putting a drop of water into it. This bowl he offered to the giant, who had never heard of wine. He drank one bowl after another, and when he was merry he said that he would make Ulysses a present. 'What is your name?' he asked. 'My name is Nobody,' said Ulysses. 'Then I shall eat the others first and Nobody last,' said the giant. 'That shall be your gift.' Then he fell asleep.

Ulysses took his bar of wood, and made the point red-hot in the fire. Next his four men rammed it into the giant's one eye, and held it down, while Ulysses twirled it round, and the eye hissed like red-hot iron when men dip it into cold water, which is the strength of iron. The Cyclops roared and leaped to his feet, and shouted for help to the other giants who lived in the neighbouring caves. 'Who is troubling you, Polyphemus,' they answered. 'Why do you wake us out of our sleep?' The giant answered, 'Nobody is killing me by his cunning, not at all in fair fight.' 'Then if nobody is harming you nobody can help you', shouted a giant. 'If you are ill pray to your father, Poseidon, who is the god of the sea.' So the giants all went back to bed, and Ulysses laughed low to see how his cunning had deceived them. Then the giant went and took down his door and sat in the doorway, stretching out his arms, so as to catch his prisoners as they went out.

But Ulysses had a plan. He fastened sets of three rams together with twisted withies, and bound a man to each ram in the middle, so that the blind giant's hands would only feel the two outside rams. The biggest and strongest ram Ulysses seized, and held on by his hands and feet to its fleece, under its belly, and then all the sheep went out through the doorway, and the giant felt them, but did not know that they were carrying out the men. 'Dear ram!' he said to the biggest, which carried Ulysses, 'you do not come out first, as usual, but last, as if you were slow with sorrow for your master, whose eye Nobody has blinded!'

Then all the rams went out into the open country, and Ulysses unfastened his men, and drove the sheep down to his ship and so on board. His crew wept when they heard of the death of six of their friends, but Ulysses made them row out to sea. When he was just so far

From Andrew Lang, *Tales of Troy and Greece*. Illustrated by Edward Bawden. (London: Faber & Faber, 1962), 121.

away from the cave as to be within hearing distance he shouted at the Cyclops and mocked him. Then that giant broke off the rocky peak of a great hill and threw it in the direction of the sound. The rock fell in front of the ship, and raised a wave that drove it back to shore, but Ulysses punted it off with a long pole, and his men rowed out again, far out. Ulysses again shouted to the giant, 'If anyone asks who blinded you, say that it was Ulysses, Laertes's son, of Ithaca, the stormer of cities.'

Then the giant prayed to the sea god, his father, that Ulysses might never come home, or if he did, that he might come late and lonely, with loss of all his men, and find sorrow in his house. Then the giant heaved and threw another rock, but it fell at the stern of the ship, and the wave drove the ship further out to sea, to the shore of the island. There Ulysses and his men landed, and killed some of the giant's sheep, and took supper, and drank wine.

But the sea god heard the prayer of his son the blind giant.

Ulysses and his men sailed on, in what direction and for how long we do not know, till they saw far off an island that shone in the sea. When they came nearer they found that it had a steep cliff of bronze, with a palace on the top. Here lived Aeolus, the King of the Winds, with his six sons and six daughters. He received Ulysses kindly on his island, and entertained him for a whole month. Then he gave him a leather bag, in which he had bound the ways of all the noisy winds. This bag was fastened with a silver cord, and Aeolus left no wind out except the West Wind, which would blow Ulysses straight home to Ithaca. Where he was we cannot guess, except that he was to the west of his own island.

So they sailed for nine days and nights towards the east, and Ulysses always held the helm and steered, but on the tenth day he fell asleep. Then his men said to each other, 'What treasure is it that he keeps in the leather bag, a present from King Aeolus? No doubt the bag is full of gold and silver, while we have only empty hands.' So they opened the bag when they were so near Ithaca that they could see people lighting fires on the shore. Then out rushed all the winds, and carried the ship into unknown seas, and when Ulysses woke he was so miserable that he had a mind to drown himself. But he was of an enduring heart, and he lay still, and the ship came back to the isle of Aeolus, who cried, 'Away with you! You are the most luckless of living men: you must be hated by the Gods.'

Thus Aeolus drove them away, and they sailed for seven days and nights, till they saw land, and came to a harbour with a narrow entrance, and with tall steep rocks on either side. The other eleven ships sailed into the haven, but Ulysses did not venture in; he fastened his ship to a rock at the outer end of the harbour. The place must have been very far north, for, as it was summer, the sun had hardly set till dawn began again, as it does in Norway and Iceland, where there are many such narrow harbours within walls of rock. These places are called fjords. Ulysses sent three men to spy out the country, and at a well outside the town they met a damsel drawing water; she was the child of the king of the people, the Laestrygonians. The damsel led them to her father's house; he was a giant and seized one of the men of Ulysses, meaning to kill and eat him. The two other men fled to the ships, but the Laestrygonians ran along the tops of the cliffs and threw down great rocks, sinking the vessels and killing the sailors. When Ulysses saw this he drew his sword and cut the cable that fastened his ship to the rock outside the harbour, and his crew rowed for dear life and so escaped, weeping for the death of their friends. Thus the prayer of the blind Cyclops was being fulfilled, for now out of twelve ships Ulysses had but one left.

———

From *Tales of Troy and Greece*, by Andrew Lang (London: Faber and Faber, 1962).

The Crooked Tote Road

Stories of the lumberjack Paul Bunyan are an outgrowth of the popular nineteenth century tall-tale tradition. Stories of this type may deal with real people, but the adventures are humourously exaggerated so that the characters seem almost bigger than life. Of the most famous tall-tale heroes, only Paul Bunyan is international; his adventures take place throughout both his home country, the United States, and Canada. During the time of the booming lumber industry of the last half of the nineteenth century, the stories no doubt originated as yarns told by loggers on

Saturday nights, with each yarn-spinner trying to out-exaggerate the others. Canadian author John D. Robins, who worked in the woods in the early twentieth century, retells many of the standard adventures but adds an ironic tone that seems at times to deflate the view of Bunyan as a super hero. In 'The Crooked Tote Road', which recounts one of Paul's best-known feats, the narrator, Ed, recalls his boss's practical solution to a problem that was lowering the efficiency of the logging operation. However, the narrator's tendency to exaggerate his account casts doubt on the truth of the event. His apparent admiration of the hero may be the author's way of deflating the grandness of the great logger. No one could be as ingenious or as strong as Ed's hero. This story also functions as a modern *pourquoi* tale, explaining the origin of the northern lights and the formation of Silver Peak in northern Ontario.

One night last winter when I was sittin' by the stove the tote-teamster came into the bunkhouse cursin' all the ruddy road-makers who ever lived. I can't tell you exactly what he said, but the gen'ral idee was if they had known enough to pound sand in a rat-hole, they'd have made the tote road at least reason'bly straight, then a man wouldn't have to get up before he struck the hay almost and drive forty-seven miles to cover fifteen. As it was, he didn't get in until an hour and a half after he went to bed. That was the last time he was goin' to do it. They could stick their old job up their coat-sleeve.

He don't do so bad at that, I thought to myself. Give that boy time an' he might get to be as good at cursin' as Louis Mafraw hisself.

Louis made a bet once that he could keep her goin' steady without sayin' anythin' twicet for eighteen hours, countin' three off for eatin'. I guess maybe he'd a won it too, only just as luck would have it, the priest come to camp that very afternoon.

I don't know, though. He was doin' some funny work all right, an' I heerd a lot then I ain't heerd very often, an' one or two I hadn't never though of even myself, but I had a notion he was weakenin' a little before the priest got there. Even with the bet on, an' his name to keep up, he was doin' it cold, you might say. He didn't have no mad on.

No, the boy didn't do so bad, but he didn't know what a crooked tote road was. They was one tote road that Paul had oncet that would of made his'n seem like it been drawed along a straight-edge. Paul was cuttin' pine near Collins Inlet that winter, an' 'course he had to have a tote road to haul grub an' supplies in to camp from outside. An' she was some tote road I'm tellin' you.

Seems Paul had a kind of second cousin by marriage that was a surveyor for the Grand Trunk Railroad when she was first built. Well, in them days it seems the railroads got so much land on each side of the right-of-way. So the crookeder she was the more land they got, an' of course the more mileage they had to charge for too. So this here surveyor he got into the habit of layin' every thin' out as crooked as a ram's horn, an' I'll be jiggered if he didn't get it down so fine he run hisself out of a job. He laid out the first Algoma Central so crooked that the freight trains that was anyways long, the engines would run smash head-on into their own cabooses at the rear end. So they fired him an' scrapped the whole road an' they didn't build her ag'in for a long time.

So Paul give him a job till he'd get on his feet ag'in, an' he set him to layin' out the tote road from Blind River into his limit, that was down Collins Inlet way. I s'pose Paul had ought to of knowed better, but I guess he thought a surveyor couldn't go far wrong on just buildin' a tote road to take supplies in on. Well, that fool couldn't get out of the notion he was buildin' a railroad right-of-way, an' he made that road so crooked it made you dizzy walkin' on it. She wasn't too bad the first twelve miles, follerin' the concession lines, but after that she was a humdinger. Paul cussed around considerable when he seen her, an' then he got his cousin a job puttin' a road up Pike's Peak.

We had the most almighty job gettin' Babe in to camp. It took us three weeks an' a half. Or was it four weeks an' a half? Let's see. We started in from Blind River on a Monday, an' I think it was the eighteenth of October, an' we gets there on a Thursday afternoon about four o'clock in November. That makes it four an' a half, don't it? But after all that, I didn't drive

Babe on the road. I druv the tote team, one of the first teams of horses I guess ever was used in the bush. But it was no cinch. I had to get up thirty-six hours before sunrise to do the round trip in a day.

Fact is, there was so much night-drivin' that Paul rigged up a set of lights for me to see by. They used to shine as steady as a lamp. When Paul got through with 'em he sent a green-horn out one night to blow 'em out, but the poor boob ain't got 'em blowed out yet. He got the chimley off, an' they went kind of wavy-like, an' sometimes it looks like he's made it, an' then they'll start up again. Some folks got a fancy name for 'em, but we just call 'em the Northern Lights an' let it go at that.

Well, things kinda went along till one day Paul he looks at me pretty sharp an' he says, 'Ed, old timer,' he says, 'what's the matter? You look like you been drawed through a knot-hole. Gettin' distemper?'

'No, Paul,' I says, 'I ain't gettin' distemper, an' I ain't got the heaves, an' I ain't goin' off my feed. But I can't get no sleep.'

'The hell you can't,' he says. 'What's the itch? Greybacks too big this winter?'

'Say, Paul,' I says, 'I ain't in my bunk long enough for a greyback to find me,' I says. I'm on that eternal tote road of your'n twenty-six hours out of the twenty-four.'

Paul looked at me, but he didn't say a word. Then he pulls up a smallish pine that was standin' there an' he strips off the branches through his teeth, an' then he begins to chaw on her. He knowed he was wastin' at least four sixteen-foot logs in the clear, but Paul was that kind. He didn't care one way or the other about a couple of hunderd thousan' feet of timber. 'Course they was lots of timber in them days, an' it didn't look as if she'd ever be all cut.

I didn't say nothin'. I knowed Paul was thinkin'. Maybe he stood there a couple of hours, chewin' on that pine an' spittin' her out an' thinkin'.

Then he stops all of a sudden an' he says, 'What day of the month is this?'

'I dunno,' I says. 'Goin' by the tobacco I've used, I guess maybe it might be about the last week in November or somethin' like that.'

'I guess Johnny Inkslinger is about the only man in camp that knows for sure,' says Paul. 'I gotta know when New Year's comes. Ed,' he says, 'do you think you could stick her out till New Year's?'

For the life of me I couldn't think what was in Paul's mind, but I knowed he had fig-gered out somethin' or other, an' that was good enough for me.

Well, I didn't hear nothin' more about it till one day I heerd Paul tellin' Ole the Blacksmith to make him up a couple of half-mile chains an make 'em strong, an' for him to have 'em ready for the next night.

Well, when the next night come, Paul calls me an' Ole out an' gets Babe, an' we heads off to the end of the tote road—that was five miles past camp, on account of that fool sur-veyor'd gone an' laid out five extra miles on top of all the crookedness.

You know, it was kind a nice out there that night. The old moon was a-comin' up through them pines an' she was the biggest, an' yellerest I ever seen her, an' she had a kind of friendly look, just like she felt she belonged with them great big fellers standin' there. Babe a-chewin' away at his cud. Ole the Blacksmith with the one half-mile of chain, an' old Paul hisself with the other chain hangin' down over his shoulder an' his big red mackinaw an' him a-facin' into that moonlight an' them good old pines standin' up there tall an' straight an' clean, an' the frost a-cracklin'. Doggone if it don't make my old backbone feel kinda ticklish right now when I think about it.

Pretty soon Paul hauls out his turnip an' looks at the time. 'Boys,' he says, 'it's just three minutes past eleven. I set her tonight by Johnny Inkslinger's watch, an' everybody knows it reg'lates the sun, moon, an' stars an' tells the price of potatoes in Orillia. Now how long is that tote road all told?'

'Well,' I says, 'I ain't never paced her off, an' I can't say to the odd half mile, but I'd judge her to be rough around a hunderd an' twenty-five mile, not countin' the straight part at the other end,' I says.

'I think I'll go through the bush,' Paul says. 'Now there's that big rock at the place where the road begins to bend, an' I'll hitch that old road to that there rock there. An' when I get her all set, I'll whistle. Then you hitch Babe on to this end. Ole, did you double-temper them chains like I said?'

'Yass, I did,' says Ole, an' that was 'bout the longest speech I ever heerd Ole make.

'All right,' says Paul. 'Now I'm goin' to whistle so's the sound'll get to you boys about ten seconds after midnight. That'll be New Year's an' ten seconds. When you hear that whistle, let Babe lay into her like all get out—'Pon my soul, I b'lieve the old flea-bitten geezer knows what I'm sayin'.'

What's more, the old critter did. He reaches out with his tongue an' licked a whole week's growth of beard off of Paul with one lick. Paul tickled Babe in the ear with the butt end of a log an' then he puts off through the bush, a-gatherin' up the chain he was carryin' in his hand so it wouldn't catch on the trees an' things—that was three-eighths of a mile of chain he was totin'.

Ole an' me hitched Babe up to our end of the road an' waited. She was quiet as a graveyard, 'cept for the trees poppin' an' crackin' in the frost an' Babe chewin' his cud. All at once, Babe stopped chewin' an' settled into his harness an' let out a low beller. Then we heerd it too, that whistle. But before we'd even heerd it, Babe, he straightens away into the yoke.

Well, sir, I thought he wouldn't make it. That road was froze solid about twenty feet down an' it jerked Babe right back on his tail. He tried her ag'in an' still no go. Then Ole took out his plug of chewin' tobacco an' held it out to Babe. Babe reached out his tongue an' gathered it in an' chewed a minute. Then he shook his head an' snorted.

Then that old ox pawed the ground a minute or two, an' fetched a beller from way down in his insides somewheres, an' then he h'isted his tail up an'—pulled. Boys, I'm a-settin' here tellin' you I seen then an' there the biggest pull that was ever made on this earth since creation begun.

That old road heaved a little at first, an' then she settled back a little, an' then she come. An' did she come! Boys oh boys, didn't she come? She come with such a jerk Babe went right over on his snoot.

That tote road was straight as a yard ruler an' it was only thirty-five mile long an' a couple of hunderd foot or so. Johnny Inkslinger figgered that left a hunderd an' ninety-three miles of loose road to get rid of. Some said they was more'n that left over. Like enough they was. Johnny was usin' his payroll measurin' stick, an' it might of been a little short.

Some of the boys was for leavin' it lyin' around anyways, but that wasn't Paul Bunyan's way of doin' things.

'She's in the road,' he says, 'an' she'll be a hell of a mess when the break-up comes. An' what's more,' he says, 'I wants things kinda tidy round here. Coil her up', he says.

So we sets Babe to work to coil up that slack. When we got her coiled up she made a hill that high it took a man with specs four days to see to the top of her. An' that was in the summer, when the days was long. It took a week an' a half in January.

They ain't scarcely anythin' left of that coiled-up road now. It's about all washed away an' wore away. But what they is left of it is still up there somewheres nigh Collins Inlet or Killarney. They calls it Silver Peak.

The day after the big pull I asked Paul what made him so partic'lar about this New Year's business.

'Well,' says Paul, 'I'll tell you. You know how old folks like to keep things the way they always was. I figgered the Old Year'd maybe feel that way about that tote road, an' the only sure way to get that road straightened would be to get her the minute the Old Year kicked the bucket an' before the New Year had time to look around much.'

Well, that sounded pretty reasonable—an' anyway, it worked.

From *Paul Bunyan: Superhero of the Lumberjacks*, by John D. Robins, edited by Edith Fowke (Toronto: NC Press, 1980).

Robin Hood Turns Butcher

Among the English hero Robin Hood's most significant deeds are his fights against evil oppressors. Like Ulysses, he is a trickster, often disguising himself to outwit his enemies. Frequently, as is the case in this episode, his escapades result as much from his restless, adventure-loving spirit as from necessity. The ironies arise not only because of Robin's clever manipulations, but also because of the character of the Sheriff who, led by his greed, agrees to travel to the home of his unknown dinner guest. As in all of the Robin Hood tales, Sherwood Forest is seen in double perspective. For the hero and his honest outlaws, it is a sanctuary and home; for the conniving Sheriff and other evil hypocrites, it is a place to be feared. Howard Pyle, a well-known nineteenth-century American author-illustrator, has consciously used an archaic style to capture the medieval flavor of the original Robin Hood stories.

*N*ow after all these things had happened, and it became known to Robin Hood how the Sheriff had tried three times to make him captive, he said to himself: 'If I have the chance, I will make our worshipful Sheriff pay right well for that which he hath done to me. Maybe I may bring him some time into Sherwood Forest, and have him to a right merry feast with us.' For when Robin Hood caught a baron or a squire, or a fat abbot or bishop, he brought them to the greenwood tree and feasted them before he lightened their purses.

But in the meantime Robin Hood and his band lived quietly in Sherwood Forest, without showing their faces abroad, for Robin knew that it would not be wise for him to be seen in the neighbourhood of Nottingham, those in authority being very wroth with him. But though they did not go abroad, they lived a merry life within the woodlands, spending the days in shooting at garlands hung upon a willow wand at the end of the glade, the leafy aisles ringing with merry jests and laughter: for whoever missed the garland was given a sound buffet, which, if delivered by Little John, never failed to topple over the unfortunate yeoman. Then they had bouts of wrestling and of cudgel play, so that every day they gained in skill and strength.

Thus they dwelt for nearly a year, and in that time Robin Hood often turned over in his mind many means of making an even score with the Sheriff. At last he began to fret at his confinement; so one day he took up his stout cudgel and set forth to seek adventure, strolling blithely along until he came to the edge of Sherwood. There, as he rambled along the sunlit road, he met a lusty young Butcher driving a fine mare, and riding in a stout new cart, all hung about with meat. Merrily whistled the Butcher as he jogged along, for he was going to the market, and the day was fresh and sweet, making his heart blithe within him.

'Good morrow to thee, jolly fellow,' quoth Robin; 'thou seemest happy this merry morn.'

'Ay, that am I,' quoth the jolly Butcher; 'and why should I not be so? Am I not hale in wind and limb? Have I not the bonniest lass in all Nottinghamshire? And lastly, am I not to be married to her on Thursday next in sweet Locksley Town?'

'Ha,' said Robin, 'comest thou from Locksley Town? Well do I know that fair place for miles about, and well do I know each hedgerow and gentle pebbly stream, and even all the bright little fishes therein, for there I was born and bred. Now, where goest thou with thy meat, my fair friend?'

'I go to the market at Nottingham Town to sell my beef and my mutton,' answered the Butcher. 'But who art thou that comest from Locksley Town?'

'A yeoman am I, good friend, and men do call me Robin Hood.'

'Now, by Our Lady's grace,' cried the Butcher, 'well do I know thy name, and many a time have I heard thy deeds both sung and spoken of. But Heaven forbid that thou shouldst take ought of me! An honest man am I, and have wronged neither man nor maid; so trouble me not, good master, as I have never troubled thee.'

'Nay, Heaven forbid, indeed,' quoth Robin, 'that I should take from such as thee, jolly fellow! Not so much as one farthing would I take from thee, for I love a fair Saxon face like thine right well; more especially when it cometh from Locksley Town, and most especially when the man that owneth it is to marry a bonny lass on Thursday next. But come, tell me for what price thou wilt sell all thy meat and thy horse and cart.'

'At four marks do I value meat, cart, and mare,' quoth the Butcher; 'but if I do not sell all my meat I will not have four marks in value.'

Then Robin Hood plucked the purse from his girdle, and quoth he, 'Here in this purse are six marks. Now, I would fain be a butcher for the day and sell my meat in Nottingham Town, wilt thou close a bargain with me and take six marks for thine outfit?'

'Now may the blessings of all the saints fall on thine honest head!' cried the Butcher right joyfully, as he leaped down from his cart and took the purse that Robin held out to him.

'Nay,' quoth Robin, laughing loudly, 'many do like me and wish me well, but few call me honest. Now get thee gone back to thy lass, and give her a sweet kiss from me.' So saying, he donned the Butcher's apron, and, climbing into the cart, he took the reins in his hand, and drove off through the forest to Nottingham Town.

When he came to Nottingham, he entered that part of the market where butchers stood, and took up his inn[1] in the best place he could find. Next, he opened his stall and spread his meat upon the bench, then, taking his cleaver and steel and clattering them together, he trolled aloud, in merry tones:—

> 'Now come, ye lasses, and eke, ye dames,
>   And buy your meat from me;
> For three pennyworths of meat I sell
>   For the charge of one penny.

---

1. Stand for selling.

Lamb have I that hath fed upon nought
   But the dainty daisies pied,
And the violet sweet, and the daffodil
   That grow fair streams beside.

And beef have I from the heathery wolds,
   And mutton from dales all green,
And veal as white as a maiden's brow,
   With its mother's milk, I ween.

Then come ye lasses, and eke, ye dames,
   Come, buy your meat from me;
For three pennyworths of meat I sell
   For the charge of one penny.'

Thus he sang blithely, while all who stood near listened amazedly; then, when he had finished, he clattered the steel and cleaver still more loudly, shouting lustily, 'Now, who'll buy? who'll buy? Four fixed prices have I. Three pennyworths of meat I sell to a fat friar or priest for sixpence, for I want not their custom; stout aldermen I charge threepence, for it doth not matter to me whether they buy or not; to buxom dames I sell three pennyworths of meat for one penny, for I like their custom well; but to the bonny lass that hath a liking for a good tight butcher I charge nought but one fair kiss, for I like her custom the best of all.'

Then all began to stare and wonder, and crowd around, laughing, for never was such selling heard of in all Nottingham Town; but when they came to buy they found it as he had said, for he gave good wife or dame as much meat for one penny as they could buy else-where for three, and when a widow or a poor woman came to him, he gave her flesh for nothing; but when a merry lass came and gave him a kiss, he charged not one penny for his meat; and many such came to his stall, for his eyes were as blue as the skies of June, and he laughed merrily, giving to each full measure. Thus he sold his meat so fast that no butcher that stood near him could sell anything.

Then they began to talk among themselves, and some said, 'This must be some thief who has stolen cart, horse, and meat'; but others said, 'Nay, when did ye ever see a thief who parted with his goods so freely and merrily? This must be some prodigal who hath sold his father's land, and would fain live merrily while the money lasts.' And these latter being the greater number, the others came round, one by one, to their way of thinking.

Then some of the butchers came to him to make his acquaintance. 'Come, brother,' quoth one who was the head of them all, 'we be all of one trade, so wilt thou go dine with us? For this day the Sheriff hath asked all the Butcher Guild to feast with him at the Guild Hall. There will be stout fare, and much to drink, and that thou likest, or I much mistake thee.'

'Now, beshrew his heart,' quoth jolly Robin, 'that would deny a butcher. And, more-over, I will go dine with you all, my sweet lads, and that as fast as I can hie.' Whereupon, having sold all his meat, he closed his stall, and went with them to the great Guild Hall.

There the Sheriff had already come in state, and with him many butchers. When Robin and those that were with him came in, all laughing at some merry jest he had been telling them, those that were near the Sheriff whispered to him, 'Yon is a right mad blade, for he hath sold more meat for one penny this day than we could sell for three, and to whatsoever merry lass gave him a kiss he gave meat for nought.' And others said, 'He is some prodigal that hath sold his land for silver and gold, and meaneth to spend all right merrily.'

From Howard Pyle, *The Merry Adventures of Robin Hood*. (New York: Charles Scribner's Sons, 1946), 43.

Then the Sheriff called Robin to him, not knowing him in his butcher's dress, and made him sit close to him on his right hand; for he loved a rich young prodigal—especially when he thought that he might lighten that prodigal's pockets into his own most worshipful purse. So he made much of Robin, and laughed and talked with him more than with any of the others.

At last the dinner was ready to be served and the Sheriff bade Robin say grace, so Robin stood up and said: 'Now Heaven bless us all and eke good meat and good sack within this house, and may all butchers be and remain as honest men as I am.'

At this all laughed, the Sheriff loudest of all, for he said to himself, 'Surely this is indeed some prodigal, and perchance I may empty his purse of some of the money that the fool throweth about so freely.' Then he spake aloud to Robin, saying: 'Thou art a jolly young blade, and I love thee mightily'; and he smote Robin upon the shoulder.

Then Robin laughed loudly too. 'Yea,' quoth he, 'I know thou dost love a jolly blade, for didst thou not have jolly Robin Hood at thy shooting-match and didst thou not gladly give him a bright golden arrow for his own?'

At this the Sheriff looked grave and all the guild of butchers too, so that none laughed but Robin, only some winked slyly at each other.

'Come, fill us some sack!' cried Robin. 'Let us e'er be merry while we may, for man is but dust, and he hath but a span to live here till the worm getteth him, as our good gossip Swanthold sayeth; so let life be merry while it lasts, say I. Nay, never look down i' the mouth, Sir Sheriff. Who knowest but that thou mayest catch Robin Hood yet if thou drinkest less good sack and Malmsey, and bringest down the fat about thy paunch and the dust from out thy brain. Be merry, man.'

Then the Sheriff laughed again, but not as though he liked the jest, while the butchers said, one to another, 'Before Heaven, never have we seen such a mad rollicking blade. Mayhap, though, he will make the Sheriff mad.'

'How now, brothers,' cried Robin, 'be merry! nay, never count over your farthings, for by this and by that I will pay this shot myself, e'en though it cost two hundred pounds. So let no man draw up his lip, nor thrust his forefinger into his purse, for I swear that neither butcher nor Sheriff shall pay one penny for this feast.'

'Now thou art a right merry soul,' quoth the Sheriff, 'and I wot thou must have many a head of horned beasts and many an acre of land, that thou dost spend thy money so freely.'

'Ay, that have I,' quoth Robin, laughing loudly again, 'five hundred and more horned beasts have I and my brothers, and none of them have we been able to sell, else I might not have turned butcher. As for my land, I have never asked my steward how many acres I have.'

At this the Sheriff's eyes twinkled, and he chuckled to himself. 'Nay, good youth,' quoth he, 'if thou canst not sell thy cattle it may be I will find a man that will lift them from thy hands; perhaps that man may be myself, for I love a merry youth and would help such a one along the path of life. Now how much dost thou want for thy horned cattle?'

'Well,' quoth Robin, 'they are worth at least five hundred pounds.'

'Nay,' answered the Sheriff, slowly, and as if he were thinking within himself; 'well do I love thee, and fain would I help thee along, but five hundred pounds in money is a good round sum; beside I have it not by me. Yet I will give thee three hundred pounds for them all, and that in good hard silver and gold.'

'Now thou old Jew!' quoth Robin; 'well thou knowest that so many horned cattle are worth seven hundred pounds and more, and even that is but small for them, and yet thou, with thy grey hairs and one foot in the grave, wouldst trade upon the folly of a wild youth.'

At this the Sheriff looked grimly at Robin. 'Nay,' quoth Robin, 'look not on me as though thou hadst sour beer in thy mouth, man. I will take thine offer, for I and my brothers do need the money. We lead a merry life, and no one leads a merry life for a farthing, so I will close the bargain with thee. But mind that thou bringest a good three hundred pounds with thee, for I trust not one that driveth so shrewd a bargain.'

'I will bring the money,' said the Sheriff. 'But what is thy name, good youth?'

'Men call me Robert o' Locksley,' quoth bold Robin.

'Then, good Robert o' Locksley,' quoth the Sheriff, 'I will come this day to see thy horned beasts. But first my clerk shall draw up a paper in which thou shalt be bound to the sale, for thou gettest not my money without I get thy beasts in return.'

Then Robin Hood laughed again. 'So be it', he cried, smiting his palm upon the Sheriff's hand. 'Truly my brothers will be thankful to thee for thy money.'

Thus the bargain was closed; but many of the butchers talked among themselves of the Sheriff, saying that it was but a scurvy trick to beguile a poor spendthrift youth in this way.

The afternoon had come when the Sheriff mounted his horse and joined Robin Hood, who stood outside the gateway of the paved court waiting for him, for he had sold his horse and cart to a trader for two marks. Then they set forth upon their way, the Sheriff riding upon his horse and Robin running beside him. Thus they left Nottingham Town and travelled forward along the dusty highway, laughing and jesting together as though they had been old friends; but all the time the Sheriff said within himself, 'Thy jest to me of Robin Hood shall cost thee dear, good fellow, even four hundred pounds, thou fool.' For he thought he would make at least that much by his bargain.

So they journeyed onward till they came within the verge of Sherwood Forest, when presently the Sheriff looked up and down and to the right and to the left of him and then grew quiet and ceased his laughter. 'Now,' quoth he, 'may Heaven and its saints preserve us this day from a rogue men call Robin Hood.'

Then Robin laughed aloud. 'Nay,' said he, 'thou mayst set thy mind at rest, for well do I know Robin Hood and well do I know that thou art in no more danger from him this day than thou art from me.'

At this the Sheriff looked askance at Robin, saying to himself, 'I like not that thou seemest so well acquainted with this bold outlaw, and I wish that I were well out of Sherwood Forest.'

But still they travelled deeper into the forest shades, and the deeper they went the more quiet grew the Sheriff. At last they came to where the road took a sudden bend, and before them a herd of dun deer went tripping across the path. Then Robin Hood came close to the Sheriff and pointing his finger he said, 'These are my horned beasts, good Master Sheriff. How dost thou like them? Are they not fat and fair to see?'

At this the Sheriff drew rein quickly. 'Now fellow,' quoth he, 'I would I were well-out of this forest, for I like not thy company. Go thou thine own path, good friend, and let me but go mine.'

But Robin only laughed and caught the Sheriff's bridle rein. 'Nay,' cried he, 'stay a while, for I would thou shouldst see my brothers who own these fair horned beasts with me.' So saying he clapped his bugle to his mouth and winded three merry notes, and presently up the path came leaping fivescore good stout yeomen with Little John at their head.

'What wouldst thou have, good master?' quoth Little John.

'Why,' answered Robin, 'dost thou not see that I have brought goodly company to feast with us today? Fye, for shame! do you not see our good and worshipful master, the Sheriff of Nottingham? Take thou his bridle, Little John, for he has honoured us today by coming to feast with us.'

Then all doffed their hats humbly, without smiling, or seeming to be in jest, whilst Little John took the bridle rein and led the palfrey still deeper into the forest, all marching in order, with Robin Hood walking beside the Sheriff, hat in hand.

All this time the Sheriff said never a word but only looked about him like one suddenly awakened from sleep; but when he found himself going within the very depth of Sherwood his heart sank within him, for he thought, 'Surely my three hundred pounds will be taken from me, even if they take not my life itself, for I have plotted against their lives more than once.' But all seemed humble and meek and not a word was said of danger, either to life or money.

So at last they came to that part of Sherwood Forest where a noble oak spread its branches wide, and beneath it was a seat all made of moss, on which Robin sat down, placing the Sheriff at his right hand. 'Now busk ye, my merry men all,' quoth he, 'and bring forth the best we have, both of meat and wine, for his worship, the Sheriff, hath feasted me in Nottingham Guild Hall to-day, and I would not have him go back empty.'

All this time nothing had been said of the Sheriff's money, so presently he began to pluck up heart. 'For,' said he to himself, 'maybe Robin Hood hath forgotten all about it.'

Then, whilst beyond in the forest bright fires crackled and savory smells of sweetly roasting venison and fat capons filled the glade, and brown pasties warmed beside the blaze, did Robin Hood entertain the Sheriff right royally. First, several couples stood forth at quarterstaff, and so shrewd were they at the game, and so quickly did they give stroke and parry, that the Sheriff, who loved to watch all lusty sports of the kind, clapped his hands, forgetting where he was, and crying aloud, 'Well struck! well struck, thou fellow with the black beard!' little knowing that the man he called upon was the Tinker that tried to serve his warrant upon Robin Hood.

Then the best archers of the band set up a fair garland of flowers at eightscore paces distance, and shot at it with the cunningest archery practice. But the Sheriff grew grave, for he did not like this so well, the famous meeting at the butts in Nottingham Town being still green in his memory, and the golden arrow that had been won there hanging close behind him. Then, when Robin saw what was in the Sheriff's mind, he stopped the sport, and called forth some of his band, who sang merry ballads, while others made music upon the harp.

When this was done, several yeomen came forward and spread cloths upon the green grass, and placed a royal feast; while others still broached barrels of sack and Malmsey and good stout ale, and set them in jars upon the cloth, with drinking-horns about them. Then all sat down and feasted and drank merrily together until the sun was low and the half-moon glimmered with a pale light betwixt the leaves of the trees overhead.

Then the Sheriff arose and said, 'I thank you all, good yeomen, for the merry entertainment ye have given me this day. Right courteously have ye used me, showing therein that ye have much respect for our glorious King and his deputy in brave Nottinghamshire. But the shadows grow long, and I must away before darkness comes, lest I lose myself within the forest.'

Then Robin Hood and all his merry men arose also, and Robin said to the Sheriff, 'If thou must go, worshipful sir, go thou must; but thou hast forgotten one thing.'

'Nay, I forgot nought,' said the Sheriff; yet all the same his heart sank within him.

'But I say thou hast forgot something', quoth Robin. 'We keep a merry inn here in the greenwood, but whoever becometh our guest must pay his reckoning.'

Then the Sheriff laughed, but the laugh was hollow. 'Well, jolly boys,' quoth he, 'we have had a merry time together today, and even if ye had not asked me, I would have given you a score of pounds for the sweet entertainment I have had.'

'Nay,' quoth Robin seriously, 'it would ill beseem us to treat your worship so meanly. By my faith, Sir Sheriff, I would be ashamed to show my face if I did not reckon the King's deputy at three hundred pounds. Is it not so, my merry men all?'

Then 'Ay!' cried all, in a loud voice.

'Three hundred devils!' roared the Sheriff. 'Think ye that your beggarly feast was worth three pounds, let alone three hundred?'

'Nay,' quoth Robin gravely. 'Speak not so roundly, your worship. I do love thee for the sweet feast thou hast given me this day in merry Nottingham Town; but there be those here who love thee not so much. If thou wilt look down the cloth thou wilt see Will Stutely, in whose eyes thou hast no great favour; then two other stout fellows are there here that thou knowest not, that were wounded in a brawl nigh Nottingham Town, some time ago—thou wottest when; one of them was sore hurt in one arm, yet he hath got the use of it again. Good Sheriff, be advised by me; pay thy score without more ado, or maybe it may fare ill with thee.'

As he spoke the Sheriff's ruddy cheeks grew pale, and he said nothing more but looked upon the ground and gnawed his nether lip. Then slowly he drew forth his fat purse and threw it upon the cloth in front of him.

'Now take the purse, Little John,' quoth Robin Hood, 'and see that the reckoning be right. We would not doubt our Sheriff, but he might not like it if he should find he had not paid his full score.'

Then Little John counted the money, and found that the bag held three hundred pounds in silver and gold. But to the Sheriff it seemed as if every clink of the bright money was a drop of blood from his veins; and when he saw it all counted out in a heap of silver and gold, filling a wooden platter, he turned away and silently mounted his horse.

'Never have we had so worshipful a guest before!' quoth Robin; 'and, as the day waxeth late, I will send one of my young men to guide thee out of the forest depths.'

'Nay, heaven forbid!' cried the Sheriff, hastily. 'I can find mine own way, good man, without aid.'

'Then I will put thee on the right track mine own self,' quoth Robin; and, taking the Sheriff's horse by the bridle rein, he led him into the main forest path; then, before he let him go, he said, 'Now, fare thee well, good Sheriff, and when next thou thinkest to despoil some poor prodigal, remember thy feast in Sherwood Forest. "Ne'er buy a horse, good friend, without first looking into its mouth," as our good gaffer Swanthold says. And so, once more, fare thee well.' Then he clapped his hand to the horse's back, and off went nag and Sheriff through the forest glades.

Then bitterly the Sheriff rued the day that first he meddled with Robin Hood, for all men laughed at him and many ballads were sung by folk throughout the country, of how the Sheriff went to shear and came home shorn to the very quick. For thus men sometimes overreach themselves through greed and guile.

From *The Merry Adventures of Robin Hood*, by Howard Pyle (New York: Charles Scribner's Sons, 1946).

The Last Journey of Gilgamesh

The Sumerian epic of *Gilgamesh*, first written on clay tablets four thousand years ago, has been called the oldest piece of written literature in the world. However, the epic was lost for several centuries and was only rediscovered in 1853. Gilgamesh, who is most likely based on an historical king, ruled with extreme rigidity and spent much of his time consorting with women. Only after he had encountered, fought with, and then befriended Enkidu, a man of nature, did he change his ways. Together, the two had many adventures. The present selection takes place after the death of Enkidu, who had fallen victim to a goddess he had insulted. Grieving over the loss of his closest friend, Gilgamesh, the son of a goddess and a mortal man, sets out on his greatest quest: a search for immortality. Although he fails twice in his journey, he reveals the strength, courage, and determination that make him so heroic and that earn him the help he receives along the way. Scholars have noted the parallels between the flood described by the wise old man Utnapishtim and that recounted in the Bible, an account believed to have been recorded sometime after the Gilgamesh story.

Then Gilgamesh took a cloth and veiled the face of Enkidu, even as men veil a bride on the day of her espousal. And he paced to and fro and cried aloud, and his voice was the voice of a lioness robbed of her whelps. And he stripped off his garments and tore his hair and gave himself up to mourning.

All night long he gazed upon the prostrate form of his companion and saw him grow stiff and wizened, and all the beauty was departed from him. 'Now,' said Gilgamesh, 'I have seen the face of death and am sore afraid. One day I too shall be like Enkidu.'

When morning came he had made a bold resolve.

On an island at the far ends of the earth, so rumour had it, lived the only mortal in the world who had ever escaped death—an old, old man, whose name was Utnapishtim. Gilgamesh decided to seek him out and to learn from him the secret of eternal life.

As soon as the sun was up he set out on his journey, and at last, after travelling long and far, he came to the end of the world and saw before him a huge mountain whose twin peaks touched the sky and whose roots reached down to nethermost hell. In front of the mountain there was a massive gate, and the gate was guarded by fearsome and terrible creatures, half man and half scorpion.

Gilgamesh flinched for a moment and screened his eyes from their hideous gaze. Then he recovered himself and strode boldly to meet them.

When the monsters saw that he was unafraid, and when they looked on the beauty of his body, they knew at once that no ordinary mortal was before them. Nevertheless they challenged his passage and asked the purpose of his coming.

Gilgamesh told them that he was on his way to Utnapishtim, to learn the secret of eternal life.

'That,' replied their captain, 'is a thing which none has ever learned, nor was there ever a mortal who succeeded in reaching that ageless sage. For the path which we guard is the path of the sun, a gloomy tunnel twelve leagues long, a road where the foot of man may not tread.'

'Be it never so long,' rejoined the hero, 'and never so dark, be the pains and the perils never so great, be the heat never so searing and the cold never so sharp, I am resolved to tread it!'

At the sound of these words the sentinels knew for certain that one who was more than a mortal was standing before them, and at once they threw open the gate.

Boldly and fearlessly Gilgamesh entered the tunnel, but with every step he took the path became darker and darker, until at last he could see neither before nor behind. Yet still he strode forward, and just when it seemed that the road would never end, a gust of wind fanned his face and a thin streak of light pierced the gloom.

When he came out into the sunlight a wondrous sight met his eyes, for he found himself in the midst of a faery garden, the trees of which were hung with jewels. And even as he stood rapt in wonder the voice of the sun-god came to him from heaven.

'Gilgamesh,' it said, 'go no farther. This is the garden of delights. Stay awhile and enjoy it. Never before have the gods granted such a boon to a mortal, and for more you must not hope. The eternal life which you seek you will never find.'

But even these words could not divert the hero from his course and, leaving the earthly paradise behind him, he proceeded on his way.

Presently, footsore and weary, he saw before him a large house which had all the appearance of being a hospice. Trudging slowly toward it, he sought admission.

But the alewife, whose name was Siduri, had seen his approach from afar and, judging by his grimy appearance that he was simply a tramp, she had ordered the postern barred in his face.

Gilgamesh was at first outraged and threatened to break down the door, but when the lady called from the window and explained to him the cause of her alarm his anger cooled, and he reassured her, telling her who he was and the nature of his journey and the reason he was so disheveled. Thereupon she raised the latch and bade him welcome.

Later in the evening they fell to talking, and the alewife attempted to dissuade him from his quest. 'Gilgamesh,' she said, 'that which you seek you will never find. For when the gods created man they gave him death for his portion; life they kept for themselves. Therefore enjoy your lot. Eat, drink, and be merry; for *that* were you born!'

But still the hero would not be swerved, and at once he proceeded to inquire of the alewife the way to Utnapishtim.

'He lives,' she replied, 'on a faraway isle, and to reach it you must cross an ocean. But the ocean is the ocean of death, and no man living has sailed it. Howbeit, there is at present in this hospice a man named Urshanabi. He is the boatman of that aged sage, and he has come hither on an errand. Maybe you can persuade him to ferry you across.'

So the alewife presented Gilgamesh to the boatman, and he agreed to ferry him across.

'But there is one condition,' he said. 'You must never allow your hands to touch the waters of death, and when once your pole has been dipped in them you must straightway discard it and use another, lest any of the drops fall upon your fingers. Therefore take your ax and hew down six-score poles; for it is a long voyage, and you will need them all.'

Gilgamesh did as he was bidden, and in a short while they had boarded the boat and put out to sea.

But after they had sailed a number of days the poles gave out, and they had well nigh drifted and foundered, had not Gilgamesh torn off his shirt and held it aloft for a sail.

Meanwhile, there was Utnapishtim, sitting on the shore of the island, looking out upon the main, when suddenly his eyes descried the familiar craft bobbing precariously on the waters.

'Something is amiss,' he murmured. 'The gear seems to have been broken.'

And as the ship drew closer he saw the bizarre figure of Gilgamesh holding up his shirt against the breeze.

'That is not my boatman,' he muttered. 'Something is surely amiss.'

When they touched land Urshanabi at once brought his passenger into the presence of Utnapishtim, and Gilgamesh told him why he had come and what he sought.

'Young man,' said the sage, 'that which you seek you will never find. For there is nothing eternal on earth. When men draw up a contract they set a term. What they acquire today, tomorrow they must leave to others. Age-long feuds in time die out. Rivers which rise and swell, in the end subside. When the butterfly leaves the cocoon it lives but a day. Times and seasons are appointed for all.'

'True,' replied the hero. 'But you yourself are a mortal, no whit different from me; yet you live forever. Tell me how you found the secret of life, to make yourself like the gods.'

A faraway look came into the eyes of the old man. It seemed as though all the days of all the years were passing in procession before him. Then, after a long pause, he lifted his head and smiled.

'Gilgamesh,' he said slowly, 'I will tell you the secret—a secret high and holy, which no one knows save the gods and myself.' And he told him the story of the great flood which the gods had sent upon the earth in the days of old, and how Ea, the kindly lord of wisdom, had sent him warning of it in the whistle of the wind which soughed through the wattles of his hut. At Ea's command he had built an ark, and sealed it with pitch and asphalt, and loaded his kin and his cattle within it, and sailed for seven days and seven nights while the waters rose and the storms raged and the lightnings flashed. And on the seventh day the ark had grounded on a mountain at the end of the world, and he had opened a window in the ark and sent out a dove, to see if the waters had subsided. But the dove had returned, for want of place to rest. Then he had sent out a swallow, and the swallow too had come back. And at last he had sent out a raven, and the raven had not returned. Then he had led forth his kinsmen and his cattle and offered thanksgiving to the gods. But suddenly the god of the winds had come down from heaven and led him back into the ark, along with his wife, and set it afloat upon the waters once more, until it came to the island on the far horizon, and there the gods had set him to dwell forever.

When Gilgamesh heard the tale he knew at once that his quest had been vain, for now it was clear that the old man had no secret formula to give him. He had become immortal, as he now revealed, by special grace of the gods and not, as Gilgamesh had imagined, by possession of some hidden knowledge. The sun-god had been right, and the scorpion men had been right, and the alewife had been right: that which he had sought he would never find—at least on this side of the grave.

When the old man had finished his story he looked steadily into the drawn face and tired eyes of the hero. 'Gilgamesh,' he said kindly, 'you must rest awhile. Lie down and sleep for six days and seven nights.' And no sooner had he said these words than, lo and behold, Gilgamesh was fast asleep.

Then Utnapishtim turned to his wife. 'You see,' said he, 'this man who seeks to live forever cannot even go without sleep. When he awakes he will, of course, deny it—men were liars ever—so I want you to give him proof. Every day that he sleeps bake a loaf of bread and place it beside him. Day by day those loaves will grow staler and mouldier, and after seven nights, as they lie in a row beside him, he will be able to see from the state of each how long he has slept.'

So every morning Utnapishtim's wife baked a loaf, and she made a mark on the wall to show that another day had passed; and naturally, at the end of six days, the first loaf was dried out, and the second was like leather, and the third was soggy, and the fourth had white specks on it, and the fifth was filled with mould, and only the sixth looked fresh.

When Gilgamesh awoke, sure enough, he tried to pretend that he had never slept. 'Why,' said he to Utnapishtim, 'the moment I take a nap you go jogging my elbow and waking me up!' But Utnapishtim showed him the loaves, and then Gilgamesh knew that he had indeed been sleeping for six days and seven nights.

Thereupon Utnapishtim ordered him to wash and cleanse himself and make ready for the journey home. But even as the hero stepped into his boat to depart Utnapishtim's wife drew near.

'Utnapishtim,' said she, 'you cannot send him away empty-handed. He has journeyed hither with great effort and pain, and you must give him a parting gift.'

The old man raised his eyes and gazed earnestly at the hero. 'Gilgamesh,' he said, 'I will tell you a secret. In the depths of the sea lies a plant. It looks like a buckthorn and pricks like a rose. If any man come into possession of it, he can, by tasting it, regain his youth!'

When Gilgamesh heard these words he tied heavy stones to his feet and let himself down into the depths of the sea; and there, on the bed of the ocean, he espied the plant. Caring little that it pricked him, he grasped it between his fingers, cut the stones from his feet, and waited for the tide to wash him ashore.

Then he showed the plant to Urshanabi the boatman. 'Look,' he cried, 'it's the famous plant called Greybeard-grow-young! Whoever tastes it, gets a new lease on life! I will carry it back to Erech and give it to the people to eat. So will I at least have some reward for my pains!'

After they had crossed the perilous waters and reached land, Gilgamesh and his companion began the long journey on foot to the city of Erech. When they had travelled fifty leagues the sun was already beginning to set, and they looked for a place to pass the night. Suddenly they came upon a cool spring.

'Here let us rest,' said the hero, 'and I will go bathe.'

So he stripped off his clothes and placed the plant on the ground and went to bathe in the cool spring. But as soon as his back was turned a serpent came out of the waters and, sniffing the fragrance of the plant, carried it away. And no sooner had it tasted of it than at once it sloughed off its skin and regained its youth.

When Gilgamesh saw that the precious plant had now passed from his hands forever he sat down and wept. But soon he stood up and, resigned at last to the fate of all mankind, he returned to the city of Erech, back to the land whence he had come.

From *The Oldest Stories in the World*, by Theodore H. Gaster (New York: Viking, 1952).

The Death of Beowulf

The death of the hero marks the final stage of his linear journey through life. Although Beowulf, the great Anglo-Saxon hero, has performed almost superhuman feats as a young man—killing the cannibalistic monster Grendel and his equally fearsome mother—he is mortal. After fifty years of wise and peaceful rule, the aging king is called to fight what becomes his final battle. He faces a dragon, or fire-drake, who, because one piece of his ill-begotten treasure has been stolen, devastates the countryside. The late Rosemary Sutcliff, a renowned creator of young adult novels about early English history, provides a vivid account of the action of the battle. Equally important, she relates the event to the cultural beliefs of the Anglo-Saxons. One of the most important aspects is the *comitatus* bond, the mutually supportive relationship between a leader and his followers. Beowulf and Wiglaf follow the duties expected of each other; however, the rest of the followers do not, fleeing in terror when they see the great danger facing their leader. In her retelling, Sutcliff approximates the rhythmic alliteration and the word-kennings (creation of new compound words) found in heroic Anglo-Saxon poetry.

As Beowulf drew near to the gigantic rock-tumble under the Whale's Ness, he saw in the midst of it the dark mouth of a cave about which the smoke hung more thickly than elsewhere. A stream broke out from the darkness of it, flowing away down the slope of the valley, the water boiling as it came, and flickered over with the vapourous flame of dragon's breath; and Beowulf, with his shield before his face, forced his way up beside it until he reached the trampled ground before the cave mouth and could go no further for the choking fumes and smoke that poured out from the darkness under the flank of the hill.

There he stood, and beat sword upon shield and shouted his defiance to the fire-drake within. His shout rose like a storm, the war-cry that his thanes had heard above the clamour of many and many a battlefield; it pierced in through the opening among the rocks, and the fire-drake heard it and awoke. A great cloud of fiery breath belched out from the cave mouth, and within there sounded the clapping of mighty wings; and even as the King flung up his shield to guard his face, the earth shook and roared and the dragon came coiling from its lair.

Heat played over its scales so that they changed colour, green and blue and gold, as the colours play on a sword-blade heated for tempering, and all the air danced and quivered about him. Fire was in his wings and a blasting flame leapt from his eyes. With wings spread, he half-flew half-sprang at Beowulf, who stood firm to meet him and swung up his sword for a mighty blow. The bright blade flashed down, wounding the monster in the head: but though the skin gaped and the stinking blood sprang forth, the bones of the skull turned the blow so that the wound was not mortal. Bellowing, the creature crouched back, then sprang again, and Beowulf was wrapped from head to heel in a cloud of fire. The iron rings of his mail seared him to the bone and the great shield of smith's work glowed red-hot as he strove to guard his face and bring up his blade for another blow.

On the hill above the watching thanes saw the terrible figure of their lord in its rolling shroud of flame, and brave men though they had been in battle, terror seized them and they turned to fly; all save one. Wiglaf, grandson of Waegmund, and the youngest of them all, stood firm. For one despairing moment he tried to rally the rest, crying after them to remember their loyalty to their House-Lord. 'Brave things we promised in the King's hall when we drank his mead and took the gifts he gave us! Often we swore ourselves his men to the death—and now the death comes, we forget! Shame to us for ever if we bear home our shields in safety from this day; but I will not share the shame!' And snatching up his shield and dragging his sword from its sheath, he began to run also, not back towards the safety of the woods, but forward and down into the smoke-filled valley.'

Head down and shield up, he plunged into the fiery reek, shouting, 'Beowulf, beloved lord, I come! Remember the battles of your youth and stand strong—I am here beside you!'

Beowulf heard his young kinsman's voice and felt him at his shoulder, yellow linden shield beside that of glowing iron, and his heart took new strength within him. But the sound of another voice roused the dragon to yet greater hatred, and the earth groaned and the rocks shivered to his fury, while he drove out blast on blast of searing flame. Wiglaf's shield blackened and flamed like a torch, and he flung the blazing remnant from him and sprang to obey his lord as Beowulf shouted to him, 'Here! Behind my targe—it shall serve to cover us both!' And steady and undismayed they fought on behind the red-hot shield of iron.

But at last, as it came whistling down in mighty blow, Beowulf's sword that had seen the victory in a hundred battles shivered into fragments on the dragon's head.

With a great cry, the King threw the useless hilt away from him, but before he could snatch the saex from his belt, the fire-drake was upon him, rearing up under the flailing darkness of its wings, the poisonous foreclaws slashing at his throat above the golden collar.

In the same instant, while the King's life blood burst out in a red wave, Wiglaf sprang clear of the iron targe and, diving low under the fire-drake, stabbed upward with shortened blade into its scaleless underparts.

A convulsive shudder ran through all the lashing coils of the dragon's body, and instantly the fire began to fade, and as it faded, Beowulf with the last of his battle strength, tore the saex from his belt and hurling himself forward, hacked the great brute almost in two.

The dragon lay dead, with the brightness of its fires darkening upon it. But Beowulf also had got his death hurt, and now as he stood swaying above the huge carcass, his wounds began to burn and swell, the venom from the monster's talons boiled in his breast and all his limbs seemed on fire. Blindly he staggered towards a place where the rocks made a natural couch close beside the cave entrance, and sank down upon it, gasping for air.

Wiglaf with his own burns raw upon him bent over his lord, loosened the thongs of his helmet and lifted it away so that the cool sea wind was on his forehead; brought water in his own helmet from the stream, which now ran cool and clear, to bathe Beowulf's face and wounds, all the while calling to him, calling him back from somewhere a long way off. By and by Beowulf's head cleared a little, and for a while the scalding tide of poison seemed to ebb, and the old King gathered up strength to speak, knowing that his time for speaking would soon be done. 'Now I wish in my heart that the All-Father had granted me a son to take my war-harness after me; but since that may not be, you must be son to me in this, and take my helm and good saex, and my battle-sark from my body after I am dead, and wear them worthily for my sake.'

He felt Wiglaf's tears upon his face, and gathered himself again. 'Na, na, here is no cause for weeping. I am an old man and have lived my life and fought my battles. Fifty winters I have held rule over my people and made them strong so that never a war-host dared to cross our frontiers. I have not sought out feuds, nor sworn many oaths and lightly broken them; and when my life goes out from my body I shall not have to answer to the All-Father for slain kinsfolk or unjust rule.'

He propped himself on to his elbow and looked about him, and his gaze came to rest on the carcass of the fire-drake lying sprawled before the entrance to the cave. 'I have paid away my life to slay the thing which would have slain my people, and now I see it lying dead before me. But if the thief's tale be true, then I have won for them in my last battle some store of treasure also, and that too I would see before the light goes from my eyes. Go now, Wiglaf, my kinsman, and bring out to me what you can carry.'

Wiglaf, who had been kneeling at his lord's side, got to his feet and stumbling past the still twitching coils of the dead monster, went into the cave.

From Rosemary Sutcliff, *Dragon Slayer, the Story of Beowulf*. Illustrated by Charles Keeping. (London: Bodley Head, 1961), 101.

Within the entrance he came to a halt, staring with scarce-believing eyes at the piled-up wonders of the fire-drake's hoard. Golden cups and pitchers, jewelled collars for a king's throat, ancient ring-mail and boar-masked helmets and swords eaten through with rust; and upreared high above the rest, a golden banner curiously wrought with long-forgotten magic, which shone of itself, and shed about it a faint light in which he saw all the rest. But he had neither the time nor the heart for much marvelling. In frantic haste, he loaded himself with cups and armrings and weapons, and the banner last of all, and carried them out into the daylight, and flung them clanging down at the old man's feet.

Beowulf lay still with his eyes closed, and the blood still flowing from his wounds. But when Wiglaf fetched more water from the stream and again bathed his face he revived once more, and opened his eyes to gaze upon the treasure as it lay glittering among the rocks. 'A fine bright gleam of gold to light me on my way,' he said. 'Glad am I that since the time has come for me to go I may leave behind me such treasure for my people.' Then his gaze abandoned the glitter of the dragon's hoard, and went out and upward to where the great bluff forehead of the Whale's Ness upreared itself against the sky. 'After the bale-fire is burned out, bid them raise me a burial howe on the Whale's Ness yonder, a tall howe on the cliff edge, that it may serve as a mark for seafaring men such as I was in my youth. So they may see it from afar as they pass on the Sail-Road, and say, "There stands Beowulf's Barrow" and remember me.'

For the last time his gaze went to young Wiglaf's face, and his hands were at his wounded throat, fumbling off the golden collar of the Kingship. 'Take this also, with my war-gear.' His voice was only a whisper now. 'Use it well, for you are the last of our kindred. One by one, Wyrd has swept them all away at their fated hour; and now it is time for me to go to them.'

And with the words scarce spoken, a great sigh broke from him and he fell back into the young warrior's arms. And Wiglaf laid him down.

He was still sitting at his dead lord's shoulder when a shadow fell across them both and, looking up slowly, he saw that the King's Hearth Companions had come stealing down from the high woods of their refuge, and were standing about him staring down in shame at slain hero and slain monster. He did not trouble to rise, but sitting drearily where he was, stony-eyed, he flayed them with all the bitter scorn that was in his heart. 'So you come, do you, now that the fire is spent! Well may men say, seeing you safe and unmarked in the war-gear that Beowulf gave you, that he made a bad bargain with his gifts. When his sorest need came upon him he had no cause to boast of his companions in arms. Small honour will Geatland have in her foremost warriors, when the princes of other lands hear of this day's work! Aye, you have kept whole your skins under your bright battle-sarks; but it may be that death is better for a warrior than a life of shame!'

And the thanes stood silent about their dead lord, enduring the lash of Wiglaf's scorn, for there was nothing that they could say.

Presently a scout sent out by the following war-host came riding over the wooded ridge and looked down into the valley. One long look was enough, and then wheeling his horse he galloped back to tell what he had seen. 'The fight is over, and our King lies dead among the rocks with the fire-drake dead beside him. Now the joy and honour that he gave us are fled from the land, and the War Chieftains will come against us as they have not dared to do for fifty years, and Beowulf who should have led us against them is dead.'

A groan ran through the host at his words, and at an increased pace they pressed on towards the dragon's lair.

When they came down into the blackened valley they found all as the messenger had told them, the grey-headed King lying dead with his broken sword beside him, and the carcass of the fire-drake outstretched on the burned and blood-soaked turf nearby; the shamed thanes standing at a distance, and Wiglaf sitting bowed with grief at his lord's shoulder; the golden gleam of the dragon's hoard among the rocks and, upreared over all, the great gold-wrought banner curving to the sea wind like the curved sail of a ship.

Sadly the warriors gathered about their King, and then at last Wiglaf stirred and rose to his feet, stiffly as though he too were an old man. He took up the golden collar of the Kingship, stained as it was with the dead hero's blood, and standing there before the sorrowing war-host he fastened it about his own neck. And with it he put on the King's authority. 'Beowulf is dead, and plainly you may see how he met his end. Gladly he paid away his life to save his people from the Terror-that-flew-by-Night, and in his dying he bade me greet you and pray you, after the bale-fire is burned out, to build him a worthy barrow for his resting-place—a great barrow high on the Whale's Ness, to be a guiding-mark hereafter for all who sail the sea. Now make ready the funeral pyre, and bring something to serve as a bier, that we may carry our old King to his chosen place. And meanwhile let seven of you come with me into the cave and bring out into the daylight all that yet remains there of the fire-drake's hoard.'

So while Wiglaf and the seven toiled to and fro, bringing out from the dark the treasure that had not seen the sun for a thousand years, others set themselves to gather wood and build a pyre high on the Whale's Ness and hand it round with war helms and fine weapons and ring-mail sarks, as befitted a King's funeral pyre. And yet others dragged the carcass of the fire-drake to the cliff's edge and heaved it over into the surf that creamed below. They brought a farm wain drawn by oxen and hung it round with shields as though its sides were the bulwarks of a warboat, and when all was ready they laid the dead King in it, and piled about him the wrought gold and wondrous weapons of the dragon's hoard— for Wiglaf said, 'As Beowulf alone won all these things, so let them go back with him into the dark from which they came,' and in all the war-host no man lifted a voice against him.

Then they set the four slow yoke of oxen straining up the steep slope to the headland, where the pyre stood waiting against the sky. They laid the body of Beowulf on the stacked brushwood and thrust in the torches, and presently all men far and wide saw the red fire on the Whale's Ness, and knew that Beowulf had gone to join his kindred.

All night long the fire burned, and when it sank at dawn they piled about the ashes the precious things of the dragon's hoard, and upreared the golden banner over all. Then they set themselves to raise the barrow as the old King had bidden them. For ten days they laboured, building it high and strong for the love that they had borne him, and on the tenth day the great howe of piled stones stood finished, notching the sky for all time on the uttermost height of the Whale's Ness, where the cliffs plunged sheer to the sea.

Then twelve chieftains of his bodyguard rode sunwise about it, singing the death song that the harpers had made for him. And when the song was sung, all men went away, and left Beowulf's barrow alone with the sea wind and the wheeling gulls and the distant ships that passed on the Sail-Road.

———

From *Dragon Slayer: The Story of Beowulf*, by Rosemary Sutcliff (Harmondsworth, England: Puffin Books, 1966).

Joan the Maid

This story of the peasant girl who rose to great glory leading the French against the English illustrates how the life of an historical figure (Joan lived in the fifteenth century) takes on legendary aspects. Although Andrew Lang makes use of historical sources, he tends to emphasize the miraculous elements of Joan's linear journey to a martyr's death: her voices and visions, her discovery of a hidden sword, the miracles she performed, her capture by betrayal, and her heroic death. His references to the Trojan War further add to her heroic stature. It is important to notice the fear Joan created in many people; she was considered unnatural not only because of her visions, but also because she assumed a male role.

Four hundred and seventy years ago, the children of Domremy, a little village near the Meuse, on the borders of France and Lorraine, used to meet and dance and sing beneath a beautiful beech-tree, 'lovely as a lily'. They called it 'The Fairy Tree', or 'The Good Ladies' Lodge', meaning the fairies by the words 'Good Ladies'. Among these children was one named Jeanne (born 1412), the daughter of an honest farmer, Jacques d'Arc. Jeanne sang more than she danced, and though she carried garlands like the other boys and girls, and hung them on the boughs of the Fairies' Tree, she liked better to take the flowers into the parish church, and lay them on the altars of St Margaret and St Catherine. It was said among the villagers that Jeanne's godmother had once seen the fairies dancing; but though some of the older people believed in the Good Ladies, it does not seem that Jeanne and the other children had faith in them or thought much about them. They only went to the tree and to a neighbouring fairy well to eat cakes and laugh and play. Yet these fairies were destined to be fatal to Jeanne d'Arc, JOAN THE MAIDEN, and her innocent childish sports were to bring her to the stake and the death by fire. For she was that famed Jeanne la Pucelle, the bravest, kindest, best, and wisest of women, whose tale is the saddest, the most wonderful, and the most glorious page in the history of the world. It is a page which no good Englishman and no true Frenchman can read without sorrow and bitter shame, for the English burned Joan with the help of bad Frenchmen, and the French of her party did not pay a *sou*, or write a line, or strike a stroke to save her.

The English were besieging Orleans; Joan the Maid drove them from its walls. How did it happen that a girl of seventeen, who could neither read nor write, became the greatest general on the side of France? How did a woman defeat the hardy English soldiers who used to chase the French before them like sheep?

We must say that France could only be saved by a miracle, and by a miracle she was saved. This is a mystery; we cannot understand it. Joan the Maiden was not as other men and women are. But, as a little girl, she was a child among children, though better, kinder, stronger than the rest, and, poor herself, she was always good and helpful to those who were poorer still.

Joan's parents were not indigent; they had lands and cattle, and a little money laid by in case of need. Her father was, at one time, *doyen*, or head-man, of Domremy. Their house was hard by the church, and was in the part of the hamlet where the people were better off; and had more freedom and privileges than many of their neighbours. They were devoted to the Royal House of France, which protected them from the tyranny of lords and earls further east. As they lived in a village under the patronage of St Remigius, they were much interested in Reims, his town, where the kings of France were crowned, and were anointed with Holy Oil, which was believed to have been brought in a sacred bottle by an angel.

In the Middle Ages, the king was not regarded as really king till this holy oil had been poured on his head. Thus we shall see, later, how anxious Joan was that Charles VII, then the Dauphin, should be crowned and anointed in Reims, though it was still in the possession of the English. It is also necessary to remember that Joan had once an elder sister named Catherine, whom she loved dearly. Catherine died, and perhaps affection for her made Joan more fond of bringing flowers to the altar of her namesake, St Catherine, and of praying often to that saint.

Joan was brought up by her parents, as she told her judges, to be industrious, to sew and spin. She did not fear to match herself at spinning and sewing, she said, against any woman in Rouen. When very young she sometimes went to the fields to watch the cattle, like the goose-girl in the fairy tale. As she grew older, she worked in the house, she did not any longer watch sheep and cattle. But the times were dangerous, and, when there was an alarm of soldiers or robbers in the neighbourhood, she sometimes helped to drive the flock into a fortified island, or peninsula, for which her father was responsible in the river near her home. She learned her creed, she said, from her mother. Twenty years after her death, her neighbours, who remembered her, described her as she was when a child. Jean Morin said that she was a good industrious girl, but that she would often be praying in church when her father and mother did not know it. Beatrix Estellin, an old widow of eighty, said Joan was a good girl. When Domremy was burned, Joan would go to church at Greux, 'and there was not a better girl in the two towns'. A priest, who had known her, called her 'a good, simple, well-behaved girl'. Jean Waterin, when he was a boy, had seen Joan in the fields, 'and when they were all playing together, she would go apart, and pray to God, as he thought, and he and the others used to laugh at her. She was good and simple, and often in churches and holy places. And when she heard the church bell ring, she would kneel down in the fields.' She used to bribe the sexton to ring the bells (a duty which he rather neglected) with presents of knitted wool.

All those who had seen Joan told the same tale: she was always kind, simple, industrious, pious, and yet merry and fond of playing with the others round the Fairy Tree. They say that the singing birds came to her, and nestled in her breast.

Thus, as far as anyone could tell, Joan was a child like other children, but more serious and more religious. One of her friends, a girl called Mengette, whose cottage was next to that of Joan's father, said: 'Joan was so pious that we other children told her she was too good.'

In peaceful times Joan would have lived and married and died and been forgotten. But the times were evil. The two parties of Burgundy and Armagnac divided town from town and village from village. It was in the days of the Douglas Wars in Scotland, when the very children took sides for Queen Mary and King James, and fought each other in the streets. Domremy was for the Armagnacs—that is, against the English and for the Dauphin, the son of the mad Charles VI. But at Maxey, on the Meuse, a village near Domremy, the people were all for Burgundy and the English. The boys of Domremy would go out and fight the Maxey boys with fists and sticks and stones. Joan did not remember having taken part in those battles, but she had often seen her brothers and the Domremy boys come home all bruised and bleeding.

Once Joan saw more of war than these schoolboy bickers. It was in 1425, when she was a girl of thirteen. There was a kind of robber chief on the English side, a man named

Henri d'Orly, from Savoy, who dwelt in the castle of Doulevant. There he and his band of armed men lived and drank and plundered far and near. One day there galloped into Domremy a squadron of spearmen, who rode through the fields driving together the cattle of the villagers, among them the cows of Joan's father. The country people could make no resistance; they were glad enough if their houses were not burned. So off rode Henri d'Orly's men, driving the cattle with their spear-points along the track to the castle of Doulevant. But cows are not fast travellers, and when the robbers had reached a little village called Dommartin le France they rested, and went to the tavern to make merry. But by this time a lady, Madame d'Ogévillier, had sent in all haste to the Count de Vaudemont to tell him how the villagers of Domremy had been ruined. So he called his squire, Barthélemy de Cleftmont, and bade him summon his spears and mount and ride. It reminds us of the old Scottish ballad, where Jamie Telfer of the Fair Dodhead has seen all his cattle driven out of his stalls by the English; and he runs to Branxholme and warns the water, and they with Harden pursue the English, defeat them, and recover Telfer's kye, with a great spoil out of England. Just so Barthélemy de Clefmont, with seven or eight lances, galloped down the path to Dommartin le France. There they found the cattle, and D'Orly's men fled like cowards. So Barthélemy with his comrades was returning very joyously, when Henri d'Orly rode up with a troop of horse and followed hard after Barthélemy. He was wounded by a lance, but he cut his way through d'Orly's men, and also brought the cattle back safely—a very gallant deed of arms. We may fancy the delight of the villagers when 'the kye cam' home'. It may have been now that an event happened, of which Joan does not tell us herself, but which was reported by the king's seneschal, in June 1429, when Joan had just begun her wonderful career. The children of the village, says the seneschal, were running races and leaping in wild joy about the fields; possibly their gladness was caused by the unexpected rescue of their cattle. Joan ran so much more fleetly than the rest, and leaped so far, that the children believed she actually *flew*, and they told her so! Tired and breathless, 'out of herself', says the seneschal, she paused, and in that moment she heard a Voice, but saw no man; the Voice bade her go home, because her mother had need of her. And when she came home the Voice said many things to her about the great deeds which God bade her do for France. We shall later hear Joan's own account of how her visions and Voices first came to her.

Three years later there was an alarm, and the Domremy people fled to Neufchâteau, Joan going with her parents. Afterwards her enemies tried to prove that she had been a servant at an inn in Neufchâteau, and lived roughly with grooms and soldiers, and had learned to ride. But this was absolutely untrue. An ordinary child would have thought little of war and of the sorrows of her country in the flowery fields of Domremy and Vaucouleurs; but Joan always thought of the miseries of *France la bele*, fair France, and prayed for her country and her king. A great road, on the lines of an old Roman way, passed near Domremy, so Joan would hear all the miserable news from travellers. Probably she showed what was in her mind, for her father dreamed that she 'had gone off with soldiers', and this dream struck him so much, that he told his sons that he, or they, must drown Joan if she so disgraced herself. For many girls of bad character, lazy and rude, followed the soldiers, as they always have done, and always will. Joan's father thought that his dream meant that Joan would be like these women. It would be interesting to know whether he was in the habit of dreaming true dreams. For Joan, his child, dreamed when wide awake, dreamed dreams immortal, which brought her to her glory and her doom.

When Joan was between twelve and thirteen, a wonderful thing befell her. We have already heard one account of it, written when Joan was in the first flower of her triumph, by the seneschal of the King of France. A Voice spoke to her and prophesised of what she was to do. But about all these marvellous things it is more safe to attend to what Joan always said herself. She told the same story both to friends and foes; to the learned men who, by the king's desire, examined her at Poictiers, before she went to war (April 1429); and to her deadly foes at Rouen. No man can read her answers to them and doubt that she spoke what she believed. And she died for this belief. Unluckily the book that was kept of what she said at Poictiers is lost. Before her enemies at Rouen there were many things which she did not think it right to say. On one point, after for long refusing to speak, she told her foes a kind of parable, which we must not take as part of her real story.

When Joan was between twelve and thirteen (1424), so she swore, '*a Voice came to her from God for her guidance*', but when first it came, she was in great fear. And it came, that Voice, about noonday, in the summer season, she being in her father's garden. And Joan had not fasted the day before that, but was fasting when the Voice came. And she heard the Voice on her right side, towards the church, and rarely did she hear it but she also saw 'a great light'. These are her very words. They asked her if she heard the Voices there, in the hall of judgment, and she answered, 'If I were in a wood, I should well hear these Voices coming to me.' The Voices at first only told her 'to be a good girl, and go to church'. She thought it was a holy Voice, and that it came from God; and the third time she heard it she knew it was the voice of an angel. The Voice told her of 'the great pity there was in France', and that one day she must go into France and help the country. She had visions with the Voices; visions first of St Michael, and then of St Catherine and St Margaret. She hated telling her hypocritical judges anything about these heavenly visions, but it seems that she really believed in their appearance, believed that she had embraced the knees of St Margaret and St Catherine, and she did reverence to them when they came to her. 'I saw them with my bodily eyes, as I see you,' she said to her judges, 'and when they departed from me I wept, and well I wished that they had taken me with them.'

What are we to think about these visions and these Voices which were with Joan to her death?

It was in 1424 that the Voices first came to Joan the Maid. The years went on; bringing more and more sorrow to France. In 1428 only a very few small towns in the east still held out for the Dauphin, and these were surrounded on every side by enemies. Meanwhile the Voices came more frequently, urging Joan to go into France, and help her country. She asked how she, a girl, who could not ride or use sword and lance, could be of any help? Rather would she stay at home and spin beside her dear mother. At the same time she was encouraged by one of the vague old prophecies which were as common in France as in Scotland. A legend ran 'that France was to be saved by a Maiden from the Oak Wood', and there was an Oak Wood, *le bois chênu*, near Domremy. Some such prophecy had an influence on Joan, and probably helped people to believe her. The Voices, moreover, instantly and often commanded her to go to Vaucouleurs, a neighbouring town which was loyal, and there meet Robert de Baudricourt, who was captain of the French garrison. Now, Robert de Baudricourt was not what is called a romantic person. Though little over thirty, he had already married, one after the other, two rich widows. He was a gallant soldier, but a plain practical man, very careful of his own interest, and cunning enough to hold his own among his many enemies, English, Burgundian, and Lorrainers. It was to him that Joan must go, a country girl to a great noble, and tell him that she, and she alone, could save France! Joan knew what manner of man Robert de Baudricourt was, for her father had been obliged to visit him, and speak for the people of Domremy when they were oppressed. She could hardly hope that he would listen to her, and it was with a heavy heart that she found a good reason for leaving home to visit Vaucouleurs. Joan had a cousin, a niece of her mother's, who was married to one Durand Lassois, at Burey en Vaux, a village near Vaucouleurs. This cousin invited Joan to visit her for a week. At the end of that time she spoke to her cousin's husband. There was an old saying, as we saw, that France would be rescued by a Maid, and she, as she told Lassois, was that Maid. Lassois listened, and, whatever he may have thought of her chances, he led her to Robert de Baudricourt.

Joan came, on May 13, 1428, in her simple red dress, and walked straight up to the captain among his men. She knew him, she said, by what her Voices had told her, but she may also have heard him described by her father. She told him that the Dauphin must keep quiet, and risk no battle, for before the middle of Lent next year (1429) God would send him succour. She added that the kingdom belonged, not to the Dauphin, but to her Master, who willed that the Dauphin should be crowned, and she herself would lead him to Reims, to be anointed with the holy oil.

'And who is your Master?' said Robert.

'The King of Heaven!'

Robert, very naturally, thought that Joan was crazed, and shrugged his shoulders. He bluntly told Lassois to box her ears, and take her back to her father. So she had to go home; but here new troubles awaited her. The enemy came down on Domremy and burned it; Joan and her family fled to Neufchâteau, where they stayed for a few days. It was perhaps about this time that a young man declared that Joan had promised to marry him, and he actually brought her before a court of justice, to make her fulfil her promise.

Joan was beautiful, well-shaped, dark-haired, and charming in her manner.

We have a letter which two young knights, André and Guy de Laval, wrote to their mother in the following year. 'The Maid was armed from neck to heel,' they say, 'but unhelmeted; she carried a lance in her hand. Afterwards, when we lighted down from our horses at Selles, I went to her lodging to see her, and she called for wine for me, saying she would soon make me drink wine in Paris' (then held by the English), 'and, indeed, she seems a thing wholly divine, both to look on her and to hear her sweet voice.'

It is no wonder that the young man of Domremy wanted to marry Joan; but she had given no promise, and he lost his foolish lawsuit. She and her parents soon went back to Domremy.

In Domremy they found that the enemy had ruined everything. Their cattle were safe, for they had been driven to Neufchâteau, but when Joan looked from her father's garden to the church, she saw nothing but a heap of smoke ruins. She had to go to say her prayers now at the church of Greux. These things only made her feel more deeply the sorrows of her country. The time was drawing near when she had prophesied that the Dauphin was to receive help from heaven—namely, in the Lent of 1429. On that year the season was held more than commonly sacred, for Good Friday and the Annunciation fell on the same day. So, early in January, 1429, Joan the Maid turned her back on Domremy, which she was never to see again. Her cousin Lassois came and asked leave for Joan to visit him again; she said good-bye to her father and mother, and to her friend Mengette, but to her dearest friend Hauvette she did not even say good-bye, for she could not bear it. She went to her cousin's house at Burey, and there she stayed for six weeks, hearing bad news of the siege of Orleans by the English. Meanwhile, Robert de Baudricourt, in Vaucouleurs, was not easy in his mind, for he was likely to lose the protection of René of Anjou, the Duc de Bar, who was on the point of joining the English. Thus Robert may have been more inclined to listen to Joan than when he bade her cousin box her ears and take her back to her father. A squire named Jean de Nouillompont met Joan one day.

'Well, my lass,' said he, 'is our king to be driven from France, and are we all to become English?'

'I have come here,' said Joan, 'to bid Robert de Baudricourt lead me to the king, but he will not listen to me. And yet to the king I must go, even if I walk my legs down to the knees; for none in all the world—king, nor duke, nor the King of Scotland's daughter—can save France, but myself only. *Certes*, I would rather stay and spin with my poor mother, for to fight is not my calling; but I must go and I must fight, for so my Lord will have it.'

'And who is your Lord?' said Jean de Nouillompont.

'He is God,' said the Maiden.

'Then, so help me God, I shall take you to the king,' said Jean, putting her hands in his. 'When do we start?'

'To-day is better than to-morrow,' said the Maid.

Joan was now staying in Vaucouleurs with Catherine le Royer. One day, as she and Catherine were sitting at their spinning-wheels, who should come in but Robert de Baudricourt with the *curé* of the town. Robert had fancied that perhaps Joan was a witch! He told the priest to perform some rite of the Church over her, so that if she were a witch she would be obliged to run away. But when the words were spoken, Joan threw herself at the knees of the priest, saying, 'Sir, this is ill done of you, for you have heard my confession and know that I am not a witch.'

Robert was now half disposed to send her to the king and let her take her chance. But days dragged on, and when Joan was not working she would be on her knees in the crypt or underground chapel of the chapel Royal in Vaucouleurs. Twenty-seven years later a chorister boy told how he often saw her praying there for France. Now people began to hear of Joan, and the Duke of Lorraine asked her to visit him at Nancy, where she bade him lead a better life. He is said to have given her a horse and some money. On February 12 the story goes that she went to Robert de Baudricourt.

'You delay too long,' she said. 'On this very day, at Orleans, the gentle Dauphin has lost a battle.'

This was, in fact, the Battle of Herrings, so called because the English defeated and cut off a French and Scottish force which attacked them as they were bringing herrings into camp for provisions in Lent. If this tale is true, Joan cannot have known of the battle by any common means; but though it is vouched for by the king's secretary, Joan has told us nothing about it herself.

Now the people of Vaucouleurs bought clothes for Joan to wear on her journey to the Dauphin. They were such clothes as men wear—doublet, hose, surcoat, boots, and spurs— and Robert de Baudricourt gave Joan a sword.

On February 23, 1429, the gate of the little castle of Vaucouleurs, 'the Gate of France', which is still standing, was thrown open. Seven travellers rode out, among them two squires, Jean de Nouillompont and Bertrand de Poulengy, with their attendants, and Joan the Maid. 'Go, and let what will come of it come!' said Robert de Baudricourt. He did not expect much to come of it. It was a long journey—they were eleven days on the road—and a dangerous one. But Joan laughed at danger. 'God will clear my path to the king, for to this end I was born.' Often they rode by night, stopping at monasteries when they could. Sometimes they slept out under the sky. Though she was so young and so beautiful, with the happiness of her long desire in her eyes, and the glory of her future shining on her, these two young gentlemen never dreamed of paying their court to her and making love, as in romances they do, for they regarded her 'as if she had been an angel.' 'They were in awe of her,' they said, long afterwards, long after the angels had taken Joan to be with their company in heaven. And all the knights who had seen her said the same. Dunois and d'Aulon and the beautiful Duc d'Alençon, 'le beau Duc' as Joan called him, all said that she was 'a thing enskied and sainted'. So on they rode, six men and a maid, through a country full of English and Burgundian soldiery. There were four rivers to cross, Marne, Aube, Seine, and Yonne, and the rivers were 'great and mickle o' spate,' running red with the rains from bank to bank, so that they could not ford the streams, but must go by unfriendly towns, where alone there were bridges. Joan would have liked to stay and go to church in every town, but this might not be. However, she heard mass thrice at the church of her favourite saint, Catherine de Fierbois, between Loches and Chinon, in a friendly country. And a strange thing happened later in that church.

From Fierbois Joan made some clerk write to the king that she was coming to help him, and that she would know him among all his men. Probably it was here that she wrote to beg her parents' pardon, and they forgave her, she says. Meanwhile news reached the people then besieged in Orleans that a marvellous Maiden was riding to their rescue. On March 6 Joan arrived in Chinon, where for two or three days the king's advisers would not let him see her. At last they yielded, and she went straight up to hill, and when he denied that he was the king, she told him that she knew well who he was.

'There is the king,' said Charles, pointing to a richly dressed noble.

'No, fair sire. You are he!'

Still, it was not easy to believe. Joan stayed at Chinon in the house of a noble lady. The young Duc d'Alençon was on her side from the first, bewitched by her noble horsemanship, which she had never learned. Great people came to see her, but, when she was alone, she wept and prayed. The king sent messengers to inquire about her at Domremy, but time was going on, and Orleans was not relieved.

Weeks had passed, and Joan had never yet seen a blow struck in war. She used to exercise herself in horsemanship, and knightly sports of tilting, and it is wonderful that a peasant girl became, at once, one of the best riders among the chivalry of France. The young Duc d'Alençon, lately come from captivity in England, saw how gallantly she rode, and gave her a horse. He and his wife were her friends from the first, when the politicians and advisers were against her. But, indeed, whatever the Maid attempted, she did better than others, at once, without teaching or practice. It was now determined that Joan should be taken to Poictiers, and examined before all the learned men, bishops, doctors, and higher clergy who still were on the side of France. There was good reason for this delay. It was plain to all, friends and foes, that the wonderful Maid was not like other men and women, with her Voices, her visions, her prophecies, and her powers. All agreed that she had some strange help given to her; but who gave it? This aid must come, people thought then, either from heaven or hell—either from God and his saints, or from the devil and his angels. Now, if any doubt could be thrown on the source whence Joan's aid came, the English might argue (as of course they did), that she was a witch and a heretic. If she was a heretic and a witch, then her king was involved in her wickedness, and so he might be legally shut out from his kingdom. It was necessary, therefore, that Joan should be examined by learned men. They must find out whether she had always been good, and a true believer, and whether her Voices always agreed in everything with the teachings of the Church. Otherwise her angels must be devils in disguise. For these reasons Joan was carried to Poictiers. During three long weeks the learned men asked her questions, and, no doubt, they wearied her terribly. But they said it was wonderful how wisely this girl, 'who did not know A from B', replied to their puzzling inquiries. She told the story of her visions, of the command laid upon her to rescue Orleans. Said Guillaume Aymeri, 'You ask for men-at-arms, and you say that God will have the English to leave France and go home. If that is true, no men-at-arms are needed; God's pleasure can drive the English out of the land.'

'In God's name,' said the Maid, 'the men-at-arms will fight, and God will give the victory.' Then came the learned Seguin; 'a right sour man was he,' said those who knew him.

Seguin was a Limousin, and the Limousins spoke in a queer accent at which the other French were always laughing.

'In what language do your Voices speak?' asked he.

'In a better language than *yours*,' said Joan, and the bishops smiled at the country quip.

'We may not believe in you,' said Seguin, 'unless you show us a sign.'

'I did not come to Poictiers to work miracles,' said Joan; 'take me to Orleans, and I shall show you the signs that I am sent to do.' And show them she did.

Joan never pretended to work miracles. Though, in that age, people easily believed in miracles, it is curious that none worth mentioning were invented about Joan in her own time. She knew things in some strange way sometimes, but the real miracle was her extraordinary wisdom, genius, courage, and power of enduring hardship.

At last, after examining witnesses from Domremy, and the Queen of Sicily and other great ladies to whom Joan was entrusted, the clergy found nothing in her but 'goodness, humility, frank maidenhood, piety, honesty, and simplicity.' As for her wearing a man's dress, the Archbishop of Embrun said to the king, 'It is more becoming to do these things in man's gear, since they have to be done amongst men.'

The king therefore made up his mind at last. Jean and Pierre, Joan's brothers, were to ride with her to Orleans; her old friends, her first friends, Jean de Nouillompont and Bertrand de Poulengy, had never left her. She was given a squire, Jean d'Aulon, a very good man, and a page, Louis de Coutes, and a chaplain. The king gave Joan armour and horses, and offered her a sword. But her Voices told her that, behind the altar of St Catherine de Fierbois, where she heard mass on her way to Chinon, there was an old sword, with five crosses on the blade, buried in the earth. That sword she was to wear. A man whom Joan did not know, and had never seen, was sent from Tours, and found the sword in the place which she described. The sword was cleaned of rust, and the king gave her two sheaths, one of velvet, one of cloth of gold, but Joan had a leather sheath made for use in war. She also commanded a banner to be made, with the Lilies of France on a white field. There was also a picture of God, holding the round world, and two angels at the sides, with the sacred words, JHESU MARIA. On another flag was the Annunciation, the Virgin holding a lily, and the angel coming to her. In battle, when she led a charge, Joan always carried her standard, that she might not be able to use her sword. She wished to kill nobody, and said 'she loved her banner forty times more than her sword'. Joan afterwards broke St Catherine's sword, when slapping a girl (who richly deserved to be slapped) with the flat of the blade. Her enemies, at her trial, wished to prove that her flag was a kind of magical talisman, but Joan had no belief in anything of that kind. What she believed in was God, her Voices, and her just cause. When once it was settled that she was to lead an army to relieve Orleans, she showed her faith by writing a letter addressed to the King of England; Bedford, the Regent; and the English generals at Orleans. This letter was sent from Blois, late in April. It began JHESU MARIA. Joan had no ill-will against the English. She bade them leave France, 'and if you are reasonable, you yet may ride in the Maid's company, where the French will do the fairest feat of arms that ever yet was done for Christentie.' Probably she had in her mind some Crusade. But, before France and England can march together, 'do ye justice to the King of Heaven and the Blood Royal of France. Yield to the Maid the keys of all the good towns which ye have taken and assailed in France.' If they did not yield to the Maid and the king, she will come on them to their sorrow. 'Duke of Bedford, the Maid prays and entreats you not to work your own destruction!'

We may imagine how the English laughed and swore when they received this letter. They threw the heralds of the Maid into prison, and threatened to burn them as heretics. From the very first, the English promised to burn Joan as a witch and a heretic. This fate was always before her eyes. But she went where her Voices called her.

At last the men-at-arms who were to accompany Joan were ready. She rode at their head, as André de Laval and Guy de Laval saw her, and described her in a letter to their mother. She was armed in white armour, but unhelmeted, a little axe in her hand, riding a great black charger, that reared at the door of her lodging and would not let her mount. 'Lead him to the Cross!' cried she, for a Cross stood on the roadside, by the church. There he stood as if he had been stone, and she mounted. Then she turned to the church, and said, in her girlish voice, 'You priests and churchmen, make prayers and processions to God.' Then she cried 'Forwards Forwards!' and on she rode, a pretty page carrying her banner, and with her little axe in her hand. And so Joan went to war. She led, she says, ten or twelve thousand soldiers. Among the other generals were Xaintrailles and La Hire. Joan made her soldiers confess themselves; as for La Hire, a brave rough soldier, she forbade him to swear, as he used to do, but, for his weakness, she permitted him to say, *By my bâton!* This army was to defend a great convoy of provisions, of which the people of Orleans stood in sore need. Since November they had been besieged, and now it was late April. The people in Orleans were not yet starving, but food came in slowly, and in small quantities. From the first the citizens had behaved well; a Scottish priest describes their noble conduct. They had burned all the outlying suburbs, beyond the wall, that they might not give shelter to the English. They had plenty of cannon, which carried large rough stone balls, and usually did little harm. But a gun was fired, it is said by a small boy, which killed Salisbury, the English general, as he looked out of an arrow-slit in a fort that the English had taken.

The French general-in-chief was the famous Dunois, then called the Bastard of Orleans. On the English side was the brave Talbot, who fought under arms for sixty years, and died fighting when he was over eighty. There were also Suffolk, Pole, and Glasdale, whom the French called 'Classidas'. The English had not soldiers enough to surround and take so large a town, of 30,000 people, in ordinary war. But as Dunois said, 'two hundred English could then beat a thousand French'—that is, as the French were before the coming of the Maid.

About half-past six in the morning the fight began. The French and Scottish leaped into the fosse, they set ladders against the walls, they reached the battlements, and were struck down by English swords and axes. Cannon-balls and great stones and arrows rained on them. 'Fight on!' cried the Maid; 'the place is ours.' At one o'clock she set a ladder against the wall with her own hands, but was deeply wounded by an arrow, which pierced clean through between neck and shoulder. Joan wept, but seizing the arrow with her own hands she dragged it out. The men-at-arms wished to say magic spells over the wound to 'charm' it, but this the Maid forbade as witchcraft. 'Yet,' says Dunois, 'she did not withdraw from the battle, nor took any medicine for the wound; and the onslaught lasted from morning till eight at night, so that there was no hope of victory. Then I desired that the army should go back to the town, but the Maid came to me and bade me wait a little longer. Next she mounted her horse and rode into a vine-yard, and there prayed for the space of seven minutes or eight. Then she returned, took her banner, and stood on the brink of the fosse. The English trembled when they saw her, but our men returned to the charge and met with no resistance. The English fled or were slain, and Glasdale who had insulted the Maid, was drowned' (by the burning of the drawbridge between the redoubt and Les Tourelles. The Maid in vain besought him, with tears, to surrender and be ransomed), 'and we returned gladly into Orleans.' The people of Orleans had a great share in this victory. Seeing the

English hard pressed, they laid long beams across the broken arches of the bridge, and charged by this perilous way. The triumph was even more that of the citizens than of the army. Homer tells us how Achilles, alone and unarmed, stood by the fosse and shouted, and how all the Trojans fled. But here was a greater marvel; and the sight of the wounded girl, bowed beneath the weight of her banner, frighted stouter hearts than those of the men of Troy.

Joan returned, as she had prophesied, by the bridge, but she did not make her supper off the fish: she took a little bread dipped in wine and water, her wound was dressed, and she slept. Next day the English drew up their men in line of battle. The French went out to meet them, and would have begun the attack. Joan said that God would not have them fight.

'If the English attack, we shall defeat them; we are to let them go in peace if they will.'

Mass was then said before the French army.

When the rite was done, Joan asked: 'Do they face us, or have they turned their backs?'

It was the English backs that the French saw that day: Talbot's men were in full retreat on Meun.

From that hour May 8 is kept a holiday at Orleans in honour of Joan the Maiden. Never was there such a deliverance. In a week the Maid had driven a strong army, full of courage and well led, out of forts like Les Tourelles. The Duc d'Alençon visited it, and said that with a few men-at-arms he would have felt certain of holding it for a week against any strength however great. But Joan not only gave the French her spirit: her extraordinary courage in leading a new charge after so terrible a wound, 'six inches deep', says d'Alençon, made the English think that they were fighting a force not of this world. And that is exactly what they were doing.

The Maid had shown her sign, as she promised; she had rescued Orleans. Her next desire was to lead Charles to Reims, through a country occupied by the English, and to have him anointed there with the holy oil. Till this was done she could only regard him as Dauphin—king, indeed, by blood, but not by consecration.

Here are the exploits which the Maid and the loyal French did in one week. She took Jargeau on June 11; on June 15 she seized the bridge of Meun; Beaugency yielded to her on June 17; on June 18 she defeated the English army at Pathay. Now sieges were long affairs in those days, as they are even to-day, when cannon are so much more powerful than they were in Joan's time. Her success seemed a miracle to the world.

This miracle, like all miracles, was wrought by faith. Joan believed in herself, in her country, and in God. It was not by visions and by knowing things strangely that she conquered, but by courage, by strength (on one occasion she never put off her armour for six days and six nights), and by inspiring the French with the sight of her valour. Without her visions, indeed, she would never have gone to war. She often said so. But, being at war, her word was 'Help yourselves, and God will help you.' Who could be lazy or a coward when a girl set such an example?

The King of France and his favourites could be indolent and cowards. Had Charles VII been such a man as Charles Stuart was in 1745, his foot would have been in the stirrup, and his lance in rest. In three months the English would have been driven into the sea. But the king loitered about the castles of the Loire with his favourites, La Tremouille, and his adviser, the Archbishop of Reims. They wasted the one year of Joan. There were jealousies against the Constable de Richemont of Brittany who had come with all his lances to follow the lily flag. If once Charles were king indeed and the English driven out, La Tremouille would cease to be powerful. This dastard sacrificed the Maid in the end, as he was ready to sacrifice France to his own private advantage.

At last, with difficulty, Charles was brought to visit Reims, and consented to be crowned like his ancestors. Seeing that he was never likely to move, Joan left the town where he was and went off into the country. This retreat brought Charles to his senses. The towns which he passed by yielded to him; Joan went and summoned each. 'Now she was with the king in the centre, now with the rearguard, now with the van.' The town of Troyes, where there was an English garrison, did not wish to yield. There was a council in the king's army: they said they could not take the place.

'In two days it shall be yours, by force or by good will,' said the Maid.

'Six days will do,' said the chancellor, 'if you are sure you speak truth.'

Joan made ready for an attack. She was calling 'Forward!' when the town surrendered. Reims, after some doubts, yielded also, on July 16, and all the people, with shouts of 'Noel!' welcomed the king. On July 17 the king was crowned and anointed with the Holy Oil by that very Archbishop of Reims who always opposed Joan. The Twelve Peers of France were not all present—some were on the English side—but Joan stood by Charles, her banner in her hand. 'It bore the brunt, and deserved to share the renown,' she said later to her accusers.

When the ceremony was ended, and the Dauphin Charles was a crowned and anointed king, the Maid knelt weeping at his feet.

'Gentle king', she said, 'now is accomplished the will of God, who desired that you should come to Reims to be consecrated, and to prove that you are the true king and the kingdom is yours.'

Then all the knights wept for joy.

The king bade Joan choose her reward. Already horses, rich armour, jeweled daggers, had been given to her. These, adding to the beauty and glory of her aspect, had made men follow her more gladly, and for that she valued them. She, too, made gifts to noble ladies, and gave much to the poor. She only wanted money to wage the war with, not for herself. Her family was made noble; on their shield, between two lilies, a sword upholds the crown. Her father was at Reims, and saw her in her glory. What reward, then, was Joan to choose? She chose nothing for herself, but that her native village of Domremy should be free from taxes. This news her father carried home from the splendid scene at Reims.

The name of Joan was now such a terror to the English that men deserted rather than face her in arms. At this time the truce with Burgundy ended, and the duke openly set out to besiege the strong town of Compiègne, held by de Flavy for France. Joan hurried to Compiègne, whence she made two expeditions which were defeated by treachery. Perhaps she thought of this, perhaps of the future, when in the church of Compiègne she declared one day to a crowd of children whom she loved that she knew she was sold and betrayed. Old men who had heard her told this tale long afterwards.

Burgundy had invested Compiègne, when Joan, with four hundred men, rode into the town secretly at dawn. That day Joan led a sally against the Burgundians. Her Voices told her nothing, good or bad, she says. The Burgundians were encamped at Margny and at Clairoix, the English at Venette, villages on a plain near the walls. Joan crossed the bridge on a grey charger, in a surcoat of crimson silk, rode through the redoubt beyond the bridge, and attacked the Burgundians. Flavy in the town was to prevent the English from attacking her in the rear. He had boats on the river to secure Joan's retreat if necessary.

Joan swept through Margny, driving the Burgundians before her; the garrison of Clairoix came to their help; the battle was doubtful. Meanwhile the English came up; they could not have reached the Burgundians, to aid them, but some of the Maid's men, seeing the English standards, fled. The English followed them under the walls of Compiègne; the gate of the redoubt was closed to prevent the English from entering with the runaways. Like Hector under Troy, the Maid was shut out from the town which she came to save.

Joan was with her own foremost line when the rear fled. They told her of her danger, she heeded not. For the last time rang out in that girlish voice: 'Allez avant! Forward, they are ours!'

Her men seized her bridle and turned her horse's head about. The English held the entrance from the causeway; Joan and a few men (her brother was one of them) were driven into a corner of the outer wall. A rush was made at Joan. 'Yield! yield! give your faith to me!' each man cried.

'I have given my faith to Another,' she said, 'and I will keep my oath.'

Her enemies confess that on this day Joan did great feats of arms, covering the rear of her force when they had to fly.

Some French historians hold that the gates were closed by treason that the Maid might be taken. We may hope that this was not so; the commander of Compiègne held his town successfully for the king, and was rescued by Joan's friend, the brave Pothon de Xaintrailles.

The sad story that is still to tell shall be shortly told. There is no word nor deed of the Maid's, in captivity as in victory, that is not to her immortal honour. But the sight of the wickedness of men, their cowardice, cruelty, greed, ingratitude, is not a thing to linger over.

Joan was now kept in a high tower at Beaurevoir, and was allowed to walk on the leads. She knew she was sold to England, she had heard that the people of Compiègne were to be massacred. She would rather die than fall into English hands, 'rather give her soul to God, than her body to the English.' But she hoped to escape and relieve Compiègne. She, therefore, prayed for counsel to her Saints; might she leap from the top of the tower? Would they not bear her up in their hands? St Catherine bade her not to leap; God would help her and the people of Compiègne

Then, for the first time as far as we know, the Maid willfully disobeyed her Voices. She leaped from the tower. They found her, not wounded, not a limb was broken, but stunned. She knew not what had happened; they told her she had leaped down. For three days she could not eat, 'yet was she comforted by St Catherine, who bade her confess and seek pardon of God, and told her that, without fail, they of Compiègne should be relieved before Martinmas.' This prophecy was fulfilled.

About the trial and the death of the Maid, I have not the heart to write a long story. Some points are to be remembered. The person who conducted the trial, itself illegal, was her deadly enemy, the false Frenchman, the Bishop of Beauvais, Cauchon, whom she and her men had turned out of his bishoprick. It is most unjust and unheard of, that any one should be tried by a judge who is his private enemy. Next, Joan was kept in strong irons day and night, and she, the most modest of maidens, was always guarded by five brutal English soldiers of the lowest rank. Again, she was not allowed to receive the Holy Communion as she desired with tears. Thus weakened by long captivity and ill usage, she, an untaught girl, was questioned repeatedly for three months, by the most cunning and learned doctors in law of the Paris University. Often many spoke at once, to perplex her mind. But Joan always showed a wisdom which confounded them, and which is at least as extraordinary as her skill in war. She would never swear an oath to answer all their questions. About herself, and all matters bearing on her own conduct, she would answer. About the king and the secrets of the king, she would not answer. If they forced her to reply about these things, she frankly said, she would not tell them the truth. The whole object of the trial was to prove that she dealt with powers of evil, and that her king had been crowned and aided by the devil. Her examiners, therefore, attacked her day by day, in public and in her dungeon, with questions about these visions which she held sacred, and could only speak of with a blush among her friends. Had she answered (as a lawyer said at the time), 'it seemed to me I saw a saint,' no man could have condemned her. Probably she did not know this, for she was not allowed to have an advocate of her own party, and she, a lonely girl, was opposed to the keenest and most learned lawyers of France. But she maintained that she certainly did see, hear, and touch her Saints, and that they came to her by the will of God. This was called blasphemy and witchcraft. And now came in the fatal Fairies! She was accused of dealing with devils under the Tree of Domremy.

Most was made of her refusal to wear woman's dress. For this she seems to have had two reasons; first, that to give up her old dress would have been to acknowledge that her mission was ended; next, for reasons of modesty, she being alone in prison among ruffianly men. She would wear woman's dress if they would let her take the Holy Communion; but this they refused. To these points she was constant, she would not deny her visions; she would not say one word against her king, 'the noblest Christian in the world' she called him who had deserted her. She would not wear woman's dress in prison. We must remember that, as she was being tried by churchmen, she should have been, as she often prayed to be, in a prison of the church, attended by women. They set a spy on her, a caitiff priest named L'Oyseleur, who pretended to be her friend, and who betrayed her. The English soldiers were allowed to bully, threaten, and frighten away everyone who gave her any advice. They took her to the torture-chamber; and threatened her with torture, but from this even these priests shrunk, except a few more cruel and cowardly than the rest. Finally, they put her up in public, opposite a pile of wood ready for burning, and then set a priest to preach at her. All through her trial, her Voices bade her 'answer boldly.' In three months she would give her last answer, in three months 'she would be free with great victory, and come into the Kingdom of Paradise.' In three months from the first day of her trial she went free through the gate of fire. Boldly she answered, and wisely. She would submit the truth of her visions to the Church, that is, to God, and the Pope. But she would not submit them to 'the Church', if that meant the clergy round her. At last, in fear of fire, and the stake before her, and on promise of being taken to a kindlier prison among women, and released from chains, she promised to 'abjure', to renounce her visions, and submit to the Church, that is to Cauchon, and her other priestly enemies. Some little note on paper she now signed with a cross, and repeated 'with a smile', poor child, a short form of words. By some trick this signature was changed for a long document, in which she was made to confess all her visions false. It is certain that she did not understand her words in this sense.

Cauchon had triumphed. The blame of heresy and witchcraft was cast on Joan, and on her king as an accomplice. But the English were not satisfied; they made an uproar, they threatened Cauchon, for Joan's life was to be spared. She was to be in prison all her days, on bread and water, but, while she lived, they dared scarcely stir against the French. They were soon satisfied.

Joan's prison was not changed. There soon came news that she had put on man's dress again. The judges went to her. She told them (they say), that she put on this dress of her own free will. In confession, later, she told her priest that she had been refused any other dress, and had been brutally treated both by the soldiers and by an English lord. In self-defence, she dressed in the only attire within her reach. In any case, the promises made to her had been broken. The judge asked her if her Voices had been with her again?

'Yes.'

'What did they say?'

'God told me by the voices of St Catherine and St Margaret of the great sorrow of my treason, when I abjured to save my life; that I was damning myself for my life's sake.'

'Do you believe the Voices come from St Margaret and St Catherine?'

'Yes, and that they are from God.'

She added that she had never meant to deny this, had not understood that she had denied it.

All was over now; she was a 'relapsed heretic'.

The judges said that they visited Joan again on the morning of her death, and that she withdrew her belief in her Voices; or, at least, left it to the Church to decide whether they were good or bad, while she still maintained that they were *real*. She had expected release, and, for the first time, had been disappointed. At the stake she understood her Voices: they had foretold her martyrdom, 'great victory' over herself, and her entry into rest. But the document of the judges is not signed by the clerks, as all such documents must be. One of them, Manchon, who had not been present, was asked to sign it; he refused. Another, Taquel, is said to have been present, but he did not sign. The story is, therefore, worth nothing.

Enough. They burned Joan the Maid. She did not suffer long. Her eyes were fixed on a cross which a priest, Martin L'Advenu, held up before her. She maintained, he says, to her dying moment, the truth of her Voices. With a great cry of JESUS! she gave up her breath, and her pure soul was with God.

From *The True Red Storybook*, edited by Andrew Lang (London: Longman's, Green, and Company, 1895).

Ned Kelly—Iron Man

The greatest of Australia's folk-heroes, Ned Kelly was the son of an Irishman who had been exiled from his homeland for stealing two pigs. His family was frequently in trouble with the law and, at one time, even his mother was imprisoned. Ned, who had been born in 1854 as the eldest of eight children, joined a gang that stole horses and cattle, robbed banks, and reportedly killed policemen. His country's most renowned 'Bushranger', a term used to describe outlaws hiding in the outback, he was only twenty-five years old when he was captured, tried, and hanged. During his lifetime, he was feared and reviled, but also revered, particularly by poor people. Since his death, he has become a national hero to many, a kind of 'Robin Hood' figure, a symbol of the downtrodden who was finally destroyed by the establishment. Michael and Christopher Stuart-Clark stress the ambiguity of the character in their narrative of the hero's last stand. Although Ned and his band have been treated like 'wild dogs', many of the people in the town of Glenrowan have a kind of admiration for him. He seems in part motivated by an egotism, refusing to acquiesce to entreaties to flee. Ned is brought down because his cast iron armour does not cover his legs. In this regard, he resembles the Greek hero Achilles, a proud warrior whose only vulnerable spot was his heel.

This was going to be the 'Big One'. Ned Kelly and his outlaws had been hunted like wild dogs by the police for too long. This time they would be the hunters—or so they thought. In any event it was Kelly's last stand.

It was Saturday evening in Glenrowan, a small town just north of Broken River. After the last train came through Ned and his men planned to tear up some of the track just outside the station. No trains came through on a Sunday, except the special police train. They would ambush this when it was forced to stop, round up the police—who, after all, usually rounded other people up—and then they could raid the banks freely.

There was talk in the town that a whole load of cast-iron had gone missing. Nobody could explain the theft—except Ned Kelly. He had his gang busy making strong metal armour for themselves. They made breast-plates, back-plates, and helmets: a suit weighed about forty-five kilos in all! They left their legs unprotected as they would need to be mobile and legs do not need armour when you are up close raiding a bank.

Ned called to his men, 'Round up all the townsfolk and bring them to the hotel. I am going to check the rails being ripped up.'

Some of the people of Glenrowan were happy to go along with Ned's gang. Many had heard of his daring and his humour, of how he often entertained his prisoners, of how he was quite a ladies' man. Often the poor of the community received money from his raids themselves.

When he came to the hotel Ned saw the local schoolteacher among his prisoners.

'Good to see you, teacher. I am sure you can keep all these people in order,' he joked.

'I'll certainly try to, sir,' came the reply. But the schoolteacher was watching Ned and his men carefully. And when Ned suggested that they should start up some dancing to pass the time, the schoolteacher took his chance and slipped out of a back window—and telegraphed a warning message to the police.

The dancing started and just as Ned was beginning to enjoy himself, knowing that the police would soon be coming up the track, a message was handed to him. 'So you thought you would ambush us. We are on our way—not by train—and we know where you are. See you soon!'

Ned was stunned. He released the local people at once, and his own men were keen to make a run for it.

'Come on, Ned. Those lawmen have never caught us yet.'

'. . . and they aren't going to now. Let's go!'

'Wait!' shouted Ned. 'Now is the time to stand and fight and prove they can't beat us. We have our armour, we'll take them on. We won't be hunted like dingos any more.'

Suddenly a blazing torch flew through the hotel window, and a fire started. Ned's men found it difficult to move in their heavy armour and were gradually overcome by the flames. Only Ned could move.

Ned heard a call from outside the hotel. 'Come on out, Ned Kelly. We've got you at last.' The police were waiting, with rifles raised. But they were astonished by the sight that met their eyes. Ned stood in the doorway, a huge man in armour of solid iron.

Through his helmet he shouted, 'Fire away, you can't hurt me. I'm made of iron.' And as he walked slowly forward bullets bounced off him.

But one of the policemen, realizing the armour did not protect his legs, aimed at the knees, and the wounds and the weight of the armour brought Ned Kelly down. They stripped him of his armour and took him to hospital to tend his wounds.

A doctor got talking to him. 'So they got you at last. How come you didn't try to escape this time? You always managed to before.'

From Michael Harrison and Christopher Stewart-Clark, *The Oxford Treasury of World Stories*. Illustrated by Paul Dainton. (Oxford: Oxford University Press, 1998), 73.

Ned looked at him wearily. 'A man gets tired of being hunted like a dog in his native land. I wanted to see the thing end.'

Ned was soon moved to prison. The guards there knew all about Ned's exploits. They too were curious about his capture.

'Your gang were all dead in the hotel—why didn't you leave them there and escape yourself?'

Ned looked them in the eye and said slowly, 'A man would be a nice sort of dingo to walk out on his mates.'

From *The Oxford Treasury of World Stories*, by Michael Harrison and Christopher Stuart-Clark (London: Oxford University Press, 1998).

John Henry

The threat of machines and progress has been a major theme in literature since the Industrial Revolution. In the well-known story from African-American folklore, the railroad construction worker John Henry is determined to assert the dignity of man in the face of the new steam drills. Ironically, he is a victim of the progress he helps to create; he collapses after having completed the driving of steel through the Big Bend Tunnel in the early 1870s. Whether the hero was an actual person or a symbol of the hard-working labourer is unknown. However, stories and songs about episodes in his life, particularly the one that led to his death, became popular in the last quarter of the nineteenth century and folksongs and written accounts of his deeds have appeared throughout the twentieth century. His hammer, with which he labours and with which he dies, becomes a symbol of his character and his way of life.

John Henry was born way down south. Yes, down south in the cotton country, where the Mississippi flows. And yet he wasn't a cotton-picker in the fields. Nor yet was he a roustabout, rolling bales of cotton on the steamboats.

Oh, he could pick cotton, and he could roust cotton. He could, better than the best. But he was meant to drive steel on the railroad, because he was a natural man. Yes, yes, he was a natural man.

John Henry knew what he was meant for. He knew, even when he was a little baby. Sitting on his pappy's knee, he said:

'I'm goin' to drive steel. Goin' to whop it on down with a big hammer. And that hammer will be the death of me. Yes, that hammer will be the death of me.'

John Henry's pappy smiled.

'Son, you're just makin' foolish talk,' he said.

But John Henry's mama looked at John Henry. She gave him a long, slow look. His skin was as dark as deep night, and his eyes shone like two bright stars.

'I'm a natural man,' he said. 'And I'm a steel-drivin' man. And I'll die with my hammer in my hand.'

John Henry's mama made up her mind he wouldn't. She wouldn't allow John Henry to end his days that way. She would raise him so he wouldn't go to driving steel. She would take care that he never held a hammer in his hand.

John Henry's mama didn't let on what she was thinking. But anything she made up her mind to, she did. Instead of going out to pick cotton, she took in washing from the white folks. She tied John Henry to her apron strings. She kept him close to her side. She watched him and looked after him. And he never held a hammer in his hand.

Then one day John Henry's pappy was picking on the banjo. John Henry took the banjo from his pappy's hands. He picked out a tune, the same as his pappy. He really made that banjo ring.

'That's it! That's surely it!' said John Henry's mama.

'What's it?' said his pappy.

'That's what the boy's going to be,' his mama said. 'A music man. And then he'll never hold a hammer in his hand.'

'Music man,' said John Henry's pappy. 'Well, he could try.'

Going out of the cabin, he hitched his mule to the wagon. He and John Henry's mama got on the seat, with John Henry between. And they took John Henry to New Orleans, to the professor on Perdido Street.

Soon as he was in the professor's house, John Henry ran to the piano. He played that piano, the black and white keys, both. He didn't miss a one.

'Child,' said the professor, 'you can sure tickle them ivories. Where did you learn to play like that?'

'It just come to me natural,' John Henry said. 'Because I'm a natural man.' Then John Henry beat out a roll on the professor's drums. He played the drums fast time, slow time, double time, ragtime, and no time. Then he picked up the slide trambone. He played it sweet and he played it low. Then he picked up the clarinet. He played it hot as fire and cool as ice. And then he picked up the trumpet. He made it laugh and cry, snicker and sob. Why, he almost made that horn talk.

Folks crowded around the door, listening.

'Play it, boy,' they said. 'Play it!'

And John Henry played. He played everything from *Mushrat Ramble* to *High Society*, and plenty in between. The professor picked up the slide trambone and joined in. Somebody took the drums, and somebody else the clarinet. From the house next door a man brought a bass horn. Folks came running from everywhere, singing and clapping hands. They followed John Henry down the street, dancing, marching, high-stepping. John Henry blew glory on his trumpet, while the folks sang:

'Oh, when the saints,
Oh, when the saints,
Oh, when the saints go march in' in,
I want to be in that number,
When the saints go march in' in.'

'That's surely it,' said John Henry's mama. 'John Henry is goin' to be a music man.'

But it didn't turn out that way. Because John Henry was growing, faster than any weed. He grew until he was eight feet tall, and he was still growing. There wasn't a trumpet or a trambone made to match his size. And John Henry was strong. He didn't dare put a finger on a piano, or beat a drum. He would just smash and crash them to bits.

'Well, you can sing, maybe,' his mama told him.

'I beg to differ, mama,' said John Henry. 'I can't sing, unless it's outdoors and far from a house. For every time I let loose with a song, it raises the roof.'

To show his mama, he sang out 'Mi, mi, mi, mi!'

And the roof raised.

'Well, then,' his mama said, 'you can just stay home, the way you've been. No need to trouble yourself about anything.'

John Henry shook his head. 'No, mama, I don't mean to cross you, but I can't stay home. Not with pappy's back bent from pickin' the cotton, and you worn and weary from washin' the clothes.'

'I'm not lettin' you go to work on the railroad,' John Henry's mama said. 'I'm not lettin' you drive steel with a hammer in your hand.'

'I could pick the cotton. That wouldn't do any harm,' said John Henry.

His mama thought, 'No. It might not do harm. But do you pick cotton, you'll see the roustabouts on the river. And you'll want to roust cotton. And do you roust cotton, you'll see the steel-drivin' men drivin' steel on the railroad. And you'll want to drive steel. And do you drive steel, you'll die with your hammer in your hand.'

That's what John Henry's mama thought. But she didn't let on. She knew she couldn't hold John Henry back. Couldn't anybody hold him back, because he was a natural man. Yes, yes, he was a natural man.

And so John Henry went to picking cotton in the fields. His pappy and his mama went with him. At first they were faster than John Henry. He picked cotton and put it in his sack, picked cotton, put it in his sack. After a while, though, John Henry's hands moved like lightning. It was pick and put, pick and put, pick and put. And while he worked, he sang:

> 'You got to jump down, turn around,
> Pick a bale of cotton,
> You got to jump down, turn around,
> To pick a bale a day.'

John Henry picked more than a bale a day—lots more. From sun-up to sun-down—from can-see to can't-see—he worked in the fields. It was pick cotton the livelong day, until all the crop was picked.

It was time, then, to take the bales of cotton to town. Time for the roustabouts to roll the bales a board the steamboats. They dug their hooks into the cotton, taking the bales up the gangplank. John Henry watched them. While he did, a white man eyed him every which way.

He was the captain of the roustabouts, that white man was.

He said, 'Where you come from, boy? How did you get so big?'

'It just come natural, cap'n,' said John Henry. 'Because I'm a natural man.'

'Boy, think you can roust cotton?' asked the captain.

'Think I could, cap'n,' John Henry said.

The captain handed him a cotton-hook, and John Henry rousted that cotton. Soon he was rousting cotton every day, just as his mama feared. At first he used one hook, and then he used two. Sometimes he carried a bale or two on his head, besides. He rousted more cotton than any ten men, piling it up on the steamboats. Folks came from miles around just to see the sight.

Among the folks was a pretty little girl by the name of Polly Ann. She liked John Henry and John Henry liked her. They kept company for a while. Then they were married, setting up housekeeping in New Orleans. Polly Ann was a good wife. When John Henry came home from his work, she had his supper waiting. There was side meat and corn pone, turnip greens and black-eyed peas. Or there might be chicken and biscuits and maybe pot licker. Even John Henry's mama couldn't do better than that.

With a wife to keep, John Henry rousted more cotton than ever. But one day he passed a place where the railroad was being built. He saw a crew putting down the wooden ties, and the rails on the ties. He saw the gandy dancers, packing down the crushed stone. And he saw the steel drivers, driving in spikes with big hammers.

John Henry had picked the cotton, and rousted the cotton. He'd done both, better than the best. But he knew now he'd only been biding his time.

'Cap'n,' he said to the captain, 'could I heft one of those hammers? Just to sort of get the feel.'

The captain gave him a hammer to heft.

'Cap'n,' he said to the captain, 'could I drive in one of those spikes? Just to sort of see if I can.'

The captain gave him a spike to drive. John Henry raised the hammer, and it made a rainbow around his shoulder. He brought the hammer down, and there was an awful rumbling sound. He hit the spike and whopped that steel on down. Yes, yes, he whopped that steel on down.

'Boy,' said the captain, 'where did you learn to drive steel like that?'

'Never had to learn, cap'n,' said John Henry. 'It just come natural. Because I'm a natural man.'

John Henry hefted the hammer again.

'Cap'n,' he said, 'you got a job of work for me?'

The captain said, 'Boy, you're workin' now. I hired you two minutes ago. Now line out those rails! Let me see you whop that steel on down!'

And so John Henry went to driving steel. He had a hammer in his hands at last. It came about just the way his mama feared. The tears sprang to her eyes when she heard the news.

'I tried to hold you back, John Henry,' she said. 'I tried and I tried. But couldn't anybody keep the hammer from your hand. And that hammer will be the death of you.'

'Now who told you that, mama?' John Henry asked, though he remembered.

'You did. When you were a little baby, sittin' on your pappy's knee.'

'A little baby don't know,' said Polly Ann. 'A baby says anything comes into its little head.'

'Why, sure,' said John Henry's pappy. 'Just fool talk. I said it then, and I say it now. No cause to fret.'

'Maybe,' said John Henry's mama. 'Maybe so. I hope, I hope and I pray. But I won't try to stop you, son, because I can't.'

After that, John Henry drove steel every day. At first he used one hammer, and then he used two-one in each hand. Sometimes the railroad men couldn't wait until all the track was laid. It didn't worry John Henry any. He'd run out on the ties, with a train chug-chugging right behind him. He'd have his two hammers, and a mouthful of spikes. He'd spit out the spikes and drive 'em in, keeping just ahead of the train. When all the track was fixed, he'd jump aside, and the train would rush on.

John Henry traveled around some himself. He worked in eastern Virginia and western Virginia. He did the same in Georgia, Alabama, and Mississippi, too. Not that he had an itch in his heel. Oh, no, he wasn't the rambling kind. But he was a steel-driving fool. Wherever track was laid, John Henry was wanted. The captain told him to go, and he went.

So John Henry wasn't surprised when he was sent to western Virginia again. This time his job was a little different. A tunnel had to be built, to get the C. & O. Railroad through a stone mountain. To make the tunnel, dynamite had to be used. To use the dynamite, holes had to made in the rock. The dynamite would be dropped in the holes, and *blam-te-blam!* it would blow up the stone on the mountain. John Henry's job was to make the holes in the rock, driving in a big steel drill. The drill would be held by a man called a shaker, while John Henry whopped it on down.

John Henry took Polly Ann with him to western Virginia. She was a big help. Whenever John Henry was sick and took to his bed, Polly drove steel like a man. Yes, yes, Polly drove steel like a man.

It didn't happen often, though. John Henry was strong, and he wasn't sick more than once or twice. From the dark of morn to the dark of night he drove steel on the mountain. Then he hurried home to Polly Ann. They had a little son now, and John Henry liked to hold him on his knee. The little tyke would grab John Henry's big finger in his little fist. He'd hold on and he wouldn't let go.

'I do declare,' said John Henry. 'This baby got a power of strength. He's goin' to be a natural man, and a steel drivin' man, just like his pappy.'

Some days Polly Ann would take the baby and bring a lunch to John Henry on the mountain. She was there when the stranger came around, with his fast talk and his fancy clothes. He carried a strange contraption, and was looking for the captain.

'What's that you've got there?' asked the captain.

'Glad you asked,' the stranger said. 'For I'm here to tell you. And you'll be happy I did. For never, sir, have you seen the like. It's the marvel of the age. It's what you've been needing. It's what you've been wanting. It's what you must have. Try it, sir, and you'll say the same.'

'I might. And then again I might not.'

'You will, sir!' the stranger said. 'You'll see, sir! It's bound to please. And to amaze and astound you as well.'

'But what is it?' the captain said.

'Aha,' said the stranger. 'I was coming to that. I was, indeed. This, sir—' and he waved his hand—'this is a steam drill. It does the work of three men in half the time.'

'I don't need it, then,' the captain said. 'I don't want it. I don't have to have it. Because I've got a boy here does the work of six men in hardly no time at all. Name of John Henry. He can beat any machine that ever was.'

The stranger threw back his head and laughed. He laughed and he laughed.

'Know when John Henry will beat this steam drill?' he said. 'When the rocks on this mountain turn to gold.'

The captain turned to John Henry.

'You hear that, John Henry?' he said.

'I hear it, cap'n,' said John Henry. 'I hear the words, but I don't hear the sense. Cap'n, a man ain't nothin' but a man. But before I'd let that steam drill beat me down, I'd die with my hammer in my hand.'

'Huh! No man can beat a machine,' the stranger said.

'He can if he's a natural man,' John Henry said.

The stranger wasn't laughing now. He looked mean.

'Uppity, ain't he?' he said to the captain. 'Talks big. Acts big. Mighty biggety and uppity. But I've got just the thing to put him in his place.' He patted the steamdrill with one hand. 'How about a race, sir? My steam drill against John Henry. I'll give you a steam drill, free and for nothing, if John Henry can beat it down.'

'And what if he can't?'

'Then you'll buy a steam drill from me.'

'You hear that, boy?' the captain said to John Henry. 'What do you say?'

'Don't you do it, John Henry! You got no call to beat a steam drill!' Polly Ann said.

It was John Henry's turn to laugh.

'Cap'n,' he said, 'I'll beat that steam drill to the bottom, or I'll die.'

'Good boy,' the captain said. He told the stranger, 'You've got yourself a race. Week from today suit you?'

'Suits me fine,' the stranger answered.

And, shaking hands with the captain, he took his leave.

All that week folks kept coming from everywhere, to see the race. John Henry's mama came, and his pappy. His mama was afraid. And this time his pappy and Polly Ann were afraid, too.

'John Henry,' said his mama, 'you goin' to die with your hammer in your hand. You said so yourself.'

'That was just fool talk,' John Henry said. 'When I was a little baby, and didn't know A from izzard.'

'I'm not so sure,' said his pappy.

'I've been driving steel some time,' John Henry said. 'And I'm still here. Still alive and kickin'.'

'Now see here, John Henry,' Polly Ann said. 'You never raced a steam drill before. Don't do it, John Henry.'

'Don't do it, son,' said his mama and his pappy.

'Why, I couldn't back out now,' John Henry said. 'Not with all the folks here to see me. Besides, the cap'n wouldn't like it. And all the drivers and shakers would laugh. So stop your frettin' and your fussin'. Little ol' steam drill can't do me any harm.'

John Henry wouldn't talk about it any more. He laughed, and ate good, and played with his little son. The morning of the race, he joked while they walked up the mountain. When they reached the top, he waved his hand to the crowd.

'How you feelin' boy?' the captain asked him.

'Feelin' mighty spry,' said John Henry.

The sun was coming up over the mountain, blazing hot. Not a breeze of air stirred. John Henry took off his shirt and picked up his hammer. He lifted it a few times, just to limber up his muscle. The crowd cheered, and he looked around.

There was his shaker, holding the steel drill. There was the steam drill, with the stranger beside it. There was the crowd watching, and the captain. There was his mama. There was his pappy, and Polly Ann holding his little son. And there was the mayor of the town in his high hat, his gold watch and chain in his hand.

'Ready with the steam drill, sir?' the mayor asked the stranger.

'More than ready,' the stranger said.

'You ready, boy?' the mayor asked John Henry.

'Yes, sir,' John Henry said.

The mayor looked down at his gold watch and chain.

'Then go!' he said.

John Henry raised his hammer, and the ground shook underfoot.

'The mountain's sinkin' in!' the stranger cried.

'Why, that's just my hammer suckin' wind,' John Henry said.

The crowd laughed and cheered.

'That's it, boy!' they said. 'Whop that steel, John Henry! Beat that steam drill down!'

And John Henry drove steel—wham! wham! wham! And the steam drill hissed and drove steel—bam! bam! bam! The race was on. It was the machine against John Henry, and John Henry was a man. Yes, yes, he was a natural man.

His hammer flashed like lightning, as he sang:

> 'There ain't no hammer,
> Upon this mountain,
> Ring-a like mine, boys,
> Ring-a like mine!'

The drill cut into the rock, and John Henry sang to his shaker:

> 'Shaker, why don't you sing?
> I'm throwin' twelve pounds
> from my hips on down,
> Just listen to the cold steel ring,
> Just listen to the cold steel ring!'

John Henry kept bringing his hammer down, faster and faster. Then, after a while, his hammer wasn't so fast any more. But still he kept driving steel. Near him, the steam drill kept turning. And the sun went high in the sky, and the sun went low in the sky. And the steam drill kept turning, and John Henry kept whopping that steel on down.

Then the sun went down behind the mountain, and the mayor looked at his gold watch and chain.

'Stop!' he said. 'I declare this race over.'

He counted the holes John Henry had drilled, and the holes the steam drill had drilled. He measured to see how deep they were, every one. He cleared his throat, took off his high hat, and said: 'John Henry's drilled more holes! And he's drilled them deeper. I declare John Henry the winner. He's beat the steam drill down!'

Well, the crowd cheered. Well, they stomped and yelled and carried on. John Henry smiled, but he didn't smile for long. He pressed his hand to his heart, and he laid him on the ground.

'Where's my mama?' he said. 'Where's my pappy? Where's my sweet Polly Ann? And where's my son?'

They all gathered round him, and Polly put John Henry's son in the palm of his hand. John Henry held him up. The little tyke reached for the evening star, as, if he could pluck it from the sky.

'You got a power of strength in you,' John Henry said. 'A power of strength.'

He gave his son back to Polly Ann. Then a trembling came over him, and the mountain shook. And he died with his hammer in his hand—died with his hammer in his hand.

Well, they took and buried John Henry. And every time the people passed his grave, they said, 'There was a natural man. Yes, yes, John Henry was a natural man.'

From *Tall Tales of America*, by Irwin Shapiro (Poughkeepsie, NY: Guild Press, 1958).

LINKS TO OTHER STORIES

Part Four

*U*nlikely *H*eroes
Triumphs of the Underdog

In *Anatomy of Criticism*, Northrop Frye suggested a useful method of categorizing stories. He distinguished among narratives in which the characters, in their abilities and encounters with their human and natural environments, are superior, equal, or inferior to normal readers. Two of his classifications, 'high mimetic' and 'low mimetic', are appropriate to children's literature. The former was a 'mode of literature, in which, as in most epics and tragedies, the central characters are above our own level and authority, though within the order of nature and subject to social criticism' (366). The latter was 'a mode of literature in which the characters exhibit a power of action which is roughly on our own level' (366).

The first category can be applied to the stories in Part Three, 'Larger than Life: Tales of Heroes'. In those narratives, the characters are generally adults, occupy positions of power, and have physical and or psychological attributes superior to those of child audiences. The second can be applied to the stories in this section. Most of the characters here are, at the beginning of their stories, restricted because of age, physical abilities, experience, skills, and knowledge, and because of social, economic, or family status. As a result of such restrictions, they seem most unlikely to accomplish significant feats, and, therefore, resemble many child readers. However, because of their actions, these characters frequently rise in status and, indeed, become individuals to whom children can look up. If 'high mimetic' heroes embody ideal adults whom children can admire from afar, these 'low mimetic' heroes represent qualities young readers can strive to emulate.

At the beginning of stories about unlikely heroes, or, to use a popular term, 'underdogs', the central characters are generally marginalized. That is, they have little power in relation to the family, political, or social groups on the edges of which they live. Not only are they unable to influence others, but also they are themselves controlled by the people who have marginalized them. In this respect, it is not surprising that stories about unlikely heroes have been popular with children, who are generally controlled by those who have the physical, psychological, and economic power to direct their lives.

The marginalization of the central characters and their apparent lack of heroic potential is generally set forth in descriptions early in the tales. Their size and lack of either strength or other conventionally heroic physical attributes initially place them at a disadvantage. From Thumbelina, a tiny girl living in a world of normal-sized human beings and other creatures, to Tortoise, who is now very old and very slow, but who eventually comes to the aid of his starving friends in 'How the Tortoise Got His Shell', the title characters appear at first more likely to become victims than heroes. Encountering dragons, giants, and ogres, all larger, fiercer, and stronger than they are, Jack, Belinda the Practical Princess, or Momotaro, Little Peachling, would seem to be doomed to defeat.

Many unlikely heroes are placed at great disadvantage because of their young age. Molly Whuppie, Súmac from 'The Search for the Magic Lake', and the only child in 'The Fly' are children and, as such, not only smaller and less powerful, but also far less knowledgeable and experienced than their adult adversaries. Given their apparent naiveté and innocence, how can they be expected to succeed in the tasks or quests in which they have become involved? In addition, Súmac, like the biblical David, is the youngest member of her family and, within the social structures of her society, the most marginalized. In European societies, only the first-born male could be expected to assume power and wealth within the family structure. The youngest was not only the baby, but also the least likely to acquire a role of power or influence. Jack and Aladdin are without fathers and, as such, live in families with little power. In the case of Thumbelina, the heroine is essentially an orphan; after the opening paragraphs, the normal-sized woman with whom she initially lives disappears from the story.

If the youngest child is a girl, she is even more powerless, because males usually held all the legal and economic power. Additionally, people in many cultures considered that females were intellectually inferior and believed that they lacked the powers of reasoning needed to develop the survival strategies necessary in a male dominated world. Molly and Súmac are, therefore, doubly disadvantaged. Interestingly Perrault's Cinderella, who could be considered an unlikely hero, is relatively passive, as European women were traditionally expected to be, and depends in considerable part on a magical helper and the passions of an actively pursuing prince. She is, thus, a different kind of unlikely hero: she does little, she just is. As such, she is a contrast to Molly Whuppie, the Practical Princess, and Súmac, who actively shape their destinies.

Many unlikely heroes are economically marginalized. Jack, Molly, and the hero of 'The Fly' live with poor adults and in positions in which the acquisition of wealth—along with the security and power it could bring—appears impossible. These economic situations are part of the social and political exclusions. The poor had little opportunity to acquire the financial security that could provide upward social mobility. Their lives were constant struggles to fulfill day-to-day needs. Add to this the characters' youth and, in some cases, their gender and one can see that those unlikely child heroes faced even greater exclusion and powerlessness.

If the unlikely heroes' chances of victory appear slight because of their personal and social situations, they are rendered even less probable because of the nature of their adversaries. Both Belinda, the Practical Princess, and the unnamed heroine of 'The Last of the Dragons' must face huge, fierce, flame-throwing dragons who reportedly enjoy devouring human beings, particularly princesses. The biblical David, Jack, and Molly Whuppie encounter giants who are enemies of their people and, for the latter two, devourers of children. The 'valiant' Chattee-Maker apparently confronts a fierce tiger and an invading army, defeating both. Momotaro confronts ogres who, it seems, horde ill-begotten wealth in their island fortress. And Thumbelina, the boy in 'The Fly', and Aladdin face adults in positions of power.

Finally, unlikely heroes must often face opponents whom others, both children and adults, have unsuccessfully encountered. Adults are powerless against the moneylender in 'The Fly'. The armies of Israel have failed to defeat Goliath. The young sister engages in a search for the magic lake after many others, including her brothers, have not succeeded.

Many boys have preceded Jack into the giant's house and none have returned. Younger, quicker animals than Tortoise have died trying to gain food from the willy-wagtail.

Marginalized and faced with defeating adversaries that supposedly more able individuals have not overcome, the unlikely heroes emerge victorious. Their successes seem to result in part because of their motivations and inherent character traits, and because of their abilities to understand their adversaries and to use this understanding to overcome them. Certainly the majority of the protagonists possess courage. This courage is evident in their decisions to take the initiative, to enter perilous places, and to confront dangerous adversaries. Jack decides to climb the beanstalk, David to meet Goliath in single combat, the youngest sister to make the dangerous journey in search of the magic lake and her missing brothers, and Momotaro to attack the ogres. Ironically, the Chattee-Maker is praised because he appears to have courageously undertaken the initiative to tame a dangerous tiger and single-handedly to confront enemy armies. Because others do not understand what has actually happened, they accord him heroic status. He is thus a special case; while he remains unheroic in reality, he is a hero in the eyes of society.

The successes of the unlikely heroes frequently depend on their motivations. Generally, their actions are taken for the sake of others, rather than for their own good. Momotaro thinks of his parents' well-being; Tortoise considers his starving fellow animals; Molly makes her first two trips back to the giant's home so that her sisters can marry princes; Súmac heads to the magic lake so that she can help both the ailing prince and her imprisoned brothers; David wishes to destroy the enemy of his people.

Closely linked to such selfless, altruistic motives are the kindnesses that many of the unlikely heroes display during their encounters. Both Momotaro and Súmac share their food with characters they encounter on their journeys and, as a result, gain allies who help them in their quests. The princess in 'The Last of the Dragons' decides not to kill, but to tame her adversary with kindness, and, by doing so, she acquires a devoted pet.

The most frequently displayed characteristic of these protagonists is cleverness, a quality they use to emerge victorious over larger, stronger, more experienced enemies. Caught by the giant on her third trip to his home, Molly Whuppie gives her slow-thinking adversary what he thinks is advice on how to punish her, but what is really part of her plan of escape. And the small boy in 'The Fly' tricks the evil moneylender by using the tactics of the adult. He uses a lie to catch the usurer in a lie and so saves his parents. Belinda, the Practical Princess, remembers that kings often used impossible tests to discourage young suitors and uses the same technique to rid herself of an old and undesirable suitor.

Their victories complete, the unlikely heroes often experience a change in their social and economic status: Molly and Jack marry into royal families and Thumbelina not only receives a gift of wings that makes her a member of the fairy group, but also marries the prince. Acclaimed by the members of the Israeli army, David has made the first step toward becoming the leader of his people. Interestingly, however, other heroes return to their homes which have been made more secure, and even prosperous because of their actions. In 'The Search for the Magic Lake', Súmac, after she has delivered the potion that will cure the prince, asks that her family be given a prosperous farm and that she be allowed to return to it. The loyal son in 'The Fly', having lifted the burden of debt from his parents, will accompany them back to their house.

Although all of the characters in the stories in this section appear to be unlikely heroes, triumphing over superior adversaries, it can be argued that such is not the case in three of the tales. These may be seen as wholly or partially ironic; the storytellers may be creating the appearance of unlikely heroism while, at the same time, subtly and implicitly under-cutting the heroic portrayals. Jack, for example, could be seen as a lucky opportunist whose last trip up the beanstalk is implicitly motivated more by curiosity, boredom, and greed than by need. Aladdin, the poor fatherless boy who opposes an evil magician and wins the hand of the sultan's daughter, is introduced in the story's first sentences as 'a careless, little boy who would do nothing but play all day long in the streets with idle boys like himself'. He discovers the powers of a magic ring only by accident, uses the power of the genie of the lamp to provide wealth, voyeuristically gazes at the princess in defiance of law, and earns her hand because of the actions of the genie. Indeed, even though he exhibits qualities that endear him to the people after his marriage, he depends on his magical ring to assist him in defeating his adversaries at the story's climax.

The most obviously unheroic unlikely hero, however, is the title character of the iron-ically labeled 'The Valiant Chattee-Maker'. The humble potter, who finds himself raised to a caste he could never have reached in real life, achieves his first fame because of too much alcohol and a series of misunderstandings. This renown is increased when the Rajah, acting on the erroneous reports arriving at his palace, confers wealth and honour on him, raising the simple man above his humble origins. Through the help of his wife, the Chatte-Maker finds himself in a situation where his actions are again misunderstood and his fame, rank, and wealth, increased. The focus of the tale seems to be on satirizing those uninformed peo-ple who conferred the unlikely hero status on the Chattee-Maker. As such, it deals with a theme frequently found in traditional stories from India: the consequences of acting on the basis of rumour or incorrect information.

Works Cited

Frye, Northrop. 1957. *Anatomy of Criticism*. Princeton, NJ: Princeton University Press.

Molly Whuppie

This English folktale has frequently been compared to another English tale, 'Jack and the Beanstalk', because it is about a child's successful confrontation with a giant. Molly is, however, far more than a 'female Jack'. Her initial situation, like that of Hansel and Grethel, is a realization of one of the deepest fears of children: abandonment by parents. Moreover, like Grethel, she uses her courage and cleverness to rescue her siblings. Signifi-cantly, Molly's first two return trips to the giant's home are not motivated by greed or a love of daring-do, but by a desire to help her sisters marry royally. Only after they are cared for does she return to benefit herself. Molly is also not a giant-killer. While mod-ern readers have frequently commented on Molly's heroism, some have noted that, in marrying the youngest prince, she will have very little chance of becoming a queen. Perhaps this marriage is an indication of her selflessness: power and wealth were never her principal objectives.

Once upon a time there was a man and a wife had too many children, and they could not get meat for them, so they took the three youngest and left them in a wood. They travelled and travelled and could see never a house. It began to be dark, and they were hungry. At last they saw a light and made for it; it turned out to be a house. They knocked at the door, and a woman came to it, who said: 'What do you want ?' They said: 'Please let us in and give us something to eat.' The woman said: 'I can't do that, as my man is a giant, and he would kill you if he comes home.' They begged hard. 'Let us stop for a little while,' said they, 'and we will go away before he comes.' So she took them in, and set them down before the fire, and gave them milk and bread; but just as they had begun to eat a great knock came to the door, and a dreadful voice said:

> 'Fee, fie, fo, fum,
> I smell the blood of some earthly one.'

'Who have you there wife?' 'Eh,' said the wife, 'it's three poor lassies cold and hungry, and they will go away. Ye won't touch 'em, man.' He said nothing, but ate up a big supper, and ordered them to stay all night. Now he had three lassies of his own, and they were to sleep in the same bed with the three strangers. The youngest of the three strange lassies was called Molly Whuppie, and she was very clever. She noticed that before they went to bed the giant put straw ropes round her neck and her sisters', and round his own lassies' necks he put gold chains. So Molly took care and did not fall asleep, but waited till she was sure every one was sleeping sound. Then she slipped out of the bed, and took the straw ropes off her own and her sisters' necks, and took the gold chains off the giant's lassies. She then put the straw ropes on the giant's lassies and the gold on herself and her sisters, and lay down. And in the middle of the night up rose the giant, armed with a great club, and felt for the necks with the straw. It was dark. He took his own lassies out of bed on to the floor, and battered them until they were dead, and then lay down again, thinking he had managed finely, Molly thought it time she and her sisters were off and away, so she wakened them and told them to be quiet, and they slipped out of the house. They all got out safe, and they ran and ran, and never stopped until morning, when they saw a grand house before them. It turned out to be a king's house: so Molly went in, and told her story to the king. He said: 'Well, Molly, you are a clever girl, and you have managed well; but, if you would manage better, and go back, and steal the giant's sword that hangs on the back of his bed, I would give your eldest sister my eldest son to marry.' Molly said she would try. So she went back, and managed to slip into the giant's house, and crept in below the bed. The giant came home, and ate up a great supper, and went to bed. Molly waited until he was snoring, and she crept out, and reached over the giant and got down the sword; but just as she got it out over the bed it gave a rattle, and up jumped the giant, and Molly ran out at the door and the sword with her; and she ran, and he ran, till they came to the 'Bridge of one hair'; and she got over, but he couldn't, and he says, 'Woe worth ye, Molly Whuppie! never ye come again.' And she says: 'Twice yet, carle,' quoth she, 'I'll come to Spain.' So Molly took the sword to the king, and her sister was married to his son.

Well, the king he says: 'Ye've managed well, Molly; but if ye would manage better, and steal the purse that lies below the giant's pillow, I would marry your second sister to my second son.' And Molly said she would try. So she set out for the giant's house, and slipped in, and hid again below the bed, and waited till the giant had eaten his supper, and was snoring sound asleep. She slipped out, and slipped her hand below the pillow, and got out the purse; but just as she was going out the giant wakened, and ran after her; and she ran, and he ran, till they came to the 'Bridge of one hair', and she got over, but he couldn't, and he

From Joseph Jacobs, *English Fairy Tales*. Illustrated by John D. Batten. (London: David Nutt, 1989), 128.

said, 'Woe worth ye, Molly Whuppie! never you come again.' 'Once yet, carle,' quoth she, 'I'll come to Spain.' So Molly took the purse to the king, and her second sister was married to the king's second son.

After that the king says to Molly: 'Molly, you are a clever girl, but if you would do better yet, and steal the giant's ring that he wears on his finger, I will give you my youngest son for yourself.' Molly said she would try. So back she goes to the giant's house, and hides herself below the bed. The giant wasn't long ere he came home, and, after he had eaten a great big supper, he went to his bed, and shortly was snoring loud. Molly crept out and reached over the bed, and got hold of the giant's hand, and she pulled and she pulled until she got off the ring; but just as she got it off the giant got up, and gripped her by the hand, and he says: 'Now I have caught you, Molly Whuppie, and, if I had done as much ill to you as ye have done to me, what would ye do to me?'

Molly says: 'I would put you into a sack, and I'd put the cat inside wi' you, and the dog aside you, and a needle and thread and a shears, and I'd hang yon up upon the wall, and I'd go to the wood, and choose the thickest stick I could get, and I would come home, and take you down, and bang you till you were dead.'

'Well, Molly,' says the giant, 'I'll just do that to you.'

So he gets a sack, and puts Molly into it, and the cat and the dog beside her, and a needle and thread and shears, and hangs her up upon the wall, and goes to the wood to choose a stick.

Molly she sings out: 'Oh, if ye saw what I see.'

'Oh,' says the giant's wife, 'what do ye see Molly?'

But Molly never said a word but, 'Oh, if ye saw what I see!'

The giant's wife begged that Molly would take her up into the sack till she would see what Molly saw. So Molly took the shears and cut a hole in the sack, and took out the needle and thread with her, and jumped down and helped the giant's wife up into the sack, and sewed up the hole.

The giant's wife saw nothing, and began to ask to get down again; but Molly never minded, but hid herself at the back of the door. Home came the giant, and a great big tree in his hand, and he took down the sack, and began to batter it. His wife cried, 'It's me, man'; but the dog barked and the cat mewed, and he did not know his wife's voice. But Molly came out from the back of the door, and the giant saw her, and he ran after her; and he ran and she ran, till they came to the 'Bridge of one hair', and she got over but he couldn't; and he said, 'Woe worth you, Molly Whuppie! never you come again.' 'Never more, carle,' quoth she, 'will I come again to Spain.'

So Molly took the ring to the king, and she was married to his youngest son, and she never saw the giant again.

————

From *English Fairy Tales*, collected by Joseph Jacobs (London: David Nutt, 1898).

Jack and the Beanstalk

One of the best-known English folktales, 'Jack and the Beanstalk' focuses on the actions of the child-hero. Jack is small and the only child of a poor widow; his adversary is a giant who has eaten many children. If he is to live, Jack must succeed where other children have failed and died. Jack passes his first test when he successfully answers a riddle and earns the magic objects: the beans. Each of his three trips up the beanstalk is more dangerous than the last, and Jack must exhibit both increasing courage and cleverness. It is interesting to note, however, that, although heroic, Jack's second and third trips are motivated partly by self-interest and greed. The narrative develops a contrast between the optimistic and opportunistic child hero and the pessimistic mother, who, at the crucial moment, is incapable of action.

𝒯here was once upon a time a poor widow who had an only son named Jack, and a cow named Milky-white. And all they had to live on was the milk the cow gave every morning which they carried to the market and sold. But one morning Milky-white gave no milk and they didn't know what to do.

'What shall we do, what shall we do?' said the widow, wringing her hands.

'Cheer up, mother, I'll go and get work somewhere,' said Jack.

'We've tried that before, and nobody would take you,' said his mother; 'we must sell Milky-white and with the money start shop, or something.'

'All right, mother,' says Jack; 'it's market-day today, and I'll soon sell Milky-white, and then we'll see what we can do.'

So he took the cow's halter in his hand, and off he started. He hadn't gone far when he met a funny-looking old man who said to him: 'Good morning, Jack.'

'Good morning to you,' said Jack, and wondered how he knew his name.

'Well, Jack, and where are you off to?' said the man.

'I'm going to market to sell our cow here.'

'Oh, you look the proper sort of chap to sell cows,' said the man; 'I wonder if you know how many beans make five.'

'Two in each hand and one in your mouth,' says Jack, as sharp as a needle.

'Right you are,' says the man, 'and here they are, the very beans themselves,' he went on, pulling out of his pocket a number of strange-looking beans. 'As you are so sharp,' says he, 'I don't mind doing a swap with you—your cow for these beans.'

'Go along,' says Jack; 'wouldn't you like it?'

'Ah! you don't know what these beans are,' said the man; 'if you plant them over-night, by morning they grow right up to the sky.'

'Really?' says Jack; 'you don't say so.'

'Yes, that is so, and if it doesn't turn out to be true you can have your cow back.'

'Right,' says Jack, and hands him over Milky-white's halter and pockets the beans.

Back goes Jack home, and as he hadn't gone very far it wasn't dusk by the time he got to his door.

'Back already, Jack?' said his mother; 'I see you haven't got Milky-white, so you've sold her. How much did you get for her?'

'You'll never guess, mother,' says Jack.

'No, you don't say so. Good boy! Five pounds, ten, fifteen, no, it can't be twenty.'

'I told you you couldn't guess; what do you say to these beans; they're magical, plant them over-night and—'

'What!' says Jack's mother, 'have you been such a fool, such a dolt, such an idiot, as to give away my Milky-white, the best milker in the parish, and prime beef to boot, for a set of paltry beans. Take that! Take that! Take that! And as for your precious beans here they go out of the window. And now off with you to bed. Not a sup shall you drink, and not a bit shall you swallow this very night.'

So Jack went upstairs to his little room in the attic, and sad and sorry he was, to be sure, as much for his mother's sake, as for the loss of his supper.

At last he dropped off to sleep.

When he woke up, the room looked so funny. The sun was shining into part of it, and yet all the rest was quite dark and shady. So Jack jumped up and dressed himself and went to the window. And what do you think he saw? Why, the beans his mother had thrown out of the window into the garden had sprung up into a big beanstalk which went up and up and up till it reached the sky. So the man spoke truth after all.

The beanstalk grew up quite close past Jack's window, so all he had to do was to open it and give a jump on to the beanstalk which ran up just like a big ladder. So Jack climbed, and he climbed and he climbed and he climbed and he climbed and he climbed and he climbed till at last he reached the sky. And when he got there he found a long broad road going as straight as a dart. So he walked along and he walked along and he walked along till he came to a great big tall house, and on the doorstep there was a great big tall woman.

'Good morning, mum,' says Jack, quite polite-like. 'Could you be so kind as to give me some breakfast?' For he hadn't had anything to eat, you know, the night before and was a hungry as a hunter.

'It's breakfast you want, is it?' says the great big tall woman, 'it's breakfast you'll be if you don't move off from here. My man is an ogre and there's nothing he likes better than boys broiled on toast. You'd better be moving on or he'll soon be coming.'

'Oh! please mum, do give me something to eat, mum. I've had nothing to eat since yesterday morning, really and truly, mum,' says Jack, 'I may as well be broiled as die of hunger.'

Well, the ogre's wife was not half so bad after all. So she took Jack into the kitchen, and gave him a junk of bread and cheese and a jug of milk. But Jack hadn't half finished these when thump! thump! thump! the whole house began to tremble with the noise of someone coming.

'Goodness gracious me! It's my old man,' said the ogre's wife, 'what on earth shall I do? Come along quick and jump in here.' And she bundled Jack into the oven just as the ogre came in.

He was a big one, to be sure. At his belt he had three calves strung up by the heels, and he unhooked them and threw them down on the table and said: 'Here, wife, broil me a couple of these for breakfast. Ah! What's this I smell?

'Fee-fi-fo-fum,
I smell the blood of an Englishman,
Be he alive, or be he dead
I'll have his bones to grind my bread.'

'Nonsense, dear,' said his wife, 'you're dreaming. Or perhaps you smell the scraps of that little boy you liked so much for yesterday's dinner. Here, you go and have a wash and tidy up, and by the time you come back your breakfast'll be ready for you.'

So off the ogre went, and Jack was just going to jump out of the oven and run away when the woman told him not. 'Wait till he's asleep,' says she; 'he always has a doze after breakfast.'

Well, the ogre had his breakfast, and after that he goes to a big chest and takes out of it a couple of bags of gold, and down he sits and counts till at last his head began to nod and he began to snore till the whole house shook again.

Then Jack crept out on tiptoe from his oven, and as he was passing the ogre he took one of the bags of gold under his arm, and off he pelters till he came to the beanstalk, and then he threw down the bag of gold, which of course fell in to his mother's garden, and then he climbed down and climbed down till at last he got home and told his mother and showed her the gold and said: 'Well, mother, wasn't I right about the beans. They are really magical, you see.'

So they lived on the bag of gold for some time, but at last they came to the end of it, and Jack made up his mind to try his luck once more up at the top of the beanstalk. So one fine morning he rose up early, and got on to the beanstalk, and he climbed and he climbed and he climbed and he climbed and he climbed and he climbed till at last he came out on to the road again and up to the great big tall house he had been to before. There, sure enough, was the great big tall woman a-standing on the door-step.

'Good morning, mum,' says Jack, as bold as brass, 'could you be so good as to give me something to eat?'

'Go away, my boy,' said the big tall woman, 'or else my man will eat you up for breakfast. But aren't you the youngster who came here once before? Do you know, that very day, my man missed one of his bags of gold.'

'That's strange, mum,' says Jack, 'I dare say I could tell you something about that, but I'm so hungry I can't speak till I've had something to eat.'

Well the big tall woman was so curious that she took him in and gave him something to eat. But he had scarcely begun munching it as slowly as he could when thump! thump! thump! they heard the giant's footstep, and his wife hid Jack away in the oven.

All happened as it did before. In came the ogre as he did before, said: 'Fee-fi-fo-fum', and had his breakfast of three broiled oxen. Then he said: 'Wife, bring me the hen that lays the golden eggs.' So she brought it, and the ogre said: 'Lay,' and it laid an egg all of gold. And then the ogre began to nod his head, and to snore till the house shook.

Then Jack crept out of the oven on tiptoe and caught hold of the golden hen, and was off before you could say 'Jack Robinson'. But this time the hen gave a cackle which woke the ogre, and just as Jack got out of the house he heard him calling: 'Wife, wife, what have you done with my golden hen?'

And the wife said: 'Why, my dear?'

But that was all Jack heard, for he rushed off to the beanstalk and climbed down like a house on fire. And when he got home he showed his mother the wonderful hen and said 'Lay', to it; and it laid a golden egg every time he said 'Lay'.

Well, Jack was not content, and it wasn't very long before he determined to have another try at his luck up there at the top of the beanstalk. So one fine morning, he rose up early, and got on to the beanstalk, and he climbed and he climbed and he climbed and he climbed till he got to the top. But this time he knew better than to go straight to the ogre's house. And when he got near it he waited behind a bush till he saw the ogre's wife come out with a pail to get some water, and then he crept into the house and got into the copper. He hadn't been there long when he heard thump! thump! thump! as before, and in come the ogre and his wife.

'Fee-fi-fo-fum, I smell the blood of an Englishman,' cried out the ogre; 'I smell him, wife, I smell him.'

'Do you, my dearie?' says the ogre's wife. 'Then if it's that little rogue that stole your gold and the hen that laid the golden eggs he's sure to have got into the oven.' And they both rushed to the oven. But Jack wasn't there, luckily, and the ogre's wife said: 'There you are again with your fee-fi-fo-fum. Why of course it's the boy you caught last night that I've just broiled for your breakfast. How forgetful I am, and how careless you are not to know the difference between live and dead after all these years.'

So the ogre sat down to the breakfast and ate it, but every now and then he would mutter: 'Well, I could have sworn—' and he'd get up and search the larder and the cupboards, and everything, only luckily he didn't think of the copper.

After breakfast was over, the ogre called out: 'Wife, wife, bring me my golden harp.' So she brought it and put it on the table before him. Then he said: 'Sing!' and the golden harp sang most beautifully. And it went on singing till the ogre fell asleep, and commenced to snore like thunder.

Then Jack lifted up the copper-lid very quietly and got down like a mouse and crept on hands and knees till he came to the table when up he crawled, caught hold of the golden harp and dashed with it towards the door. But the harp called out quite loud: 'Master! Master!' and the ogre woke up just in time to see Jack running off with his harp.

Jack ran as fast as he could, and the ogre came rushing after, and would soon have caught him only Jack had a start and dodged him a bit and knew where he was going. When he got to the beanstalk the ogre was not more than twenty yards away when suddenly he saw Jack disappear like, and when he came to the end of the road he saw Jack underneath climbing down for dear life. Well, the ogre didn't like trusting himself to such a ladder, and he stood and waited, so Jack got another start. But just then the harp cried out: 'Master! master!' and the ogre swung himself down on to the beanstalk which shook with his weight. Down climbs Jack, and after him climbed the ogre. By this time Jack had climbed down and climbed down and climbed down till he was very nearly home. So he called out: 'Mother!

mother! bring me an axe, bring me an axe.' And his mother came rushing out with the axe in her hand, but when she came to the beanstalk she stood stock still with fright for there she saw the ogre with his legs just through the clouds.

But Jack jumped down and got hold of the axe and gave a chop at the beanstalk which cut it half. The ogre felt the beanstalk shake and quiver so he stopped to see what was the matter. Then Jack gave another chop with the axe, and the beanstalk was cut in two and began to topple over. Then the ogre fell down and broke his crown, and the beanstalk came toppling after.

Then Jack showed his mother his golden harp, and what with showing that and selling the golden eggs, Jack and his mother became very rich, and he married a great princess, and they lived happily ever after.

From *English Fairy Tales*, collected by Joseph Jacobs (London: David Nutt, 1898).

David and Goliath

In the European tradition, one of the best-known unlikely heroes is David, the Old Testament youngest son who defeats the giant Goliath. David, in his role as the youngest son, had been regulated to performing menial tasks while his brothers went to war. From his humble origins he rises to become a great leader, proving himself by using his cleverness and courage to perform an amazing feat that benefits his people. Drawing on II Samuel, Chapter 17, reteller Sara Cone Bryant uses the measured prose rhythms of the Bible, but includes 'slight interpolations, changes of order, and omissions'.

A long time ago, there was a boy named David, who lived in a country far east of this. He was good to look upon, for he had fair hair and ruddy skin; and he as very strong and brave and modest. He was a shepherd-boy for his father, and all day—often all night— he was out in the fields, far from home, watching over the sheep. He had to guard them from wild animals, and lead them to the right pastures, and care for them.

By and by, war broke out between the people of David's country and a people that lived near at hand; these men were called Philistines, and the people of David's country were named Israel. All the strong men of Israel went up to the battle, to fight for their king. David's three older brothers went, but he was only a boy, so he was left behind to care for the sheep.

After the brothers had been gone some time, David's father longed very much to hear from them, and to know if they were safe; so he sent for David, from the fields, and said to him, 'Take now for thy brothers an ephah of this parched corn, and these ten loaves, and run to the camp, where thy brothers are; and carry these ten cheeses to the captain of their thousand, and see how thy brothers fare, and bring me word again.' (An ephah is about three pecks.)

David rose early in the morning, and left the sheep with a keeper, and took the corn and the loaves and the cheeses, as his father had commanded him, and went to the camp of Israel.

The camp was on a mountain; Israel stood on a mountain on the one side, and the Philistines stood on a mountain on the other side; and there was a valley between them. David came to the place where the Israelites were, just as the host was going forth to the fight, shouting for the battle. So he left his gifts in the hands of the keeper of the baggage, and ran into the army, amongst the soldiers, to find his brothers. When he found them, he saluted them and began to talk with them.

But while he was asking them the questions his father had commanded, there arose a great shouting and tumult among the Israelites, and men came running back from the front line of battle; everything became confusion. David looked to see what the trouble was, and he saw a strange sight: on the hillside of the Philistines, a warrior was striding forward, calling out something in a taunting voice; he was a gigantic man, the largest David had ever seen, and he was all dressed in armour, that shone in the sun: he had a helmet of brass upon his head, and he was armed with a coat of mail, and he had greaves of brass upon his legs, and a target of brass between his shoulders; his spear was so tremendous that the staff of it was like a weaver's beam, and his shield so great that a man went before him, to carry it.

'Who is that?' asked David.

'It is Goliath, of Gath, champion of the Philistines,' said the soldiers about. 'Every day, for forty days, he has come forth, so, and challenged us to send a man against him, in single combat; and since no one dares to go out against him alone, the armies cannot fight.' (That was one of the laws of warfare in those times.)

'What!' said David, 'does none dare go out against him?'

As he spoke, the giant stood still, on the hillside opposite the Israelitish host, and shouted his challenge, scornfully. He said, 'Why are ye come out to set your battle in array? Am I not a Philistine, and ye servants of Saul? Choose you a man for you, and let him come down to me. If he be able to fight with me, and to kill me, then will we be your servants; but if I prevail against him, and kill him, then shall ye be our servants, and serve us. I defy the armies of Israel this day; give me a man, that we may fight together!'

When King Saul heard these words, he was dismayed, and all the men of Israel, when they saw the man, fled from him and were sore afraid. David heard them talking among themselves, whispering and murmuring. They were saying, 'Have ye seen this man that is come up? Surely if any one killeth him that man will the king make rich; perhaps he will give him his daughter in marriage, and make his family free in Israel!'

David heard this, and he asked the men if it were so. It was surely so, they said.

'But,' said David, 'who is this Philistine, that he should defy the armies of the living God?' And he was stirred with anger.

Very soon, some of the officers told the king about the youth who was asking so many questions, and who said that a mere Philistine should not be let defy the armies of the living God. Immediately Saul sent for him. When David came before Saul, he said to the king, 'Let no man's heart fail because of him; thy servant will go and fight with this Philistine.'

But Saul looked at David, and said, 'Thou art not able to go against this Philistine, to fight with him, for thou art but a youth, and he has been a man of war from his youth.'

Then David said to Saul, 'Once I was keeping my father's sheep, and there came a lion and a bear, and took a lamb out of the flock; and I went out after the lion, and struck him, and delivered the lamb out of his mouth, and when he arose against me, I caught him by the beard, and struck him, and slew him! Thy servant slew both the lion and the bear; and this Philistine shall be as one of them, for he hath defied the armies of the living God. The Lord, who delivered me out of the paw of the lion and out of the paw of the bear, he will deliver me out of the hand of this Philistine.'

'Go,' said Saul, 'and the Lord be with thee!'

And he armed David with his own armour,—he put a helmet of brass upon his head, and armed him with a coat of mail. But when David girded his sword upon his armour, and tried to walk, he said to Saul, 'I cannot go with these, for I am not used to them.' And he put them off.

Then he took his staff in his hand and went and chose five smooth stones out of the brook, and put them in a shepherd's bag which he had; and his sling was in his hand; and he went out and drew near to the Philistine.

And the Philistine came on and drew near to David; and the man that bore his shield went before him. And when the Philistine looked about and saw David, he disdained him, for he was but a boy, and ruddy, and of a fair countenance. And he said to David, 'Am I a dog, that thou comest to me with a cudgel?' And with curses he cried out again, 'Come to me, and I will give thy flesh unto the fowls of the air, and to the beasts of the field.'

But David looked at him, and answered, 'Thou comest to me with a sword, and with a spear, and with a shield; but I come to thee in the name of the Lord of hosts, the God of the armies of Israel, whom thou hast defied. This day will the Lord deliver thee into my hand; and I will smite thee, and take thy head from thee, and I will give the carcasses of the host of the Philistines this day unto the fowls of the air, and to the wild beasts of the earth, that all the earth may know that there is a God in Israel! And all this assembly shall know that the Lord saveth not with a sword and spear; for the battle is the Lord's, and he will give you into our hands.'

And then, when the Philistine arose, and came, and drew nigh to meet David, David hasted, and ran towards the army to meet the Philistine. And when he was a little way from him, he put his hand in his bag, and took thence a stone, and put it in his sling, and slung it, and smote the Philistine in the forehead, so that the stone sank into his forehead; and he fell on his face to the earth.

And David ran, and stood upon the Philistine, and took his sword, and drew it out of its sheath, and slew him with it.

Then, when the Philistines saw that their champion was dead, they fled. But the army of Israel pursued them, and victory was with the men of Israel.

And after the battle, David was taken to the king's tent, and made a captain over many men; and he went no more to his father's house, to herd the sheep, but became a man, in the king's service.

———

From *Stories to Tell to Children*, by Sara Cone Bryant (Boston: Houghton Mifflin, 1907).

The Last of the Dragons

Early twentieth-century British children's writer E. Nesbit has created both a humourous parody of the traditional dragon-slayer tale, in which a brave knight rescues a helpless princess, and a serious commentary about socially imposed roles. The princess of this story is brave, athletic, and unconventional; she proposes that the prince, a dreamy philosopher, become her partner in confronting the dragon, who, it turns out, would rather be left alone and does not want to devour the princess. The humour arises because each character refuses to fit into a role defined by a centuries-old genre. Nesbit, who lived an unconventional life herself, uses the parody to illustrate the restrictions that society tries to impose on its members. The characters achieve real happiness only when they act according to their true natures, not according to the expectations of those around them. Because the prince, princess, and dragon accept each other as they are, they lead fulfilled lives. The story's conclusion also parodies the *pourquoi* tale, offering a far-fetched explanation for the origin of the first airplane.

Of course you know that dragons were once as common as motor-omnibuses are now, and almost as dangerous. But as every well-brought-up prince was expected to kill a dragon, and rescue a princess, the dragons grew fewer and fewer, till it was often quite hard for a princess to find a dragon to be rescued from. And at last there were no more dragons in France and no more dragons in Germany, or Spain, or Italy, or Russia. There were some left in China, and are still, but they are cold and bronzy, and there were never any, of course, in America. But the last real live dragon left was in England, and of course that was a very long time ago, before what you call English History began. This dragon lived in Cornwall in the big caves amidst the rocks, and was a very fine big dragon, quite seventy feet long from the tip of its fearful snout to the end of its terrible tail. It breathed fire and smoke, and rattled when it walked, because its scales were made of iron. Its wings were like half-umbrellas—or like bat's wings, only several thousand times bigger. Everyone was very frightened of it, and well they might be.

Now the King of Cornwall had one daughter, and when she was sixteen, of course she would have to go and face the dragon: such tales are always told in royal nurseries at twilight, so the Princess knew what she had to expect. The dragon would not eat her, of course—because the prince would come and rescue her. But the Princess could not help thinking it would be much pleasanter to have nothing to do with the dragon at all—not even to be rescued from him.

'All the princes I know are such very silly little boys,' she told her father. 'Why must I be rescued by a prince?'

'It's always done, my dear,' said the King; taking his crown off and putting it on the grass, for they were alone in the garden, and even kings must unbend sometimes.

'Father, darling,' said the Princess presently, when she had made a daisy chain and put it on the King's head, where the crown ought to have been. 'Father, darling, couldn't we tie up one of the silly little princes for the dragon to look at—and then I could go and kill the dragon and rescue the Prince? I fence much better than any of the princes we know.'

'What an unladylike idea!' said the King, and put his crown on again, for he saw the Prime Minister coming with a basket of new-laid Bills for him to sign. 'Dismiss the thought, my child. I rescued your mother from a dragon, and you don't want to set yourself up above her, I should hope?'

'But this is the *last* dragon. It is different from all other dragons.'

'How?' asked the King.

'Because he is the last,' said the Princess, and went off to her fencing lessons, with which she took great pains. She took great pains with all her lessons—for she could not give up the idea of fighting the dragon. She took such pains that she became the strongest and boldest and most skilful and most sensible princess in Europe. She had always been the prettiest and nicest.

And the days and years went on, till at last the day came which was the day before the Princess was to be rescued from the dragon. The prince who was to do this deed of valour was a pale prince, with large eyes and a head full of mathematics and philosophy, but he had unfortunately neglected his fencing lessons. He was to stay the night at the palace, and there was a banquet.

After supper the Princess sent her pet parrot to the Prince with a note. It said:

'Please, Prince, come on to the terrace. I want to talk to you without anybody else hearing—The Princess.'

So, of course he went—and he saw her gown of silver a long way off shining among the shadows of the trees like water in starlight. And when he came quite close to her he said:

'Princess, at your service,' and bent his cloth-of-gold-covered knee and put his hand on his cloth-of-gold-covered heart.

'Do you think,' said the Princess earnestly, 'that you will be able to kill the dragon?'

'I will kill the dragon,' said the Prince firmly, 'or perish in the attempt.'

'It's no use your perishing,' said the Princess.

'It's the least I can do,' said the Prince.

'What I'm afraid of is that it'll be the most you can do,' said the Princess.

'It's the only thing I can do,' said he, 'unless I kill the dragon.'

'Why you should do anything for me is what I can't see,' said she.

'But I want to,' he said. 'You must know that I love you better than anything in the world.'

When he said that he looked so kind that the Princess began to like him a little.

'Look here,' she said, 'no one else will go out tomorrow. You know they tie me to a rock, and leave me—and then everybody scurries home and puts up the shutters and keeps them shut till you ride through the town in triumph shouting that you've killed the dragon, and I ride on the horse behind you weeping for joy.'

'I've heard that that is how it is done,' said he.

'Well, do you love me well enough to come very quickly and set me free,—and we'll fight the dragon together?'

'It wouldn't be safe for you.'

'Much safer for both of us for me to be free, with a sword in my hand, than tied up and helpless. *Do* agree.'

He could refuse her nothing. So he agreed. And next day everything happened as she had said.

When he had cut the cords that tied her to the rocks they stood on the lonely mountainside looking at each other.

'It seems to me,' said the Prince, 'that this ceremony could have been arranged without the dragon.'

'Yes,' said the Princess, 'but since it has been arranged with the dragon—'

'It seems such a pity to kill the dragon—the last in the world,' said the Prince.

'Well, then, don't let's,' said the Princess; 'let's tame it not to eat princesses but to eat out of their hands. They say everything can be tamed by kindness.'

'Taming by kindness means giving them things to eat,' said the Prince. 'Have you got anything to eat?'

She hadn't, but the Prince owned that he had a few biscuits. 'Breakfast was so very early,' said he, 'and I thought you might have felt faint after the fight.'

'How clever,' said the Princess, and they took a biscuit in each hand. And they looked here and they looked there, but never a dragon could they see.

'But here's its trail,' said the Prince, and pointed to where the rock was scarred and scratched so as to make a track leading to the mouth of a dark cave. It was like cart-ruts in a Sussex road, mixed with the marks of sea-gulls' feet on the sea-sand. 'Look, that's where it dragged its brass tail and planted its steel claws.'

'Don't let's think how hard its tail and its claws are,' said the Princess, 'or I shall begin to be frightened—and I know you can't tame anything, even by kindness, if you're frightened of it. Come on. Now or never.'

She caught the Prince's hand in hers and they ran along the path towards the dark mouth of the cave. But they did not run into it. It really was so very *dark*.

So they stood outside, and the Prince shouted: 'What ho! Dragon there! What ho within!' And from the cave they heard an answering voice and great clattering and creaking. It sounded as though a rather large cotton-mill were stretching itself and waking up out of its sleep.

The Prince and the Princess trembled, but they stood firm.

'Dragon—I say, Dragon!' said the Princess, 'do come out and talk to us. We've brought you a present.'

'Oh, yes—I know your presents,' growled the dragon in a huge rumbling voice. 'One of those precious princesses, I suppose? And I've got to come out and fight for her. Well, I tell you straight, I'm not going to do it. A fair fight I wouldn't say no to—a fair fight and no favour—but one of these put-up fights where you've got to lose—No. So I tell you. If I wanted a princess I'd come and take her, in my own time—but I don't. What do you suppose I'd do with her, if I'd got her?'

'Eat her, wouldn't you?' said the Princess in a voice that trembled a little.

'Eat a fiddle-stick end,' said the dragon very rudely. 'I wouldn't touch the horrid thing.'

The Princess' voice grew firmer.

'Do you like biscuits?' she asked.

'No,' growled the dragon.

'Not the nice little expensive ones with sugar on the top?'

'*No*,' growled the dragon.

'Then what *do* you like?' asked the Prince.

'You go away and don't bother me,' growled the dragon, and they could hear it turn over, and the clang and clatter of its turning echoed in the cave like the sound of the steam-hammers in the Arsenal at Woolwich.

The Prince and Princess looked at each other. What *were* they to do? Of course it was no use going home and telling the King that the dragon didn't want princesses—because His Majesty was very old-fashioned and would never have believed that a new-fashioned dragon could ever be at all different from an old-fashioned dragon. They could not go into the cave and kill the dragon. Indeed, unless he attacked the Princess it did not seem fair to kill him at all.

'He must like something,' whispered the Princess, and she called out in a voice as sweet as honey and sugar-cane:

'Dragon! Dragon dear!'

'WHAT?' shouted the dragon. 'Say that again!' and they could hear the dragon coming towards them through the darkness of the cave. The Princess shivered, and said in a very small voice:

'Dragon—Dragon dear!'

And then the dragon came out. The Prince drew his sword, and the Princess drew hers—the beautiful silver-handled one that the Prince had brought in his motor-car. But they did not attack; they moved slowly back as the dragon came out, all the vast scaly length of him, and lay along the rock—his great wings half-spread and his silvery sheen gleaming like diamonds in the sun. At last they could retreat no further—the dark rock behind them stopped their way—and with their backs to the rock they stood swords in hand and waited.

The dragon drew nearer and nearer—and now they could see that he was not breathing fire and smoke as they had expected—he came crawling slowly towards them wriggling a little as a puppy does when it wants to play and isn't quite sure whether you're not cross with it.

And then they saw that great tears were coursing down its brazen cheek.

'Whatever's the matter?' said the Prince.

'Nobody,' sobbed the dragon, 'ever called me "dear" before!'

'Don't cry, dragon dear,' said the Princess. 'We'll call you "dear" as often as you like. We want to tame you.'

'I *am* tame,' said the dragon—'that's just it. That's what nobody but you has ever found out. I'm so tame that I'd eat out of your hands.'

'Eat what, dragon dear?' said the Princess. 'Not biscuits?'

The dragon slowly shook its heavy head.

'Not biscuits?' said the Princess tenderly. 'What, then, dragon dear?'

'Your kindness quite undragons me,' it said. 'No one has ever asked any of us what we like to eat—always offering us princesses, and then rescuing them—and never once, "What'll you take to drink the King's health in?" Cruel hard I call it,' and it wept again.

'But what would you like to drink our health in?' said the Prince. 'We're going to be married today, aren't we, Princess?'

She said that she supposed so.

'What'll I take to drink your health in?' asked the dragon. 'Ah, you're something like a gentleman, you are, sir. I don't mind if I do, sir. I'll be proud to drink your and your good lady's health in a tiddy drop of'—its voice faltered—'to think of you asking me so friendly like,' it said. 'Yes, sir, just a tiddy drop of puppuppuppuppupetrol—tha—that's what does a dragon good, sir—'

'I've lots in the car,' said the Prince, and was off down the mountain like a flash. He was a good judge of character, and he knew that with this dragon the Princess would be safe.

'If I might make so bold,' said the dragon, 'while the gentleman's away—p'raps just to pass the time you'd be so kind as to call me Dear again, and if you'd shake claws with a poor old dragon that's never been anybody's enemy but his own—well, the last of the dragons'll be the proudest dragon there's ever been since the first of them.'

It held out an enormous paw, and the great steel hooks that were its claws closed over the Princess's hand as softly as the claws of the Himalayan bear will close over the bit of bun you hand it through the bars at the Zoo.

And so the Prince and Princess went back to the palace in triumph, the dragon following them like a pet dog. And all through the wedding festivities no one drank more earnestly to the happiness of the bride and bridegroom than the Princess' pet dragon—whom she had at once named Fido.

And when the happy pair were settled in their own kingdom, Fido came to them and begged to be allowed to make himself useful.

'There must be some little thing I can do,' he said, rattling his wings and stretching his claws. 'My wings and claws and so on ought to be turned to some account—to say nothing of my grateful heart.'

So the Prince had a special saddle or howdah made for him—very long it was—like the tops of many tramcars fitted together. One hundred and fifty seats were fitted to this, and the dragon, whose greatest pleasure was now to give pleasure to others, delighted in taking parties of children to the seaside. It flew through the air quite easily with its hundred and fifty little passengers—and would lie on the sand patiently waiting till they were ready to return. The children were very fond of it and used to call it dear, a word which never failed to bring tears of affection and gratitude to its eyes. So it lived, useful and respected, till quite the other day—when some one happened to say, in his hearing, that dragons were out-of-date, now so much new machinery had come in. This so distressed him that he asked the King to change him into something less old-fashioned, and the kindly monarch at once changed him into a mechanical contrivance. The dragon, indeed, became the first aeroplane.

From *Five of Us—and Madeline*, by E. Nesbit (London: Ernest Benn, 1958).

The Practical Princess

Princess Bedelia, whose name is derived from Bridget—the name of an Irish goddess associated with wisdom—has the qualities of common sense and practicality, traits that, in earlier centuries, it was believed women did not possess. In a world that is run according to conventions found in traditional folk tales, this particular young woman takes responsibility for her own destiny. Her father believes that she must be sacrificed to a dragon. However, recognizing the dragon's inherent stupidity, she devises a plan to destroy it. When an unsuitable suitor is presented, she uses the conventions to her advantage, creating impossible tasks in order to reveal him as a fraud. Imprisoned in a tower, she does not wait for a rescuing prince; instead, she saves a prince and escapes using his incredibly long hair as a ladder. Written in the late 1970s, near the end of the first major decade of the modern feminist movement, Jay Williams's story not only satirizes conventional portrayals of women in folktales but also implicitly criticizes the view of real women these stories embody.

*P*rincess Bedelia was as lovely as the moon shining upon a lake full of waterlilies. She was as graceful as a cat leaping. And she was also extremely practical.

When she was born, three fairies had come to her cradle to give her gifts as was usual in that country. The first fairy had given her beauty. The second had given her grace. But the third who was a wise old creature, had said, 'I give her common sense.'

'I don't think much of that gift,' said King Ludwig, raising his eyebrows. 'What good is common sense to a princess? All she needs is charm.'

Nevertheless, when Bedelia was eighteen years old, something happened which made the king change his mind.

A dragon moved into the neighbourhood. He settled in a dark cave on top of a mountain, and the first thing he did was to send a message to the king. 'I must have a princess to devour,' the message said, 'or I shall breathe out my fiery breath and destroy the kingdom.'

Sadly, King Ludwig called together his councillors and read them the message. 'Perhaps,' said the Prime Minister, 'we had better advertise for a knight to slay the dragon? That is what is generally done in these cases.'

'I'm afraid we haven't time,' answered the king. 'The dragon has only given us until tomorrow morning. There is no help for it. We shall have to send him the princess.' Princess Bedelia had come to the meeting because, as she said, she liked to mind her own business and this was certainly her business.

'Rubbish!' she said. 'Dragons can't tell the difference between princesses and anyone else. Use your common sense. He's just asking for me because he's a snob.'

'That may be so,' said her father, 'but if we don't send you along, he'll destroy the kingdom.'

'Right!' said Bedelia. 'I see I'll have to deal with this myself.' She left the council chamber. She got the largest and gaudiest of her state robes and stuffed it with straw, and tied it together with string. Into the centre of the bundle she packed about a hundred pounds of gunpowder. She got two strong young men to carry it up the mountain for her. She stood in front of the dragon's cave, and called, 'Come out! Here's the princess!'

The dragon came blinking and peering out of the darkness. Seeing the bright robe covered with gold and silver embroidery, and hearing Bedelia's voice, he opened his mouth wide.

At Bedelia's signal, the two young men swung the robe and gave it a good heave, right down the dragon's throat. Bedelia threw herself flat on the ground, and the two young men ran.

As the gunpowder met the flames inside the dragon, there was a tremendous explosion.

Bedelia got up, dusting herself off. 'Dragons,' she said, 'are not very bright.'

She left the two young men sweeping up the pieces, and she went back to the castle to have her geography lesson.

The lesson that morning was local geography. 'Our kingdom, Arapathia, is bounded on the north by Istven,' said the teacher. 'Lord Garp, the ruler of Istven, is old, crafty, rich, and greedy.' At that very moment, Lord Garp of Istven was arriving at the castle. Word of Bedelia's destruction of the dragon had reached him. 'That girl,' said he, 'is just the wife for me.' And he had come with a hundred finely-dressed courtiers and many presents to ask King Ludwig for her hand.

The king sent for Bedelia. 'My dear,' he said, clearing his throat nervously, 'just see who this is here.'

'I see. It's Lord Garp,' said Bedelia. She turned to go.

'He wants to marry you,' said the king.

Bedelia looked at Lord Garp. His face was like an old napkin, crumpled and wrinkled. It was covered with warts, as if someone had left crumbs on the napkin. He had only two teeth. Six long hairs grew from his chin, and none on his head. She felt like screaming.

However, she said, 'I'm very flattered. Thank you, Lord Garp. Just let me talk to my father in private for a minute.' When they had retired to a small room behind the throne, Bedelia said to the king, 'What will Lord Garp do if I refuse to marry him?'

'He is rich, greedy, and crafty,' said the king unhappily. 'He is also used to having his own way in everything. He will be insulted. He will probably declare war on us, and then there will be trouble.'

'Very well,' said Bedelia. 'We must be practical.'

She returned to the throne room. Smiling sweetly at Lord Garp, she said, 'My lord, as you know, it is customary for a princess to set tasks for anyone who wishes to marry her. Surely you wouldn't like me to break the custom. And you are bold and powerful enough, I know, to perform any task.'

'That is true,' said Lord Garp smugly, stroking the six hairs on his chin. 'Name your task.'

'Bring me,' said Bedelia, 'a branch from the Jewel Tree of Paxis.'

Lord Garp bowed, and off he went. 'I think,' said Bedelia to her father, 'that we have seen the last of him. For Paxis is a thousand miles away, and the Jewel Tree is guarded by lions, serpents, and wolves.'

But in two weeks, Lord Garp was back. With him he bore a chest, and from the chest he took a wonderful twig. Its bark was of rough gold. The leaves that grew from it were of fine silver. The twig was covered with blossoms, and each blossom had petals of mother-of-pearl and centres of sapphires, the colour of the evening sky.

Bedelia's heart sank as she took the twig. But then she said to herself, 'Use your common sense, my girl! Lord Garp never travelled two thousand miles in two weeks, nor is he the man to fight his way through lions, serpents, and wolves.'

She looked more carefully at the branch. Then she said, 'My lord, you know that the Jewel Tree of Paxis is a living tree, although it is all made of jewels.'

'Why, of course,' said Lord Garp. 'Everyone knows that.'

'Well,' said Bedelia, 'then why is it that these blossoms have no scent?'

Lord Garp turned red.

'I think,' Bedelia went on, 'that this branch was made by the jewellers of Istven, who are the best in the world. Not very nice of you, my lord. Some people might even call it cheating.'

Lord Garp shrugged. He was too old and rich to feel ashamed. But like many men used to having their own way, the more Bedelia refused him, the more he was determined to have her.

'Never mind all that,' he said. 'Set me another task. This time, I swear I will perform it.'

Bedelia sighed. 'Very well. Then bring me a cloak made from the skins of the salamanders who live in the Volcano of Scoria.'

Lord Garp bowed, and off he went. 'The Volcano of Scoria,' said Bedelia to her father, 'is covered with red-hot lava. It burns steadily with great flames, and pours out poisonous smoke so that no one can come within a mile of it.'

'You have certainly profited by your geography lessons,' said the king, with admiration.

Nevertheless, in a week, Lord Garp was back. This time, he carried a cloak that shone and rippled like all the colours of fire. It was made of scaly skins, stitched together with golden wire as fine as a hair; and each scale was red and orange and blue, like a tiny flame.

Bedelia took the splendid cloak. She said to herself, 'Use your head, miss! Lord Garp never climbed the red-hot slopes of the Volcano of Scoria.'

A fire was burning in the fireplace of the throne room. Bedelia hurled the cloak into it. The skins blazed up in a flash, blackened, and fell to ashes.

Lord Garp's mouth fell open. Before he could speak, Bedelia said, 'That cloak was a fake, my lord. The skins of salamanders who can live in the Volcano of Scoria wouldn't burn in a little fire like that one.'

Lord Garp turned pale with anger. He hopped up and down, unable at first to do anything but splutter.

'Ub—ub—ub!' he cried. Then, controlling himself, he said, 'So be it. If I can't have you, no one shall!'

He pointed a long, skinny finger at her. On the finger was a magic ring. At once, a great wind arose. It blew through the throne room. It sent King Ludwig flying one way and his guards the other. It picked up Bedelia and whisked her off through the air. When she could catch her breath and look about her, she found herself in a room at the top of a tower.

Bedelia peered out of the window. About the tower stretched an empty, barren plain. As she watched, a speck appeared in the distance. A plume of dust rose behind it. It drew nearer and became Lord Garp on horseback.

He rode to the tower and looked up at Bedelia. 'Aha!' he croaked. 'So you are safe and snug, are you? And will you marry me now?'

'Never,' said Bedelia, firmly.

'Then stay there until never comes,' snarled Lord Garp.

Away he rode.

For the next two days, Bedelia felt very sorry for herself. She sat wistfully by the window, looking out at the empty plain. When she was hungry, food appeared on the table. When she was tired, she lay down on the narrow cot and slept. Each day, Lord Garp rode by and asked if she had changed her mind, and each day she refused him. Her only hope was that, as so often happens in old tales, a prince might come riding by who would rescue her.

But on the third day, she gave herself a shake.

'Now, then, pull yourself together,' she said, sternly. 'If you sit waiting for a prince to rescue you, you may sit here forever. Be practical! If there's any rescuing to be done, you're going to have to do it yourself.'

She jumped up. There was something she had not yet done, and now she did it. She tried the door.

It opened.

Outside, were three other doors. But there was no sign of a stair, or anyway down from the top of the tower.

She opened two of the doors and found that they led into cells just like hers, but empty.

Behind the fourth door, however, lay what appeared to be a haystack.

From beneath it came the sound of snores. And between snores, a voice said, 'Sixteen million and twelve . . . *snore* . . . sixteen million and thirteen . . . *snore* . . . sixteen million and fourteen . . .'

Cautiously, she went closer. Then she saw that what she had taken for a haystack was in fact an immense pile of blond hair. Parting it, she found a young man, sound asleep.

As she stared, he opened his eyes. He blinked at her. 'Who—?' he said. Then he said, 'Sixteen million and fifteen,' closed his eyes, and fell asleep again.

Bedelia took him by the shoulder and shook him hard. He awoke, yawning, and tried to sit up. But the mass of hair made this difficult.

'What on earth is the matter with you?' Bedelia asked. 'Who are you?'

'I am Prince Perian,' he replied, 'the rightful ruler of—oh, dear, here I go again. Sixteen million and . . .' His eyes began to close.

Bedelia shook him again. He made a violent effort and managed to wake up enough to continue, '—of Istven. But Lord Garp has put me under a spell. I have to count sheep jumping over a fence, and this puts me to slee—ee—ee—'

He began to snore lightly.

'Dear me,' said Bedelia. 'I must do something.'

She thought hard. Then she pinched Perian's ear, and this woke him with a start. 'Listen,' she said. 'It's quite simple. It's all in your mind, you see. You are imagining the sheep jumping over the fence—No! Don't go to sleep again!'

'This is what you must do. Imagine them jumping backwards. As you do, count them backwards and when you get to one you'll be wide awake.'

The prince's eyes snapped open. 'Marvellous!' he said. 'Will it work?'

'It's bound to,' said Bedelia. 'For if the sheep going one way will put you to sleep, their going back again will wake you up.'

Hastily, the prince began to count, 'Six million and fourteen, six million and thirteen, six million and twelve . . .'

'Oh, my goodness,' cried Bedelia, 'count by hundreds, or you'll never get there.'

He began to gabble as fast as he could, and with each moment that passed, his eyes sparkled more brightly, his face grew livelier, and he seemed a little stronger, until at last, he shouted, 'Five, four, three, two, ONE!' and awoke completely.

He struggled to his feet, with a little help from Bedelia.

'Heavens!' he said. 'Look how my hair and beard have grown. I've been here for years. Thank you, my dear. Who are you, and what are you doing here?'

Bedelia quickly explained.

Perian shook his head. 'One more crime of Lord Garp's,' he said. 'We must escape and see that he is punished.'

'Easier said than done,' Bedelia replied. 'There is no stair in this tower, as far as I can tell, and the outside wall is much too smooth to climb.'

Perian frowned. 'This will take some thought,' he said. 'What we need is a long rope.'

'Use your common sense,' said Bedelia. 'We haven't any rope.'

Then her face brightened, and she clapped her hands. 'But we have your beard,' she laughed.

Perian understood at once, and chuckled. 'I'm sure it will reach almost to the ground,' he said. 'But we haven't any scissors to cut it off with.'

'That is so,' said Bedelia. 'Hang it out of the window and let me climb down. I'll search the tower and perhaps I can find a ladder, or a hidden stair. If all else fails, I can go for help.'

She and the prince gathered up great armfuls of the beard and staggered into Bedelia's room, which had the largest window. The prince's long hair trailed behind and nearly tripped him.

He threw the beard out of the window, and sure enough the end of it came to within a few feet of the ground.

Perian braced himself, holding the beard with both hands to ease the pull on his chin. Bedelia climbed out of the window and slid down the beard. She dropped to the ground and sat for a moment, breathless.

And as she sat there, out of the wilderness came the drumming of hoofs, a cloud of dust, and then Lord Garp on his swift horse.

With one glance, he saw what was happening. He shook his fist up at Prince Perian.

'Meddlesome fool!' he shouted. 'I'll teach you to interfere.'

He leaped from the horse and grabbed the beard. He gave it a tremendous yank. Headfirst came Perian, out of the window. Down he fell, and with a thump, he landed right on top of old Lord Garp.

This saved Perian, who was not hurt at all. But it was the end of Lord Garp.

Perian and Bedelia rode back to Istven on Lord Garp's horse.

In the great city, the prince was greeted with cheers of joy—once everyone had recognized him after so many years and under so much hair.

And of course, since Bedelia had rescued him from captivity, she married him. First, however, she made him get a haircut and a shave so that she could see what he really looked like.

For she was always practical.

———

From *The Practical Princess and Other Liberating Fairy Tales*, by Jay Williams (New York: Scholastic Book Services, 1978).

⚜

The Search for the Magic Lake

Told to the adaptor by Ecuadorian Indians who were the descendents of the original pre-contact tellers, this story reveals the influence of the culture of the Spanish conquerors on Native tales. Although the subject matter—including Inca rulers and the raising of llamas—is indigenous, the narrative includes many European motifs. These include the mysterious illness of the ruler's son, the promise of great rewards to the suppliers of a cure, the discovery of the deception of two claimants for that reward, the long and dangerous quest of an unlikely hero, and the importance of a special, almost magical substance. In spite of her age and gender, the heroine is successful in saving both her brothers and the king's son because of her courage and consideration of others. Unlike female heroes in similar European tales, she is not rewarded with marriage into the royal family. In Inca society, the imperial family married among themselves. The emperor's gift of land and llamas, however, would have socially elevated the girl's originally poor family.

*L*ong ago there was a ruler of the vast Inca Empire who had an only son. This youth brought great joy to his father's heart but also a sadness, for the prince had been born in ill health.

As the years passed the prince's health did not improve, and none of the court doctors could find a cure for his illness.

One night the aged emperor went down on his knees and prayed at the altar.

'O Great Ones,' he said, 'I am getting older and will soon leave my people and join you in the heavens. There is no one to look after them but my son, the prince. I pray you make him well and strong so he can be a fit ruler for my people. Tell me how his malady can be cured.'

The emperor put his head in his hands and waited for an answer. Soon he heard a voice coming from the fire that burned constantly in front of the altar.

'Let the prince drink water from the magic lake at the end of the world,' the voice said, 'and he will be well.'

At that moment the fire sputtered and died. Among the cold ashes lay a golden flask.

But the emperor was much too old to make the long journey to the end of the world, and the young prince was too ill to travel. So the emperor proclaimed that whosoever should fill the golden flask with the magic water would be greatly rewarded.

Many brave men set out to search for the magic lake, but none could find it. Days and weeks passed and still the flask remained empty.

In a valley, some distance from the emperor's palace, lived a poor farmer who had a wife, two grown sons, and a young daughter.

One day the older son said to his father, 'Let my brother and me join in the search for the magic lake. Before the moon is new again, we shall return and help you harvest the corn and potatoes.'

The father remained silent. He was not thinking of the harvest, but feared for his sons' safety.

When the father did not answer, the second son added, 'Think of the rich reward, Father!'

'It is their duty to go,' said his wife, 'for we must all try to help our emperor and the young prince.'

After his wife had spoken, the father yielded.

'Go if you must, but beware of the wild beasts and evil spirits,' he cautioned.

With their parents' blessing, and an affectionate farewell from their young sister, the sons set out on their journey.

They found many lakes, but none where the sky touched the water.

Finally the younger brother said, 'Before another day has passed we must return to help father with the harvest.'

'Yes,' agreed the other, 'but I have thought of a plan. Let us each carry a jar of water from any lake along the way. We can say it will cure the prince. Even if it doesn't, surely the emperor will give us a small reward for our trouble.'

'Agreed,' said the younger brother.

On arriving at the palace, the deceitful youths told the emperor and his court that they brought water from the magic lake. At once the prince was given a sip from each of the brothers' jars, but of course he remained as ill as before.

'Perhaps the water must be sipped from the golden flask,' one of the high priests said.

But the golden flask would not hold the water. In some mysterious way, the water from the jars disappeared as soon as it was poured into the flask.

In despair the emperor called for his magician and said to him, 'Can you break the spell of the flask so the water will remain for my son to drink?'

'I cannot do that, your majesty,' replied the magician. 'But, I believe,' he added wisely, 'that the flask is telling us that we have been deceived by the two brothers. The flask can be filled only with water from the magic lake.'

When the brothers heard this they trembled with fright, for they knew their falsehood was discovered.

So angry was the emperor that he ordered the brothers thrown into chains. Each day they were forced to drink water from their jars as a reminder of their false deed. News of their disgrace spread far and wide.

Again the emperor sent messengers throughout the land pleading for someone to bring the magic water before death claimed him and the young prince.

Súmac, the little sister of the deceitful youths, was tending her flock of llamas when she heard the sound of the royal trumpet. Then came the voice of the emperor's servant with his urgent message from the court.

Quickly the child led her llamas home and begged her parents to let her go in search of the magic water.

'You are too young,' her father said. 'Besides, look at what has already befallen your brothers. Some evil spirit must have taken hold of them to make them tell such a lie.'

And her mother said, 'We could not bear to be without our precious Súmac!'

'But think how sad our emperor will be if the young prince dies,' replied the innocent child. 'And if I can find the magic lake, perhaps the emperor will forgive my brothers and send them home.'

'Dear husband,' said Súmac's mother, 'maybe it is the will of the gods that we let her go.'

Once again the father gave his permission.

'It is true,' he murmured, 'I must think of our emperor.'

Súmac was overjoyed, and went skipping out to the corral to harness one of her pet llamas. It would carry her provisions and keep her company.

Meanwhile her mother filled a little woven bag with food and drink for Súmac—toasted golden kernels of corn and a little earthen jar of *chicha*, a beverage made from crushed corn.

The three embraced each other tearfully before Súmac set out bravely on her mission, leading her pet llama along the trail.

The first night she slept, snug and warm against her llama, in the shelter of a few rocks. But when she heard the hungry cry of the puma, she feared for her pet animal and bade it return safely home.

The next night she spent in the top branches of a tall tree, far out of reach of the dreadful puma. She hid her provisions in a hole in the tree trunk.

At sunrise she was aroused by the voices of gentle sparrows resting on a nearby limb.

'Poor child,' said the oldest sparrow, 'she can never find her way to the lake.'

'Let us help her,' chorused the others.

'Oh please do!' implored the child, 'and forgive me for intruding in your tree.'

'We welcome you,' chirped another sparrow, 'for you are the same little girl who yesterday shared your golden corn with us.'

'We shall help you,' continued the first sparrow, who was the leader, 'for you are a good child. Each of us will give you a wing feather, and you must hold them all together in one hand as a fan. The feathers have magic powers that will carry you wherever you wish to go. They will also protect you from harm.'

Each sparrow then lifted a wing, sought out a special feather hidden underneath, and gave it to Súmac. She fashioned them into the shape of a little fan, taking the ribbon from her hair to bind the feathers together so none would be lost.

'I must warn you,' said the oldest sparrow, 'that the lake is guarded by three terrible creatures. But have no fear. Hold the magic fan up to your face and you will be unharmed.'

Súmac thanked the birds over and over again. Then, holding up the fan in her chubby hands, she said politely, 'Please, magic fan, take me to the lake at the end of the world.'

A soft breeze swept her out of the top branches of the tree and through the valley. Then up she was carried, higher and higher into the sky, until she could look down and see the great mountain peaks covered with snow.

At last the wind put her down on the shore of a beautiful lake. It was, indeed, the lake at the end of the world, for, on the opposite side from where she stood, the sky came down so low it touched the water.

Súmac tucked the magic fan into her waistband and ran to the edge of the water. Suddenly her face fell. She had left everything back in the forest. What could she use for carrying the precious water back to the prince?

'Oh, I do wish I had remembered the jar!' she said, weeping.

Suddenly she heard a soft thud in the sand at her feet. She looked down and discovered a beautiful golden flask—the same one the emperor had found in the ashes.

Súmac took the flask and kneeled at the water's edge. Just then a hissing voice behind her said, 'Get away from my lake or I shall wrap my long, hairy legs around your neck.'

Sumac turned around. There stood a giant crab as large as a pig and as black as night.

With trembling hands the child took the magic fan from her waistband and spread it open in front of her face. As soon as the crab looked at it, he closed his eyes and fell down on the sand in a deep sleep.

Once more Súmac started to fill the flask. This time she was startled by a fierce voice bubbling up from the water.

'Get away from my lake or I shall eat you,' gurgled a giant green alligator. His long tail beat the water angrily.

Súmac waited until the creature swam closer. Then she held up the fan. The alligator blinked. He drew back. Slowly, quietly, he sank to the bottom of the lake in a sound sleep.

Before Súmac could recover from her fright, she heard a shrill whistle in the air. She looked up and saw a flying serpent. His skin was red as blood. Sparks flew from his eyes.

'Get away from my lake or I shall bite you,' hissed the serpent as it batted its wings around her head.

Again Súmac's fan saved her from harm. The serpent closed his eyes and drifted to the ground. He folded his wings and coiled up on the sand. Then he began to snore.

Súmac sat for a moment to quiet herself. Then, realizing that the danger was past, she sighed with great relief.

'Now I can fill the golden flask and be on my way,' she said to herself.

When this was done, she held the flask tightly in one hand and clutched the fan in the other.

'Please take me to the palace,' she said.

Hardly were the words spoken, when she found herself safely in front of the palace gates. She looked at the tall guard.

'I wish to see the emperor,' Súmac uttered in trembling tones.

'Why, little girl?' the guard asked kindly.

'I bring water from the magic lake to cure the prince.'

The guard looked down at her in astonishment.

'Come!' he commanded in a voice loud and deep as thunder.

In just a few moments Súmac was led into a room full of sadness. The emperor was pacing up and down in despair. The prince lay motionless on a huge bed. His eyes were closed and his face was without colour. Beside him knelt his mother, weeping.

Without wasting words, Súmac went to the prince and gave him a few drops of magic water. Soon he opened his eyes. His cheeks became flushed. It was not long before he sat up in bed. He drank same more.

'How strong I feel!' the prince cried joyfully.

The emperor and his wife embraced Súmac. Then Súmac told them of her adventurous trip to the lake. They praised her courage. They marvelled at the reappearance of the golden flask and at the powers of the magic fan.

'Dear child,' said the emperor, 'all the riches of my empire are not enough to repay you for saving my son's life. Ask what you will and it shall be yours.'

'Oh, generous emperor,' said Súmac timidly, 'I have but three wishes.'

'Name them and they shall be yours,' urged the emperor.

'First, I wish my brothers to be free to return to my parents. They have learned their lesson and will never be false again. I know they were only thinking of a reward for my parents. Please forgive them.'

'Guards, free them at once!' ordered the emperor.

'Secondly, I wish the magic fan returned to the forest so the sparrows may have their feathers again.'

This time the emperor had no time to speak. Before anyone in the room could utter a sound, the magic fan lifted itself up, spread itself wide open, and floated out the window towards the woods. Everyone watched in amazement. When the fan was out of sight, they applauded.

'What is your last wish, dear Súmac?' asked the queen mother.

'I wish that my parents be given a large farm and great flocks of llamas, vicuñas, and alpacas, so they will not be poor any longer.'

'It will be so,' said the emperor, 'but I am sure your parents never considered themselves poor with so wonderful a daughter.'

'Won't you stay with us in the palace?' ventured the prince.

'Yes, stay with us!' urged the emperor and his wife. 'We will do everything to make you happy.'

'Oh thank you,' said Súmac blushing happily, 'but I must return to my parents and to my brothers. I miss them as I know they have missed me. They do not even know I am safe, for I came directly to your palace.'

The royal family did not try to detain Súmac any longer.

'My own guard will see that you get home safely', said the emperor.

When she reached home, she found that all she had wished for had come to pass: her brothers were waiting for her with their parents; a beautiful house and huge barn were being constructed; her father had received a deed granting him many acres of new, rich farmland.

Súmac ran into the arms of her happy family.

At the palace, the golden flask was never empty. Each time it was used, it was refilled. Thus the prince's royal descendants never suffered ill health and the kingdom remained strong.

But it is said that when the Spanish conqueror of the ancient Incas demanded a room filled with golden gifts, the precious flask was among them. Whatever happened to this golden treasure is unknown, for the conqueror was killed and the Indians wandered over the mainland in search of a new leader. Some say the precious gifts—including the golden flask—are buried at the bottom of the lake at the end of the world, but no one besides Súmac has ever ventured to go there.

From *Best Loved Folktales of the World*, selected by Joanna Cole (Garden City, New York: Anchor Press/Doubleday, 1982). Reprinted from *Latin American Tales*, by Genevieve Barlow, 1966.

The Fly

Many Chinese and Vietnamese folktales deal with the defeat of a powerful figure who uses his authority to bully those who are poor, weak, or socially inferior. In this story, the usurer, who has acquired great wealth because of the exorbitant interest he charges, is not content and wishes to gain more wealth. To achieve this, he often bullies his unfortunate debtors to exhort payments. The object of his bullying in this story is a small child whose cleverness is not recognized by the adults until the story's conclusion. His skill is with words: he knows when to be silent, when to speak in riddles, and when to lie to achieve his ends. The double irony arises from the fact that the powerful adult is beaten at his own game by the child he considered powerless. The boy has been able to save his parents from a man against whom they had no defense.

Everyone in the village knew the usurer, a rich and smart man. Having accumulated a fortune over the years, he settled down to a life of leisure in his big house surrounded by an immense garden and guarded by a pack of ferocious dogs. But still unsatisfied with what he had acquired, the man went on making money by lending it to people all over the county at exorbitant rates. The usurer reigned supreme in the area, for numerous were those who were in debt to him.

One day, the rich man set out for the house of one of his peasants. Despite repeated reminders, the poor labourer just could not manage to pay off his long-standing debt. Working himself to a shadow, the peasant barely succeeded in making ends meet. The moneylender was therefore determined that if he could not get his money back this time, he would proceed to confiscate some of his debtor's most valuable belongings. But the rich man found no one at the peasant's house but a small boy of eight or nine playing alone in the dirt yard.

'Child, are your parents home?' the rich man asked.

'No, sir,' the boy replied, then went on playing with his sticks and stones, paying no attention whatever to the man.

'Then, where are they?' the rich man asked, somewhat irritated, but the little boy went on playing and did not answer.

When the rich man repeated his query, the boy looked up, and answered, with deliberate slowness, 'Well, sir, my father has gone to cut living trees and plant dead ones and my mother is at the market place selling the wind and buying the moon.'

'What? What in heaven are you talking about?' the rich man commanded. 'Quick, tell me where they are, or you will see what this stick can do to you!' The bamboo walking stick in the big man's hand looked indeed menacing.

After repeated questioning, however, the boy only gave the same reply. Exasperated, the rich man told him, 'All right, little devil, listen to me! I came here today to take the money your parents owe me. But if you tell me where they really are and what they are doing, I will forget all about the debt. Is that clear to you?'

'Oh, sir, why are you joking with a poor little boy? Do you expect me to believe what you are saying?' For the first time the boy looked interested.

'Well, there is heaven and there is earth to witness my promise,' the rich man said, pointing up to the sky and down to the ground.

But the boy only laughed. 'Sir, heaven and earth cannot talk and therefore cannot testify. I want some living thing to be our witness.'

Catching sight of a fly alighting on a bamboo pole nearby, and laughing inside because he was fooling the boy, the rich man proposed, 'There is a fly. He can be our witness. Now, hurry and tell me what you mean when you say that your father is out cutting living trees and planting dead ones, while your mother is at the market selling the wind and buying the moon.'

Looking at the fly on the pole, the boy said, 'A fly is a good enough witness for me. Well, here it is, sir. My father has simply gone to cut down bamboos and make a fence with them for a man near the river. And my mother . . . oh, sir, you'll keep your promise, won't you? You will free my parents of all their debts? You really mean it?'

'Yes, yes, I do solemnly swear in front of this fly here.' The rich man urged the boy to go on.

'Well, my mother, she has gone to the market to sell fans so she can buy oil for our lamps. Isn't that what you would call selling the wind to buy the moon?'

Shaking his head, the rich man had to admit inwardly that the boy was a clever one. However, he thought, the little genius still had much to learn, believing as he did that a fly could be a witness for anybody. Bidding the boy good-by, the man told him that he would soon return to make good his promise.

A few days had passed when the moneylender returned. This time he found the poor peasant couple at home, for it was late in the evening. A nasty scene ensued, the rich man claiming his money and the poor peasant apologizing and begging for another delay. Their argument awakened the little boy who ran to his father and told him, 'Father, father, you don't have to pay your debt. This gentleman here has promised me that he would forget all about the money you owe him.'

'Nonsense,' the rich man shook his walking stick at both father and son. 'Nonsense, are you going to stand there and listen to a child's inventions? I never spoke a word to this boy. Now, tell me, are you going to pay or are you not?'

The whole affair ended by being brought before the mandarin who governed the county. Not knowing what to believe, all the poor peasant and his wife could do was to bring their son with them when they went to court. The little boy's insistence about the rich man's promise was their only encouragement.

The mandarin began by asking the boy to relate exactly what had happened between himself and the moneylender. Happily, the boy hastened to tell about the explanations he gave the rich man in exchange for the debt.

'Well,' the mandarin said to the boy, 'if this man here has indeed made such a promise, we have only your word for it. How do we know that you have not invented the whole story yourself? In a case such as this, you need a witness to confirm it, and you have none.' The boy remained calm and declared that naturally there was a witness to their conversation.

'Who is that, child?' the mandarin asked.

'A fly, Your Honour.'

'A fly? What do you mean, a fly? Watch out, young man, fantasies are not to be tolerated in this place!' The mandarin's benevolent face suddenly became stern.

'Yes, Your Honour, a fly. A fly which was alighting on this gentleman's nose!' The boy leapt from his seat.

'Insolent little devil, that's a pack of lies!' The rich man roared indignantly, his face like a ripe tomato. 'The fly was not on my nose; he was on the housepole . . .' But he stopped dead. It was, however, too late.

The majestic mandarin himself could not help bursting out laughing. Then the audience burst out laughing. The boy's parents too, although timidly, laughed. And the boy, and the rich man himself, also laughed. With one hand on his stomach, the mandarin waved the other hand toward the rich man:

'Now, now, that's all settled. You have indeed made your promises, dear sir, to the child. *Housepole or no housepole, your conversation did happen after all!* The court says you must keep your promise.'

And still chuckling, he dismissed all parties.

From *The Toad is the Emperor's Uncle: Animal Folktales from Viet-Nam*, told and illustrated by Vo-Dinh (Garden City, New York: Doubleday, 1970).

How the Tortoise Got His Shell

This story, originally collected by David Unaipon, a member of the southern Australian Nagarrindjeri tribe, is a version of a story told around the world: the explanation of the origin of the tortoise's shell. The unlikely hero of the tale—old, slow, and generally mocked by others—succeeds where more apparently capable birds and animals fail. As in many stories in which a group seeks an essential object or substance, such as fire or, in this case, food, the object is protected by a clever and dangerous adversary. The tortoise's opponent is a willy-wagtail, a small, quickly moving bird that is a trickster in many Australian folktales. The tortoise, though much slower, proves to be wiser, killing the bird and thereby saving the members of his group. His reward is the right to wear in perpetuity the curved shell like the one he carved from the wood of the coolamon tree. People seeing the shell are reminded of the story and the virtues it embodies: selflessness, cleverness, and humility.

Long, long ago all the bush birds and animals lived in a big, deep valley that was hemmed in on every side by high, rough hills. Food had become very scarce, and all the birds and animals held a special meeting to discuss how it could be procured. They all talked and talked, but they came to no decision as to how to obtain more food. At last the tortoise rose to speak, and all the animals laughed. Everybody made fun of the tortoise, for he was so slow and ungainly; and everybody looked upon him as a fool, because he was always either asleep or sleepy. However, the tortoise proposed that the big eagle-hawk, the fierce king of birds, who was a great hunter, should fly over the ranges and find food. 'Oh, yes,' said the big eagle-hawk; and away he flew.

When the eagle-hawk had gone a long way over on the other side of the ranges he saw a beautiful country full of all kinds of food, but he saw no birds or animals there, except one little willy-wagtail. So the eagle-hawk said to the little willy-wagtail, 'May I fetch my brothers and sisters, who are starving, into this beautiful country of yours?' 'Oh, yes,' said the willy-wagtail, 'but you must wrestle with me first.'

Of course, the big, strong eagle-hawk thought this was easy, but the cunning little willy-wagtail had placed some sharp fish-bones like spikes in the ground where he proposed that they should wrestle. When they began to wrestle the willy-wagtail was very quick and nimble, and hopped and jumped about just as he does to-day. Suddenly the willy-wagtail tripped up the eagle-hawk, who fell among the sharp spikes and was pinned to the ground, where he was at the mercy of the willy-wagtail, who at once pecked him to death.

Meantime, all the other birds and animals over the ranges waited for the eagle-hawk to return. By and by they became tired of waiting, and they sent out the kite-hawk. But the kite-hawk met the same fate as the eagle-hawk. Then the magpie, the wombat, the dingo, and others were sent out in turn, but the wicked little willy-wagtail tripped them all on to his spikes, and then pecked them to death. All the birds and animals became very much alarmed, because none returned.

At last the position became serious, for food had to be found somewhere. Then the old tortoise volunteered to go. He went away, crawling slowly and painfully, over the ranges and into the land of the willy-wagtail. As usual the willy-wagtail invited his visitor to wrestle.

'Oh, yes, willingly,' replied the tortoise, 'but just wait a while.' The tortoise went into the bush, and cut a *coolamon* and a thick strip of bark out of a gum-tree. The tortoise placed the *coolamon* on his back, and he tied on the thick sheet of bark as a breastplate; then he went to wrestle with the willy-wagtail.

The quick, lively willy-wagtail hopped round and soon tripped up the slow old tortoise, who, when he fell on the spikes, was protected by the *coolamon*. Again and again the willy-wagtail threw the tortoise, but he was always saved either by the *coolamon* on his back or by his bark breastplate. After a while the willy-wagtail became exhausted, and then the tortoise was able to catch and kill the cunning little bird.

Of course the tortoise let all the birds and animals know as quickly as he could where there was plenty of food. What the eagle-hawk, the dingo, the kangaroo, and all the other animals failed to accomplish by main force the slow moving old tortoise achieved through wisdom and cunning, and to this day he is allowed to carry the *coolamon* and the breastplate as a memorial of a great victory in overcoming a cunning and wicked enemy. He is to be seen during the long years of his lifetime seeking no applause, but humbly bearing his shield of service.

From *Myths and Legends of the Australian Aboriginals*, by W. Ramsay Smith (London: George G. Harrap & Company, 1930).

The Adventures of Little Peachling

Adapted by Lord Redesdale, a nineteenth-century British official posted in Japan, the story of Momotaro—Little Peachling—is one of the best-known Japanese hero narratives. The tale's elements bear resemblance to stories from other cultures. The hero has a mysterious birth: he is born out of a peach, hence his name: Momo—meaning peach—and Taro, son. He becomes the child of an old, poor, and heretofore childless couple; leaves to prove himself on a long, hazardous journey; acquires, because of his generosity, a number of companions; and defeats a dangerous enemy acquiring its ill-begotten wealth. In spite of its similarities to tales of other lands, 'The Adventures of Little Peachling' embodies Japanese cultural values and uses details that have symbolic significance for Japanese audiences. For example, the hero returns to his family, bringing them wealth and happiness. His acquisition of companions illustrates the value of cooperation. This cooperation is seen in the fact that two of his companions are an ape and a dog, which, in Japan, are traditionally depicted as enemies. Additionally, in Japanese culture apes symbolized wisdom; dogs, loyalty; and pheasants, protectiveness. Momotaro acquires these virtues and, as such, is able to be a benefactor to his aging parents. The peach is a Japanese symbol for fertility and good fortune.

Many hundred years ago there lived an honest old woodcutter and his wife. One fine morning the old man went off to the hills with his billhook, to gather a faggot of sticks, while his wife went down to the river to wash the dirty clothes. When she came to the river, she saw a peach floating down the stream; so she picked it up, and carried it home with her, thinking to give it to her husband to eat when he should come in. The old man

From Lord Redesdale, *Tales of Old Japan*. (London: Macmillan, 1908), 185.

soon came down from the hills, and the good wife set the peach before him, when, just as she was inviting him to eat it, the fruit split in two, and a little puling baby was born into the world. So the old couple took the babe, and brought it up as their own; and, because it had been born in a peach, they called it *Momotarô*[1] or Little Peachling.

By degrees Little Peachling grew up to be strong and brave, and at last one day he said to his old foster-parents—

'I am going to the ogres' island to carry off the riches that they have stored up there. Pray, then, make me some millet dumplings for my journey.'

So the old folks ground the millet, and made the dumplings for him; and Little Peachling, after taking an affectionate leave of them, cheerfully set out on his travels.

As he was journeying on, he fell in with an ape, who gibbered at him, and said, 'Kia! kia! kia! where are you off to, Little Peachling?'

'I'm going to the ogres' island, to carry off their treasure,' answered Little Peachling.

'What are you carrying at your girdle?'

'I'm carrying the very best millet dumplings in all Japan.'

'If you'll give me one, I will go with you,' said the ape. So Little Peachling gave one of his dumplings to the ape, who received it and followed him. When he had gone a little further, he heard a pheasant calling—

'Ken! ken! ken![2] where are you off to, Master Peachling?'

Little Peachling answered as before; and the pheasant, having begged and obtained a millet dumpling, entered his service, and followed him. A little while after this, they met a dog, who cried—

1. Momo means a peach, and Tarô is the termination of the names of eldest sons, as Hikotarô, Tokutarô, etc. In modern times, however, the termination has been applied indifferently to any male child.
2. The country folk in Japan pretend that the pheasant's call is a sign of an approaching earthquake.

'Bow! wow! wow! whither away, Master Peachling?'

'I'm going off to the ogres' island, to carry off their treasure.'

'If you will give me one of those nice millet dumplings of yours, I will go with you,' said the dog.

'With all my heart,' said Little Peachling. So he went on his way, with the ape, the pheasant, and the dog following after him.

When they got to the ogres' island, the pheasant flew over the castle gate, and the ape clambered over the castle wall, while Little Peachling, leading the dog, forced in the gate, and got into the castle. Then they did battle with the ogres, and put them to flight, and took their king prisoner. So all the ogres did homage to Little Peachling, and brought out the treasures which they had laid up. There were caps and coats that made their wearers invisible, jewels which governed the ebb and flow of the tide, coral, musk, emeralds, amber, and tortoiseshell, besides gold and silver. All these were laid before Little Peachling by the conquered ogres.

So Little Peachling went home laden with riches, and maintained his foster-parents in peace and plenty for the remainder of their lives.

———

From *Tales of Old Japan*, by Lord Redesdale (London: Macmillan, 1908).

Thumbelina

In creating the story about Thumbelina, one of his best-known heroines, Danish author Hans Christian Andersen drew on many of the elements of traditional European folklore. The vulnerable, tiny heroine has a mysterious birth; she is soon 'orphaned' and begins a long and dangerous journey; she is helped by a bird and, after having passed a series of tests, marries a prince. Only at the story's conclusion does Thumbelina relate to someone her own size; throughout the story she has been surrounded by frightening, often large, and frequently controlling individuals. Andersen used settings, characters, and objects symbolically in presenting the story's conflicts. Born out of a flower, the heroine is associated with daylight, summer, flowers, and birds. Two of her adversaries—the toad and mole, who are also suitors—are creatures of darkness, living below the earth. The mole, in particular, dislikes daylight and birds and plans for a late fall marriage. Because of her courage, consideration, and life-giving qualities, the heroine finally arrives at a paradise of flowers, a land of perpetual spring and summer. She receives an appropriate new name and literally, as well as symbolically, 'earns her wings'.

There was once a woman who wanted to have quite a tiny, little child, but she did not know where to get one from. So one day she went to an old witch and said to her:

'I should so much like to have a tiny, little child. Can you tell me where I can get one?'

'Oh, we have just got one ready!' said the witch. 'Here is a barleycorn for you, but it's not the kind the farmer sows in his field or feeds the cocks and hens with, I can tell you. Put it in a flower-pot, and then you will see something happen.'

'Oh, thank you!' said the woman, and gave the witch a shilling, for that was what it cost. Then she went home and planted the barleycorn. Immediately there grew out of it a large and beautiful flower which looked like a tulip, but the petals were tightly closed as if it were still only a bud.

'What a beautiful flower!' exclaimed the woman, and she kissed the red and yellow petals; but as she kissed them the flower burst open. It was a real tulip, such as one can see any day, but in the middle of the blossom, on the green velvety petals, sat a little girl, quite tiny, trim, and pretty. She was scarcely half a thumb in height, so they called her Thumbelina. An elegant polished walnutshell served Thumbelina as a cradle, the blue petals of a violet were her mattress, and a rose-leaf her coverlid. There she lay at night, but in the day-time she used to play about on the table. Here the woman had put a bowl, surrounded by a ring of flowers, with their stalks in water, in the middle of which floated a great tulip petal, and on this Thumbelina sat and sailed from one side of the bowl to the other, rowing herself with two white horsehairs for oars. It was such a pretty sight! She could sing, too, with a voice more soft and sweet than had ever been heard before.

One night, when she was lying in her pretty little bed, an old toad crept in through a broken pane in the window. She was very ugly, clumsy, and clammy; she hopped on to the table where Thumbelina lay asleep under the red roseleaf.

'This would make a beautiful wife for my son,' said the toad, taking up the walnut-shell, with Thumbelina inside, and hopping with it through the window into the garden.

There flowed a great wide stream, with slippery and marshy banks; here the toad lived with her son. Ugh! how ugly and clammy he was, just like his mother! 'Croak! croak! croak!' was all he could say when he saw the pretty little girl in the walnut-shell.

'Don't talk so loud or you'll wake her,' said the old toad. 'She might escape us even now; she is as light as a feather. We will put her at once on a broad water-lily leaf in the stream. That will be quite an island for her; she is so small and light. She can't run away from us there while we are preparing the guest-chamber under the marsh where she shall live.'

Outside in the brook grew many water-lilies, with broad green leaves, which looked as if they were swimming about on the water. The leaf furthest away was the largest, and to this the old toad swam with Thumbelina in her walnut-shell.

The tiny Thumbelina woke up very early in the morning, and when she saw where she was she began to cry bitterly; for on every side of the great green leaf was water, and she could not get to the land.

The old toad was down under the marsh decorating her room with rushes and yellow marigold leaves, to make it very grand for her new daughter-in-law; then she swam out with her ugly son to the leaf where Thumbelina lay. She wanted to fetch the pretty cradle to put it into her room before Thumbelina herself came there. The old toad bowed low in the water before her and said: 'Here is my son; you shall marry him and live in great magnificence down under the marsh.'

'Croak! croak! croak!' was all that the son could say. Then they took the neat little cradle and swam away with it; but Thumbelina sat alone on the great green leaf and wept, for she did not want to live with the clammy toad or marry her ugly son. The little fishes swimming about under the water had seen the toad quite plainly and heard what she had said, so they put up their heads to see the little girl. When they saw her they thought her so pretty that they were very sorry she should go down with the ugly toad to live. No, that must not happen. They assembled in the water round the green stalk which supported the leaf on which she was sitting and nibbled the stem in two. Away floated the leaf down the stream, bearing Thumbelina far beyond the reach of the toad.

Thumbelina rides on the waterlily-leaf

From Andrew Lang, *The Yellow Fairy Book*. Illustrated by H.J. Ford. (London: A.L. Burt, 1894), 300.

On she sailed past several towns, and the little birds sitting in the bushes saw her and sang: 'What a pretty little girl!' The leaf floated further and further away; thus Thumbelina left her native land.

A beautiful little white butterfly fluttered above her and at last settled on the leaf. Thumbelina pleased him, and she, too, was delighted, for now the toads could not reach her, and it was so beautiful where she was traveling; the sun shone on the water and made it sparkle like the brightest silver. She took off her sash and tied one end round the butterfly; the other end she fastened to the leaf so that now it glided along with her faster than ever.

A great cockchafer came flying past. He caught sight of Thumbelina, and in a moment had put his arms round her slender waist and had flown off with her to a tree. The green leaf floated away down the stream, and the butterfly with it, for he was fastened to the leaf and could not get loose from it. Oh, dear! how terrified poor little Thumbelina was when the cockchafer flew off with her to the tree! But she was especially distressed on the beautiful white butterfly's account, as she had tied him fast, so that if he could not get away he must starve to death. But the cockchafer did not trouble himself about that. He sat down with her on a large green leaf, gave her the honey out of the flowers to eat, and told her that she was very pretty, although she wasn't in the least like a cockchafer. Later on all the other cockchafers who lived in the same tree came to pay calls. They examined Thumbelina closely and remarked:

'Why, she has only two legs! How very miserable!'

'She has no feelers!' cried another.

'How ugly she is!' said all the lady chafers—and yet Thumbelina was really very pretty.

The cockchafer who had stolen her knew this very well, but when he heard all the ladies saying she was ugly, he began to think so too and would not keep her; she might go wherever she liked. So he flew down from the tree with her and put her on a daisy. There she sat and wept, because she was so ugly that the cockchafer would have nothing to do with her; and yet she was the most beautiful creature imaginable, so soft and delicate, like the loveliest rose-leaf.

The whole summer poor little Thumbelina lived alone in the great wood. She plaited a bed for herself of blades of grass and hung it up under a clover-leaf, so that she was protected from the rain; she gathered honey from the flowers for food and drank the dew on the leaves every morning. Thus the summer and autumn passed, but then came winter—the long, cold winter. All the birds who had sung so sweety about her had flown away; the trees shed their leaves, the flowers died; the great cloverleaf under which she had lived curled up, and nothing remained of it but the withered stalk. She was terribly cold, for her clothes were ragged and she herself was so small and thin. Poor little Thumbelina! she would surely be frozen to death. It began to snow, and every snowflake that fell on her was to her as a whole shovelful thrown on one of us, for we are so big, and she was only an inch high. She wrapped herself round in a dead leaf, but it was torn in the middle and gave her no warmth; she was trembling with cold.

Just outside the wood where she was now living lay a great corn-field. But the corn had been gone a long time; only the dry, bare stubble was left standing in the frozen ground. This made a forest for her to wander about in. All at once she came across the door of a fieldmouse who had a little hole under a corn-stalk. There the mouse lived warm and snug, with a store-room full of corn, a splendid kitchen, and dining-room. Poor little Thumbelina went up to the door and begged for a little piece of barley, for she had not had anything to eat for the last two days.

'Poor little creature!' said the field-mouse, for she was a kind-hearted old thing at the bottom. 'Come into my warm room and have some dinner with me.'

As Thumbelina pleased her she said: 'As far as I am concerned you may spend the winter with me; but you must keep my room clean and tidy and tell me stories, for I like that very much.'

And Thumbelina did all that the kind old field-mouse asked, and did it remarkably well too.

'Now I am expecting a visitor,' said the field-mouse. 'My neighbour comes to call on me once a week. He is in better circumstances than I am, has great big rooms, and wears a fine black-velvet coat. If you could only marry him you would be well provided for. But he is blind. You must tell him all the prettiest stories you know.'

But Thumbelina did not trouble her head about him, for he was only a mole. He came and paid them a visit in his black-velvet coat.

'He is so rich and so accomplished,' the field-mouse told her. 'His house is twenty times larger than mine. He possesses great knowledge, but he cannot bear the sun and the beautiful flowers and speaks slightingly of them; for he has never seen them.'

Thumbelina had to sing to him, so she sang 'Lady-bird, lady-bird, fly way home!' and other songs so prettily that the mole fell in love with her; but he did not say anything—he was a very cautious man. A short time before he had dug a long passage through the ground from his own house to that of his neighbour; in this he gave the fieldmouse and Thumbelina permission to walk as often as they liked. But he begged them not to be afraid of the dead bird that lay in the passage: it was a real bird with beak and feathers, and must have died a little time ago, and now laid buried just where he had made his tunnel. The mole took a piece of rotten wood in his mouth, for that glows like fire in the dark, and went in front, lighting them through the long dark passage. When they came to the place where the dead bird lay the mole put his broad nose against the ceiling and pushed a hole through, so that the daylight could shine down. In the middle of the path lay a dead swallow, his pretty wings pressed close to his sides, his claws and head drawn under his feathers; the poor bird had evidently died of cold. Thumbelina was very sorry, for she was very fond of all little birds; they had sung and twittered so beautifully to her all through the summer. But the mole kicked him with his bandy legs and said:

'Now he can't sing any more! It must be very miserable to be a little bird! I'm thankful that none of my little children are. Birds always starve in winter.'

'Yes, you speak like a sensible man,' said the field-mouse. 'What has a bird, in spite of all his singing, in the winter time? He must starve and freeze, and that must be very pleasant for him, I must say!'

Thumbelina did not say anything; but when the other two had passed on she bent down to the bird, brushed aside the feathers from his head, and kissed his closed eyes gently. 'Perhaps it was he that sang to me so prettily in the summer,' she thought. 'How much pleasure he did give me, dear little bird!'

The mole closed up the hole again which let in the light and then escorted the ladies home. But Thumbelina could not sleep that night; so she got out of bed and plaited a great big blanket of straw, and carried it off and spread it over the dead bird, and piled upon it thistledown as soft as cotton-wool which she had found in the field-mouse's room, so that the poor little thing should lie warmly buried.

'Farewell, pretty little bird!' she said. 'Farewell, and thank you for your beautiful songs in the summer, when the trees were green and the sun shone down warmly on us!' Then she laid her head against the bird's heart. But the bird was not dead: be had been frozen, but now that she had warmed him he was coming to life again.

In autumn the swallows fly away to foreign lands, but there are some who are late in starting, and then they get so cold that they drop down as if dead, and the snow comes and covers them over.

Thumbelina trembled, she was so frightened, for the bird was very large in comparison with herself—only an inch high. But she took courage, piled up the down more closely over the poor swallow, and fetched her own coverlid and laid it over his head.

Next night she crept out again to him. There he was alive, but very weak. He could only open his eyes for a moment and look at Thumbelina, who was standing in front of him with a piece of rotten wood in her hand, for she had no other lantern.

'Thank you, pretty little child!' said the swallow to her. 'I am so beautifully warm! Soon I shall regain my strength, and then I shall be able to fly out again into the warm sunshine.'

'Oh!' she said, 'it is very cold outside; it is snowing and freezing! Stay in your warm bed; I will take care of you!'

Then she brought him water in a petal, which he drank, after which he related to her how he had torn one of his wings on a bramble, so that he could not fly as fast as the other swallows, who had flown far away to warmer lands. So at last he had dropped down exhausted, and then he could remember no more. The whole winter he remained down there, and Thumbelina looked after him and nursed him tenderly. Neither the mole nor the field-mouse learned anything of this, for they could not bear the poor swallow.

When the spring came and the sun warmed the earth again, the swallow said farewell to Thumbelina, who opened the hole in the roof for him which the mole had made. The sun shone brightly down upon her, and the swallow asked her if she would go with him; she could sit upon his back. Thumbelina wanted very much to fly far away into the greenwood, but she knew that the old field-mouse would be sad if she ran away.

'No, I mustn't come!' she said.

'Farewell, dear good little girl,' said the swallow, and flew off into the sunshine. Thumbelina gazed after him with the tears standing in her eyes, for she was very fond of the swallow.

'Tweet! tweet!' sang the bird, and flew into the greenwood. Thumbelina was very unhappy. She was not allowed to go out into the warm sunshine. The corn which had been sowed in the field over the field-mouse's home grew up high into the air, and made a thick forest for the poor little girl, who was only an inch high.

'Now you are to be a bride, Thumbelina!' said the field-mouse, 'for our neighbour has proposed for you! What a piece of fortune for a poor child like you! Now you must set to work at your linen for your dowry, for nothing must be lacking if you are to become the wife of our neighbour, the mole!'

Thumbelina had to spin all day long, and every evening the mole visited her and told her that when the summer was over the sun would not shine so hot; now it was burning the earth as hard as a stone. Yes, when the summer had passed they would keep the wedding.

But she was not at all pleased about it, for she did not like the stupid mole. Every morning when the sun was rising and every evening when it was setting she would steal out of the house door, and when the breeze parted the ears of corn so that she could see the blue sky through them, she thought how bright and beautiful it must be outside, and longed to see her dear swallow again. But he never came; no doubt he had flown away far into the great greenwood.

By the autumn Thumbelina had finished the dowry.

'In four weeks you will be married!' said the field-mouse. 'Don't be obstinate or I shall bite you with my sharp white teeth! You will get a fine husband! The king himself has not such a velvet coat. His store-room and cellar are full, and you should be thankful for that.'

Well, the wedding-day arrived. The mole had come to fetch Thumbelina to live with him deep down under the ground, never to come out into the warm sun again, for that was what he didn't like. The poor little girl was very sad, for now she must say good-by to the beautiful sun.

'Farewell, bright sun!' she cried, stretching out her arms toward it and taking another step outside the house, for now the corn had been reaped and only the dry stubble was left standing. 'Farewell! farewell!' she said, and put her arms round a little red flower that grew there. 'Give my love to the dear swallow when you see him!'

'Tweet! tweet!' sounded in her ear all at once. She looked up. There was the swallow flying past! As soon as he saw Thumbelina he was very glad. She told him how unwilling she was to marry the ugly mole, as then she had to live underground where the sun never shone, and she could not help bursting into tears.

'The cold winter is coming now,' said the swallow. 'I must fly away to warmer lands. Will you come with me? You can sit on my back, and we will fly far away from the ugly mole and his dark house, over the mountains to the warm countries where the sun shines more brightly than here, where it is always summer and there are always beautiful flowers. Do come with me, dear little Thumbelina, who saved my life when I lay frozen in the dark tunnel!'

'Yes, I will go with you,' said Thumbelina, and got on the swallow's back, with her feet on one of his outstretched wings. Up he flew into the air, over woods and seas, over the great mountains where the snow is always lying. And if she was cold she crept under his warm feathers, only keeping her little head out to admire all the beautiful things in the world beneath. At last they came to warm lands. There the sun was brighter, the sky seemed twice as high, and in the hedges hung the finest green and purple grapes; in the woods grew oranges and lemons; the air was scented with myrtle and mint, and on the roads were pretty little children running about and playing with great gorgeous butterflies. But the swallow flew on further, and it became more and more beautiful. Under the most splendid green trees beside a blue lake stood a glittering white marble castle. Vines hung about the high pillars; there were many swallows' nests, and in one of these lived the swallow who was carrying Thumbelina.

'Here is my house!' said he. 'But it won't do for you to live with me; I am not tidy enough to please you. Find a home for yourself in one of the lovely flowers that grow down there. Now I will set you down, and you can do whatever you like.'

'That will be splendid!' said she, clapping her little hands.

There lay a great white marble column which had fallen to the ground and broken into three pieces, but between these grew the most beautiful white flowers. The swallow flew down with Thumbelina and set her upon one of the broad leaves. But there, to her astonishment, she found a tiny little man sitting in the middle of the flower, as white and transparent as if he were made of glass. He had the prettiest golden crown on his head and the most beautiful wings on his shoulders; he himself was no bigger than Thumbelina. He was the spirit of the flower. In each blossom there dwelt a tiny man or woman; but this one was the king over the others.

'How handsome he is!' whispered Thumbelina to the swallow.

The little prince was very much frightened at the swallow, for in comparison with one so tiny as himself he seemed a giant. But when he saw Thumbelina he was delighted, for she was the most beautiful girl he had ever seen. So he took his golden crown from off his head and put it on hers, asking her her name and if she would be his wife, and then she would be queen of all the flowers. Yes! he was a different kind of husband to the son of the toad and the mole with the black-velvet coat. So she said 'Yes' to the noble prince. And out of each flower came a lady and gentleman, each so tiny and pretty that it was a pleasure to see them. Each brought Thmnbelina a present, but the best of all was a beautiful pair of wings which were fastened on to her back, and now she too could fly from flower to flower. They all wished her joy, and the swallow sat above in his nest and sang the wedding march, and that he did as well as he could: but he was sad because he was very fond of Thumbelina and did not want to be separated from her.

'You shall not be called Thumbelina!' said the spirit of the flower to her. 'That is an ugly name, and you are much too pretty for that. We will call you May Blossom.'

'Farewell! Farewell!' said the little swallow with a heavy heart, and flew away to further lands, far, far away, right back to Denmark. There be had a little nest above a window, where his wife lived, who can tell fairy-stories. 'Tweet! tweet!' he sang to her. And that is the way he learned the whole story.

From *The Yellow Fairy Book*, edited by Andrew Lang (London: A.L. Burt Company, [1894]).

The Valiant Chattee-Maker

During an 1865 trip through southern India with her colonial administrator father, Mary Frere recorded stories told by her native maid and travelling companion, Anna Liberata de Souza. The collection, the first in English of what she called 'Hindu Fairy Legends', went through many editions and was widely translated. 'The Valiant Chattee-Maker'—the adventures of a humble maker of pots—recounts the consequences of people's acting on the basis of rumour or misinformation. Although this theme is found around the world, the humour of this tale arises in part because it reveals a series of inversions of the highly ordered caste system of India. The tiger, the embodiment of power and fearlessness, and a regal emblem, is frightened of a humble man who has mistaken it for a donkey. The Chattee-Maker, a member of a lower caste, is elevated to the status of warrior because the actions in which he is involved are misinterpreted. This accidental hero, who is bumbling and fearful, must seek assistance from his wife.

Long long ago, in a violent storm of thunder, lightning, wind, and rain, a tiger crept for shelter close to the wall of an old woman's hut. This old woman was very poor, and her hut was but a tumble-down place, through the roof of which the rain came drip, drip, drip, on more sides than one. This troubled her much, and she went running about from side to side, dragging first one thing and then another out of the way of the leaky places in the roof, and as she did so, she kept saying to herself, 'Oh, dear! oh, dear! how tiresome this is! I'm sure the roof will come down! If an elephant, or a lion, or a tiger were to walk in, he wouldn't frighten me half as much as this perpetual dripping.' And then she would begin dragging the bed and all the other things in the room about again, to get them out of the way of the rain. The Tiger, who was crouching down just outside, heard all that she said, and thought to himself, 'This old woman says she would not be afraid of an elephant, or a lion, or a tiger, but that this perpetual dripping frightens her more than all. What can this "perpetual dripping" be? it must be something very dreadful.' And, hearing her immediately afterwards dragging all the things about the room again, he said to himself, 'What a terrible noise! Surely that must be the "*perpetual dripping*".'

At this moment a Chattee-maker,[1] who was in search of his donkey which had strayed away, came down the road. The night being very cold, he had, truth to say, taken a little more toddy[2] than was good for him, and seeing, by the light of a flash of lightning, a large animal lying down close to the old woman's hut, mistook it for the donkey he was looking for. So, running up to the Tiger, he seized hold of it by one ear, and commenced beating, kicking, and abusing it, with all his might and main. 'You wretched creature,' he cried, 'is this the way you serve me, obliging me to come out and look for you in such pouring rain, and on such a dark night as this? Get up instantly, or I'll break every bone in your body;' and he went on scolding and thumping the Tiger with his utmost power, for he had worked himself up into a terrible rage.

1. Potter.
2. An intoxicating drink made of palm juice.

The Tiger did not know what to make of it all, but he began to feel quite frightened, and said to himself, 'Why, this must be the "perpetual dripping"; no wonder the old woman said she was more afraid of it than of an elephant, a lion, or a tiger, for it gives most dreadfully hard blows.'

The Chattee-maker, having made the Tiger get up, got on his back, and forced him to carry him home, kicking and beating him the whole way (for all this time he fancied he was on his donkey), and then he tied his fore feet and his head firmly together, and fastened him to a post in front of his house, and when he had done this he went to bed.

Next morning, when the Chattee-maker's wife got up and looked out of the window, what did she see but a great big Tiger tied up in front of their house, to the post to which they usually fastened the donkey; she was very much surprised, and running to her husband, awoke him, saying, 'Do you know what animal you fetched home last night?' 'Yes, the donkey, to be sure,' he answered. 'Come and see,' said she, and she showed him the great Tiger tied to the post. The Chattee-maker at this was no less astonished than his wife, and felt himself all over to find out if the Tiger had not wounded him. But no! there he was, safe and sound, and there was the Tiger tied to the post, just as he had fastened it up the night before.

News of the Chattee-maker's exploit soon spread through the village, and all the people came to see him and hear him tell how he had caught the Tiger and tied it to the post; and this they thought so wonderful, that they sent a deputation to the Rajah, with a letter to tell him how a man of their village had, alone and unarmed, caught a great Tiger, and tied it to a post.

When the Rajah read the letter he also was much surprised, and determined to go in person and see this astonishing sight. So he sent for his horses and carriages, his lords and attendants, and they all set off together to look at the Chattee-maker and the Tiger he had caught.

Now the Tiger was a very large one, and had long been the terror of all the country round, which made the whole matter still more extraordinary; and this being represented to the Rajah, he determined to confer every possible honour on the valiant Chattee-maker. So he gave him houses and lands, and as much money as would fill a well, made him lord of his court, and conferred on him the command of ten thousand horse.

It came to pass, shortly after this, that a neighbouring Rajah, who had long had a quarrel with this one, sent to announce his intention of going instantly to war with him; and tidings were at the same time brought that the Rajah who sent the challenge had gathered a great army together on the borders, and was prepared at a moment's notice to invade the country.

In this dilemma no one knew what to do. The Rajah sent for all his generals, and inquired which of them would be willing to take command of his forces and oppose the enemy. They all replied that the country was so ill-prepared for the emergency, and the case was apparently so hopeless, that they would rather not take the responsibility of the chief command. The Rajah knew not whom to appoint in their stead. Then some of his people said to him, 'You have lately given command of ten thousand horse to the valiant Chattee-maker who caught the Tiger, why not make him Commander-in-Chief? A man who could catch a Tiger and tie him to a post must surely be more courageous and clever than most.' 'Very well,' said the Rajah, 'I will make him Commander-in-Chief.' So he sent for the Chattee-maker and said to him, 'In your hands I place all the power of the kingdom; you must put our enemies to flight.' 'So be it,' answered the Chattee-maker, 'but, before I lead the whole army against the enemy, suffer me to go by myself and examine their position; and, if possible, find out their numbers and strength.'

The Rajah consented, and the Chattee-maker returned home to his wife, and said, 'They have made me Commander-in-Chief, which is a very difficult post for me to fill, because I shall have to ride at the head of all the army, and you know I never was on a horse in my life. But I have succeeded in gaining a little delay, as the Rajah has given me permission to go first alone, and reconnoitre the enemy's camp. Do you, therefore, provide a very quiet pony, for you know I cannot ride, and I will start to-morrow morning.'

But, before the Chattee-maker had started, the Rajah sent over to him a most magnificent charger, richly caparisoned, which he begged he would ride when going to see the enemy's camp. The Chattee-maker was frightened almost out of his life, for the charger that the Rajah had sent him was very powerful and spirited, and he felt sure that, even if he ever got on it, he should very soon tumble off; however, he did not dare to refuse it, for fear of offending the Rajah by not accepting his present. So he sent him back a message of dutiful thanks, and said to his wife, 'I cannot go on the pony now that the Rajah has sent me this fine horse, but how am I ever to ride it?' 'Oh, don't be frightened,' she answered, 'you've only got to get upon it, and I will tie you firmly on, so that you cannot tumble off, and if you start at night no one will see that you are tied on.' 'Very well,' he said. So that night his wife brought the horse that the Rajah had sent him to the door. 'Indeed,' said the Chattee-maker, 'I can never get into that saddle, it is so high up.' 'You must jump,' said his wife. Then he tried to jump several times, but each time he jumped he tumbled down again. 'I always forget when I am jumping,' said he, 'which way I ought to turn.' 'Your face must be towards the horse's head,' she answered. 'To be sure, of course,' he cried, and giving one great jump he jumped into the saddle, but with his face towards the horse's tail. 'This won't do at all,' said his wife as she helped him down again; 'try getting on without jumping.' 'I never can remember,' he continued, 'when I have got my left foot in the stirrup, what to do with my right foot, or where to put it.' 'That must go in the other stirrup,' she answered; 'let me help you.' So, after many trials, in which he tumbled down very often, for the horse was fresh and did not like standing still, the Chattee-maker got into the saddle; but no sooner had he got there than he cried, 'Oh, wife, wife! tie me very firmly as quickly as possible, for I know I shall jump down if I can.' Then she fetched some strong rope and tied his feet firmly into the stirrups, and fastened one stirrup to the other, and put another rope round his waist, and another round his neck, and fastened them to the horse's body, and neck, and tail.

When the horse felt all these ropes about him he could not imagine what queer creature had got upon his back, and he began rearing, and kicking, and prancing, and at last set off full gallop, as fast as he could tear, right across country. 'Wife, wife,' cried the Chattee-maker, 'you forgot to tie my hands.' 'Never mind,' said she; 'hold on by the mane.' So he caught hold of the horse's mane as firmly as he could. Then away went horse, away went Chattee-maker, away, away, away, over hedges, over ditches, over rivers, over plains, away, away, like a flash of lightning, now this way, now that, on, on, on, gallop, gallop, gallop, until they came in sight of the enemy's camp. The Chattee-maker did not like his ride at all, and when he saw where it was leading him he liked it still less, for he thought the enemy would catch him and very likely kill him. So he determined to make one desperate effort to be free, and stretching out his hand as the horse shot past a young banyan tree, seized hold of it with all his might, hoping the resistance it offered might cause the ropes that tied him to break. But the horse was going at his utmost speed, and the soil in which the banyan tree grew was loose, so that when the Chattee-maker caught hold of it and gave it such a violent pull, it came up by the roots, and on he rode as fast as before, with the tree in his hand.

All the soldiers in the camp saw him coming, and having heard that an army was to be sent against them, made sure that the Chattee-maker was one of the vanguard. 'See,' cried they, 'here comes a man of gigantic stature on a mighty horse! He rides at full speed across the country, tearing up the very trees in his rage! He is one of the opposing force; the whole army must be close at hand. If they are such as he, we are all dead men.' Then, running to their Rajah, some of them cried again, 'Here comes the whole force of the enemy' (for the story had by this time become exaggerated), 'they are men of gigantic stature, mounted on mighty horses; as they come they tear up the very trees in their rage; we can oppose men, but not monsters such as these.' These were followed by others, who said, 'It is all true,' for by this time the Chattee-maker had got pretty near the camp, 'they're coming! they're coming! let us fly! let us fly! fly, fly for your lives!' And the whole panic-stricken multitude fled from the camp (those who had seen no cause for alarm going because the others did, or because they did not care to stay by themselves), after having obliged their Rajah to write a letter to the one whose country he was about to invade, to say that he would not do so, and propose terms of peace, and to sign it, and seal it with his seal. Scarcely had all the people fled from the camp, when the horse on which the Chattee-maker was came galloping into it, and on his back rode the Chattee-maker, almost dead from fatigue, with the banyan tree in his hand. Just as he reached the camp the ropes by which he was tied broke, and he fell to the ground. The horse stood still, too tired with his long run to go further. On recovering his senses, the Chattee-maker discovered, to his surprise, that the whole camp, full of rich arms, clothes, and trappings, was entirely deserted. In the principal tent, moreover, he found a letter addressed to his Rajah, announcing the retreat of the invading army, and proposing terms of peace.

So he took the letter, and returned home with it as fast as he could, leading his horse all the way, for he was afraid to mount him again. It did not take him long to reach his house by the direct road, for whilst riding he had gone a more circuitous journey than was necessary, and he got there just at nightfall. His wife ran out to meet him, overjoyed at his speedy return. As soon as he saw her, he said, 'Ah, wife, since I saw you last I've been all round the world, and had many wonderful and terrible adventures. But never mind that now, send this letter quickly to the Rajah by a messenger, and also the horse that he sent for me to ride. He will then see, by the horse looking so tired, what a long ride I've had, and if he is sent on beforehand, I shall not be obliged to ride him up to the palace-door to-morrow morning, as I otherwise should, and that would be very tiresome, for most likely I should tumble off.' So his wife sent the horse and the letter to the Rajah, and a message that her husband would be at the palace early next morning, as it was the late at night. And next day he went down there as he had said he would, and when the people saw him coming, they said, 'This man is as modest as he is brave after having put our enemies to flight, he walks quite simply to the door, instead of riding here in state, as any other man would.' [For they did not know that the Chattee-maker walked because he was afraid to ride.]

The Rajah came to the palace-door to meet him, and paid him all possible honour. Terms of peace were agreed upon between the two countries, and the Chattee-maker was rewarded for all he had done by being given twice as much rank and wealth as he had before, and he lived very happily all the rest of his life.

From *Old Deccan Days or Hindu Fairy Legends Current in Southern India*, collected from Oral Tradition by Mary Frere (London: John Murray, 1881).

Aladdin and the Wonderful Lamp

The story of Aladdin follows the rags-to-riches linear journey pattern found not only in European, but also Persian and Indian folktales. The tale has generally been associated with *The Thousand and One Nights*, an ancient Persian text that first appeared in a European translation in 1704. Now, however, the eighteenth-century narrative is thought to be a highly Europeanized version of the original text. As such, it reflects popular eighteenth-century fairy tales in which a poor, but deserving, hero acquires wealth and is married to royalty. It also embodies European notions prevalent in the eighteenth and early nineteenth centuries of the East as an exotic, opulent place of magic and adventure. Although on the surface Andrew Lang's 1889 adaptation appears to reflect the 'oriental' characteristics and tone of earlier European retellings, it can also be interpreted ironically. The young hero is referred to as a 'careless idle boy'. Like many folktale characters, he falls in love at first sight, but his first sight comes from disobeying the sultan's orders and spying on the princess as she prepares to bathe. Aladdin passes his tests mainly because he relies on magical objects to perform actions that would otherwise be impossible for him to do. His actions reveal little that is heroic.

There once lived a poor tailor, who had a son called Aladdin, a careless, idle, boy who would do nothing but play all day long in the streets with idle boys like himself. This so grieved the father that he died, yet in spite of his mother's tears and prayers Aladdin did not mend his ways. One day when he was playing in the streets as usual, a stranger asked him his age and if he was not the son of Mustapha the tailor. 'I am, sir,' replied Aladdin; 'but he died a long while ago.' The stranger, who was a famous African magician fell on his neck and kissed him, saying: 'I am your uncle and knew you from your likeness to my brother. Go to your mother and tell her that I am coming.' Aladdin ran home and told his mother of his newly found uncle. 'Indeed child,' she said, 'your father had a brother, but I always thought he was dead.' She prepared supper and bade Aladdin seek his uncle, who came laden with wine and fruit. He presently fell down and kissed the place where Mustapha used to sit, bidding Aladdin's mother not to be surprised at not having seen him before, as he had been forty years out of the country. He then turned to Aladdin and asked him his trade, at which the boy hung his head, while his mother burst into tears. On learning that Aladdin was idle and would learn no trade, he offered to take a shop for him and stock it with merchandise. Next day he bought Aladdin a fine suit of clothes and took him all over the city, showing him the sights, and brought him home at nightfall to his mother, who was overjoyed to see her son so fine.

Next day the magician led Aladdin into some beautiful gardens a long way outside the city gates. They sat down by a fountain and the magician pulled a cake from his girdle, which he divided between them. They then journeyed onward till they almost reached the mountains. Aladdin was so tired that he begged to go back, but the magician beguiled him with pleasant stories and led him on in spite of himself. At last they came to two mountains divided by a narrow valley. 'We will go no further,' said the false uncle. 'I will show you something wonderful; only do you gather up sticks while I kindle a fire.'

When it was lit the magician threw on it a powder he had about him, at the same time saying some magical words. The earth trembled a little and opened in front of them, disclosing a square flat stone with a brass ring in the middle to raise it by. Aladdin tried to run away, but the magician caught him and gave him a blow that knocked him down. 'What have I done, uncle?' he said piteously; whereupon the magician said more kindly: 'Fear nothing, but obey me. Beneath this stone lies a treasure which is to be yours, and no one else may touch it; so you must do exactly as I tell you.'

At the word treasure Aladdin forgot his fears and grasped the ring as was told, saying the names of his father and grandfather. The stone came up easily and some steps appeared. 'Go down,' said the magician. 'At the foot of those steps you will find an open door leading into three large halls. Tuck up your gown and go through them, without touching anything, or you will die instantly. These halls lead into a garden of fine fruit-trees. Walk on till you come to a niche in a terrace where stands a lighted lamp. Pour out the oil it contains and bring it to me.' He drew a ring from his finger and gave it to Aladdin, bidding him prosper.

Aladdin found everything as the magician had said, gathered some fruit off the trees, and having got the lamp arrived at the mouth of the cave. The magician cried out in a great hurry: 'Make haste and give me the lamp.' This Aladdin refused to do until he was out of the cave. The magician flew into a terrible passion, and throwing some more powder on to the fire, he said something and the stone rolled back into its Place.

The magician left Persia forever, which plainly showed that he was no uncle of Aladdin's, but a cunning magician who had read in his magic books of a wonderful lamp which would make him the most powerful man in the world. Though he alone knew where to find it, he could only receive it from the hand of another. He had picked the foolish Aladdin for this purpose, intending to get the lamp and kill him afterward.

For two days Aladdin remained in the dark, crying and lamenting. At last he clasped his hands in prayer, and in so doing rubbed the ring, which the magician had forgotten to take from him. Immediately an enormous and frightful genie rose out of the earth, saying: 'What wouldst thou of me? I am the slave of the ring and will obey thee in all things.' Aladdin fearlessly replied, 'Deliver me from this place!' whereupon the earth opened and he found himself outside. As soon as his eyes could bear the light he went home, but fainted on the threshold. When he came to himself he told his mother what had passed and showed her lamp and the fruits he had gathered in the garden, which were in reality precious stones. He then asked for some food. 'Alas! child,' she said, 'I have nothing in the house, but I have spun a little cotton and will go and sell it.' Aladdin bade her keep her cotton, for he would sell the lamp instead. As it was very dirty she began to rub it, that it might bring a higher price. Instantly a hideous genie appeared and asked what she would have. She fainted away, but Aladdin, snatching the lamp, said boldly 'Fetch me something to eat!' The genie returned with a silver bowl, twelve silver plates containing rich meats, two silver cups, and two bottles of wine. Aladdin's mother, when she came to herself, said: 'Whence comes this splendid feast?' 'Ask not, but eat,' replied Aladdin. So they sat at breakfast till it was dinner-time, and Aladdin told his mother about the lamp. She begged him to sell it and have nothing to do with devils. 'No,' said Aladdin. 'Since chance hath made us aware of its virtues, we will use it, and the ring likewise, which I shall always wear on my finger.' When they had eaten all that the genie had brought Aladdin sold one of the silver plates, and so on until none was left. He then had recourse to the genie, who gave him another set of plates, and thus they lived for many years.

One day Aladdin heard an order from the sultan proclaimed that everyone was to stay at home and close his shutters while the princess, his daughter, went to and from the bath.

Aladdin was seized by a desire to see her face, which was very difficult, as she always went veiled. He hid himself behind the door of the bath and peeped through a chink. The princess lifted her veil as she went in, and looked so beautiful that Aladdin fell in love with her at first sight. He went home so changed that his mother was frightened. He told her that he loved the princess so deeply that he could not live without her, and meant to ask her hand in marriage of her father. His mother, on hearing this, burst out laughing, but Aladdin at last prevailed upon her to go before the sultan and carry his request. She fetched a napkin and laid in it the magic fruits from the enchanted garden, which sparkled and shone like the most beautiful jewels. She took these with her to please the sultan, and set out, trusting in the lamp. The grand vizier and the lords of council had just gone in as she entered the hall and placed herself in front of the sultan. He took no notice of her. She went every day for a week and stood in the same place. When the council broke up on the sixth day the sultan said to his vizier: 'I see a certain woman in the audience chamber every day carrying something in a napkin. Call her next time that I may find out what she wants.' Next day, at a sign from the vizier, she went up to the foot of the throne and remained kneeling till the sultan said to her: 'Rise, good woman, and tell me what you want.' She hesitated, so the sultan sent away all but the vizier and bade her speak freely, promising to forgive her beforehand for anything she might say. She then told him of her son's violent love for the princess. 'I prayed him to forget her,' she said, 'but in vain. He threatened to do some very desperate deed if I refused to go and ask your majesty for the hand of the princess. Now I pray you to forgive not me alone, but my son Aladdin.' The sultan asked her kindly what she had in the napkin, whereupon she unfolded the jewels and presented them. He was thunderstruck, and turning to the vizier said: 'What sayest thou? Ought I not to bestow the princess on one who values her at such a price?' The vizier, who wanted her for his own son, begged the sultan to withhold her for three months, in the course of which he hoped his son would contrive to make him a richer present. The sultan granted this, and told Aladdin's mother that though he consented to the marriage, she must not appear before him again for three months.

Aladdin waited patiently for nearly three months, but after two had elapsed his mother, going into the city to buy oil, found everyone rejoicing and asked what was going on.

'Do you not know,' was the answer, 'that the son of the grand vizier is to marry the sultan's daughter to-night?' Breathless, she ran and told Aladdin, who was overwhelmed at first, but presently bethought him of the lamp. He rubbed it, and the genie appeared, saying: 'What is thy will?' Aladdin replied: 'The sultan, as thou knowest, has broken his promise to me, and the vizier's son is to have the princess. My command is that to-night you bring hither the bride and bridegroom.' 'Master, I obey,' said the genie. Aladdin then went to his chamber, where, sure enough, at midnight the genie transported the bed containing the vizier's son and the princess. 'Take this new-married man,' he said, 'and put him outside in the cold, and return at daybreak.' Whereupon the genie took the vizier's son out of bed, leaving Aladdin with the princess. 'Fear nothing,' Aladdin said to her. 'You are my wife, promised to me by your unjust father, and no harm shall come to you.' The princess was too frightened to speak, and passed the most miserable night of her life, while Aladdin lay down beside her and slept soundly. At the appointed hour the genie fetched in the shivering bridegroom, laid him in his place, and transported the bed back to the palace.

Presently the sultan came to wish his daughter good-morning. The unhappy vizier's son jumped up and hid himself, while the princess could not say a word and was very sorrowful. The sultan sent her mother to her, who said: 'How comes it, child, that you will not speak to your Father? What has happened?' The princess sighed deeply, and at last told her mother how, during the night, the bed had been carried into some strange house, and what had passed there. Her mother did not believe her in the least, but bade her rise and consider it an idle dream.

The following night exactly the same thing happened, and next morning, on the princess' refusing to speak, the sultan threatened to cut off her head. She then confessed all, bidding him ask the vizier's son if it were not so. The sultan told the vizier to ask his son, who owned the truth, adding that, dearly as he loved the princess, he had rather die than go through another such fearful night, and wished to be separated from her. His wish was granted, and there was an end of feast and rejoicing.

When the three months were over Aladdin sent his mother to remind the sultan of his promise. She stood in the same place as before, and the sultan, who had forgotten Aladdin, at once remembered him and sent for her. On seeing her poverty the sultan felt less inclined than ever to keep his word, and asked his vizier's advice, who counseled him to set so high a value on the princess that no man living could come up to it. The sultan then turned to Aladdin's mother saying: 'Good woman, a sultan must remember his promises, and I will remember mine, but your son must first send me forty basins of gold brimful of jewels, carried by forty black slaves, led by as many white ones, splendidly dressed. Tell him that I await his answer.' The mother of Aladdin bowed low and went home, thinking all was lost. She gave Aladdin the message, adding: 'He may wait long enough for your answer!' 'Not so long, mother, as you think,' her son replied. 'I would do a great deal more than that for the princess.' He summoned the genie, and in a few moments the eighty slaves arrived and filled up the small house and garden. Aladdin made them set out to the palace, two and two, followed by his mother. They were so richly dressed, with such splendid jewels in their girdles, that everyone crowded to see them and the basins of gold they carried on their heads. They entered the palace and, after kneeling before the sultan, stood in a half-circle round the throne with their arms crossed, while Aladdin's mother presented them to the sultan. He hesitated no longer, but said: 'Good woman, return and tell your son that I wait for him with open arms.' She lost no time in telling Aladdin, bidding him make haste. But Aladdin first called the genie, 'I want a scented bath,' he said, 'a richly embroidered habit, a horse surpassing the sultan's, and twenty slaves to attend me. Besides this, six slaves, beautifully dressed, to wait on my mother; and lastly, ten thousand pieces of gold in ten purses.' No sooner said than done. Aladdin mounted his horse and passed through the streets, the slaves strewing gold as they went. Those who had played with him in childhood knew him not, he had grown so handsome. When the sultan saw him he came down from his throne, embraced him, and led him into a hall where a feast was spread, tending to marry him to the princess that very day. But Aladdin refused, saying, 'I must build a palace fit for her,' and took his leave. Once home, he said to the genie: 'Build me a palace of the finest marble, set with jasper, agate, and other precious stones. In the middle you shall build me a large hall with a dome, its four walls of massive gold and silver, each side having six windows, whose lattices, all except one which is to be left unfinished, must be set with diamonds and rubies. There must be stables and horses and grooms and slaves. Go and see about it!'

The palace was finished by next day, and the genie carried him there and showed him all his orders faithfully carried out, even to the laying of a velvet carpet from Aladdin's palace to the sultan's. Aladdin's mother then dressed herself carefully and walked to the palace with her slaves, while he followed her on horseback. The sultan sent musicians with trumpets and cymbals to meet them, so that the air resounded with music and cheers. She was taken to the princess, who saluted her and treated her with great honour. At night the princess said good-by to her father and set out on the carpet for Aladdin's palace, with his mother at her side and followed by the hundred slaves. She was charmed at the sight of Aladdin, who ran to receive her. 'Princess,' he said, 'blame your beauty for my boldness if I have displeased you.' She told him that, having seen him, she willingly obeyed her father in this matter. After the wedding had taken place Aladdin led her into the hall, where a feast was spread, and she supped with him, after which they danced till midnight.

Next day Aladdin invited the sultan to see the palace. On entering the hall with the twenty-four windows, with their rubies, diamonds, and emeralds, he cried: 'It is a world's wonder! There is only one thing that surprises me. Was it by accident that one window was left unfinished?' 'No, sir, by design,' returned Aladdin. 'I wished your majesty to have the glory of finishing this palace.' The sultan was pleased and sent for the best jewelers in the city. He showed them the unfinished window and bade them fit it up like the others. 'Sir,' replied their spokesman, 'we cannot find jewels enough.' The sultan had his own fetched, which they soon used, but to no purpose, for in a month's time the work was not half-done. Aladdin, knowing that their task was in vain, bade them undo their work and carry the jewels back, and the genie finished the window at his command. The sultan was surprised to receive his jewels again, and visited Aladdin, who showed him the window finished. The sultan embraced him, the envious vizier meanwhile hinting that it was the work of enchantment.

Aladdin had won the hearts of the people by his gentle bearing. He was made captain of the sultan's armies and won several battles for him, but remained modest and courteous as before, and lived thus in peace and content for several years.

But far away in Africa the magician remembered Aladdin, and by his magic arts discovered that Aladdin, instead, of perishing miserably in the cave, had escaped and had married a princess, with whom he was living in great honour and wealth. He knew that the poor tailor's son could only have accomplished this by means of the lamp, and traveled night and day till he reached the capital of China, bent on Aladdin's ruin. As he passed through the town he heard people talking everywhere about a marvelous palace. 'Forgive my ignorance,' he said. 'What is this palace you speak of?' 'Have you not heard of Prince Aladdin's palace,' was the reply, 'the greatest wonder of the world! I will direct you if you have a mind to see it.' The magician thanked him who spoke, and having seen the palace, knew that it had been raised by the genie of the lamp and became half-mad with rage. He determined to get hold of the lamp and again plunge Aladdin into the deepest poverty.

Unluckily, Aladdin had gone a-hunting for eight days, which gave the magician plenty of time. He bought a dozen copper lamps, put them in a basket, and went to the palace, crying, 'New lamps for old!' followed by a jeering crowd. The princess, sitting in the hall of twenty-four windows, sent a slave to find out what the noise was about, who came back laughing, so that the princess scolded her. 'Madam,' replied the slave, 'who can help laughing to see an old fool offering to exchange fine new lamps for old ones?' Another slave, hearing this, said: 'There is an old one in the cornice there which he can have.' Now, this was the magic lamp, which Aladdin had left there, as he could not take it out hunting with him. The princess, not knowing its value, laughingly bade the slave take it and make the exchange. She went and said to the magician, 'Give me a new lamp for this.' He snatched it and bade the slave take her choice, amid the jeers of the crowd. Little he cared, but left off crying his lamps, and went out of the city gates to a lonely place where he remained till nightfall, when he pulled out the lamp and rubbed it. The genie appeared, and at the magician's command carried him, together with the palace and the princess in it, to a lonely place in Africa.

Next morning the sultan looked out of the window toward Aladdin's palace and rubbed his eyes, for it was gone. He sent for the vizier and asked what had become of the palace. The

From Marianna Mayer, *Aladdin and the Enchanted Lamp*. Illustrated by Gerald McDermott. (New York: Macmillan, 1985), 59.

vizier looked out too and was lost in astonishment. He again put it down to enchantment, and this time the sultan believed him and sent thirty men on horseback to fetch Aladdin in chains. They met him riding home, bound him, and forced him to go with them on foot. The people, who loved him, followed, armed, to see that he came to no harm. He was carried before the sultan, who ordered the executioner to cut off his head. The executioner made

Aladdin kneel down, bandaged his eyes, and raised his scimitar to strike. At that instant the vizier, who saw that the crowd had forced their way into the court-yard and were scaling the walls to rescue Aladdin, called to the executioner to stay his hand. The people, indeed, looked so threatening that the sultan gave way and ordered Aladdin to be unbound, and pardoned him in the sight of the crowd.

Aladdin now begged to know what he had done. 'False wretch!' said the sultan, 'come hither,' and showed him from the window the place where his palace had stood. Aladdin was so amazed that he could not say a word. 'Where is your palace and my daughter?' demanded the sultan. 'For the first I am not so deeply concerned, but my daughter I must have, and you must find her or lose your head.' Aladdin begged for forty days in which to find her, promising, if he failed, to return and suffer death at the sultan's pleasure. His prayer was granted, and he went forth sadly from the sultan's presence.

For three days he wandered about like a madman, asking everyone what had become of his palace, but they only laughed and pitied him. He came to the banks of a river and knelt down to say his prayers before throwing himself in. In so doing he rubbed the magic ring he still wore. The genie he had seen in the cave appeared and asked his will. 'Save my life, genie,' said Aladdin, 'and bring my palace back.' 'That is not in my power,' said the genie. I am only the slave of the ring; you must ask him of the lamp.' 'Even so,' said Aladdin, 'but thou canst take me to the palace and set me down under my dear wife's window.' He at once found himself in Africa, under the window of the princess, and fell asleep out of sheer weariness.

He was awakened by the singing of the birds, and his heart was lighter. He saw plainly that all his misfortunes were owing to the loss of the lamp, and vainly wondered who had robbed him of it.

That morning the princess rose earlier than she had done since she had been carried into Africa by the magician, whose company she was forced to endure once a day. She treated him so harshly that he dared not live there altogether. As she was dressing, one of her women looked out and saw Aladdin. The princess ran and opened the window, and at the noise she made Aladdin looked up. She called to him to come to her, and great was the joy of these lovers at seeing each other again. After he had kissed her Aladdin said: 'I beg of you, princess, in God's name, before we speak of anything else, for your own sake and mine, tell me what has become of the old lamp I left on the cornice in the hall of twenty-four windows when I went hunting.' 'Alas!' she said, 'I am the innocent cause of our sorrows,' and told him of the exchange of that lamp. 'Now I know,' cried Aladdin, 'that we have to thank the African magician for this! Where is the lamp?' 'He carries it about with him,' said the princess. 'I know, for he pulled it out of his breast to show me. He wishes me to break my faith with you and marry him, saying that you were beheaded by my father's command. He is forever speaking ill of you, but I only reply by my tears. If I persist, I doubt not but he will use violence.'

Aladdin comforted her and left her for awhile. He changed clothes with the first person he met in the town, and having bought a certain powder returned to the princess, who let him in by a little side door. 'Put on your most beautiful dress,' he said to her, 'and receive the magician with smiles, leading him to believe that you have forgotten me. Invite him up to sup with you and say you wish to taste the wine of his country. He will go for some, and while he is gone I will tell you what to do.' She listened carefully to Aladdin, and when he left her arrayed herself gaily for the first time since she left China. She put on a girdle and head-dress of diamonds, and seeing in a glass that she was more beautiful than ever, received the magician, saying, to his great amazement: 'I have made up my mind that Aladdin is dead and that all my tears will not bring him back to me, so I am resolved to mourn no more, and have therefore invited you to sup with me; but I am tired of the wines of China, and would fain taste those of Africa.'

The magician flew to his cellar, and the princess put the powder Aladdin had given her into her cup. When he returned she asked him to drink her health in the wine of Africa, handing him her cup in exchange for his, as a sign she was reconciled to him. Before drinking the magician made her a speech in praise of her beauty, but the princess cut him short, saying: 'Let us drink first, and you shall say what you will afterward.' She set her cup to her lips and kept it there, while the magician drained his to the dregs and fell back lifeless. The princess then opened the door to Aladdin and flung her arms round his neck; but Aladdin put her away, bidding her leave him, as he had more to do. He then went to the dead magician, took the lamp out of his vest, and bade the genie carry the palace and all in it back to China. This was done, and the princess in her chamber only felt two little shocks, and little thought that she was at home again.

The sultan, who was sitting in his closet mourning for his lost daughter, happened to look up, and rubbed his eyes, for there stood the palace as before! He hastened thither, and Aladdin received him in the hall of the twenty-four windows, with the princess at his side. Aladdin told him what had happened and showed him the dead body of the magician, that he might believe. A ten days' feast was proclaimed, and it seemed as if Aladdin might now live the rest of his life in peace; but it was not to be.

The African magician had a younger brother, who was, if possible, more wicked and more cunning than himself. He traveled to China to avenge his brother's death, and went to visit a pious woman called Fatima, thinking she might be of use to him. He changed clothes with her, coloured his face like hers, put on her veil, and murdered her, that she might tell no tales. Then he went toward the palace of Aladdin, and all the people, thinking he was the holy woman, gathered round him kissing his hands and begging his blessing. When he got to the palace there was such a noise going on round him that the princess bade her slave look out of the window and ask what was the matter. The slave said it was the holy woman, curing people by her touch of their ailments, whereupon the princess, who had long desired to see Fatima, sent for her. On coming to the princess the magician offered up a prayer for her health and prosperity. When he had done the princess made him sit by her and begged him to stay with her always. The false Fatima, who wished for nothing better, consented, but kept his veil down for fear of discovery. The princess showed him the hall and asked him what he thought of it. 'It is truly beautiful,' said the false Fatima. 'In my mind it wants but one thing.' 'And what is that?' said the princess. 'If only a roc's egg,' replied he, 'were hung up from the middle of this dome, it would be the wonder of the world.'

After this the princess could think of nothing but the roc's egg, and when Aladdin returned from hunting he found her in a very ill humour. He begged to know what was amiss, and she told him that all her pleasure in the hall was spoiled for the want of a roc's egg hanging from the dome. 'If that is all,' replied Aladdin, 'you shall soon be happy.' He left her and rubbed the lamp, and when the genie appeared commanded him to bring a roc's egg. The genie gave such a loud and terrible shriek that the hall shook. 'Wretch!' he cried, 'is it not enough that I have done everything for you but you must command me to bring my master and hang him up in the midst of this dome? You and your wife and your palace deserve to be burned to ashes, but that this request does not come from you, but from the brother of the African magician whom you destroyed. He is now in your palace disguised as the holy woman—whom he murdered. He it was who put that wish into your wife's head. Take care of yourself, for he means to kill you.' So saying, the genie disappeared.

Aladdin went back to the princess, saying that his head ached, and requesting that the holy Fatima should be fetched to lay her hands on it. But when the magician came near, Aladdin, seizing his dagger, pierced him to the heart. 'What have you done?' cried the princess. 'You have killed the holy woman!' 'Not so,' replied Aladdin, 'but a wicked magician,' and told her of how she had been deceived.

After this Aladdin and his wife lived in peace. He succeeded the sultan when he died and reigned for many years, leaving behind him a long line of kings.

———

From *The Blue Fairy Book*, edited by Andrew Lang (New York: Grosset and Dunlap, 1889).

LINKS TO OTHER STORIES

Part Five

Purposeful Journeys
Errands and Quests

In *Sounder* (1969), William H. Armstrong's classic novel about growing up in the Depression-era South, a boy intent on leaving home to find his imprisoned father thinks of an argument to allay his mother's fears: 'In Bible stories everybody's always goin' on a long journey. Abraham goes on a long journey. Jacob goes into a strange land where his uncle lives, and he don't know where he lives, but he finds him easy. Joseph goes on the longest journey of all and has more troubles, but the Lord watches over him. And in Bible-story journeys, ain't no journey hopeless. Everybody finds what they supposed to find' (78). Although this passage sets up the irony of his own journey, which does not end happily, it also demonstrates that the young boy has developed an admirable comprehension of literature, understanding one of its most important organizing devices.

In a great many oral tales, and in the written tales inspired by them, the journey is a plot device that provides obvious starting and stopping points, as well as places between that can be the scenes of danger and adventure. The significance of the journey device, however, extends far beyond its value as a plotting mechanism. In many instances, the journey is a powerful symbol. Since ancient times, for example, people have declared that life itself is a journey from cradle to grave. Fictional journeys seldom, however, cover the entire span of a life. Rather, they tend to represent stages in the larger journey from birth to death, such as the transition from childhood to adulthood. In doing so, these journeys are frequently outward manifestations of inward development. In moving from one physical location to another, characters suggest changes to such things as their level of understanding, their maturation, their sense of self-worth, and their spiritual values. Additionally, the journey may signal, and be the occasion for, changes in social status. Many folktales, for instance, symbolize happiness and autonomy through upward social mobility, sending a protagonist from a hovel to the palace, where he or she marries royalty.

The reasons that characters undertake journeys differ significantly. In many tales, however, the characters have one of two definite and positive purposes in setting out. Sometimes, the characters undertake errands: they deliver a message or object to others, or they perform an important commission. In 'Henny Penny', included in the section on animal tales, for example, the hen sets out to tell the king that the sky is falling. Although the shorter tales included in this anthology tend to involve simple errands, readers should be aware that errands often have the kind of significant moral and social dimensions that the

American Puritans expressed by calling their endeavours in the New World an 'errand in the wilderness'. Such dimensions appear, for example, when Frodo Baggins, in the fantasy trilogy *The Lord of the Rings*, performs the gruelling errand of carrying the 'one ring' to its destruction in the volcanic Mount Doom.

The second purpose that characters have in setting out on journeys is the undertaking of quests: they seek an object or person whom they usually must rescue from some enemy. In the romance 'Of Sir Gareth of Orkney', for example, a knight sets out to free the Lady Lyoness from her captor. Regardless of whether a character undertakes a quest or an errand,[1] however, the journey itself becomes a device for displaying the qualities and values of the protagonist. In other words, the purposeful journey is a test of inner worth and resolve as much as it is a test of physical abilities.

In 'The Quest Hero', W.H. Auden identifies six basic elements in quest stories. His list is most applicable to myths, epics, romances, and long fantasies, but this list is useful, even if it occasionally demands modification, in studying tales that, technically speaking, involve errands, not quests. The first element that Auden identifies is the precious object to be found or the special person who is to be rescued (and then married). As the goal of the journey, this object or person not only gives purpose to the protagonist's actions in literal terms but also symbolizes purpose in life itself (see Auden 372–3). *Little Badger and the Fire Spirit*, a literary myth, provides an example of a quest for a precious object. In this case, the object is fire, precious because it will give people comfort during the cold winter. The precious object is not a tangible thing in the Norse myth 'Odin Goes to Mimir's Well': it is wisdom, specifically the power to foresee the future. The second kind of quest, the rescue of a person, appears in 'Of Sir Gareth of Orkney', an Arthurian romance adapted for nineteenth-century children by the American Sidney Lanier. In this tale, a fledgling knight must rescue a lady whom another knight is holding prisoner. His quest becomes a testimonial to and demonstration of his identity as a truly worthy knight

Tales about errands do not involve obtaining precious objects or rescuing people, but they do have a goal—the delivery of messages or objects, or the performance of a task—that gives meaning to the journey and its obstacles, even in simple tales. In Perrault's 'Little Red Riding-hood', for example, the girl's errand is to deliver food promptly, a duty demanding obedience to and respect for her elders.

As different as they are in form, the quests noted above reveal a similar motivation. These questers all confer benefits on others.[2] Their endeavours may give quest heroes some personal benefit, such as a bride, but in such cases the hero almost always gives a greater benefit to the community. Sometimes, though, the tale may only imply this benefit. As Auden suggests, for example, the protagonist's marriage to a princess actually promises peace, at least with the kingdom of the bride's father, and the stability that comes through the wife's provision of an heir (373). Many tales, even those involving the winning of a bride, are more explicit about the benefit accruing to the community. In the Blackfoot legend 'Scarface: Origin of the Medicine Lodge', for example, Scarface sets out only on a personal quest to gain permission to marry a maiden already promised to the Sun. When he finally returns with signs that the Sun has given him permission to marry, he also brings significant knowledge, most notably about establishing the Medicine Lodge, which becomes a central element of Blackfoot culture and well-being.

The second basic element of quest tales is a long journey, which Auden sees as a spatial representation of our consciousness of time as 'a continuous irreversible process of change' (373). The folk tale's propensity to be concrete uses movement between physical places to represent the development that occurs over time. In 'Scarface: Origin of the Medicine Lodge', for example, Scarface is initially a pathetic and pitiful character, but after his arduous journey to the sun's home, he changes into a braver and more confident individual.

The third essential element in Auden's list is the hero who undertakes the quest. Auden notes that, especially in epics, the heroism of the protagonist may be obvious (373). In such cases he or she is a hero with an established public reputation and the expectations that such a reputation brings. Such heroes include Beowulf, Perseus, Krishna, and Robin Hood. On the other hand, the heroism may be concealed (373), in which case the character is an unlikely hero whose inner qualities do not become evident until circumstances reveal them. In folk tales and fairy tales, such unlikely heroes, especially children, are numerous. The lassie in 'East o' the Sun and West o' the Moon', who undertakes what she is told is an impossible journey to save her beloved from imprisonment by trolls, and Little Badger, the blind boy who journeys to the forbidden home of the Fire Spirit, are two such unlikely heroes found in tales in this section.

It should be noted, however, that for various reasons, those who would seem likely to be heroic may disguise themselves in order to accomplish their goals. Such is the case in 'Of Sir Gareth of Orkney', in which a knight hides his true abilities so that he can establish the virtues of his noble lineage through deeds and thereby become a hero of renown. Similarly, in 'Odin Goes to Mimir's Well', the god disguises himself as part of a trick to gain information essential to his quest's success. In such instances the treatment that the hero receives when in disguise may be important in revealing both his or her own character and that of those with whom the hero interacts.

The demonstration or revelation of heroic qualities comes through the fourth element that Auden identifies, the tests or series of tests that screen out those unworthy of the quest (372). Auden argues that the hero who passes the test symbolizes our sense of uniqueness and that the rivals who fail represent our sense of uncertainty about the future (373). Be that as it may, the tests may establish the physical prowess of the hero, as do Sir Gareth's encounters with the various knights hindering his way. Frequently, however, they reveal, sometimes symbolically, the psychological, moral, or spiritual status of the protagonist. In addition to revealing the physical prowess of Sir Gareth of Orkney, for example, his battles and other tests of his identity establish his dedication to such chivalric ideals as the display of courtesy, the defense of honour, and fitting obedience to the commands of women. In 'Odin Goes to Mimir's Well', events challenge Odin's wit and compassion, not his physical power. His compassionate nature as a good ruler is made particularly poignant when he enters into a sacrificial bargain and plucks out his eye so that he may receive the object of the quest, a draught from the well of wisdom. The third son in 'The Wonderful Brocade', a tale from one of China's minority cultures, shows his commitment to familial duty when, although offered wealth to abandon his quest, he unhesitatingly knocks out his teeth, which he is told is necessary to do if he is to continue. In the literary myth 'Cupid and Psyche', the tests are a series of quests and tasks that initially seem impossible. By attempting them, Psyche reveals her unwavering desire to be a faithful partner to Cupid.

Much the same is true in 'East o' the Sun and West o' the Moon', in which the lassie endures hardships while trying to make her way to the castle of the trolls. Her story clearly shows, however, the difference between two kinds of tests that quests present. The first is the informal test, a situation in which the hero is unaware that he or she is being tested. The three hags, whom she meets, for instance, tell the lassie that she will never arrive at the castle east of the sun and west of the moon, or that she will arrive too late. Although the undiscouraged lassie is unaware of the fact, the hags thereby test her spirit and determination. At the castle, the lassie endures the second kind of test, the formal test, a situation in which the hero is aware that he or she is being tested and, furthermore, is usually aware of the consequence of failure and success. By successfully washing her beloved's shirt in the formal bridal test, the lassie demonstrates that she has the abilities of a good wife; more importantly, she literally undoes the harm of the past by removing the stain that she caused.

The remaining elements in Auden's list are two major roles that characters may play in the quest. What Auden calls 'The Guardians of the Object' (372) may represent opposition or even the hero's inner doubts, or they may represent some form of evil. The guardians may constitute the only test or they may provide the ultimate test on the journey. By challenging the hero, the guardians reveal the hero's determination, bravery, and resourcefulness. In *Little Badger and the Fire Spirit*, the blind boy gets past a series of animals because of his compassion, courage, and wit. When he reaches the chamber of the Fire Spirit, his apparent infirmity, his blindness, becomes a source of strength because it prevents him from violating the injunction that forbids anyone from seeing the home of the Fire Spirit. The guardians thus reveal this hero's inner qualities, his insight, rather than his external ones, such as his blindness. In 'Of Sir Gareth of Orkney', the red knight of the red lawns is the guardian, the one who holds Lyoness prisoner. He differs from the other knights who tested Gareth primarily in the intensity of his physical opposition. When he begs for mercy and reveals his motivation for holding Lyoness prisoner, however, he adds to the physical test something of an ethical one; he appeals to Gareth's understanding of the code of chivalry.

The other role that Auden identifies is that of the helper. Helpers provide knowledge or magical powers without which the hero cannot succeed (372). Helpers, whether animal or human, also provide a sense of community for the quester, who must leave his fixed community in order to achieve his goal. Furthermore, the mere presence of helpers signals the quester's special status, an especially important signal when the quester is an unlikely hero. Helpers indicate that the quester has a special destiny to fulfill, that the character will be able to prove him or herself worthy of that destiny, and that the quester will have, at the appropriate moment, the resources to fulfill that destiny. Helpers appear in various forms. During her trials, Psyche receives help from ants, a green reed, an eagle, and a tower. Little Badger also depends on several helpers. He requires the help of runners to carry him to the mountain home of the Fire Spirit, Grey Coyote to give him courage by drumming, and the spirits of rock and wind to assist him on his climb up the mountain. In *Simon and the Golden Sword*, a Canadian quest tale, the hero receives help from an innkeeper, who must be technically classified as a donor because he helps Simon by giving him objects that become essential to the successful completion of his quest. The lassie in 'East o' the Sun and West o' the Moon' also receives help from donors, the three hags whose words test her determination, as well as well as from the four winds. In 'The Magic Brocade', the white-haired old woman has a complex role similar to that of the lassie's hags. This woman, an archetype of the Wise Old Woman, not only provides each son with information about completing the quest, but she also tests them by telling them that they cannot succeed and offering them gold if they abandon the quest. Only for the third son, who passes the test by refusing the temptation of the gold, does she become the true helper. In other words, she tests the quester to ensure that he is worthy of help. Although the helper is essential to the success of many quests, the quester must have the wit or courage to use the help appropriately. Furthermore, the quester invariably faces the ultimate test alone, thus ensuring that victory reveals his or her abilities and qualities.

Not surprisingly, tales about simple errands do not necessarily contain all of the elements that Auden lists. In Perrault's cautionary 'Little Red Riding-hood', for example, the eponymous hero certainly faces a test on the way to fulfilling her commission to deliver a basket of food to her grandmother. The wolf who tests her and exposes her naïveté may also play the role of the guardian because he is the final obstacle, even though he has already eaten the grandmother and made it impossible for Little Red Riding-hood to complete her errand. Furthermore, partly because Little Red Riding-hood has no helpers, she fails to complete her errand. A helper does, however, appear in 'Little Red-Cap', the version of this tale by the Brothers Grimm. By rescuing both the girl and the grandmother from the belly of the wolf, the huntsman ensures that Little Red-Cap can succeed when given a second errand. The helper thus gives this version of the cautionary tale a different meaning than exists in Perrault's tale: this version suggests that one can redeem oneself after making errors if one will only learn from painful experience.

This part concludes with two animal tales. Auden contends that quests involve seeking things of which we have not yet had experience, so animals cannot go on quests. Because they humanize their animal characters, however, traditional stories belie Auden's comments. The purpose of the journey in 'The Three Billy-Goats Gruff', to eat, certainly aligns this tale with Auden's contention that, when animals hunt, 'the object of their search is determined by what they already are and its purpose is to restore a disturbed equilibrium' (370). Nevertheless, these sentient goats must use their special talents to overcome obstacles and transform themselves physically into fat goats, a symbol of contentment when we consider what a fat goat would mean to the peasants among whom the story probably originated. Their adventure takes on the quality of a compact quest not simply for a hillside of grass but for life and happiness. The goats have no helpers—the first two do, however, mention the existence of another goat, thereby indirectly enlisting a helper—but the troll who blocks their way is the guardian who tests their worthiness to survive.

Because the animals undertaking journeys in many other tales are not really animals but representatives of various human qualities or human types we may similarly analyze their actions as elements of quests. We close this part, however, with an ironic quest story, 'The Half-Chick'. In this Spanish *pourquoi* tale, the protagonist, a malformed chick, seeks out the king for unworthy reasons. Because of his arrogance, he proves himself unworthy of helpers and therefore ends up in a state that he did not anticipate.

Notes

1. In practice, scholars generally discuss arduous, dangerous, and important purposeful journeys as quests, even if, as is the case with Frodo Baggins, the protagonist is not seeking any object or person but is performing an important commission. One reason for this general lack of critical distinction is that when errands require long and dangerous journeys, they inevitably involve seeking (the word *quest* comes from the Latin *quaerere*, 'to seek'); characters performing significant errands often have to seek places of safety, helpers, or the location where they can fulfill their commission.

2. Auden notes that sometimes, as in a Grail Quest, the goal is important only to the quester (373). In such cases, we may argue that the achievement of the goal symbolizes attainment of a particular spiritual or psychological state. Because they symbolize complex interior states, traditional stories of this sort are seldom included in collections aimed at child readers.

Works Cited

Armstrong, William H. [1969] 1972. *Sounder*. New York: Perennial Library/Harper & Row.

Auden, W.H. 1968. 'The Quest Hero'. *Perspectives in Contemporary Criticism: A Collection of Recent Essays by American, English, and European Literary Critics*. Ed. Sheldon Norman Grebstein. New York: Harper & Row.

Of Sir Gareth of Orkney

In this tale, which the nineteenth-century American writer Sidney Lanier adapted for children from *Le Morte d'Arthur*, Sir Thomas Malory's fifteenth-century collection of stories about the Knights of the Round Table, the quest and the tests that it inevitably occasions constitute an initiation into manhood. As a result, the quest not only benefits the lady whom Gareth rescues, but it also acts as a formal rite of passage, one made more dramatic by the fact that Gareth moves from the kitchen to a seat at the Round Table. As is the case with many young heroes, including King Arthur, Gareth's identity is not known at first. In fact, Sir Kay, blinded by false appearances, disparagingly assigns him the name Beaumains ('Fair Hands'), a name that challenges Gareth's manliness and his right to take on quests. By concealing his name, however, Gareth gives himself the opportunity to prove his character in action. During the quest, he therefore shows his gentility—an essential element of chivalry—by enduring the insults of the Lady Linet, and his manliness by defeating the arrogant Sir Kay, the noble Sir Launcelot, and the knights whom he meets on his journey. Having defeated his foes and rescued the Lady Lyoness, Gareth has earned a new identity as both a man and a proven knight.

Chapter I: How Beaumains came to King Arthur's Court and demanded Three Petitions of King Arthur.

When Arthur held his Round Table most fully, it fortuned that he commanded that the high feast of Pentecost should be holden at a city and a castle, the which in those days was called King-Kenadon, upon the sands that marched [*bordered*] nigh Wales. So ever the king had a custom that at the feast of Pentecost, in especial afore other feasts in the year, he would not go that day to meat until he had heard or seen of a great marvel. And for that custom all manner of strange adventures came before Arthur as at that feast before all other feasts. And so Sir Gawaine, a little tofore noon of the day of Pentecost, espied at a window three men upon horseback and a dwarf on foot. And so the three men alighted, and the dwarf kept their horses, and one of the three men was higher than the other twain by a foot and an half. Then Sir Gawaine went unto the king and said, 'Sir, go to your meat, for here at the hand come strange adventures.'

So Arthur went unto his meat with many other kings. And there were all the knights of the Round Table, save those that were prisoners or slain at a recounter. Then at the high feast evermore they should be fulfilled the whole number of an hundred and fifty, for then was the Round Table fully accomplished. Right so came into the hall two men well beseen and richly, and upon their shoulders there leaned the goodliest young man and the fairest that ever they all saw, and he was large and long, and broad in the shoulders, and well visaged, and the fairest and the largest handed that ever man saw, but he fared as though he might not go nor bear himself but if he leaned upon their shoulders. Anon as Arthur saw him there was made peace [*silence*] and room, and right so they went with him unto the high dais, without saying of any words. Then this much big man pulled him aback, and easily stretched up straight, saying, 'King Arthur, God you bless, and all your fair fellowship, and in especial the fellowship of the Table Round. And for this cause I am come hither, to pray you and require you to give me three gifts, and they shall not be unreasonably asked, but that ye may worshipfully and honourably grant them me, and to you no great hurt nor loss. And as for the first gift I will ask now, and the other two gifts I will ask this day twelve-month, wheresoever ye hold your high feast.

'Now ask,' said Arthur, 'and ye shall have your asking.'

'Now, sir, this is my petition for this feast, that ye will give me meat and drink suffi-ciently for this twelvemonth, and at that day I will ask mine other two gifts.'

'My fair son,' said Arthur, 'ask better, I counsel thee, for this is but a simple asking, for my heart giveth me to thee greatly that thou art come of men of worship, and greatly my conceit faileth me but thou shalt prove a man of right great worship.'

'Sir,' he said, 'thereof be as it be may, I have asked that I will ask.'

'Well,' said the king, 'ye shall have meat and drink enough, I never defended that none, neither my friend nor my foe. But what is thy name I would wit?'

'I cannot tell you,' said he.

'That is marvel,' said the king, 'that thou knowest not thy name, and thou art the good-liest young man that ever I saw.'

Then the king betook him to Sir Kay, the steward, and charged him that he should give him of all manner of meats and drinks of the best, and also that he had all manner of find-ing as though he were a lord's son.

'That shall little need,' said Sir Kay, 'to do such cost upon him; for I dare undertake he is a villain born, and never will make man, for and he had come of gentlemen he would have asked of you horse and armour, but such as he is, so he asketh. And since he hath no name, I shall give him a name: that shall be Beaumains, that is Fairhands, and into the kitchen I shall bring him, and there he shall have fat browis [*broth*] every day, that he shall be as fat by the twelvemonth's end as a pork hog.'

Right so the two men departed, and left him to Sir Kay, that scorned him and mocked him.

Chapter II: How Sir Launcelot and Sir Gawaine were wroth because Sir Kay mocked Beaumains, and of a Damsel which desired a Knight to fight for a Lady.

Thereat was Sir Gawaine wroth, and in especial Sir Launcelot bade Sir Kay leave his mock-ing, 'for I dare lay my head he shall prove a man of great worship.'

'Let be,' said Sir Kay, 'it may not be, by no reason, for as he is, so he hath asked.'

'Beware,' said Sir Launcelot; 'so ye gave the good knight Brewnor, Sir Dinadan's brother, a name, and ye called him La Cote Male Taile, and that turned you to anger afterward.'

'As for that,' said Sir Kay, 'this shall never prove none such; for Sir Brewnor desired ever worship, and this desireth bread and drink and broth; upon pain of my life he was fostered up in some abbey, and, howsoever it was, they failed meat and drink, and so hither he is come for his sustenance.'

And so Sir Kay bade get him a place and sit down to meat, so Beaumains went to the hall door, and set him down among boys and lads, and there he eat sadly. And then Sir Launcelot after meat bade him come to his chamber, and there he should have meat and drink enough. And so did Sir Gawaine, but he refused them all; he would do none other but as Sir Kay commanded him, for no proffer. But as touching Sir Gawaine, he had reason to proffer him lodging, meat, and drink, for that proffer came of his blood, for he was nearer kin to him than he wist. But that as Sir Launcelot did was of his great gentleness and cour-tesy. So thus he was put into the kitchen, and lay nightly as the boys of the kitchen did. And so he endured all that twelvemonth, and never displeased man nor child, but always he was meek and mild. But ever when he saw any jousting of knights, that would he see and he might. And ever Sir Launcelot would give him gold to spend, and clothes, and so did Sir Gawaine. And where were any masteries done thereat would he be, and there might none cast the bar or stone to him by two yards. Then would Sir Kay say, 'How like you my boy of the kitchen?' So it passed on till the feast of Pentecost, and at that time the king held it at Carleon, in the most royallest wise that might be, like as yearly he did. But the king would eat no meat upon the Whitsunday till he heard of some adventure. And then came there a squire to the king, and said, 'Sir, ye may go to your meat, for here cometh a damsel with some strange adventure.' Then was the king glad, and set him down. Right so there came in a damsel, and saluted the king, and prayed him for succor.

'For whom?' said the king: 'what is the adventure?'

'Sir,' said she, 'I have a lady of great worship and renown, and she is besieged with a tyrant, so that she may not go out of her castle, and because that here in your court are called the noblest knights of the world, I come unto you and pray you for succor.'

'What call ye your lady, and where dwelleth she, and who is he and what is his name that hath besieged her?'

'Sir king,' said she, 'as for my lady's name, that shall not be known for me as at this time; but I let you wit she is a lady of great worship, and of great lands. And as for the tyrant that besiegeth her and destroyeth her land, he is called the Red Knight of the Red Lawns.'

'I know him not,' said the king.

'Sir,' said Sir Gawaine, 'I know him well, for he is one of the perilous knights of the world; men say that he hath seven men's strength, and from him I escaped once full hard with my life.'

'Fair damsel,' said the king, 'there be knights here that would do their power to rescue your lady, but because ye will not tell her name nor where she dwelleth, therefore none of my knights that be here now shall go with you by my will.'

'Then must I speak further,' said the damsel.

Chapter III: How Beaumains desired the Battle, and how it was granted to him. And how he desired to be made Knight of Sir Launcelot.

Then with these words came before the king Beaumains, while the damsel was there; and thus he said: 'Sir king, God thank you, I have been this twelve months in your kitchen, and have had my full sustenance, and now I will ask my two gifts that be behind.'

'Ask upon my peril,' said the king.

'Sir, these shall be my two gifts: first, that ye will grant me to have this adventure of the damsel, for it belongeth to me.'

'Thou shalt have it,' said the king; 'I grant it thee.'

'Then, sir, this is the other gift: that ye shall bid Launcelot du Lake to make me a knight, for of him I will be made knight, and else of none; and when I am passed, I pray you let him ride after me, and make me knight when I require him.'

'All this shall be done,' said the king.

'Fie on thee,' said the damsel, 'shall I have none but one that is your kitchen page?'

Then was she wroth, and took her horse and departed. And with that there came one to Beaumains, and told him that his horse and armour was come for him, and there was a dwarf come with all things that him needed in the richest manner. Thereat all the court had much marvel from whence came all that gear. So when he was armed, there was none but few so goodly a man as he was. And right so as he came into the hall, and took his leave of King Arthur and of Sir Gawaine, and Sir Launcelot, and prayed him that he would hie after him; and so departed and rode after the damsel.

Chapter IV: How Beaumains departed, and how he got of Sir Kay a Spear and a Shield, and how he jousted with Sir Launcelot.

But there went many after to behold how well he was horsed and trapped in cloth of gold, but he had neither shield nor spear. Then Sir Kay said openly in the hall : 'I will ride after my boy of the kitchen, for to wit [*know*] whether he will know me for his better.'

Sir Launcelot and Sir Gawaine said, 'Yet abide at home.'

So Sir Kay made him ready, and took his horse and his spear, and rode after him. And right as Beaumains overtook the damsel, right so came Sir Kay, and said, 'Beaumains, what sir, know ye not me?'

Then he turned his horse, and knew it was Sir Kay, that had done him all the despite as ye have heard afore.

'Yea,' said Beaumains, 'I know you for an ungentle knight of the court, and therefore beware of me.'

Therewith Sir Kay put his spear in the rest and ran straight upon him, and Beaumains came as fast upon him with his sword in his hand; and so he put away his spear with his sword, and with a foin [*feint*] thrust him through the side, that Sir Kay fell down as he had been dead, and he alighted down and took Sir Kay's shield and his spear, and started upon his own horse, and rode his way. All that saw Sir Launcelot, and so did the damsel. And then he bade his dwarf start upon Sir Kay's horse, and so he did. By that Sir Launcelot was come. Then he proffered Sir Launcelot to joust, and either made them ready, and came together so fiercely that either bare down other to the earth, and sore were they bruised. Then Sir Launcelot arose and helped him from his horse. And then Beaumains threw his shield from him, and proffered to fight with Sir Launcelot on foot; and so they rushed together like boars, tracing, racing, and foining to the mountenance [*amount*] of an hour, and Sir Launcelot felt him so big that he marvelled of his strength, for he fought more like a giant than a knight, and that his fighting was durable and passing perilous. For Sir Launcelot had so much ado with him that he dreaded himself to be shamed, and said, 'Beaumains, fight not so sore, your quarrel and mine is not so great but we may leave off.'

'Truly, that is truth,' said Beaumains, 'but it doth me good to feel your might, and yet, my lord, I showed not the uttermost.'

Chapter V: How Beaumains told to Sir Launcelot his Name, and how he was dubbed Knight of Sir Launcelot, and after overtook the Damsel.

'Well,' said Sir Launcelot, 'for I promise you by the faith of my body I had as much to do as I might to save myself from you unshamed, and therefore have ye no doubt of none earthly knight.'

'Hope ye so that I may any while stand a proved knight?' said Beaumains.

'Yea,' said Launcelot, 'do as ye have done, and I shall be your warrant.'

'Then, I pray you,' said Beaumains, 'give me the order of knighthood.'

'Then must ye tell me your name,' said Launcelot, 'and of what kin ye be born.'

'Sir, so that ye will not discover me I shall,' said Beaumains.

'Nay,' said Sir Launcelot, 'and that I promise you by the faith of my body, until it be openly known.'

'Then, Sir,' he said, 'my name is Gareth, and brother unto Sir Gawaine, of father and mother.'

'Ah! Sir,' said Sir Launcelot, 'I am more gladder of you than I was, for ever me thought ye should be of great blood, and that ye came not to the court neither for meat nor for drink.'

And then Sir Launcelot gave him the order of knighthood. And then Sir Gareth prayed him for to depart, and let him go. So Sir Launcelot departed from him and came to Sir Kay, and made him to be borne home upon his shield, and so he was healed hard with the life, and all men scorned Sir Kay, and in especial Sir Gawaine and Sir Launcelot said it was not his part to rebuke [any] young man, for full little knew he of what birth he is come, and for what cause he came to this court. And so we leave off Sir Kay and turn we unto Beaumains. When he had overtaken the damsel anon she said, 'What dost thou here? thou stinkest all of the kitchen, thy clothes be foul of the grease and tallow that thou gainedst in King Arthur's kitchen; weenest thou,' said she, 'that I allow thee, for yonder knight that thou killedst? Nay truly, for thou slewest him unhappily and cowardly, therefore return again, kitchen page. I know thee well, for Sir Kay named thee Beaumains. What art thou but a turner of broaches and a washer of dishes!'

'Damsel,' said Sir Beaumains, 'say to me what ye list, I will not go from you whatsoever ye say, for I have undertaken of King Arthur for to achieve your adventure, and I shall finish it to the end, or I shall die therefore.'

'Fie on thee, kitchen knave. Wilt thou finish mine adventure? thou shalt anon be met withal, that thou wouldest not, for all the broth that ever thou suppest, once look him in the face.'

'I shall assay,' said Beaumains. So as they thus rode in the wood, there came a man flying all that ever he might.

'Whither wilt thou?' said Beaumains.

'O lord,' said he, 'help me, for hereby in a slade are six thieves that have taken my lord and bound him, and I am afraid lest they will slay him.'

'Bring me thither,' said Beaumains.

And so they rode together till they came there as the knight was bound; and then he rode unto the thieves, and struck one at the first stroke to death, and then another, and at the third stroke he slew the third thief; and then the other three fled, and he rode after and overtook them, and then those three thieves turned again and hard assailed Sir Beaumains; but at the last he slew them; and returned and unbound the knight. And the knight thanked him, and prayed him to ride with him to his castle there a little beside, and he should worshipfully reward him for his good deeds.

'Sir,' said Beaumains, 'I will no reward have; I was this day made knight of noble Sir Launcelot, and therefore I will have no reward, but God reward me. And also I must follow this damsel.'

And when he came nigh her, she bade him ride from her, 'for thou smellest all of the kitchen. Weenest thou that I have joy of thee? for all this deed that thou hast done is but mishappened thee. But thou shalt see a sight shall make thee turn again, and that lightly.'

Chapter VI: How Sir Beaumains fought with the Knight of the Black Lawns, and fought so long with him that the Black Knight fell down and died.

[Then all the next day] this Beaumains rode with that lady till even-song time, and ever she chid him and would not rest. And then they came to a black lawn, and there was a black hawthorn, and thereon hung a black banner, and on the other side there hung a black shield, and by it stood a black spear and a long, and a great black horse covered with silk, and a black stone fast by.

There sat a knight all armed in black harness, and his name was the Knight of the Black Lawns. When the damsel saw the black knight, she bade Sir Beaumains flee down the valley, for his horse was not saddled.

'I thank you,' said Sir Beaumains, 'for always ye will have me a coward.'

With that the Black Knight came to the damsel, and said, 'Fair damsel, have ye brought this knight from King Arthur's court to be your champion?'

'Nay, fair knight,' said she, 'this is but a kitchen knave, that hath been fed in King Arthur's kitchen for alms.'

'Wherefore cometh he in such array?' said the kinght: 'it is great shame that he beareth you company.'

'Sir, I cannot be delivered of him,' said the damsel, 'for with me he rideth maugre [*in spite of*] mine head; would to God ye would put him from me, or else to slay him if ye may, for he is an unhappy knave, and unhappy hath he done to-day through misadventure; for I saw him slay two knights at the passage of the water, and other deeds he did before right marvellous and through unhappiness.'

'That marvelleth me,' said the Black Knight, 'that any man the which is of worship will have to do with him.'

'Sir, they know him not,' said the damsel, 'and because he rideth with me, they think he is some man of worship born.'

'That may be,' said the Black Knight, 'howbeit, as ye say that he be no man of worship, he is a full likely person, and full like to be a strong man; but thus much shall I grant you,' said the Black Knight, 'I shall put him down upon his feet, and his horse and his harness he shall leave with me, for it were shame to me to do him any more harm.'

When Sir Beaumains heard him say thus, he said, 'Sir knight, thou art full liberal of my horse and my harness. I let thee wit it cost thee nought, and whether it liketh thee or not this lawn will I pass, maugre thine head, and horse nor harness gettest thou none of me, but if thou win them with thy hands; and therefore let see what thou canst do.'

'Sayest thou that?' said the black knight, 'now yield thy lady from thee, for it beseemeth never a kitchen page to ride with such a lady.'

'Thou liest,' said Beaumains, 'I am a gentleman born, and of more high lineage than thou, and that will I prove on thy body.'

Then in great wrath they departed with their horses, and came together as it had been the thunder; and the black knight's spear brake, and Beaumains thrust him through both his sides, and therewith his spear brake, and the truncheon left still in his side. But nevertheless the black knight drew his sword, and smote many eager strokes and of great might, and hurt Beaumains full sore. But at the last the black knight within an hour and an half he fell down off his horse in a swoon, and there he died. And then Beaumains saw him so well horsed and armed, then he alighted down, and armed him in his armour, and so took his horse and rode after the damsel.

When she saw him come nigh, she said, 'Away, kitchen knave, out of the wind, for the smell of thy foul clothes grieveth me. Alas,' she said, 'that ever such a knave as thou art should by mishap slay so good a knight as thou hast done, but all this is thine unhappiness. But hereby is one shall pay thee all thy payment, and therefore yet I counsel thee, flee.'

'It may happen me,' said Beaumains, 'to be beaten or slain, but I warn you, fair damsel, I will not flee away for him, nor leave your company for all that ye can say; for ever ye say that they slay me or beat me, but how soever it happeneth I escape, and they lie on the ground, and therefore it were as good for you to hold you still, than thus to rebuke me all day, for away will I not till I feel the uttermost of this journey, or else I will be slain or truly beaten; therefore ride on your way, for follow you I will, whatsoever happen.'

Chapter VII: How the Brother of the Knight that was Slain met with Sir Beaumains, and fought with Sir Beaumains, which yielded him at the last.

Thus as they rode together they saw a knight come driving by them all in green, both his horse and his harness, and when he came nigh the damsel he asked of her, 'Is that my brother, the black knight, that ye have brought with you?'

'Nay, nay,' said she, 'this unhappy kitchen knave hath slain your brother through unhappiness.'

'Alas!' said the green knight, 'that is great pity that so noble a knight as he was should so unhappily be slain, and namely of a knave's hand, as ye say he is. Ah, traitor!' said the green knight, 'thou shalt die for slaying of my brother; he was a full noble knight, and his name was Sir Periard.'

'I defy thee,' said Sir Beaumains, 'for I let thee to wit I slew him knightly, and not shamefully.'

Therewithal the green knight rode unto an horn that was green, and it hung upon a thorn, and there he blew three deadly notes, and there came three damsels that lightly armed him. And then took he a great horse, and a green shield and a green spear. And then they ran together with all their mights; and brake their spears unto their hands. And then they drew their swords, and gave many sad strokes, and either of them wounded other full ill. And at the last at an overthwart Beaumains' horse struck the green knight's horse upon the side [that] he fell to the earth. And then the green knight avoided his horse lightly, and dressed him upon foot. That saw Beaumains, and therewithal he alighted, and they rushed together like two mighty champions a long while, and sore they bled both. With that came the damsel and said, ' My lord the green knight, why for shame stand ye so long fighting with the kitchen knave? Alas, it is shame that ever ye were made knight, to see such a lad match such a knight, as the weed overgrew the corn.'

Therewith the green knight was ashamed, and therewithal he gave a great stroke of might, and clave his shield through. When Beaumains saw his shield cloven asunder he was a little ashamed of that stroke, and of her language; and then he gave him such a buffet upon the helm that he fell on his knees; and so suddenly Beaumains pulled him upon the ground grovelling. And then the green knight cried him mercy, and yielded him unto Sir Beaumains, and prayed him to slay him not.

'All is in vain,' said Beaumains, 'for thou shalt die, but if this damsel that came with me pray me to save thy life.'

And therewithal he unlaced his helm, like as he would slay him.

'Fie upon thee, false kitchen page, I will never pray thee to save his life, for I never will be so much in thy danger.'

'Then shall he die,' said Beaumains.

'Not so hardy, thou foul knave,' said the damsel, 'that thou slay him.'

'Alas,' said the green knight, 'suffer me not to die, for a fair word may save my life. O fair knight,' said the green knight, 'save my life, and I will forgive the death of my brother, and forever to become thy man, and thirty knights that hold of me forever shall do you service.'

Said the damsel, 'That such a kitchen knave should have thee and thirty knights' service!'

'Sir knight,' said Sir Beaumains, 'all this availeth not, but if my damsel speak with me for thy life.'

And therewithal he made resemblance to slay him.

'Let be,' said the damsel, 'thou knave, slay him not, for if thou do, thou shalt repent it.'

'Damsel,' said Sir Beaumains, 'your charge is to me a pleasure, and at your commandment his life shall be saved, and else not.'

Then he said, 'Sir knight with the green arms, I release thee quit [*acquitted*] at this damsel's request, for I will not make her wroth, I will fulfil all that she chargeth me.'

And then the green knight kneeled down and did him homage with his sword.

Chapter VIII: How the Damsel always rebuked Sir Beaumains, and would not suffer him to sit at her Table, but called him Kitchen Page.

And always the damsel rebuked Sir Beaumains. And so that night they went unto rest, and all that night the green knight commanded thirty knights privily to watch Beaumains, for to keep him from all treason. And so on the morn they all arose, and heard their mass and brake their fast, and then they took their horses and rode on their way, and the green knight conveyed them through the forest, and there the green knight said, 'My lord Beaumains, I and these thirty knights shall be always at your summons, both early and late, at your calling, and where that ever ye will send us.'

'It is well said,' said Beaumains; 'when that I call upon you ye must yield you unto King Arthur and all your knights.'

'If that ye so command us, we shall be ready at all times,' said the green knight.

'Fie, fie, upon thee,' said the damsel, 'that any good knights should be obedient unto a kitchen knave.'

So then departed the green knight and the damsel. And then she said unto Beaumains, 'Why followest thou me, thou kitchen boy, cast away thy shield and thy spear and flee away, yet I counsel thee betimes, or thou shalt say right soon, Alas!'

Chapter IX: How Sir Beaumains suffered Great Rebukes of the Damsel, and he suffered it patiently.

'Damsel,' said Sir Beaumains, 'ye are uncourteous so to rebuke me as ye do, for meseemeth I have done you great service, and ever ye threaten me for I shall be beaten with knights that we meet, but ever for all your boast they lie in the dust or in the mire, and therefore I pray you rebuke me no more; and when ye see me beaten or yielden as recreant, then may ye bid me go from you shamefully, but first I let you wit I will not depart from you, for I were worse than a fool and I would depart from you all the while that I win worship.'

'Well,' said she, 'right soon there shall meet a knight shall pay thee all thy wages, for he is the most man of worship of the world, except King Arthur.'

'I will well,' said Beaumains; 'the more he is of worship the more shall be my worship to have ado with him.'

Then anon they were ware where was before them a city rich and fair. And betwixt them and the city a mile and a half there was a fair meadow that seemed new mown, and therein were many pavilions fair to behold.

'Lo,' said the damsel, 'yonder is a lord that owneth yonder city, and his custom is when the weather is fair to lie in this meadow to joust and tourney; and ever there be about him five hundred knights and gentlemen of arms, and there be all manner of games that any gentleman can devise.'

'That goodly lord,' said Beaumains, 'would I fain see.'

'Thou shalt see him time enough,' said the damsel.

And so as she rode near she espied the pavilion where he was.

'Lo,' said she, 'seest thou yonder pavilion, that is all of the colour of Inde, and all manner of thing that there is about, men and women, and horses trapped, shields and spears, all of the colour of Inde, and his name is Sir Persant of Inde, the most lordliest knight that ever thou lookedest on.'

'It may well be,' said Beaumains, 'but be he never so stout a knight, in this field I shall abide till that I see him under his shield.'

'Ah, fool,' said she, 'thou were better flee betimes.'

'Why,' said Beaumains, 'and he be such a knight as ye make him, he will not set upon me with all his men, or with his five hundred knights. For and there come no more but one at once, I shall him not fail whilst my life lasteth.'

'Fie, fie,' said the damsel, 'that ever such a dirty knave should blow such a boast.'

'Damsel,' he said, 'ye are to blame so to rebuke me, for I had liever do five battles than so to be rebuked; let him come, and then let him do his worst.'

'Sir,' she said, 'I marvel what thou art, and of what kin thou art come: boldly thou speakest, and boldly thou has done, that have I seen: therefore I pray thee save thyself and thou mayest, for thy horse and thou have had great travail, and I dread we dwell over long from the siege, for it is but hence seven mile, and all perilous passages we are past, save all only this passage, and here I dread me sore lest ye shall catch some hurt, therefore I would ye were hence, that ye were not bruised nor hurt with this strong knight. But I let you wit this Sir Persant of Inde is nothing of might nor strength unto the knight that laid the siege about my lady.'

'As for that,' said Sir Beaumains, 'be it as it may; for since I am come so nigh this knight I will prove his might or [*ere*] I depart from him, and else I shall be, shamed and [*if*] I now withdraw me from him. And therefore, damsel, have ye no doubt by the grace of God I shall so deal with this knight, that within two hours after noon I shall deliver him, and then shall we come to the siege by daylight.'

'Oh, mercy, marvel have I,' said the damsel, 'what manner a man ye be for it may never be otherwise but that ye be come of a noble blood, for so foul and shamefully did never woman rule a knight as I have done you, and ever courteously ye have suffered me, and that came never but of a gentle blood.'

'Damsel,' said Beaumains, 'a knight may little do that may not suffer a damsel; for whatsoever ye said unto me I took none heed to your words, for the more ye said the more ye angered me, and my wrath I wreaked upon them that I had ado withal. And therefore all the missaying that ye missayed me furthered me in my battle, and caused me to think to show and prove myself at the end what I was; for peradventure though I had meat in King Arthur's kitchen, yet I might have had meat enough in other places; but all that I did for to prove my friends; and whether I be a gentleman born or no, fair damsel, I have done you gentleman's service, and peradventure better service yet will I do you or [*before*] I depart from you.'

'Alas,' said she, 'fair Beaumains, forgive me all that I have missaid and misdone against you.'

'With all my heart,' said Sir Beaumains, 'I forgive it you, for ye did nothing but as ye ought to do, for all your evil words pleased me; and, damsel,' said Sir' Beaumains, 'sith [*since*] it liketh you to speak thus fair to me, wit ye well it gladdeth greatly mine heart; and now meseemeth there is no knight living but I am able enough for him.'

Chapter X: How Sir Beaumains fought with Sir Persant of Inde, and made him to be yielden.

With this Sir Persant of Inde had espied them, as they hoved [*hovered*] in the field, and knightly he sent to them to know whether he came in war or in peace.

'Say unto thy lord,' said Sir Beaumains, 'I take no force,[1] but whether as him list[2] himself.'

---

1. 'I take no force', I care not.
2. 'Him list', he wishes, he pleases.

So the messenger went again unto Sir Persant, and told him all his answer.

'Well,' said he, 'then will I have ado with him to the uttermost;' and so he purveyed him [*prepared himself*], and rode against him. And when Sir Beaumains saw him, he made him ready, and there they met with all the might that their horses might run, and brake their spears either in three pieces, and their horses rashed so together that both their horses fell dead to the earth; and lightly they avoided their horses, and put their shields before them, and drew their swords, and gave each other many great strokes, that sometime they so hurled together that they fell both grovelling on the ground. Thus they fought two hours and more, that their shields and their hauberks were all forhewen [*hew to pieces*] and in many places they were sore wounded. So at the last Sir Beaumains smote him through the cost [*rib part*] of the body, and then he retrayed him [*drew back*] here and there, and knightly maintained his battle long time. And at the last Sir Beaumains smote Sir Persant on the helm that he fell grovelling to the earth, and then he leaped overthwart [*across*] upon him, and unlaced his helm for to have slain him. Then Sir Persant yielded him, and asked him mercy. With that came the damsel and prayed him to save his life.

'I will well,' said Sir Beaumains, 'for it were pity that this noble knight should die.'

'Gramercy,' said Sir Persant, 'gentle knight and damsel, for certainly now I know well it was you that slew the black knight my brother at the blackthorn; he was a full noble knight, his name was Sir Periard. Also I am sure that ye are he that won mine other brother the green knight: his name was Sir Pertolope. Also ye won the red knight, my brother, Sir Perimones. And now, sir, sith ye have won these knights, this shall I do for to please you: ye shall have homage and fealty of me, and an hundred knights to be always at your command, to go and ride where ye will command us.'

And so they went unto Sir Persant's pavilion, and there he drank wine and eat spices. And afterward Sir Persant made him to rest upon a bed till it was supper time, and after supper to bed again. And so we leave him there till on the morrow.

Chapter XI: How the Damsel and Beaumains came to the Siege, and came to a Sycamore Tree, and there Beaumains blew a Horn, and then the Knight of the Red Lawns came to fight with him.

Now leave we the knight and the dwarf, and speak we of Beaumains, that all night lay in the hermitage, and upon the morn he and the damsel Linet heard their mass, and brake their fast. And then they took their horses and rode throughout a fair forest, and then they came to a plain, and saw where were many pavilions and tents, and a fair castle, and there was much smoke and great noise. And when they came near the siege Sir Beaumains espied upon great trees, as he rode, how there hung full goodly armed knights by the neck, and their shields about their necks with their swords, and gilt spurs upon their heels, and so there hung shamefully nigh forty knights with rich arms. Then Sir Beaumains abated his countenance, and said, 'What thing meaneth this?'

'Fair sir,' saith the damsel, 'abate not your cheer for all this sight, for ye must encourage yourself, or else ye be all shent [*ruined*], for all these knights came hither unto this siege to rescue my sister dame Lyoness, and when the red knight of the red lawns had overcome them, he put them to this shameful death, without mercy and pity, and in the same wise he will serve you, but if ye quit [*acquit*] you the better.'

'Now Jesu defend me,' said Sir Beaumains, 'from such a villanous death and shenship [*disgrace*] of arms! for rather than thus I should fare withal, I would rather be slain manfully in plain battle.'

From Sidney Lanier, 'Of Sir Gareth of Orkney', *The Boy's King Arthur*. Illustrated by N.C. Wyeth. (New York: Scribner, 1917), facing 82.

'So were ye better,' said the damsel, 'trust not in him, for in him is no courtesy, but all goeth to the death or shameful murder, and that is great pity, for he is a full likely man and well made of body, and a full noble knight of prowess, and a lord of great lands and possessions.'

'Truly,' said Sir Beaumains, 'he may well be a good knight, but he useth shameful customs, and it is great marvel that he endureth so long, that none of the noble knights of my lord King Arthur's court have not dealt with him.'

And then they rode unto the ditches, and saw them double ditched with full strong walls, and there were lodged many great estates and lords nigh the walls, and there was great noise of minstrels, and the sea beat upon the one side of the walls, where as were many ships and mariners' noise with hale and how.[3] And also there was fast by a sycamore tree, and thereon hung an horn, the greatest that ever they saw, of an elephant's bone.

'And this knight of the red lawns hath hanged it up there, that if there come any errant knight, he must blow that horn, and then will he make him ready, and come to him to do battle. But sir, I pray you,' said the damsel Linet, 'blow ye not the horn till it be high noon, for now it is about prime, and now increaseth his might, that, as men say, he hath seven men's strength.'

'Ah, fie for shame, fair damsel, say ye never so more to me, for, and he were as good a knight as ever was, I shall never fail him in his most might, for either I will win worship worshipfully, or die knightly in the field.'

And therewith he spurred his horse straight to the sycamore tree and blew the horn so eagerly that all the siege and the castle rang thereof. And then there leaped out knights out of their tents and pavilions, and they within the castle looked, over the walls and out at windows. Then the red knight of the red lawns armed him hastily, and two barons set on his spurs upon his heels, and all was blood-red, his armour, spear, and shield. And an earl buckled his helm upon his head, and then they brought him a red spear and a red steed, and so he rode into a little vale under the castle, that all that were in the castle and at the siege might behold the battle.

Chapter XII: How the two knights met together, and of their talking, and how they began their battle.

'Sir,' said the damsel Linet unto Sir Beaumains, 'look ye be glad and light, for yonder is your deadly enemy, and at yonder window is my lady my sister, dame Lyoness.'

'Where?' said Beaumains.

'Yonder,' said the damsel, and pointed with her finger.

'That is truth,' said Beaumains. 'She seemeth afar the fairest lady that ever I looked upon, and truly,' he said, 'I ask no better quarrel than now for to do battle, for truly she shall be my lady, and for her I will fight.'

And ever he looked up to the window with glad countenance. And the lady Lyoness made courtesy to him down to the earth, with holding up both her hands. With that the red knight of the red lawns called to Sir Beaumains, 'Leave, sir knight, thy looking, and behold me, I counsel thee, for I warn thee well she is my lady, and for her I have done many strong battles.'

'If thou have so done,' said Beaumains, 'meseemeth it was but waste labour, for she loveth none of thy fellowship, and thou to love that loveth not thee, is a great folly. For if I understood that she were not glad of my coming, I would be advised or I did battle for her, but I understand by the besieging of this castle she may forbear thy company. And therefore wit thou well, thou red knight of the red lawns, I love her and will rescue her, or else die in the quarrel.'

'Sayst thou that?' said the red knight; 'me seemth thou ought of reason to beware by yonder knights that thou sawest hang upon yonder great elms.'

'Fie, fie, for shame,' said Sir Beaumains, 'that ever thou shouldest say or do so evil and such shamefulness, for in that thou shamest thyself and the order of knighthood, and

---

3. 'Hale and how', haul and ho: the sailors' cries in hoisting away, etc.

than mayst be sure there will no lady love thee that knoweth thy detestable customs. And now thou weenest [*thinkest*] that the sight of these hanged knights should fear [*scare*] me and make me aghast, nay truly not so, that shameful sight causeth me to have courage and hardiness against thee, more than I would have had against thee and if thou be a well ruled knight.'

'Make thee ready,' said the red knight of the red lawns, 'and talk no longer with me.'

Then Sir Beaumains bade the damsel go from him, and then they put their spears in their rests, and came together with all the might they had, and either smote other in the midst of their shields, that the paytrels [*breast-plates*], surcingles, and cruppers burst, and fell both to the ground with the reins of their bridles in their hands, and so they lay a great while sore astonied, and all they that were in the castle and at the siege wend [*thought*] their necks had been broken, and then many a stranger and other said that the strange knight was a big man and a noble jouster, 'for or [*ere*] now we saw never no knight match the red knight of the red lawns;' thus they said both within the castle and without. Then they lightly avoided their horses and put their shields afore them, and drew their swords and ran together like two fierce lions, and either gave other such buffets upon their helms that they reeled both backward two strides; and then they recovered both, and, hewed great pieces from their harness and their shields that a great part fell in the fields.

Chapter XIII: How after Long Fighting Beaumains overcame the Knight, and would have slain him, but at the Request of the Lords he saved his Life, and made him to yield him to the Lady.

And then thus they fought till it was past noon and never would stint till at last they lacked wind both, and then they stood wagging and scattering, panting, blowing and bleeding, that all that beheld them for the most part wept for pity. So when they had rested them a while they went to battle again, tracing, racing, foining [*feinting*], as two boars. And at some time they took their run as it had been two rams, and hurtled together that sometimes they fell grovelling to the earth; and at some time they were so amazed that either took other's sword instead of his own.

Thus they endured till even-song time [*vespers*], that there was none that beheld them might know whether was like to win the battle; and their armour was so far hewn that men might see their naked sides, and in other places they were naked, but ever the naked places they did defend. And the red knight was a wily knight of war, and his wily fighting taught Sir Beaumains to be wise; but he abought [*paid for*] it full sore ere he did espy his fighting. And thus by assent of them both, they granted either other to rest; and so they set them down upon two mole-hills there beside the fighting place, and either of them unlaced his helm, and took the cold wind, for either of their pages was fast by them, to come when they called to unlace their harness and to set it on again at their command. And then when Sir Beaumains' helm was off, he looked up unto the window, and there he saw the fair lady dame Lyoness. And she made to him such countenance that his heart was light and joyful. And therewith he started up suddenly, and bade the red knight make him ready to do the battle to the uttermost.

'I will well,' said the red knight.

And then they laced up their helms, and their pages avoided [*got out of the way*], and they stepped together and fought freshly. But the red knight of the red lawns awaited him, and at an overthwart [*crosswise*] smote him within the hand, that his sword fell out at his hand; and yet he gave him another buffet on the helm that he fell grovelling to the earth, and the red knight fell over him for to hold him down.

Then cried the maiden Linet on high, 'O Sir Beaumains, where is thy courage become! Alas, my lady my sister beholdeth thee, and she sobbeth and weepeth, that maketh mine heart heavy.'

When Sir Beaumains heard her say so, he started up with a great might and gat him upon his feet, and lightly he leaped to his sword and griped it in his hand, and doubled his pace unto the red knight, and there they fought a new battle together. But Sir Beaumains then doubled his strokes, and smote so thick that he smote the sword out of his hand, and then he smote him upon the helm that he fell to the earth, and Sir Beaumains fell upon him, and unlaced his helm to have slain him; and then he yielded him and asked mercy, and said with a loud voice, 'O noble knight, I yield me to thy mercy.'

Then Sir Beaumains bethought him upon the knights that he had made to be hanged shamefully, and then he said, 'I may not with my worship save thy life, for the shameful deaths thou hast caused many full good knights to die.'

'Sir,' said the red knight of the red lawns, 'hold your hand, and ye shall know the causes why I put them to so shameful a death.'

'Say on,' said Sir Beaumains.

'Sir, I loved once a lady, a fair damsel, and she had her brother slain, and she said it was Sir Launcelot du Lake, or else Sir Gawaine, and she prayed me as that I loved her heartily that I would make her a promise by the faith of my knighthood for to labour daily in arms until I met with one of them, and all that I might overcome I should put them unto a villanous death; and this is the cause that I have put all these knights to death, and so I ensured her to do all the villany unto King Arthur's knights, and that I should take vengeance upon all these knights. And, sir, now I will thee tell that every day my strength increaseth till noon, and all this time have I seven men's strength.'

Chapter XIV: How the Knight yielded him, and how Beaumains made him to go unto King Arthur's Court, and to cry Sir Launcelot Mercy.

Then came there many earls, and barons, and noble knights, and prayed that knight to save his life, and take him to your prisoner: and all they fell upon their knees and prayed him of mercy, and that he would save his life, and, 'Sir,' they all said, 'it were fairer of him to take homage and fealty, and let him hold his lands of you, than for to slay him: by his death ye shall have none advantage, and his misdeeds that be done may not be undone; and therefore he shall make amends to all parties, and we all will become your men, and do you homage and fealty.'

'Fair lords,' said Beaumains, 'wit you well I am full loth to slay this knight, nevertheless he hath done passing ill and shamefully. But insomuch all that he did was at a lady's request, I blame him the less, and so for your sake I will release him, that he shall have his life upon this covenant, that he go within the castle and yield him there to the lady, and if she will forgive and quit [acquit] him, I will well; with this that he make her amends of all the trespass he hath done against her and her lands. And also, when that is done, that ye go unto the court of King Arthur, and there that ye ask Sir Launcelot mercy, and Sir Gawaine, for the evil will ye have had against them.'

'Sir,' said the red knight of the red lawns, 'all this will I do as ye command, and certain assurance and sureties ye shall have.'

And so then when the assurance was made, he made his homage and fealty, and all those earls and barons with him. And then the maiden Linet came to Sir Beaumains and unarmed him, and searched his wounds, and stinted his blood, and in likewise she did to the red knight of the red lawns. And so they sojourned ten days in their tents. And the red knight made his lords and servants to do all the pleasure that they might unto Sir Beaumains.

And within a while after, the red knight of the red lawns went unto the castle and put him in the lady Lyoness' grace, and so she received him upon sufficient sureties, and all her hurts were well restored of all that she could complain. And then he departed and went unto the court of King Arthur, and there openly the red knight of the red lawns put him in the mercy of Sir Launcelot and Sir Gawaine, and there he told openly how he was overcome, and by whom, and also he told of all the battles, from the beginning to the ending.

'Jesus, mercy,' said King Arthur and Sir Gawaine, 'we marvel much of what blood he is come, for he is a full noble knight.'

'Have ye no marvel,' said Sir Launcelot, 'for ye shall right well wit that he is come of a full noble blood, and, as for his might and hardiness, there be but few now living that is so mighty as he is and so noble of prowess.'

'It seemeth by you,' said King Arthur, 'that ye know his name, and from whence he is come, and of what blood he is.'

'I suppose I do so,' said Sir Launcelot, 'or else I would not have given him the order of knighthood; but he gave me at that time such charge that I should never discover him until he required me, or else it be known openly by some other.'

Now return we unto Sir Beaumains, which desired of the damsel Linet that he might see her sister his lady.

'Sir,' said she, 'I would fain ye saw her.'

Then Sir Beaumains armed him at all points, and took his horse and his spear, and rode straight to the castle. And when he came to the gate, he found there many men armed, that pulled up the drawbridge and drew the port close. Then marvelled he why they would not suffer him to enter in. And then he looked up to the window, and there he saw the fair lady dame Lyoness, that said on high: 'Go thy way, Sir Beaumains, for as yet thou shalt not wholly have my love, until the time thou be called one of the number of the worthy knights; and therefore go and labour in arms worshipfully these twelve months, and then ye shall hear new tidings; and perdé [per dieu, truly] a twelvemonth will be soon gone, and trust you me, fair knight, I shall be true unto you, and shall never betray you, but unto my death I shall love you and none other.'

And therewithal she turned her from the window. And Sir Beaumains rode away from the castle in making great moan and sorrow; and so he rode here and there, and wist not whither he rode, till it was dark night; and then it happened him to come to a poor man's house, and there he was harboured all that night: But Sir Beaumains could have no rest, but wallowed and writhed for the love of the lady of the castle. And so on the morrow he took his horse and his armour, and rode till it was noon; and then he came unto a broad water, and thereby was a great lodge, and there he alighted to sleep, and laid his head upon his shield, and betook his horse to the dwarf, and commanded him to watch all night.

Now turn we to the lady of the castle, that thought much upon Sir Beaumains; and then she called unto her Sir Gringamor her brother, and prayed him in all manner, as he loved her heartily, that he would ride after Sir Beaumains, 'and ever have him in a wait [look after him] till that ye may find him sleeping, for I am sure in his heaviness he will alight down in some place and lie down to sleep, and therefore have your watch upon him, and, in the priviest wise [softest way] that ye can, take his dwarf from him, and go your way with him as fast as ever ye may or Sir Beaumains awake; for my sister Linet hath showed me that the dwarf can tell of what kindred he is come, and what his right name is; and in the meanwhile I and my sister will ride to your castle to await when ye shall bring with you this dwarf, and then when ye have brought him to your castle, I will have him in examination myself; unto the time I know what his right name is, and of what kindred he is come, shall I never be merry at my heart.'

'Sister,' said Sir Gringamor, 'all this shall be done after your intent.' And so he rode all the other day and the night till that he found Sir Beaumains lying by a water, and his head upon his shield, for to sleep. And then when he saw Sir Beaumains fast on sleep, he came stilly stalking behind the dwarf, and plucked him fast under his arm, and so he rode away with him as fast as ever he might unto his own castle. But ever as he rode with the dwarf toward his castle he cried unto his lord and prayed him of help. And therewith awoke Sir Beaumains, and up he leaped lightly, and saw where Sir Gringamor rode his way with the dwarf, and so Sir Gringamor rode out of his sight.

Chapter XV: How Sir Gareth, otherwise called Beaumains, came to the Presence of his Lady, and how they took Acquaintance, and of their Love.

Then Sir Beaumains put on his helm anon, and buckled his shield, and took his horse and rode after him all that ever he might ride, through marshes and fields and great dales, that many times his horse and he plunged over the head in deep mires, for he knew not the way, but he took the next [*nearest*] way in that woodness [*madness*] that many times he was like to perish. [And so he came following his dwarf to Sir Gringamor's castle. But aforetime the lady Lyoness had come and had the dwarf in examination; and the dwarf had told the lady how that Sir Beaumains was the son of a king, and how his mother was sister to King Arthur, and how his right name was Sir Gareth of Orkney.]

And as they sat thus talking, there came Sir Beaumains at the gate with an angry countenance, and his sword drawn in his hand, and cried aloud that all the castle might hear it, saying, 'Thou traitor, Sir Gringamor, deliver me my dwarf again, or by the faith that I owe to the order of knighthood, I shall do thee all the harm that I can.'

Then Sir Gringamor looked out at a window, and said, 'Sir Gareth of Orkney, leave thy boasting words, for thou gettest not thy dwarf again,'

'Thou coward knight,' said Sir Gareth, 'bring him with thee, and come and do battle with me, and win him, and take him.'

'So will I do,' said Sir Gringamor, 'and me list [*if it please me*], but for all thy great words thou gettest him not.'

'Ah, fair brother,' said dame Lyoness, 'I would he had his dwarf again, for I would not he were wroth, for how he hath told me all my desire I will no longer keep the dwarf, And also, brother, he hath done much for me, and delivered me from the red knight of the red lawns, and therefore, brother, I owe him my service afore all knights living; and wit ye well I love him above all other knights, and full fain would I speak with him, but in no wise I would he wist what I were, but that I were another strange lady.'

'Well,' said Sir Gringamor, 'sith [*since*] that I know your will, I will now obey unto him.'

And therewithal he went down unto Sir Gareth, and said, 'Sir, I cry you mercy, and all that I have misdone against your person I will amend it at your own will, and therefore I pray you that you will alight, and take such cheer as I can make you here in this castle.'

'Shall I then have my dwarf again?' said Sir Gareth.

'Yea, sir, and all the pleasure that I can make you, for as soon as your dwarf told me what ye were and of what blood that ye are come, and what noble deeds ye have done in these marches [*borders*], then I repent me of my deeds.'

And then Sir Gareth alighted down from his horse, and therewith came his dwarf and took his horse.

'O my fellow,' said Sir Gareth, 'I have had many evil adventures for thy sake.'

And so Sir Gringamor took him by the hand, and led him into the hall, and there was Sir Gringamor's wife.

And then there came forth into the hall dame Lyoness arrayed like a princess, and there she made him passing good cheer, and he her again. And they had goodly language and lovely countenance together. And Sir Gareth many times thought in himself, 'Would to God that the lady of the Castle Perilous were so fair as she is!' There were all manner of games and plays, both of dancing and leaping; and ever the more Sir Gareth beheld the lady, the more he loved her; and so he burned in love that he was past himself in his understanding. And forth toward night they went to supper, and Sir Gareth might not eat, for his love was so hot that he wist not where he was. All these looks Sir Gringamor espied, and after supper he called his sister dame Lyoness unto a chamber, and said: 'Fair sister, I have well espied your countenance between you and this knight, and I will, sister, that ye wit that he is a full noble knight, and if ye can make him to abide here, I will do to him all the pleasure that I can, for and ye were better than ye be, ye were well bestowed upon him.'

'Fair brother,' said dame Lyoness, 'I understand well that the knight is good, and come he is of a noble house; notwithstanding I will assay him better, for he hath had great labour for my love, and hath passed many a dangerous passage.'

Right so Sir Gringamor went unto Sir Gareth, and said: 'Sir, make ye good cheer; for wist [*know*] ye well that she loveth you as well as ye do her, and better if better may be.'

'And I wist that,' said Sir Gareth, 'there lived not a gladder man than I would be.'

'Upon my worship,' said Sir Gringamor, 'trust unto my promise; and as long as it liketh you ye shall sojourn with me, and this lady shall be with us daily and nightly to make you all the cheer that she can.'

'I will well,' said Sir Gareth, 'for I have promised to be nigh this country this twelvemonth. And well I am sure King Arthur and other noble knights will find me where that I am within this twelvemonth. For I shall be sought and found, if that I be on live.'

And then the noble knight Sir Gareth went unto the dame Lyoness, which he then much loved, and kissed her many times, and either made great joy of other. And there she promised him her love, certainly to love him and none other the days of her life. Then this lady, dame Lyoness, by the assent of her brother, told Sir Gareth all the truth what she was, and how she was the same lady that he did battle for, and how she was lady of the Castle Perilous. And there she told him how she caused her brother to take away his dwarf, 'For this cause, to know the certainty what was your name, and of what kin ye were come.'

And then she let fetch before him Linet the damsel, which had ridden with him many dreary ways. Then was Sir Gareth more gladder than he was tofore. And then they troth plight[4] each other to love, and never to fail while their life lasted.

From *The Boy's King Arthur*, by Sidney Lanier (New York: Scribner, 1884).

---

4. 'Troth', *truth*, and 'plight', *wove*: 'troth plight', *wove their truth together*.

Odin Goes to Mimir's Well

Unlike immortal Zeus, the selfish, tyrannical, and foul-tempered leader of the Greek gods, Odin, king of the Aesir, or Norse gods, took his responsibilities seriously. In addition to being the god of war, he was the god of wisdom, and he used his wisdom to be a good ruler. As a mortal, however, Odin faced danger in every adventure. Padraic Colum emphasizes both Odin's sense of responsibility and his bravery by altering and linking two episodes from the *Poetic Edda* (also known as the *Elder Edda*), a collection of poems recounting the adventures of Norse gods and heroes. Colum characterizes Odin as being motivated by a feeling that he could benefit his subjects if he could gain the ability to see into the future by drinking from Mimir's well of wisdom. He makes Odin's riddling contest with the giant Vafthrudner—an independent episode in the *Poetic Edda*—a major test of worthiness during Odin's quest. By answering the riddles correctly, the disguised Odin avoids death, foreshadows the ability of the Aesir to ultimately defeat the Giants, and demonstrates that he has the cleverness necessary to continue the journey towards wisdom. When he finally reaches the well, Odin pays an excruciating price for the right to drink: he plucks out his own eye. Symbolically, he trades physical sight for inner sight, or wisdom.

*A*nd so Odin, no longer riding on Sleipner, his eight-legged steed; no longer wearing his golden armour and his eagle-helmet, and without even his spear in his hand, travelled through Midgard, the World of Men, and made his way towards Jötunheim, the Realm of the Giants.

No longer was he called Odin All-Father, but Vegtam the Wanderer. He wore a cloak of dark blue and he carried a traveller's staff in his hands. And now, as he went towards Mimir's Well, which was near to Jötunheim, he came upon a Giant riding on a great Stag.

Odin seemed a man to men and a giant to giants. He went beside the Giant on the great Stag and the two talked together. 'Who art thou, O brother?' Odin asked the Giant.

'I am Vafthrudner, the wisest of the Giants,' said the one who was riding on the Stag. Odin knew him then. Vafthrudner was indeed the wisest of the Giants, and many went to strive to gain wisdom from him. But those who went to him had to answer the riddles Vafthrudner asked, and if they failed to answer the Giant took their heads off.

'I am Vegtam the Wanderer,' Odin said, 'and I know who thou art, O Vafthrudner. I would strive to learn something from thee.'

The Giant laughed, showing his teeth. 'Ho, ho,' he said, 'I am ready for a game with thee. Dost thou know the stakes? My head to thee if I cannot answer any question thou wilt ask. And if thou canst not answer any question that I may ask, then thy head goes to me. Ho, ho, ho. And now let us begin.'

'I am ready,' Odin said.

'Then tell me,' said Vafthrudner, 'tell me the name of the river that divides Asgard from Jötunheim?'

'Ifling is the name of that river,' said Odin. 'Ifling that is dead cold, yet never frozen.'

'Thou hast answered rightly, O Wanderer,' said the Giant. 'But thou hast still to answer other questions. What are the names of the horses that Day and Night drive across the sky?'

Odin The Wanderer

From Colum Padraic, *The Children of* Odin. Illustrated by Willy Pogany. (New York: Macmillan, 1920), 78.

'Skinfaxe and Hrimfaxe,' Odin answered. Vafthrudner was startled to hear one say the names that were known only to the Gods and to the wisest of the Giants. There was only one question now that he might ask before it came to the stranger's turn to ask him questions.

'Tell me,' said Vafthrudner, 'what is the name of the plain on which the last battle will be fought?'

'The Plain of Vigard,' said Odin, 'the plain that is a hundred miles long and a hundred miles across.'

It was now Odin's turn to ask Vafthrudner questions. 'What will be the last words that Odin will whisper into the ear of Baldur, his dear son?' he asked.

Very startled was the Giant Vafthrudner at that question. He sprang to the ground and looked at the stranger keenly.

'Only Odin knows what his last words to Baldur will be,' he said, 'and only Odin would have asked that question. Thou art Odin, O Wanderer, and thy question I cannot answer.'

'Then,' said Odin, 'if thou wouldst keep thy head, answer me this: what price will Mimir ask for a draught from the Well of Wisdom that he guards?'

'He will ask thy right eye as a price, O Odin,' said Vafthrudner.

'Will he ask no less a price than that?' said Odin.

'He will ask no less a price. Many have come to him for a draught from the Well of Wisdom, but no one yet has given the price Mimir asks. I have answered thy question, O Odin. Now give up thy claim to my head and let me go on my way.'

'I give up my claim to thy head,' said Odin. Then Vafthrudner, the wisest of the Giants, went on his way, riding on his great Stag.

It was a terrible price that Mimir would ask for a draught from the Well of Wisdom, and very troubled was Odin All-Father when it was revealed to him. His right eye! For all time to be without the sight of his right eye! Almost he would have turned back to Asgard, giving up his quest for wisdom.

He went on, turning neither to Asgard nor to Mimir's Well. And when he went towards the South he saw Muspelheim, where stood Surtur with the Flaming Sword, a terrible figure, who would one day join the Giants in their war against the Gods. And when he turned North he heard the roaring of the cauldron Hvergelmer as it poured itself out of Niflheim, the place of darkness and dread. And Odin knew that the world must not be left between Surtur, who would destroy it with fire, and Niflheim, that would gather it back to Darkness and Nothingness. He, the eldest of the Gods, would have to win the wisdom that would help to save the world.

And so, with his face stern in front of his loss and pain, Odin All-Father turned and went towards Mimir's Well. It was under the great root of Ygdrassil—the root that grew out of Jötunheim. And there sat Mimir, the Guardian of the Well of Wisdom, with his deep eyes bent upon the deep water. And Mimir, who had drunk every day from the Well of Wisdom, knew who it was that stood before him.

'Hail, Odin, Eldest of the Gods,' he said.

Then Odin made reverence to Mimir, the wisest of the world's beings. 'I would drink from your well, Mimir,' he said.

'There is a price to be paid. All who have come here to drink have shrunk from paying that price. Will you, Eldest of the Gods, pay it?'

'I will not shrink from the price that has to be paid, Mimir,' said Odin All-Father.

'Then drink,' said Mimir. He filled up a great horn with water from the well and gave it to Odin.

Odin took the horn in both his hands and drank and drank. And as he drank all the future became clear to him. He saw all the sorrows and troubles that would fall upon Men and Gods. But he saw, too, why the sorrows and troubles had to fall, and he saw how they might be borne so that Gods and Men, by being noble in the days of sorrow and trouble, would leave in the world a force that one day, a day that was far off indeed, would destroy the evil that brought terror and sorrow and despair into the world.

Then when he had drunk out of the great horn that Mimir had given him, he put his hand to his face and he plucked out his right eye. Terrible was the pain that Odin All-Father endured. But he made no groan nor moan. He bowed his head and put his cloak before his face, as Mimir took the eye and let it sink deep, deep into the water of the Well of Wisdom. And there the Eye of Odin stayed, shining up through the water, a sign to all who came to that place of the price that the Father of the Gods had paid for his wisdom.

From *The Children of Odin: A Book of Northern Myth*, by Padraic Colum (New York: Macmillan, 1920).

The Wonderful Brocade

This elaborate quest tale comes from China's Zhuang people, an ethnic minority that did not have a written language until the 1950s. One source of the tale's appeal is that the object of the quest, the brocade, makes concrete the Oriental aesthetic that graphic art should invite the viewer into a scene. At the same time, the brocade symbolizes the magic and life-transforming power of all art. Other quest elements contribute to the development of a morality tale. For example, the white-haired woman offers help that both tests the brothers' dedication to their mother and reveals their inner qualities. The two older sons show that they put self-love, in the form of greed, ahead of duty to family, an obligation considered to be of exceptional importance to Oriental cultures. As is the case in folk tales from many other cultures, the third son, the one who would at first glance seem the least likely to succeed, reveals that he is the one possessing the love, determination, courage, and wit to become the true hero of the quest. The final ironic scene of the tale develops, in images, a powerful moral lesson: selfless love leads to wealth and happiness whereas selfishness and greed lead to both spiritual and physical poverty.

*O*nce upon a time on the plain at the foot of a huge mountain, there lived an old widow and her three sons.

The woman was very good at weaving brocades. The flowers, trees, birds, and animals she wove on cloth were so lively that everyone wanted to buy her work.

One day, when the woman went to town to sell her brocades, she spied a wonderful picture in a shop. Coloured on that picture was a big house set in a pretty garden, with land stretching into the distance. There was an orchard, a vegetable plot, a fish pond, and lots of farm animals. She couldn't stop looking at it. The more she looked, the happier she felt. Usually she spent all her money on rice, but that day she bought less and took that wonderful picture home.

On her way home she sat down many times to look at the picture. She said to herself, 'How happy I should be if I could live in a wonderful place like this.'

When she got home she showed the picture to her sons, and they too got all excited by it.

The mother asked her biggest son, 'Do you think we could live in this good place?'
He said, 'That is just a dream.'

The mother turned to her second son. 'Do you think we could live in this good place?'
He said, 'Not yet. Perhaps when we die we shall be born again there for a second life.

' The mother said to the youngest son, 'I *shall* die if I cannot live in that good place. '

The youngest son thought for a while and comforted his mother with these words: 'You are such a good weaver, mother. You can almost make a picture come alive. Copy this scene onto a cloth. When you look at it, you will feel as though you are living in the good place.'

She said, 'You are right. I will do it or I shall die.'

The mother bought some colourful silk thread, set up the loom and started to weave the wonderful picture.

Day followed day, month followed month, and still she wove.

The biggest son and the second son didn't like it. They often stopped their mother saying, 'You have woven for months and sold nothing. Why should we do all the work, gathering firewood to sell for rice? We are tired and want to rest.'

But the youngest son said to them, 'Let mother alone. She will die if she doesn't weave. If you think that getting firewood is too heavy or too much trouble for you, leave that job to me.'

And from then on the two older brothers stayed at home, while the youngest boy went far and wide to get firewood, by day and night. Only he kept the four of them alive.

The mother also kept on weaving by day and night. In the evenings, instead of lighting a lamp, they burned some of the wood which the youngest son had fetched. The smoke was so thick that the mother's eyes hurt. In spite of that, the old woman kept on weaving ceaselessly. After a year her tears dropped on the cloth, and where they fell she wove a little river and a round pond. Two years later, blood dropped down from her eyes, and there she wove a red sun and many fresh flowers.

She worked and worked for three years before the brocade was finished.

What a beautiful brocade it was!

The large house had blue tiles, green walls and red pillars. Behind a yellow gate there was a big garden full of flowers in bloom. In the middle of the garden there was a pond with fish swimming to and fro. To the left of the house there was an orchard. The trees were full of red fruit, and on their branches were all kinds of birds. To the right of the house there was a vegetable plot, bursting with green vegetables and yellow melons. Behind the house were fields of rice and corn. A clean stream passed in front of the house, and the red sun shone above it.

'Oh, this cloth is really very beautiful,' the three brothers praised.

The mother gave her waist a stretch and rubbed her aching eyes to look at the cloth. She began to smile.

But just then a strong wind gusted from the west and snatched the wonderful brocade up into the sky, and carried it away to the east.

The woman rushed after it, waving her arms. She was crying. She watched the wonderful brocade disappear, till there was only blue sky to be seen.

The old woman fainted outside the door.

The three brothers helped her into bed. She drank a bowl of herbal tea, and felt a bit better. She said to the biggest son, 'Go to the east and find the cloth. It is as precious as my life.'

The biggest son agreed to go. He put on a pair of straw sandals and set out for the east. After a month's walk he arrived at the foot of a huge mountain.

There he found a cave, and on the right side of the cave there was a stone horse with its mouth wide open as if it wanted to eat the red berries from a nearby tree. A white-haired old woman was sitting at the cave entrance. She asked, 'Boy, where are you going?'

The biggest son replied, 'I am looking for a wonderful brocade. My mother spent three years weaving it, and it was taken away to the east by a strong wind.'

The white-haired old woman said, 'That beautiful brocade was stolen by the spirit maidens of the Sun Mountain of the East. They saw your mother had woven a wonderful brocade and sent the wind to fetch it to them, so they could copy it. It is very hard to find their palace. First, you must pull out two of your teeth and put them into the mouth of my stone horse. With the teeth, it can eat the berries, and when it has eaten ten berries you may ride on its back and it will take you to the Sun Mountain of the East.

'On the way, you must cross a fiery mountain. Oh, the fierce flames of that mountain cannot be described. Do not flinch as the stone horse carries you through the flames: you must bear all hardship, and be silent. You'll be burnt to a little flake of ash if you utter a sound.

'After you get through the flames, you'll come to a wide sea. Gales will buffet you, and rough ice will stab at you. All this you'll have to bear and say nothing. If you shiver or if you speak you'll be buried at the bottom of the sea.

'Beyond the sea is the Sun Mountain of the East. There you may ask the spirit maidens to return your mother's brocade.'

The white-haired old woman looked at his face, and said with a smile, 'My boy, you cannot stand these hardships. Don't go. I'm going to give you a box of gold with which to lead a better life.'

She brought an iron box full of gold from the cave. The biggest boy took it and turned back.

As he walked home, he thought, With this little box of gold, I could lead a rich life. But if I take it home, there is not enough to make four people rich. It is much better for one person to have all of it than to let four people share it.

And so, instead of taking the box of gold home, he made up his mind to go to the big city. The mother's illness grew worse. She waited in bed for two months, but the biggest son didn't come back. Calling the second son, she said, 'Go to the east to search for the wonderful brocade. That cloth is my life-work.'

The second son nodded. He put on his straw sandals and set out for the east. After a month's journey, he reached the mountain. There the old woman still sat near the cave mouth. She told him of the dangerous journey as before. The second son touched his teeth, imagining the scorching flames and the roaring waves, and his face quivered.

The old woman gave him another box of gold. He took it and went to the city, just as his brother did.

The mother lay in bed for another two months. She couldn't eat, and she was as skinny as a stick. She just sobbed bitterly as she lay looking to the east. She looked so hard and cried so much she went blind.

One day the youngest son said to her, 'Mother, my two brothers have gone and nothing has been heard of them. Some unlucky thing must have happened to them on the way. Let me go: I'm sure to bring the beautiful brocade back.'

The mother thought for a while and then said, 'All right. You go but you must take good care of yourself on the way. The neighbours will look after me.'

The youngest son put on his straw sandals and marched bravely to the east. In less than a month, he arrived at the foot of the mountain and found the old woman, still sitting in front of the cave.

The old woman told him what she had told his brothers. She said, 'My child, your two brothers have taken a box of gold each. You can have a box just like theirs. '

But the youngest son struck his breast and said, 'No, I'm going to get the beautiful cloth.' Then he picked up a rock and hit himself in the mouth with it. He took out two of his teeth and put them into the mouth of the stone horse. The big stone horse stirred. It began to eat the berries, and when it had eaten ten, the youngest boy leapt up on its back, gripping fast to its mane. The stone horse neighed a long neigh and off they started for the east.

After three days they reached the blazing mountain. The flames shot upwards. They licked him fiercely, but the boy stood the pain and said nothing. It took them about half an hour to get through the fire. After the fire came the roaring sea, with its sharp and freezing waves coming one after another. They sank icy teeth in him, but the boy stood the pain and said nothing. And at last the stone horse stepped from the sea onto the slopes of the Sun Mountain. The boy stood in the warm sunlight and smiled and smiled.

A cheerful clatter was coming from the palace of the Sun Mountain. The boy walked into the hall, and saw a group of ravishing spirit maidens clustered around a cloth. His mother's brocade was displayed in front of them, and they were copying it.

They were very surprised to see him. He told them he had come for the brocade. One of them said, 'Our work will be finished this evening. You can have the cloth back tomorrow morning. But for tonight, please, stay here.'

The boy said, 'Yes.' The maiden gave him magic fruits to eat. Oh, they had such a tang!

The boy was so tired that he fell asleep on a chair. The spirit maidens worked on. When dark fell, they just hung a pearl from the ceiling, which made the hall as bright as daytime. They were all kept busy in their hurry to finish the cloth.

A maiden dressed in red was quicker than the rest, and she finished her job first. She went to compare her work with the mother's brocade, and she thought the mother's skill was much greater than hers. Just look: the sun was redder, the fish pond was clearer, the flowers fresher and the animals more life-like.

The maiden dressed in red said to herself, 'How nice it would be if I could live in the good place shown on this brocade.' As the other maidens were still busy, she took some more silk thread and embroidered a picture of her own on the old woman's cloth. It was a picture of herself, standing next to the pond and looking at the fresh flowers.

It was very late in the evening when the boy woke up. All the spirit maidens had gone to bed. Under the bright light of the pearl, he could see his mother's cloth on display. The maidens' copy was not finished. He thought, What if they do not give me the cloth? My mother has been sick for so long. I cannot wait. I'd better take it and leave before they get up.

The boy stood up, folded the cloth and put it in his shirt. He walked out and jumped onto the horse's back. In the moonlight, they made their escape.

Once again, the boy and the stone horse crossed the raging sea and climbed over the fiery mountain. Soon enough, and not too soon, they found themselves back at the mouth of the cave.

The old woman was still there. She smiled, and said, 'Get down, my child.'

The boy dismounted. The old woman pulled out two teeth from the stone horse and fixed them back into the boy's mouth. The stone horse stiffened. It stood motionless by the tree, its mouth open by the berries.

The old woman gave the youngest son a pair of deerskin shoes. He put them on, and after a few paces he was home. His mother was lying in bed, so skinny and shrivelled as a piece of dry firewood. She was moaning a little. Truly the old woman was going to die soon.

The youngest boy came to her bed and called, 'Mother.' He pulled out the wonderful brocade from his shirt. And as the cloth was unfolded before her, his mother found that she could see it. She got up then and there to look at the brocade on which she had worked for three whole years. She said, 'My boy, it is too dark to appreciate it. Let's go out and look at it under the sunlight.'

The mother and the boy walked out of the door and unfolded the cloth on the ground. There came a fragrant wind, and the wonderful cloth billowed and grew, getting wider and longer until it covered the ground for many miles.

The cottage they used to live in was gone. Instead of that poor shed, there was a grand building surrounded by a garden, an orchard and a vegetable plot, with crops and herds of cattle. Everything was just the same as in the wonderful picture. The mother and her youngest son were standing in front of the main gate.

Suddenly, the woman noticed a girl dressed in red looking at the flowers near the pond. She hurried to ask the girl who she was and what she was doing. The girl replied, 'I am a spirit maiden. I embroidered my own picture onto the cloth. I would like to live here.'

'You are welcome,' said the mother.

And in time the youngest brother and the spirit maiden were married, and they all lived a happy life together. They invited all the poor people who lived nearby to come and share the good place, especially those who helped the mother when she was so ill.

One day two beggars came to the edge of the good place. These two beggars were the very same brothers who had gone to the city to spend their boxes of gold. They had enjoyed themselves eating and drinking whatever they wanted. Very soon their gold was gone, and they had to become beggars.

They saw the good place, and their mother smiling, and their young brother singing with his beautiful wife. They were ashamed to go in. Dragging their sticks in the dust, they walked away and away.

From *The Spring of Butterflies and Other Folktales of China's Minority Peoples*, translated by He Liyi, edited by Neil Philip (New York: Lothrop, Lee & Shepard, 1986).

Simon and the Golden Sword

Like 'The Wonderful Brocade', this Canadian quest story from New Brunswick compares the honesty of the youngest brother with the selfishness and duplicity of the older brothers. Although it lacks the symbolic and moral depth of the Chinese tale, *Simon and the Golden Sword* has an equally elaborate plot. This plot requires that Simon, in order to succeed in his quest for the Sword of Light, must first succeed in two others. Simon's helper, the old innkeeper who subtly tests his kindness by having him do chores, provides Simon with magical helping objects, especially the black book, a symbol of the very wisdom his brothers think that he lacks. Simon would never have succeeded without these objects, but his dedication is equally important. Simon's circular journey culminates in an identity test that is reminiscent of the young King Arthur establishing his right to rule by pulling a sword from a stone. In this instance, Simon pulls a sword from a scabbard, thereby establishing that he, not his greedy brothers, is the son worthy of his father's acceptance. Simon's marriage to the princess, which forms a kind of epilogue to the quest tale, symbolically indicates both his achievement of happiness and his status as a mature man.

Once upon a time there lived a farmer who had three sons. As he neared the end of his days he called them to him and said that he would leave his farm to only one of them, since the farm was small.

'In the land of Tetagouche lives a wealthy king who owns three swords. One of them is made of gold and is called the Sword of Light. The possessor of this sword, it is said, will have good fortune all his days. Whoever brings it back to me will show that he deserves to inherit this farm.'

The two older brothers sneered at Simon, their young stepbrother.

'You can't come!' said one.

'You are a fool!' said the other. 'You'll never get anything from the king.'

Simon replied: 'Maybe not. But I'll try my luck anyway.'

So the three brothers set out to look for the kingdom of Tetagouche. That night they came to a town with two inns. Each inn had a large sign by the entrance. The first sign read:

> COME IN! BE WELCOME!
> PAY NOTHING!

The eldest brother said: 'Here's the place to stay. Why pay when you can get something for nothing?'

The other sign read:

> COME IN! BE WELCOME!
> PAY WHAT YOU CAN!

That was the inn Simon chose.

When he entered he found it deserted but for an old man in a rocking chair. 'Do you take boarders for the night?' Simon asked him.

'Yes,' the innkeeper replied, 'but my servants have all left because I can't pay them and my rheumatism is so bad I can hardly leave my rocking-chair. But there is a little food to eat. Prepare a meal for me, if you please, and one for yourself.'

Simon cooked the supper. While they ate he told the innkeeper of his quest for the Sword of Light. At bedtime he helped the old man to his room and found another for himself. He soon fell fast asleep.

The next morning Simon helped the innkeeper back to his chair.

After making breakfast, he prepared to leave.

'You are a good boy,' said the innkeeper. 'You need not pay me anything. Go out to the barn and bring me back a barley straw and an egg laid by my white hen.'

When Simon did this, the old man put the barley straw and the egg and a little black book in a round box.

'I will lend you this box,' he said. 'Whenever you need help in your quest, consult the little book.'

After Simon left the innkeeper, the first thing he did was to open the box and examine the little book. Printed on the cover was the following:

> IF BY DOUBT YOU ARE PERPLEXED
> OPEN ME AND HEED MY TEXT.

'Well, I must try this,' Simon said to himself. 'I want to go to Tetagouche and I don't know where it is.'

He opened the book and on the first page he read these words:

STRADDLE THY BARLEY STRAW

'That seems a silly thing to do,' thought Simon. 'But what have I got to lose?' As soon as he threw one leg over the barley straw, it turned into a beautiful grey horse.

Simon barely had time to grab hold of the horse's reins before the stallion flew over hill and dale until it came to rest outside a great castle.

It turned back into a barley straw as soon as Simon dismounted.

Simon walked through the open gate and found himself in a large hall. Hanging on the far wall he saw the three swords and beneath them three scabbards: one of leather, one of silver, and one of gold.

Leaning against the wall were two guards asleep.

'I'd better consult my book,' said Simon to himself.

On the second page he read:

TAKE THE SWORD YOUNG MAN, BE BOLD
AND ANY SCABBARD BUT THE GOLD

Simon carefully took down the golden sword. Nothing happened. The gold scabbard glittered so temptingly on the wall that he decided to take that too. But as soon as he touched it, the guards awoke.

They fell upon Simon; put him in chains, and dragged him before the king.

The king was furious.

'How dare you steal my Sword of Light!' he thundered.

Simon told him his story. The king thought awhile, then said:

'One year ago today my daughter Cybelle was captured by a giant who lives in the neighbouring kingdom. She has been put under a spell and is imprisoned in a cage on Glass Mountain. Only the sound of a golden bell will free her. Bring her back to me and I will give you the Sword of Light.'

'I will look for her gladly, Your Majesty,' said Simon.

Before you could say Tetagouche, Simon caught sight of a tree that glistened brightly in the sun. Over it a flock of blackbirds flew round and round. As he drew nearer he saw that the tree was hung with golden bells. Stretched beneath it, fast asleep, was the giant. He was so huge that his arm was longer than the tree was high.

Simon landed on the giant's elbow. The giant did not stir. Slowly Simon reached out for a bell. But as he took it off the tree, *all* the bells began to ring. The giant instantly woke up. He lifted Simon in one hand and demanded to know why he had tried to steal thebell.

Simon thought quickly. 'Why wouldn't I want to pick a beautiful golden bell?' he said. 'If your tree grew apples, you would surely let me pick one fruit.' The giant thought awhile before he said: 'Perhaps you're right. I wish my tree *did* grow apples. You can't eat bells.' Then he brightened. 'Do you see those birds up there?' he asked, pointing above the tree. 'They will soon have eaten all my crops. If you can rid me of them, you may keep that bell.'

Simon consulted the book. On the second page he read:

AROUND YOUR NECK HANG THE BELL
BREAK THE EGG AND EAT THE SHELL

Simon did as the book told him to do. The pieces of egg-shell were nasty things to swallow, but as soon as he ate them all, an amazing thing happened.

From Frank Newfeld, *Simon and the Golden Sword*. (Toronto: Oxford University Press, 1976).

He turned into a beautiful bird. As he flew into the air, all the blackbirds left the tree and followed him.

As he flew towards Glass Mountain, he saw the cage perched on top. He looked with horror at the girl inside. She had the ugliest face he had ever seen, a misshapen body, and scraggly black hair.

'Could this be the King's daughter?' he wondered.

He landed beside the cage, while the blackbirds flew off into the distance, and he immediately turned back into himself.

He rang the bell, and before his eyes the ugly face turned young and beautiful, the body straight and slender, the black hair sleek and shining.

'Are you Cybelle, the king's daughter?' he asked.

'Oh, yes, I am,' she said. 'Thank you for breaking my spell. Please open the cage and let me out.'

'How shall I do that?' thought Simon. 'Perhaps the book will tell me.' He turned its pages until he read:

TAKE THE KEY FROM OFF THE TREE
TURN THE LOCK AND SHE'LL BE FREE

He looked up and sure enough, hanging from a tree above the cage was a key. Simon undid the lock.

He and the princess mounted the barley straw and the stallion carried them off.

They waved at the giant as they passed over the tree of bells.

On they went until they reached Tetagouche.

The king was beside himself with delight at having his daughter back.

He handed Simon the Sword of Light. 'It is yours now,' he said. 'Only you can draw it from its scabbard.'

Simon thanked the king. He was not as happy as he thought he would be because he had to leave Cybelle, but there was nothing else to do. So he bade farewell, bowed to the king, and set off on foot with his sword.

He first stopped at the inn, where he placed the wooden box in the sleeping innkeeper's lap. Then he walked for several more hours. As twilight descended, he felt tired and decided to rest by the roadside.

While he slept, his brothers happened by. 'What? Is that the Sword of Light?' whispered the eldest brother.

'I'll attend to this,' said the middle one. He hit Simon on the head. 'Now he won't wake up until we're home.'

His brother took the sword from between Simon's arms and the two thieves ran off with it.

The old farmer was overjoyed to see them with the golden sword.

'Which one of you does it belong to?'

'I found it,' said the eldest brother. But when he pulled at the sword, it would not leave the scabbard.

'Let me try,' said the middle brother. But still it would not move.

'How strange!' said their father. 'Well, let us eat supper and you can tell me about your journey. Maybe then I can see the sword.'

Two hours later, as the brothers were telling their seventeenth lie about their journey, they heard a great bang at the door.

When the father opened it, there stood Simon, his head all bruised. 'What is this?' said the old man. 'What happened to you?'

Without a word, Simon walked over to the sword and pulled it from its scabbard with the greatest of ease.

'Look, father,' he said. 'The sword is mine. My brothers stole it from me.' The old man embraced Simon.

Then he turned to his other sons.

'You might have benefited from the good fortune that will come to Simon with this sword,' he said to them, 'but you have proved yourselves unworthy. Leave this house forever!'

Soon afterwards he died, leaving Simon with the farm and the sword.

Simon did not forget the innkeeper. Every Saturday he delivered fresh vegetables to the inn.

Did the sword bring him good fortune? It certainly did.

Remember Cybelle, the king's daughter? The sword gave Simon courage to return to Tetagouche and pay court to her. A year to the day after he had freed her from the giant's spell, they were married . . . and lived happily ever after.

From *Simon and the Golden Sword*, by Frank Newfeld (Toronto: Oxford University Press, 1976).

Little Badger and the Fire Spirit

This literary *pourquoi* myth by Canadian Métis writer Maria Campbell employs several elements common in traditional Native literature: the four-fold pattern of testing, the relay runners, the final solitary journey, and the rapport between humans and animals. Although helpers play a prominent role, Little Badger must undertake the final stage of the journey alone in order to demonstrate his worthiness. His confrontations with the four animals and the final guardian of the quest object, the Fire Spirit himself, reveal Little Badger's courage and consideration for others. The restoration of his sight is a poetic symbol of recompense: because he had inner sight—a compassionate understanding of others—he receives physical sight. Campbell develops her myth within a narrative frame that serves an important purpose: it recounts the attempts of contemporary young people to discover their cultural heritage from the old people who have preserved it.

*A*hsinee was going to visit her grandparents, Mooshoom and Kookoom. She was so happy she could hardly wait to get there. It was her eighth birthday and for a present she could spend the whole summer with them. How lucky could a little girl be!

Mooshoom and Kookoom lived in a little log house right beside a huge lake called Lac La Biche. Here Mooshoom spent his days mending nets for the fishermen who fished in the big lake, and making snow shoes for the trappers who went far into the wilderness to trap when the first snows came.

Kookoom, too, had much work to keep her busy. She had a small garden to look after, and fish and meat to smoke and dry on the racks set up outside. She also had hides to tan, and plenty of sewing and beading to do. She had many grandchildren who wore the beautiful moccasins she sewed and decorated with dyed porcupine quills and beads.

Ahsinee lived only ten miles from Mooshoom and Kookoom. For a little girl, it was like a million miles away.

She talked excitedly as she and her father bounced along the rough dirt road in the old pick-up truck. They arrived just as the sun was going down over the lake, the last rays casting a golden glow over the calm water.

Mooshoom's old dog, Ma-he-kun, limped out to meet them as they stopped in the yard. He wagged his tail in welcome. There was a light in the kitchen window, and as Ahsinee jumped from the truck, she could smell freshly baked bannock and rabbit stew, which was her very favourite. She had not realized she was so hungry.

Kookoom bustled around the old black wood stove warming the stew and bannock, which she served with steaming cups of tea. Ahsinee sat down and ate and ate, until Mooshoom reminded her that Kookoom had baked some fresh Saskatoon pie. Ahsinee was so full she could only smile and nod her head. Yes, she had room for pie.

Soon they were all done and Kookoom got up to wash the dishes and clean the table. This was the time of day that Ahsinee loved best.

It was always the same in the evening with the two old people. When Kookoom finished cleaning the supper dishes, she took her sewing to the table and began her work. Mooshoom built up the fire to take away the chill of evening. Then he sat across from Kookoom to mend his nets. Kookoom smiled at Ahsinee because they both knew that Mooshoom would soon fall asleep.

Ahsinee sat between them, and after a time of silence, she would go to the cupboard where Mooshoom kept his pipe and tobacco. Giving the pipe to the old man, she would ask for a story.

This evening Ahsinee could hardly wait. She had something special to ask Mooshoom. Maybe the old man would not have a story for this question, but Ahsinee rushed over to the cupboard for the pipe and tobacco. In her hurry, she forgot old Ma-he-kun lying by the stove, and tripped over him. What a commotion! The old dog yelped so loudly that Mooshoom, who was sleeping soundly, woke up with a start. Kookoom began to laugh.

'Waa-hi,' said Mooshoom, as he helped Ahsinee up. 'You must not always be in such a hurry. Here, sit down and rest before you get us all tired. We are old, remember, and our days of hurry are over.'

Old Ma-he-kun growled in agreement.

Kookoom smiled as she bit the thread from the needle and said, 'Speak for yourself and your dog, Old Man.'

Mooshoom filled his pipe. As he packed the tobacco, he looked at Ahsinee.

'Your Kookoom makes jokes about my old bones. Pay her no mind for she has loved them for many years now.'

Kookoom smiled and did not reply.

'Now, my girl,' said Mooshoom, 'what is it you want to know? It must be very important if you could not sit still for a moment and let your belly rest.'

'Fire, Mooshoom,' said Ahsinee at last. 'How did our people get fire?'

'Aaah . . . that is a good question. Let me think for a while. Perhaps I will remember.'

The old man sat back and puffed on his pipe.

He puffed and puffed. Finally he laid down his pipe and began to mend the net. He worked for a long time, then he looked across at Kookoom.

'Do you remember the animal's name?' he asked her.

Animal? Ahsinee looked at them. What did animals have to do with fire? Perhaps Mooshoom had forgotten.

'Mas-cha-can-is una,' Kookoom replied.

'Aaah,' interrupted Mooshoom, raising his hand. 'Ni-kis-kis-in aqua, the Grey Coyote.' He took a big puff from his pipe and began to speak.

It was a long time ago when our mother, the earth, was young. In those days, people and animals all spoke one language. There was one animal who was a very good friend of the people and he often came to visit them. His name was Grey Coyote.

Now, Grey Coyote was a gentle and considerate creature. He was also very wise. When he visited, the people all gathered around and listened to him speak. Grey Coyote had one friend who was special, a boy named Little Badger.

Grey Coyote and Little Badger spent many hours talking. You see, Little Badger was blind. Grey Coyote took him on many long walks in the forest. He taught Little Badger about the earth he could not see, and how to smell, hear and touch all the things around him. He taught him that everything on the earth—human, animal, insect or plant—had a purpose. This purpose was to serve and help each other.

Little Badger's people lived in a world of plenty. Mother earth give them all they needed. There was never any want. However, with so much good, there had to be some bad. For Little Badger's people, the bad was the long, cold winters. On winter days, the people took refuge in their teepees, huddled together for warmth.

One cold day, as Little Badger shivered under his robe, he thought: *There must be some way for us to be warm. But how? Grey Coyote will know what to do. I will go and find him.*

And he set off to find Grey Coyote.

Outside, the wind howled in rage and blew snow around Little Badger's head. He pulled his robe tightly around himself and started for the forest.

Grey Coyote told me if I ever needed him, I was to sit under the pine tree and think very hard. He said he would hear me and come, thought Little Badger. He sat down under the tall pine and began to concentrate on Grey Coyote.

Grey Coyote was trotting through the forest when he heard a voice calling to him. He stopped and listened.

It is Little Badger, he thought. *I must hurry. He sounds very weak.*

Grey Coyote headed for the pine tree as fast as he could run. When he arrived, Little Badger was so cold his teeth rattled when he tried to talk.

'What is wrong, Little Brother?' asked Grey Coyote.

'My people are freezing to death,' chattered Little Badger. 'You must help us.'

'How thoughtless of me,' said Grey Coyote. 'I have a warm coat, and I never thought of my brothers and sisters. Here, I will shield you from the cold.' Grey Coyote wrapped himself around Little Badger.

'You must help us, Grey Coyote,' Little Badger pleaded. 'You are wise. There must be some way for us to keep warm in the winter.'

Grey Coyote thought and thought. Slowly he said, 'Yes, there is a way, Little Brother, but it is very dangerous.'

'Tell me, Grey Coyote, before my people perish,' cried Little Badger.

'There is a mountain far away from our land. Inside the mountain is fire. This fire is strange. It feeds on wood and rock and it burns forever. It would provide warmth for the people. But someone must go inside the mountain to get it.'

'I will go,' said Little Badger.

'Wait. I am not finished,' warned Grey Coyote. 'Inside the mountain lives the Fire Spirit. He has four strange creatures who stand guard for him.

'There is Mountain Goat who can stab you with his horns, Mountain Lion who can tear you apart with his claws, Grizzly Bear who can kill you with one slap of his mighty paw, and Rattlesnake whose teeth hold deadly poison. And remember, Little Brother, you are blind and will not be able to see these dangers.'

'I will still go,' insisted Little Badger. 'Will you take me to this place?'

Grey Coyote thought for a while.

'Yes, I will take you. Go back to your people. Find among them one hundred of the fastest runners. Bring them here tomorrow when the sun comes up.'

'Where are you going?' asked Little Badger as Grey Coyote turned to leave.

'I am going to call the spirits to help us,' said Grey Coyote as he trotted away.

The next morning, when Little Badger met Grey Coyote by the pine tree, he had with him one hundred of the fastest runners and the wise men of the tribe. They held council, and the wise men asked the Great Spirit for strength, endurance, and courage for Little Badger, Grey Coyote and the runners.

Then Grey Coyote spoke.

'I have talked to the spirits and they have given me guidance for our journey. They will do all in their power to help us reach the great mountain. Once we are there, Little Badger must go into the mountain alone. No power can help him until he has climbed back outside with the fire.'

Now Grey Coyote said to the runners: 'You must follow the direction in which I am pointing. That is where the mountain is.'

He turned to the first runner. 'You must run with Little Badger on your shoulders. When you have run as far as you can, the second runner will take Little Badger and do the same thing. You must wait where you are. When the last runner has gone as far as he can, I will meet him. From there, Little Badger and I will go on alone.

'I have told you of the journey there,' continued Grey Coyote. 'Now I will tell you of the journey back. Instead of carrying Little Badger, you will carry a stick of burning wood. You will bring it back here the same way you carried Little Badger. When you arrive here, the people of the tribe will feed the fire with small pieces of wood and keep it burning until Little Badger and I return.'

The runners nodded and, picking up Little Badger, the first one started off. He ran so fast Little Badger felt he was flying through the air.

Finally, after many days, the last runner went as far he could go. When he stopped, Grey Coyote appeared and led Little Badger to the foot of the mountain.

'Here is the mountain, Little Brother,' said Grey Coyote. 'From here the spirits will guide and help you to the top. Once you reach the top, you must climb down the hole and get the fire yourself. When you have the fire and have climbed out, the spirits will help you down again. I will beat this drum and sing until you return.'

Little Badger took a deep breath. He was frightened, but he knew that if he failed, his people would continue to die from the cold. He listened to the beat of the drum. Suddenly, he did not feel frightened anymore and he began to climb. As he climbed, he felt the spirit of the wind steadying him, and the spirit of the rocks made the way smooth. When he reached the top, he stopped to rest. He felt a last breath of air, then it was gone and he knew he was alone. The spirits had left him.

Little Badger stood wondering how he was going to find the opening in the mountain. He began to move around slowly and to feel with his hands. A wave of warm air touched him and he knew he had found the entrance to the place of fire. He stopped and listened for a moment. When he again heard the drum Grey Coyote was beating, he carefully started down.

Suddenly, Little Badger heard a gruff voice: 'WHAT ARE YOU DOING HERE? THIS PLACE IS FORBIDDEN TO YOU!'

Almost paralyzed with fear, he stayed very still. He knew he had come upon one of the guardians of the fire as it was told to him by Grey Coyote, but he did not know which one.

'I have come to see the Fire Spirit,' he said, his voice shaking. 'My people are cold and he is the only one who can help us.'

'NO ONE CAN SEE THE FIRE SPIRIT,' said the gruff voice. 'YOU CANNOT PASS BY ME. IF YOU TRY, THEN I WILL KILL YOU.'

Little Badger's heart pounded with fear. He had no weapons. He could not even see his enemy. As he clung to the rock ledge, he could hear Grey Coyote's drum beating. The sound comforted him, and his fear was gone. He reached out towards the voice. When he touched the creature, it trembled, and Little Badger could feel coarse hair.

'WHY DO YOU DO THAT?' grumbled the creature. 'NO ONE TOUCHES ME. MY HORNS COULD TEAR YOU APART.' The words were angry, but the voice was frightened.

'Do not be afraid,' said Little Badger gently. 'I will not hurt you. As you can see, I have no weapons. I am blind. To know who you are, I must touch you. Ah, you are the Mountain Goat.'

When Little Badger touched the Mountain Goat, he felt peace come over them. He told the creature of his mission.

The goat listened, then said, 'I WILL LET YOU GO BY, BUT I CANNOT HELP YOU GO BACK. BEWARE. THERE ARE THREE MORE GUARDIANS YOU MUST PASS BEFORE YOU REACH THE FIRE SPIRIT. I WISH YOU GOOD FORTUNE, LITTLE BROTHER.'

Little Badger continued climbing down inside of the mountain. As he descended, he could feel the heat of the fire. When he heard a soft growl, he knew he had met the Mountain Lion.

Little Badger reached out and touched the animal. As he stroked the smooth fur, he told the Lion of his people. They could hear the drum far off in the distance and again peace settled over both of them. The Lion growled softly, 'YOU MAY GO ON.'

Little Badger continued his slow climb down. He knew he still had to meet the Grizzly Bear and the Rattlesnake, but he was no longer afraid. If things went on as they had, he knew he would make two new friends.

It was true. When he met the Grizzly Bear and touched him, they became friends. The Bear warned him that the Rattlesnake was very dangerous.

'YOU MUST BE VERY CAREFUL, LITTLE BROTHER,' he rumbled in his great voice, as the boy turned to go. 'YOU MUST USE WISDOM TO GET BY RATTLER, FOR HIS MEDICINE IS VERY POWERFUL.'

Little Badger continued his climb down towards the fire. Soon he met the Rattlesnake. The Snake coiled, rattled his tail, and raised his mighty head up to strike.

When Little Badger heard the sound of the rattle, he quickly said, 'You must be the Snake. What a beautiful rattle you have.'

Rattlesnake was so surprised that someone, especially a small boy, would dare to talk to him, and find him beautiful, that he relaxed without even realizing he had done so.

'WHY ARE YOU NOT AFRAID OF ME?' he hissed.

'I do not want to hurt you, so why should you want to hurt me?' replied Little Badger.

Rattlesnake was astonished at the little boy's words. He was thinking about what the boy had said and did not notice him leave to continue his climb.

Little Badger had almost finished his journey to meet the Fire Spirit. It was so hot, he felt his braids must be singed. He was also very tired and he stumbled. As he tried to catch his balance, a voice crackled, 'NO HUMAN BEING HAS EVER SEEN THE HOME OF THE FIRE SPIRIT. WHY ARE YOU HERE?'

Little Badger knew that at last he had met the Fire Spirit.

'I cannot see your home,' replied Little Badger, 'for I am blind. It is very warm. If my people lived here, they would never be cold.'

'COLD? COLD?' said the Fire Spirit. 'WHAT IS COLD?'

As he talked, he flamed up and all the colours of the rainbow seemed to glow around him.

Little Badger could not see the flames but he felt a gust of warm air as the Spirit spoke.

'When the snows come,' explained Little Badger, 'my people are very cold. There is not enough warmth from the sun, so many of them die. I have come to ask you for fire to warm my people.'

'TELL ME MORE,' said the Fire Spirit. 'I HAVE NEVER TALKED TO A HUMAN BEFORE AND THERE IS MUCH I DO NOT KNOW.'

Little Badger sat down. He told the Fire Spirit about his land and his people. He told of his journey into the heart of the mountain and of the friends he had made along the way. The Fire Spirit was quiet for a long time. All that Little Badger could hear was the hiss of his flames.

Finally the Spirit spoke: 'HOW LONG HAVE YOU BEEN BLIND?'

'All my life,' replied Little Badger. 'But I can feel and hear very well. Grey Coyote has taught me. He is like my eyes.'

'GREY COYOTE? WHO IS HE?' asked the Spirit.

'Grey Coyote is my friend,' said Little Badger. He told the Fire Spirit how his friend had taught him about the world.

'He brought me to this mountain and he is waiting for me now. Listen. Can you hear him? He is beating a drum.'

The Fire Spirit listened. 'YES, I CAN HEAR HIM,' he replied.

'The drum gave me courage and strength,' said Little Badger. 'It helped me make new friends.'

Little Badger and the Fire Spirit sat together for a long time and listened to the faint beating of the drum.

'IT IS STRONG AND BEAUTIFUL MUSIC,' said the Fire Spirit. 'I WILL NEVER FORGET IT . . . HERE, TAKE THIS BURNING STICK. IT IS THE WARMTH OF FRIENDSHIP THAT YOU BROUGHT TO THIS PLACE. IT WILL KEEP YOUR PEOPLE WARM FOREVER.'

Little Badger was bursting with gratitude.

'DO NOT THANK ME FOR IT, LITTLE BROTHER. YOU SHARED YOUR WARMTH WITH ME, AND I WILL SHARE MINE WITH YOU. WHEN YOU REACH THE TOP OF THE MOUNTAIN, YOU WILL NO LONGER BE BLIND. YOU WILL SEE THE WORLD THAT YOUR FRIEND, GREY COYOTE, HAS TAUGHT YOU ABOUT. GO NOW, HE WAITS FOR YOU.'

Little Badger took the stick, said goodbye to the Fire Spirit and began to climb up out of the mountain. As he climbed, he met his friends and said goodbye to them also.

When he reached the top, with the stick of fire in his hand, he saw a great light. He saw the world for the first time in his life.

He stopped for a long time and looked and looked at the world. It was so beautiful. His eyes filled with tears of happiness. He felt the Spirit of the wind touch his hair gently and whisper, 'Listen, Little Brother.'

From far below, at the foot of the mountain, came the beating of the drum. As Little Badger listened, he heard two drums, then three.

How can there be three drums? he wondered. He listened again. Now there were four, five, then six drums. Soon the air was filled with the sound of many drums, all of different sizes, making different and beautiful sounds.

Suddenly Little Badger smiled. He knew. Grey Coyote's magic drum was his heartbeat. The other drums were the beating hearts of all living things.

Little Badger laughed as he climbed down the mountain. Around him was the sound of the drums, the pulse of the world, the music of the universe.

The story was finished, and Ahsinee's eyes were shining as she said, 'Oh, Mooshoom, it was a beautiful story. But what happened to the fire?'

Mooshoom struck a match to light his pipe, then answered her.

'Little Badger brought the fire home to his people, and we have it to this day.'

'Tell me another story about Little Badger,' Ahsinee pleaded.

'It is time for bed, my girl,' Kookoom said. 'There will be many more stories later. We have all summer, remember.'

Ahsinee could hear a loon calling from across the lake as she snuggled down in the soft feather bed.

Yes, they had all summer together, and Mooshoom and Kookoom had so many stories to tell.

From *Little Badger and the Fire Spirit*, by Maria Campbell (Toronto: McClelland and Stewart, 1977).

Scarface: Origin of the Medicine Lodge

Collected at the end of the nineteenth century by George Bird Grinell, who lived among the peoples of the Great Plains for more than twenty years, this tale, which combines myth, legend, and hero story, embodies specific elements of Blackfoot life and culture. It evokes fundamental elements of that culture such as the importance of the Sun as the prime source of life, the close relationship between humans and animals, and the nature and origin of the Medicine Lodge. As a circular journey quest story, however, it also incorporates many of the features found in heroic adventures from other cultures: the hero's humble origins and early life, his long and arduous journey, his support from helper figures, his success in passing tests, his receipt of gifts from a supernatural power, and his reintegration into the community, to which he brings a great boon, most notably the institution of the Medicine Lodge. Scarface emerges from his ordeals as a culture bringer but he does so only because these adventures allow him to establish an identity that he could not achieve in mundane society.

I

In the earliest times there was no war. All the tribes were at peace. In those days there was a man who had a daughter, a very beautiful girl. Many young men wanted to marry her, but every time she was asked, she only shook her head and said she did not want a husband.

'How is this?' asked her father. 'Some of these young men are rich, handsome, and brave.'

'Why should I marry?' replied the girl. 'I have a rich father and mother. Our lodge is good. The parfleches are never empty. There are plenty of tanned robes and soft furs for winter. Why worry me, then?'

The Raven Bearers held a dance; they all dressed carefully and wore their ornaments, and each one tried to dance the best. Afterwards some of them asked for this girl, but still she said no. Then the Bulls, the Kit-foxes, and others of the *I-kun-uh'-kah-tsi* held their dances, and all those who were rich, many great warriors, asked this man for his daughter, but to every one of them she said no. Then her father was angry, and said: 'Why, now, this way? All the best men have asked for you, and still you say no. I believe you have a secret lover.'

'Ah!' said her mother. 'What shame for us should a child be born and our daughter still unmarried!' 'Father! mother!' replied the girl, 'pity me. I have no secret lover, but now hear the truth. That Above Person, the Sun, told me, "Do not marry any of those men, for you are mine; thus you shall be happy, and live to great age"; and again he said, "Take heed. You must not marry. You are mine."'

'Ah!' replied her father. 'It must always be as he says.' And they talked no more about it.

There was a poor young man, very poor. His father, mother, all his relations, had gone to the Sand Hills. He had no lodge, no wife to tan his robes or sew his moccasins. He stopped in one lodge to-day, and to-morrow he ate and slept in another; thus he lived. He was a good-looking young man, except that on his cheek he had a scar, and his clothes were always old and poor.

After those dances some of the young men met this poor Scarface, and they laughed at him, and said: 'Why don't you ask that girl to marry you? You are so rich and handsome!' Scarface did not laugh; he replied: 'Ah! I will do as you say. I will go and ask her.' All the young men thought this was funny. They laughed a great deal. But Scarface went down by the river. He waited by the river, where the women came to get water, and by and by the girl came along. 'Girl,' he said, 'wait. I want to speak with you. Not as a designing person do I ask you, but openly where the Sun looks down, and all may see.'

'Speak then,' said the girl.

'I have seen the days,' continued the young man 'You have refused those who are young, and rich, and brave. Now, to-day, they laughed and said to me, "Why do you not ask her?" I am poor, very poor. I have no lodge, no food, no clothes, no robes and warm furs. I have no relations; all have gone to the Sand Hills; yet, now, to-day, I ask you, take pity, be my wife.'

The girl hid her face in her robe and brushed the ground with the point of her moccasin, back and forth, back and forth; for she was thinking. After a time she said: 'True. I have refused all those rich young men, yet now the poor one asks me, and I am glad. I will be your wife, and my people will be happy. You are poor, but it does not matter. My father will give you dogs. My mother will make us a lodge. My people will give us robes and furs. You will be poor no longer.'

Then the young man was happy, and he started to kiss her, but she held him back, and said: 'Wait! The Sun has spoken to me. He says I may not marry; that I belong to him. He says if I listen to him, I shall live to great age. But now I say: Go to the Sun. Tell him, "She whom you spoke with heeds your words. She has never done wrong, but now she wants to marry. I want her for my wife." Ask him to take that scar from your face. That will be his sign. I will know he is pleased. But if he refuses, or if you fail to find his lodge, then do not return to me.'

'Oh!' cried the young man, 'at first your words were good. I was glad. But now it is dark. My heart is dead. Where is that far-off lodge? where the trail, which no one yet has travelled?'

'Take courage, take courage!' said the girl; and she went to her lodge.

II

Scarface was very sad. He sat down and covered his head with his robe and tried to think what to do. After a while he got up, and went to an old woman who had been kind to him. 'Pity me,' he said. 'I am very poor. I am going away now on a long journey. Make me some moccasins.'

'Where are you going?' asked the old woman. 'There is no war; we are very peaceful here.'

'I do not know where I shall go,' replied Scarface. 'I am in trouble, but I cannot tell you now what it is.'

So the old woman made him some moccasins, seven pairs, with parfleche soles, and also she gave him a sack of food,—pemmican of berries, pounded meat, and dried back fat; for this old woman had a good heart. She liked the young man.

All alone, and with a sad heart, he climbed the bluffs and stopped to take a last look at the camp. He wondered if he would ever see his sweetheart and the people again. 'Hai'-yu! Pity me, O Sun,' he prayed, and turning, he started to find the trail.

For many days he travelled on, over great prairies, along timbered rivers and among the mountains, and every day his sack of food grew lighter; but he saved it as much as he could, and ate berries, and roots, and sometimes he killed an animal of some kind. One night he stopped by the home of a wolf. 'Hai-yah!' said that one; 'what is my brother doing so far from home?'

'Ah!' replied Scarface, 'I seek the place where the Sun lives; I am sent to speak with him.'

'I have travelled far,' said the wolf. 'I know all the prairies, the valleys, and the mountains, but I have never seen the Sun's home. Wait; I know one who is very wise. Ask the bear. He may tell you.'

The next day the man travelled on again, stopping now and then to pick a few berries, and when night came he arrived at the bear's lodge.

'Where is your home?' asked the bear. 'Why are you travelling alone, my brother?'

'Help me! Pity me!' replied the young man; 'because of her words[1] I seek the Sun. I go to ask him for her.'

'I know not where he stops,' replied the bear. 'I have travelled by many rivers, and I know the mountains, yet I have never seen his lodge. There is some one beyond, that striped-face, who is very smart. Go and ask him.'

The badger was in his hole. Stooping over, the young man shouted: 'Oh, cunning striped-face! Oh, generous animal! I wish to speak with you.'

'What do you want?' said the badger, poking his head out of the hole.

'I want to find the Sun's home,' replied Scarface. 'I want to speak with him.'

'I do not know where he lives,' replied the badger. 'I never travel very far. Over there in the timber is a wolverine. He is always traveling around, and is of much knowledge. Maybe he can tell you.'

Then Scarface went to the woods and looked all around for the wolverine, but could not find him. So he sat down to rest 'Hai'-yu! Hai'-yu!' he cried. 'Wolverine, take pity on me. My food is gone, my moccasins worn out. Now I must die.'

'What is it, my brother?' he heard, and looking around, he saw the animal sitting near.

'She whom I would marry,' said Scarface, 'belongs to the Sun; I am trying to find where he lives, to ask him for her.'

'Ah!' said the wolverine. 'I know where he lives. Wait; it is nearly night. To-morrow I will show you the trail to the big water. He lives on the other side of it.'

Early in the morning, the wolverine showed him the trail, and Scarface followed it until he came to the water's edge. He looked out over it, and his heart almost stopped. Never before had any one seen such a big water. The other side could not be seen, and there was no end to it. Scarface sat down on the shore. His food was all gone, his moccasins worn out. His heart was sick. 'I cannot cross this big water,' he said. 'I cannot return to the people. Here, by this water, I shall die.'

Not so. His Helpers were there. Two swans came swimming up to the shore. 'Why have you come here?' they asked him. 'What are you doing? It is very far to the place where your people live.'

'I am here,' replied Scarface, 'to die. Far away, in my country, is a beautiful girl. I want to marry her, but she belongs to the Sun. So I started to find him and ask for her. I have travelled many days. My food is gone. I cannot go back. I cannot cross this big water, so I am going to die.'

'No,' said the swans; 'it shall not be so. Across this water is the home of that Above Person. Get on our backs, and we will take you there.'

Scarface quickly arose. He felt strong again. He waded out into the water and lay down on the swans' backs, and they started off. Very deep and black is that fearful water. Strange people live there, mighty animals which often seize and drown a person. The swans carried

---

1. A Blackfoot often talks of what this or that person said, without mentioning names.

him safely, and took him to the other side. Here was a broad hard trail leading back from the water's edge.

'Kyi' said the swans. 'You are now close to the Sun's lodge. Follow that trail, and you will soon see it.'

III

Scarface started up the trail, and pretty soon he came to some beautiful things, lying in it. There was a war shirt, a shield, and a bow and arrows. He had never seen such pretty weapons; but he did not touch them. He walked carefully around them, and travelled on. A little way further on, he met a young man, the handsomest person he had ever seen. His hair was very long, and he wore clothing made of strange skins. His moccasins were sewn with bright coloured feathers. The young man said to him, 'Did you see some weapons lying on the trail?'

'Yes,' replied Scarface; 'I saw them.'

'But did you not touch them?' asked the young man.

'No; I thought some one had left them there, so I did not take them.'

'You are not a thief,' said the young man. 'What is your name?'

'Scarface.'

'Where are you going?'

'To the Sun.'

'My name,' said the young man, 'is A-pi-su'-ahts.[2] The Sun is my father; come, I will take you to our lodge. My father is not now at home, but he will come in at night.'

Soon they came to the lodge. It was very large and handsome; strange medicine animals were painted on it. Behind, on a tripod, were strange weapons and beautiful clothes— the Sun's. Scarface was ashamed to go in, but Morning Star said, 'Do not be afraid, my friend; we are glad you have come.'

They entered. One person was sitting there, Ko-ko-mik'-e-is,[3] the Sun's wife, Morning Star's mother. She spoke to Scarface kindly, and gave him something to eat. 'Why have you come so far from your people?' she asked.

Then Scarface told her about the beautiful girl he wanted to marry. 'She belongs to the Sun,' he said. 'I have come to ask him for her.'

When it was time for the Sun to come home, the Moon hid Scarface under a pile of robes. As soon as the Sun got to the doorway, he stopped, and said, 'I smell a person.'

'Yes, father,' said Morning Star; 'a good young man has come to see you. I know he is good, for he found some of my things on the trail and did not touch them.'

Then Scarface came out from under the robes, and the Sun entered and sat down. 'I am glad you have come to our lodge,' he said. 'Stay with us as long as you think best. My son is lonesome sometimes; be his friend.'

The next day the Moon called Scarface out of the lodge, and said to him: 'Go with Morning Star where you please, but never hunt near that big water; do not let him go there. It is the home of great birds which have long sharp bills; they kill people. I have had many sons, but these birds have killed them all. Morning Star is the only one left.'

So Scarface stayed there a long time and hunted with Morning Star. One day they came near the water, and saw the big birds.

'Come,' said Morning Star; 'let us go and kill those birds.'

---

2. Early Riser, i.e. The Morning Star.
3. Night red light, the Moon.

'No, no!' replied Scarface; 'we must not go there. Those are very terrible birds; they will kill us.'

Morning Star would not listen. He ran towards the water, and Scarface followed. He knew that he must kill the birds and save the boy. If not, the Sun would be angry and might kill him. He ran ahead and met the birds, which were coming towards him to fight, and killed every one of them with his spear: not one was left. Then the young men cut off their heads, and carried them home. Morning Star's mother was glad when they told her what they had done, and showed her the birds' heads. She cried, and called Scarface 'my son'. When the Sun came home at night, she told him about it, and he too was glad. 'My son,' he said to Scarface, 'I will not forget what you have this day done for me. Tell me now, what can I do for you?'

'Hai'-yu' replied Scarface. 'Hai'-yu, pity me. I am here to ask you for that girl. I want to marry her. I asked her, and she was glad; but she says you own her, that you told her not to marry.'

'What you say is true,' said the Sun. 'I have watched the days, so I know it. Now, then, I give her to you; she is yours. I am glad she has been wise. I know she has never done wrong. The Sun pities good women. They shall live a long time. So shall their husbands and children. Now you will soon go home. Let me tell you something. Be wise and listen: I am the only chief. Everything is mine. I made the earth, the mountains, prairies, rivers, and forests. I made the people and all the animals. This is why I say I alone am the chief. I can never die. True, the winter makes me old and weak, but every summer I grow young again.'

Then said the Sun: 'What one of all animals is smartest? The raven is, for he always finds food. He is never hungry. Which one of all the animals is most Nat-o'-ye[4]? The buffalo is. Of all animals, I like him best. He is for the people. He is your food and your shelter. What part of his body is sacred? The tongue is. That is mine. What else is sacred? Berries are. They are mine too. Come with me and see the world.' He took Scarface to the edge of the sky, and they looked down and saw it. It is round and flat, and all around the edge is the jumping-off place [or walls straight down]. Then said the Sun: 'When any man is sick or in danger, his wife may promise to build me a lodge, if he recovers. If the woman is pure and true, then I will be pleased and help the man. But if she is bad, if she lies, then I will be angry. You shall build the lodge like the world, round, with walls, but first you must build a sweat house of a hundred sticks. It shall be like the sky [a hemisphere], and half of it shall be painted red. That is me. The other half you will paint black. That is the night.'

Further said the Sun: 'Which is the best, the heart or the brain? The brain is. The heart often lies, the brain never.' Then he told Scarface everything about making the Medicine Lodge, and when he had finished, he rubbed a powerful medicine on his face, and the scar disappeared. Then he gave him two raven feathers, saying: 'These are the sign for the girl, that I give her to you. They must always be worn by the husband of the woman who builds a Medicine Lodge.'

The young man was now ready to return home. Morning Star and the Sun gave him many beautiful presents. The Moon cried and kissed him, and called him 'my son'. Then the Sun showed him the short trail. It was the Wolf Road (Milky Way). He followed it, and soon reached the ground.

---

4. This word may be translated as 'of the Sun', having Sun power', or more properly, 'something sacred'.

IV

It was a very hot day. All the lodge skins were raised, and the people sat in the shade. There was a chief, a very generous man, and all day long people kept coming to his lodge to feast and smoke with him. Early in the morning this chief saw a person sitting out on a butte near by, close wrapped in his robe. The chief's friends came and went, the sun reached the middle, and passed on, down towards the mountains. Still this person did not move. When it was almost night, the chief said: 'Why does that person sit there so long? The heat has been strong, but he has never eaten nor drunk. He may be a stranger; go and ask him in.'

So some young men went up to him, and said: 'Why do you sit here in the great heat all day? Come to the shade of the lodges. The chief asks you to feast with him.'

Then the person arose and threw off his robe, and they were surprised. He wore beautiful clothes. His bow, shield, and other weapons were of strange make. But they knew his face, although the scar was gone, and they ran ahead, shouting, 'The scarface poor young man has come. He is poor no longer. The scar on his face is gone.'

All the people rushed out to see him. 'Where have you been?' they asked. 'Where did you get all these pretty things?' He did not answer. There in the crowd stood that young woman; and taking the two raven feathers from his head, he gave them to her, and said: 'The trail was very long, and I nearly died, but by those Helpers, I found his lodge. He is glad. He sends these feathers to you. They are the sign.'

Great was her gladness then. They were married, and made the first Medicine Lodge, as the Sun had said. The Sun was glad. He gave them great age. They were never sick. When they were very old, one morning, their children said: 'Awake! Rise and eat.' They did not move. In the night, in sleep, without pain, their shadows had departed for the Sand Hills.

From *Blackfoot Lodge Tales*, by George Bird Grinnell (Lincoln, NE: University of Nebraska Press, 1962).

Cupid and Psyche

A folktale that Lucius Apuleius transformed into an elegant literary myth in his Latin novel *The Golden Ass* (c. 170), 'Cupid and Psyche' is allegorical at its core. Essentially, it represents the union of Love (Cupid) and the soul (Psyche), a concept still important in literature. Incidentally, the offspring of their union is a daughter named Volupta (Pleasure). The vehicle for the allegory, however, is also an interesting errand and quest narrative. The quest arises from a conflict between Psyche and Venus that exposes a number of emotionally-charged attitudes: the jealousy of the gods, their domineering attitudes towards mortals, the jealousy of an older woman who feels supplanted by a younger rival, and a mother's protective hostility towards a woman whom she believes is unworthy of her son. The supposedly impossible tasks that Venus assigns to Psyche constitute the trials that she must endure to redeem herself for her faithless betrayal of her husband. Her quest to win back the love of Cupid thus becomes a symbol of her own development and a concrete demonstration of her virtues.

ℐhere was once a king who had three daughters, all lovely maidens, but the youngest, Psyche, excelled her sisters so greatly that beside them she seemed a very goddess consorting with mere mortals. The fame of her surpassing beauty spread over the earth, and everywhere men journeyed to gaze upon her with wonder and adoration and to do her homage as though she were in truth one of the immortals. They would even say that Venus herself could not equal this mortal. As they thronged in ever-growing numbers to worship her loveliness no one any more gave a thought to Venus herself. Her temples were neglected; her altars foul with cold ashes; her favourite towns deserted and falling in ruins. All the honours once hers were now given to a mere girl destined some day to die.

It may well be believed that the goddess would not put up with this treatment. As always when she was in trouble she turned for help to her son, that beautiful winged youth whom some call Cupid and others Love, against whose arrows there is no defense, neither in heaven nor on the earth. She told him her wrongs and as always he was ready to do her bidding. 'Use your power,' she said, 'and make the hussy fall madly in love with the vilest and most despicable creature there is in the whole world.' And so no doubt he would have done, if Venus had not first shown him Psyche, never thinking in her jealous rage what such beauty might do even to the God of Love himself. As he looked upon her it was as if he had shot one of his arrows into his own heart. He said nothing to his mother, indeed he had no power to utter a word, and Venus left him with the happy confidence that he would swiftly bring about Psyche's ruin.

What happened, however, was not what she had counted on. Psyche did not fall in love with a horrible wretch, she did not fall in love at all. Still more strange, no one fell in love with her. Men were content to look and wonder and worship—and then pass on to marry someone else. Both her sisters, inexpressibly inferior to her, were splendidly married, each to a king. Psyche, the all-beautiful, sat sad and solitary, only admired, never loved. It seemed that no man wanted her.

This was, of course, most disturbing to her parents. Her father finally traveled to an oracle of Apollo to ask his advice on how to get her a good husband. The god answered him, but his words were terrible. Cupid had told him the whole story and had begged for his help. Accordingly Apollo said that Psyche, dressed in deepest mourning, must be set on the summit of a rocky hill and left alone, and that there her destined husband, a fearful winged serpent, stronger than the gods themselves, would come to her and make her his wife.

The misery of all when Psyche's father brought back this lamentable news can be imagined. They dressed the maiden as though for her death and carried her to the hill with greater sorrowing than if it had been to her tomb. But Psyche herself kept her courage. 'You should have wept for me before,' she told them, 'because of the beauty that has drawn down upon me the jealousy of Heaven. Now go, knowing that I am glad the end has come.' They went in despairing grief, leaving the lovely helpless creature to meet her doom alone, and they shut themselves in their palace to mourn all their days for her.

On the high hilltop in the darkness Psyche sat, waiting for she knew not what terror. There, as she wept and trembled, a soft breath of air came through the stillness to her, the gentle breathing of Zephyr, sweetest and mildest of winds. She felt it lift her up. She was floating away from the rocky hill, and down until she lay upon a grassy meadow soft as a bed and fragrant with flowers. It was so peaceful there, all her trouble left her and she slept. She woke beside a bright river; and on its bank was a mansion stately and beautiful as though built for a god, with pillars of gold and walls of silver and floors inlaid with precious stones. No sound was to be heard; the place seemed deserted and Psyche drew near, awestruck at the sight of such splendour. As she hesitated on the threshold, voices sounded in her ear. She could see no one, but the words they spoke came clearly to her. The house was for her, they told her. She must enter without fear and bathe and refresh herself. Then a banquet table would be spread for her. 'We are your servants,' the voices said, 'ready do whatever you desire.'

The bath was the most delightful, the food the most delicious, she had ever enjoyed. While she dined, sweet music breathed around her: a great choir seemed to sing to a harp, but she could only hear, not see, them. Throughout the day, except for the strange companionship of the voices, she was alone, but in some inexplicable way she felt sure that with the coming of the night her husband would be with her. And so it happened. When she felt him beside her and heard his voice softly murmuring in her ear, all her fears left her. She knew without seeing him that here was no monster or shape of terror, but the lover and husband she had longed and waited for.

This half-and-half companionship could not fully content her; still she was happy and the time passed swiftly. One night, however, her dear though unseen husband spoke gravely to her and warned her that danger in the shape of her two sisters was approaching. 'They are coming to the hill where you disappeared, to weep for you,' he said; 'but you must not let them see you or you will bring great sorrow upon me and ruin to yourself.' She promised him she would not, but all the next day she passed in weeping, thinking of her sisters and herself unable to comfort them. She was still in tears when her husband came and even his caresses could not check them. At last he yielded sorrowfully to her great desire. 'Do what you will,' he said, 'but you are seeking your own destruction.' Then he warned her solemnly not to be persuaded by anyone to try to see him, on pain of being separated from him forever. Psyche cried out that she would never do so. She would die a hundred times over rather than live without him. 'But give me this joy,' she said: 'to see my sisters.' Sadly he promised her that it should be so.

The next morning the two came, brought down from the mountain by Zephyr. Happy and excited, Psyche was waiting for them. It was long before the three could speak to each other; their joy was too great to be expressed except by tears and embraces. But when at last they entered the palace and the elder sisters saw its surpassing treasures; when they sat at the rich banquet and heard the marvelous music, bitter envy took possession of them and a devouring curiosity as to who was the lord of all this magnificence and their sister's husband. But Psyche kept faith; she told them only that he was a young man, away now on a hunting expedition. Then filling their hands with gold and jewels, she had Zephyr bear them back to the hill. They went willingly enough, but their hearts were on fire with jealousy. All their own wealth and good fortune seemed to them nothing compared with Psyche's, and their envious anger so worked in them that they came finally to plotting how to ruin her.

That very night Psyche's husband warned her once more. She would not listen when he begged her not to let them come again. She never could see him, she reminded him. Was she also to be forbidden to see all others, even her sisters so dear to her? He yielded as before, and very soon the two wicked women arrived, with their plot carefully worked out.

Already, because of Psyche's stumbling and contradictory answers when they asked her what her husband looked like they had become convinced that she had never set eyes on him and did not really know what he was. They did not tell her this, but they reproached her for hiding her terrible state from them, her own sisters. They had learned, they said, and knew for a fact, that her husband was not a man, but the fearful serpent Apollo's oracle had declared he would be. He was kind now, no doubt, but he would certainly turn upon her some night and devour her.

Psyche, aghast, felt terror flooding her heart instead of love. She had wondered so often why he would never let her see him. There must be some dreadful reason. What did she really know about him? If he was not horrible to look at, then he was cruel to forbid her ever to behold him. In extreme misery, faltering and stammering, she gave her sisters to understand that she could not deny what they said, because she had been with him only in the dark. 'There must be something very wrong,' she sobbed, 'for him so to shun the light of day.' And she begged them to advise her.

They had their advice all prepared beforehand. That night she must hide a sharp knife and a lamp near her bed. When her husband was fast asleep she must leave the bed, light the lamp, and get the knife. She must steel herself to plunge it swiftly into the body of the frightful being the light would certainly show her. 'We will be near,' they said, 'and carry you away with us when he is dead.'

Then they left her torn by doubt and distracted what to do. She loved him; he was her dear husband. No; he was a horrible serpent and she loathed him. She would kill him—She would not. She must have certainty—She did not want certainty. So all day long her thoughts fought with each other. When evening came, however, she had given the struggle up. One thing she was determined to do: she would see him.

When at last he lay sleeping quietly, she summoned all her courage and lit the lamp. She tiptoed to the bed and holding the light high above her she gazed at what lay there. Oh, the relief and the rapture that filled her heart. No monster was revealed, but the sweetest and fairest of all creatures, at whose sight the very lamp seemed to shine brighter. In her first shame at her folly and lack of faith, Psyche fell on her knees and would have plunged the knife into her own breast if it had not fallen from her trembling bands. But those same unsteady hands that saved her betrayed her, too, for as she hung over him, ravished at the sight of him and unable to deny herself the bliss of filling her eyes with his beauty, some hot oil fell from the lamp upon his shoulder. He started awake: he saw the light and knew her faithlessness, and without a word he fled from her.

She rushed out after him into the night. She could not see him, but she heard his voice speaking to her. He told her who he was, and sadly bade her farewell. 'Love cannot live where there is no trust,' he said, and flew away. 'The God of Love!' she thought. 'He was my husband, and I, wretch that I am, could not keep faith with him. Is he gone from me forever? . . . At any rate,' she told herself with rising courage, 'I can spend the rest of my life searching for him. If he has no more love left for me, at least I can show him how much I love him.' And she started on her journey. She had no idea where to go; she knew only that she would never give up looking for him.

He meanwhile had gone to his mother's chamber to have his wound cared for, but when Venus heard his story and learned that it was Psyche whom he had chosen, she left him angrily alone in his pain, and went forth to find the girl of whom he had made her still more jealous. Venus was determined to show Psyche what it meant to draw down the displeasure of a goddess.

Poor Psyche in her despairing wanderings was trying to win the gods over to her side. She offered ardent prayers to them perpetually, but not one of them would do anything to make Venus their enemy. At last she perceived that there was no hope for her, either in heaven or on earth, and she took a desperate resolve. She would go straight to Venus; she would offer herself humbly to her as her servant, and try to soften her anger. 'And who knows,' she thought, 'if he himself is not there in his mother's house.' So she set forth to find the goddess who was looking everywhere for her.

From Edith Hamilton, *Mythology*. Illustrated by Steele Savage. (Boston: Little, Brown: 1942), 127.

When she came into Venus' presence the goddess laughed aloud and asked her scornfully if she was seeking a husband since the one she had had would have nothing to do with her because he had almost died of the burning wound she had given him. 'But really,' she said, 'you are so plain and ill-favoured a girl that you will never be able to get you a lover except by the most diligent and painful service. I will therefore show my good will to you by training you in such ways.' With that she took a great quantity of the smallest of the seeds, wheat and poppy and millet and so on, and mixed them all together in a heap. 'By nightfall these must all be sorted,' she said. 'See to it for your own sake.' And with that she departed.

Psyche, left alone, sat still and stared at the heap. Her mind was all in a maze because of the cruelty of the command; and indeed, it was of no use to start a task so manifestly impossible. But at this direful moment she who had awakened no compassion in mortals or immortals was pitied by the tiniest creatures of the field, the little ants, the swift-runners. They cried to each other, 'Come, have mercy on this poor maid and help her diligently.' At once they came, waves of them, one after another, and they laboured separating and dividing, until what had been a confused mass lay all ordered, every seed with its kind. This was what Venus found when she came back, and very angry she was to see it. 'Your work is by no means over,' she said. Then she gave Psych a crust of bread and bade her sleep on the ground while she herself went off to her soft, fragrant couch. Surely if she could keep the girl at hard labour and half starve her, too, that hateful beauty of hers would soon be lost. Until then she must see that her son was securely guarded in his chamber where he was still suffering from his wound. Venus was pleased at the way matters were shaping.

The next morning she devised another task for Psyche, this time a dangerous one. 'Down there near the riverbank,' she said, 'where the bushes grow thick, are sheep with fleeces of gold. Go fetch me some of their shining wool.' When the worn girl reached the gently flowing stream, a great longing seized her to throw herself into it and end all her pain and despair. But as she was bending over the water she heard a little voice from near her feet, and looking down saw that it came from a green reed. She must not drown herself, it said. Things were not as bad as that. The sheep were indeed very fierce, but if Psyche would wait until they came out of the bushes toward evening to rest beside the river, she could go into the thicket and find plenty of the golden wool hanging on the sharp briars.

So spoke the kind and gentle reed, and Psyche, following the directions, was able to carry back to her cruel mistress a quantity of the shining fleece. Venus received it with an evil smile. 'Someone helped you,' she said sharply. 'Never did you do this by yourself. However, I will give you an opportunity to prove that you really have the stout heart and the singular prudence you make such a show of. Do you see that black water which falls from the hill yonder? It is the source the terrible river which is called hateful, the river Styx. You are to fill this flask from it.' That was the worst task yet, as Psyche saw when she approached the waterfall. Only a winged creature could reach it, so steep and slimy were the rocks on all sides, and so fearful the onrush of the descending waters. But by this time it must be evident to all the readers of this story (as, perhaps, deep in her heart it had become evident to Psyche herself) that although each of her trials seemed impossibly hard, an excellent way out would always be provided for her. This time her saviour was an eagle, who poised on his great wings beside her, seized the flask from her with his beak and brought it back to her full of the black water.

But Venus kept on. One cannot but accuse her of some stupidity. The only effect of all that had happened was to make her try again. She gave Psyche a box which she was to carry to the underworld and ask Proserpine to fill with some of her beauty. She was to tell her that

Venus really needed it, she was so worn-out from nursing her sick son. Obediently as always Psyche went forth to look for the road to Hades. She found her guide in a tower she passed. It gave her careful directions how to get to Proserpine's palace, first through a great hole in the earth, then down to the river of death, where she must give the ferryman, Charon, a penny to take her across. From there the road led straight to the palace. Cerberus, the three-headed dog, guarded the doors, but if she gave him a cake he would be friendly and let her pass.

All happened, of course, as the tower had foretold. Proserpine was willing to do Venus a service, and Psyche, greatly encouraged, bore back the box, returning far more quickly than she had gone down.

Her next trial she brought upon herself through her curiosity and, still more, her vanity. She felt that she must see what that beauty-charm in the box was; and, perhaps, use a little of it herself. She knew quite as well as Venus did that her looks were not improved by what she had gone through, and always in her mind was the thought that she might suddenly meet Cupid. If only she could make herself more lovely for him! She was unable to resist the temptation; she opened the box. To her sharp disappointment she saw nothing there; it seemed empty. Immediately, however, a deadly languor took possession of her and she fell into a heavy sleep.

At this juncture the God of Love himself stepped forward. Cupid was healed of his wound by now and longing for Psyche. It is a difficult matter to keep Love imprisoned. Venus had locked the door, but there were the windows. All Cupid had to do was to fly out and start looking for his wife. She was lying almost beside the palace, and he found her at once. In a moment he had wiped the sleep from her eyes and put it back into the box. Then waking her with just a prick from one of his arrows, and scolding her a little for her curiosity, he bade her take Proserpine's box to his mother and he assured her that all thereafter would be well.

While the joyful Psyche hastened on her errand, the god flew up to Olympus. He wanted to make certain that Venus would give them no more trouble, so he went straight to Jupiter himself. The Father of Gods and Men consented at once to all that Cupid asked— 'Even though,' he said, 'you have done me great harm in the past—seriously injured my good name and my dignity by making me change myself into a bull and a swan and, so on . . . However, I cannot refuse you.'

Then he called a full assembly of the gods, and announced to all, including Venus, that Cupid and Psyche were formally married, and that he proposed to bestow immortality upon the bride. Mercury brought Psyche into the palace of the gods, and Jupiter himself gave her the ambrosia to taste which made her immortal. This, of course, completely changed the situation. Venus could not object to a goddess for her daughter-in-law; the alliance had become eminently suitable. No doubt she reflected also that Psyche, living up in heaven with a husband and children to care for, could not be much on the earth to turn men's heads and interfere with her own worship.

So all came to a most happy end. Love and the Soul (for that is what Psyche means) had sought and, after sore trials, found each other; and that union could never be broken.

———

From *Mythology*, by Edith Hamilton (Boston: Little, Brown, 1942).

✤

East o' the Sun and West o' the Moon

This Nowegian folktale, which shares plot similarities with the literary myth 'Cupid and Psyche', falls into three main parts. In the first, the maiden, who has previously been a benefactor to her family by agreeing to marry the White Bear, loses everything because she breaks a taboo by demonstrating a lack of faith in her husband. In the middle part, she undertakes an arduous and seemingly impossible quest to rescue her imprisoned husband. Like most questers, she receives aid from helpers. In the final stage, when she has completed her seemingly impossible journey, she must pass one more test alone. Washing the shirt that she herself had previously soiled is both a formal test of her worthiness to be a bride and a symbolic redemptive act in which she literally undoes the harm that she caused. As in many Scandinavian tales, the villains are trolls and, like evil characters in a number of European tales, they destroy themselves—they literally burst—because of their strong negative emotions.

*O*nce on a time there was a poor husbandman who had so many children that he hadn't much of either food or clothing to give them. Pretty children they all were, but the prettiest was the youngest daughter, who was so lovely there was no end to her loveliness.

So one day, 'twas on a Thursday evening late at the fall of the year, the weather was so wild and rough outside, and it was so cruelly dark, and rain fell and wind blew, till the walls of the cottage shook again. There they all sat round the fire busy with this thing and that. But just then, all at once something gave three taps on the window-pane. Then the father went out to see what was the matter; and, when he got out of doors, what should he see but a great big White Bear.

'Good evening to you,' said the White Bear.

'The same to you,' said the man.

'Will you give me your youngest daughter? If you will, I'll make you as rich as you are now poor,' said the Bear.

Well, the man would not be at all sorry to be so rich; but still he thought he must have a bit of a talk with his daughter first; so he went in and told them how there was a great White Bear waiting outside, who had given his word to make them so rich if he could only have the youngest daughter.

The lassie said 'No!' outright. Nothing could get her to say anything else; so the man went out and settled it with the White Bear, that he should come again the next Thursday evening and get an answer. Meantime he talked his daughter over, and kept on telling her of all the riches they would get, and how well off she would be herself; and so at last she thought better of it, and washed and mended her rags, made herself as smart as she could, and was ready to start. I can't say her packing gave her much trouble.

Next Thursday evening came the White Bear to fetch her, and she got upon his back with her bundle, and off they went. So, when they had gone a bit of the way, the White Bear said—'Are you afraid?'

'No!' she wasn't.

'Well! mind and hold tight by my shaggy coat, and then there's nothing to fear,' said the Bear.

So she rode a long, long way, till they came to a great steep hill. There, on the face of it, the White Bear gave a knock, and a door opened, and they came into a castle, where there were many rooms all lit up; rooms gleaming with silver and gold; and there too was a table ready laid, and it was all as grand as grand could be. Then the White Bear gave her a silver bell; and when she wanted anything, she was only to ring it, and she would get it at once.

Well, after she had eaten and drunk, and evening wore on, she got sleepy after her journey, and thought she would like to go to bed, so she rang the bell; and she had scarce taken hold of it before she came into a chamber, where there was a bed made; as fair and white as any one would wish to sleep in, with silken pillows and curtains, and gold fringe. All that was in the room was gold or silver; but when she had gone to bed, and put out the light, a man came and laid himself alongside her. That was the White Bear, who threw off his beast shape at night; but she never saw him, for he always came after she had put out the light, and before the day dawned he was up and off again. So things went on happily for a while, but at last she began to get silent and sorrowful; for there she went about all day alone, and she longed to go home to see her father and mother, and brothers and sisters. So one day, when the White Bear asked what it was that she lacked, she said it was so dull and lonely there, and how she longed to go home to see her father and mother, and brothers and sisters, and that was why she was so sad and sorrowful, because she couldn't get to them.

'Well, well!' said the Bear, 'perhaps there's a cure for all this; but you must promise me one thing, not to talk alone with your mother, but only when the rest are by to hear; for she'll take you by the hand and try to lead you into a room alone to talk; but you must mind and not do that, else you'll bring bad luck on both of us.'

So one Sunday the White Bear came and said now they could set off to see her father and mother. Well, off they started, she sitting on his back; and they went far and long. At last they came to a grand house, and there her brothers and sisters were running about out of doors at play, and everything was so pretty, 'twas a joy to see.

'This is where your father and mother live now,' said the White Bear but don't forget what I told you, else you'll make us both unlucky.'

'No! bless her, she'd not forget'; and when she had reached the house, the White Bear turned right about and left her.

Then when she went in to see her father and mother, there was such joy, there was no end to it. None of them thought they could thank her enough for all she had done for them. Now, they had everything they wished, as good as good could be, and they all wanted to know how she got on where she lived.

Well, she said, it was very good to live where she did; she had all she wished. What she said beside I don't know; but I don't think any of them had the right end of the stick, or that they got much out of her. But so in the afternoon, after they had done dinner, all happened as the White Bear had said. Her mother wanted to talk with her alone in her bed-room; but she minded what the White Bear had said, and wouldn't go up stairs.

'Oh, what we have to talk about will keep,' she said, and put her mother off. But somehow or other, her mother got round her at last, and she had to tell her the whole story. So she said, how every night, when she had gone to bed, a man came and lay down beside her as soon as she had put out the light, and how she never saw him, because he was always up and away before the morning dawned; and how she went about woeful and sorrowing, for she thought she should so like to see him, and how all day long she walked about there alone, and how dull, and dreary, and lonesome it was.

'My!' said her mother; 'it may well be a Troll you slept with! But now I'll teach you a lesson how to set eyes on him. I'll give you a bit of candle, which you can carry home in your bosom; just light that while he is asleep, but take care not to drop the tallow on him.'

Yes! she took the candle, and hid it in her bosom, and as night drew on, the White Bear came and fetched her away.

But when they had gone a bit of the way, the White Bear asked if all hadn't happened as he had said?

'Well, she couldn't say it hadn't.'

'Now, mind,' said he, 'if you have listened to your mother's advice, you have brought bad luck on us both, and then, all that has passed between us will be as nothing.'

'No,' she said, 'she hadn't listened to her mother's advice.'

So when she reached home, and had gone to bed, it was the old story over again. There came a man and lay down beside her; but at dead of night, when she heard he slept, she got up and struck a light, lit the candle, and let the light shine on him, and so she saw that he was the loveliest Prince one ever set eyes on, and she fell so deep in love with him on the spot, that she thought she couldn't live if she didn't give him a kiss there and then. And so she did, but as she kissed him, she dropped three hot drops of tallow on his shirt, and he woke up.

'What have you done?' he cried; 'now you have made us both unlucky, for had you held out only this one year, I had been freed. For I have a stepmother who has bewitched me, so that I am a White Bear by day, and a Man by night. But now all ties are snapt between us; now I must set off from you to her. She lives in a castle which stands East o' the Sun and West o' the Moon, and there, too, is a Princess, with a nose three ells long, and she's the wife I must have now.'

She wept and took it ill, but there was no help for it; go he must.

'Then she asked if she mightn't go with him?'

No, she mightn't.

'Tell me the way, then,' she said, 'and I'll search you out; *that* surely I may get leave to do.'

'Yes, she might do that,' he said; 'but there was no way to that place. It lay East o' the Sun and West o' the Moon, and thither she'd never find her way.'

So next morning, when she woke up, both Prince and castle were gone, and then she lay on a little green patch, in the midst of the gloomy thick wood, and by her side lay the same bundle of rags she had brought with her from her old home.

So when she had rubbed the sleep out of her eyes, and wept till she was tired, she set out on her way, and walked many, many days, till she came to a lofty crag. Under it sat an old hag, and played with a gold apple which she tossed about. Her the lassie asked if she knew the way to the Prince, who lived with his stepmother in the castle that lay East o' the Sun and West o' the Moon, and who was to marry the Princess with a nose three ells long.

'How did you come to know about him?' asked the old hag; 'but maybe you are the lassie who ought to have had him?'

Yes, she was.

'So, so; it's you, is it?' said the old hag. 'Well, all I know about him is, that he lives in the castle that lies East o' the Sun and West o' the Moon, and thither you'll come, late or never; but still you may have the loan of my horse, and on him you can ride to my next neighbour. Maybe she'll be able to tell you; and when you get there, just give the horse a switch under the left ear, and beg him to be off home; and, stay, this gold apple you may take with you.'

So she got upon the horse, and rode a long long time, till she came to another crag, under which sat another old hag, with a gold carding-comb. Her the lassie asked if she knew the way to the castle that lay East o' the Sun and West o' the Moon, and she answered, like the first old hag, that she knew nothing about it, except it was east o' the sun and west o' the moon.

'And thither you'll come, late or never; but you shall have the loan of my horse to my next neighbour; maybe she'll tell you all about it; and when you get there, just switch the horse under the left ear, and beg him to be off home.'

And this old hag gave her the golden carding-comb; it might be she'd find some use for it, she said. So the lassie got up on the horse, and rode a far far way, and a weary time; and so at last she came to another great crag, under which sat another old hag, spinning with a golden spinning-wheel. Her, too, she asked if she knew the way to the Prince, and where the castle was that lay East o' the Sun and West o' the Moon. So it was the same thing over again.

'Maybe it's you who ought to have had the Prince?' said the old hag.

Yes, it was.

But she, too, didn't know the way a bit better than the other two. 'East o' the sun and west o' the moon it was,' she knew—that was all.

'And thither you'll come, late or never; but I'll lend you my horse, and then I think you'd best ride to the East Wind and ask him; maybe he knows those parts, and can blow you thither. But when you get to him, you need only give the horse a switch under the left ear, and he'll trot home of himself.'

And so, too, she gave her the gold spinning-wheel. 'Maybe you'll find a use for it,' said the old hag.

Then on she rode many many days, a weary time, before she got to the East Wind's house, but at last she did reach it, and then she asked the East Wind if he could tell her the way to the Prince who dwelt east o' the sun and west o' the moon. Yes, the East Wind had often heard tell of it, the Prince and the castle, but he couldn't tell the way, for he had never blown so far.

'But, if you will, I'll go with you to my brother the West Wind, maybe he knows, for he's much stronger. So, if you will just get on my back, I'll carry you thither.'

Yes, she got on his back, and I should just think they went briskly along.

So when they got there, they went into the West Wind's house, and the East Wind said the lassie he had brought was the one who ought to have had the Prince who lived in the castle East o' the Sun and West o' the Moon; and so she had set out to seek him, and how he had come with her, and would be glad to know if the West Wind knew how to get to the castle.

'Nay,' said the West Wind, 'so far I've never blown; but if you will, I'll go with you to our brother the South Wind, for he's much stronger than either of us, and he has flapped his wings far and wide. Maybe he'll tell you. You can get on my back, and I'll carry you to him.'

Yes! she got on his back, and so they travelled to the South Wind, and weren't so very long on the way, I should think.

When they got there, the West Wind asked him if he could tell her the way to the castle that lay East o' the Sun and West o' the Moon, for it was she who ought to have had the Prince who lived there.

'You don't say so! That's she, is it?' said the South Wind.

'Well, I have blustered about in most places in my time, but so far have I never blown; but if you will, I'll take you to my brother the North Wind; he is the oldest and strongest of the whole lot of us, and if he don't know where it is, you'll never find any one in the world to tell you. You can get on my back, and I'll carry you thither.'

Yes! she got on his back, and away he went from his house at a fine rate. And this time, too, she wasn't long on her way.

So when they got to the North Wind's house, he was so wild and cross, cold puffs came from him a long way off.

'BLAST YOU BOTH, WHAT DO YOU WANT?' he roared out to them ever so far off so that it struck them with an icy shiver.

'Well,' said the South Wind, 'you needn't be so foul-mouthed, for here I am, your brother, the South Wind, and here is the lassie who ought to have had the Prince who dwells in the castle that lies East o' the Sun and West o' the Moon, and now she wants to ask you if you ever were there, and can tell her the way, for she would be so glad to find him again.'

'YES, I KNOW WELL ENOUGH WHERE IT IS,' said the North Wind; 'once in my life I blew an aspen-leaf thither but I was so tired I couldn't blow a puff for ever so many days after. But if you really wish to go thither, and aren't afraid to come along with me, I'll take you on my back and see if I can blow you thither.'

Yes! with all her heart; she must and would get thither if it were possible in any way; and as for fear, however madly he went, she wouldn't be at all afraid.

'Very well, then,' said the North Wind, 'but you must sleep here to-night, for we must have the whole day before us, if we're to get thither at all.'

Early next morning the North Wind woke her, and puffed himself up, and blew himself out, and made himself so stout and big, 'twas gruesome to look at him; and so off they went high up through the air, as if they would never stop till they got to the world's end.

Down here below there was such a storm; it threw down long tracts of wood and many houses, and when it swept over the great sea, ships foundered by hundreds.

So they tore on and on,—no one can believe how far they went,—and all the while they still went over the sea, and the North Wind got more and more weary, and so out of breath he could scarce bring out a puff, and his wings drooped and drooped, till at last he sunk so low that the crests of the waves dashed over his heels.

'Are you afraid?' said the North Wind.

'No!' she wasn't.

But they weren't very far from land; and the North Wind had still so much strength left in him that he managed to throw her up on the shore under the windows of the castle which lay East o' the Sun and West o' the Moon; but then he was so weak and worn out, he had to stay there and rest many days before he could get home again.

Next morning the lassie sat down under the castle window, and began to play with the gold apple; and the first person she saw was the Long-nose who was to have the Prince.

'What do you want for your gold apple, you lassie?' said the Long-nose, and threw up the window.

'It's not for sale, for gold or money,' said the lassie.

'If it's not for sale for gold or money, what is it that you will sell it for? You may name your own price,' said the Princess.

'Well! if I may get to the Prince, who lives here, and be with him to-night, you shall have it,' said the lassie whom the North Wind had brought.

Yes! she might; that could be done. So the Princess got the gold apple; but when the lassie came up to the Prince's bed-room at night he was fast asleep; she called him and shook him, and between whiles she wept sore; but all she could do she couldn't wake him up. Next morning as soon as day broke, came the Princess with the long nose, and drove her out again.

So in the daytime she sat down under the castle windows and began to card with her golden carding-comb, and the same thing happened. The Princess asked what she wanted for it; and she said it wasn't for sale for gold or money, but if she might get leave to go up to the Prince and be with him that night, the Princess should have it. But when she went up she found him fast asleep again, and all she called, and all she shook, and wept, and prayed, she couldn't get life into him; and as soon as the first gray peep of day came, then came the Princess with the long nose, and chased her out again.

So in the day time the lassie sat down outside under the castle window, and began to spin with her golden spinning-wheel, and that, too, the Princess with the long nose wanted to have. So she threw up the window and asked what she wanted for it. The lassie said, as she had said twice before, it wasn't for sale for gold or money; but if she might go up to the Prince who was there, and be with him alone that night, she might have it.

Yes! she might do that and welcome. But now you must know there were some Christian folk who had been carried off thither, and as they sat in their room, which was next the Prince, they had heard how a woman had been in there, and wept and prayed, and called to him two nights running, and they told that to the Prince.

That evening, when the Princess came with her sleepy drink, the Prince made as if he drank, but threw it over his shoulder, for he could guess it was a sleepy drink. So, when the lassie came in, she found the Prince wide awake; and then she told him the whole story how she had come thither.

'Ah,' said the Prince, 'you've just come in the very nick of time, for to-morrow is to be our wedding-day; but now I won't have the Long-nose, and you are the only woman in the world who can set me free. I'll say I want to see what my wife is fit for, and beg her to wash the shirt which has the three spots of tallow on it; she'll say yes, for she doesn't know 'tis you who put them there; but that's a work only for Christian folk, and not for such a pack of Trolls, and so I'll say that I won't have any other for my bride than the woman who can wash them out, and ask you to do it.'

So there was great joy and love between them all that night. But next day, when the wedding was to be, the Prince said—

'First of all, I'd like to see what my bride is fit for.'

'Yes!' said the stepmother, with all her heart.

'Well,' said the Prince, 'I've got a fine shirt which I'd like for my wedding shirt, but some how or other it has got three spots of tallow on it, which I must have washed out; and I have sworn never to take any other bride than the woman who's able to do that. If she can't, she's not worth having.'

Well, that was no great thing they said, so they agreed, and she with the long nose began to wash away as hard as she could, but the more she rubbed and scrubbed, the bigger the spots grew.

'Ah!' said the old hag, her mother, 'you can't wash; let me try.'

But she hadn't long taken the shirt in hand, before it got far worse than ever, and with all her rubbing, and wringing and scrubbing the spots grew bigger and blacker, and the darker and uglier was the shirt.

Then all the other Trolls began to wash, but the longer it lasted, the blacker and uglier the shirt grew, till at last it was as black all over as if it had been up the chimney.

'Ah!' said the Prince, 'you're none of you worth a straw: you can't wash. Why there, outside, sits a beggar lassie I'll be bound she knows how to wash better than the whole lot of you. Come in, Lassie!' he shouted.

Well, in she came.

'Can you wash this shirt clean, lassie, you?' said he.

'I don't know,' she said, 'but I think I can.'

And almost before she had taken it and dipped it in the water, it was as white as driven snow, and whiter still.

'Yes; you are the lassie for me,' said the Prince.

At that the old hag flew into such a rage, she burst on the spot, and the Princess with the long nose after her, and the whole pack of Trolls after her,—at least I've never heard a word about them since.

As for the Prince and Princess, they set free all the poor Christian folk who had been carried off and shut up there; and they took with them all the silver and gold, and flitted away as far as they could from the castle that lay East o' the Sun and West o' the Moon.

From *Popular Tales from the Norse*, by George Webbe Dasent (Edinburgh: Edmonston and Douglas, 1859).

Little Red Riding-hood

A failed errand gives this tale an ironic ending: what should have been a circular journey from home to the grandmother's cottage and back, unexpectedly becomes a linear one with the demise of the heroine. The first moral that Perrault appended to the conclusion suggests that this is a cautionary tale illustrating the grave dangers awaiting the naïve and innocent. Contemporary critics have, however, argued about whether the mother, who is guilty of educational neglect because she failed to give sufficient warnings, or Little Red Riding-hood, who is quite willing to be led astray, is more to blame for the wolf's success. Perrault's second moral, which talks about smooth-talking wolves who pursue girls, has bolstered the case of those psychological critics who point to the tale's implicit sexual content and who view the tale as one about seduction. Both the moral and psychological readings, however, reaffirm the status of the wolf as an archetype of destructive evil.

Once upon a time there lived in a certain village a little country girl, the prettiest creature that ever was seen. Her mother was very fond of her, and her grandmother loved her still more. This good woman made for her a little red riding hood, which became the girl so well that everybody called her Little Red Riding-hood.

One day her mother, having made some custards, said to her:—

'Go, my dear, and see how your grandmother does, for I hear she has been very ill; carry her a custard and this little pot of butter.'

Little Red Riding-hood set out immediately to go to her grandmother's, who lived in another village.

As she was going through the wood, she met Gaffer Wolf, who had a very great mind to eat her up; but he dared not, because of some fagot-makers hard by in the forest. He asked her whither she was going. The poor child, who did not know that it was dangerous to stay and hear a wolf talk, said to him:—

'I am going to see my grandmother, and carry her a custard and a little pot of butter from my mamma.'

'Does she live far off? ' said the Wolf.

From A.E. Johnson, trans., *Perrault's Fairy Tales*. Illustrated by Gustave Dore. (Paris: Libraire-Editeure, 1867).

'Oh, yes,' answered Little Red Riding-hood; 'it is beyond that mill you see there, the first house you come to in the village.'

'Well,' said the Wolf, 'and I'll go and see her, too. I'll go this way, and you go that, and we shall see who will be there first.'

The Wolf began to run as fast as he could, taking the shortest way, and the little girl went by the longest way, amusing herself by gathering nuts, running after butterflies, and making nosegays of such little flowers as she met with. The Wolf was not long before he reached the old woman's house. He knocked at the door—tap, tap, tap.

'Who's there?' called the grandmother.

'Your grandchild, Little Red Riding-hood,' replied the Wolf, imitating her voice, 'who has brought a custard and a little pot of butter sent to you by mamma.'

The good grandmother, who was in bed, because she was somewhat ill, cried out:

'Pull the bobbin, and the latch will go up.'

The Wolf pulled the bobbin, and the door opened. He fell upon the good woman and ate her up in no time, for he had not eaten anything for more than three days. He then shut the door, went into the grandmother's bed, and waited for Little Red Riding-hood, who came sometime afterward and knocked at the door—tap, tap, tap.

'Who's there? ' called the Wolf.

Little Red Riding-hood, hearing the big voice of the Wolf, was at first afraid; but thinking her grandmother had a cold, answered:

''Tis your grandchild, Little Red Riding-hood, who has brought you a custard and a little pot of butter sent to you by mamma.'

The Wolf cried out to her, softening his voice a little: —

'Pull the bobbin, and the latch will go up.'

Little Red Riding-hood pulled the bobbin, and the door opened.

The Wolf, seeing her come in, said to her, hiding himself under the bedclothes:—

'Put the custard and the little pot of butter upon the stool, and come and lie down with me.'

Little Red Riding-hood undressed herself, and went into bed, where she was much surprised to see how her grandmother looked in her night-clothes.

She said to her :—

'Grandmamma, what great arms you have got!'

'That is the better to hug thee, my dear.'

'Grandmamma, what great legs you have got!'

'That is to run the better, my child.'

'Grandmamma, what great ears you have got!'

'That is to hear the better, my child.'

'Grandmamma, what great eyes you have got!'

'It is to see the better, my child.'

'Grandmamma, what great teeth you have got.'

'That is to eat thee up.'

And, saying these words, this wicked Wolf fell upon Little Red Riding-hood, and ate her all up.

———

From *The Tales of Mother Goose as First Collected by Charles Perrault in 1696*, translated by Charles Welsh (New York: D.C. Heath, 1901).

☙

Little Red-Cap

Published more than a century after Perrault's 'Little Red Riding-hood', the version of this famous cautionary tale by the Brothers Grimm presents an optimistic conclusion that insists on the need for, and value of, education. Although a wolf devours Little Red-Cap, like Little Red Riding-hood, Little Red Cap gets a second chance when the huntsman releases her from its belly. Having returned home much wiser, she displays a far different attitude when she undertakes her second errand through the perilous forest to her grandmother's cottage. Some mythological critics once suggested that this tale is a debased solar myth: the red-clad heroine represents the sun, which disappears into the maw of the wolfish night but is reborn each morning. Most contemporary critics of this tale, however, conduct the same kind of social, moral, or psychological analysis that they do when examining Perrault's version

Once upon a time there was a dear little girl who was loved by every one who looked at her, but most of all by her grandmother, and there was nothing that she would not have given to the child. Once she gave her a little cap of red velvet, which suited her so well that she would never wear anything else; so she was always called 'Little Red-Cap'.

One day her mother said to her, 'Come, Little Red-Cap, here is a piece of cake and a bottle of wine; take them to your grandmother, she is ill and weak, and they will do her good. Set out before it gets hot, and when you are going, walk nicely and quietly and do not run off the path, or you may fall and break the bottle, and then your grandmother will get nothing; and when you go into her room, don't forget to say, 'Good-morning,' and don't peep into every corner before you do it.'

'I will take great care,' said Little Red-Cap to her mother, and gave her hand on it.

The grandmother lived out in the wood, half a league from the village, and just as Little Red-Cap entered the wood, a wolf met her. Red-Cap did not know what a wicked creature he was, and was not at all afraid of him.

'Good-day, Little Red-Cap,' said he.

'Thank you kindly, wolf.'

'Whither away so early, Little Red-Cap?'

'To my grandmother's.'

'What have you got in your apron?'

'Cake and wine; yesterday was baking-day, so poor sick grandmother is to have something good, to make her stronger.'

'Where does your grandmother live, Little Red-Cap?'

'A good quarter of a league farther on in the wood; her house stands under the three large oak-trees, the nut-trees are just below; you surely must know it,' replied Little Red-Cap.

The wolf thought to himself, 'What a tender young creature! what a nice plump mouthful—she will be better to eat than the old woman. I must act craftily, so as to catch both.' So he walked for a short time by the side of Little Red-Cap, and then he said, 'See Little Red-Cap, how pretty the flowers are about here—why do you not look round? I believe, too, that you do not hear how sweetly the little birds are singing; you walk gravely along as if you were going to school, while everything else out here in the wood is merry.'

Little Red-Cap raised her eyes, and when she saw the sunbeams dancing here and there through the trees, and pretty flowers growing everywhere, she thought, 'Suppose I take grandmother a fresh nosegay; that would please her too. It is so early in the day that I shall still get there in good time;' and so she ran from the path into the wood to look for flowers. And whenever she had picked one, she fancied that she saw a still prettier one farther on, and ran after it, and so got deeper and deeper into the wood.

Meanwhile the wolf ran straight to the grandmother's house and knocked at the door.

'Who is there?'

'Little Red-Cap,' replied the wolf. 'She is bringing cake and wine; open the door.'

'Lift the latch,' called out the grandmother, 'I am too weak, and cannot get up.'

The wolf lifted the latch, the door flew open, and without saying a word he went straight to the grandmother's bed, and devoured her. Then he put on her clothes, dressed himself in her cap, laid himself in bed and drew the curtains.

Little Red-Cap, however, had been running about picking flowers, and when she had gathered so many that she could carry no more, she remembered her grandmother, and set out on the way to her.

She was surprised to find the cottage-door standing open, and when she went into the room, she had such a strange feeling that she said to herself, 'Oh dear! how uneasy I feel to-day, and at other times I like being with grandmother so much.' She called out, 'Good morning,' but received no answer; so she went to the bed and drew back the curtains. There lay her grandmother with her cap pulled far over her face, and looking very strange.

'Oh! grandmother,' she said, 'what big ears you have!'

'The better to hear you with, my child,' was the reply.

'But, grandmother, what big eyes you have!' she said.

'The better to see you with, my dear.'

'But, grandmother, what large hands you have!'

'The better to hug you with.'

'Oh! but, grandmother, what a terrible big mouth you have!'

'The better to eat you with!'

And scarcely had the wolf said this, than with one bound he was out of bed and swallowed up Red-Cap.

When the wolf had appeased his appetite, he lay down again in the bed, fell asleep and began to snore very loud. The huntsman was just passing the house, and thought to himself, 'How the old woman is snoring! I must just see if she wants anything.' So he went into the room, and when he came to the bed, he saw that the wolf was lying in it. 'Do I find thee here, thou old sinner!' said he. 'I have long sought thee!' Then just as he was going to fire at him, it occurred to him that the wolf might have devoured the grandmother, and that she might still be saved, so he did not fire, but took a pair of scissors, and began to cut open the stomach of the sleeping wolf. When he had made two snips, he saw the little Red-Cap shining, and then he made two snips more, and the little girl sprang out, crying, 'Ah, how frightened I have been! How dark it was inside the wolf;' and after that the aged grandmother came out alive also, but scarcely able to breathe. Red-Cap, however, quickly fetched great stones with which they filled the wolf's body, and when he awoke, he wanted to run away, but the stones were so heavy that he fell down at once, and fell dead.

Then all three were delighted. The huntsman drew off the wolf's skin and went home with it; the grandmother ate the cake and drank the wine which Red-Cap had brought, and revived, but Red-Cap thought to herself, 'As long as I live, I will never by myself leave the path, to run into the wood, when my mother has forbidden me to do so.'

It is also related that once when Red-Cap was again taking cakes to the old grandmother, another wolf spoke to her, and tried to entice her from the path. Red-Cap, however, was on her guard, and went straight forward on her way, and told her grandmother that she had met the wolf, and that he had said 'good-morning' to her, but with such a wicked look in his eyes, that if they had not been on the public road she was certain he would have eaten her up. 'Well,' said the grandmother, 'we will shut the door, that he may not come in.' Soon afterwards the wolf knocked, and cried, 'Open the door, grandmother, I am little Red-Cap, and am fetching you some cakes.' But they did not speak, or open the door, so the grey-beard stole twice or thrice round the house, and at last jumped on the roof, intending to wait until Red-Cap went home in the evening, and then to steal after her and devour her in the darkness. But the grandmother saw what was in his thoughts. In front of the house was a great stone trough, so she said to the child, 'Take the pail, Red-Cap; I made some sausages yesterday, so carry the water in which I boiled them to the trough.' Red-Cap carried until the great trough was quite full. Then the smell of the sausages reached the wolf, and he sniffed and peeped down, and at last stretched out his neck so far that he could no longer keep his footing and began to slip, and slipped down from the roof straight into the great trough, and was drowned. But Red-Cap went joyously home, and never did anything to harm any one.

From *Grimm's Household Tales*, Vol. 1, translated by Margaret Hunt (London: George Bell and Sons, 1884).

The Three Billy-Goats Gruff

This popular Norwegian tale presents an extremely simple and compact quest. The goats undertake a linear journey from a place of want to one in which they can eat their fill. Their quest, then, is for life itself. In their journey they encounter the troll as an equally hungry enemy who tests their ability to survive. The goats pass this test of worthiness because they possess wit, in the case of the first two goats, and physical strength, in the case of the last goat. In addition, the evil troll, who stands between them and their goal, reveals himself to be stereotypically greedy and, therefore, stupid. The tale's structure, containing three-fold repetitions, each of which concludes with a dramatic variation, is not simply a stylistic feature: these varied repetitions both advance the conflict and reveal character.

Once on a time there were three Billy-goats, who were to go up to the hill-side to make themselves fat, and the name of all three was 'Gruff.'

On the way up was a bridge over a burn they had to cross; and under the bridge lived a great ugly Troll, with eyes as big as saucers, and a nose as long as a poker.

So first of all came the youngest billy-goat Gruff to cross the bridge.

'Trip, trap; trip, trap!' went the bridge.

'WHO'S THAT tripping over my bridge?' roared the Troll.

'Oh! it is only I, the tiniest billy-goat Gruff; and I'm going up to the hill-side to make myself fat,' said the billy-goat, with such a small voice.

'Now, I'm coming to gobble you up,' said the Troll.

'Oh, no! pray don't take me. I'm too little, that I am,' said the billy-goat; 'wait a bit till the second billy-goat Gruff comes, he's much bigger.'

'Well! be off with you,' said the Troll.

A little while after came the second billy-goat Gruff to cross the bridge.

'TRIP, TRAP! TRIP, TRAP! TRIP, TRAP!' went the bridge.

'WHO'S THAT tripping over my bridge?' roared the Troll.

'Oh, it's the second billy-goat Gruff, and I'm going up to the hill-side to make myself fat,' said the billy-goat, who hadn't such a small voice.

'Now I'm coming to gobble you up,' said the Troll.

'Oh, no! don't take me, wait a little till the big billy-goat Gruff comes, he's much bigger.'

'Very well! be off with you,' said the Troll.

But just then up came the big billy-goat Gruff.

'TRIP, TRAP! TRIP, TRAP! TRIP, TRAP!' went the bridge, for the billy-goat was so heavy that the bridge creaked and groaned under him.

'WHO'S THAT tramping over my bridge?' roared the Troll.

'IT'S I! THE BIG BILLY-GOAT GRUFF,' said the billy-goat, who had an ugly hoarse voice of his own.

'Now I'm coming to gobble you up,' roared the Troll,

'Well, come along! I've got two spears,
And I'll poke your eyeballs out at your ears;
I've got besides two curling-stones,
And I'll crush you to bits, body and bones.'

That was what the big billy-goat said; and so he flew at the Troll, and poked his eyes out with his horns, and crushed him to bits, body and bones, and tossed him out into the burn, and after that he went up to the hill-side. There the billy-goats got so fat they were scarce able to walk home again; and if the fat hasn't fallen off them, why, they're still fat; and so,—

'Snip, snap, snout
This tale's told out.'

From *Popular Tales from the Norse*, by George Webbe Dasent (Edinburgh: Edmonston and Douglas, 1859).

The Half-Chick

In this Spanish tale, the errand does not originate out of necessity for survival or for the betterment of the community. Medio Pollito, the half-chick, inaugurates a trivial errand to see the king for no other reason than that he is bored and egotistical. His journey presents unwitting tests, episodes in which Medio Pollito does not know that he is being tested. Having ignored his mother's warning, he fails his tests, demonstrating insensitivity and egotism by refusing to help those who ask him for it. Fittingly, after the cook grabs him, the ones he condescendingly ignored reject his own requests for help. The tale's conclusion blends the moral lessons with a *pourquoi* element. Instead of rising socially, as he planned, Medio Pollito rises physically, ending up on the roof of a Madrid church. This conclusion simultaneously uses Medio Politto as a warning to those who have similar faults and offers a fanciful explanation of the origin of the weather-cock found on Spanish churches.

Once upon a time there was a handsome black Spanish hen, who had a large brood of chickens. They were all fine, plump little birds, except the youngest, who was quite unlike his brothers and sisters. Indeed, he was such a strange, queer-looking creature, that when he first chipped his shell his mother could scarcely believe her eyes, he was so different from the twelve other fluffy, downy, soft little chicks who nestled under her wings. This one looked just as if he had been cut in two. He had only one leg, and one wing, and one eye, and he had half a head and half a beak. His mother shook her head sadly as she looked at him and said:

'My youngest born is only a half-chick. He can never grow up a tall handsome cock like his brothers. They will go out into the world and rule over poultry yards of their own; but this poor little fellow will always have to stay at home with his mother.' And she called him Medio Pollito, which is Spanish for half-chick.

Now though Medio Pollito was such an odd, helpless-looking little thing, his mother soon found that he was not at all willing to remain under her wing and protection. Indeed, in character he was as unlike his brothers and sisters as he was in appearance. They were good, obedient chickens, and when the old hen chicked after them, they chirped and ran back to her side. But Medio Pollito had a roving spirit in spite of his one leg, and when his mother called to him to return to the coop, he pretended that he could not hear, because he had only one ear.

When she took the whole family out for a walk in the fields, Medio Pollito would hop away by himself, and hide among the Indian corn. Many an anxious minute his brothers and sisters had looking for him, while his mother ran to and fro cackling in fear and dismay.

As he grew older he became more self-willed and disobedient, and his manner to his mother was often very rude, and his temper to the other chickens very disagreeable.

One day he had been out for a longer expedition than usual in the fields. On his return he strutted up to his mother with the peculiar little hop and kick which was his way of walking, and cocking his one eye at her in a very bold way he said:

'Mother, I am tired of this life in a dull farmyard, with nothing but a dreary maize field to look at. I'm off to Madrid to see the King.'

'To Madrid, Medio Pollito!' exclaimed his mother; 'why, you silly chick, it would be a long journey for a grown-up cock, and a poor little thing like you would be tired out before you had gone half the distance. No, no, stay at home with your mother, and some day, when you are bigger, we will go a little journey together.'

But Medio Pollito had made up his mind, and he would not listen to his mother's advice, nor to the prayers and entreaties of his brothers and sisters.

'What is the use of our all crowding each other up in this poky little place?' he said. 'When I have a fine courtyard of my own at the King's palace, I shall perhaps ask some of you to come and pay me a short visit,' and scarcely waiting to say good-bye to his family, away he stumped down the high road that led to Madrid.

'Be sure that you are kind and civil to everyone you meet,' called his mother, running after him; but he was in such a hurry to be off, that he did not wait to answer her, or even to look back.

A little later in the day, as he was taking a short cut through a field, he passed a stream. Now the stream was all choked up, and overgrown with weeds and water-plants, so that its waters could not flow freely.

'Oh! Medio Pollito,' it cried, as the half-chick hopped along its banks, 'do come and help me by clearing away these weeds.'

'Help you, indeed!' exclaimed Medio Pollito, tossing his head, and shaking the few feathers in his tail. 'Do you think I have nothing to do but to waste my time on such trifles? Help yourself, and don't trouble busy travellers. I am off to Madrid to see the King,' and hoppity-kick, hoppity-kick, away stumped Medio Pollito.

A little later he came to a fire that had been left by some gipsies in a wood. It was burning very low, and would soon be out.

'Oh! Medio Pollito,' cried the fire, in a weak, wavering voice as the half-chick approached, 'in a few minutes I shall go quite out, unless you put some sticks and dry leaves upon me. Do help me, or I shall die!'

'Help you, indeed!' answered Medio Pollito. 'I have other things to do. Gather sticks for yourself, and don't trouble me. I am off to Madrid to see the King,' and hoppity-kick, hoppity-kick, away stumped Medio Pollito.

The next morning, as he was getting near Madrid, he passed a large chestnut tree, in whose branches the wind was caught and entangled. 'Oh! Medio Pollito,' called the wind, 'do hop up here, and help me to get free of these branches. I cannot come away, and it is so uncomfortable.'

'It is your own fault for going there,' answered Medio Pollito. 'I can't waste all my morning stopping here to help you. Just shake yourself off, and don't hinder me, for I am off to Madrid to see the King,' and hoppity-kick, hoppity-kick, away stumped Medio Pollito in great glee, for the towers and roofs of Madrid were now in sight. When he entered the town he saw before him a great splendid house, with soldiers standing before the gates. This he knew must be the King's palace, and he determined to hop up to the front gate and wait there until the King came out. But as he was hopping past one of the back windows the King's cook saw him:

'Here is the very thing I want,' he exclaimed, 'for the King has just sent a message to say that he must have chicken broth for his dinner,' and opening the window he stretched out his arm, caught Medio Pollito, and popped him into the broth-pot that was standing near the fire. Oh! how wet and clammy the water felt as it went over Medio Pollito's head, making his feathers cling to his side.

'Water, water!' he cried in his despair, 'do have pity upon me and do not wet me like this.'

'Ah! Medio Pollito,' replied the water, 'you would not help me when I was a little stream away on the fields, now you must be punished.'

Then the fire began to burn and scald Medio Pollito, and he danced and hopped from one side of the pot to the other, trying to get away from the heat, and crying out in pain:

'Fire, fire! do not scorch me like this; you can't think how it hurts.'

'Ah! Medio Pollito,' answered the fire, 'you would not help me when I was dying away in the wood. You are being punished.'

At last, just when the pain was so great that Medio Pollito thought he must die, the cook lifted up the lid of the pot to see if the broth was ready for the King's dinner.

'Look here!' he cried in horror, 'this chicken is quite useless. It is burnt to a cinder. I can't send it up to the royal table;' and opening the window he threw Medio Pollito out into the street. But the wind caught him up, and whirled him through the air so quickly that Medio Pollito could scarcely breathe, and his heart beat against his side till he thought it would break.

'Oh, wind!' at last he gasped out, 'if you hurry me along like this you will kill me. Do let me rest a moment, or—' but he was so breathless that he could not finish his sentence.

'Ah! Medio Pollito,' replied the wind, 'when I was caught in the branches of the chestnut tree you would not help me; now you are punished.' And he swirled Medio Pollito over the roofs of the houses till they reached the highest church in the town, and there he left him fastened to the top of the steeple.

And there stands Medio Pollito to this day. And if you go to Madrid, and walk through the streets till you come to the highest church, you will see Medio Pollito perched on his one leg on the steeple, with his one wing drooping at his side, and gazing sadly out of his one eye over the town.

———

From *The Green Fairy Book*, by Andrew Lang (London: Longmans, Green, and Co., 1892).

LINKS TO OTHER STORIES

Part Six

Loves Won and Lost
Tales of Courtship and Marriage

In *The Folktale*, Stith Thompson says that 'We see the lowly hero or heroine win a royal mate so frequently in folktales that this revolution of fortune has come to seem the most characteristic sign of the "fairy tale"' (87). As he makes clear through his examples, cultures all over the world tell stories about attempts to win or recover a mate. Although some tales do present marriages in which the couple does not live 'happily ever after', the vast majority of courtship and marriage tales end happily. Regardless of the ending, however, tales about love seldom, if ever, make overt statements about the significance of their plots because they operate under what literary critic James M. McGlathery terms the folk tale's 'requirement of silence about the action's meaning' (3). McGlathery indicates that this tendency to avoid commentary about feelings and experiences limits the romantic atmosphere in such tales:

> When the princess meets her charming prince, in the stereotypical fairy tale situation, there is almost never much romantic about it, in the way of lovers' talk or description of the reactions. The characters typically appear almost not to feel, only to act. The lovers meet; external obstacles to their union are overcome; and they marry—all rather prosaic, except for magical realm in which the action may be imagined to take place. (4)

This lack of overt emotion in tales treating what is probably the most emotional of all human experiences leads many critics to regard such tales as being about something other than love. In other words, many critics view tales about love as symbolic representations of general psychological or social phenomena.

Western psychological critics, in particular, have found the symbolic tendencies of fairy tales about love and courtship especially attractive. Marie von Franz, a disciple of Carl Jung, argues that 'fairy tales actually tell us about figures of the unconscious, of the other world' (6), that the characters are 'archetypal figures lacking human amplification', and that, consequently, such tales are about the 'Anima, Ego, and Self' (15). Although he does it from a Freudian perspective, Bruno Bettelheim makes a similar point, contending 'Each fairy tale is a magic mirror which reflects some aspects of our inner world, and of the steps required by our evolution from immaturity to maturity' (309). He can thus argue, for example, that '"Beauty and the Beast" begins with an immature view which posits man to have a dual existence as animal and as mind—symbolized by Beauty' (308) and that it concludes with a marriage that 'is a symbolic expression of the healing of the pernicious break between the animal and the higher aspects of man . . .' (308–9).

Although Bettelheim confidently asserts that their symbolic language makes fairy tales 'an ideal way for the child to learn about sex in a fashion appropriate to his age and developmental understanding' (279), sociological and feminist critics have forcefully opposed this benign view of the use of tales. The Marxist critic Jack Zipes, for example, argues that, 'In essence, Bettelheim's book discusses the use of the folk tale to compensate for social repression' (Zipes 1979, 174). Denying that a tale can act as a guide for children to order their internal worlds, he seizes on one of the tales Bettelheim praises to assert that 'the ideological and psychological pattern and message of Cinderella do nothing more than reinforce sexist values and a Puritan ethos that serves a society which fosters competition and achievement for survival' (173). Concentrating his argument on European examples, Zipes notes that many romantic fairy tales took form in the salon culture of seventeenth-century France. Intended for an adult audience 'The fairy tale was used in refined discourse as a means through which women imagined their lives might be improved (Zipes 1994, 23). He further argues that the reception of these tales and their acceptance by the upper levels of society transformed them: 'the tales were changed to introduce morals to children that emphasized the enforcement of a patriarchal code of civilité to the detriment of women, even though women were originally the major writers of the tales' (24).

Feminist critics have similarly refused to view fairy tale characters as symbolic abstractions. Instead, like Zipes, they view the heroines of tales about love and courtship as agents of a patriarchal system that has repressed women. For example, Andrea Dworkin says

> Cinderella, Sleeping Beauty, Snow-white, Rapunzel—all are characterized by passivity, beauty, innocence, and victimization. They are archetypal good women—victims by definition. They never think, act, initiate, confront, resist, challenge, feel, care, or question. . . . They are moved, as if inert, from the house of the mother to the house of the prince. First they are objects of malice, then they are objects of romantic adoration. They do nothing to warrant either. (42)

Feminist critics also point out that the active women in these tales tend to be evil: wicked stepmothers and witches. Because they believe that these tales praise female passivity and condemn female activity, they argue that the fairy tales about love have a far from benign effect in fostering images of ideal female character.

It is important, however, to note that these psychological, social, and feminist critics come from a Western intellectual tradition and that the ideas that they express may not be entirely applicable to tales from non-European cultures. For instance, in The Japanese Psyche: Major Motifs in the Fairy Tales of Japan, Hayao Kawai, a Japanese Jungian, says that 'In symbolism, some areas are universal while others are influenced by cultural differences. One who fails to keep this in mind is apt to err seriously in interpreting Japanese fairy tales' (26). He even makes the controversial assertion that Japanese tales differ so markedly from Western ones that readers need to view them through 'female eyes' because 'the ego of a Japanese is properly symbolized by a female and not by a male' (26). Until more resources for understanding them become available, Western readers must, therefore, take exceptional care not to impose their cultural beliefs and habits of mind in interpreting highly symbolic love stories from other cultures.

Although traditional romantic tales seem to some Western critics to be conservative because they preserve a patriarchal vision of gender roles, they continue to appeal to children and adults alike. Perhaps this appeal comes from the fact that these tales also probe deep-seated human emotions and express fantasies of wish fulfillment. Such fantasies do rely on oft-criticized stereotypes, such as the beautiful princess and the handsome prince. It is possible, however, that these stereotypes appeal as idealizations, symbols of social, psychological, and spiritual excellence for which people long. Furthermore, although in most cultures females historically had few options other than marriage, we, even in an age when multiple marriages or sequential common-law relationships are nearly the norm, can still appreciate the symbolic power of marriage. In fairy tales, getting married is the ultimate symbol of successful maturation. In these tales, marriage marks an acceptance by others and provides a couple with both personal and social purpose. As a result, it marks the end of irrelevance, solitariness, or alienation. Marriage, in other words, is the prime symbol of accord and fulfillment.

Folk and fairy tales treat the love, courtship, and marriage motifs in a variety of ways. The love interest may be incidental in a tale, a shorthand way of symbolizing personal and social success, as is the sudden marriage at the end of Joseph Jacobs' 'Jack and the Beanstalk'. On the other hand, the love interest may be at the core of a tale, as it is in the tales gathered here, and in most of those collected in the 'Cinderella and Her Cousins' section. Such tales portray lovers in a variety of roles. In the majority of Cinderella tales, for example, the female lover appears initially as a victim who, through her own wiles, or magical help that symbolizes her virtue (in the sense of both power and moral excellence), or a combination of each of these, wins the hand of a handsome prince. Marriage thus symbolizes loving acceptance of the once-scorned girl.

Another common figure of victimization is the enchanted female lover, the central motif in the first two tales of this section. This figure, because she is acted upon rather than acting, is a device for focusing attention of the visions and desires of those who encounter her. Both Charles Perrault's 'The Sleeping Beauty in the Woods' and the Grimm Brothers' 'Little Briar-Rose' thus turn on issues of desire. The female is first a long-desired child and then a much-desired maiden. In between is the desire for respect and revenge exhibited by the slighted fairy, the desire to protect children evident in the parents' attempts to destroy all spindles, the young girl's desire to learn about spinning because it is a novel activity, and the desire of the old woman to teach her spinning, presumably because such knowledge has traditionally been part of a girl's education. Of course, the majority of critics have seen the issue of sexual desire as foremost, citing the phallic spindle and the adolescent girl's drop of blood as symbols of either her sexual initiation or her maturation into puberty through menstruation. No matter how one interprets such details, however, it is clear that the story is about awakening, an act that gives fresh vision. Because Sleeping Beauty is passive and is literally not her conscious self until the moment when her true love arrives, this tale foregrounds love as that which awakens one into consciousness of self and others.

Females are not the only victims in romantic tales: enchanted male lovers also figure prominently. 'Beauty and the Beast', in which a curse has transformed a handsome prince into a frightening monster, is probably the most famous of the group of animal groom tales. This particular tale contains echoes of the Greek literary myth of 'Cupid and Psyche', which critic Marina Warner has called 'a founding myth of sexual difference' (274). Unlike the myth, however, this fairy tale has a theme of dual transformation: Beauty's inward transformation occurs when she learns to value character more than appearance. Her transformation precipitates the physical transformation of the Beast, who resumes his true shape as a handsome prince. Because it is symbolic—Iona and Peter Opie have called it 'The most symbolic of the fairy tales after Cinderella, and the most intellectually satisfying' (137)—'Beauty and the Beast' has provoked a variety of readings. Bettelheim interprets it as an illustration of psychological development in which the female moves from oedipal attachment to the father, through revulsion at the idea of male sexuality, to mature acceptance of sexuality. Marina Warner also sees erotic desire as a major subject, but she places the tale within a historical social context of arranged marriages. For her, this tale explores the feelings of a girl forced to leave home and experience a 'terrifying encounter with Otherness' (276) in the house to which her father sends her. Jack Zipes argues that 'Beauty and the Beast' tries 'to legitimize the aristocratic standard of living in contrast to the allegedly crass, vulgar values of the emerging bourgeoisie'. For him, 'The theme of this aristocratic tale involves "putting the bourgeoisie in their place"' (Zipes 1979, 10).

Exogamy, marrying outside of one's home group, which Warner and anthropological critics see as symbolically presented in 'Beauty and the Beast', is a much more overt concern in another tale about an animal groom, 'The Story of Five Heads'. This didactic South African tale contrasts the fates of two sisters to illustrate both the value of traditional social practices and the necessity for women to be respectful and to heed advice. The prince, who appears only at the climax of each of the tale's two sections, is not a victim of enchantment. He voluntarily assumes the shape of a five-headed snake. Nevertheless, he is like the Beast in that his outward appearance reveals the inner nature of the females who encounter him and his ultimate transformation into a handsome prince symbolizes the life-altering power of love.

Exogamy and arranged marriage are also themes in a famous European tale that shows female victimization continuing past the marriage ceremony. In 'Rumpelstiltskin' the young woman is a victim of the desires of three males. Her father's bragging, evidence of his desire for notoriety or importance, forces her to leave home and eventually to enter into marriage. The King's desire for gold forces her into attempting to pass the impossible marriage test of spinning straw into gold. The little man's mysterious desire for her child (perhaps symbolizing social practices in which children were taken away from the mother to be wet-nursed and even raised by others) forces her into another seemingly impossible task, the guessing of her tormentor's name.

The young woman in 'Rumpelstiltskin' is not alone in having to pass a bridal test. Tests of a person's worthiness for marriage frequently display society's assumptions about gender roles. Females most often have to pass tests of domestic competence, as does the lassie in 'East o' the Sun and West o' the Moon' when she washes her beloved's shirt, or of social propriety, as does the second daughter in 'The Story of Five Heads', when she follows tradition by having relatives and drummers escort her, displays humility by accepting advice from others, and refrains from displaying her fear when she first sees her groom's ferocious appearance. For men, marriage tests frequently involve bravery and physical prowess, such as the dragon-slaying episode at the end of the male Cinderella tale 'Billy Beg and the Bull'.

One of the most common tests to establish worthiness for marriage involves impossible tasks. The Slav tale 'The Maid with Hair of Gold' employs the device in an unusual way: George, the young man, does not undertake the impossible tasks for his own benefit but for that of the King. Naturally, he himself falls in love with the princess, who is the prize for success in the test. Just as conventionally, magical intervention provokes the King's worst traits and leads to the conventional happy ending of the marriage of the young man and the bride whom he had truly won.

Another kind of marriage test involves riddling, an activity that may display the participants' wit and knowledge of the world. Of all the tales involving a contest of wits with a princess, the one that Stith Thompson cites as having 'the widest distribution as an oral narrative and the most extensive literary history' (156) presents a clever princess who is offered to the man who can formulate a riddle that she cannot solve. The version of this widespread tale that that we include in this part, the Puerto Rican 'Juan Bobo and the Princess Who Answered Riddles', focuses on a character who is a simpleton in most tales about him. In this tale, Juan Bobo displays his worthiness for marriage, first, by stumping the princess with his questionable riddle, and, second, by outwitting her when he obtains proof that he told her the answer to his riddle.

Another group of tales involving tests has females succeeding where males fail miserably. In the Jewish-American 'The Innkeeper's Wise Daughter', the young woman passes riddling tests to establish that she is intellectually superior to older men. After her marriage, she proves to her husband that she worthy of respect but is also capable of deep love. 'The Frog Maiden', a Burmese tale, has the frog-like bride secretly performing the tasks that allow her husband to pass the succession tests that defeat his brothers. The story concludes, however, as a transformation tale, with the animal bride, like the groom in 'Beauty and the Beast', shedding her animal appearance once she receives a sign of his worthiness to have her.

As both 'Beauty and the Beast' and 'The Frog Maiden' show, the beloved in romantic tales is not always an ordinary human. In many instances, the wife has a supernatural origin or is the offspring of an ogre. The eponymous heroine of 'Rosalie', a tale from Mexico, is the daughter of a giant. Much of the tale, in which she saves her beloved from her parents' attempts to kill him, symbolically dramatizes her maturation through her assertion of her right to choose her own husband. In a sense, her parents' attempts on her beloved's life, their pursuit of the fleeing couple, and her rescue of her beloved just before he marries another constitute informal bridal tests: by using her wit and her magic, and by showing courage and determination, she shows that she is worthy of becoming a happy bride

Although, as we noted earlier, most tales dramatize the successful union of lovers, some romantic tales end ironically with loss, rather than this traditional life of unalloyed happiness. In 'The Crane Wife', a tale from Japan, and 'The Goodman of Wastness and His Selkie Wife', from the Orkney Islands, men encounter shape shifters, animals who can transform into humans. Unlike the Beast, the normal and desirable state for these brides is not as human but as Other. Both tales agree that such transgressive unions cannot endure, so, eventually, the females recover their own identity and leave their husbands. In both instances, the animal-bride may symbolize the idea that a lasting marriage cannot be built upon any kind of coercion, and both may symbolize the devastation and longings for return that beset brides forced by exogamy to leave their home group. Furthermore, as a symbolic representation of psychological states, 'The Crane Wife' offers the opposite lesson of 'East o' the Sun and West o' the Moon' and 'Cupid and Psyche': in those tales, females drove away males by prying too deeply into their identities; in this tale, the male drives away his wife by prying into her female identity.

Another Japanese tale of loss is the legend of 'Urashima Taro', in which the male, like Rosalie's fiancé or the lassie in 'East o' the Sun and West o' the Moon', violates a taboo and thereby loses a marriage partner. Unlike these two, however, Urashima Taro is not given a chance to redeem himself. His attachment to his home and his failure to curtail curiosity suggests that his very humanity, the source of these attributes, limits his capacity to achieve happiness through permanent change. The Australian Aboriginal myth 'The Moon', which concludes this collection, also denies the central character a second chance. Having failed to understand how to court females properly, the personified Moon forever loses his chances of a happy union. Although it seems to imply that some males may never learn, this comical myth suggests that understanding of and respect for females is a necessary prerequisite to satisfying male desire and achieving happiness.

Works Cited

Bettleheim, Bruno. 1976. 'Cinderella', *The Uses of Enchantment*. New York: Alfred A. Knopf.

Dworkin, Andrea. 1974. *Woman Hating*. New York: Dutton.

Franz, Marie-Louise von. [1972] 1976. *Problems of the Feminine in Fairytales*. New York: Spring Publications.

Kawai, Hayao. 1988. *The Japanese Psyche, Major Motifs in the Fairy Tales of Japan*. Trans. Hayao Kawai and Sachiko Reece. Dallas, Texas: Spring Publications.

Thompson, Stith. [1946] 1967. *The Folktale*. New York: Holt, Rinehart and Winston; Berkley: University of California Press.

Warner, Marina. 1995. *From the Beast to the Blonde: On Fairy Tales and Their Tellers*. London: Vintage.

Zipes, Jack. 1979. *Breaking the Magical Spell: Radical Theories of Folk and Fairy Tales*. Austin: University of Texas Press.

———. 1994. *Fairy Tale as Myth, Myth as Fairy Tale*. Lexington: University of Kentucky Press.

The Sleeping Beauty in the Woods

As the introduction to this section notes, the plot of the Sleeping Beauty story depends of various kinds of desire. Critics who see the tale as symbolizing female maturation emphasize that Beauty awakens both to recognize and to consummate her erotic desire. It is important to note, however, that in 'The Sleeping Beauty in the Woods' ('La Belle au Bois Dormis'), Charles Perrault does not end the story, as do the Brothers Grimm, with a marriage that symbolizes happiness and fulfillment of desire. Instead, Perrault makes the young bride once again a victim of an older female, her husband's mother, who is inflamed with a diabolical desire to destroy her and her children. The account of the princess's persecution at the hands of her mother-in-law may seem to modern readers like a puzzling continuation to a love story. This plot becomes much more understandable, however, when we take into account the fact that Perrault was sanitizing for the French court his earthy source text, 'Sun, Moon, and Talia', the fifth tale of the fifth day in Giambattista Basile's *Pentamerone* (1636). In Basile's narrative, the Prince raped the sleeping maiden, who gave birth to children named Sun and Moon, and the vicious queen, who was actually the Prince's wife, became so enraged at his infidelity that she wanted to make her husband dine on his illegitimate children. Perrault's transformation of Basile's tale makes the second part both a symbolic account of the jealousy an older woman feels when she is supplanted by a younger one and a story of rescue, for the Prince, who merely arrived at the appropriate time when Beauty awoke, now arrives at the appropriate time to save her from his mother's evil scheme.

Once upon a time there was a king and a queen, who were very sorry that they had no children,—so sorry that it cannot be told.

At last, however, the Queen had a daughter. There was a very fine christening; and the Princess had for her godmothers all the fairies they could find in the whole kingdom (there were seven of them), so that every one of them might confer a gift upon her, as was the custom of fairies in those days. By this means the Princess had all the perfections imaginable.

After the christening was over the company returned to the King's palace, where was prepared a great feast for the fairies. There was placed before every one of them a magnificent cover with a case of massive gold, wherein were a spoon, and a knife and fork, all of pure gold set with diamonds and rubies. But as they were all sitting down at table they saw a very old fairy come into the hall. She had not been invited, because for more than fifty years she had not been out of a certain tower, and she was believed to be either dead or enchanted.

The King ordered her a cover, but he could not give her a case of gold as the others had, because seven only had been made for the seven fairies. The old fairy fancied she was slighted, and muttered threats between her teeth. One of the young fairies who sat near heard her, and, judging that she might give the little Princess some unlucky gift, hid herself behind the curtains as soon as they left the table. She hoped that she might speak last and undo as much as she could the evil which the old fairy might do.

In the meanwhile all the fairies began to give their gifts to the Princess. The youngest gave her for her gift that she should be the most beautiful person in the world; the next, that she should have the wit of an angel; the third, that she should be able to do everything she did gracefully; the fourth, that she should dance perfectly; the fifth, that she should sing like a nightingale; and the sixth, that she should play all kinds of musical instruments to the fullest perfection.

The old fairy's turn coming next, her head shaking more with spite than with age, she said that the Princess should pierce her hand with a spindle and die of the wound. This terrible gift made the whole company tremble, and everybody fell a-crying.

At this very instant the young fairy came from behind the curtains and said these words in a loud voice:—

'Assure yourselves, O King and Queen, that your daughter shall not die of this disaster. It is true, I have no power to undo entirely what my elder has done. The Princess shall indeed pierce her hand with a spindle; but, instead of dying, she shall only fall into a deep sleep, which shall last a hundred years, at the end of which a king's son shall come and awake her.'

The King, to avoid the misfortune foretold by the old fairy, issued orders forbidding any one, on pain of death, to spin with a distaff and spindle, or to have a spindle in his house. About fifteen or sixteen years after, the King and Queen being absent at one of their country villas, the young Princess was one day running up and down the palace; she went from room to room, and at last she came into a little garret on the top of the tower, where a good old woman, alone, was spinning with her spindle. This good woman had never heard of the King's orders against spindles.

'What are you doing there, my good woman?' said the Princess.

'I am spinning, my pretty child,' said the old woman, who did not know who the Princess was.

'Ha!' said the Princess, 'this is very pretty; how do you do it? Give it to me. Let me see if I can do it.'

She had no sooner taken it into her hand than, either because she was too quick and heedless, or because the decree of the fairy had so ordained, it ran into her hand, and she fell down in a swoon.

The good old woman, not knowing what to do, cried out for help. People came in from every quarter; they threw water upon the face of the Princess, unlaced her, struck her on the palms of her hands, and rubbed her temples with cologne water; but nothing would bring her to herself.

Then the King, who came up at hearing the noise, remembered what the fairies had foretold. He knew very well that this must come to pass, since the fairies had foretold it, and he caused the Princess to be carried into the finest room in his palace, and to be laid upon a bed all embroidered with gold and silver. One would have taken her for a little angel, she was so beautiful; for her swooning had not dimmed the brightness of her complexion: her cheeks were carnation, and her lips coral. It is true her eyes were shut, but she was heard to breathe softly, which satisfied those about her that she was not dead.

The King gave orders that they should let her sleep quietly till the time came for her to awake. The good fairy who had saved her life by condemning her to sleep a hundred years was in the kingdom of Matakin, twelve thousand leagues off, when this accident befell the Princess; but she was instantly informed of it by a little dwarf, who had seven-leagued boots, that is, boots with which he could stride over seven leagues of ground at once. The fairy started off at once, and arrived, about an hour later, in a fiery chariot drawn by dragons.

The King handed her out of the chariot, and she approved everything he had done; but as she had very great foresight, she thought that when the Princess should awake she might not know what to do with herself, if she was all alone in this old palace. This was what she did: she touched with her wand everything in the palace (except the King and Queen),— governesses, maids of honour, ladies of the bedchamber, gentlemen, officers, stewards, cooks, undercooks, kitchen maids, guards with their porters, pages, and footmen; she like-wise touched all the horses which were in the stables, the cart horses, the hunters and the saddle horses, the grooms, the great dogs in the outward court, and little Mopsey, too, the Princess's spaniel, which was lying on the bed.

As soon as she touched them they all fell asleep, not to awake again until their mistress did, that they might be ready to wait upon her when she wanted them. The very spits at the fire, as full as they could hold of partridges and pheasants fell asleep, and the fire itself as well. All this was done in a moment. Fairies are not long in doing their work.

And now the King and Queen, having kissed their dear child without waking her, went out of the palace and sent forth orders that nobody should come near it. These orders were not necessary; for in a quarter of an hour's time there grew up all round about the park such a vast number of trees, great and small, bushes and brambles, twining one within another, that neither man nor beast could pass through; so that nothing could be seen but the very top of the towers of the palace; and that, too, only from afar off. Everyone knew that this also was the work of the fairy in order that while the Princess slept she should have noth-ing to fear from curious people.

After a hundred years the son of the King then reigning, who was of another family from that of the sleeping Princess, was a-hunting on that side of the country, and he asked what those towers were which he saw in the middle of a great thick wood. Everyone answered according as they had heard. Some said that it was an old haunted castle, others that all the witches of the country held their midnight revels there, but the common opin-ion was that it was an ogre's dwelling, and that he carried to it all the little children he could catch, so as to eat them up at his leisure, without anyone being able to follow him, for he alone had the power to make his way through the wood.

The Prince did not know what to believe, and presently a very aged countryman spake to him thus:—

'May it please your royal Highness, more than fifty years since I heard from my father that there was then in this castle the most beautiful princess that was ever seen; that she must sleep there a hundred years, and that she should be waked by a king's son, for whom she was reserved.'

The young Prince on hearing this was all on fire. He thought, without weighing the matter, that he could put an end to this rare adventure; and, pushed on by love and the desire of glory, resolved at once to look into it.

As soon as he began to get near to the wood, all the great trees, the bushes, and brambles gave way of themselves to let him pass through. He walked up to the castle which he saw at the end of a large avenue; and you can imagine he was a good deal surprised when he saw none of his people following him, because the trees closed again as soon as he had passed through them. However, he did not cease from continuing his way; a young prince in search of glory is ever valiant.

He came into a spacious outer court, and what he saw was enough to freeze him with horror. A frightful silence reigned over all; the image of death was everywhere, and there was nothing to be seen but what seemed to be the outstretched bodies of dead men and animals. He, however, very well knew, by the ruby faces and pimpled noses of the porters, that they were only asleep; and their goblets, wherein still remained some drops of wine, showed plainly that they had fallen asleep while drinking their wine.

He then crossed a court paved with marble, went up the stairs, and came into the guard chamber, where guards were standing in their ranks, with their muskets upon their shoulders, and snoring with all their might. He went through several rooms fun of gentlemen and ladies, some standing and others sitting, but all were asleep. He came into a gilded chamber, where he saw upon a bed, the curtains of which were all open, the most beautiful sight ever beheld—a princess who appeared to be about fifteen or sixteen years of age, and whose bright and resplendent beauty had something divine in it. He approached with trembling and admiration, and fell down upon his knees before her.

Then, as the end of the enchantment was come, the Princess awoke, and looking on him with eyes more tender than could have been expected at first sight, said;

'Is it you, my Prince? You have waited a long while.'

The Prince, charmed with these words, and much more with the manner in which they were spoken, knew not how to show his joy and gratitude; he assured her that he loved her better than he did himself. Their discourse was not very connected, but they were the better pleased, for where there is much love there is little eloquence. He was more at a loss than she, and we need not wonder at it; she had had time to think of what to say to him; for it is evident (though history says nothing of it) that the good fairy, during so long a sleep, had given her very pleasant dreams. In short, they talked together for four hours, and then they said not half they had to say. In the meanwhile all the palace had woke up with the Princess; everyone thought upon his own business, and as they were not in love, they were ready to die of hunger. The lady of honour being as sharp set as the other folks, grew very impatient, and told the Princess aloud that the meal was served. The Prince helped the Princess to rise. She was entirely and very magnificently dressed; but his royal Highness took care not to tell her that she was dressed like his great-grandmother, and had a high collar. She looked not a bit the less charming and beautiful for all that.

They went into the great mirrored hall, where they supped, and were served by the officers of the Princess's household. The violins and hautboys played old tunes, but they were excellent, though they had not been played for a hundred years; and after supper, without losing any time, the lord almoner married them in the chapel of the castle. They had but very little sleep—the Princess scarcely needed any; and the Prince left her next morning to return into the city, where his father was greatly troubled about him.

The Prince told him that he lost his way in the forest, as he was hunting, and that he had slept in the cottage of a charcoal-burner, who gave him cheese and brown bread.

The King, his father, who was a good man, believed him; but his mother could not be persuaded that it was true; and seeing that he went almost every day a-hunting, and that he always had some excuse ready for so doing, though he had been out three or four nights together, she began to suspect that he was married; for he lived thus with the Princess above two whole years, during which they had two children, the elder, a daughter, was named Dawn, and the younger, a son, they called Day, because he was a great deal handsomer than his sister.

The Queen spoke several times to her son, to learn after what manner he was passing his time, and told him that in this he ought in duty to satisfy her. But he never dared to trust her with his secret; he feared her, though he loved her, for she was of the race of the Ogres, and the King married her for her vast riches alone. It was even whispered about the Court that she had Ogreish inclinations, and that, whenever she saw little children passing by, she had all the difficulty in the world to prevent herself from falling upon them. And so the Prince would never tell her one word.

But when the King was dead, which happened about two years afterward, and he saw himself lord and master, he openly declared his marriage; and he went in great state to conduct his Queen to the palace. They made a magnificent entry into the capital city, she riding between her two children.

Soon after, the King made war on Emperor Cantalabutte, his neighbour. He left the government of the kingdom to the Queen, his mother, and earnestly commended his wife and children to her care. He was obliged to carry on the war all the summer, and as soon as he left, the Queen-mother sent her daughter-in-law and her children to a country house among the woods, that she might with the more ease gratify her horrible longing. Some few days afterward she went thither herself, and said to her head cook:—

'I intend to eat little Dawn for my dinner to-morrow.'

'O! madam!' cried the head cook.

'I will have it so,' replied the Queen (and this she spoke in the tone of an Ogress who had a strong desire to eat fresh meat), 'and will eat her with a sharp sauce.'

The poor man, knowing very well that he must not play tricks with Ogresses, took his great knife and went up into little Dawn's chamber. She was then nearly four years old, and came up to him, jumping and laughing, to put her arms round his neck, and ask him for some sugar-candy. Upon which he began to weep, the great knife fell out of his hand, and he went into the back yard and killed a little lamb, and dressed it with such good sauce that his mistress assured him she had never eaten anything so good in her life. He had at the same time taken up little Dawn and carried her to his wife, to conceal her in his lodging at the end of the courtyard.

Eight days afterwards the wicked Queen said to the chief cook, 'I will sup upon little Day.'

He answered not a word, being resolved to cheat her again as he had done before. He went to find little Day, and saw him with a foil in his hand, with which he was fencing with a great monkey: the child was then only three years of age. He took him up in his arms and carried him to his wife, that she might conceal him in her chamber along with his sister, and instead of little Day he served up a young and very tender kid, which the Ogress found to be wonderfully good.

All had gone well up to now; but one evening this wicked Queen said to her chief cook:—

'I will eat the Queen with the same sauce I had with her children.'

Now the poor chief cook was in despair and could not imagine how to deceive her again. The young Queen was over twenty years old, not reckoning the hundred years she had been asleep; and how to find something to take her place greatly puzzled him. He then decided, to save his own life, to cut the Queen's throat; and going up into her chamber, with intent to do it at once, he put himself into as great fury as he possibly could, and came into the young Queen's room with his dagger in his hand. He would not, however, deceive her, but told her with a great deal of respect, the orders he had received from the Queen-mother.

'Do it; do it,' she said, stretching out her neck. 'Carry out your orders, and then I shall go and see my children, my poor children, whom I loved so much and so tenderly.'

For she thought them dead, since they had been taken away without her knowledge.

'No, no, madam,' cried the poor chief cook, all in tears: 'you shall not die; and you shall see your children again at once. But then you must go home with me to my lodgings, where I have concealed them, and I will deceive the Queen once more, by giving her a young hind in your stead.'

Upon this he forthwith conducted her to his room, where, leaving her to embrace her children, and cry along with them, he went and dressed a young hind, which the Queen had for her supper, and devoured with as much appetite as if it had been the young Queen. She was now well satisfied with her cruel deeds, and she invented a story to tell the King on his return, of how the Queen his wife and her two children had been devoured by mad wolves.

One evening, as she was, according to her custom, rambling round about the courts and yards of the palace to see if she could smell any fresh meat, she heard, in a room on the ground floor, little Day crying, for his mamma was going to whip him, because he had been naughty; and she heard, at the same time, little Dawn begging mercy for her brother.

The Ogress knew the voice of the Queen and her children at once, and being furious at having been thus deceived, she gave orders (in a most horrible voice which made everybody tremble) that, next morning by break of day, they should bring into the middle of the great court a large tub filled with toads, vipers, snakes, and all sorts of serpents, in order to have the Queen and her children, the chief cook, his wife, and maid, thrown into it, all of whom were to be brought thither with their hands tied behind them.

They were brought out accordingly, and the executioners were just going to throw them into the tub, when the King, who was not so soon expected, entered the court on horseback and asked, with the utmost astonishment, what was the meaning of that horrible spectacle.

No one dared to tell him, when the Ogress, all enraged to see what had happened, threw herself head foremost into the tub, and was instantly devoured by the ugly creatures she had ordered to be thrown into it to kill the others. The King was of course very sorry, for she was his mother; but he soon comforted himself with his beautiful wife and his pretty children.

From *The Tales of Mother Goose as First Collected by Perrault in 1697*, translated by Charles Welsh. (New York: D.C. Heath & Co., 1901).

Little Briar-Rose

'Little Briar-Rose' turns on the same motifs of desire as Perrault's 'The Sleeping Beauty in the Woods.' In fact, the tale is essentially the same as the first part of Perrault's tale, but it differs in some its details, such as the number of fairies invited to the celebratory feast. Perhaps the most significant difference, however, lies in the manner in which the enchanted princess awakens. Whereas in Perrault's version she wakens because the spell has run its course, the Grimms have her awaken as the direct result of the Prince's kiss. The romantic symbolism of this kiss as the beginning of love and its erotic symbolism as an act that leads to an awakening and a new consciousness have made this version the most popular of the Sleeping Beauty variants.

A long time ago there were a King and Queen who said every day, 'Ah, if only we had a child!' but they never had one. But it happened that once when the Queen was bathing, a frog crept out of the water on to the land, and said to her, 'Your wish shall be fulfilled; before a year has gone by you shall have a daughter.'

What the frog had said came true, and the Queen had a little girl who was so pretty that the King could not contain himself for joy, and ordered a great feast. He invited not only his kindred, friends, and acquaintance, but also the Wise Women, in order that they might be kind and well-disposed towards the child. There were thirteen of them in his kingdom, but, as he had only twelve golden plates for them to eat out of, one of them had to be left at home.

The feast was held with all manner of splendour, and when it came to an end the Wise Women bestowed their magic gifts upon the baby: one gave virtue, another beauty, a third riches, and so on with everything in the world that one can wish for.

When eleven of them had made their promises, suddenly the thirteenth came in. She wished to avenge herself for not having been invited, and without greeting, or even looking at anyone, she cried with a loud voice, 'The King's daughter shall in her fifteenth year prick herself with a spindle, and fall down dead.' And, without saying a word more, she turned round and left the room.

They were all shocked; but the twelfth, whose good wish still remained unspoken, came forward, and as she could not undo the evil sentence, but only soften it, she said, 'It shall not be death, but a deep sleep of a hundred years, into which the princess shall fall.'

The King, who would fain keep his dear child from the misfortune, gave orders that every spindle in the whole kingdom should be burnt. Meanwhile the gifts of the Wise Women were plenteously fulfilled on the young girl, for she was so beautiful, modest, good-natured, and wise, that everyone who saw her was bound to love her.

It happened that on the very day when she was fifteen years old, the King and Queen were not at home, and the maiden was left in the palace quite alone. So she went round into all sorts of places, looked into rooms and bedchambers just as she liked, and at last came to an old tower. She climbed up the narrow winding-staircase, and reached a little door. A rusty key was in the lock, and when she turned it the door sprang open, and there in a little room sat an old woman with a spindle, busily spinning her flax.

'Good day, old dame,' said the King's daughter; 'what are you doing there?' 'I am spinning,' said the old woman, and nodded her head. 'What sort of thing is that, that rattles round so merrily?' said the girl, and she took the spindle and wanted to spin too. But scarcely had she touched the spindle when the magic decree was fulfilled, and she pricked her finger with it.

And, in the very moment when she felt the prick, she fell down upon the bed that stood there, and lay in a deep sleep. And this sleep extended over the whole palace; the King and Queen who had just come home, and had entered the great hall, began to go to sleep, and the whole of the court with them. The horses, too, went to sleep in the stable, the dogs in the yard, the pigeons upon the roof, the flies on the wall; even the fire that was flaming on the hearth became quiet and slept, the roast meat left off frizzling, and the cook, who was just going to pull the hair of the scullery boy, because he had forgotten something, let him go, and went to sleep. And the wind fell, and on the trees before the castle not a leaf moved again.

But round about the castle there began to grow a hedge of thorns, which every year became higher, and at last grew close up round the castle and all over it, so that there was nothing of it to be seen, not even the flag upon the roof. But the story of the beautiful sleeping 'Briar-rose', for so the princess was named, went about the country, so that from time to time kings' sons came and tried to get through the thorny hedge into the castle.

But they found it impossible, for the thorns held fast together, as if they had hands, and the youths were caught in them, could not get loose again, and died a miserable death.

After long, long years a King's son came again to that country, and heard an old man talking about the thorn-hedge, and that a castle was said to stand behind it in which a wonderfully beautiful princess, named Briar-rose, had been asleep for a hundred years; and that the King and Queen and the whole court were asleep likewise. He had heard, too, from his grandfather, that many kings' sons had already come, and had tried to get through the thorny hedge, but they had remained sticking fast in it, and had died a pitiful death. Then the youth said, 'I am not afraid, I will go and see the beautiful Briar-rose.' The good old man might dissuade him as he would, he did not listen to his words.

But by this time the hundred years had just passed, and the day had come when Briar-rose was to awake again. When the King's son came near to the thorn-hedge, it was nothing but large and beautiful flowers, which parted from each other of their own accord, and let him pass unhurt, then they closed again behind him like a hedge. In the castle-yard he saw the horses and the spotted hounds lying asleep; on the roof sat the pigeons with their heads under their wings. And when he entered the house, the flies were asleep upon the wall, the cook in the kitchen was still holding out his hand to seize the boy, and the maid was sitting by the black hen which she was going to pluck.

He went on farther, and in the great hall he saw the whole of the court lying asleep, and up by the throne lay the King and Queen.

Then he went on still farther, and all was so quiet that a breath could be heard, and at last he came to the tower, and opened the door into the little room where Briar-rose was sleeping. There she lay, so beautiful that he could not turn his eyes away; and he stooped down and gave her a kiss. But as soon as he kissed her, Briar-rose opened her eyes and awoke, and looked at him quite sweetly.

Then they went down together, and the King awoke, and the Queen, and the whole court, and looked at each other in great astonishment. And the horses in the courtyard stood up and shook themselves; the hounds jumped up and wagged their tails; the pigeons upon the roof pulled out their heads from under their wings, looked round, and flew into the open country; the flies on the wall crept again; the fire in the kitchen burned up and flickered and cooked the meat; the joint began to turn and frizzle again, and the cook gave the boy such a box on the ear that he screamed, and the maid plucked the fowl ready for the spit.

And then the marriage of the King's son with Briar-rose was celebrated with all splendour, and they lived contented to the end of their days.

From *Grimm's Household Tales*, Vol. 1, translated by Margaret Hunt (London: George Bell and Sons, 1884).

Beauty and the Beast

'Beauty and the Beast' was first published as one of two fairy tales included in *Le jeune amériquaine et les contes marin* (1740), by Madame Gabrielle-Suzanne de Barbot de Villeneuve. In 1756 Madame Leprince de Beaumont, a Frenchwoman working in London as a tutor and writer of educational books, adapted this elaborate 362-page tale to make it suitable for children. She published her version in her *Magasin des enfans, ou dialogues entre une sage gouvernante at plusiers de ses élèves de lat première distinction* (translated into English as *The Young Misses Magazine* in 1761). Her adaptation formed the basis for later versions, such as that by Victorian novelist Dinah Maria Mulock Craik, of what has become probably the most famous of all literary fairy tales. Although it has some of the elaborate description characteristic of the *contes*, or tales, that were a hallmark of eighteenth-century Parisian salon culture, it also contains some folkloric archetypes: Beauty is the youngest and best of three sisters; she undertakes a journey that involves tests of her character; the Prince is victim of a magical spell that requires a seemingly impossible condition to be fulfilled before it can be lifted; and the conclusion has the significant characters receiving either rewards or stern, but appropriate, punishments.

There was once a very rich merchant who had six children, three boys and three girls. As he was himself a man of great sense, he spared no expense for their education. The three daughters were all handsome, but particularly the youngest; indeed, she was so very beautiful, that in her childhood every one called her the Little Beauty; and being equally lovely when she was grown up, nobody called her by any other name, which made her sisters very jealous of her. This youngest daughter was not only more handsome than her sisters, but also was better tempered. The two eldest were vain of their wealth and position. They gave themselves a thousand airs, and refused to visit other merchants' daughters; nor would they condescend to be seen except with persons of quality. They went every day to balls, plays, and public walks, and always made game of their youngest sister for spending her time in reading or other useful employments. As it was well known that these young ladies would have large fortunes, many great merchants wished to get them for wives; but the two eldest always answered, that, for their parts, they had no thoughts of marrying anyone below a duke or an earl at least. Beauty had quite as many offers as her sisters; but she always answered, with the greatest civility, that though she was much obliged to her lovers, she would, rather live some years longer with her father, as she thought herself too young to marry.

It happened that, by some unlucky accident, the merchant suddenly lost all his fortune, and had nothing left but a small cottage in the country. Upon this he said to his daughters, while the tears ran down his cheeks, 'My children, we must now go and dwell in the cottage, and try to get a living by labour, for we have no other means of support.' The two eldest replied that they did not know how to work, and would not leave town; for they had lovers enough who would be glad to marry them, though they had no longer any fortune. But in this they were mistaken; for when the lovers heard what had happened, they said, 'The girls were so proud and ill-tempered, that all we wanted was their fortune: we are not sorry at all to see their pride brought down: let them show off their airs to their cows and sheep.' But everybody pitied poor Beauty, because she was so sweet-tempered and kind to all; and several gentlemen offered to marry her, though she had not a penny; but Beauty still refused, and said she could not think of leaving her poor father in this trouble. At first Beauty could not help sometimes crying in secret for the hardships she was now obliged to suffer; but in a very short time she said to herself, 'All the crying in the world will do me no good, so I will try to be happy without a fortune.'

When they had removed to their cottage, the merchant and his three sons employed themselves in ploughing and sowing the fields, and working in the garden. Beauty also did her part, for she rose by four o'clock every morning, lighted the fires, cleaned the house, and got ready the breakfast for the whole family. At first she found all this very hard; but she soon grew quite used to it, and thought it no hardship; indeed, the work greatly benefited her health. When she had done, she used to amuse herself with reading, playing her music, or singing while she spun. But her two sisters were at a loss what to do to pass the time away: they had their breakfast in bed, and did not rise till ten o'clock. Then they commonly walked out, but always found themselves very soon tired; when they would often sit down under a shady tree, and grieve for the loss of their carriage and fine clothes, and say to each other, 'What a mean-spirited poor stupid creature our young sister is, to be so content with this low way of life!' But their father thought differently: and loved and admired his youngest child more than ever.

After they had lived in this manner about a year, the merchant received a letter, which informed him that one of his richest ships, which he thought was lost, had just come into port. This news made the two eldest sisters almost mad with joy; for they thought they should now leave the cottage, and have all their finery again. When they found that their father must take a journey to the ship, the two eldest begged he would not fail to bring them back some new gowns, caps, rings, and all sorts of trinkets. But Beauty asked for nothing; for she thought in herself that all the ship was worth would hardly buy everything her sisters wished for. 'Beauty,' said the merchant, 'how comes it that you ask for nothing: what can I bring you, my child?'

'Since you are so kind as to think of me, dear father,' she answered, 'I should be glad if you would bring me a rose, for we have none in our garden.' Now Beauty did not indeed wish for a rose, nor anything else, but she only said this that she might not affront her sisters; otherwise they would have said she wanted her father to praise her for desiring nothing. The merchant took his leave of them, and set out on his journey; but when he got to the ship, some persons went to law with him about the cargo, and after a deal of trouble he came back to his cottage as poor as he had left it. When he was within thirty miles of his home, and thinking of the joy of again meeting his children, he lost his way in the midst of a dense forest. It rained and snowed very hard, and, besides, the wind was so high as to throw him twice from his horse. Night came on, and he feared he should die of cold and hunger, or be torn to pieces by the wolves that he heard howling round him. All at once, he cast his eyes towards a long avenue; and saw at the end a light, but it seemed a great way off. He made the best of his way towards it, and found that it came from a splendid palace, the windows of which were all blazing with light. It had great bronze gates, standing wide open, and fine court-yards, through which the merchant passed; but not a living soul was to be seen. There were stables too, which his poor, starved horse, less scrupulous than himself, entered at once, and took a good meal of oats and hay. His master then tied him up, and walked towards the entrance hall, but still without seeing a single creature. He went on to a large dining-parlour, where he found a good fire, and a table covered with some very nice dishes, but only one plate with a knife and fork. As the snow and rain had wetted him to the skin, he went up to the fire to dry himself. 'I hope,' said he, 'the master of the house or his servants will excuse me, for it surely will not be long now before I see them.' He waited some time, but still nobody came: at last the clock struck eleven, and the merchant, being quite faint for the want of food, helped himself to a chicken, and to a few glasses of wine, yet all the time trembling with fear. He sat till the clock struck twelve, and then, taking courage, began to think he might as well look about him: so he opened a door at the end of the hall, and went through it into a very grand room, in which there was a fine bed; and as he was feeling very weary, he shut the door, took off his clothes, and got into it.

It was ten o'clock in the morning before he awoke, when he was amazed to see a handsome new suit of clothes laid ready for him, instead of his own, which were all torn and spoiled; 'To be sure,' said he to himself, 'this place belongs to some good fairy, who has taken pity on my ill luck.' He looked out of the window, and instead of the snow-covered wood, where he had lost himself the previous night, he saw the most charming arbours covered with all kinds of flowers. Returning to the hall where he had supped, he found a breakfast table, ready prepared. 'Indeed, my good fairy,' said the merchant aloud, 'I am vastly obliged to you for your kind care of me.' He then made a hearty breakfast, took his hat, and was going to the stable to pay his horse a visit; but as he passed under one of the arbours, which was loaded with roses, he thought of what Beauty had asked him to bring back to her, and so he took a bunch of roses to carry home. At the same moment he heard a loud noise, and saw coming towards him a beast, so frightful to look at that he was ready to faint with fear. 'Ungrateful man!' said the beast in a terrible voice, 'I have saved your life by admitting you into my palace, and in return you steal my roses, which I value more than anything I possess. But you shall atone for your fault: you shall die in a quarter of an hour.'

The merchant fell on his knees, and, clasping his hands, said, 'Sir, I humbly beg your pardon: I did not think it would offend you to gather a rose for one of my daughters, who had entreated me to bring her one home. Do not kill me, my lord!'

'I am not a lord, but a beast!' replied the monster; 'I hate false compliments: so do not fancy that you can coax me by any such ways. You tell me that you have daughters; now I will suffer you to escape, if one of them will come and die in your stead. If not, promise that you will yourself return in three months, to be dealt with as I may choose.

The tender-hearted merchant had no thoughts of letting anyone of his daughters die for his sake; but he knew that if he seemed to accept the beast's terms, he should at least have the pleasure of seeing them once again. So he gave his promise, and was told he might then set off as soon as he liked. 'But,' said the beast, 'I do not wish you to go back empty-handed. Go to the room you slept in, and you will find a chest there; fill it with whatsoever you like best, and I will have it taken to your own house for you.'

When the beast had said this, he went away. The good merchant, left to himself, began to consider that as he must die—for he had no thought of breaking a promise, made even to a beast—he might, as well have the comfort of leaving his children provided for. He returned to the room he had slept in, and found there heaps of gold pieces lying about. He filled the chest with them, to the very brim, locked it, and, mounting his horse, left the palace as sorrowful as he had been glad when he first beheld it. The horse took a path across the forest of its own accord, and in a few hours they reached the merchant's house. His children came running around him, but, instead of kissing them with joy, he could not help weeping as he looked at them. He held in his hand the bunch of roses, which he gave to Beauty, saying, 'Take these roses, Beauty; but little do you think how dear they have cost your poor father;' and then he gave them an account of all that he had seen or heard in the palace of the beast.

The two eldest sisters now began to shed tears, and to lay the blame upon Beauty, who, they said, would be the cause of her father's death. 'See,' said they, 'what happens from the pride of the little wretch; why did not she ask for such things as we did? But, to be sure, Miss must not be like other people; and though she will be the cause of her father's death, yet she does not shed a tear.'

'It would be useless,' replied Beauty, 'for my father shall not die. As the beast will accept of one of his daughters, I will give myself up, and be only too happy to prove my love for the best of fathers.'

'No, sister,' said the three brothers with one voice, 'that cannot be; we will go in search of this monster, and either he or we will perish.'

'Do not hope to kill him,' said the merchant, 'his power is far too great. But Beauty's young life shall not be sacrificed: I am old and cannot expect to live much longer; so I shall but give up a few years of my life, and shall only grieve for the sake of my children.'

'Never father!' cried Beauty: 'If you go back to the palace, you cannot hinder my going after you; though young, I am not over-fond of life; and I would much rather be eaten up by the monster, than die of grief for your loss.'

The merchant in vain tried to reason with Beauty, who still obstinately kept to her purpose; which, in truth, made her two sisters glad; for they were jealous of her, because everybody loved her.

The merchant was so grieved at the thoughts of losing his child, that he never once thought of the chest filled with gold, but at night, to his great surprise, he found it standing by his bedside. He said nothing about his riches to his eldest daughters; for he knew very well it would at once make them want to return to town; but he told Beauty his secret, and she then said, that while he was away, two gentlemen had been on a visit at their cottage, who had fallen in love with her two sisters. She entreated her father to marry them without delay, for she was so sweet-natured, she only wished them to be happy.

Three months went by, only too fast; and then the merchant and Beauty got ready to set out for the palace of the beast: Upon this, the two sisters rubbed their eyes with an onion, to make believe they were crying; both the merchant and his sons cried in earnest. Only Beauty shed no tears. They reached the palace in a very few hours, and the horse, without bidding, went into the same stable as before. The merchant and Beauty walked towards the large hall, where they found a table covered with every dainty, and two plates laid ready. The merchant had very little appetite; but Beauty, that she might the better hide her grief, placed herself at the table; and helped her father; she then began to eat herself, and thought all the time that, to be sure, the beast had a mind to fatten her before he ate her up, since he had provided such good cheer for her. When they had done their supper they heard a great noise, and the good old man began to bid his poor child farewell, for he knew it was the beast coming to them. When Beauty first saw that frightful form, she was very much terrified, but tried to hide her fear. The creature walked up to her, and eyed her all over—then asked her in a dreadful voice if she had come quite of her own accord.

'Yes,' said Beauty.

'Then you are a good girl, and I am very much obliged to you.'

This was such an astonishingly civil answer that Beauty's courage rose: but it sank again when the beast, addressing the merchant, desired him to leave the palace next morning; and never return to it again. 'And so good night, merchant. And good night, Beauty.'

'Good night, beast,' she answered, as the monster shuffled out of the room.

'Ah! my dear child,' said the merchant, kissing his daughter, 'I am half dead already, at the thought of leaving you with this dreadful beast; you shall go back and let me stay in your place.'

'No,' said Beauty, boldly, 'I will never agree to that; you must go home to-morrow morning.'

They then wished each other good night, and went to bed, both of them thinking they should not be able to close their eyes; but as soon as ever they had lain down, they fell into a deep sleep, and did not awake till the morning. Beauty dreamed that a lady came up to her, who said, 'I am very much pleased, Beauty, with the goodness you have shown, in being willing to give your life to save that of your father. Do not be afraid of anything; you shall not go without a reward.'

As soon as Beauty awoke, she told her father this dream; but though it gave him some comfort, he was a long time before he could be persuaded to leave the palace. At last Beauty succeeded in getting him safely away.

When her father was out of sight, poor Beauty began to weep sorely; still, having naturally a courageous spirit, she soon resolved not to make her sad case still worse by sorrow, which she knew was vain, but to wait and be patient. She walked about to take a view of all the palace, and the elegance of every part of it much charmed her.

But what was her surprise, when she came to a door on which was written, BEAUTY'S ROOM! She opened it in haste, and her eyes were dazzled by the splendour and taste of the apartment. What made her wonder more than all the rest, was a large library filled with books, a harpsichord, and many pieces of music. 'The beast surely does not mean to eat me up immediately,' said she, 'since he takes care I shall not be at a loss how to amuse myself.' She opened the library and saw these verses written in letters of gold on the back of one of the books:—

> 'Beauteous lady, dry your tears,
> Here's no cause for sighs or fears.
> Command as freely as you may.
> For you command and I obey.'

'Alas!' said she, sighing; 'I wish I could only command a sight of my poor father, and to know what he is doing at this moment.' Just then, by chance, she cast her eyes on a looking glass that stood near her, and in it she saw a picture of her old home, and her father riding mournfully up to the door. Her sisters came out to meet him, and although they tried to look sorry, it was easy to see that in their hearts, they were very glad. In a short time all this picture disappeared, but it caused Beauty to think that the beast, besides being very powerful, was also very kind. About the middle of the day she found a table laid ready for her, and a sweet concert of music played all the time she was dining, without her seeing anybody. But, at supper, when she was going to seat herself at table, she heard the noise of the beast, and could not help trembling with fear.

'Beauty,' said he, 'will you give me leave to see you sup?'

'That is as you please,' answered she, very much afraid.

'Not in the least,' said the beast; 'you alone command in this place. If you should not like my company, you need only say so, and I will leave you that moment; But tell me, Beauty, do you not think me very ugly?'

'Why, yes,' said she, 'for I cannot tell a falsehood; but then I think you are very good.'

'Am I?' sadly replied the beast; 'yet, besides being ugly, I am also very stupid: I know well enough that I am but a beast.'

'Very stupid people,' said Beauty, 'are never aware of it themselves.'

At which kindly speech the beast looked pleased, and replied, not without an awkward sort of politeness, 'Pray do not let me detain you from supper, and be sure that you are well served. All you see is your own, and I should be deeply grieved if you wanted for any thing.'

'You are very kind—so kind that I almost forgot you are so ugly,' said Beauty, earnestly.

'Ah! yes,' answered the beast, with a great sigh; 'I hope I am good-tempered, but still I am only a monster.'

'There is many a monster who wears the form of a man; it is better of the two to have the heart of a man and the form of a monster.'

'I would thank you, Beauty, for this speech, but I am too senseless to say anything that would please you,' returned the beast in a melancholy voice; and altogether he seemed so gentle and so unhappy, that Beauty, who had the tenderest heart in the world, felt her fear of him gradually vanish.

She ate her supper with a good appetite, and conversed in her own sensible and charming way, till at last, when the beast rose to depart, he terrified her more than ever by saying abruptly, in his gruff voice, 'Beauty, will you marry me!'

Now Beauty, frightened as she was, would speak only the exact truth; besides, her father had told her that the beast liked only to have the truth spoken to him. So she answered, in a very firm tone, 'No, beast.'

He did not go into a passion, or do anything but sigh deeply, and depart.

When Beauty found herself alone, she began to feel pity for the poor beast. 'Oh!' said she, 'what a sad thing it is that he should be so very frightful, since he is so good-tempered!'

Beauty lived three months in this palace very well pleased. The beast came to see her every night, and talked with her while she supped and though what he said was not very clever, yet, as she saw in him every day some new goodness, instead of dreading the time of his coming, she soon began continually looking at her watch, to see if it were nine o'clock; for that was the hour when he never failed to visit her. One thing only vexed her, which was that every night before he went away, he always made it a rule to ask her if she would be his wife, and seemed very much grieved at her steadfastly replying 'No.' At last, one night, she said to him, 'You wound me greatly, beast, by forcing me to refuse you so often; I wish I could take such a liking to you as to agree to marry you: but I must tell you plainly, that I do not think it will ever happen. I shall always be your friend; so try to let that content you.'

'I must,' sighed the beast, 'for I know well enough how frightful I am; but I love you better than myself. Yet I think I am very lucky in your being pleased to stay with me: now promise me, Beauty, that you will never leave me.'

Beauty would almost have agreed to this, so sorry was she for him, but she had that day seen in her magic glass, which she looked at constantly, that her father was dying of grief for her sake.

'Alas!' she said, 'I long so much to see my father, that if you do not give me leave to visit him, I shall break my heart.'

'I would rather break mine, Beauty,' answered the beast; 'I will send you to your father's cottage: you shall stay there, and your poor beast shall die of sorrow.'

'No,' said Beauty, crying, 'I love you too well to be the cause of your death; I promise to return in a week. You have shown me that my sisters are married, and my brothers are gone for soldiers, so that my father is left all alone. Let me stay a week with him.'

'You shall find yourself with him to-morrow morning,' replied the beast; 'but mind, do not forget your promise. When you wish to return, you have nothing to do but to put your ring on a table when you go to bed. Good-bye, Beauty!' The beast sighed as he said these words, and Beauty went to bed very sorry to see him so much grieved. When she awoke in the morning, she found herself in her father's cottage. She rang a bell that was at her bedside, and a servant entered; but as soon as she saw Beauty, the woman gave a loud shriek; upon which the merchant ran upstairs, and when he beheld his daughter he ran to her, and kissed her a hundred times. At last Beauty began to remember that she had brought no clothes with her to put on but the servant told her she had just found in the next room a large chest full of dressees, trimmed all over with gold and adorned with pearls and diamonds.

Beauty, in her own mind, thanked the beast for his kindness, and put on the plainest gown she could find among them all. She then desired the servant to lay the rest aside, for she intended to give them to her sisters; but, as soon as she had spoken these words, the chest was gone out of sight in a moment. Her father then suggested, perhaps the beast chose for her to keep them all for herself: and as soon as he had said this, they saw the chest standing again in the same place. While Beauty was dressing herself, a servant brought word to her that her sisters were come with their husbands to pay her a visit. They both lived unhappily with the gentlemen they had married. The husband of the eldest was very handsome, but was so proud of this, that he thought of nothing else from morning till night, and did not care a pin for the beauty of his wife. The second had married a man of great learning; but he made no use of it, except to torment and affront all his friends, and his wife more than any of them. The two sisters were ready to burst with spite when they saw Beauty dressed like a princess, and looking so very charming. All the kindness that she showed them was of no use; for they were vexed more than ever when she told them how happy she lived at the palace of the beast. The spiteful creatures went by themselves into the garden, where they cried to think of her good fortune.

'Why should the little wretch be better off than we?' said they. 'We are much handsomer than she is.'

'Sister!' said the eldest, 'a thought has just come into my head: let us try to keep her here longer than the week for which the beast gave her leave; and then he will be so angry, that perhaps when she goes back to him he will eat her up in a moment.'

'That is well thought of,' answered the other, 'but to do this, we must pretend to be very kind.'

They then went to join her in the cottage, where they showed her so much false love, that Beauty could not help crying for joy.

When the week was ended, the two sisters began to pretend such grief at the thought of her leaving them, that she agreed to stay a week more: but all that time Beauty could not help fretting for the sorrow that she knew her absence would give her poor beast; for she tenderly loved him, and much wished for his company again. Among all the grand and clever people she saw, she found nobody who was half so sensible, so affectionate, so thoughtful, or so kind. The tenth night of her being at the cottage, she dreamed she was in the garden of the palace, that the beast lay dying on a grass-plot; and with his last breath put her in mind of her promise, and laid his death to her forsaking him. Beauty awoke in a great fright, and burst into tears. 'Am not I wicked,' said she, 'to behave so ill to a beast who has shown me so much kindness? Why will not I marry him? I am sure I should be more happy with him than my sisters are with their husbands. He shall not be wretched any longer on my account; for I should do nothing but blame myself all the rest of my life.'

From Walter Crane, *Beauty and the Beast and Other Tales*. (London: Thames and Hudson, 1982). The illustration originally appeared in 1875.

She then rose, put her ring on the table, got into bed again, and soon fell asleep. In the morning she with joy found herself in the palace of the beast. She dressed herself very carefully, that she might please him the better, and thought she had never known a day pass away so slowly. At last the clock struck nine, but the beast did not come. Beauty, dreading lest she might truly have caused his death, ran from room to room, calling out, 'Beast, dear beast;' but there was no answer. At last she remembered her dream, rushed to the grass-plot, and there saw him lying apparently dead beside the fountain. Forgetting all his ugliness, she threw herself upon his body, and, finding his heart still beat, she fetched some water and sprinkled it over him, weeping and sobbing the while.

The beast opened his eyes: 'You forgot your promise, Beauty, and so I determined to die; for I could not live without you. I have starved myself to death, but I shall die content since I have seen your face once more.'

'No, dear beast,' cried Beauty, passionately, 'you shall not die; you shall live to be my husband. I thought it was only friendship I felt for you, but now I know it was love.'

The moment Beauty had spoken these words, the palace was suddenly lighted up, and all kinds of rejoicings were heard around them, none which she noticed, but hung over her dear beast with the utmost tenderness. At last, unable to restrain herself, she dropped her head over her hands, covered her eyes, and cried for joy; and, when she looked up again, the beast was gone. In his stead she saw at her feet a handsome, graceful young prince, who thanked her with the tenderest expressions for having freed him from enchantment.

'But where is my poor beast? I only want him and nobody else,' sobbed Beauty.

'I am he,' replied the Prince. 'A wicked fairy condemned me to this form, and forbade me to show that I had any wit or sense, till a beautiful lady should consent to marry me. You alone, dearest Beauty, judged me neither by my looks nor by my talents, but by my heart alone. Take it then, and all that I have besides, for all is yours.'

Beauty, full of surprise, but very happy, suffered the prince to lead her to his palace, where she found her father and sisters, who had been brought there by the fairy-lady whom she had seen in a dream the first night she came:

'Beauty,' said the fairy, 'you have chosen well, and you have your reward, for a true heart is better than either good looks or clever brains. As for you, ladies,' and she turned to the two elder sisters, 'I know all your ill deeds, but I have no worse punishment for you than to see your sister happy. You shall stand as statues at the door of her palace, and when you repent of and have amended your faults, you shall become women again. But, to tell you the truth, I very much fear you will remain statues for ever.'

From *The Fairy Book: The Best Popular Stories Selected and Rendered Anew*, by Dinah Maria Mulock Craik (1863; New York: Harper, n.d).

The Story of Five Heads

This tale from the Xosa people of South Africa reinforces cultural practices by combining a cautionary tale with one of wish fulfillment. Mpunzikazi, the first daughter to undertake the marriage journey, meets disaster precisely because she refuses to follow tradition, to act charitably, or to accept advice. In contrast, her sister, Mpunzanyana, is the model of female virtues and therefore wins happiness. The groom in this tale is a shape-shifter who, in the manner of Strong Wind in 'The Indian Cinderella', uses his ability to take on another form to test those who wish to marry him. He appears as a snake, a common symbol of sexuality in animal groom tales from various cultures. Unlike snakes in many tales within the Christian tradition of Western Europe, however, this snake does not carry connotations of evil. Rather, because the Xosa believe that the spirits of ancestors may assume the shape of snakes, it is a figure that commands respect. Furthermore, because it keeps rodents and small marauding animals from cultivated ground, the Xosa also regard it as an agent of good fortune.

𝒯here was once a man living in a certain place, who had two daughters big enough to be married.

One day the man went over the river to another village, which was the residence of a great chief. The people asked him to tell them the news. He replied, that there was no news in the place that he came from. Then the man inquired about the news of their place. They said the news of their place was that the chief wanted a wife.

The man went home and said to his two daughters: 'Which of you wishes to be the wife of a chief?'

The eldest replied: 'I wish to be the wife of a chief, my father.' The name of that girl was Mpunzikazi.

The man said 'At that village which I visited, the chief wishes for a wife; you, my daughter, shall go.'

The man called all his friends, and assembled a large company to go with his daughter to the village of the chief. But the girl would not consent that those people should go with her.

She said: 'I will go alone to be the wife of the chief.'

Her father replied: 'How can you, my daughter, say such a thing? Is it not so that when a girl goes to present herself to her husband she should be accompanied by others? Be not foolish, my daughter.'

The girl still said: 'I will go alone to be the wife of the chief.'

Then the man allowed his daughter to do as she chose. She went alone, no bridal party accompanying her, to present herself at the village of the chief who wanted a wife.

As Mpunzikazi was in the path, she met a mouse.

The mouse said: 'Shall I show you the way?'

The girl replied: 'Just get away from before my eyes.'

The mouse answered: 'If you do like this, you will not succeed.'

Then she met a frog.

The frog said: 'Shall I show you the way?'

Mpunzikazi replied: 'You are not worthy to speak to me, as I am to be the wife of a chief.'

The frog said: 'Go on then; you will see afterwards what will happen.'

When the girl got tired, she sat down under a tree to rest. A boy who was herding goats in that place came to her, he being very hungry.

The boy said: 'Where are you going to, my eldest sister?'

Mpunzikazi replied in an angry voice: 'Who are you that you should speak to me? Just get away from before me.'

The boy said: 'I am very hungry; will you not give me of your food?'

She answered: 'Get away quickly.'

The boy said: 'You will not return if you do this.'

She went on her way again, and met with an old woman sitting by a big stone.

The old woman said: 'I will give you advice. You will meet with trees that will laugh at you: you must not laugh in return. You will see a bag of thick milk: you must not eat of it. You will meet a man whose head is under his arm: you must not take water from him.'

Mpunzikazi answered: 'You ugly thing! who are you that you should advise me?'

The old woman continued in saying those words.

The girl went on. She came to a place where were many trees. The trees laughed at her, and she laughed at them in return. She saw a bag of thick milk, and she ate of it. She met a man carrying his head under his arm, and she took water to drink from him.

She came to the river of the village of the chief. She saw a girl there dipping water from the river. The girl said: 'Where are you going to, my sister?'

Mpunzikazi replied: 'Who are you that you should call me sister? I am going to be the wife of a chief.'

The girl drawing water was the sister of the chief. She said: 'Wait, I will give you advice. Do not enter the village by this side.'

Mpunzikazi did not stand to listen, but just went on.

She reached the village of the chief. The people asked her where she came from and what she wanted.

She answered: 'I have come to be the wife of the chief.'

They said: 'Who ever saw a girl go without a retinue to be a bride?'

They said also: 'The chief is not at home; you must prepare food for him, that when he comes in the evening he may eat.'

They gave her millet to grind. She ground it very coarse, and made bread that was not nice to eat.

In the evening she heard the sound of a great wind. That wind was the coming of the chief. He was a big snake with five heads and large eyes. Mpunzikazi was very much frightened when she saw him. He sat down before the door and told her to bring his food. She brought the bread which she had made. Makanda Mahlanu (Five Heads) was not satisfied with that bread. He said: 'You shall not be my wife,' and he struck her with his tail and killed her.

Afterwards the sister of Mpunzikazi said to her father: 'I also wish to be the wife of a chief.'

Her father replied: 'It is well, my daughter; it is right that you should wish to be a bride.'

The man called all his friends, and a great retinue prepared to accompany the bride. The name of the girl was Mpunzanyana.

In the way they met a mouse.

The mouse said: 'Shall I show you the road?'

Mpunzanyana replied: 'If you will show me the way I shall be glad.'

Then the mouse pointed out the way.

She came into a valley, where she saw an old woman standing by a tree.

The old woman said to her: 'You will come to a place where two paths branch off. You must take the little one, because if you take the big one you will not be fortunate.'

Mpunzanyana replied: 'I will take the little path, my mother.' She went on.

Afterwards she met a cony.

The cony said: 'The village of the chief is close by. You will meet a girl by the river: you must speak nicely to her. They will give you millet to grind: you must grind it well. When you see your husband, you must not be afraid.'

She said: 'I will do as you say, cony.'

In the river she met the chief's sister carrying water.

The chief's sister said: 'Where are you going to?'

Mpunzanyana replied: 'This is the end of my journey.'

The chief's sister said: 'What is the object of your coming to this place?'

Mpunzanyana replied: 'I am with a bridal party.'

The chief's sister said: 'That is right, but will you not be afraid when you see your husband?'

Mpunzanyana answered: 'I will not be afraid.'

The chief's sister pointed out the hut in which she should stay. Food was given to the bridal party. The mother of the chief took millet and gave to the bride, saying: 'You must prepare food for your husband. He is not here now, but he will come in the evening.'

In the evening she heard a very strong wind, which made the hut shake. The poles fell, but she did not run out. Then she saw the chief Makanda Mahlanu coming. He asked for food. Mpunzanyana took the bread which she had made, and gave it to him. He was very much pleased with that food, and said:

'You shall be my wife.' He gave her very many ornaments.

Afterwards Makanda Mahlanu became a man, and Mpunzanyana continued to be the wife he loved best.

————

From *Kaffir Folk-lore: A Selection from the Traditional Tales Current among the People Living on the Eastern Border of the Cape Colony*, by Geo. McCall Theal (London: S. Sonnenschein, Le Bas, & Lowry, 1886).

Rumpelstiltskin

'Rumpelstiltskin' employs two common folkloric motifs. The first is a bargain with the devil or another magical character. 'Rumpelstiltskin' differs from most tales employing this motif, however, because the girl who enters into the contract is not motivated by pride or greed, the flaws that beset such characters as the legendary Dr Faust, who sold his soul to the devil for a temporary satisfaction of his desires. Instead, the pride of her father and the greed of the prince drive her to make a deal with the strange little man who appears when she is most desperate for help. The second common motif is the gaining of power over another by using that person's true name. As a tale of courtship, however, 'Rumpelstiltskin' is unusual among European tales because, after passing the bridal test and marrying royalty, the girl does not gain perpetual happiness. Rather, she still faces problems that she, with timely help from others, must solve.

Once there was a miller who was poor, but who had a beautiful daughter. Now it happened that he had to go and speak to the King, and in order to make himself appear important he said to him, 'I have a daughter who can spin straw into gold.' The King said to the miller, 'That is an art which pleases me well; if your daughter is as clever as you say, bring her to-morrow to my palace, and I will try what she can do.'

And when the girl was brought to him he took her into a room which was quite full of straw, gave her a spinning-wheel and a reel, and said, 'Now set to work, and if by to-morrow morning early you have not spun this straw into gold during the night, you must die.' Thereupon he himself locked up the room, and left her in it alone. So there sat the poor miller's daughter, and for her life could not tell what to do; she had no idea how straw could be spun into gold, and she grew more and more miserable, until at last she began to weep.

But all at once the door opened, and in came a little man, and said, 'Good evening, Mistress Miller; why are you crying so?' 'Alas!' answered the girl, 'I have to spin straw into gold, and I do not know how to do it.' 'What will you give me,' said the manikin, 'if I do it for you?' 'My necklace,' said the girl. The little man took the necklace, seated himself in front of the wheel, and 'whirr, whirr, whirr,' three turns, and the reel was full; then he put another on, and whirr, whirr, whirr, three times round, and the second was full too. And so it went on until the morning, when all the straw was spun, and all the reels were full of gold. By daybreak the King was already there, and when he saw the gold he was astonished and delighted, but his heart became only more greedy. He had the miller's daughter taken into

From Edgar Taylor, ed., *German Popular Stories*. Illustrated by Walter Cruikshank. (London: Chatto and Windus, 1869), facing 150.

another room full of straw, which was much larger, and commanded her to spin that also in one night if she valued her life. The girl knew not how to help herself, and was crying, when the door again opened, and the little man appeared, and said, 'What will you give me if I spin the straw into gold for you?' 'The ring on my finger,' answered the girl. The little man took the ring, again began to turn the wheel, and by morning had spun all the straw into glittering gold.

The King rejoiced beyond measure at the sight, but still he had not gold enough; and he had the miller's daughter taken into a still larger room full of straw, and said, 'You must spin this, too, in the course of this night; but if you succeed, you shall be my wife.' 'Even if she be a miller's daughter,' thought he, 'I could not find a richer wife in the whole world.'

When the girl was alone the manikin came again for the third time, and said, 'What will you give me if I spin the straw for you this time also?' 'I have nothing left that I could give,' answered the girl. 'Then promise me, if you should become Queen, your first child.' 'Who knows whether that will ever happen?' thought the miller's daughter; and, not knowing how else to help herself in this strait, she promised the manikin what he wanted, and for that he once more span the straw into gold.

And when the King came in the morning, and found all as he had wished, he took her in marriage, and the pretty miller's daughter became a Queen.

A year after, she had a beautiful child, and she never gave a thought to the manikin. But suddenly he came into her room, and said, 'Now give me what you promised.' The Queen was horror-struck, and offered the manikin all the riches of the kingdom if he would leave her the child. But the manikin said, 'No, something that is living is dearer to me than all the treasures in the world.' Then the Queen began to weep and cry, so that the manikin pitied her. 'I will give you three days' time,' said he; 'if by that time you find out my name, then shall you keep your child.'

So the Queen thought the whole night of all the names that she had ever heard, and she sent a messenger over the country to inquire, far and wide, for any other names that there might be. When the manikin came the next day, she began with Caspar, Melchior, Balthazar, and said all the names she knew, one after another; but to every one the little man said, 'That is not my name.' On the second day she had inquiries made in the neighbourhood as to the names of the people there, and she repeated to the manikin the most uncommon and curious. 'Perhaps your name is Shortribs, or Sheepshanks, or Laceleg?' but he always answered, 'That is not my name.'

On the third day the messenger came back again, and said, 'I have not been able to find a single new name, but as I came to a high mountain at the end of the forest, where the fox and the hare bid each other good night, there I saw a little house, and before the house a fire was burning, and round about the fire quite a ridiculous little man was jumping: he hopped upon one leg, and shouted—

> 'To-day I bake, to-morrow brew,
>   The next I'll have the young Queen's child.
> Ha! glad am I that no one knew
>   That Rumpelstiltskin I am styled.'

You may think how glad the Queen was when she heard the name! And when soon afterwards the little man came in, and asked, 'Now, Mistress Queen, what is my name?' at first she said, 'Is your name Conrad?' 'No.' 'Is your name Harry?' 'No.'

'Perhaps your name is Rumpelstiltskin?'

'The devil has told you that! the devil has told you that!' cried the little man, and in his anger he plunged his right foot so deep into the earth that his whole leg went in; and then in rage he pulled at his left leg so hard with both hands that he tore himself in two.

From *Grimm's Household Tales*, translated by Margaret Hunt, Vol. 1 (London: George Bell and Sons, 1884).

The Maid with Hair of Gold

In this Slav tale, two common folkloric plot devices—a man's acquisition of the knowledge of animal languages and the reciprocating actions of animals grateful for help—provide the framework for the familiar story of a servant who both marries a beautiful princess and becomes king. By secretly acquiring knowledge of animal speech, George gains the same power that the king possesses, symbolically usurping the king's rights and foreshadowing his later replacement of the king. His use of his power reveals his truly noble character and earns him the help that is essential when he undertakes a quest to win a bride for the king. By passing the suitor tests, including the identification of the true bride, another very common motif in tales in both Europe and the Middle East, George establishes that he himself is worthy of happiness. He ultimately gains this happiness because the princess proves to be more than a passive object of courtship: she takes action to restore the life of the one she truly loves.

There was once a king so wise and clever that he understood the language of all animals. You shall hear how he gained this power.

One day an old woman came to the palace and said, 'I wish to speak to his majesty, for I have something of great importance to tell him.' When admitted to his presence she presented him with a curious fish, saying, 'Have it cooked for yourself, and when you have eaten it you will understand all that is said by the birds of the air, the animals that walk the earth, and the fishes that live under the waters.'

The king was delighted to know that which everyone else was ignorant of, so he rewarded the old woman generously, and told a servant to cook the fish very carefully.

'But take care,' said the monarch, 'that you do not taste it yourself, for if you do you will be killed.'

George, the servant, was astonished at such a threat, and wondered why his master was so anxious that no one else should eat any of the fish. Then examining it curiously he said, 'Never in all my life have I seen such an odd-looking fish; it seems more like a reptile. Now where would be the harm if I did take some? Every cook tastes of the dishes he prepares.'

When it was fried he tasted a small piece, and while taking some of the sauce heard a buzzing in the air and a voice speaking in his ear.

'Let us taste a crumb: let us taste a little,' it said.

He looked round to see where the words came from, but there were only a few flies buzzing about in the kitchen. At the same moment some one out in the yard said in a harsh jerky voice, 'Where are we going to settle? Where?'

And another answered, 'In the miller's barley-field; ho! for the miller's field of barley.' When George looked towards where this strange talk came he saw a gander flying at the head of a flock of geese.

'How lucky,' thought he; 'now I know why my master set so much value on this fish and wished to eat it all himself.'

George had now no doubt that by tasting the fish he had learnt the language of animals, so after having taken a little more he served the king with the remainder as if nothing had happened.

When his majesty had dined he ordered George to saddle two horses and accompany him for a ride. They were soon off, the master in front, the servant behind.

While crossing a meadow George's horse began to prance and caper, neighing out these words, 'I say, brother, I feel so light and in such good spirits to-day that in one single bound I could leap over those mountains yonder.'

'I could do the same,' answered the king's horse, 'but I carry a feeble old man on my back; he would fall like a log and break his skull.'

'What does that matter to you? So much the better if he should break his head, for then, instead of being ridden by an old man you would probably be mounted by a young one.'

The servant laughed a good deal upon hearing this conversation between the horses, but he took care to do so on the quiet, lest the king should hear him. At that moment his majesty turned round, and, seeing a smile on the man's face, asked the cause of it.

'Oh nothing, your majesty, only some nonsense that came into my head.'

The king said nothing, and asked no more questions, but he was suspicious, and distrusted both servant and horses; so he hastened back to the palace.

When there he said to George, 'Give me some wine, but mind you only pour out enough to fill the glass, for if you put in one drop too much, so that it overflows, I shall certainly order my executioner to cut off your head.'

While he was speaking two birds flew near the window, one chasing the other, who carried three golden hairs in his beak.

'Give them me,' said one, 'you know they are mine.'

'Not at all, I picked them up myself.'

'No matter, I saw them fall while the Maid with Locks of Gold was combing out her hair. At least, give me two, then you can keep the third for yourself.'

'No, not a single one.'

Thereupon one of the birds succeeded in seizing the hairs from the other bird's beak, but in the struggle he let one fall, and it made a sound as if a piece of metal had struck the ground. As for George, he was completely taken off his guard, and the wine overflowed the glass.

The king was furious, and feeling convinced that his servant had disobeyed him and had learnt the language of animals, he said, ' You scoundrel, you deserve death for having failed to do my bidding, nevertheless, I will show you mercy upon one condition, that you bring me the Maid with the Golden Locks, for I intend to marry her.'

Alas, what was to be done? Poor fellow, he was willing to do anything to save his life, even run the risk of losing it on a long journey. He therefore promised to search for the Maid with the Golden Locks: but he knew not where or how to find her.

When he had saddled and mounted his horse he allowed it to go its own way, and it carried him to the outskirts of a dark forest, where some shepherds had left a bush burning. The sparks of fire from the bush endangered the lives of a large number of ants which had built their nest close by, and the poor little things were hurrying away in all directions, carrying their small white eggs with them.

'Help us in our distress, good George,' they cried in a plaintive voice; 'do not leave us to perish, together with our children whom we carry in these eggs.'

George immediately dismounted, cut down the bush, and put out the fire.

'Thank you, brave man: and remember, when you are in trouble you have only to call upon us, and we will help you in our turn.' The young fellow went on his way far into the forest until he came to a very tall fir tree. At the top of the tree was a raven's nest, while at the foot, on the ground, lay two young ones who were calling out to their parents and saying, 'Alas, father and mother, where have you gone? You have flown away, and we have to seek our food, weak and helpless as we are. Our wings are as yet without feathers, how then shall we be able to get anything to eat? Good George,' said they, turning to the young man, 'do not leave us to starve.'

Without stopping to think, the young man dismounted, and with his sword slew his horse to provide food for the young birds. They thanked him heartily, and said, 'If ever you should be in distress, call to us and we will help you at once.'

After this George was obliged to travel on foot, and he walked on for a long time, ever getting further and further into the forest. On reaching the end of it, he saw stretching before him an immense sea that seemed to mingle with the horizon. Close by stood two men disputing the possession of a large fish with golden scales that had fallen into their net.

'The net belongs to me,' said one, 'therefore the fish must be mine.'

'Your net would not have been of the slightest use, for it would have been lost in the sea, had I not come with my boat just in the nick of time.'

'Well, you shall have the next haul I make.'

'And suppose you should catch nothing? No; give me this one and keep the next haul for yourself.'

'I am going to put an end to your quarrel,' said George, addressing them. 'Sell me the fish: I will pay you well, and you can divide the money between you.'

Thereupon he put into their hands all the money the king had given him for the journey, without keeping a single coin for himself. The fishermen rejoiced at the good fortune which had befallen them, but George put the fish back into the water. The fish, thankful for this unexpected freedom, dived and disappeared, but returning to the surface, said, 'Whenever you may need my help you have but to call me, I shall not fail to show my gratitude.'

'Where are you going?' asked the fisherman.

'I am in search of a wife for my old master; she is known as the Maid with the Golden Locks; but I am at a loss where to find her.'

'If that be all, we can easily give you information,' answered they. 'She is Princess Zlato Vlaska, and daughter of the king whose crystal palace is built on that island yonder. The golden light from the princess's hair is reflected on sea and sky every morning when she combs it. If you would like to go to the island we will take you there for nothing, in return for the clever and generous way by which you made us stop quarrelling. But beware of one thing: when in the palace do not make a mistake as to which is the princess, for there are twelve of them, but only Zlato Vlaska has hair of gold.'

When George reached the island he lost no time in making his way to the palace, and demanded from the king the hand of his daughter, Princess Zlato Vlaska, in marriage to the king his master.

'I will grant the request with pleasure,' said his majesty, 'but only on one condition, namely, that you perform certain tasks which I will set you. These will be three in number, and must be done in three days, just as I order you. For the present you had better rest and refresh yourself after your journey.'

On the next day the king said, 'My daughter, the Maid with the Golden Hair, had a string of fine pearls, and the thread having broken, the pearls were scattered far and wide among the long grass of this field. Go and pick up every one of the pearls, for they must all be found.'

George went into the meadow, which was of great length and stretched away far out of sight. He went down on his knees and hunted between the tufts of grass and bramble from morning until noon, but not a single pearl could he find.

From Emily J. Harding, *Fairy Tales of the Slav Peasants and Herdsmen, from the French of Alx. Chodsko.* (London: George Allen, 1896), 75.

'Ah, if I only had my good little ants here,' he cried, 'they would be able to help me.' 'Here we are, young man, at your service,' answered the ants, suddenly appearing. Then they all ran round him, crying out, 'What is the matter? What do you want?'

'I have to find all the pearls lost in this field, and cannot see a single one: can you help me?'

'Wait a little, we will soon get them for you.'

He had not to wait very long, for they brought him a heap of pearls, and all he had to do was to thread them on the string. Just as he was about to make a knot he saw a lame ant coming slowly towards him, for one of her feet had been burned in the bush fire.

'Wait a moment, George,' she called out; 'do not tie the knot before threading this last pearl I am bringing you.'

When George took his pearls to the king, his majesty first counted them to make sure they were all there, and then said, 'You have done very well in this test, to-morrow I will give you another.'

Early next morning the king summoned George to him and said, 'My daughter, the Princess with the Golden Hair, dropped her gold ring into the sea while bathing. You must find the jewel and bring it me to-day.'

The young fellow walked thoughtfully up and down the beach. The water was pure and transparent, but he could not see beyond a certain distance into its depths, and therefore could not tell where the ring was lying beneath the water.

'Ah, my golden fishling, why are you not here now? You would surely be able to help me,' he said to himself, speaking aloud.

'Here I am,' answered the fish's voice from the sea, 'what can I do for you?'

'I have to find a gold ring which has been dropped in the sea, but as I cannot see to the bottom there is no use looking.'

The fish said, 'Fortunately I have just met a pike, wearing a gold ring on his fin. Just wait a moment, will you?'

In a very short time he reappeared with the pike and the ring. The pike willingly gave up the jewel.

The king thanked George for his cleverness, and then told him the third task. 'If you really wish me to give the hand of my daughter with the golden hair to the monarch who has sent you here, you must bring me two things that I want above everything: the Water of Death and the Water of Life.'

George had not the least idea where to find these waters, so he determined to trust to chance and 'follow his nose', as the saying is. He went first in one direction and then in another, until he reached a dark forest.

'Ah, if my little ravens were but here, perhaps they would help me,' he said aloud. Suddenly there was heard a rushing noise, as of wings overhead, and then down came the ravens calling 'Krâk, krâk, here we are, ready and willing to help you. What are you look-ing for?'

'I want some of the Water of Death and the Water of Life: it is impossible for me to find them, for I don't know where to look.'

'Krâk, krâk, we know very well where to find some. Wait a moment.'

Off they went immediately, but soon returned, each with a small gourd in his beak. One gourd contained the Water of Life, the other the Water of Death.

George was delighted with his success, and went back on his way to the palace. When nearly out of the forest, he saw a spider's web hanging between two fir trees, while in the centre was a large spider devouring a fly he had just killed. George sprinkled a few drops of the Water of Death on the spider; it immediately left the fly, which rolled to the ground like a ripe cherry, but on being touched with the Water of Life she began to move, and stretch-ing out first one limb and then another, gradually freed herself from the spider's web. Then she spread her wings and took flight, having first buzzed these words in the ears of her deliverer: 'George, you have assured your own happiness by restoring mine, for without my help you would never have succeeded in recognizing the Princess with the Golden Hair when you choose her to-morrow from among her twelve sisters.'

And the fly was right, for though the king, on finding that George had accomplished the third task, agreed to give him his daughter Zlato Vlaska, he yet added that he would have to find her himself.

He then led him to a large room and bade him choose from among the twelve charm-ing girls who sat at a round table. Each wore a kind of linen head-dress that completely hid the upper part of the head, and in such a way that the keenest eye could not discover the colour of the hair.

'Here are my daughters,' said the king, 'but only one among them has golden hair. If you find her you may take her with you; but if you make a mistake she will remain with us, and you will have to return empty-handed.'

George felt much embarrassed, not knowing what course to take.

'Buzz, Buzz, come walk round these young girls, and I will tell you which is yours.'

Thus spoke the fly whose life George had saved.

Thus reassured he walked boldly round, pointing at them one after the other and saying, 'This one has not the golden hair, nor this one either, nor this. . . .'

Suddenly, having been told by the fly, he cried, 'Here we are: this is Zlato Vlaska, even she herself. I take her for my own, she whom I have won, and for whom I have paid the price with many cares. You will not refuse her me this time.'

'Indeed, you have guessed aright,' replied the king.

The princess rose from her seat, and letting fall her head-dress, exposed to full view all the splendour of her wonderful hair, which seemed like a waterfall of golden rays, and covered her from head to foot. The glorious light that shone from it dazzled the young man's eyes, and he immediately fell in love with her.

The king provided his daughter with gifts worthy of a queen, and she left her father's palace in a manner befitting a royal bride. The journey back was accomplished without any mishaps.

On their arrival the old king was delighted at the sight of Zlato Vlaska, and danced with joy. Splendid and costly preparations were made for the wedding. His majesty then said to George, 'You robbed me of the secret of animal language. For this I intended to have your head cut off and your body thrown to birds of prey. But as you have served me so faithfully and won the princess for my bride I will lessen the punishment—that is, although you will be executed, yet you shall be buried with all the honours worthy of a superior officer.'

So the sentence was carried out, cruelly and unjustly. After the execution the Princess with the Golden Hair begged the king to make her a present of George's body, and the monarch was so much in love that he could not refuse his intended bride anything.

Zlato Vlaska with her own hands replaced the head on the body, and sprinkled it with the Water of Death. Immediately the separated parts became one again. Upon this she poured the Water of Life, and George returned to life, fresh as a young roebuck, his face radiant with health and youth.

'Ah me! How well I have slept,' said he, rubbing his eyes.

'Yes; no one could have slept better,' answered the princess, smiling, 'but without me you would have slept through eternity.'

When the old king saw George restored to life, and looking younger, handsomer, and more vigorous than ever, he too wanted to be made young again. He therefore ordered his servants to cut off his head and sprinkle it with the Life-Giving Water. They cut it off, but he did not come to life again, although they sprinkled his body with all the water that was left. Perhaps they made some mistake in using the wrong water, for the head and body were joined, but life itself never returned, there being no Water of Life left for that purpose. No one knew where to get any, and none understood the language of animals.

So, to make a long story short, George was proclaimed king, and the Princess with Hair of Gold, who really loved him, became his queen.

***

From *Fairy Tales of the Slav Peasants and Herdsmen*, from the French of Alx. Chodsko, translated by Emily J. Harding (London: George Allen, 1896).

Juan Bobo and the Princess Who Answered Riddles

The tale of a contest of wits with a princess who is herself the prize goes back as far as Greek romances and appears in the oral and literary collections of many countries. In the following version of this popular courtship tale, Juan Bobo (Simple John), normally a simpleton in Puerto Rican stories, proves to be quite intellectually resourceful. Of course, his riddle is just as unfair as Rumpelstiltskin's request that the miller's daughter guess his name: both answers depend on biographical knowledge that the one questioned could hardly be expected to know. If the source of his riddle is genuine naiveté, Juan Bobo's subsequent action in obtaining proof that he has told the princess the answer shows remarkable foresight. By acquiring her ring and the shoe as evidence of their meeting, Juan Bobo demonstrates that he is too wise to be bested by either a woman's seductive tricks or her emotional wiles.

Once upon a time there was a king who was very fond of riddles. He had a talented daughter who was clever at solving them, no matter how difficult they might be.

The King wanted his daughter to marry a man who was as intelligent as she was, so he decided that she should marry the first man who could ask her a riddle that she could not solve. He posted a proclamation to this effect all over the kingdom, but he also made it clear that any man who failed in the test should have his head cut off.

As the Princess was very beautiful, ever so many princes and noblemen were eager to marry her, so there were great numbers of applicants. But, alas! The beautiful Princess was able to solve all of their riddles. It wasn't long before the castle walls were covered with the heads of those who had failed to win the Princess.

In this country there lived a poor widow who had an only son named Juan. Because he was a rather foolish fellow who didn't seem to know his right hand from his left, people called him Juan Bobo, which means Simple John. One day as Juan Bobo was walking by the castle walls, he looked at the heads of the princes and noblemen who had failed to win the Princess by their cleverness. It occurred to him that he might be able to succeed where they had failed. That day Juan Bobo came home earlier than usual and told his mother that he was going to try his luck at the castle and see if he could win the Princess. His mother cried and begged him not to think of it, reminding him of the numbers who had tried and failed and lost their heads, princes and noblemen and all much more intelligent than Juan Bobo; so, how could he think of doing such a foolish thing! But neither her arguments nor her tears were of any avail. Juan Bobo insisted that the next morning early he would leave on his donkey for the King's castle, and he knew he would be able to catch the beautiful Princess with a riddle.

When his mother saw that it was useless to try to dissuade him, she stopped trying and prepared two cakes for Juan to take with him—all the food she had in the house. She was so upset and her eyes were so filled with tears that she could not see clearly, and she seasoned them with a poisonous powder instead of sprinkling salt upon them.

Early the next morning, after saying good-by to his mother, who was still crying that she would never see her son again, Juan Bobo mounted his old donkey, named Panda, and set out for the castle. After several hours of travel, he dismounted and stretched out on the grass at the edge of the road to rest and to think up a riddle that the Princess would not be able to solve. While Juan Bobo lay there dreaming, the donkey broke open the lunch basket and ate the poisoned cakes. In no time at all she rolled over and died. Three vultures, flying overhead, swooped down and made a meal of the dead donkey, and since she had been poisoned, they, too, died.

When Juan Bobo awoke and saw them lying there—the dead donkey and the three dead vultures—he knew immediately what had happened because the cakes were gone. Since he was hungry, he took his gun to hunt for food. He spied a wild rabbit and shot at it, but missed and killed another rabbit, which at that moment jumped in the path of his bullet. Juan Bobo cooked and ate it and found he was thirsty. As he had no water, he climbed a coconut tree, cut off one of the nuts, and drank the juice. He had to go the rest of the way to the castle on foot. As he walked along, his mind was filled with thoughts of his donkey, Panda, the vultures, the rabbit, and the coconut. Since he had as yet thought of no riddle, he decided to make one up out of the adventures that had befallen him that morning.

When Juan Bobo reached the castle and told the guards what he had come for, they laughed and laughed. They knew him and how stupid he was, and they were not going to let him in. But Juan Bobo insisted that the proclamation applied to everyone, and he was within his rights in accepting the King's invitation. So the guards finally went to the King and told him that Juan Bobo was outside with a riddle for the Princess. At first the King was indignant that a country bumpkin should dare think himself worthy of marrying his daughter. Then he remembered his promise that she should marry the man, rich or poor, nobleman or commoner, whose riddle she could not solve, and he ordered the guards to bring Juan Bobo in.

Juan Bobo walked into the throne room, past the King and his court, over to where the Princess was waiting for him. He greeted her and said:

> 'I left home with Panda,
> And two killed her;
> But Panda killed three.
> I shot at what I saw,
> But killed what I didn't see.
> I was thirsty and drank
> Water which never sank
> Into earth nor fell from sky.
> If you guess my conundrum,
> Princess, I'm done-drum!'

The Princess thought and thought and thought, and, to the great surprise of the King and the court, she could not find the answer. Now, according to the rules the King had made, she was allowed three days in which to find the solution. So Juan Bobo was lodged in the castle for three days while she was thinking.

The first night the Princess sent one of her handmaidens to Juan's room to see if she could get the answer from him. The girl was very beautiful, but Juan Bobo paid no attention to her chatter.

The second night the Princess sent her lady-in-waiting, who was even more beautiful. But her efforts, too, were futile. Juan would say nothing.

The third night the Princess, in desperation, went herself and begged him to tell her the solution to his riddle. After she had begged a long time, Juan Bobo agreed to tell her the answer if she, in turn, would give him her ring and one of her shoes. The Princess did not hesitate—she gave him her ring and a shoe. Then Juan Bobo explained how he had left home on his donkey, Panda; how she had died after eating the poisoned cakes; how the three vultures had also been poisoned when they ate Panda; how he had fired at a rabbit, missed it, and killed another; and how he had quenched his thirst with coconut water.

As soon as the Princess heard this, she clapped her hands and ran from the room.

The next day the court assembled in the throne room to hear the Princess solve Juan Bobo's riddle. She had no trouble at all. Before them all, she gave the explanation Juan had given her the night before.

The King was very happy when he saw that he would not have to be the father-in-law of an ignorant country bumpkin. He called the headsman and ordered him to cut off Juan Bobo's head and put it on the wall with the others.

As the headsman started to carry out the order, Juan Bobo asked permission to speak, and the King granted his request. Then Juan told how the Princess had obtained the answer from him and how she had come to his room begging for it the night before. As proof, he showed the ring and the shoe that the Princess had given him.

The King was a just man. He ordered that the sentence of execution be suspended and that a wedding be celebrated instead of a beheading.

Thus it was that the fool of the town married the Princess and, after a while, became the King of the country.

From *The Three Wishes: A Collection of Puerto Rican Folktales*, by Ricardo E. Alegería, translated by Elizabeth Culbert (New York: Harcourt, Brace & World, 1969).

The Innkeeper's Wise Daughter

This Jewish-American tale belongs to a widely known group of tales about clever riddle solvers. The focus in the 'The Innkeeper's Wise Daughter', however, is not so much on the ingenious solution to the riddles, but on the way that males perceive, and thus judge, females. In the initial section of the story, the young woman is a kind of unlikely hero. She easily passes the riddle tests that completely stump her older and ostensibly wiser father, thereby proving that she, not her father or his rival, is truly wise.

In the second part of the tale, she shows that she is more than an equal to the nobleman whom she marries. Having had the foresight to make her husband accept her condition for marriage, she refuses to hide either her compassion or intelligence when someone in need comes to her. Subsequently, she uses her wit and her understanding of her husband to change his views. She compels him, that is, to see her as an individual who is worthy of both his respect and his love.

$\mathcal{M}$any years ago, in a small village in Russia, there were two friends, a tailor and an innkeeper. One day, as they were drinking glasses of tea, they began to talk about their philosophies of life. As their discussion went on, they began to argue more and more intensely—each one claiming to know more about life than the other one—and they almost came to blows. They realized that neither one would win the argument, so they decided to bring the matter to the local nobleman, who was respected for his wisdom and honesty and who often served as a judge in disputes. The two friends finished their tea in silence and set out to see the nobleman.

When the nobleman heard the case, he said to the two men, 'Whoever answers these three questions correctly will be the one who knows more about life: What is the quickest thing in the world? What is the fattest in the world? And what is the sweetest? Return in three day's time with your answers and I will settle your disagreement!'

The tailor returned home and spent the three days thinking about these riddles, but found no answers to them. When the innkeeper returned to his home, he sat down holding his head in his hands. Just then, his daughter saw him and cried out, 'What's wrong, Father?' The innkeeper told her about the three questions. She answered, 'Father, when you go back to the nobleman, give him these answers: The quickest thing in the world is thought. The fattest thing is the earth. The sweetest is sleep.'

When three days had passed, the tailor and the innkeeper came before the nobleman. 'Have you found answers to my questions?' he asked. The tailor stood there silently.

But when the innkeeper gave his answers, the nobleman exclaimed, 'Wonderful! Those are wonderful answers! But tell me, how did you think of those answers?'

'I must tell you truthfully that those answers were told to me by my daughter,' replied the innkeeper.

'Since your daughter knows so much about life, I will test her further. Give her this dozen eggs and see if she can hatch them all in three days. If she does so, she will have a great reward.'

The innkeeper carefully took the eggs and returned home. When his daughter saw him carrying a large basket, and she also saw how he stumbled, she asked him, 'What is wrong, Father?' He showed her the eggs and told her what she must do in order to receive a reward and prove her wisdom again.

The daughter took the eggs, and she weighed them, each one, in her hands. 'Dear Father, how can these eggs be hatched when they are cooked? Boiled eggs indeed! But wait, Father, I have a plan as to how to answer this riddle.' The daughter boiled some beans and waited three days. Then she instructed her father to go to the nobleman's house and ask permission to plant some special beans.

'Beans?' asked the nobleman. 'What sort of special beans?' Taking the beans from his pocket, the innkeeper showed them to the nobleman and said, 'These are boiled beans, your honour, that I want to plant.'

The nobleman burst out laughing and said, 'Well, you certainly are not wise to the ways of the world if you don't even know that beans can't grow from boiled beans— only from seeds.'

'Well then,' replied the innkeeper, 'neither can chickens hatch from boiled eggs!'

The nobleman immediately sensed the clever mind of the innkeeper's daughter in the answer. So he said to the innkeeper, 'Tell your daughter to come here in three days. And she must come neither dressed nor undressed, neither walking nor riding, neither hungry nor overfed, and she must bring me a gift that is not a gift.'

The innkeeper returned home even more perplexed than before. When his daughter heard what she had to do in three days' time, she laughed and said, 'Father, tomorrow I will tell you what to do.'

The next day, the daughter said to her father, 'Go to the marketplace and buy these things—a large net, some almonds, a goat, and a pair of pigeons.' The father was puzzled by these requests, but as he loved his daughter and knew her to be wise, he did not question her. Instead he went to the marketplace and bought all that she had requested.

On the third day, the innkeeper's daughter prepared for her visit to the nobleman. She did not eat her usual morning meal. Instead, she got undressed and wrapped herself in the transparent net, so she was neither dressed nor undressed.

Then she took two almonds in one hand and the pair of pigeons in the other. Leaning on the goat, she held on so that one foot dragged on the ground while she hopped on the other one. In this way, she was neither walking nor riding.

As she approached the nobleman's house, he saw her and came out to greet her.

At the gate, she ate the two almonds to show she was neither hungry nor overfed.

Then the innkeeper's daughter extended her hand showing the pigeons she intended to give as a gift. The nobleman reached out to take them, but just at that moment the young woman opened her hand to release the pigeons—and they flew away. So she had brought a gift that was not a gift.

The nobleman gave a laugh of approval and called out, 'You are a clever woman! I want to marry you, but on one condition. You must promise never to interfere with any of my judgments.'

'I will marry you,' said the innkeeper's daughter, 'but I also have one condition: If I do anything that will cause you to send me away, you must promise to give me whatever I treasure most in your house.' They each agreed to the other's condition, and they were married.

Some time passed, and one day a man came to speak with the young wife, who had become known for her wisdom, 'Help me, please,' the man begged, 'for I know you are wise and understand things in ways your husband does not.'

'Tell me what is wrong, for you look very troubled, sir,' she answered. And the man told her his story.

'Last year,' said the man, 'my partner and I bought a barn which we now share. He keeps his wagon there, and I keep my horse there. Well, last night my horse gave birth to a pony under the wagon. So my partner says the pony belongs to him. We began to argue and fight, so we brought our dispute to the nobleman. The nobleman judged that my partner was right. I protested, but to no avail. What can I do?'

The young woman gave him certain advice and instructions to follow. As she had told him to do, he took a fishing pole and went over to the nobleman's well and pretended he was fishing there. The nobleman rode by the well, just as his wife had predicted, and when he saw the man, he stopped and asked, 'What are you doing?' The man replied, 'I am fishing in the well.' The nobleman started to laugh. 'Are you really so stupid that you do not know that you can't catch fish in a well?' 'No sir,' said the man, 'not any more than I know that a wagon cannot give birth to a pony.'

At this answer, the nobleman stopped laughing. Understanding that his wife must be involved in this case after all, he got out of his carriage and went looking for his wife. When he found her he said, 'You did not keep your promise not to interfere with my judgments, so I must send you back to your father's home.'

'You are right, my husband. But before I leave, let us dine together one last time.' The nobleman agreed to this request.

At dinner, the nobleman drank a great deal of wine, for his wife kept refilling his cup, and, as a result, he soon became very sleepy. As soon as he was asleep, the wife signaled to the servants to pick him up and put him in the carriage next to her, and so they returned to her father's home.

The next morning, when the nobleman woke up, he looked around and realized where he was. 'But how did I get here? What is the meaning of this?' he shouted.

'You may remember, dear husband, that you also made an agreement with me. You promised that if you sent me away, I would be able to pick whatever I treasured most in your house to take with me. There is nothing that I treasure more than you. So that is how you come to be here with me.'

The nobleman laughed, embraced his wife, and said, 'Knowing how much you love me, I now realize how much I love you. Let us return to our home.'

And they did go home, where they lived with love and respect for many happy years.

From *Jewish Stories One Generation Tells Another*, by Peninnah Schram (London: Jason Aronson, 1987).

The Frog Maiden

This Burmese tale combines several story types before concluding as a romantic tale of wish fulfillment. It begins as an unusual child tale in which a longed-for baby looks like a frog. It then becomes a Cinderella tale, with Little Miss Frog enduring hardship at the hands of her stepmother and stepsisters. Unlike the French and German Cinderellas, who attend a ball where a prince chooses them to be his bride, Little Miss Frog finds herself chosen at the hair-washing ceremony. Typically a part of the Burmese New Year's Water Festival, this ceremony reflects Buddhist belief that, as the noblest part of the body, the head should be clean for the new year. It also marks a time when people strive to obey the Five Precepts of Zen Buddhism, as does the prince when he keeps his word about marrying the one who catches the flowers.

After Little Miss Frog's marriage, the tale becomes a succession test story, and she uses mysterious abilities to enable her husband to show his worthiness to inherit the kingdom. The final test, however, involves a transformation similar to that in 'Beauty and the Beast'. As soon as her husband publicly declares that she is the most beautiful woman in the world, she removes her frog skin to reveal that he has indeed spoken the truth. In this animal bride tale, then, the female has implicitly tested the husband; he has passed by displaying kindness and faith in her, and he has thereby earned the reward of a wife who becomes what he desires her to be. As in 'Beauty and the Beast', the outward transformation, which produces a figure of ideal beauty, is the external sign of inward nature.

*A*n old couple was childless, and the husband and the wife longed for a child. So when the wife found that she was with child, they were overjoyed; but to their great disappointment, the wife gave birth not to a human child, but to a little she-frog. However, as the little frog spoke and behaved as a human child, not only the parents but also the neighbours came to love her and called her affectionately 'Little Miss Frog'.

Some years later the woman died, and the man decided to marry again. The woman he chose was a widow with two ugly daughters and they were very jealous of Little Miss Frog's popularity with the neighbours. All three took a delight in illtreating Little Miss Frog.

One day the youngest of the king's four sons announced that he would perform the hair-washing ceremony on a certain date and he invited all young ladies to join in the ceremony, as he would choose at the end of the ceremony one of them to be his princess.

On the morning of the appointed day the two ugly sisters dressed themselves in fine raiment, and with great hopes of being chosen by the Prince they started for the palace. Little Miss Frog ran after them, and pleaded, 'Sisters, please let me come with you.'

The sisters laughed and said mockingly, 'What, the little frog wants to come? The invitation is to young ladies and not to young frogs.' Little Miss Frog walked along with them towards the palace, pleading for permission to come. But the sisters were adamant, and so at the palace gates she was left behind. However, she spoke so sweetly to the guards that they allowed her to go in. Little Miss Frog found hundreds of young ladies gathered round the pool full of lilies in the palace grounds; and she took her place among them and waited for the Prince.

The Prince now appeared, and washed his hair in the pool. The ladies also let down their hair and joined in the ceremony. At the end of the ceremony, the Prince declared that as the ladies were all beautiful, he did not know whom to choose and so he would throw a posy of jasmines into the air; and the lady on whose head the posy fell would be his princess. The Prince then threw the posy into the air, and all the ladies present looked up expectantly. The posy, however, fell on Little Miss Frog's head, to the great annoyance of the ladies, especially the two stepsisters. The Prince also was disappointed, but he felt that he should keep his word. So little Miss Frog was married to the Prince, and she became Little Princess Frog.

Some time later, the old king called his four sons to him and said, 'My sons, I am now too old to rule the country, and I want to retire to the forest and become a hermit. So I must appoint one of you as my successor. As I love you all alike, I will give you a task to perform, and he who performs it successfully shall be king in my place. The task is, bring me a golden deer at sunrise on the seventh day from now.'

The Youngest Prince went home to Little Princess Frog and told her about the task. 'What, only a golden deer!' exclaimed Princess Frog. 'Eat as usual, my Prince, and on the appointed day I will give you the golden deer.' So the Youngest Prince stayed at home, while the three elder princes went into the forest in search of the deer. On the seventh day before sunrise, Little Princess Frog woke up her husband and said, 'Go to the palace, Prince, and here is your golden deer.' The young Prince looked, then rubbed his eyes, and looked again. There was no mistake about it; the deer which Little Princess Frog was holding by a lead was really of pure gold. So he went to the palace, and to the great annoyance of the elder princes who brought ordinary deer, he was declared to be the heir by the king. The elder princes, however, pleaded for a second chance, and the king reluctantly agreed.

'Then perform this second task,' said the king. 'On the seventh day from now at sunrise, you must bring me the rice that never becomes stale, and the meat that is ever fresh.'

The Youngest Prince went home and told Princess Frog about the new task. 'Don't you worry, sweet Prince,' said Princess Frog. 'Eat as usual, sleep as usual, and on the appointed day I will give you the rice and meat.' So the Youngest Prince stayed at home, while the three elder princes went in search of the rice and meat. On the seventh day at sunrise, Little Princess Frog woke up her husband and said, 'My Lord, go to the palace now, and here is your rice and meat.' The Youngest Prince took the rice and meat, and went to the palace, and to the great annoyance of the elder princes who brought only well-cooked rice and meat, he was again declared to be the heir. But the three elder princes again pleaded for one more chance, and the king said, 'This is positively the last task. On the seventh day from now at sunrise, bring me the most beautiful woman on this earth.'

'Ho, ho!' said the three elder princes to themselves in great joy. 'Our wives are very beautiful, and we will bring them. One of us is sure to be declared heir, and our good-for-nothing brother will be nowhere this time.' The Youngest Prince overheard their remark, and felt sad, for his wife was a frog and ugly. When he reached home, he said to his wife, 'Dear Princess, I must go and look for the most beautiful woman on this earth. My brothers will bring their wives, for they are really beautiful, but I will find someone who is more beautiful.'

'Don't you fret, my Prince,' replied Princess Frog. 'Eat as usual, sleep as usual, and you can take me to the palace on the appointed day; surely I shall be declared to be the most beautiful woman.'

The Youngest Prince looked at the Princess in surprise; but he did not want to hurt her feelings, and he said gently, 'All right, Princess, I will take you with me on the appointed day.'

On the seventh day at dawn, Little Princess Frog woke up the Prince and said, 'My Lord, I must make myself beautiful. So please wait outside and call me when it is nearly time to go.' The Prince left the room as requested. After some moments, the Prince shouted from outside, 'Princess, it is time for us to go.'

'Please wait, my Lord,' replied the Princess, 'I am just powdering my face.'

After some moments the Prince shouted, 'Princess, we must go now.'

'All right, my Lord,' replied the Princess, 'please open the door for me.'

The Prince thought to himself, 'Perhaps, just as she was able to obtain the golden deer and the wonderful rice and meat, she is able to make herself beautiful,' and he expectantly opened the door, but he was disappointed to see Little Princess Frog still a frog and as ugly as ever. However, so as not to hurt her feelings, the Prince said nothing and took her along to the palace. When the Prince entered the audience-chamber with his Frog Princess the three elder princes with their wives were already there. The king looked at the Prince in surprise and said, 'Where is your beautiful maiden?'

'I will answer for the prince, my king,' said the Frog Princess. 'I am his beautiful maiden.' She then took off her frog skin and stood a beautiful maiden dressed in silk and satin. The king declared her to be the most beautiful maiden in the world, and selected the Prince as his successor on the throne. The Prince asked his Princess never to put on the ugly frog skin again, and the Frog Princess, to accede to his request, threw the skin into the fire.

From *Burmese Folk-Tales*, by Maung Htin Aung (London: Oxford University Press, 1948).

Rosalie

Although 'Rosalie', a tale from the Mayan people of Mexico, shows obvious signs of European influence, it reverses the pattern found in most romantic European tales. Unlike many of the females in the classic romantic fairy tales, Rosalie is active and aware, whereas the male whom she loves is dependent and unconscious of what is happening. Furthermore, she is the one who must guide and ultimately save him. In the first part of the tale, Rosalie, the daughter of giants, uses both wit and magic to enable her beloved to pass the series of seemingly impossible suitor tests that her father sets. Realizing that her parents will never consent to the marriage, Rosalie then plans their escape, again using her powers to thwart her parents' pursuit. Her beloved jeopardizes their happiness, however, when, like the lassie in 'East o' the Sun and West o' the Moon', he violates a prohibition during a visit with his relatives. Ultimately, Rosalie must rescue him from his enchanted state so that he can become conscious of his love for an active and extraordinary woman.

𝒯ravelling far, a young man who had started out from home to earn some money came to a hut where a giant lived with three daughters, and falling in love with the youngest, he made up his mind to stay. 'You may stay and be my son-in-law,' said the giant, 'but only if you can perform the four tasks that I will give you.' The young man agreed.

'First,' said the giant, 'I have a great desire to take my bath the moment I get out of bed instead of having to go all the way down to the lake. Tonight you will bring the lake up to the hut, so that when I wake in the morning I can sit on my bed and put my feet in water. Use this basket to carry it.'

The young man hardly knew what to think. But the giant's youngest daughter, whose name was Rosalie, told him not to worry. That night, while everyone else was sleeping, Rosalie went down to the lake, and with her skirt she swept the water up to her father's bedside. When the giant awoke, he was astonished to find the water lapping the leg posts of his bed.

Next the giant took a large pot, threw it into the deepest river he could find, and told his future son-in-law to bring it back home. After diving many times, the young man was about to give up, for the river was so deep he could not reach the bottom. Then Rosalie told him to go with her to the riverbank that night, and she would dive. But he must call her name when she reached the bottom, otherwise she would be unable to rise to the surface again. This they did, and the following morning the giant found the pot once more in the house.

The next task was to make a cornfield of a hundred mecates. The young man must clear and burn the forest, do the planting, and at midnight, of the same day bring back a load of fresh young ears. He set to work at daybreak but by sunset had accomplished practically nothing.

Then Rosalie stretched out her skirt, and all the forest was immediately felled. Using the same magic, she dried the brush, burned it, sowed the corn, raised the plants, and harvested the young ears, so that the young man was able to take them to her father at midnight.

Furious, the giant went to his wife to ask her how they could get rid of this would-be son-in-law. 'We'll have him thrown from a horse,' said his wife, and they arranged that she herself would turn into a mare, the giant would become the saddle and stirrups, and Rosalie would be the bridle. Rosalie, however, overheard their conversation and warned the one who loved her to treat the bridle carefully and not to spare the horse and the saddle.

Next morning the giant told the young man to go out into the savanna, where he would find a mare already saddled. He was to mount her and bring her back to the house. Meanwhile the giant and his wife and Rosalie took a short cut through the forest, and by the time the young man arrived, they had changed themselves into the fully saddled mare.

The young man, who had brought along a stout club, jumped onto the mare's back, and before she had a chance to buck, he began beating her as hard as he could. All but paralyzed by the blows, the mare was unable to throw her rider, and after a few moments she sank exhausted to the ground.

The young man returned to the hut, where a little later he was joined by the giant and his wife, bruised all over and worn out.

The son-in-law had now completed his four tasks, but the giant, going back on his word, told him there were yet more. That night Rosalie decided they must run away, while the giant and his wife would still be sore from the beating. When the two were asleep, Rosalie took a needle, a grain of white earth, and a grain of salt, and spitting on the floor, slipped quietly out of the house to meet the young man.

At daybreak the giant called to Rosalie to get up. 'It's all right, Papa. I'm getting up. I'm combing my hair,' replied the spittle. It spoke with the voice of the giant's daughter, so he suspected nothing.'

A little later the giant again called to Rosalie, asking her if she was dressed yet. Again the spittle replied: 'I'm combing my hair.' By this time, however, the spittle was almost dry and could only answer in a whisper. Suspicious, the old lady went into Rosalie's room and discovered the trick that had been played on them.

Then the giant set out in pursuit of the fleeing couple, rapidly gaining on them. When he had nearly overtaken them, Rosalie turned herself into an orange tree, and her companion disguised himself as an old man. Stopping next to the tree, the giant asked if a young couple had gone by.

'No,' replied the old man, 'but stay a moment and rest, and eat some of these oranges.' The giant tasted the oranges and immediately lost his desire to run after his daughter and the young man. Returning to his hut, he explained to his wife that he had been unable to overtake them.

'You fool!' cried the old lady. 'That orange tree was Rosalie.'

Again the giant set out in pursuit. When he was once more at the point of overtaking them, Rosalie turned the horse they were riding into a church, her young man into the door-keeper, and herself into an image of the Virgin. When the giant reached the church, he asked the doorkeeper if he had seen any sign of the missing pair.

'Hush!' replied the doorkeeper. 'You must not talk here, the priest is just about to sing mass. Come inside and see our beautiful Virgin.'

The giant entered the church, and the moment he laid eyes on the statue he lost all thought of pursuing the young couple. Returning once again to his hut, he told his wife how he had seen the Virgin and had decided to come home.

'You fool, you fool!' cried the old lady. 'The Virgin was Rosalie. You are too dim-witted to be of any use. I'll catch them myself.'

The giant's wife set out at full speed. Rosalie and the young man travelled as fast as they could, but the old lady ran faster, and gradually she caught up with them. When she was almost within reach, Rosalie cried out, 'We can't fool her, we'll have to use the needle.'

Stooping down, she planted the needle in the ground, and immediately a dense thicket grew up. For the moment they were out of danger. As the old lady cut her way through the thicket, the young couple fled on. At last she got clear of the thicket and began gaining on them once more.

When her mother had nearly caught up with them, Rosalie threw down the grain of white earth, and immediately a mountain rose up. Again the couple fled away, as the old lady, half out of breath, scrambled to the top of the steep slope, then made her way down the other side.

Clear of the mountain at last, she continued on, rapidly gaining on her daughter and the young man. When she had almost overtaken them, Rosalie threw down the grain of salt, and it became an enormous sea. Rosalie herself became a sardine, the young man a shark, and their horse a crocodile. The old lady waded into the water, trying to catch the sardine, but the shark drove her off.

'Very well,' said the old lady. 'But you must remain in the water seven years.'

When the seven years were up and they were free at last, they came out on dry land and returned to the town where the young man's grandparents lived. Rosalie, however, could not enter the town, because she had not been baptized. She sent the young man ahead telling him to return with half a bottle of holy water, and on no account was he to embrace his grandparents, or then he would instantly forget his Rosalie.

The young man arrived at his old home, and greeted his grandparents, but he would not permit them to embrace him. Feeling tired, he decided to rest awhile before returning to Rosalie with the holy water. Soon he was fast asleep, whereupon his grandmother bending over him, softly kissed him. When he awoke, therefore, he no longer had any recollection of Rosalie.

For days Rosalie waited for him to come back. At last, one morning, seeing a little boy playing at the edge of the town, she called to him and asked him to get her some holy water. The boy brought it to her, and she bathed herself with it and entered the town. There she learned that the one she loved, at the urging of his grandparents, was about to marry another young woman.

Rosalie went straight to the grandparents' house, but the young man did not know who she was. Nevertheless, she succeeded in having the marriage postponed three days. Then she prepared a great feast and invited all the elders of the town as well as the young man she loved. In the centre of the table she placed two dolls she had made: one that resembled herself; the other, the young man.

The guests arrived and sat down to the feast. Then Rosalie pulled out a whip and began thrashing the doll that represented the man.

'Don't you remember how you were told to carry water in a basket?' she cried, and 'Whang!' the whip cut through the air. As it struck the doll, the man himself cried out in pain.

Again she spoke to the doll: 'Don't you remember the pot at the bottom of the river and how I brought it up for you?' 'Whang!' and again the young man cried out in pain.

'Don't you remember the cornfield you had to make and the fresh young ears I grew for you?'

'Whang!'

'And the seven years we spent in the sea?'

'Whang!'

Again the young man shrieked in pain. Then the memory of the past returned to him, and forgetting his bride-to-be, and with a cry of joy, he threw himself into Rosalie's arms.

From *The Monkey's Haircut and Other Stories Told by the Maya*, edited by John Bierhorst (New York: William Morrow, 1986).

The Crane Wife

A number of tales about a shape-shifting bride do not end with the unalloyed happiness common to animal groom tales. The Japanese tale of 'The Crane Wife' initially makes use of the crane as a symbol of good fortune. Having been kind to nature, in the form of the trapped crane, Karoku receives the reward of a wife with remarkable talents as a weaver. Unfortunately, when Karoku violates his wife's instructions and sees her in her true state, his luck and happiness end because she insists that she must leave him. Although he follows her to her world, they never reunite. This ending may seem strange to Western readers, but in *The Japanese Psyche: Major Motifs in the Fairy Tales of Japan*, Hayao Kawai says that the Japanese feel that it has 'a fine ending' because, after the man and crane separate 'They can coexist by "living in divided territory". There is no sense of controlling each other' (121).

Once there was a man named Karoku. He lived with his seventy-year-old mother far back in the mountains, where he made charcoal for a living. One winter, as he was going to the village to buy some *futon* [bedding], he saw a crane struggling in a trap where it had been caught.

Just as Karoku was stooping to release the poor crane, the man who had set the trap came running up. 'What are you doing, interfering with other people's business?' he cried.

'I felt so sorry for the crane I thought I would let it go. Will you sell it to me? Here, I have the money I was going to use to buy *futon*. Please take the money, and let me have the crane.' The man agreed, and Karoku took the crane and immediately let it flyaway free.

'Well,' thought Karoku, returning home, 'we may get cold tonight, but it can't be helped.' When he got home, his mother asked what he had done with the futon. He replied, 'I saw a crane caught in a trap. I felt so sorry for it that I used all the money to buy it and set it free.'

'Well,' his mother said, 'since you have done it, I suppose that it is all right.'

The next evening, just as night was falling, a beautiful young lady such as they had never seen before came to Karoku's house. 'Please let me spend the night here,' she asked, but Karoku refused, saying, 'My little hut is too poor.' She replied, 'No, I do not mind; please, I implore you, let me stay,' until finally he consented, and she was allowed to spend the night.

During the evening she said, 'I have something I should like to discuss with you,' and when Karoku asked what it was, she replied, 'I beg of you, please make me your wife.'

Karoku, greatly surprised, said: 'This is the first time in my life that I have seen such a beautiful woman as you. I am a very poor man; I do not even know where my next meal is coming from; how could I ever take you as my wife?'

'Please do not refuse,' she pleaded; 'please take me as your wife.'

'Well, you beg me so much, I don't know what to do,' he replied. When his mother heard this, she said to her, 'Since you insist, you may become my son's bride. Please stay here and work hard.' Soon preparations were made, and they were married.

Some time after this his wife said, 'Please put me in a cabinet and leave me there for three days. Close the door tightly and be sure not to open it and look at me.' Her husband put her in a cabinet, and on the fourth day, she came out. 'It must have been very unpleasant in there,' he said. 'I was worried about you. Hurry and have something to eat.'

'All right,' she said. After she finished eating she said, 'Karoku, Karoku, please take the cloth that I wove while in the cabinet and sell it for two thousand *ryo*.' Saying this, she took a bolt of cloth from the cabinet and gave it to her husband. He took it to the lord of the province, who, when he saw it, said, 'This is very beautiful material, I will pay you two or even three thousand *ryo* for it. Can you bring me another bolt like it?'

'I must ask my wife if she can weave another,' Karoku replied.

'Oh, you need not ask her; it is all right if only you agree. I will give you the money for it now,' the lord said.

Karoku returned home and told his wife what the lord had said. 'Just give me time and I'll weave another bolt,' she said. 'This time please shut me in the cabinet for one week. During that time you must be sure not to open the door and look at me.' And so he shut her in the cabinet again.

By the time the week was nearly over, Karoku became very worried about his wife. On the last day of the week, he opened the door to see if she were all right. There inside the cabinet was a crane, naked after having pulled out all her beautiful long feathers. She was using her feathers to weave the cloth and was just at the point of finishing it.

The crane cried out, 'I have finished the cloth, but since you have seen who I really am, I am afraid that you can no longer love me. I must return to my home. I am not a person but the crane whom you rescued. Please take the cloth to the lord as you promised.'

After she had said this, the crane silently turned toward the west. When she did this, thousands of cranes appeared, and taking her with them, they all flew out of sight.

Karoku had become a rich man, but he wanted to see his beloved wife so badly that he could not bear it. He searched for her throughout Japan until he was exhausted. One day as he was sitting on the seashore resting, he saw an old man alone in a rowboat, approaching from the open ocean. 'How strange,' thought Karoku. 'Where could he be coming from; there are no islands near here.' As he sat in bewilderment, the boat landed on the beach. Karoku called out, 'Grandfather, where did you come from?'

'I came from an island called "The Robe of Crane Feathers,"' the old man replied.

'Would you please take me to that island?' asked Karoku.

The old man quickly agreed, and Karoku climbed into the boat. The boat sped over the water, and in no time they had arrived at a beautiful white beach. They landed, and when Karoku got out of the boat and turned around, the boat and the old man had vanished from sight.

Karoku walked up the beach and soon came to a beautiful pond. In the middle of the pond was an island, and there on the island was the naked crane. She was surrounded by a myriad of cranes, for she was queen of the cranes.

Karoku stayed a short while and was given a feast. Afterward the old man with the boat returned, and Karoku was taken back to his home.

From *Folktales of Japan*, by Keigo Seki, translated by Robert J. Adams (Chicago: University of Chicago Press, 1963).

⚜

The Goodman of Wastness and His Selkie Wife

Stories of shape-shifting selkies (the Orcadian word for 'seal') abound in the Orkney Islands, a group of more than seventy mostly uninhabited islands off the north coast of Scotland. Legends have it that the seals are a magical race able to shed their skins to become beautiful human beings. Humans, both women and men, are irresistibly attracted to these shape shifters who frequently have romantic dalliances with them and then put on their skins, become seals again, and return to the sea. Although tales of selkie males wooing human females

and then disappearing are common, the most popular tales about selkies focus on a human man who keeps a female selkie as his wife by hiding her seal skin, thus compelling her to remain in her human form. In these tales the marriage seldom endures: usually, as in the story of the goodman of Wastness, a child finds the skin and gives it to her mother, who returns to the sea, sometimes with her children but just as frequently without them. These haunting tales suggest that coercion can never change the female Other, nor can it result in enduring love.

𝒯he goodman of Wastness was a handsome young man with a good, profitable farm. Many pretty lasses on the island had set their caps at him, but none could catch him. Eventually, the pretty lasses began to have contempt for the goodman, calling him 'an old young man' and declaring that he was committing the unpardonable sin of refusing marriage.

He did not worry about what the lasses said, and when his friends urged him to take a wife, he would say, 'Women are like many another thing in this weary world, only sent for a trial to man; and I have trials enough without being tried by a wife. If that old fool Adam had not been bewitched by his wife, he might have been a happy man in the Garden of Eden to this day.'

One old woman who heard him make this speech wagged her finger and replied, 'Take heed of what you say, for one day you yourself may become bewitched.'

'Ay,' he laughed, 'that will be the same day that you walk from island to island without getting your feet wet.'

Well, it happened one day that the goodman of Wastness was walking along the shore at low tide when he saw at a little distance a number of selkie folk on a flat rock. Some were lying down and sunning themselves, while others jumped and played about in great glee. They were all naked, and had skins as white as his own. The rock on which they amused themselves had deep water on its seaward side, and on its shore side a shallow pool. The goodman of Wastness crept unseen right to the edge of the shallow pool; he then rose and dashed through the pool to the rock. The alarmed selkie folk seized their seal skins, and, in mad haste, jumped into the sea. They were quick, but so was the goodman. He seized the skin belonging to an unfortunate lass, who in her terror, had been unable to grab it when she sprang into the water.

The selkie folk swam out a little distance, then turning, raised their heads and gazed at the goodman. He noticed that one of them did not, like the others, appear to be a seal. Tucking the captured skin under his arm, he started home. Before he even got off the beach, however, he heard someone weeping behind him. He turned to see a woman following him. She was the one whose seal skin he had taken. She was a pitiful sight: she sobbed in bitter grief, the big tears flowing down her beautiful cheeks, while she held out both hands and begged the goodman to return her precious skin. Over and over she cried out, 'O handsome man, if you have any mercy in your human breast, give me back my seal skin. I cannot live in the sea without it. I cannot live among my own people without my seal skin. Have pity on a poor lass in her distress if ever you have hope for mercy for yourself.'

The goodman was not soft-hearted, but he could not help pitying her. With this pity came other feelings. Soon, his heart, which had never before loved a woman, was bewitched by the selkie-lass's beauty. Consequently, he absolutely refused to give back her skin. Because she could not return to the sea without it, the lass reluctantly gave in to his pleadings and agreed to be his wife.

The sea-lass therefore went with the goodman and stayed with him for many years, proving herself to be a thrifty, frugal, and kindly goodwife. She bore her goodman seven children, four boys and three lasses, and there were not prettier lasses nor handsomer boys in all the Orkneys. The goodwife of Wastness appeared happy, and sometimes she was genuinely merry. At other times, however, she would sit by the window and stare longingly at the sea; if she then saw seals near the shore, her eyes would cloud over, and she would have to wipe away tears. Unaware of these moods, the goodman led a happy life with her.

One fine day, the goodman and his three eldest sons were out in his boat fishing. The goodwife sent three of the other children to the shore to gather limpits and whelks. The youngest lass, who had hurt her foot on a sharp rock, stayed at home with her mother. Pretending to be cleaning house, the goodwife did what she always did when she was alone: she searched for her long-lost skin. She searched up, and she searched down; she searched out, and she searched in, but she could not find a trace of her skin.

The sun began to sink into the west. Finally, the youngest lass, who had sat all this time in a chair with her sore foot on a low stool, asked, 'Mam, what are you looking for?'

'Oh, my dear child, don't tell anyone,' said her mother, 'but I am looking for a pretty skin from which I can make a shoe that will cure your sore foot.'

'But, Mam,' replied the lass, 'I know where there is just such a skin. One day when you were out and Dad thought that I was sleeping in my bed, he took down a pretty skin, stared at it for awhile, and then put it up under the aisins above the bed.'

When her mother heard this, she rushed to the aisins, the space between the sloping roof and the top of the wall, and pulled out her longed-for skin. 'Farewell, my dear beauty,' she said to her child, and ran out. She rushed to the shore, flung on her skin, and plunged into the sea with a wild cry of joy. A male of the selkie folk met her and greeted her with every token of delight. The goodman, who was just then rowing home, saw them both from his boat. His wife, removing the seal skin to show her beautiful human face, cried out to him: 'Goodman of Wastness, farewell! I liked you well enough, for you were good to me, but I love better my own man of the sea!' With that, she and her seal companion plunged beneath the waves.

In the years that followed, the goodman of Wastness wandered often on the sea-shore, hoping to meet once more his lost love, but never again did he see her fair face.

———

Adapted for children by Raymond E. Jones from an account in *The Scottish Antiquary* 5.7 (1893), by Walter Traill Dennison.

Urashima Taro

Often called the Japanese Rip Van Winkle, this tale is among the most popular in Japan, where it has inspired a variety of stories. The tale first appears in print in the eighth-century AD *Nihongi*, which chronicles the history of Japan from the earliest times to AD 697. According to the *Nihongi*, the first-born son of a fisherman named Urashima (*Taro* is a name given to first-born Japanese males) made his remarkable journey in the autumn of AD 478. Several coastal locales claim to be the burial site of this adventurer, and the temples in Kanagawa reputedly have his fishing line and the casket given him by the sea-maiden. Now treated in Japan more as the equivalent of a fairy tale than an historical legend, the tale of Urashima Taro contains the familiar motifs of receipt of a reward for being kind to an animal, transformation of an animal into a bride, and punishment for breaking of a taboo.

One day Urashima, who lived in a little fishing village called Midzunoe, in the province of Tango, went out to fish. It so happened that he caught a tortoise, and as tortoises are said to live many thousands of years, the thoughtful Urashima allowed the creature to return to the sea, rebaited his hook, and once more waited for the bite of a fish. Only the sea gently waved his line to and fro. The sun beat down upon his head till at last Urashima fell asleep. He had not been sleeping long when he heard some one calling his name: 'Urashima, Urashima!'

It was such a sweet, haunting voice that the fisher-lad stood up in his boat and looked around in every direction, till he chanced to see the very tortoise he had been kind enough to restore to its watery home. The tortoise, which was able to speak quite fluently, profusely thanked Urashima for his kindness, and offered to take him to the *ryūkyū*, or Palace of the Dragon King.

The invitation was readily accepted, and getting on the tortoise's back, Urashima found himself gliding through the sea at a tremendous speed, and the curious part about it was he discovered that his clothes remained perfectly dry.

In the Sea King's Palace
Arriving at the Sea King's Palace, red bream, flounder, sole, and cuttlefish came out to give Urashima a hearty welcome. Having expressed their pleasure, these vassals of the Dragon King escorted the fisher-lad to an inner apartment, where the beautiful Princess Otohime and her maidens were seated. The Princess was arrayed in gorgeous garments of red and gold, all the colours of a wave with the sunlight upon it.

This Princess explained that she had taken the form of a tortoise by way of testing his kindness of heart. The test had happily proved successful, and as a reward for his virtue she offered to become his bride in a land where there was eternal youth and ever-lasting summer.

Urashima bashfully accepted the high honour bestowed upon him. He had no sooner spoken than a great company of fishes appeared, robed in long ceremonial garments, their fins supporting great coral trays loaded with rare delicacies. Then the happy couple drank the wedding cup of *saké,* and while they drank, some of the fishes played soft music, others sang, and not a few, with scales of silver and golden tails, stepped out a strange measure on the white sand.

After the festivities were over, Otohime showed her husband all the wonders of her father's palace. The greatest marvel of all was to see a country where all the seasons lingered together. Looking to the east, Urashima saw plum- and cherry-trees in full bloom, with bright-winged butterflies skimming over the blossom, and away in the distance it seemed that the pink petals and butterflies had suddenly been converted into the song of a wondrous nightingale. In the south he saw trees in their summer glory, and heard the gentle note, of the cricket. Looking to the west, the autumn maples made a fire in the branches, so that if Urashima had been other than a humble fisher-lad he might have recalled the following poem:

> 'Fair goddess of the paling Autumn skies,
> Fain would I know how many looms she plies,
> Wherein through skilful tapestry she weaves
> Her fine brocade of fiery maple leaves—
> Since on each hill, with every gust that blows,
> In varied hues her vast embroidery glows?'
>
> Trans. by Clara A. Walsh

It was, indeed, a 'vast embroidery', for when Urashima looked toward the north he saw a great stretch of snow and a mighty pond covered with ice. All the seasons lingered together in that fair country where Nature had yielded to the full her infinite variety of beauty.

After Urashima had been in the Sea King's Palace for three days, and seen many wonderful things, he suddenly remembered his old parents, and felt a strong desire to go and see them. When he went to his wife, and told her of his longing to return home, Otohime began to weep, and tried to persuade him to stop another day. But Urashima refused to be influenced in the matter. 'I must go,' said he, 'but I will leave you only for a day. I will return again, dear wife of mine.'

The Homecoming of Urashima

Then Otohime gave her husband a keepsake in remembrance of their love. It was called the *Tamate-Bako* ('Box of the Jewel Hand'). She explained that he was on no account to open the box, and Urashima, promising to fulfil her wish, said farewell, mounted a large tortoise, and soon found himself in his own country. He looked in vain for his father's home. Not a sign of it was to be seen. The cottage had vanished, only the little stream remained.

Still much perplexed, Urashima questioned a passerby, and he learnt from him that a fisher-lad, named Urashima, had gone to sea three hundred years ago and was drowned, and that his parents, brothers, and their grandchildren had been laid to rest for a long time. Then Urashima suddenly remembered that the country of the Sea King was a divine land, where a day, according to mortal reckoning, was a hundred years.

Urashima's reflections were gloomy in the extreme, for all whom he had loved on earth were dead. Then he heard the murmur of the sea, and recalled the lovely Otohime, as well as the country where the seasons joined hands and made a fourfold pageant of their beauty—the land where trees had emeralds for leaves and rubies for berries, where the fishes wore long robes and sang and danced and played. Louder the sea sounded in Urashima' s ears. Surely Otohime called him? But no path opened out before him, no obliging tortoise appeared on the scene to carry him to where his wife waited for him. 'The box! the box!' said Urashima softly, 'if I open my wife's mysterious gift, it may reveal the way.'

Urashima untied the red silk thread and slowly, fearfully opened the lid of the box. Suddenly there rushed out a little white cloud; it lingered a moment, and then rolled away far over the sea. But a sacred promise had been broken, and Urashima from a handsome youth became old and wrinkled. He staggered forward, his white hair and beard blowing in the wind. He looked out to sea, and then fell dead upon the shore.

From *Myths and Legends of Japan*, by F. Hadland Davis (London: George G. Harrap, 1912).

The Moon

The aboriginal tribes of Australia, for whom all of nature is animate, explain natural phenomena through tales that give every element of nature human characteristics. This etiological myth accounting for the phases of the moon is set in the dream time, the time before phenomena assumed the form or characteristics they now possess and when the spirits of the celestial bodies freely walked among humans. Amusingly, the moon appears as a figure familiar in many cultures: a dull-witted and immature male, who simply does not understand how to court females successfully and is doomed never to learn.

*A*t one time the moon was a man. He was a happy-go-lucky fellow, spending much of his time in whistling and singing and laughing. There were occasions, however, when he would have very despondent moods. The reason of this was that he was unable to win the affection of any one of the beautiful girls with whom he associated. In spite of his merry disposition he failed to attract these girls. They would only laugh and make jokes about him because he was so fat, and very dull-witted. Every night he would travel from place to place, always hoping that he would find a wife. But the tribe that saw him set out on his journey would send abroad a message, 'Look out, the moon is on his way, seeking a wife. Tell the girls.'

One clear, cloudless night the stars were shining brightly, giving tidings of plenty of food, plenty of enjoyment, and plenty of strength to resist the Evil Spirit. The moon was singing merrily as he sauntered along the banks of a river, and he attracted the attention of the two daughters of a widowed mother. Though full of excitement, they sat quietly awaiting his approach. They thought, 'This person who is possessed of such a lovely voice must be handsome!' Presently he came within their range of vision, and lo! they saw a very fat man, with short legs, and arms that were very thin, and a big head with shining eyes. 'What a funny man!' laughed the girls. They ran to the riverside and leaped into a canoe, and began to paddle across the stream. The moon shouted and called out piteously, begging them to take him across the water. In mid-stream the girls stopped paddling, and called to him, 'We have heard of you, and have been told that you are a flirt. All of us have been warned not to have anything to do with you. Swim across the stream.' 'Oh,' said the moon, 'I am hungry and weary; have pity on me. Oh, for the sake of the Pleiades, who have set all girls an example of how to think of others, look at yonder sky. How disappointed they must be to see you treating me thus!'

Then the sisters remembered how all the aboriginal girls were striving to imitate the beautiful characters of those lovely maidens who now shine from the sky to remind them to do good to friend and foe alike. They thought for a while, and, responding to the spirit call of the Pleiades, they rowed back to the bank, and both leaped ashore. Then they invited the moon to go on board the canoe, and he stepped into it. They said, 'We will lend you the canoe, but you must row yourself across the stream.' 'But,' said he, 'I am unable to row.' 'All right,' said the good-hearted girls, 'we will take you across.'

So, plunging into the stream, each grasped a side of the canoe, intending to tow it across. Before they had swum a quarter of the distance the moon began tickling the girls under the arms. They became angry at this proceeding, and told him to cease his rude behaviour. He desisted for a while, but when they had arrived in midstream he once more commenced to tickle them. This time, without more ado, they tipped him into the deep, clear river, and as he sank into the depths they could see his shining face looking at them. The farther he sank the smaller he grew, until only one part of his face could be seen, and then that too gradually diminished, until there was only a small crescent visible. Eventually even that disappeared from view.

The girls went home and told their mother and the whole tribe the story of the flirting moon, and how he had sunk to the bottom of the river. The news was spread all over the country by smoke signals, and when the crow heard it he sent this message throughout the length and breadth of the land:

'The moon will no longer shine constantly. From this time onward you will see him coming out of the Land of Spirits in the west, with only part of his face visible, but increasing in size night after night, until the whole of it is seen. Then he will gradually disappear into the east, and he will be invisible for a season. Then he will appear again as a thin crescent in the west, peeping expectantly, as if ashamed to show his face. Gradually, as he regains confidence, he will show a more ample face. By and by he will look down with a countenance wholly visible, and try with his silvery smile to win the affections of some young girl. In this he will fail, and so he will gradually fade away to hide his disappointment.'

From *Myths and Legends of the Australian Aboriginals,* by W. Ramsay Smith (London: George G. Harrap, [1930]).

LINKS TO OTHER STORIES

Part Seven

It's All Relative
The Trials and Triumphs of Family Life

Relationships between family members figure into the plots of numerous folktales and fairy tales from all cultures. Sometimes these relationships merely precipitate the major action. In such tales as 'The Story of the Three Little Pigs' and 'Molly Whuppie', for example, the mother sow and the girls' parents, respectively, are mentioned merely as instruments for launching the pigs and the girls on their journeys of maturation. In many other tales, however, family relationships are vital to the plot. In stories from all cultures, relationships between mothers or stepmothers and children, fathers and their children, mothers-in-law and married couples, children and their siblings, and husbands and wives are often the focus or cause of conflict. The tales in this section are primarily of this kind. They turn upon the relationships between various family members and the values that those relationships demonstrate.

By far the most prominent family relationships in folktales and fairy tales are those between children and their mothers or stepmothers. Perhaps because these tales need conflict in order to develop interest, the mothers and stepmothers tend to be evil. Good mothers do appear, but in many of the tales they die, providing the opportunity for the entrance of a stepmother who will make both the child's life miserable and the tale's plot interesting. What continuing influence the good mother exerts is through memory and a supernatural presence that is often expressed symbolically. In the Haitian tale 'The Magic Orange Tree', for instance, the good birth mother, like the birth mother in the German 'Aschenputtel', continues her role of caring for her daughter through the agency of the tree growing from her grave. In the Russian tale 'Vasilisa the Beautiful', to cite another example, the birth mother dies, but she continues to assist her daughter by means of the doll that she had given to the girl.

Tales most frequently characterize as evil those mothers who deviate from expectations that maternity is accompanied by the desire to nurture and to protect one's offspring. Culturally specific expectations can, however, also influence the characterization of the evil mother. The mother in the Inuit legend 'The Blind Boy and the Loon', for example, becomes evil when she rebels against a role her culture assigns to females. Seeing her son's great hunting skill as a personal burden because she must turn the product of the hunt into food and clothing, she causes misery and poverty by blinding him. She also shows selfishness by giving her son old fox meat while herself eating the more favoured meat of the bear that her son kills. In other words, she abandons the culturally-determined duties of both a woman and a mother. Her death may seem harsh and cruel to people outside of Inuit culture, but the boy upholds the traditional Inuit values that find it just to restore order by killing those whose selfishness imperils the family or the group.

More prominent than evil birth mothers, however, are evil stepmothers. In fact, in *The Hard Facts of the Grimms' Fairy Tales*, Maria Tatar has said that 'Folklorists would be hard pressed to name a single good stepmother, for in fairy tales the very title "stepmother" pins the badge of iniquity on a figure' (141). Historical factors may play some role in the characterization of stepmothers. In the eighteenth and early nineteenth centuries, for example, European women, especially widows with children of their own, had few resources for survival outside of marriage. Men, because mortality rates among women of child-bearing age were relatively high, frequently needed someone to raise their children. Social and financial need thus compelled people to marry. It is probable that a number of those women would feel something less than maternal affection for the children of the men they married out of economic necessity. The psychoanalytic critic Bruno Bettelheim, however, offers a different explanation for the prominence of evil stepmothers. He argues that fairy tales reflect a psychological process that divides the nurturing and the disciplinary phases of motherhood into two figures. In *The Uses of Enchantment*, he asserts that 'the typical fairy-tale splitting of the mother into a good (usually dead) mother and an evil stepmother serves the child well' (69) because it preserves the good mother while allowing the child to feel angry towards those acts of the mother that the child hates.

This division is apparent in the Haitian tale 'The Magic Orange Tree', which, as we noted above, employs the motif of a tree growing from the mother's grave. The tree is a helper figure, a symbol of the continuing nurturance of the birth mother. Typically, this tale offers no sympathy for or understanding of the stepmother, who may be a woman lashing out because of economic victimization. Rather, the stepmother appears as morally flawed, a mean and cruel woman who violates the most basic duty of maternity, that of feeding one's children. Her selfishness and greed appear when she demands her stepdaughter's oranges. As our headnote to this tale indicates, Haitian tradition decrees that the fruit, which usually would grow from a seed buried with her placenta, belongs solely to the girl; it is her birthright. By trying to seize the oranges, the stepmother is robbing the girl of her right to autonomy and independence. Such a transgression thus deserves the punishment that the good mother, acting through the tree growing from her grave, visits upon the stepmother.

This division of the mother into separate good and evil figures has not, however, always arisen because of what Bettleheim posits as a natural psychological tendency of children. In a number of documented instances, it is the result of deliberate editorial manipulation. 'Snow White', a tale that has, arguably, the most famous and diabolical of wicked stepmothers, was in the first edition of the Grimms' Nursery and Household Tales (1812) about a mother who wanted to destroy her daughter. In the second edition of 1819, the Grimms changed the tale, ostensibly to make it less offensive to middle-class purchasers who would be reading the collection to their children.[1] In their revised version, the mother dies after giving birth, and it is the stepmother who tries to murder Snow White. After detailing the changes that the Grimms made to the tale, John M. Ellis thus criticizes Bettelheim by noting that his theory is 'of somewhat limited relevance to the fairy tales of the Grimms, where the malevolent side of mothers was often faced squarely until the Grimms—not the symbolic imagination of children—tried in a mechanical way to cover it up' (202n2). Maria Tatar, who also notes these changes, concurs, asking, 'What easier way is there to depict maternal abuse of children and at the same time preserve the sanctity of mothers than by turning the evil mother into an alien interloper whose goal is to disturb the harmony of family life?' (1987, 143).

Tatar also seems correct when she says that 'Even when a stepmother stands in for the mother, it has not been difficult for most readers and critics to recognize that "Snow White" is a story about mother-daughter conflict' (1992, 231–2). Bettleheim, focusing primarily on what he perceives as the jealousy of an oedipal, adolescent girl, examines this mother–daughter rivalry and claims that 'The story of Snow White warns of the evil consequences of narcissism for both parent and child' (203). In *The Madwoman in the Attic*, feminist critics Sandra M. Gilbert and Susan Gubar counter that historical conditions gave women no alternatives to such narcissism because women existed in 'a state from which all outward prospects have been removed' (37). They view the tale as enacting a masculine schema, for they note that it has the two females competing for the approval of the King, who is 'the voice of the looking glass, the patriarchal voice of judgment that rules the Queen's—and every woman's—self-evaluation' (38).

The tale thus may use the stepmother's hostility to symbolize problems historically facing aging woman. In a patriarchal culture in which beauty is the one power that women can wield to control their lives, the fading of that beauty might lead a woman to become hostile to the person who is gaining sexual power, the young and developing girl who, in this case at least, is her stepdaughter. Indeed, most interpreters locate the conflict in the stepmother's jealousy and fear of the girl's emerging beauty, the physical sign of the sexuality that will give her more power than the Queen. Gilbert and Gubar, however, go further: 'the Queen and Snow White are in some sense one' (41). For them the key is not the split between phases of motherhood, as with Bettleheim, but the split between what women desire themselves and what men force them to be like and to think that they desire. From this point of view, the tale pits the Queen, who represents the artistic and creative energy of the female, against Snow White, who symbolizes the male constructs of the ideal female: passivity, innocence, and purity. The Queen must kill Snow White because Snow White is the part of her that denies meaningful action to the female. Snow White's survival, therefore, marks the triumph of a patriarchal formulation, or 'framing', of what it means to be feminine.

Like a number of other tales, 'Snow White' amplifies the evil nature of the stepmother by connecting her to witchcraft. The Queen resorts to witchcraft to make the poisoned comb and apple that she uses in her plot to kill Snow White. In 'The Six Swans', the stepmother has learned witchcraft from her mother. Impelled by what may be jealousy of the time that her husband spends with the children he had by his first wife, she sews charms into shirts that she has made and transforms six of his children into swans. In 'Hänsel and Grethel', the connection is more tenuous: the witch, who captures the children and feeds them only so that she can eat them, functions as a diabolic exaggeration of the stepmother, who abandoned the children so that she herself could eat. The parallel between them is strengthened by the fact that both die, possibly at the same time, near the end of the tale.

'The Six Swans' also introduces another stock female villain, the mother-in-law. In folk tales and fairy tales, mothers-in-law tend to poison the trust that good marriages require. In 'East o' the Sun and West o' the Moon', for example, the mother of the lassie makes her daughter doubt her husband, necessitating the quest that will redeem their faith in each other. In 'The Six Swans', the King's 'wicked' mother, who has declared that his wife is not worthy of her son, devises a plot that has her daughter-in-law condemned to death as a cannibal. In these tales, the mother–daughter and mother–son relationships, respectively, reveal another negative side of the mother figure: in both cases the mother essentially does not allow her child to mature as a separate and independent person.[2]

In most traditional tales given to children, the roles of fathers are not as dramatic as those of mother figures. Fathers can, of course, be so egotistical that they become oppressively and unreasonably demanding, as does the father in 'Cap o' Rushes', a tale discussed in the Cinderella section. As we also note in that section, fathers sometimes express incestuous desires for their daughters, but these traditional tales are not normally included in collections for children. For the most part, fathers permit evil deeds simply because they are absent or disengaged. 'The Magic Orange Tree' is typical in this regard: after noting that the father married a cruel woman, it makes no further mention of him.

In some cases, however, fathers become partners with mothers in victimizing their children. In the Thai tale 'Chet Huat Chet Hai (Seven Pot, Seven Jar)', the impoverished father and mother together agree that they must abandon their son because he has a voracious appetite. The father then takes the active role in trying to kill the boy because he does not want him to suffer. The father does not appear as a monster, however, because the tale turns his attempts to kill his son into absurdly comical episodes. Furthermore, the naïve son never resents his father. In fact, he behaves as the ideal dutiful son. Thus, in keeping with traditional Thai values, he honours his parents by taking care of them once he becomes wealthy. The German tale of 'Hänsel and Grethel', in which the parents also decide to abandon their children, blames the father less than the stepmother (who was the birth mother until the fourth edition), presumably because his wife must talk him into the deed. Interestingly, the tale does not fault him for being a weak and ineffective example of a patriarch. In fact, whereas the callous stepmother (or mother) dies, he lives happily, his children returning from the witch's house to share with him their newly acquired wealth.

Good, active fathers do, however, appear in some tales, such as the Scottish legend 'The Smith and the Fairies'. This heroic father is so devoted to his only son that he embarks on an uncanny quest to rescue him from the fairies holding him prisoner. The father's success depends on two traits. First, he has humility to seek wise advice. Secondly, he is brave enough not to lose his composure when he enters the fairies' underground kingdom. His physical success on the quest also enables a later success. His son, freeing himself from the lingering enchantment, joins in the work at his forge and anvil, quintessential symbols of masculine creativity. Using what he remembers of work in the Fairyland, the son is able to craft superb weapons, thus earning wealth and happiness for the pair.

More common than questing fathers, however, are testing fathers. When a father tests his daughter, as does the father in 'Cap o' Rushes', he is usually an egotist demanding excessive displays of affection. When he tests his sons, the more common situation, he is trying to ensure that they are worthy to take over from him. In other words, the task that the father assigns to his sons becomes a test of manhood. Such a test appears in *Simon and the Golden Sword*, a tale discussed in the section on purposeful journeys, in which the sibling jealousy that develops during an inheritance test becomes a sign of unworthiness. The African 'The Three Sons and Their Objects of Power', included in this section, also has three sons embark on a quest at the behest of the father. In this tale, however, none of the sons succeeds in the original goal of the quest, but all three nevertheless contribute to their father's well-being. Here, the rivalry is not enacted within the tale but, as is customary in many areas of Africa, by a discussion among audience members, who participate by advancing the relative merits of each son.

Rivalry among sisters usually involves jealousy because one is more beautiful and has opportunities for a loving relationship involving social advancement. Such rivalry appears in a number of the Cinderella tales, where the rivals are figured as stepsisters,[3] and in 'Beauty and the Beast', in which their own inferior social relationships lead Beauty's jealous sisters to plot against her. When the siblings are male and female, however, loyalty and cooperation are often prominent. In 'The Six Swans' the sister thus displays compassion for and loyalty to her brothers, enduring pain and slander while she tries to restore them to their natural forms. 'Hänsel and Grethel' shows sibling loyalty and respect in a different way. At first, Hänsel is the protector, devising the scheme that saves them when they are abandoned the first time and comforting his sister when his plan fails the second time. Grethel, however, is more than a passive female timidly following her brother's directions. After the witch imprisons Hänsel in a cage, Grethel uses her wit to destroy the witch and liberate him. Both children thus cooperate in ensuring their own survival and in bringing riches to their father.

Many traditional tales about husbands and wives are ribald and thus not appropriate for children. In some cases, however, these tales treat infidelity symbolically, making them perfectly suitable entertainment for children. Such is the case with the French-Canadian 'Jacques the Woodcutter'. Its comical treatment of appetite allows children to see it as a story about food and adults to recognize that it employs eating as a symbol for sex. Significantly, this tale neither mocks the cuckolded husband as a fool nor heaps scorn on the unfaithful wife, as do many tales for adults. Instead, it lightheartedly suggests a traditional notion that marital happiness comes when a husband asserts his authority and has his wife devote her attention to him alone. Failure to assert this kind of authority and failure to control a wife's desires frequently lead to disaster in traditional tales such as 'The Fisherman and His Wife', in which the demanding woman fails to recognize her proper place in both the marriage and the world at large.

Of course, husbands are not always strong or correct. A common enough figure in traditional tales is the wife whose intelligence is the driving force behind her husband's success. 'The Barber's Clever Wife', a story collected in the Punjab region of India during the nineteenth century affords a good example of one such woman. In this tale, the wife overcomes her husband's incompetence because of her superior knowledge of human nature, her powers of observation, and her composure, even when she faces physical danger. A wife with similar qualities appears in the Scottish tale 'The Woman Who Flummoxed the Fairies', but she is not burdened with an incompetent husband. Like the Barber's wife, the wife in this tale is a skillful trickster who succeeds because she knows how to turn the tables on those who would make her a victim. Therefore, it is she who directs her husband when he joins the plot, and it is she who, because she has a kind heart that enables her to understand the desires of the fairies, secures wealth and happiness for her family.

Notes

1. In *The Hard Facts of the Grimms' Fairy Tales*, Maria Tatar postulates that 'As successive editions of the *Nursery and Household Tales* rolled from the presses, Whilhelm Grimm [the author of the revisions] must have become acutely aware of the collection's role as a repository of bedtime stories for children rather than as a source of entertainment for adults. What might have been perfectly acceptable as adult entertainment required considerable modification for children' (37). The Grimms also inserted into their Preface for the second edition the statement that 'In this edition, we have carefully eliminated every phrase not appropriate for children' (217).

2. A similar symbolic meaning may also be seen in Perrault's 'The Sleeping Beauty in the Woods', in which the King's mother seeks to destroy her son's wife and their children because she has ogre blood in her veins. Here, as with tales about stepmothers, however, we must be aware of the possibility of deliberate textual changes. In what may have been at least one of Perrault's sources, the fifth tale of the fifth day in Giambattista Basile's *Pentamerone* (1636), for instance, relationships are significantly different. In that tale, the Prince comes upon an enchanted sleeping beauty named Talia, and he rapes her. She later gives birth to twins. His

wife, not his mother-in-law, is so enraged by this adultery that she plots revenge, serving him what she believes to be the organs of the twins. Perrault, who was probably unwilling to risk offending the court of the Sun King by telling stories of royal adultery, thus transforms a tale about marital strife into one that focuses the reluctance of a woman to allow her child to extend the family through marriage.

3. In psychological terms the figuration of the evil or nasty sibling as a stepsister performs the same function as figuring an evil mother as a stepmother: it allows the child the luxury of indulging in an intense dislike of a sibling as an interloper while yet preserving the ideal of a loving relationship with an actual sibling.

Works Cited

Bettleheim, Bruno. 1976. 'Cinderella', *The Uses of Enchantment*. New York: Alfred A. Knopf.

Ellis, John M. 1983. *One Fairy Story Too Many: The Brothers Grimm and Their Tales*. Chicago and London: University of Chicago Press.

Gilbert, Sandra M., and Susan Gubar. 1979. *The Madwoman in the Attic: The Woman Writer and the Nineteenth-Century Literary Imagination*. New Haven and London: Yale University Press.

Tatar, Maria. 1987. *The Hard Facts of the Grimms' Fairy Tales*. Princeton, NJ: Princeton University Press.

———. 1992. *Off with Their Heads! Fairy Tales and the Culture of Childhood*. Princeton, NJ: Princeton University Press.

The Blind Boy and the Loon

Collected from the Inuit group known to anthropologists as the Copper Eskimos, who inhabit primarily the coastal regions of what is now Nunavat, this tale—variants of which are also told by various West Coast tribes—dramatizes the importance of gender roles in survival. Males had to hunt in order to provide the materials for food, clothing, and fuel; females had to prepare the animals that the males caught. Both sets of tasks were arduous and time-consuming, and they required significant degrees of skill to perform adequately. When the deceitful mother rebels against the demands of her role, she imperils the lives of her family. As a result, the Inuit would regard her death not as revenge but as justice. It is appropriate that the boy receives help from a loon, because that bird has been frequently associated with shamans, the healers of the Inuit people.

A woman lived with her son and daughter in a far away land. The son, although young in years, was already a skillful hunter and the four storage platforms built around the igloo were always filled with meat. His success at hunting was so great that the family never wanted for anything.

The young hunter's sister loved him dearly but his mother gradually grew tired of his hunting activities. Each time her son returned home with some game she would have to work hard at cleaning and skinning the animals and in preparing the meat for storage. As time went on the woman wished more and more to be able to rest but as long as her son continued to hunt this was not possible. Eventually her weariness turned to hatred.

From Maurice Metayer, trans., *Tales from the Igloo*. Illustrated by Agnes Nanogak. (Edmonton, AB: Hurtig, 1972), 94.

One day, while her son was sleeping, the woman took a piece of dirty blubber and rubbed it on his eyes, wishing as she did so that he would become blind. When the young man awoke his eyesight was gone. Try as he might he could see nothing but a dim whiteness.

From that day on increasing misery became the lot of the family. The son could do nothing but sit on his bed. His mother tried to provide food for the family by trapping foxes and hunting ptarmigan and ground squirrels. Yet when food was available the woman refused to give her son anything to eat or drink but the worst parts of the meat and some foul drinking water brought from the lake. Throughout the spring and summer the three people lived in this manner.

One day shortly after the arrival of winter, the young hunter heard steps on the snow. It was a polar bear trying to get into the igloo through the thin ice window. Asking for his bow, he told his mother to aim the arrow while he pulled back the string. When all was in readiness the son let fly the arrow. Hearing the sound of the arrow as it thudded into the flesh of the bear, the son was confident that the kill had been made.

'I got him!' he cried.

'No,' retorted his mother, 'you merely struck an old piece of hide.'

Shortly thereafter the smell of bear meat boiling in the cooking pot filled the igloo. The son said nothing but kept wondering why his mother had lied to him.

When the meat was cooked the woman fed her daughter and herself. To her son, she gave some old fox meat. It was only when she had left the igloo to get water from the lake that the young hunter was brought some bear meat by his sister.

Four long years went by while the son remained blind. Then one night, as the fluttering of wings and the cries of the birds announced the coming of spring, the son heard the call of the red-throated loon. As had been his habit during his blindness he began to crawl on his hands and knees to the lake where he knew the loon would be found.

When he arrived at the water's edge the bird came close to him and said, 'Your mother made you blind by rubbing dirt into your eyes while you slept. If you wish, I can wash your eyes for you. Lie flat on my back and hold me by my neck. I shall carry you.'

The son doubted that such a small bird would be able to perform such a feat, but the loon reassured him.

'Don't think those thoughts. Climb onto my back. I am going to dive with you into deep water. When you begin to lose your breath shake your body to signal me.'

The young man did as he was told and down into the lake dove the loon with the hunter on his back. As they descended into the water the son could feel the body of the loon growing larger and larger and between his hands the neck seemed to be swelling. When he could hold his breath no longer he shook his body as he had been instructed and the loon brought him up to the surface.

'What can you see?' the loon asked.

'I can see nothing but a great light,' replied the son.

'I shall take you down into the water once more,' said the loon. 'When you begin to choke, shake your body a little.'

This time the dive lasted a long time but when they finally surfaced the young man could see clearly. He could distinguish the smallest rocks on the mountains far away. He described what he could see to the loon.

'My blindness is gone! My sight is sharper than before!'

'Your eyesight is too sharp for your own good,' the loon told him. 'Come down with me once more and your sight will be restored as it was before your blindness.'

And it was so. When the young man came out of the water for the last time his eyesight was as it had been. Now the hunter could see the loon clearly and he realized that the bird was as large as a kayak.

When they had reached the lake shore the son asked the loon what he could give to him in return for his kindness.

The loon replied, 'I do not want anything for myself other than a few fishes. Put some in the lake for me once in a while. This is the only food that I look for.'

The son agreed and proceeded to return to his home. He was painfully surprised to see the wretched conditions in which he had been forced to live while he was blind. The skins he had used to sleep in were filthy with dirt and bugs. His drinking water and food were crawling with lice. Nevertheless he sat down in the corner and waited for his mother to awaken.

When his mother awoke the young hunter asked for food and drink. 'I am hungry and thirsty. First bring me something to drink.'

His mother did as she was told but the water she brought was so dirty that her son handed the cup back to her saying, 'I will not touch such filth!'

'So you can see, my son,' said the woman. She went then to fetch some clean food and water.

In time the young hunter was his old self again and was able to resume his successful hunting trips as before. A year went by during which time the storage platforms were once more filled with an abundance of game.

The following spring the hunter made ready to go whale hunting. He put a new skin cover on his whale boat, made lines, harpoons and spears. When the sea was free of ice he launched his boat and took his mother with him in search of whales.

'Mind the helm,' he told her. 'I shall look after the harpooning.'

Here and there they saw a few whales blowing but the young hunter was waiting until they found a big one close to their boat. Eventually he called out to his mother who, not knowing what her son was about to do, came to assist him. He threw his harpoon, making certain that its head had caught in the flesh of the whale and then quickly tied the other end of the line to his mother's wrist and threw her overboard.

Caught as she was the woman was dragged through the water, bobbing up and down in the waves. She cried out and reproached her son saying, 'When you were young I gave you my breast to suckle. I fed you and kept you clean. And now you do this to me!'

Finally she disappeared from sight. For years to come hunters claimed that they saw her in the waves and heard her song of despair as it was carried far and wide by the winds.

From *Tales from the Igloo*, edited and translated by Maurice Metayer (Edmonton, AB: Hurtig, 1972).

Snow White

The major scenes of conflict in 'Snow White' represent a battle between the generations. The deadly hostility of Snow White's stepmother reflects her failure to accept that her beauty must fade, and with it, any power that beauty has given her. (This rivalry was more pointed in the first edition of the *Household Tales* because, as we noted in the introduction to this section, it was between a birth mother and her child.) As a tale about the transformative effects of time, 'Snow White' also shows positive changes with the maturation of a girl into a woman. That transformation is, however, fraught with difficulties. Forgetting the strict warnings the dwarfs have given her, a sign of her immaturity, she fails to control her impulses and therefore succumbs to the disguised stepmother's temptations, each of which—the stay-laces, the comb, and the apple—is associated with female beauty or sexuality. In essence, she becomes a victim of her own vanity. The conclusion is full of poetic justice. The girl who suffered because of an older woman's unbridled hatred, awakens from her long death-like sleep in a life of mature love. The jealous queen, on the other hand, endures a violent form of justice that might have come straight from her own destructive imagination.

Once upon a time in the middle of winter, when the flakes of snow were falling like feathers from the sky, a queen sat at a window sewing, and the frame of the window was made of black ebony. And whilst she was sewing and looking out of the window at the snow, she pricked her finger with the needle, and three drops of blood fell upon the snow. And the red looked pretty upon the white snow, and she thought to herself, 'Would that I had a child as white as snow, as red as blood, and as black as the wood of the window-frame.'

Soon after that she had a little daughter, who was as white as snow, and as red as blood, and her hair was as black as ebony; and she was therefore called Little Snow-white. And when the child was born, the Queen died.

After a year had passed the King took to himself another wife. She was a beautiful woman, but proud and haughty, and she could not bear that anyone else should surpass her in beauty. She had a wonderful looking-glass, and when she stood in front of it and looked at herself in it, and said—

'Looking-glass, Looking-glass, on the wall,
Who in this land is the fairest of all?'

the looking-glass answered—

'Thou, O Queen, art the fairest of all!'

Then she was satisfied, for she knew that the looking-glass spoke the truth.

But Snow-white was growing up, and grew more and more beautiful; and when she was seven years old she was as beautiful as the day, and more beautiful than the Queen herself. And once when the Queen asked her looking-glass—

'Looking-glass, Looking-glass, on the wall,
Who in this land is the fairest of all?'

it answered—

'Thou art fairer than all who are here, Lady Queen.
But more beautiful still is Snow-white, as I ween.'

Then the Queen was shocked, and turned yellow and green with envy. From that hour, whenever she looked at Snow-white, her heart heaved in her breast, she hated the girl so much.

And envy and pride grew higher and higher in her heart like a weed, so that she had no peace day or night. She called a huntsman, and said, 'Take the child away into the forest; I will no longer have her in my sight. Kill her, and bring me back her heart as a token.' The huntsman obeyed, and took her away; but when he had drawn his knife, and was about to pierce Snow-white's innocent heart, she began to weep, and said, 'Ah, dear huntsman, leave me my life! I will run away into the wild forest, and never come home again.'

And as she was so beautiful the huntsman had pity on her and said, 'Run away, then, you poor child.' 'The wild beasts will soon have devoured you,' thought he, and yet it seemed as if a stone had been rolled from his heart since it was no longer needful for him to kill her. And as a young boar just then came running by he stabbed it, and cut out its heart and took it to the Queen as a proof that the child was dead. The cook had to salt this, and the wicked Queen ate it, and thought she had eaten the heart of Snow-white.

But now the poor child was all alone in the great forest, and so terrified that she looked at every leaf of every tree, and did not know what to do. Then she began to run, and ran over sharp stones and through thorns, and the wild beasts ran past her, but did her no harm.

She ran as long as her feet would go until it was almost evening; then she saw a little cottage and went into it to rest herself. Everything in the cottage was small, but neater and cleaner than can be told. There was a table on which was a white cover, and seven little plates, and on each plate a little spoon; moreover, there were seven little knives and forks, and seven little mugs. Against the wall stood seven little beds side by side, and covered with snow-white counterpanes.

Little Snow-white was so hungry and thirsty that she ate some vegetables and bread from each plate and drank a drop of wine out of each mug, for she did not wish to take all from one only. Then, as she was so tired, she laid herself down on one of the little beds, but none of them suited her; one was too long, another too short, but at last she found that the seventh one was right, and so she remained in it, said a prayer and went to sleep.

When it was quite dark the owners of the cottage came back; they were seven dwarfs who dug and delved in the mountains for ore. They lit their seven candles, and as it was now light within the cottage they saw that some one had been there, for everything was not in the same order in which they had left it.

The first said, 'Who has been sitting on my chair?'

The second, 'Who has been eating off my plate?'

The third, 'Who has been taking some of my bread?'

The fourth, 'Who has been eating my vegetables?'

The fifth, 'Who has been using my fork?'

The sixth, 'Who has been cutting with my knife?'

The seventh, 'Who has been drinking out of my mug?'

Then the first looked round and saw that there was a little hole on his bed, and he said, 'Who has been getting into my bed?' The others came up and each called out, 'Somebody has been lying in my bed too.' But the seventh when he looked at his bed saw little Snow-white, who was lying asleep therein. And he called the others, who came running up, and they cried out with astonishment, and brought their seven little candles and let the light fall on little Snow-white. 'Oh, heavens! oh, heavens!' cried they, 'what a lovely child!' and they were so glad that they did not wake her up, but let her sleep on in the bed. And the seventh dwarf slept with his companions, one hour with each, and so got through the night.

When it was morning little Snow-white awoke, and was frightened when she saw the seven dwarfs. But they were friendly and asked her what her name was. 'My name is Snow-white,' she answered. 'How have you come to our house?' said the dwarfs. Then she told them that her stepmother had wished to have her killed, but that the huntsman had spared her life, and that she had run for the whole day, until at last she had found their dwelling. The dwarfs said, 'If you will take care of our house, cook, make the beds, wash, sew, and knit, and if you will keep everything neat and clean, you can stay with us and you shall want for nothing.' 'Yes,' said Snow-white, 'with all my heart,' and she stayed with them. She kept the house in order for them; in the mornings they went to the mountains and looked for copper and gold, in the evenings they came back, and then their supper had to be ready. The girl was alone the whole day, so the good dwarfs warned her and said, 'Beware of your stepmother, she will soon know that you are here; be sure to let no one come in.'

But the Queen, believing that she had eaten Snow-white's heart, could not but think that she was again the first and most beautiful of all; and she went to her looking-glass and said—

> 'Looking-glass, Looking-glass, on the wall,
> Who in this land is the fairest of all?'

and the glass answered—

> 'Oh, Queen, thou art fairest of all I see,
> But over the hills, where the seven dwarfs dwell,
> Snow-white is still alive and well,
> And none is so fair as she.'

Then she was astounded, for she knew that the looking-glass never spoke falsely, and she knew that the huntsman had betrayed her, and that little Snow-white was still alive.

And so she thought and thought again how she might kill her, for so long as she was not the fairest in the whole land, envy let her have no rest. And when she had at last thought of something to do, she painted her face, and dressed herself like an old pedler-woman, and no one could have known her. In this disguise she went over the seven mountains to the seven dwarfs, and knocked at the door and cried, 'Pretty things to sell, very cheap, very cheap.' Little Snow-white looked out of the window and called out, 'Good-day, my good woman, what have you to sell?' 'Good things, pretty things,' she answered; 'stay-laces of all colours,' and she pulled out one which was woven of bright-coloured silk. 'I may let the worthy old woman in,' thought Snow-white, and she unbolted the door and bought the pretty laces. 'Child,' said the old woman, 'what a fright you look; come, I will lace you properly for once.' Snow-white had no suspicion, but stood before her, and let herself be laced with the new laces. But the old woman laced so quickly and laced so tightly that Snow-white lost her breath and fell down as if dead. 'Now I am the most beautiful,' said the Queen to herself, and ran away.

Not long afterwards, in the evening, the seven dwarfs came home, but how shocked they were when they saw their dear little Snow-white lying on the ground, and that she neither stirred nor moved, and seemed to be dead. They lifted her up, and, as they saw that she was laced too tightly, they cut the laces; then she began to breathe a little, and after a while came to life again. When the dwarfs heard what had happened they said, 'The old pedler-woman was no one else than the wicked Queen; take care and let no one come in when we are not with you.'

But the wicked woman when she had reached home went in front of the glass and asked—

> 'Looking-glass, Looking-glass, on the wall,
> Who in this land is the fairest of all?'

and it answered as before—

> 'Oh, Queen, thou art fairest of all I see,
> But over the hills, where the seven dwarfs dwell,
> Snow-white is still alive and well,
> And none is so fair as she.'

When she heard that, all her blood rushed to her heart with fear, for she saw plainly that little Snow-white was again alive. 'But now,' she said, 'I will think of something that shall put an end to you,' and by the help of witchcraft, which she understood, she made a poisonous comb. Then she disguised herself and took the shape of another old woman. So she went over the seven mountains to the seven dwarfs, knocked at the door, and cried, 'Good things to sell, cheap, cheap!' Little Snow-white looked out and said, 'Go away; I cannot let anyone come in.' 'I suppose you can look,' said the old woman, and pulled the poisonous comb out and held it up. It pleased the girl so well that she let herself be beguiled, and opened the door. When they had made a bargain the old woman said, ' Now I will comb you properly for once.' Poor little Snow-white had no suspicion, and let the old woman do as she pleased, but hardly had she put the comb in her hair than the poison in it took effect, and the girl fell down senseless. 'You paragon of beauty,' said the wicked woman, 'you are done for now,' and she went away.

But fortunately it was almost evening, when the seven dwarfs came home. When they saw Snow-white lying as if dead upon the ground they at once suspected the stepmother, and they looked and found the poisoned comb. Scarcely had they taken it out when Snow-white came to herself, and told them what had happened. Then they warned her once more to be upon her guard and to open the door to no one.

The Queen, at home, went in front of the glass and said—

> 'Looking-glass, Looking-glass, on the wall,
> Who in this land is the fairest of all?'

then it answered as before—

> 'Oh, Queen, thou art fairest of all I see,
> But over the hills, where the seven dwarfs dwell,
> Snow-white is still alive and well,
> And none is so fair as she.'

When she heard the glass speak thus she trembled and shook with rage. 'Snow-white shall die,' she cried, 'even if it costs me my life!'

Thereupon she went into a quite secret, lonely room, where no one ever came, and there she made a very poisonous apple. Outside it looked pretty, white with a red cheek, so that every one who saw it longed for it; but whoever ate a piece of it must surely die.

When the apple was ready she painted her face, and dressed herself up as a country-woman, and so she went over the seven mountains to the seven dwarfs. She knocked at the door. Snow-white put her head out of the window and said, 'I cannot let anyone in; the seven dwarfs have forbidden me.' 'It is all the same to me,' answered the woman, 'I shall soon get rid of my apples. There, I will give you one.'

'No,' said Snow-white, 'I dare not take anything.' 'Are you afraid of poison?' said the old woman; 'look, I will cut the apple in two pieces; you eat the red cheek, and I will eat the white.' The apple was so cunningly made that only the red cheek was poisoned. Snow-white longed for the fine apple, and when she saw that the woman ate part of it she could resist no longer, and stretched out her hand and took the poisonous half. But hardly had she a bit of it in her mouth than she fell down dead. Then the Queen looked at her with a dreadful look, and laughed aloud and said, 'White as snow, red as blood, black as ebony-wood! this time the dwarfs cannot wake you up again.'

And when she asked of the Looking-glass at home—

> 'Looking-glass, Looking-glass, on the wall,
> Who in this land is the fairest of all?'

it answered at last—

> 'Oh, Queen, in this land thou art fairest of all.'

Then her envious heart had rest, so far as an envious heart can have rest.

The dwarfs, when they came home in the evening, found Snow-white lying upon the ground; she breathed no longer and was dead. They lifted her up, looked to see whether they could find anything poisonous, unlaced her, combed her hair, washed her with water and wine, but it was all of no use; the poor child was dead, and remained dead. They laid her upon a bier, and all seven of them sat round it and wept for her, and wept three days long.

Then they were going to bury her, but she still looked as if she were living, and still had her pretty red cheeks. They said, 'We could not bury her in the dark ground,' and they had a transparent coffin of glass made, so that she could be seen from all sides, and they laid her in it, and wrote her name upon it in golden letters, and that she was a king's daughter. Then they put the coffin out upon the mountain, and one of them always stayed by it and watched it. And birds came too, and wept for Snow-white; first an owl, then a raven, and last a dove.

And now Snow-white lay a long, long time in the coffin, and she did not change, but looked as if she were asleep; for she was as white as snow, as red as blood, and her hair was as black as ebony.

It happened, however, that a king's son came into the forest, and went to the dwarfs' house to spend the night. He saw the coffin on the mountain, and the beautiful Snow-white within it, and read what was written upon it in golden letters. Then he said to the dwarfs, 'Let me have the coffin, I will give you whatever you want for it.' But the dwarfs answered, 'We will not part with it for all the gold in the world.' Then he said,' Let me have it as a gift, for I cannot live without seeing Snow-white. I will honour and prize her as my dearest possession.' As he spoke in this way the good dwarfs took pity upon him, and gave him the coffin.

And now the King's son had it carried away by his servants on their shoulders. And it happened that they stumbled over a tree-stump, and with the shock the poisonous piece of apple which Snow-white had bitten off came out of her throat. And before long she opened her eyes, lifted up the lid of the coffin, sat up, and was once more alive. 'Oh, heavens, where am I?' she cried. The King's son, full of joy, said, 'You are with me,' and told her what had happened, and said, 'I love you more than everything in the world; come with me to my father's palace, you shall be my wife.'

And Snow-white was willing, and went with him, and their wedding was held with great show and splendour. But Snow-white's wicked step-mother was also bidden to the feast. When she had arrayed herself in beautiful clothes she went before the Looking-glass, and said—

> 'Looking-glass, Looking-glass, on the wall,
> Who in this land is the fairest of all?'

the glass answered—

> 'Oh, Queen, of all here the fairest art thou,
> But the young Queen is fairer by far as I trow.'

Then the wicked woman uttered a curse, and was so wretched, so utterly wretched, that she knew not what to do. At first she would not go to the wedding at all, but she had no peace, and must go to see the young Queen. And when she went in she knew Snow-white; and she stood still with rage and fear, and could not stir. But iron slippers had already been put upon the fire, and they were brought in with tongs, and set before her. Then she was forced to put on the red-hot shoes, and dance until she dropped down dead.

From *Grimm's Household Tales*, Vol. 1, translated by Margaret Hunt (London: George Bell and Sons, 1884).

The Magic Orange Tree

Diane Wolkstein has written that storytelling in rural Haiti is a communal activity. The process begins with a potential storyteller offering a tale by calling out, 'Cric?' If the audience wishes to hear the story, they answer, 'Crac!' The story then proceeds with audience members, both adults and children, actively participating. In the case of 'The Magic Orange Tree', audience members join in by singing the songs. Wolkenstein also explains that the central image in this tale may have developed from the common Haitian practice of burying a baby's dried umbilical cord and a fruit pit; the tree that develops from this planting becomes the property of the child. Wolkenstein further notes 'Trees in Haiti are thus thought to protect children and are sometimes referred to as the guardian angel of the child' (14). The tree certainly has this protective role in 'The Magic Orange Tree', but the innocent girl must also employ her wits to survive the oppression of her selfish and evil stepmother.

CRIC? CRAC!

There was once a girl whose mother died when she was born. Her father waited for some time to remarry, but when he did, he married a woman who was both mean and cruel. She was so mean there were some days she would not give the girl anything at all to eat. The girl was often hungry.

One day the girl came from school and saw on the table three round ripe oranges. *Hmmmm.* They smelled good. The girl looked around her. No one was there. She took one orange, peeled it, and ate it. *Hmmm-mmm.* It was good. She took a second orange and ate it. She ate the third orange. Oh–oh, she was happy. But soon her stepmother came home.

'Who has taken the oranges I left on the table?' she said. 'Whoever has done so had better say their prayers now, for they will not be able to say them later.'

The girl was so frightened she ran from the house. She ran through the woods until she came to her own mother's grave. All night she cried and prayed to her mother to help her. Finally she fell asleep.

In the morning the sun woke her, and as she rose to her feet something dropped from her skirt onto the ground. What was it? It was an orange pit. And the moment it entered the earth a green leaf sprouted from it. The girl watched, amazed. She knelt down and sang:

'Orange tree,
Grow and grow and grow.
Orange tree, orange tree.
Grow and grow and grow,
Orange tree.
Stepmother is not real mother,
Orange tree.'

The orange tree grew. It grew to the size of the girl. The girl sang:

'Orange tree,
Branch and branch and branch.
Orange tree, orange tree,
Branch and branch and branch,
Orange tree.
Stepmother is not real mother,
Orange tree.'

And many twisting, turning, curving branches appeared on the tree. Then the girl sang:

'Orange tree,
Flower and flower and flower.
Orange tree, orange tree,
Flower and flower and flower,
Orange tree.
Stepmother is not real mother,
Orange tree.'

From Diane Wolkstein, *The Magic Orange Tree and Other Haitian Folktales*. Illustrated by Elsa Henriquez. (New York: Alfred A. Knopf, 1978), 19.

Beautiful white blossoms covered the tree. After a time they began to fade, and small green buds appeared where the flowers had been. The girl sang:

> 'Orange tree,
> Ripen and ripen and ripen
> Orange tree, orange tree,

> Ripen and ripen and ripen,
> Orange tree.
> Stepmother is not real mother.
> Orange tree.'

The oranges ripened, and the whole tree was filled with golden oranges. The girl was so delighted she danced around and around the tree, singing:

> 'Orange tree,
> Grow and grow and grow.
> Orange tree, orange tree,
> Grow and grow and grow,
> Orange tree.
> Stepmother is not real mother,
> Orange tree.'

But then when she looked, she saw the orange tree had grown up to the sky, far beyond her reach. What was she to do? Oh she was a clever girl. She sang:

> 'Orange tree,
> Lower and lower and lower.
> Orange tree, orange tree,
> Lower and lower and lower,
> Orange tree.
> Stepmother is not real mother,
> Orange tree.'

When the orange tree came down to her height, she filled her arms with oranges and returned home.

The moment the stepmother saw the gold oranges in the girl's arms, she seized them and began to eat them. Soon she had finished them all.

'Tell me, my sweet,' she said to the girl, 'where have you found such delicious oranges?'

The girl hesitated. She did not want to tell. The stepmother seized the girl's wrist and began to twist it.

'Tell me!' she ordered.

The girl led her stepmother through the woods to the orange tree. You remember the girl was very clever? Well, as soon as the girl came to the tree, she sang:

> 'Orange tree,
> Grow and grow and grow.
> Orange tree, orange tree,
> Grow and grow and grow,
> Orange tree.
> Stepmother is not real mother,
> Orange tree.'

And the orange tree grew up to the sky. What was the stepmother to do then? She began to plead and beg.

'Please,' she said. 'You shall be my own dear child. You may always have as much as you want to eat. Tell the tree to come down and *you* shall pick the oranges for me.' So the girl quietly sang:

> 'Orange tree,
> Lower and lower and lower.
> Orange tree, orange tree,
> Lower and lower and lower,
> Orange tree.
> Stepmother is not real mother,
> Orange tree.'

The tree began to lower. When it came to the height of the stepmother, she leapt on it and began to climb so quickly you might have thought she was the daughter of an ape. And as she climbed from branch to branch, she ate every orange. The girl saw that there would soon be no oranges left. What would happen to her then? The girl sang:

> 'Orange tree,
> Grow and grow and grow.
> Orange tree, orange tree,
> Grow and grow and grow,
> Orange tree.
> Stepmother is not real mother,
> Orange tree.'

The orange tree grew and grew and grew and grew. 'Help!' cried the stepmother as she rose into the sky. 'H-E-E-lp. . . .'

The girl cried: *'Break! Orange tree, Break!'*

The orange tree broke into a thousand pieces . . . and the stepmother as well.

Then the girl searched among the branches until she found . . . a tiny orange pit. She carefully planted it in the earth. Softly she sang:

> 'Orange tree,
> Grow and grow and grow.
> Orange tree, orange tree,
> Grow and grow and grow,
> Orange tree.
> Stepmother is not real mother,
> Orange tree.'

The orange tree grew to the height of the girl. She picked some oranges and took them to market to sell. They were so sweet the people bought all her oranges.

Every Saturday she is at the marketplace selling her oranges. Last Saturday, I went to see her and asked her if she would give me a free orange. 'What?' she cried. 'After all I've been through!' And she gave me such a kick in the pants that that's how I got here today, to tell you the story—'The Magic Orange Tree.'

From *The Magic Orange Tree and Other Haitian Folktales*, by Diane Wolkstein (New York: Alfred A. Knopf, 1978).

The Six Swans

'The Six Swans' is unusual in portraying both an evil stepmother and an evil mother-in-law. Stereotypically, both of these women are filled with unwarranted and unnatural hatred, and both seek to destroy the innocent. In the first instance, the stepmother— who has knowledge of witchcraft from her mother—transforms her husband's sons into swans. In the second, the mother-in-law falsely accuses the sister of cannibalism. Opposing these hate-filled women is the girl, whose unwavering loyalty to her siblings enables her ultimate triumph over the evil older women. By transforming the swans into humans again, the girl restores the number of siblings to seven, a number associated with wholeness and completion (seven days for the creation of the world in the Bible, seven seas, seven ancient wonders, seven ages of man). Her success, which comes only because she was willing to endure great suffering while she knitted the shirts from starwort, testifies to the power of love.

Once upon a time, a certain King was hunting in a great forest, and he chased a wild beast so eagerly that none of his attendants could follow him. When evening drew near he stopped and looked around him, and then he saw that he had lost his way. He sought a way out, but could find none. Then he perceived an aged woman with a head which nodded perpetually, who came towards him, but she was a witch. 'Good woman,' said he to her, 'Can you not show me the way through the forest?' 'Oh, yes, Lord King,' she answered, 'that I certainly can, but on one condition, and if you do not fulfil that, you will never get out of the forest, and will die of hunger in it.'

'What kind of condition is it?' asked the King.

'I have a daughter,' said the old woman, 'who is as beautiful as anyone in the world, and well deserves to be your consort, and if you will make her your Queen, I will show you the way out of the forest.' In the anguish his heart the King consented, and the old woman led to her little hut, where her daughter was sitting by the fire. She received the King as if she had been expecting him, and he saw that she was very beautiful, but still she did not please him, and he could not look at her without secret horror. After he had taken the maiden up on his horse, the old woman showed him the way, and the King reached his royal palace again, where the wedding was celebrated.

The King had already been married once, and had by his first wife, seven children, six boys and a girl, whom he loved better than anything else in the world. As he now feared that the stepmother might not treat them well, and even do them some injury, he took them to a lonely castle which stood in the midst of a forest. It lay so concealed, and the way was so difficult to find, that he himself would not have found it, if a wise woman had not given him a ball of yarn with wonderful properties. When he threw it down before him, it unrolled itself and showed him his path. The King, however, went so frequently away to his dear children that the Queen observed his absence; she was curious and wanted to know what he did when he was quite alone in the forest. She gave a great deal of money to his servants, and they betrayed the secret to her, and told her likewise of the ball which alone could point out the way. And now she knew no rest until she had learnt where the King kept the ball of yarn, and then she made little shirts of white silk, and as she had learnt the art of witchcraft from her mother, she sewed a charm inside them. And once when the King had ridden forth to hunt, she took the little shirts and went into the forest, and the ball showed her the way. The children, who saw from a distance that some one was approaching, thought that their dear father was coming to them, and full of joy, ran to meet him. Then she threw one of the little shirts over each of them, and no sooner had the shirts touched their bodies than they were changed into swans, and flew away over the forest. The Queen went home quite delighted, and thought she had got rid of her step-children, but the girl had not run out with her brothers, and the Queen knew nothing about her. Next day the King went to visit his children, but he found no one but the little girl. 'Where are thy brothers?' asked the King. 'Alas, dear father,' she answered, 'they have gone away and left me alone!' and she told him that she had seen from her little window how her brothers had flown away over the forest in the shape of swans, and she showed him the feathers, which they had let fall in the courtyard, and which she had picked up. The King mourned, but he did not think that the Queen had done this wicked deed, and as he feared that the girl would also be stolen away from him, he wanted to take her away with him. But she was afraid of her stepmother, and entreated the King to let her stay just this one night more in the forest castle.

The poor girl thought, 'I can no longer stay here. I will go and seek my brothers.' And when night came, she ran away, and went straight into the forest. She walked the whole night long, and next day also without stopping, until she could go no farther for weariness. Then she saw a forest-hut, and went into it, and found a room with six little beds, but she did not venture to get into one of them, but crept under one, and lay down on the hard ground, intending to pass the night there. Just before sunset, however, she heard a rustling, and saw six swans come flying in at the window. They alighted on the ground and blew at each other, and blew all the feathers off, and their swan's skins stripped off like a shirt. Then the maiden looked at them and recognized her brothers, was glad and crept forth from beneath the bed. The brothers were not less delighted to see their little sister, but their joy was of short duration. 'Here canst thou not abide,' they said to her. 'This is a shelter for robbers, if they come home and find thee, they will kill thee.' 'But can you not protect me?' asked the little sister. 'No,' they replied, 'only for one quarter of an hour each evening can we lay aside our swan's skins and have during that time our human form; after that, we are once more turned into swans.' The little sister wept and said, 'Can you not be set free?' 'Alas, no,' they answered, ' the conditions are too hard! For six years thou mayst neither speak nor laugh, and in that time thou must sew together six little shirts of starwort for us. And if one single word falls from thy lips, all thy work will be lost.' And when the brothers had said this, the quarter of an hour was over, and they flew out of the window again as swans.

The maiden, however, firmly resolved to deliver her brothers, even if it should cost her her life. She left the hut, went into the midst of the forest, seated herself on a tree, and there passed the night. Next morning she went out and gathered starwort and began to sew. She could not speak to anyone, and she had no inclination to laugh; she sat there and looked at nothing but her work. When she had already spent a long time there it came to pass that the King of the country was hunting in the forest, and his huntsmen came to the tree on which the maiden was sitting. They called to her and said, 'Who art thou?' But she made no answer. 'Come down to us,' said they. 'We will not do thee any harm.' She only shook her head. As they pressed her further with questions she threw her golden necklace down to them, and thought to content them thus. They, however, did not cease, and then she threw her girdle down to them, and as this also was to no purpose, her garters, and by degrees everything that she had on that she could do without until she had nothing left but her shift.

The huntsmen, however, did not let themselves be turned aside by that, but climbed the tree and fetched the maiden down and led her before the King. The King asked, 'Who art thou? What art thou doing on the tree?' But she did not answer. He put the question in every language that he knew, but she remained as mute as a fish. As she was beautiful, the King's heart was touched, and he was smitten with a great love for her. He put his mantle on her, took her before him on his horse, and carried her to his castle. Then he caused her to be dressed in rich garments, and she shone in her beauty like bright daylight, but no word could be drawn from her. He placed her by his side at table, and her modest bearing and courtesy pleased him so much that he said, 'She is the one whom I wish to marry, and no other woman in the world.' And after some days he united himself to her.

The King, however, had a wicked mother who was dissatisfied with this marriage and spoke ill of the young Queen. 'Who knows,' said she, 'from whence the creature who can't speak, comes? She is not worthy of a king!' After a year had passed, when the Queen brought her first child into the world, the old woman took it away from her, and smeared her mouth with blood as she slept. Then she went to the King and accused the Queen of being a man-eater. The King would not believe it, and would not suffer anyone to do her any injury. She, however, sat continually sewing at the shirts, and cared for nothing else. The next time, when she again bore a beautiful boy, the false mother-in-law used the same treachery, but the King could not bring himself to give credit to her words. He said, 'She is too pious and good to do anything of that kind; if she were not dumb, and could defend herself, her innocence would come to light.' But when the old woman stole away the newly-born child for the third time, and accused the Queen, who did not utter one word of defense, the King could do no otherwise than deliver her over to justice, and she was sentenced to suffer death by fire.

When the day came for the sentence to be executed, it was the last day of the six years during which she was not to speak or laugh, and she had delivered her dear brothers from the power of the enchantment. The six shirts were ready, only the left sleeve of the sixth was wanting. When, therefore, she was led to the stake, she laid the shirts on her arm, and when she stood on high and the fire was just going to be lighted, she looked around and six swans came flying through the air towards her. Then she saw that her deliverance was near, and her heart leapt with joy. The swans swept towards her and sank down so that she could throw the shirts over them, and as they were touched by them, their swan's skins fell off, and her brothers stood in their own bodily form before her, and were vigorous and handsome. The youngest only lacked his left arm, and had in the place of it a swan's wing on his shoulder. They embraced and kissed each other, and the Queen went to the King, who was greatly moved, and she began to speak and said, 'Dearest husband, now I may speak and declare to thee that I am innocent, and falsely accused.' And she told him of the treachery of the old woman who had taken away her three children and hidden them. Then to the great joy of the King they were brought thither, and as a punishment, the wicked mother-in-law was bound to the stake, and burnt to ashes. But the King and the Queen with their six brothers lived many years in happiness and peace.

From *Grimm's Household Tales*, Vol. 1, translated by Margaret Hunt (London: George Bell and Sons, 1884).

Hänsel and Grethel

'Hänsel and Grethel' explores various family relationships. Its motivating event, the fear of starvation, sets off conflict between husband and wife and then between the parents and their children. The subsequent action overtly establishes the relationship between the siblings. In the early stages of the children's adventure, Hänsel dominates, taking responsibility for devising plans that will save them. When the optimistic Hänsel fails, however, Grethel develops into the unlikely child hero. Using her courage and wit, she overcomes a superior adult foe, destroying the evil witch who has previously killed the children whom she captures. Symbolically, the story explores another relationship, pitting the children against a selfish and cruel figuration of the mother in the form of the witch who inhabits the dark forest, an archetypal setting for evil. The tale concludes with the children destroying this mother figure and thereby forming a happy relationship with their father. Many adult readers have, however, objected to the violence that enables this happy ending. In terms of the stern justice that prevails in folk and fairy tales, though, the ending is appropriate because the witch has murdered other children. Furthermore, her demise is in keeping with the traditional belief that only fire could destroy a witch.

Hard by a great forest dwelt a poor wood-cutter with his wife and his two children. The boy was called Hänsel and the girl Grethel. He had little to bite and to break, and once when great scarcity fell on the land, he could no longer procure daily bread. Now when he thought over this by night in his bed, and tossed about in his anxiety, he groaned and said to his wife, 'What is to become of us? How are we to feed our poor children, when we no longer have anything even for ourselves?' 'I'll tell you what, husband,' answered the woman, 'Early to-morrow morning we will take the children out into the forest to where it is the thickest, there we will light a fire for them, and give each of them one piece of bread more, and then we will go to our work and leave them alone. They will not find the way home again, and we shall be rid of them,' 'No, wife,' said the man, 'I will not do that; how can I bear to leave my children alone in the forest?—the wild animals would soon come and tear them to pieces.' 'O, thou fool!' said she, 'Then we must all four die of hunger, thou mayest as well plane the planks for our coffins,' and she left him no peace until he consented. 'But I feel very sorry for the poor children, all the same,' said the man.

The two children had also not been able to sleep for hunger, and had heard what their stepmother had said to their father. Grethel wept bitter tears, and said to Hänsel, 'Now all is over with us.' 'Be quiet, Grethel,' said Hänsel, 'do not distress thyself, I will soon find a way to help us.' And when the old folks had fallen asleep, he got up, put on his little coat, opened the door below, and crept outside. The moon shone brightly, and the white pebbles which lay in front of the house glittered like real silver pennies. Hänsel stooped and put as many of them in the little pocket of his coat as he could possibly get in. Then he went back and said to Grethel, 'Be comforted, dear little sister, and sleep in peace, God will not forsake us,' and he lay down again in his bed. When day dawned, but before the sun had risen, the woman came and awoke the two children, saying, 'Get up, you sluggards! we are going into the forest to fetch wood.' She gave each a little piece of bread, and said, 'There is something for your dinner, but do not eat it up before then, for you will get nothing else.' Grethel took the bread under her apron, as Hänsel had the stones in his pocket. Then they all set out together on the way to the forest. When they had walked a short time, Hänsel stood still and peeped back at the house, and did so again and again. His father said, 'Hänsel, what art thou looking at there and staying behind for? Mind what thou art about, and do not forget how to use thy legs.' 'Ah, father,' said Hänsel, ' I am looking at my little white cat, which is sitting up on the roof, and wants to say good-bye to me.' The wife said, 'Fool, that is not thy little cat, that is the morning sun which is shining on the chimneys.' Hänsel, however, had not been looking back at the cat, but had been constantly throwing one of the white pebble-stones out of his pocket on the road.

When they had reached the middle of the forest, the father said, 'Now, children, pile up some wood, and I will light a fire that you may not be cold.' Hänsel and Grethel gathered brushwood together, as high as a little hill. The brushwood was lighted, and when the flames were burning very high the woman said, 'Now, children, lay yourselves down by the fire and rest, we will go into the forest and cut some wood. When we have done, we will come back and fetch you away.'

Hänsel and Grethel sat by the fire, and when noon came, each ate a little piece of bread, and as they heard the strokes of the wood-axe they believed that their father was near. It was, however, not the axe, it was a branch which he had fastened to a withered tree which the wind was blowing backwards and forwards. And as they had been sitting such a long time, their eyes shut with fatigue, and they fell fast asleep. When at last they awoke, it was already dark night. Grethel began to cry and said, 'How are we to get out of the forest now?' But Hänsel comforted her and said, 'Just wait a little, until the moon has risen, and then we will soon find the way.' And when the full moon had risen, Hänsel took his little sister by the hand, and followed the pebbles which shone like newly-coined silver pieces, and showed them the way.

They walked the whole night long, and by break of day came once more to their father's house. They knocked at the door, and when the woman opened it and saw that it was Hänsel and Grtethel, she said, 'You naughty children, why have you slept so long in the forest?—we thought you were never coming back at all!' The father, however, rejoiced, for it had cut him to the heart to leave them behind alone.

Not long afterwards, there was once more great scarcity in all parts, and the children heard their mother saying at night to their father, 'Everything is eaten again, we have one half loaf left, and after that there is an end. The children must go, we will take them farther into the wood, so that they will not find their way out again; there is no other means of saving ourselves!' The man's heart was heavy, and he thought 'it would be better for thee to share the last mouthful with thy children.' The woman, however, would listen to nothing that he had to say, but scolded and reproached him. He who says A must say B, likewise, and as he had yielded the first time, he had to do so a second time also.

The children were, however, still awake and had heard the conversation. When the old folks were asleep, Hänsel again got up, and wanted to go out and pick up pebbles, but the woman had locked the door, and Hänsel could not get out. Nevertheless he comforted his little sister, and said, 'Do not cry, Grethel, go to sleep quietly, the good God will help us.'

Early in the morning came the woman, and took the children out of their beds. Their bit of bread was given to them, but it was still smaller than the time before. On the way into the forest Hänsel crumbled his in his pocket, and often stood still and threw a morsel on the ground. 'Hänsel, why dost thou stop and look round?' said the father, 'go on.' 'I am looking back at my little pigeon which is sitting on the roof, and wants to say good-bye to me,' answered Hänsel. 'Simpleton!' said the woman, 'that is not thy little pigeon, that is the morning sun that is shining on the chimney.' Hänsel, however, little by little, threw all the crumbs on the path.

The woman led the children still deeper into the forest, where they had never in their lives been before. Then a great fire was again made, and the mother said, 'Just sit there, you children, and when you are tired you may sleep a little; we are going into the forest to cut wood, and in the evening when we are done, we will come and fetch you away.' When it was noon, Grethel shared her piece of bread with Hänsel, who had scattered his by the way. Then they fell asleep and evening came and went, but no one came to the poor children. They did not awake until it was dark night, and Hänsel comforted his little sister and said, 'Just wait, Grethel, until the moon rises, and then we shall see the crumbs of bread which I have strewn about, they will show us our way home again.' When the moon came they set out, but they found no crumbs, for the many thousands of birds which fly about in the woods and fields, had picked them all up. Hänsel said to Grethel, 'We shall soon find the way,' but they did not find it. They walked the whole night and all the next day too from morning till evening, but they did not get out of the forest, and were very hungry, for they had nothing to eat but two or three berries, which grew on the ground. And as they were so weary that their legs would carry them no longer, they lay down beneath a tree and fell asleep.

It was now three mornings since they had left their father's house. They began to walk again, but they always got deeper into the forest, and if help did not come soon, they must die of hunger and weariness. When it was mid-day, they saw a beautiful snow-white bird sitting on a bough, which sang so delightfully that they stood still and listened to it. And when it had finished its song, it spread its wings and flew away before them, and they followed it until they reached a little house, on the roof of which it alighted; and when they came quite up to the little house they saw that it was built of bread and covered with cakes, but that the windows were of clear sugar. 'We will set to work on that,' said Hänsel 'and have a good meal. I will eat a bit of the roof, and thou, Grethel, canst eat some of the window, it will taste sweet.' Hänsel reached up above, and broke off a little of the roof to try how it tasted, and Grethel leant against the window and nibbled at the panes. Then a soft voice cried from the room,

> 'Nibble, nibble, gnaw,
> Who is nibbling at my little house?'

The children answered,

> 'The wind, the wind,
> The heaven-born wind,'

and went on eating without disturbing themselves. Hänsel, who thought the roof tasted very nice, tore down a great piece of it, and Grethel pushed out the whole of one round window-pane, sat down, and enjoyed herself with it. Suddenly the door opened, and a very, very old woman, who supported herself on crutches, came creeping out. Hänsel and Grethel were so terribly frightened that they let fall what they had in their hands. The old woman, however, nodded her head, and said, 'Oh, you dear children, who has brought you here? Do come in, and stay with me. No harm shall happen to you.' She took them both by the hand, and led them into her little house. Then good food was set before them, milk and pancakes, with sugar, apples, and nuts. Afterwards two pretty little beds were covered with clean white linen, and Hänsel and Grethel lay down in them, and thought they were in heaven.

The old woman had only pretended to be so kind; she was in reality a wicked witch, who lay in wait for children, and had only built the little bread house in order to entice them there. When a child fell into her power, she killed it, cooked and ate it, and that was a feast day with her. Witches have red eyes, and cannot see far, but they have a keen scent like the beasts, and are aware when human beings draw near. When Hänsel and Grethel came into her neighbourhood, she laughed maliciously, and said mockingly, 'I have them, they shall not escape me again!' Early in the morning before the children were awake, she was already up, and when she saw both of them sleeping and looking so pretty, with their plump red cheeks, she muttered to herself, 'That will be a dainty mouthful!' Then she seized Hänsel with her shrivelled hand, carried him into a little stable, and shut him in with a grated door. He might scream as he liked, that was of no use. Then she went to Grethel, shook her till she awoke, and cried, 'Get up, lazy thing, fetch some water, and cook something good for thy brother, he is in the stable outside, and is to be made fat. When he is fat, I will eat him.' Grethel began to weep bitterly, but it was all in vain, she was forced to do what the wicked witch ordered her.

And now the best food was cooked for poor Hänsel, but Grethel got nothing but crab-shells. Every morning the woman crept to the little stable, and cried, 'Hänsel, stretch out thy finger that I may feel if thou wilt soon be fat.' Hänsel, however, stretched out a little bone to her, and the old woman, who had dim eyes, could not see it, and thought it was Hänsel's finger, and was astonished that there was no way of fattening him. When four weeks had gone by, and Hänsel still continued thin, she was seized with impatience and would not wait any longer, 'Hola, Grethel,' she cried to the girl, 'be active, and bring some water. Let Hänsel be fat or lean, to-morrow I will kill him, and cook him,' Ah, how the poor little sister did lament when she had to fetch the water, and how her tears did flow down over her cheeks! 'Dear God, do help us,' she cried. 'If the wild beasts in the forest had but devoured us, we should at any rate have died together.' 'Just keep thy noise to thyself,' said the old woman, 'all that won't help thee at all.'

Early in the morning, Grethel had to go out and hang up the cauldron with the water, and light the fire. 'We will bake first,' said the old woman, 'I have already heated the oven, and kneaded the dough.' She pushed poor Grethel out to the oven, from which flames of fire were already darting. 'Creep in,' said the witch, 'and see if it is properly heated, so that we can shut the bread in.' And when once Grethel was inside, she intended to shut the oven and let her bake in it, and then she would eat her, too. But Grethel saw what she had in her mind, and said, ' I do not know how I am to do it; how do you get in?' 'Silly goose,' said the old woman. 'The door is big enough; just look, I can get in myself!' and she crept up and thrust her head into the oven. Then Grethel gave her a push that drove her far into it, and shut the iron door, and fastened the bolt. Oh! then she began to howl quite horribly, but Grethel ran away, and the godless witch was miserably burnt to death.

Grethel, however, ran as quick as lightning to Hänsel, opened his little stable, and cried, 'Hänsel, we are saved! The old witch is dead!' Then Hänsel sprang out like a bird from its cage when the door is opened for it. How they did rejoice and embrace each other, and dance about and kiss each other! And as they had no longer any need to fear her, they went into the witch's house, and in every corner there stood chests full of pearls and jewels. 'These are far better than pebbles!' said Hänsel, and thrust into his pockets whatever could be got in, and Grethel said, 'I, too, will take something home with me,' and filled her pinafore full. 'But now we will go away,' said Hänsel, 'that we may get out of the witch's forest.'

When they had walked for two hours, they came to a great piece of water. 'We cannot get over,' said Hänsel, 'I see no foot-plank, and no bridge.' 'And no boat crosses either,' answered Grethel, 'but a white duck is swimming there; if I ask her, she will help us over.' Then she cried,

> 'Little duck, little duck, dost thou see,
> Hänsel and Grethel are waiting for thee?
> There's never a plank, or bridge in sight,
> Take us across on thy back so white.'

The duck came to them, and Hänsel seated himself on its back, and told his sister to sit by him. 'No,' replied Grethel, 'that will be too heavy for the little duck; she shall take us across, one after the other.' The good little duck did so, and when they were once safely across and had walked for a short time, the forest seemed to be more and more familiar to them, and at length they saw from afar their father's house. Then they began to run, rushed into the parlour, and threw themselves into their father's arms. The man had not known one happy hour since he had left the children in the forest; the woman, however, was dead. Grethel emptied her pinafore until pearls and precious stones ran about the room, and Hänsel threw one handful after another out of his pocket to add to them. Then all anxiety was at an end, and they lived together in perfect happiness. My tale is done, there runs a mouse, whosoever catches it, may make himself a big fur cap out of it.

From *Grimm's Household Tales*, Vol. 1, translated by Margaret Hunt (London: George Bell and Sons, 1884).

Chet Huat Chet Hai (Seven Pot, Seven Jar)

'Chet Huat Chet Hai' gives a comic twist to the abandonment motif that is found at the beginning of such Western tales as 'Hänsel and Grethel' and 'Molly Whuppie'. When the boy's father tries to kill him by felling a tree and having it land on top of him, Chet Huat Chet Hai manages to pick up the tree and return home with it. The boy's exceptional strength and his naiveté also give a comic twist to the father's second attempt to kill him. The final attempt is significantly different, however, because it involves two antagonists, a witch and a giant, and a group of unusual helper figures. Having demonstrated his wit, loyalty, and bravery in this final adventure, Chet Huat Chet Hai earns the hand of a princess, a conventional symbol of maturity and happiness. What makes the story unusual for Western readers, however, is that the boy does not punish his murderous parents. Instead, in keeping with traditional Thai values, he shows that he is an ideal son by caring for them now that he has wealth and high status.

A long, long time ago a poor couple lived near the edge of the forest. They were so poor they barely had enough rice to eat. And to make matters worse, their only son was an unusual boy with exceptional strength. He needed lots of food. Ever since he had reached the age of seven, he had eaten an enormous amount of food each day. For only one meal he consumed seven pots of rice and seven jars of salted fish! So he was called 'Chet Huat Chet Hai,' or 'Seven Pot, Seven Jar.'

The poor couple tried hard to provide for their son, but they could not seem to get ahead. Every day that son needed his seven pots of rice and seven jars of salted fish to fill his stomach. Finally, the poor couple decided they could no longer provide for their son. They quietly consulted each other.

'Let us leave him in the forest,' the father said.

'Oh, but he will be frightened and hungry at night,' the mother protested.

'Then what do you suggest?' the father asked.

'I do not want him to suffer. He is still too young to fend for himself,' the mother said.

Several nights later, the couple found themselves faced with the son's eating habit again. There was no food left in the house. They did not know where the next meal would come from. There was just no way they could feed a child with such a huge appetite. Then the father said, 'Tomorrow, I will take him into the forest with me. If it is necessary, I will kill him myself to spare him from hunger.' The mother sobbed quietly, but did not say anything. The next morning the father asked his son to go into the forest with him.

'Chet Huat Chet Hai, you are a big boy now. You can help your father fell a tree for firewood to sell at the market. So be ready in five minutes.'

Chet Huat Chet Hai was glad to be of help to his old father. He hurriedly dressed and waited excitedly for his father. Once they reached the deep forest, the father found a tall tree and started to cut it. When the tree was about to fall, the father told his son, 'Chet Huat Chet Hai, when the tree falls, you try to catch it. We do not want any marks on the tree. This tree is too beautiful to use as firewood. We can sell it as lumber to build houses with. Remember, catch the tree. Do not let it fall to the ground.'

Chet Huat Chet Hai obediently did as he was told. Unfortunately, the tree was so big that when it fell on top of Chet Huat Chet Hai, its weight pushed Chet Huat Chet Hai down under the earth. The impact was earthshattering. The sound of the falling tree was earsplitting.

Even though the father had planned this accident, now that it had happened, he began to cry uncontrollably. He ran over to where his son had disappeared but he could not see Chet Huat Chet Hai because the huge tree was on top of him. The father thought his son was surely crushed to death. He prayed quietly for his son and began the journey home to tell his wife.

Even before he reached home, he saw his son come running after him, carrying the great tree. 'I'm coming, Father! Where do you want the tree carried?' When the tree had fallen on Chet Huat Chet Hai he had been stunned by the blow for a few moments. But as soon as he had recovered, he had hurried to push the huge tree off of his body, strip off its branches, and lift it up to carry it home. The father was both glad and dismayed to see his son still alive. But he did not say anything. He went inside and asked his wife to find something for his son to eat.

The next day, the father asked his son to go into the forest with him again. This time he said he wanted his son to help him catch a horse.

'Son, if we can catch a wild horse, we can sell it in the market, or we could use it on our farm.'

Once they had reached the deep forest, the father led his son to a wide river. 'Son, this is the river where wild animals come to drink. Stay here and wait to catch a wild horse. I will go look upriver.' The father hurried home in tears, believing that wild animals would soon come and kill his son.

Chet Huat Chet Hai did not know what a horse looked like. He obediently waited by the river for a long time. When he saw a tiger coming down to drink, he thought this must be a horse. He caught the tiger bare-handed, tied the tiger's legs, and sat waiting for his father's return. When the sun set and the father did not return, he began to worry. He thought, 'I should go home and tell my mother.' So he untied the tiger, jumped on its back, and rode the tiger home.

When he arrived home, the tiger was roaring loudly. The dog and the chickens were terrified and fled into the forest. They never returned. That is why some of these domesticated animals are wild.

The couple was very frightened when they saw their son on the back of the tiger. They called out, 'Son, get away from the tiger. Let it go free in the forest. Do not bring it home!'

Chet Huat Chet Hai did not understand all this, but he obediently did as he was told.

Many months later, the couple consulted each other, 'We are so poor. There is no more rice, no more fish. We cannot provide enough food for ourselves and our eat-too-much son. How can we go on living?' They decided the only solution was to try to abandon their son again.

The next morning, the mother called her son. 'Son, we have run out of money to buy food. There is nothing left to eat. I need money to buy food and the giant owes me money. Can you go ask him to pay me now?' She thought Chet Huat Chet Hai would never return from such a trip. The son felt sorry for his poor parents. 'Do not worry, Mother. I will go to the giant and bring back the money.'

So it was that Chet Huat Chet Hai began his great adventure. He set off in search of the giant. Chet Huat Chet Hai hadn't gone far when he heard a loud rumbling sound from the road ahead. Climbing the hill, he looked down and saw a remarkable sight: A man was coming up the road pulling a cartload of bricks. But fastened behind that cart was *another* cartload of bricks, and behind *that* cart was *another*. This man was pulling 100 cartloads of bricks up the hill, all by himself!

'Good day,' said Chet Huat Chet Hai. 'My name is Chet Huat Chet Hai, and I am searching for the giant. But who on earth are *you*?'

'My name is Kwian Roi Lem, 'One Hundred Carts.' I am so strong that I can pull 100 carts at a time with ease. I also like to fight giants. Could I go with you?'

'Certainly!' Chet Huat Chet Hai was glad to have a companion. So the two set out in search of the giant.

Soon they heard a strange cracking and crashing sound ahead. There on the river bank was a man felling bamboos. But instead of cutting them, he was pulling them up like weeds. He was grabbing 100 bamboos at a time, yanking them from the soil, and tossing them aside!

'Good day, I am Chet Huat Chet Hai, and this is my companion Kwian Roi Lem, we are travelling to fight the giant. But who are you?'

'They call me Phai Roi Ko, 'One Hundred Bamboos' because I can pull 100 bamboos at a time. I would like to fight the giant too. Could I go with you?'

'Certainly, we would like another companion.'

So the three companions traveled on together. After a while they heard a loud chopping noise coming from the forest ahead. 'A woodsman is at work,' said Chet Huat Chet Hai. But when they approached the woodsman, they saw a remarkable sight. This man had no axe. He was whacking the trees with his head to fell them!

'Good day, I am Chet Huat Chet Hai and these are my companions Kwian Roi Lem and Phai Roi Ko. We are traveling to conquer the giant. But who are you?'

'Huo Tok Ki, 'Head Stronger than an Axe' is my name. As you see, my head is so strong that I don't need an axe to cut down trees. I like to fight giants too. May I go with you?' The companions were delighted with their new friend and the four set off on their way.

Clearly, these four young men were well suited for each other. They vowed to support each other come what may. If one was ever in trouble, the others would help him out. But there was no food in the land through which they were travelling.

After they had traveled for two days without food, they were so hungry they decided to dig some chingrit bugs to eat. Today, chingrit resemble large crickets. But at that time this was not a small insect as it is now. The chingrit of those days were as big as elephants! Chet Huat Chet Hai let his three friends try first to catch the chingrit. The huge insects were very strong. They kicked loose each time one of the strong men tried to hold them. But when Chet Huat Chet Hai tried, he succeeded in digging an insect from its hole and dragging it out.

However, they could not eat the chingrit raw, and they had no fire to roast their food. A house roof could be seen in the distance, so Chet Huat Chet Hai sent one of his strong companions to fetch fire from its inhabitant.

Unfortunately, that house happened to be the home of an evil sorceress. She possessed many powers, including a magic life-and-death stick. If she pointed the death end at a person, that person fell dead. If she pointed the life end at a dead person, that person came back to life. This sorceress sat all day crouched like a spider over a huge weaving of sticky silken strands. All day she wove these strands in and out, and if a stranger ventured near, she hurled the long silken strands over him, drew him near, and bound him tight in her weaving.

When the unsuspecting Kwian Roi Lem approached, the sorceress invited him in sweetly. 'But come a little closer, I will be glad to lend you some fire.' Thus she enticed him nearer and nearer to the spot where she sat weaving, then, suddenly, she lashed out with her strands and enveloped him in a mesh of silk, trapping the strong young man.

Chet Huat Chet Hai waited a long time for his friend to return with the fire, then he sent a second companion. Phai Roi Ko met the same fate. And Huo Tok Ki followed soon after. Seeing that none of his companions returned, Chet Huat Chet Hai suspected foul play. He hurried to see what had happened.

He approached the house of the sorceress carefully, looking to see what might have happened to his friends. 'Have you seen my three friends?' he called to the weaving sorceress. 'I sent them to borrow fire from you so we could cook our meat. They did not return.'

The sorceress beckoned to Chet Huat Chet Hai. 'Come closer young man. Your friends are right here. See, I am keeping them tight in my silken strands. Come closer and you will see.' She meant to capture Chet Huat Chet Hai in her silken strands also, but she was mistaken. He watched her movements carefully, and when she threw her silk threads he was ready. Chet Huat Chet Hai jumped aside nimbly. Then, before she could recoil her strands to throw again, he pounced on the sorceress and quickly wrestled her into submission. Wrapping her in her own sticky silk, he bound her tight.

Then Chet Huat Chet Hai picked up the magic life-and-death stick. 'Which end is which?' He pointed the death end toward the witch. That was the end of her. Then he reversed the stick and pointed the life end toward each of his companions. Chet Huat Chet Hai pulled his revived friends from the silken mess and the four gathered embers from the fire of the sorceress and hurried back to cook their dinner.

Made strong once more by the tasty chingrit dinner, the four friends set off to find the giant. After traveling for some time, they reached a town where everyone was huddling in fright. 'Why is everyone here so frightened?' asked the friends.

'A giant has been coming every day to eat one of us. He catches one person each day for his meal. He is so powerful we cannot conquer him.'

At last they had found the giant. 'Do not worry,' said the four companions. 'We have come to fight your giant. When he comes tomorrow he will eat no one. We guarantee it.'

'Our king has sent many brave men to fight the giant,' said the townsfolk. 'No one has succeeded. He has promised that anyone who defeats the giant will marry the princess and have the throne of the kingdom.'

'Well that is fine with us!' laughed the four companions. The next day, when the giant came stomping down the hill, drooling for his meal, the four companions were ready. Chet Huat Chet Hai leaped onto the giant and held him fast. Using his head as an axe, Huo Tok Ki, quickly chopped the giant in two in the middle. Phai Roi Ko pulled off the giant's limbs as if they had been 100 bamboos. And Kwian Roi Lem hauled away the giant's body easily, though it weighed as much as 100 cartloads of bricks.

The king and his subjects were ecstatic. 'Come and claim your prize!' they called.

The four friends consulted. It was decided that Chet Huat Chet Hai, as leader of the group, would marry the princess. The other three friends were each given an important post in the kingdom, and for many years, the town prospered under the rule of these four strong friends.

But Chet Huat Chet Hai was thinking of his poor parents. He sent for them and told them, 'Dear Father and Mother, you don't have to worry about me any more. I am capable of taking care of myself now. I am ruler of my own kingdom and I can afford to eat as much as I want. You have taken care of me for many years. Now it is my turn to take care of you.'

From then on Chet Huat Chet Hai made sure that his parents lived in comfort and had plenty of food to eat.

This is the happy ending of the tale of Chet Huat Chet Hai, the boy who ate seven pots of rice and seven jars of salted fish at one sitting.

From *Thai Tales: Folktales of Thailand*, by Supaporn Vathanaprida, edited by Margaret Read MacDonald (Englewood, Colorado: Libraries Unlimited, 1994).

The Smith and the Fairies

As John Francis Campbell explains in his notes to this Scottish tale, many of its incidents were common in tales collected in Ireland, Scotland, and Wales, but 'This smith was a famous character, and probably a real personage, to whom the story has attached itself' (50). In other words, a relatively common changeling tale—a story about the fairies kidnapping a child and leaving in its place someone from their group—here becomes a local legend. The point of this legend is to explain how the maker of the 'Swords of the Head of Islay' (*Claidheamh Ceann-Ileach*), the walls of whose house were still standing at Caonis gall, Islay, in 1860, acquired the skill to fashion such notable

and prized weapons. Aside from its interest as a West Highland legend, this tale is notable for extending the changeling tale into a quest tale about a devoted father. The smith, once he gets rid of the *sibhreach* (changeling), ventures into the underground world of the *Daoine Sith* (Little Folk), a land from which humans do not normally return. The reaction of the fairies to the crowing cock, which is crucial to the smith's victory, may puzzle contemporary readers. The fairies, who were noted for their love of harmony and beauty, may have hated its crowing because it was cacophonous and because it was identified with the coming of dawn, the time when their magic power ebbed.

$\mathcal{Y}$ears ago there lived in Crossbrig a smith of the name of MacEachern. This man had an only child, a boy of about thirteen or fourteen years of age, cheerful, strong, and healthy. All of a sudden he fell ill; took to his bed and moped whole days away. No one could tell what was the matter with him, and the boy himself could not, or would not, tell how he felt. He was wasting away fast; getting thin, old, and yellow; and his father and all his friends were afraid that he would die.

At last one day, after the boy had been lying in this condition for a long time, getting neither better nor worse, always confined to bed, but with an extraordinary appetite,—one day, while sadly revolving these things, and standing idly at his forge, with no heart to work, the smith was agreeably surprised to see an old man, well known to him for his sagacity and knowledge of out-of-the-way things, walk into his workshop. Forthwith he told him the occurrence which had clouded his life.

The old man looked grave as he listened; and after sitting a long time pondering over all he had heard, gave his opinion thus—'It is not your son you have got. The boy has been carried away by the "Daione Sith", and they have left a *Sibhreach* in his place.' 'Alas! and what then am I to do?' said the smith. 'How am I ever to see my own son again?' 'I will tell you how,' answered the old man. 'But, first, to make sure that it is not your own son you have got, take as many empty egg shells as you can get, go with them into the room, spread them out carefully before his sight, then proceed to draw water with them, carrying them two and two in your hands as if they were a great weight, and arrange, when full, with every sort of earnestness round the fire.' The smith accordingly gathered as many broken egg-shells as he could get, went into the room, and proceeded to carry out all his instructions.

He had not been long at work before there arose from the bed a shout of laughter, and the voice of the seeming sick boy exclaimed, 'I am now 800 years of age, and I have never seen the like of that before.'

The smith returned and told the old man. 'Well, now,' said the sage to him, 'did I not tell you that it was not your son you had: your son is in Borra-cheill in a digh there (that is, a round green hill frequented by fairies). Get rid as soon as possible of this intruder, and I think I may promise you your son.'

'You must light a very large and bright fire before the bed on which this stranger is lying. He will ask you, 'What is the use of such a fire as that?' Answer him at once, 'You will see that presently!' and then seize him, and throw him into the middle of it. If it is your own son you have got, he will call out to save him; but if not, this thing will fly through the roof.'

The smith again followed the old man's advice; kindled a large fire, answered the question put to him as he had been directed to do, and seizing the child flung him in without hesitation. The 'Sibhreach' gave an awful yell, and sprung through the roof, where a hole was left to let the smoke out.

On a certain night the old man told him the green round hill, where the fairies kept the boy, would be open. And on that night the smith, having provided himself with a bible, a dirk, and a crowing cock, was to proceed to the hill. He would hear singing and dancing, and much merriment going, on, but he was to advance boldly; the bible he carried would be a certain safeguard to him against any danger from the fairies. On entering the hill he was to stick the dirk in the threshold, to prevent the hill from closing upon him; 'and then,' continued the old man, 'on entering you will see a spacious apartment before you, beautifully clean, and there, standing far within, working at a forge, you will also see your own son. When you are questioned, say you come to seek him, and will not go without him.'

Not long after this, the time came round, and the smith sallied forth, prepared as instructed. Sure enough as he approached the hill, there was a light where light was seldom seen before. Soon after a sound of piping, dancing, and joyous merriment reached the anxious father on the night wind.

Overcoming every impulse to fear, the smith approached the threshold steadily, stuck the dirk into it as directed, and entered. Protected by the bible he carried on his breast, the fairies could not touch him; but they asked him, with a good deal of displeasure, what he wanted there. He answered, 'I want my son, whom I see down there, and I will not go without him.'

Upon hearing this, the whole company before him gave a loud laugh, which wakened up the cock he carried dozing in his arms, who at once leaped up on his shoulders, clapped his wings lustily, and crowed loud and long.

The fairies, incensed, seized the smith and his son, and throwing them out of the hill flung the dirk after them, 'and in an instant a' was dark.'

For a year and a day the boy never did a turn of work, and hardly ever spoke a word; but at last one day, sitting by his father and watching him finishing a sword he was making for some chief, and which he was very particular about, he suddenly exclaimed, 'That is not the way to do it;' and taking the tools from his father's hands he set to work himself in his place, and soon fashioned a sword, the like of which was never seen in the country before.

From that day the young man wrought constantly with his father, and became the inventor of a peculiarly fine and well-tempered weapon, the making of which kept the two smiths; father and son, in constant employment, spread their fame far and wide, and gave them the means in abundance, as they before had the disposition to live content with all the world and very happily with one another.

From *Popular Tales of the West Highlands*, Vol. 2, by J.F. Campbell (Edinburgh: Edmonston and Douglas, 1860).

The Three Sons and Their Objects of Power

This tale from the Krachi people of Togo is typical of one common form of African storytelling, the dilemma tale. Such tales pose an enigma but do not offer narrative closure. Instead, they seek to engage the audience in argument about the narrative. The main body of the narrative sets the sons on a quest to obtain food and clothing for their aged father. The sons do not acquire the objects they sought, but each does obtain an object that is crucial in restoring their father to life when he dies. The issue of which son has been the greatest benefactor to his father may seem beyond resolution to many Westerners, but African audiences approach the issue in a different way. As Roger D. Abrahams notes in *African Folktales: Traditional Stories of the Black World*, 'it is the flow of discussion that counts, not the finding of a solution. Through argument, the customary practices of the community are rehearsed and celebrated' (109).

*A*n old man had three children. They were all boys. When they had grown up to manhood he called them together and told them that now he was very old and no longer able to get food even for himself. He ordered them to go forth to obtain food and clothing for him.

They all set out together, and after a while came to a large river. The journey had lasted many moons, and they decided to cross and there separate. The eldest told the youngest to take the middle road, and the second to go to the right, whilst he himself would go to the left. They were all to meet at the same spot in a year's time.

So they departed, and at the end of a year as agreed upon they found their way back to the riverside.

The eldest asked the youngest what he had obtained during his travels, and the boy replied: 'I have got nothing except a mirror. But this mirror has wonderful power, and if you look into it you can see all over the country, no matter how far away.'

The eldest then turned to his second brother and asked him what he had obtained. And the second replied: 'Nothing, except a pair of sandals which are so full of power that if one puts them on one can walk at once to any place in the country at one step.'

The eldest then said: 'I too have obtained but little. A small calabash of medicine and that is all. But let us look into the mirror and see how father fares.'

The youngest produced his mirror and they all looked into it and saw their father was already dead and that even the funeral custom was finished. Then the elder said: 'Let us hasten home and see what can be done.' So the second brought out his sandals and all three placed their feet inside them and at once they went straight to their father's grave. Then the eldest took his bag and shook out his medicine. This he poured over the grave and at once their father arose, just as if nothing had been the matter with him. Now which of these three has done best?

From *Tales Told in Togoland*, by A.W Cardinall (London: Oxford University Press, 1931) (Title Supplied).

Jacques the Woodcutter

This French-Canadian tale has its roots in *fabliaux*—humourous, often bawdy, verse tales popular in medieval France. The adaptors have, however, removed the crudity of the oral original that Canadian folkorist Marius Barbeau transcribed. In giving it literary polish, they have 'aimed at achieving in our own way a literary uplifting similar to that of Grimm, Andersen, and Perrault' (141). Although it is now a text suitable for children, 'Jacques the Woodcutter' has lost none of the sly humour that characterizes *fabliaux* that detail events in the eternal battle between the sexes. Although primarily an entertainment, the tale may reflect some of the hostility that peasants felt towards oppressive and grasping aristocrats. Its major theme comes, however, after the Pedlar becomes the helper in the task of restoring domestic order. When Jacques finally confronts his unfaithful wife and the greedy prince, he secures his position as head of a stable household.

*T*his is the story of Jacques Cornaud, who lived at the edge of a forest with his pretty wife Finette.

Jacques was a woodcutter by trade. Each morning he went off into the forest to cut down trees and chop them into firewood. As soon as he left the house, his wife Finette would have a visitor—for she was not only pretty and charming, but a fine cook besides. Not far away lived a good-for-nothing Prince named Bellay, who was extremely fond of eating.

Every day while Jacques was away working in the forest, the Prince would come to the house and sit down to an enormous meal. Finette didn't mind cooking for him. She had no other company during the daytime, and besides, when the Prince had finished his meal he always left a gold piece under the plate.

But Jacques the woodcutter was not so well satisfied. At last he decided to speak to his wife about it.

'Finette,' he said, 'I have nothing against the Prince, and I don't mind his little visits to our table. But does he have to come so often?'

Finette promised she would speak to the Prince. Next morning Jacques went off to the forest, and soon afterwards Prince Bellay turned up as usual, with a smile on his lips and a flower in his buttonhole.

'And what's on the menu today?' he asked, patting his stomach.

'Savoury dumplings,' said Finette. 'But I have a message for you. My husband thinks you come to the house too often.'

Prince Bellay frowned (thinking was such hard work that it always made him frown). 'Too often?' he repeated. 'Well, you know, he's right. I'm here every day. No wonder he's annoyed! This will have to stop.'

No more gold pieces, thought Finette. What a pity, just when she was beginning to gather together quite a tidy sum! She decided she would try to change Prince Bellay's mind.

'No more onion soup,' she said.

The Prince stared at her. 'No more onion soup?' he gasped. 'Oh, I couldn't bear that. Life without onion soup wouldn't be worth living.'

'And for next week,' said Finette, 'I had planned a meal of roast pigeon. But now we'll have to give up that idea.'

'Roast pigeon!' exclaimed the Prince, licking his lips. 'But couldn't I sneak in while he's away in the forest without his knowing?'

'He might come back during the day,' said Finette. 'Imagine how annoyed he would be then.'

'You're right,' groaned the Prince. 'We must think of a plan to keep him away from the house.'

When his food was at stake the Prince could think quite fast. After a moment he stopped frowning and smiled.

'I have it!' he said. 'This will keep him away for at least two weeks, and by that time I can think of something else. Now listen carefully.'

And he told Finette his plan. Thinking of the gold pieces, she listened carefully and promised to do as he told her.

That evening, when she saw Jacques coming home from the forest with his axe on his shoulder, she stuffed a handkerchief into her cheek so that it would look swollen. Then she lay down on her bed and began to moan.

'Oh Jacques, Jacques, I feel so awful!'

The woodcutter put down his axe and hurried to her beside. 'What is it? What's the matter?'

'Toothache,' moaned Finette. 'The worst I've ever had. Ohhh—I've been in agony ever since you left this morning!'

Jacques reached for his coat. 'I'll go and fetch the doctor at once.'

Finette moaned harder than ever. 'No, the doctor can't help me. There is only one thing that will cure this toothache, and that is water from the Fountain of Paris.'

'But dear wife,' said Jacques, 'by the time I go to Paris and back you could be seven times dead with the pain.'

'No, no,' said Finette, 'I'll wait for you. But you must hurry if you are to be back soon. I've made you a sandwich for the road. It's on the kitchen table.'

Jacques was tired after a hard day in the woods, but he was so kind-hearted that he left at once and took the high road to Paris. No sooner had he gone than Finette got to work at the stove, and soon afterwards Prince Bellay was sitting down to a delicious supper of roast pigeon and artichokes with pepper sauce.

Meanwhile Jacques had gone only a little way when he met an old man with a big wicker basket on his back. It was the Pedlar who often called at his home.

'Good evening, old friend,' said the Pedlar. 'And pray, where are you going with such a sad face?'

'To Paris,' said Jacques. 'My wife Finette is dying of toothache, and I must bring her some water from the Fountain there.'

The Pedlar shut one eye and chuckled. 'Tut, tut,' he said. 'Your wife no more has the toothache than I have.'

'You don't know Finette,' said Jacques indignantly, 'If she says she has toothache, then she has. She isn't like other women.'

The Pedlar shut his other eye. 'And she wants you to go all the way to Paris? Tell me, isn't there some reason why she'd like to have you out of the house?'

The woodcutter thought for a moment. 'Well, there's that good-for-nothing Prince with the big appetite. But I can't believe she would send me all the way to Paris just for that.'

'Well, old friend,' said the Pedlar, opening both his eyes, 'never mind about the Fountain of Paris. It just so happens that I have some of its water with me now, so I can save you the trip. Here, you're too tired to stand. Jump into my basket and I'll give you a ride back home.'

So Jacques climbed into the Pedlar's basket and rode back home. When they reached the cottage there was a fine smell of cooking in the air. The Pedlar chuckled and knocked on the door.

'Who's there?' cried Finette.

'Only the Pedlar and his basket, good lady. Will you open your door to a tired and hungry man?'

'The Pedlar, at this time of night!' said Finette. 'Is a woman never to have any peace?'

Then they heard Prince Bellay's voice from the dining table.

'Let him come in, good Finette. He's an old man, and tired. If you put him in the kitchen with his basket, he won't disturb us.'

'All right,' said Finette. She let in the Pedlar and told him to sit down in the kitchen. The Pedlar thanked her and put his basket next to the stove.

At the dining table the Prince was finishing his roast pigeon. Having eaten so well himself, he felt kindly to the rest of the world.

'Poor old fellow,' he said. 'He's probably come a long way with nothing to eat. Why don't we ask him in here to sup with us? These travelling men are always good company.'

Finette was in good humour again. She invited the Pedlar to come in and share their meal.

'Bless you, good lady,' said the Pedlar. 'Never turn down an invitation, I always say. But you won't mind if I bring my basket along? It's my living, and I don't like to leave it behind.'

'That great big basket in my dining-room?' said Finette. 'What an idea!'

'Oh, let him bring it if he must,' said the Prince kindly. 'He can put it in the corner where it won't trouble anybody.'

Finette thought of the gold piece under the plate and decided not to object. So the Pedlar brought in his basket from the kitchen and put it in the corner behind his chair. He sat down to the table, smacking his lips, and soon made short work of the roast pigeon.

'Ah,' he said when he had finished. 'A fine meal, Hostess! With food like that, I'll wager you keep in good health.'

'Indeed I do,' said Finette. 'I haven't had a day's illness in years.'

At this there was a strange grumbling noise from the wicker basket in the corner. Finette turned pale, but the Pedlar chuckled in his beard and told her not to be alarmed.

'It's the heat in here,' he explained. 'Bring an old wicker basket in out of the cold, and you'll hear it grunt and creak like a live thing.'

Prince Bellay was feeling cheerful after his meal. 'No speeches after dinner here, Master Pedlar,' he said. 'Instead, let's have a jolly song or two.'

'A fine plan!' said the Pedlar. 'Nothing would suit me better. But everyone in his place. You're a prince, and the chief guest here. It's proper that you should sing first.'

The Prince was pleased, for he liked to think of himself as a gay fellow with a fine voice. He called for wine and sang a little verse that he had just made up:

> 'There is a good woman lives in a wood
> (Savoury dumplings and pigeon pie)
> Who bakes and fries as a good wife should:
> Savoury dumplings and pigeon pie—
> If Jacques won't eat them, why can't I?'

'Bless me, that was well sung,' cried the Pedlar, laughing and clapping his hands. 'Why shouldn't you, indeed?'

The Prince beamed and called for more wine. 'Now it's your turn,' he said to Finette.

'No, no,' said Finette. 'Ask the Pedlar. He's a travelling man, and he must know all kinds of songs.'

The Pedlar shook his head. 'Everyone in his place,' he said. 'First the Hostess and afterwards the Pedlar.'

Finette gave in. And here is the song she sang:

> 'My husband has gone to Paris town
> (Savoury dumplings and pigeon pie)
> So eat and drink till the moon goes down
> (Savoury dumplings and pigeon pie);
> He won't be back till the snowflakes fly.'

'Excellent, excellent!' laughed the Pedlar. 'Oh, my basket and I haven't had such a good time in a month of Sundays!'

'More wine,' said the prince. 'And now, Master Pedlar, will you warble us a tune in your turn?'

'Sir,' said the Pedlar, 'since there is nobody left but my self and my basket, I am at your service.'

And here is the song he sang:

From Marius Barbeau, as retold by Michael Hornyansky, *The Golden Phoenix and Other Fairy Tales from Quebec*. Illustrated by Arthur Price. (Toronto: Oxford University Press, 1958), 115–16.

> 'I met a man on the broad highway.
> (We travel far, my basket and I.)
> The man would go, but I made him stay
> (We're full of surprises, my basket and I):
> And where he is now, who can say?'

Finette didn't much like the sound of this song, especially when she heard another grunt from the corner where the basket stood. But Prince Bellay was too full of wine and good food to take any notice. He clapped the Pedlar on the back and shouted with laughter.

'I declare,' said the Prince, 'you talk about that old basket of yours as if it were alive! If it's as good as you say, why don't you tell it to sing the next song?'

The Pedlar shut one eye and chuckled. 'Bless me, why not?' he said. 'It doesn't do much singing in the ordinary way—just creaks and groans—but I have a notion it will sing for you.'

'We'll make sure of it,' laughed the Prince. 'Here, basket, have some wine.'

And he poured a cup of wine over the basket.

'Enough!' said the Pedlar. 'Now, basket of mine, let's hear what kind of voice you have.'

The basket creaked, and then in a muffled voice it began to sing. And this was its song:

> 'Good wife, your toothache's cured, I see.
> (What was your medicine—pigeon pie?)
> The Prince has dined; he'll pay the fee:
> For savoury dumplings and pigeon pie
> The price is a beating. Fly, Prince, fly!'

And out of the basket sprang Jacques the woodcutter, shaking his fist. Never in your life did you see a Prince leave a house so fast. He didn't stop running till he was safe in his castle, with the door locked and barred. And he never went near Finette's table again.

As for Finette, she gave up her ideas of becoming rich. Nowadays Jacques Cornaud the woodcutter has onion soup whenever he wants it, and roast pigeon with artichokes on special days. Sometimes the Pedlar calls on them, and he can be sure of a welcome and a fine dinner. While he is at the table his old wicker basket sits quietly in the corner. It creaks a little, but it doesn't say a word.

———

From *The Golden Phoenix and Other French-Canadian Fairy Tales*, by Marius Barbeau, retold by Michael Hornyansky (Toronto: Oxford University Press, 1958).

The Woman Who Flummoxed the Fairies

Knowledge is power in this comical tale about a woman who saves herself when the fairies carry her off to their land. In this case, the woman has knowledge about what fairies like and don't like. Tricking the fairies into bringing her family and its pets to fairyland, she takes charge by directing her husband in a plan that soon liberates all of them. In the end, however, it is not her unusual cleverness that secures her family's happiness but her compassion and honesty, qualities more in keeping with stereotypical portrayals of ideal females.

There was a woman once who was a master baker. Her bannocks were like wheaten cakes, her wheaten cakes were like the finest pastries, and her pastries were like nothing but Heaven itself in the mouth!

Not having her match, or anything like it, in seven counties round she made a good penny by it, for there wasn't a wedding nor a christening for miles around in the countryside but she was called upon to make the cakes for it, and she got all the trade of all the gentry as well. She was fair in her prices and she was honest, too, but she was that good-hearted into the bargain. Those who could pay well she charged aplenty, but when some poor body came and begged her to make a wee bit of a cake for a celebration and timidly offered her the little money they had for it, she'd wave it away and tell them to pay her when they got the cake. Then she'd set to and bake a cake as fine and big as any she'd make for a laird, and she'd send it to them as a gift, with the best respects of her husband and herself, to the wedding pair or the parents of the baby that was to be christened, so nobody's feelings were hurt.

Not only was she a master baker, but she was the cleverest woman in the world; and it was the first that got her into trouble, but it was the second that got her out of it.

The fairies have their own good food to eat, but they dearly love a bit of baker's cake once in a while, and will often steal a slice of one by night from a kitchen while all the folks in a house are sleeping.

In a nearby hill there was a place where the fairies lived, and of all cakes the ones the fairies liked best were the ones this master baker made. The trouble was, the taste of one was hard to come by, for her cakes were all so good that they were always eaten up at a sitting, with hardly a crumb left over for a poor fairy to find.

So then the fairies plotted together to carry the woman away and to keep her with them always just to bake cakes for them.

Their chance came not long after, for there was to be a great wedding at the castle with hundreds of guests invited, and the woman was to make the cakes. There would have to be so many of them, with so many people coming to eat them, that the woman was to spend the whole day before the wedding in the castle kitchen doing nothing but bake one cake after another!

The fairies learned about this from one of their number who had been listening at the keyhole of the baker's door. They found out, too, what road she'd be taking coming home.

When the night came, there they were by a fairy mound where the road went by, hiding in flower cups, and under leaves, and in all manner of places.

When she came by they all flew out at her. 'The fireflies are gey thick the night,' said she. But it was not fireflies. It was fairies with the moonlight sparkling on their wings.

Then the fairies drifted fern seed into her eyes, and all of a sudden she was that sleepy that she could go not one step farther without a bit of a rest!

'Mercy me' she said with a yawn. 'It's worn myself out I have this day!' And she sank down on what she took to be a grassy bank to doze just for a minute. But it wasn't a bank at all. It was the fairy mound, and once she lay upon it she was in the fairies' power.

She knew nothing about that nor anything else till she woke again, and found herself in fairyland. Being a clever woman she didn't have to be told where she was, and she guessed how she got there. But she didn't let on.

'Well now,' she said happily, 'and did you ever! It's all my life I've wanted to get a peep into fairyland. And here I am!'

They told her what they wanted, and she said to herself, indeed she had no notion of staying there the rest of her life! But she didn't tell the fairies that either.

'To be sure!' she said cheerfully. 'Why you poor wee things! To think of me baking cakes for everyone else, and not a one for you! So let's be at it,' said she, 'with no time wasted.'

Then from her kittiebag that hung at her side she took a clean apron and tied it around her waist, while the fairies, happy that she was so willing, licked their lips in anticipation and rubbed their hands for joy.

'Let me see now,' said she, looking about her. 'Well, 'tis plain you have nothing for me to be baking a cake with. You'll just have to be going to my own kitchen to fetch back what I'll need.'

Yes, the fairies could do that. So she sent some for eggs, and some for sugar, and some for flour, and some for butter, while others flew off to get a wheen of other things she told them she had to have. At last all was ready for the mixing and the woman asked for a bowl. But the biggest one they could find for her was the size of a teacup, and a wee dainty one at that.

Well then, there was nothing for it, but they must go and fetch her big yellow crockery bowl from off the shelf over the water butt. And after that it was her wooden spoons and her egg whisp and one thing and another, till the fairies were all fagged out, what with the flying back and forth, and the carrying, and only the thought of the cake to come of it kept their spirits up at all.

At last everything she wanted was at hand. The woman began to measure and mix and whip and beat. But all of a sudden she stopped.

''Tis no use!' she sighed. 'I can't ever seem to mix a cake without my cat beside me, purring.'

'Fetch the cat!' said the fairy king sharply.

So they fetched the cat. The cat lay at the woman's feet and purred, and the woman stirred away at the bowl, and for a while all was well. But not for long.

The woman let go of the spoon and sighed again. 'Well now, would you think it?' said she. 'I'm that used to my dog setting the time of my beating by the way he snores at every second beat that I can't seem to get the beat right without him.'

'Fetch the dog!' cried the king.

So they fetched the dog and he curled up at her feet beside the cat. The dog snored, the cat purred, the woman beat the cake batter, and all was well again. Or so the fairies thought.

But no! The woman stopped again. 'I'm that worried about my babe,' said she. 'Away from him all night as I've been, and him with a new tooth pushing through this very week. It seems I just can't mix . . .'

'Fetch that babe!' roared the fairy king, without waiting for her to finish what she was saying. And they fetched the babe.

So the woman began to beat the batter again. But when they brought the babe, he began to scream the minute he saw her, for he was hungry, as she knew he would be, because he never would let his dadda feed him his porridge and she had not been home to do it.

'I'm sorry to trouble you,' said the woman, raising her voice above the screaming of the babe, 'but I can't stop beating now lest the cake go wrong. Happen my husband could get the babe quiet if . . .'

The fairies didn't wait for the king to tell them what to do. Off they flew and fetched the husband back with them. He, poor man, was all in a whirl, what with things disappearing from under his eyes right and left, and then being snatched through the air himself the way he was. But here was his wife, and he knew where she was things couldn't go far wrong. But the baby went on screaming.

So the woman beat the batter, and the baby screamed, and the cat purred, and the dog snored, and the man rubbed his eyes and watched his wife to see what she was up to. The fairies settled down, though 'twas plain to see that the babe's screaming disturbed them. Still, they looked hopeful.

Then the woman reached over and took up the egg whisp and gave the wooden spoon to the babe, who at once began to bang away with it, screaming just the same. Under cover of the screaming of the babe and the banging of the spoon and the swishing of the egg whisp the woman whispered to her husband, 'Pinch the dog!'

'What?' said the man. But he did it just the same—and kept on doing it.

'Tow! ROW! ROW!' barked the dog, and added his voice to the babe's screams, and the banging of the wooden spoon, and the swishing of the egg whisp.

'Tread on the tail of the cat!' whispered the woman to her husband, and it's a wonder he could hear her. But he did. He had got the notion now and he entered the game for himself. He not only trod on the tail of the cat, but he kept his foot there while the cat howled like a dozen lost souls.

So the woman swished, and the baby screamed, and the wooden spoon banged, and the dog yelped, and the cat howled, and the whole of it made a terrible din. The fairies, king and all, flew round and round in distraction with their hands over their ears, for if there is one thing the fairies can't bear it's a lot of noise and there was a lot more than a lot of noise in fairyland that day! And what's more the woman knew what they liked and what they didn't all the time!

So then the woman got up and poured the batter into two pans that stood ready. She laid by the egg whisp and took the wooden spoon away from the babe, and picking him up she popped a lump of sugar into his mouth. That surprised him so much that he stopped screaming. She nodded to her husband and he stopped pinching the dog and took his foot

From Sorche Nic Leodhas, *Heather and Broom: Tales of the Scottish Highlands*. Illustrated by Consuelo Joerns. (New York: Holt, Rinehart, and Winston, 1960), 40.

from the cat's tail, and in a minute's time all was quiet. The fairies stopped flying round and round and sank down exhausted.

And then the woman said, 'The cake's ready for the baking. Where's the oven?'

The fairies looked at each other in dismay, and at last the fairy queen said weakly, 'There isn't any oven.'

'What!' exclaimed the woman. 'No oven? Well then, how do you expect me to be baking the cake?'

None of the fairies could find the answer to that.

'Well then,' said the woman, 'you'll just have to be taking me and the cake home to bake it in my own oven, and bring me back later when the cake's all done.'

The fairies looked at the babe and the wooden spoon and the egg whisp and the dog and the cat and the man. And then they all shuddered like one.

'You may all go!' said the fairy king. 'But don't ask us to be taking you. We're all too tired.'

'Och, you must have your cake then,' said the woman, feeling sorry for them now she'd got what she wanted, which was to go back to her own home, 'after all the trouble you've had for it! I'll tell you what I'll do. After it's baked, I'll be leaving it for you beside the road, behind the bank where you found me. And what's more I'll put one there for you every single week's end from now on.'

The thought of having one of the woman's cakes every week revived the fairies so that they forgot they were all worn out. Or almost did.

'I'll not be outdone!' cried the fairy king. 'For what you find in that same place shall be your own!'

Then the woman picked up the pans of batter, and the man tucked the bowls and spoons and things under one arm and the baby under the other. The fairy king raised an arm and the hill split open. Out they all walked, the woman with the pans of batter, the man with the bowls and the babe, and the dog and the cat at their heels. Down the road they walked and back to their own house, and never looked behind them.

When they got back to their home the woman put the pans of batter into the oven, and then she dished out the porridge that stood keeping hot on the back of the fire and gave the babe his supper.

There wasn't a sound in that house except for the clock ticking and the kettle singing and the cat purring and the dog snoring. And all those were soft, quiet sounds.

'I'll tell you what,' said the man at last. 'It doesn't seem fair on the rest of the men that I should have the master baker and the cleverest woman in the world all in one wife.'

'Trade me off then for one of the ordinary kind,' said his wife, laughing at him.

'I'll not do it,' said he. 'I'm very well suited as I am.'

So that's the way the woman flummoxed the fairies. A good thing she made out of it, too, for when the cake was baked and cooled the woman took it up and put it behind the fairy mound, as she had promised. And when she set it down she saw there a little brown bag. She took the bag up and opened it and looked within, and it was full of bright shining yellow gold pieces.

And so it went, week after week. A cake for the fairies, a bag of gold for the woman and her husband. They never saw one of the fairies again, but the bargain never was broken and they grew rich by it. So of course they lived, as why should they not, happily ever after.

From *Heather and Broom: Tales of the Scottish Highlands*, by Sorche Nic Leodhas (New York: Holt, Rinehart and Winston, 1960).

The Barber's Clever Wife

This tale, which is found all over the Punjab region of northern India, presents a wife who becomes a classic trickster out of necessity. Burdened with a weak, incompetent, and foolish husband, the wife saves them from starvation by abandoning her traditionally passive and subservient position. Once she takes control, she shows that she is both wise and brave. She thus cleverly makes the thieves serve her economic interests and then displays considerable courage, in addition to her ever-ready wit, by protecting herself when they seek revenge. The comic crowning touch comes when the King advances her husband socially solely because of her indisputable merits.

Once upon a time there lived a barber, who was such a poor silly creature that he couldn't even ply his trade decently, but snipped off his customers' ears instead of their hair, and cut their throats instead of shaving them. So of course he grew poorer every day, till at last he found himself with nothing left in his house but his wife and his razor, both of whom were as sharp as sharp could be.

For his wife was an exceedingly clever person, who was continually rating her husband for his stupidity; and when she saw they hadn't a farthing left, she fell as usual to scolding.

But the barber took it very calmly. 'What is the use of making such a fuss, my dear?' said he; 'you've told me all this before, and I quite agree with you. I never *did* work, I never *could* work, and I never *will* work. That is the fact!'

'Then you must beg!' returned his wife, 'for *I* will not starve to please you! Go to the palace, and beg something of the King. There is a wedding feast going on, and he is sure to give alms to the poor.'

'Very well, my dear!' said the barber submissively. He was rather afraid of his clever wife, so he did as he was bid, and going to the palace, begged of the King to give him something.

'Something?' asked the king; 'what thing?'

Now the barber's wife had not mentioned anything in particular, and the barber was far too addle-pated to think of anything by himself, so he answered cautiously, 'Oh, something!'

'Will a piece of land do?' said the King.

Whereupon the lazy barber, glad to be helped out of the difficulty, remarked that perhaps a piece of land would do as well as anything else.

Then the King ordered a piece of waste, outside the city, should be given to the barber, who went home quite satisfied.

'Well! what did you get?' asked the clever wife, who was waiting impatiently for his return. 'Give it me quick, that I may go and buy bread!'

And you may imagine how she scolded when she found he had only got a piece of waste land.

'But land is land!' remonstrated the barber; 'it can't run away, so we must always have something now!'

'Was there ever such a dunderhead?' raged the clever wife. 'What good is ground unless we can till it? And where are we to get bullocks and ploughs?'

But being, as we have said, an exceedingly clever person, she set her wits to work, and soon thought of a plan whereby to make the best of a bad bargain.

She took her husband with her, and set off to the piece of waste land; then, bidding her husband imitate her, she began walking about the field, and peering anxiously into the ground. But when anybody came that way, she would sit down, and pretend to be doing nothing at all.

Now it so happened that seven thieves were hiding in a thicket hard by, and they watched the barber and his wife all day, until they became convinced something mysterious was going on. So at sunset they sent one of their number to try and find out what it was.

'Well, the fact is,' said the barber's wife, after beating about the bush for some time, and with many injunctions to strict secrecy, 'this field belonged to my grandfather, who buried five pots full of gold in it, and we were just trying to discover the exact spot before beginning to dig. You won't tell anyone, will you?'

The thief promised he wouldn't, of course, but the moment the barber and his wife went home, he called his companions, and telling them of the hidden treasure, set them to work. All night long they dug and delved, till the field looked as if it had been ploughed seven times over, and they were as tired as tired could be; but never a gold piece, nor a silver piece, nor a farthing did they find, so when dawn came they went away disgusted.

The barber's wife, when she found the field so beautifully ploughed, laughed heartily at the success of her stratagem, and going to the corn-dealer's shop, borrowed some rice to sow in the field. This the corn-dealer willingly gave her, for he reckoned he would get it back threefold at harvest time. And so he did, for never was there such a crop!—the barber's wife paid her debts, kept enough for the house, and sold the rest for a great crock of gold pieces.

Now, when the thieves saw this, they were very angry indeed, and going to the barber's house, said, 'Give us our share of the harvest, for we tilled the ground, as you very well know.'

'I told you there was gold in the ground,' laughed the barber's wife, 'but you didn't find it. I have, and there's a crock full of it in the house, only you rascals shall never have a farthing of it!'

'Very well!' said the thieves; 'look out for yourself to-night. If you won't give us our share we'll take it!'

So that night one of the thieves hid himself in the house, intending to open the door to his comrades when the housefolk were asleep; but the barber's wife saw him with the corner of her eye, and determined to lead him a dance. Therefore, when her husband, who was in a dreadful state of alarm, asked her what she had done with the gold pieces, she replied, 'Put them where no one will find them,—under the sweetmeats, in the crock that stands in the niche by the door.'

The thief chuckled at hearing this, and after waiting till all was quiet, he crept out, and feeling about for the crock, made off with it, whispering to his comrades that he had got the prize. Fearing pursuit, they fled to a thicket, where they sat down to divide the spoil.

'She said there were sweetmeats on the top,' said the thief; 'I will divide them first, and then we can eat them, for it is hungry work, this waiting and watching.'

So he divided what he thought were the sweetmeats as well as he could in the dark. Now in reality the crock was full of all sorts of horrible things that the barber's wife had put there on purpose, and so when the thieves crammed its contents into their mouths, you may imagine what faces they made and how they vowed revenge.

But when they returned next day to threaten and repeat their claim to a share of the crop, the barber's wife only laughed at them.

'Have a care!' they cried; 'twice you have fooled us—once by making us dig all night, and next by feeding us on filth and breaking our caste. It will be our turn to-night!'

Then another thief hid himself in the house, but the barber's wife saw him with half an eye, and when her husband asked 'What have you done with the gold, my dear? I hope you haven't put it under the pillow?' she answered, 'Don't be alarmed; it is out of the house. I have hung it in the branches of the *nīm* tree outside. No one will think of looking for it there!'

The hidden thief chuckled, and when the housefolk were asleep he slipped out and told his companions.

'Sure enough, there it is!' cried the captain of the band, peering up into the branches. 'One of you go up and fetch it down.' Now what he saw was really a hornets' nest, full of great big brown and yellow hornets.

So one of the thieves climbed up the tree; but when he came close to the nest, and was just reaching up to take hold of it, a hornet flew out and stung him on the thigh. He immediately clapped his hand to the spot.

'Oh, you thief!' cried out the rest from below, 'you're pocketing the gold pieces, are you? Oh ! shabby! shabby!'—For you see it was very dark, and when the poor man clapped his hand to the place where he had been stung, they thought he was putting his hand in his pocket.

'I assure you I'm not doing anything of the kind!' retorted the thief; 'but there is something that bites in this tree!'

Just at that moment another hornet stung him on the breast, and he clapped his hand there.

'Fie! fie for shame ! We saw you do it that time!' cried the rest. Just you stop that at once, or we will make you!'

So they sent up another thief, but he fared no better, for by this time the hornets were thoroughly roused, and they stung the poor man all over, so that he kept clapping his hands here, there, and everywhere.

'Shame! Shabby! Ssh-sh!' bawled the rest; and then one after another they climbed into the tree, determined to share the booty, and one after another began clapping their hands about their bodies, till it came to the captain's turn. Then he, intent on having the prize, seized hold of the hornets' nest, and as the branch on which they were all standing broke at the selfsame moment, they all came tumbling down with the hornets' nest on top of them. And then, in spite of bumps and bruises, you can imagine what a stampede there was!

After this the barber's wife had some peace, for every one of the seven thieves was in hospital. In fact, they were laid up for so long a time that she began to think that they were never coming back again, and ceased to be on the look-out. But she was wrong, for one night, when she had left the window open, she was awakened by whisperings outside, and at once recognised the thieves' voices. She gave herself up for lost; but determined not to yield without a struggle, she seized her husband's razor, crept to the side of the window, and stood quite still. By and by the first thief began to creep through cautiously. She just waited till the tip of his nose was visible, and then, flash!—she sliced it off with the razor as clean as a whistle.

'Confound it!' yelled the thief, drawing back mighty quick; 'I've cut my nose on something!'

'Hush-sh-sh-sh!' whispered the others, 'you'll wake some one. Go on!'

'Not I!' said the thief; 'I'm bleeding like a pig!'

'Pooh!—knocked your nose against the shutter, I suppose,' returned the second thief. 'I'll go!'

But, swish!—off went the tip of his nose too.

'Dear me!' said he ruefully, 'there certainly is something sharp inside!'

'A bit of bamboo in the lattice, most likely,' remarked the third thief. 'I'll go!'

And, flick!—off went his nose too.

'It is most extraordinary!' he exclaimed, hurriedly retiring; 'I feel exactly as if some one had cut the tip of my nose off!'

'Rubbish!' said the fourth thief. 'What cowards you all are! Let me go!'

But he fared no better, nor the fifth thief, nor the sixth.

'My friends!' said the captain, when it came to his turn, 'you are all disabled. One man must remain unhurt to protect the wounded. Let us return another night.'—He was a cautious man, you see, and valued his nose.

So they crept away sulkily, and the barber's wife lit a lamp, and gathering up all the nose tips, put them away safely in a little box.

Now before the robbers' noses were healed over, the hot weather set in, and the barber and his wife, finding it warm sleeping in the house, put their beds outside; for they made sure the thieves would not return. But they did, and seizing such a good opportunity for revenge, they lifted up the wife's bed, and carried her off fast asleep. She woke to find herself borne along on the heads of four of the thieves, whilst the other three ran beside her. She gave herself up for lost, and though she thought, and thought, and thought, she could find no way of escape; till, as luck would have it, the robbers paused to take breath under a banyan tree. Quick as lightning, she seized hold of a branch that was within reach, and swung herself into the tree, leaving her quilt on the bed just as if she were still in it.

'Let us rest a bit here,' said the thieves who were carrying the bed; 'there is plenty of time, and we are tired. She is dreadfully heavy!'

The barber's wife could hardly help laughing, but she had to keep very still, for it was a bright moon light night; and the robbers, after setting down their burden, began to squabble as to who should take first watch. At last they determined that it should be the captain, for the others had really barely recovered from the shock of having their noses sliced off; so they lay down to sleep, while the captain walked up and down, watching the bed, and the barber's wife sat perched up in the tree like a great bird.

Suddenly an idea came into her head, and drawing her white veil becomingly over her face, she began to sing softly. The robber captain looked up, and saw the veiled figure of a woman in the tree. Of course he was a little surprised, but being a good-looking young fellow, and rather vain of his appearance, he jumped at once to the conclusion that it was a fairy who had fallen in love with his handsome face. For fairies do such things sometimes, especially on moonlight nights. So he twirled his moustaches, and strutted about, waiting for her to speak. But when she went on singing, and took no notice of him, he stopped and called out, 'Come down, my beauty! I won't hurt you!'

But still she went on singing; so he climbed up into the tree, determined to attract her attention. When he came quite close, she turned away her head and sighed.

'What is the matter, my beauty?' he asked tenderly. 'Of course you are a fairy, and have fallen in love with me, but there is nothing to sigh at in that, surely?'

'Ah—ah—ah!' I said the barber's wife, with another sigh, 'I believe you're fickle! Men with long-pointed noses always are!'

But the robber captain swore he was the most constant of men; yet still the fairy sighed and sighed, until he almost wished his nose had been shortened too.

'You are telling stories, I am sure!' said the pretended fairy. 'Just let me touch your tongue with the tip of mine, and then I shall be able to taste if there are fibs about!'

So the robber captain put out his tongue, and, snip!—the barber's wife bit the tip off clean!

What with the fright and the pain, he tumbled off the branch, and fell bump on the ground, where he sat with his legs very wide apart, looking as if he had come from the skies.

'What is the matter?' cried his comrades, awakened by the noise of his fall.

'Bul-ul-a-bul-ul-ul!' answered he, pointing up into the tree; for of course he could not speak plainly without the tip of his tongue.'

'What—is—the—matter?' they bawled in his ear, as if that would do any good.

'Bul-ul-a-bul-ul-ul!' said he, still pointing upwards.

'The man is bewitched!' cried one; 'there must be a ghost in the tree!'

Just then the barber's wife began flapping her veil and howling; whereupon, without waiting to look, the thieves in a terrible fright set off at a run, dragging their leader with them; and the barber's wife, coming down from the tree, put her bed on her head, and walked quietly home.

After this, the thieves came to the conclusion that it was no use trying to gain their point by force, so they went to law to claim their share. But the barber's wife pleaded her own cause so well, bringing out the nose and tongue tips as witnesses, that the King made the barber his Wazīr, saying, 'He will never do a foolish thing as long as his wife is alive!'

From *Tales of the Punjab, Told by the People*, by Flora Anne Steel (London: Macmillan, 1894).

LINKS TO OTHER STORIES

Part Eight

ℒiving by 𝒲it
Trickster Tales

The trickster figure appears in traditional stories of cultures from around the world. To the Ashanti of West Africa, he is Anansi; to African-Americans in the southern United States, Br'er Rabbit; for many Native American peoples, he is Coyote. Polynesian cultures from New Zealand to Hawaii recount the deeds of Maui; Indonesians, those of Mouse-Deer. Among European cultures are found the Greek god Hermes, the Norse giant Loki, and the English outlaw Robin Hood. One of the many roles of the biblical Satan is that of a trickster.

Although trickster tales reflect many of the cultural beliefs and values of the people telling the tales, tricksters from different areas of the world share a sufficient number of characteristics that analysts are able to create a general portrait. The trickster possesses a dominant trait, extreme cunning, which he sometimes uses to help others but more often employs to gratify his own appetites, the chief of which are food and sex. At times, however, his devious plans backfire, and he not only fails to achieve his goals, but he also causes harm to himself. Sometimes he dies; however, when he does, he frequently returns to life in the next story.

While studying the motivations, successes, and failures of the trickster, scholars have commented on his complex nature. Jarold Ramsey refers to him as 'all man's epitome' (25), while Gary Snyder links him to 'something within ourselves that is creative, unpredictable, contradictory' (260). Karl Kerenyi names him 'the spirit of disorder, the enemy of boundaries' (185). Keith Lincoln points out the character's 'divine demonism' (123). Many critics have noted that the trickster frequently exists on the margins of his society.

Scholars have interpreted these characteristics of the trickster in a variety of ways. Carl Jung saw traits of human beings in a lower state of moral and social evolution in the trickster character. He believed that this figure embodied qualities that a society—focusing on the general, rather than the individual—controlled. Others have advanced more positive interpretations. Ramsey believed that in societies where accepted rules and norms of behaviour restricted individuality, the personality of the trickster contained qualities of the individual that were important counterparts to conformity. All people's unique, inner personalities were valuable, even though these qualities might conflict with their socially defined roles.

Given the complexity of the character, his roles, and his motivations, it is not surprising that the stories about him involve a clash of opposites: heroism and villainy, selfishness and altruism, individuality and group identity, cleverness and foolishness, victory and defeat, order and disorder. The end of each story resolves these oppositions, tentatively at least, sometimes to the benefit of the trickster and/or other characters, sometimes to his and/or their discomfort and distress.

Why have so many cultures told stories about so contradictory and complex a character? Part of the reason, no doubt, is that the tales were entertaining and did not lose their appeal in frequent retellings. In fact, they were like oft-repeated jokes, enjoyable because they were so familiar to audiences who knew what was coming next. But people also told them because, when either the trickster or someone else was defeated, audiences could enjoy a sense of superiority, feeling that, in like situations, they could have done better. Of course, listeners may also have been expressing an uneasy laughter. 'That,' they might have been thinking, 'could have been me.'

The stories may also have provided emotional or psychological safety valves for audiences. Because the trickster so often behaved very badly, violating social restrictions and taboos, audiences participated vicariously and safely in the adventures. Moreover, when the central figure was defeated, they could approve of his punishment with a sense of relief. By breaking rules, the character had affirmed the existence of the rules, and his punishment for transgressions restored order.

The major trickster figures found in traditional stories from around the world are male. The reason for their being male may be attributable to the fact that the majority of traditional cultures were patriarchal. It may also be because common elements in trickster stories, such as wandering in search of adventure and experiencing these adventures in alien environments, are more reflective of the lives of men, who have frequently been more able than women to move away from the ties and responsibilities of home. It could also be suggested that the self-centeredness and the quest to fulfill individual appetites are more reflective of men than women.

There are stories, however, involving women and girls who play tricks. These characters are frequently portrayed as unlikely heroes, individuals who do not at first seem able to surmount the odds facing them. They rely on their cleverness and, unlike many male tricksters, do not seem to be motivated to satisfy selfish wishes or to fulfill their egos. In fact, they frequently execute their tricks to benefit others, often to make their home environments more secure.

Not only have a large number of scholars studied the trickster figure, but also many authors and illustrators have adapted trickster tales for children. Of course, those episodes that concern the sexual exploits of the character have not been retold for the young. The trickster's foolish and humorous antics, as well as his beneficial deeds, have, however, provided the basis for individual picture books and collections of tales. Appealing to children's sense of the ridiculous and their growing awareness of verbal and situational irony, authors have capitalized on events in which trickster's victims have been unknowingly outwitted, or in which the perpetrator of the tricks has found himself in unforeseen and unfortunate predicaments.

Often, children can enjoy a sense of superiority to either the victims or the out-tricked trickster and can laugh at situations and characters that have made foolish mistakes that are obvious to the young readers. At other times, they can identify with the trickster. Surrounded by large people, parents and other adults who are in apparent control of their own lives and those of children, young readers can appreciate and admire the skills and successes of seemingly disadvantaged characters. Marginalized in a sense in their own lives, they can find similarities in these marginalized story heroes.

In addition to publishers' awareness of these fairly obvious aspects of young readers' responses, another factor has influenced their publication of trickster tales. Although stories from other lands had been appearing since the later nineteenth century, the increased number of young readers from non-European cultures and the growing multi-cultural focus of education over the past four decades have created a demand for stories from so-called 'minority' cultures. In the middle of the first half of the twentieth century, African-American stories of Br'er Rabbit, collected by nineteenth-century white southern journalist Joel Chandler Harris, were readily available in somewhat simplified versions. A smattering of stories from other cultures was also available, often adapted in ways that made them resemble more familiar European tales in style, character, and plot.

In the 1960s, however, the American Civil Rights movement, followed by increased awareness about Native Indians and other minority groups in North America, created a demand for traditional stories from these cultures. Mainstream authors began to search through anthropological journals of the late nineteenth and early twentieth centuries for lesser-known traditional tales. During the 1970s and 1980s, children's authors and illustrators not only found stories that they believed appropriate for and accessible to younger readers, but also they engaged in extensive research, studying cultural beliefs and customs and artistic styles that would cast light on the meanings of the stories. They then incorporated the results of such research into their verbal and visual retellings.

Children's books on tricksters from non-European cultures met the needs of a changing market. Young readers could learn about different cultures by reading the stories that reflected these cultures' values. They could see the Cree trickster Wisahketchahk violate Native American laws about respectful hunting and the necessity of hospitality. They could notice how the Cuban hero in 'How El Bizarrón Fooled the Devil' faced an adversary who is a prominent figure in the folktales of Latin American countries influenced by Spanish Catholicism. Studying 'A Legend of Knockmany', a story from the lesser-known Celtic traditions of Europe, they could consider the possibility that the story was a satire on the mighty deeds recounted in serious tales of such celebrated Celtic heroes as Fin and Cucullin.

Having children read these stories as reflections of specific cultures will please those teachers and scholars who emphasize differences between stories from various parts of the world and who study what the tales reveal about specific groups. The stories can, however, be read in ways that focus on their similarities. Such an approach would please universalists who believe that stories reflect fundamental human realities and characteristics that are the same around the world.

In fact, in reading the stories from around the world, one is struck by similarities in their narrative structure. Basically, the stories begin with the central character facing a problem or conflict, then engaging in creative problem solving and putting plans into action, and, finally, either succeeding or failing. The problem may relate to a group, as in 'Anansi Earns the Sky-God's Stories', which is set in a time when people were without stories. Conversely, it may involve an individual, usually the trickster himself. He may find his great appetite for food unfulfilled, as in 'Wisahketchahk and the Ducks', or he may be in danger from an enemy who wishes to harm or kill him, as in 'A Legend of Knockmany' or 'The Rabbit and the Coyote', or he may have created a situation in which his adversary seeks revenge or wants to outwit him at his own game, as in 'The Wonderful Tar-Baby Story'.

The strategies the trickster devises reflect his cleverness and quick-wittedness. Anansi uses his skill with words to capture the animals he must bring to the Sky-God. In 'Jack the Giant Killer', the hero must create stories about his non-existent prowess in order to defeat giants, earn money, and avoid physical labour. In 'The Tiger, the Brâhman, and the Jackal', the jackal feigns dim-wittedness in order to trick the tiger into a cage from which he has been released. Often, the tricksters are themselves tricked. Wisahketchahk, who has killed far more ducks than he needs to satisfy his appetite, is outwitted by a fox feigning injury as a means of stealing all the fowl that Wisahketchahk had acquired through his own duplicity.

Although the main characters in the stories are usually male, they require, in some cases, the help of women. Anansi's wife provides tips that are instrumental in his fulfilling the seemingly impossible tasks set by the Sky-God. In 'A Legend of Knockmany', Oonagh, wife of the giant Fin M'Coul, practices sly manipulation to rescue him from another giant. When a husband fails to trap a rabbit in 'The Rabbit and the Coyote', his wife is the one who suggests the use of the wax doll on which the thief gets stuck.

Whether the stories are told within cultures, reinforcing the shared values of tellers and listeners, or whether they are read by children from other cultures, trickster tales retain their vitality, engaging audiences in the adventures of a lively, indefatigable character whose audacity and vitality relates to beliefs of specific groups and to qualities of character found in people around the world.

Works Cited

Jung, Carl. 1972. 'On the Psychology of the Trickster Figure', *The Trickster: A Study in American Indian Mythology*, by Paul Radin. New York: Schocken Books.

Kerényi, Karl. 1972. 'The Trickster in Relation to Greek Mythology', *The Trickster: A Study in American Indian Mythology*, by Paul Radin. New York: Schocken Books.

Lincoln, Keith. 1983. *Native American Renaissance*. Berkeley: University of California Press.

Ramsey, Jarold. 1983. *Reading the Fire: Essays in the Traditional Indian Literatures of the Far West*. Lincoln: University of Nebraska Press.

Anansi Earns the Sky-God's Stories

A well-known *pourquoi* tale explaining the origin of what the Ashanti of West Africa call Spider-Stories, this narrative reveals how the trickster Anansi—the spider—is able to complete four apparently impossible tasks through his ability with words. Initially ridiculed when he requests the stories from the Sky-God, the unlikely hero invents clever lies to capture his first three victims; he creates ironic situations that trap his dangerous opponents. In capturing the fairy, he remains silent, refusing to reply to it. Because of his ability to know how and when to use words, he receives a gift of words in the form of the stories he shares with others. In this version of the story, Anansi is aided by his wife, who seems to think up the strategies that he employs.

We do not really mean, we do not really mean, that what we are going to say is true.

Kwaku Anansi, the Spider, once went to Nyame, the Sky-God, in order to buy the Sky-God's stories. The Sky-God was surprised and said, 'Great and powerful towns have come, but they were unable to purchase them, and you think that you, who are a mere masterless man, will be able to.'

The Spider said, 'I shall be able. What is the price of the stories?'

'They cannot be bought for anything except the Onini creature, the python; Osebo, the leopard; Moatia, the fairy; and Moboro, the hornets,' the Sky-God replied.

'I will bring these things, and, in addition, I'll add my old woman, Nsia, to the lot,' Anansi said.

Anansi returned home and consulted his wife, Aso, asking her, 'What should we do to capture Onini, the python?' Aso told him to cut off a branch of a palm-tree and a length of string creeper.

When he had done this, she told him to take the objects to the stream. As he did, he began talking to himself, 'It's longer than he is, it's not so long as he; you lie, it's longer than he.' Soon he found the python, lying by the stream.

Onini, who had heard Anansi talking to himself, asked, 'What were you talking about?'

'My wife, Aso, told me that this palm branch is longer than you, and I say she is a liar,' the Spider explained.

The python ordered Anansi to measure him, and so Anansi laid the palm-branch along the python's body, telling him to stretch himself to full length. Then Anansi took the rope-creeper and wound it around and around until he came to the head of the snake. 'Fool,' he laughed, when he had finished, 'I shall take you to the Sky-God and receive the stories in exchange.'

When Anansi had delivered Onini, Nyame reminded him, 'There remains what still remains.'

The Spider returned home and told his wife what happened. She told him to look for a gourd, fill it with water, and set off with it. Anansi went through the bush with the gourd until he saw a swarm of hornets hanging there, and he poured out some of the water and sprinkled it on the hornets. He poured the remainder on himself and cut a leaf of the plantain and covered his head with it.

Now he addressed the hornets, 'As the rain has come, had you not better come and enter my gourd so that the rain will not beat you? Don't you see that I have taken a plantain leaf to cover myself?'

All the hornets thanked Anansi as they flew into the gourd. Fom! Father Spider covered the mouth and said 'Fools, I have got you, and I am taking you to receive the tales of the Sky-God in exchange.'

When the Sky-God saw the hornets, he remarked, 'What remains, still remains.'

And so Anansi once again returned to his wife and told her he had to capture Osebo, the leopard. She ordered him to dig a hole. 'I understand,' he told her and went off to look for leopard's tracks. When he found them, he dug a very deep pit, covered it over, and returned home.

The next morning, just as it was getting light, he went to where he had dug the pit, saying as he approached. 'Little father's child, little mother's child, I have told you not to get drunk, and now, just as one would expect of you, you have become intoxicated, and that's why you have fallen into the pit. If I were to say I would get you out, the next day, if you saw me or likewise any of my children, you would go and catch them.'

The leopard replied that he would never do such a thing. Then Anansi went and cut two sticks, put them across the pit, and gave directions to the leopard. 'Put one of your paws here and one here.' The leopard did as he was told and, as he was about to climb up, Anansi hit the animal over the head. It fell into the pit again and, while it was still senseless, Anansi got a ladder to descend into the pit and drag the leopard out. 'Fool,' he said to it, 'I am taking you to exchange for the stories of the Sky-God.'

He lifted the leopard up and took it to Nyame, who said, 'What remains, still remains.'

And so, the spider went home and carved a statue of a wooden doll. He tapped some sticky latex from a tree and plastered the doll's body with it. Then he mashed some yams and put them in the doll's hand. He pounded some more and placed them in a brass basin. Finally he tied a string around the doll's waist and carried it to the foot of an odum-tree, a place where the Fairies come to play.

Soon a fairy came along and, when she noticed the doll, she said, 'May I have a little of this mash?' Anansi tugged at the string, making the doll nod her head. When she had finished eating, she thanked the doll. But the doll did not answer.

The Fairy became angry and slapped the doll. Pa! Her hand stuck on the doll. She slapped her with her other hand and it, too, became stuck. So, she pushed her stomach against the doll in order to free herself. And, of course, it stuck, too. Then Anansi came out of his hiding place, tied her up, and said, 'Fool, I have got you, I shall take you to the Sky-God in exchange for his stories.

He went home where he found his mother. 'Rise up, let us go. I am taking you along with the fairy to go and give the Sky-God in exchange for his stories.'

He lifted them up and went to where the Sky-God was. 'Sky-God,' he said, 'here is a fairy, and my old mother whom I spoke about, here she is, too.'

Now the Sky-God called together the elders, the leader of the army, the major-domo, and the leader of the rear-guard. He put the matter before them, saying, 'Very great kings have come and were not able to buy the Sky-God's stories. But Kwaku Anansi, the spider, has been able to pay the price. Sing his praise.' The crowd shouted in praise.

'Kwaku Anansi,' the Sky-God said, 'from this day and going on for ever, I take my Sky-God's stories and I present them to you. Kose! Kose! Kose! My blessing, blessing, blessing. No more shall we call them the stories of the Sky-God, but we shall call them Spider Stories.'

This is my story, which I have related, if it be sweet, or if it not be sweet, take some elsewhere, and let some come back to me.

Adapted from 'How It Came About that the Sky-God's Stories Came to be Known as "Spider-Stories",' in *Akan-Ashanti Folk-Tales*, collected and translated by Capt. R.S. Rattray (Oxford: Clarendon Press, 1930).

Tricksy Rabbit

Like many tricksters, Tricksy Rabbit, who, along with Anansi and the Tortoise, is a major West African story character, uses language to defeat physically superior adversaries and to complete a successful quest. Not only does he use flattery with the women to earn a better price for his cloth than does the elephant for his, but also he escapes dangerous animals by concocting a story that appeals to their vanity. Like many traditional African tales, however, this one has an ambiguous conclusion, casting doubt on the extent of Tricksy's success. Among the questions implicitly raised are the following: 'Considering how quickly the meat would perish, was butchering the cow a wise act?' 'Wouldn't the cow be more valuable alive as a producer of milk and calves?' 'And what will be the consequences when the local deity, Mugassa, hears that Tricksy has referred to the god for his own selfish purposes?'

*I*n Uganda, deep in the heart of Africa, there once lived a clever rabbit. He was so full of fun and tricks that the forest folk called him Tricksy Rabbit.

On the trail one day Tricksy met his friend Elephant. The two stopped to chat. 'I hear,' said Tricksy, 'that the Watusi herders are in need of cloth. I would like to get a fine fat cow for myself. This may be a wise time to go trading.'

'That is a fine idea!' said Elephant.

So the two prepared bales of cloth for the journey. Tricksy gathered a rabbit-sized bundle, and Elephant an elephant-sized one.

They set out for the land of the Watusi in a gay mood. Tricksy told one funny story after another. He kept Elephant squealing with laughter.

Presently they came to a river.

Elephant, who loved the water, waded right in.

'Wait!' cried Tricksy. 'You aren't going to cross without me, I hope! Aren't we partners?'

'Of course we're partners,' said Elephant. 'But I didn't promise to carry you and your pack. Step in! The water is hardly over my feet.'

'Over your feet is over my head,' cried Tricksy. 'And you know I can't swim!'

'I can't help that,' said Elephant. 'If you can't take care of your self on the trail, then go back home.' And he splashed on across the river.

'I'll get even with him for that!' muttered Tricksy as he set about looking for a small log. He found one nearby and, placing his bundle on it, paddled across the river. He paddled so fast to catch up with Elephant that he splashed muddy water all over the cloth. Though he wiped off the mud the best he could, the cloth was ruined.

Tricksy soon overtook Elephant, and the two reached the land of the Watusi with no more trouble.

Elephant went straight to the men of the tribe and told them he had come to trade his cloth for cattle. He was so gruff about it that at first the tall proud herders refused to deal with him. At last they agreed to give him a knobby-kneed little calf for his fine bale of cloth.

Tricksy went among the women. He laughed and joked with them and told them how pretty they were. They liked him so much that when the subject of trade was brought up, the wife of the chief was happy to give him the finest cow in the herd for his muddy little bundle of cloth.

As the traders set out for home, Elephant said, 'Now if we should meet any strangers, you tell them that both animals belong to me. If anyone were to guess that such a fine cow belonged to a rabbit, it would be as good as gone. You would never be able to defend it!'

'You're right!' said Tricksy. 'I'm glad you thought of that.'

They hadn't gone far when they met some people coming home from the market. The strangers gathered around the cows to look them over.

'How beautiful the big one is,' one man said.

'How fat!' said another.

'How sleek!' said a third.

Then a man approached Elephant. 'The big cow is yours, I suppose. And does the little one belong to your small friend?' he asked.

Elephant coughed and tossed his head, preparing to boast that both belonged to him. But Tricksy was too quick for him. 'Ha!' he cried. 'The big one is mine! Elephant and I went trading. I traded a small bundle of cloth for this fine cow. But all Elephant could get for his big bundle of cloth was that scabby little calf!'

The people had a good laugh over that!

From Verna Aardema, *Tales from the Story Hat*. Illustrated by Elton Fax. (New York: Coward, McCann & Geoghegan, 1960), 12.

The two went on. When they had gone a little way, Elephant said, 'Tricksy, you shamed me in front of all those people! Next time let me do the talking.'

'Those weren't the kind of people who would steal my cow anyway,' said Tricksy.

Soon they met more people. They, too, stopped to look at the cattle. One man said, 'That sleek fat cow couldn't be the mother of that rat-eaten calf, could she?'

Elephant opened his mouth to explain, but again Tricksy was too quick for him.

'No, no relation!' cried Tricksy. 'You see, Elephant and I have been trading with the Watusi. And I, for a small bundle of muddy old cloth—'

He never finished, for Elephant swung his trunk and sent him rolling.

The people scattered in a hurry.

Elephant said, 'A fine partner you are! You can't keep a promise from here to a bend in the road. Take that cow of yours and go home by yourself!'

So, at the first branching of the path, Rabbit separated from Elephant. From then on he knew, he would never get his cow home safely unless he used his wits. He started to think.

Elephant hadn't gone far when he met a lion. 'I happen to know,' he told Lion, 'that there's a rabbit with a bigger cow than this over on the next trail.'

Soon he met a leopard, and then a hyena. He told them both the same thing. 'One of the three will relieve him of that cow, for sure!' he chuckled.

Over on the next trail the lion soon overtook Tricksy. 'Rabbit!' he roared. 'I could eat you in one bite! But go away fast—and I'll be satisfied with the cow!'

'Oh, Bwana Lion,' cried Tricksy, 'I'm sorry, but this cow isn't mine to give! She belongs to the Great Mugassa, the spirit of the forest. I'm only driving her for him to his feast. And, now I remember, Mugassa told me to invite you if I saw you!'

'Come now,' said Lion, 'are you trying to tell me that Mugassa has invited me to a feast?'

'Are you not the king of beasts?' asked Tricksy. 'Surely he must plan to honour you! Anyway, come along and see!'

Lion fell into line behind Tricksy and the cow. They hadn't gone far when the leopard overtook them.

Leopard sidled up to Lion and said in a big whisper, 'How about sharing the cow with me? You can *have* the rabbit!'

Tricksy overheard what Leopard said, and he broke in. 'Bwana Leopard, you don't understand! This cow doesn't belong to either Lion or me. It belongs to Mugassa. We're just driving it to the feast for him. And, now I remember, I was told to invite you, too!'

'I'm invited, too,' said Lion. 'Mugassa is planning to honour me.' 'Hmmm!' said Leopard. But he followed along behind the cow, the rabbit, and the lion.

Soon the hyena joined the procession in the same way.

A little farther on, a huge buffalo blocked the path. 'Out of my way!' he bellowed.

'Oh, Bwana Buffalo,' cried Tricksy, 'I'm so glad you happened along! We're taking this cow to the feast of Mugassa, and I was told to invite you. I didn't know where to look for you. Now, here you are!'

'Are all of you going?' asked Buffalo.

'Yes,' said Lion. 'Mugassa is planning to honour *me*. Perhaps I shall be crowned!'

'Hmmm!' said Leopard.

Buffalo turned around and led the procession with Tricksy riding on his head to direct him.

Soon they arrived at Tricksy's compound. Two dogs who guarded the gate yapped wildly when they saw them. Tricksy quieted the dogs and sent one streaking off to his hut in the middle of the wide compound with a pretend message for Mugassa.

In a short time the dog came back with a pretend answer, which he whispered into Tricksy's ear.

Tricksy stood on a stump and spoke importantly. 'Mugassa says that hyena is to butcher and cook the cow. Lion will carry water for the kettle. Buffalo will chop wood for the fire. Leopard will go to the banana grove yonder and watch for leaves to fall. We need fresh leaves for plates.

'Dogs will lay out mats inside the fence. Then, when the meat is cooked, all of us must help carry it in and spread it on the mats. When all is ready, Mugassa will come out and present each his portion.

'One warning—Mugassa says that if anyone steals so much as a bite, all of us will be punished!'

Tricksy gave Lion a pail with a hole in the bottom. He gave Buffalo an ax with a loose head. He told Leopard to catch the leaves with his eyelashes so as to keep them very clean. Then he climbed to the top of an anthill to watch and laugh.

The animals were so anxious to hurry the feast that Tricksy had many a chuckle over their foolish efforts.

Lion hurried back and forth from the river to the kettle with the leaky pail. Though he filled it to the top each time he dipped it into the river, there would be only a little water to pour into the kettle.

Every time Buffalo swung the ax he had to hunt for the head of it, for it always flew off into the bushes. At last he finished breaking up the wood with his feet.

Leopard fluttered his eyelashes at the long banana leaves, but not one came down.

Now, Hyena had never before in his life had a choice of meat. Always he had to eat what was left by other animals. This time he saw and smelled the choice parts. The liver smelled best to him. 'I hope Mugassa gives me the liver!' he said. 'But he won't. He'll think the rack of bones to clean is good enough for me—me, who did most of the work!'

Hyena lifted the liver out of the pot and hid it under a bush. Tricksy saw him, but said nothing.

When the meat was done, all the animals helped carry it in and spread it on the mats laid out in Rabbit's compound. Then Tricksy began to check. 'Four legs,' he said, 'back, sides, neck, tongue. . . . But where's the liver?'

Everyone began looking for the liver. 'Someone has stolen the liver!' cried Tricksy.

'Here comes Mugassa!' cried one of the dogs. 'Run! Run!'

The big animals stampeded through the gate. Tricksy slipped the bolt through the latch. Then he and his dogs rolled on the grass with laughter.

They were still laughing when Elephant poked his head over the gate. 'I see you got home, Rabbit!' he called.

'Yes!' said Tricksy. 'I got my cow home, too—and all cooked already!'

'What I should like to know,' said Elephant, 'is *how* you did it.'

'With the help of Mugassa,' laughed Tricksy.

From *Tales from the Story Hat*, by Verna Aardema (New York: Coward, McCann & Geoghegan, 1960).

The Two Fishermen

In addition to tales of the spider-trickster, the people of the West Indies frequently adapted West African stories about the rabbit trickster to the conditions of Caribbean life. This Trinidadian tale uses a familiar motif found in trickster stories from the Americas and Africa: the strategic placement of very similar looking family members along a trail. Tigercat, the dupe, is lazy, egotistical, and greedy, qualities that are unacceptable in a fishing community where men must work together at sea. The rabbit is the opposite—not only does he uncomplainingly endure the rigours of the fishing expedition, but also he works cooperatively with his family to avenge himself on Tigercat. Ironically Tigercat, for whom appearances are important, is unable to see the differences of the apparently 'dead' rabbits on the road.

*C*ompère Tigercat always felt that one day he would be lucky at the goat races, and because of this he always tried not to miss the races which took place periodically on the long stretch of Manzanilla Beach. The beach was a really good place for the races. It was extremely wide, and very, very long, so everyone—the racing goats and the spectators—could be comfortable. Tigercat enjoyed himself and could only have been happier on these occasions if he had won a large sum of money.

Often enough he would talk the matter over with his wife, who had heard her husband express these hopes so often that she had ceased to believe it could ever happen. Well, one day it did! Compère Tigercat came home with his pockets bulging with money he had won, beaming with pride and joy at his achievement.

He put the money in his usual 'safe' place, a pan under a loose floorboard of his house, and every day or so would take it out just to look at it and feel good. He soon tired of his pastime though, and began to think that there was not much use in having so much money lying around when it could easily be working for him and increasing. He began to think of what he could do with the money that would bring a sure, quick return.

After much consideration he decided to buy a boat. He had always fancied himself as a fisherman and he reasoned that this was a golden opportunity to set himself up in business. He bought a boat with oars, and an anchor, a seine, fishing tackle, hooks, lines, a big basket for holding the fish, a bucket for baling water out of the boat, and a number of other items which he was sure would prove useful.

At last everything was ready and he sat down to plan his first fishing trip. He soon realized that he would need an assistant on his trip and he promptly decided to ask Compère Rabbit to go along with him.

Compère Rabbit accepted with pleasure. He liked fishing, and thought that doing it from a boat on the sea instead of throwing a line out from the land was a considerable improvement. He also looked forward to bringing home a number of fish for his family.

Finally the wonderful day came when the two fisherman set off. Compère Rabbit rowed while Compère Tigercat lay in the bows exclaiming at the softness of the breeze against his cheek and the salty tang of the sea. He admired and exclaimed over the boat from bow to the stern and down to the anchor. Compère Rabbit listened and noticed that Tigercat did not lift a hand to help with the rowing, but he reasoned that after all it was Tigercat's boat, and although he would have liked some assistance with the rowing he didn't mind too much. And, besides, he was enjoying the sea and the gentle breezes, too.

Soon they were a long way out from the land and were approaching a group of small islands called the Five Islands. Tigercat busied himself and took his bearings. He checked out one point of land against the other and decided on the area in which he wanted to fish. Compère Rabbit didn't really understand what he was doing but he pretended to, for after all, he had no intention of letting Compère Tigercat know that this was the first time he had ever gone fishing in a boat.

Once the area was decided upon they wasted no time in throwing out their anchor, baiting their several hooks, and casting lines. Soon the fish were nibbling and in a short space of time Tigercat was reeling in a line at the end of which wiggled a beautiful Red Sanpper.

Tigercat was extremely happy. He wanted to measure the fish but there was no rule available.

'He's a beautiful fellow, eh Rabbit?'

'Yes, yes,' said Rabbit. 'I only hope I can catch one half as good as that and I'll be satisfied.'

'Yes. Well, we shall see,' Tigercat said.

Soon Rabbit got a nibble and pulled hard. His fish was not as big as Tigercat's but good enough. Then the fish started biting like mad. It was as though they had had nothing to eat for days, and the plump sardines wriggling on the fishermen's hooks were extremely tempting. Tigercat and Rabbit were reeling in fish more rapidly than they ever thought possible.

Tigercat could hardly contain himself.

From Belma Pollard, ed., *Anansesem: A Collection of Caribbean Folk-Tales, Legends and Poems for Juniors.* (Kingston: Longman Jamaica, 1985), 11.

'Look at my fish!' he exclaimed. 'Look at my beautiful fish! So many fish. So many. They're marvellous, absolutely beautiful. I told you. I told you I was a good fisherman. You see, there's the proof, Rabbit, there's the proof!'

Tigercat was in transports of joy. Rabbit listened and said nothing. He heard Tigercat's 'My fish' and would have preferred 'Our fish,' but he was always one to hold his own counsel, so he said nothing. Instead he started pulling in his line with the look of a man who had had a successful day's fishing and was tired. He really was tired too. His arms ached from rowing and casting and pulling, and he had a sneaking suspicion that Tigercat did not intend to help with the rowing on the return trip.

But Compère Tigercat was not satisfied. He couldn't leave all those fish in the ocean uncaught. He wanted to use his seine and pull them all in but Rabbit pointed out that the water was far too deep for only two of them to manage so great a task.

Compère Tigercat was forced to agree with his reasoning but he still wanted to fish some more, so Compère Rabbit obliged and threw out his line again. The fish were still biting as eagerly as ever and it was a long time before Compère Tigercat grudgingly agreed that they had caught enough. He tried counting the fish, but was forever having to start over again because he was continually distracted by the length or width or plumpness of a particular fish and left off counting to admire. Compère Rabbit was quite fed up with him, but still he said nothing. It had been an excellent day's fishing and he was eagerly looking forward to receiving his share of the catch.

He was a bit concerned because Tigercat kept saying 'my fish', 'my fish', but reasoned to himself that his friend was so beside himself with joy that he most probably didn't realize what he was saying.

He said, 'Yes Tigercat, I don't think there's very much left to be caught now. See where the sun is already, and I am willing to bet that we have almost all the fish in this area in this boat. Just look at it. We really have done well.'

'I suppose you're right,' said Tigercat.

'We have enough for both of us,' said Rabbit. 'More than enough really.'

'Hm-m-m,' said Tigercat, and lay back in the bows again. 'Hm-m-m.'

Compère Tigercat did not help with rowing on the return trip. He lay in the bows gazing about him every now and again but concentrating on the fish more than anything else.

When they reached the shore he suddenly sprang to life. He helped Rabbit to pull the boat ashore, to remove the fishing tackle and buckets and oars and store them away in an old hut.

Then he bustled about to divide the fish.

'You know, this is going to be a very technical business, Compère Rabbit. I've been sitting there in the boat all this time studying how to share these few fish between all of us.'

'All of us, Compère Tigercat!' Rabbit said. 'Which all of us? I only see two of us. Who else is there, man?'

'How do you mean who else is there, Rabbit? What about the boat, and the seine, and the anchor, and the fishing tackle, and those things. They must get their shares as well, you know!'

'But all those things are yours, Tigercat.'

'Of course they're mine, but that has nothing to do with it!' It was at this point that Compère Rabbit suddenly gave up the argument. There was not much point to it anyway.

'Okay, Compère,' he said. 'Let's see you share for the anchor, and boat, and those things!'

Compère Tigercat started sharing, 'Two for me, two for the boat, two for the anchor, two for the seine, two for you, Compère Rabbit.'

'Two for me, two for the boat, two for the anchor, two for the seine, two for you, Compère Rabbit . . .'

On and on he went until there was no longer one heap of fish but five heaps. Compère Rabbit looked at his heap and said nothing. True enough it was a decent looking heap but he had rowed and fished all day and in view of what they had caught he had expected more.

'Hm-m-m,' he said when Tigercat stopped. 'Okay then, Tigercat. Reach home safely with those fish now, eh. I have to hurry on with my batch.' And with that he was off.

Compère Tigercat lingered to put all his piles of fish in one basket and settle the basket on his head comfortably before setting off home.

Once out of Tigercat's range of vision Compère Rabbit took off as though a mad bull was chasing him. He was panting but excited when he arrived home with his fish.

'Come on, come on,' he called to three of his plumpest sons. 'I have a job for you to do and you'd better do it well.'

Down the road came Compère Tigercat, lugging his basket and whistling. He had a vision of steamed fish with coo-coo and boiled ochroes and smiled to himself. If he gave Compère Rabbit any thought at all it was only to consider how lucky he had been to be invited to go fishing and how generous he, Tigercat had been to him.

Suddenly, as he turned a bend in the dirt road he was brought up short by the sight of a plump black and white rabbit lying there.

'Hullo!' Tigercat thought to himself. 'Not a bad looking fellow. I wonder what hit him.'

But he kept on his way with his basket of fish.

Just the same a few yards down the road around another bend there was another rabbit. Compère Tigercat looked at it.

'Hm-m-m,' he said. 'Quite a coincidence, another rabbit. This one is not quite as plump as the other, yet . . . Oh well, there's no point in turning back, and one rabbit's no good to my family.'

With that he was off again, whistling even more tunelessly than before.

To his great surprise, he had only gone a short distance and covered about two bends in the road when right there in front of him almost barring his path was another plump looking rabbit.

He put down his basket and looked at it.

'Well now,' he said. 'I've got to consider this. Here's a fine looking fellow better than the first, I'd say.' He prodded the rabbit with his toe. 'And with a thick coat too.'

'One rabbit I can leave alone, two not much different, but three, well that's asking too much. I'll just leave my basket of fish here and go back for those two fellows. I'll put it in the bushes though, and this rabbit with it. One can never tell who will pass.'

So saying, he lifted the rabbit by its feet and slung it into the fish basket. In a short while he had hidden the basket in the bushes and set off to pick up the rabbits he had passed, hoping that his luck held and that no-one had come upon them after him.

No sooner was Tigercat safely out of sight than the rabbit in the fish basket suddenly came to life.

'Uh-h,' he said. 'How dare he throw me on these fresh-smelling fish of his.'

'You'd better hurry and help me get this basket out of here,' said his father, Compère Rabbit, emerging from the bushes. 'Where are your two brothers? Ah, here they come. A good little job, boys,' he said, tweaking their ears. 'But now we must hurry. Tigercat is no fool and from the time he misses that second rabbit he'll smell a rat. So come on, let's go.'

Between them they lifted the fish basket and disappeared in the high bush.

In the meantime Compère Tigercat came to the place where the second rabbit had been. He looked down at the bare spot in the road where the 'dead' rabbit had lain and was thoroughly confused.

'Someone must have found it,' he said.

And suddenly the certainty of being tricked hit him. He turned around and darted at top speed to his hidden basket of fish but when he got there it was too late. There was no rabbit and no basket of fish, and search as he could there was not a trace to be found of either.

He was sure that Compère Rabbit had tricked him and his first reaction was to dash off to his home and accuse him, but then he thought of how foolish and greedy he'd look when the story was told and decided to say nothing.

He had really been caught by his greed on both counts and there was nothing he could do.

It was a sad, very shamefaced Tigercat who shuffled off home with empty hands to a wife and children waiting for promised fish. Not too far away, the rabbit household was in high glee and Compère Rabbit was describing in the minutest detail exactly how he had caught that huge, glassy-eyed fellow there!

From *Anansesem: A Collection of Caribbean Folk Tales, Legends and Poems for Juniors*, edited by Velma Pollard (Jamaica: Longman, 1985).

The Wonderful Tar-Baby Story

The most widely known African-American tales are the stories about Br'er Rabbit and his animal friends and enemies. They were initially popularized by Joel Chandler Harris in a series of columns that published in the *Atlanta Constitution* late in the 1880s. Harris, a white man, had, as a boy, befriended old people who had been slaves and listened to their stories. The adventures of Br'er Rabbit, who must use quick thinking to escape from the hungry Br'er Fox, can be traced back to West African folktales and are often seen as portrayals of slaves using their wits against their white masters. Harris presented the stories using an aging slave telling stories to white children as the narrator, and he stated that he had 'endeavored to give the whole a genuine flavor of the old plantation'. He has been criticized for presenting an idealized, sentimentalized view of life in the slave states. In 'The Wonderful Tar-Baby Story', the narrator does not provide a satisfying conclusion to the narrative, leaving his audience to wonder about how the tale ends and, perhaps, in the manner of African dilemma tales, implicitly inviting audience response and interpretation.

'*D*idn't the fox *never* catch the rabbit, Uncle Remus?' asked the little boy the next evening.

'He come mighty nigh it, honey, sho's you born—Brer Fox did. One day atter Brer Rabbit fool 'im wid dat calamus root, Brer Fox went ter wuk en got 'im some tar, en mix it wid some turkentime, en fix up a contrapshun wat he call a Tar-Baby, en he tuck dish yer Tar-Baby en he sot 'er in de big road, en den he lay off in de bushes fer to see what de news wuz gwineter be. En he didn't hatter wait long, nudder, kaze bimeby here come Brer Rabbit pacin' down de road—lippity-clippity, clippity-lippity—dez ez sassy ez a jay-bird. Brer Fox, he lay low. Brer Rabbit come prancin' 'long twel he spy de Tar-Baby, en den he fotch up on his behime legs like he wus 'stonished. De Tar-Baby, she sot dar, she did, en Brer Fox, he lay low.

'"Mawnin'!" sez Brer Rabbit, sezee—nice wedder dis mawnin' sezee.

'Tar-Baby ain't sayin' nothin', en Brer Fox, he lay low.

'"How duz yo' sym'tuns seem ter segashuate?" sez Brer Rabbit, sezee.

'Brer Fox, he wink his eye slow, en lay low, en de Tar-Baby, she ain't sayin' nothin'.

'"How you come on, den? Is you deaf?" sez Brer Rabbit, sezee. "Kaze if you is, I kin holler louder," sezee.

'Tar-Baby stay still, en Brer Fox, he lay low.

'"Youer stuck up, dat's w'at you is," says Brer Rabbit, sezee, "en I'm gwineter kyore you, dat's w'at I'm a gwineter do," sezee.

'Brer Fox, he sorter chuckle in his stummick, he did, but Tar-Baby ain't sayin' nothin'.

'"I'm gwineter larn you howter talk ter 'pecttubble fokes ef hit's de las' ack,' sez Brer Rabbit, sezee. "Ef you don't take off dat hat en tell me howdy, I'm gwineter bus' you wide open,' sezee.

'Tar-Baby stay still, en Brer Fox, he lay low.

'Brer Rabbit keep on axin' 'im, en de Tar-Baby, she keep on sayin' nothin', twel present'y Brer Rabbit draw back wid his fis', he did, en blip he tuck 'er side er de head. Right dar's whar

From Joel Chandler Harris, *Uncle Remus: His Songs and Sayings.* New and Revised edition. Illustrated by A.B. Frost. (New York: Appleton-Century-Crofts, 1921), 9.

he broke his merlasses jug. His fis' stuck, en he can't pull loose. De tar hilt 'im. But Tar-Baby, she stay still, en Brer Fox, he lay low.

'"If you don't lemme loose, I'll knock you agin," sez Brer Rabbit, sezee, en wid dat he fotch 'er a wipe wid de udder han', en dat stuck. Tar-Baby, she ain't sayin' nothin', en Brer Fox, he lay low.

'"Tu'n me loose, fo' I kick de natal stuffin' outen you," sez Brer Rabbit, sezee, but de Tar-Baby, she ain't sayin' nothin'. She des hilt on, en den Brer Rabbit lose de use er his feet in de same way. Brer Fox, he lay low. Den Brer Rabbit squall out dat ef de Tar-Baby don't tu'n 'im loose he butt 'er cranksided. En den he butted, en his head got stuck. Den brer Fox, he sa'ntered fort', lookin' des ez innercent ez one er yo' mammy's mockin'-birds.

'"Howdy, Brer Rabbit," sez Brer Fox, sezee. "You look sorter stuck up dis mawnin",' sezee, en den he rolled on de groun', en laughed en laughed twel he couldn't laugh no mo'. "I speck you'll take dinner wid me dis time, Brer Rabbit. I done laid in some calamus root, en I ain't gwineter take no skuse," sez Brer Fox, sezee.'

Here Uncle Remus paused and drew a two-pound yam out of the ashes.

'Did the fox eat the rabbit?' asked the little boy to whom the story had been told.

'Dat's all de fur de tale goes,' replied the old man. 'He mout, en den again he moutent. Some say Jedge B'ar come long en loosed 'im—some say he didn't. I hear Miss Sally callin'. You better run 'long.'

From *Uncle Remus: His Songs and Sayings*, new and revised edition, by Joel Chandler Harris (New York: Appleton-Century-Crofts, 1921).

A Legend of Knockmany

In Irish legend, Fin M'Coul has been referred to as his country's King Arthur, a great and honourable leader of warriors. He was also a person of prodigious strength, said to have constructed the Giant's Causeway from Ireland to Scotland and to have formed the Isle of Mann when he scooped up a large piece of earth and hurled it eastward. In this tale, however, he depends on the cleverness of his wife to save him from the giant Cucullin, whose challenge to battle he is afraid to face. Joseph Jacobs, the nineteenth-century English reteller of the story, has suggested that it may be a parody of the great Irish sagas. The fearsome M'Coul must dress as a baby, sucking his thumb, traditionally said to be the source of his renowned wisdom, while his clever wife Oonagh engineers his adversary's defeat. Jacob's mock-heroic introduction, which uses the style of heroic literature for a comic subject, helps to create the humourous tone.

What Irish man, woman, or child has not heard of our renowned Hibernian Hercules, the great and glorious Fin M'Coul? Not one, from Cape Clear to the Giant's Causeway, nor from that back again to Cape Clear. And, by the way, speaking of the Giant's Causeway brings me at once to the beginning of my story. Well, it so happened that Fin and his men were all working at the Causeway, in order to make a bridge across to Scotland; when Fin, who was very fond of his wife Oonagh, took it into his head that he would go home and see how the poor woman got on in his absence. So, accordingly, he pulled up a fir-tree, and, after lopping off the roots and branches, made a walking-stick of it, and set out on his way to Oonagh.

Oonagh, or rather Fin, lived at this time on the very tiptop of Knockmany Hill, which faces a cousin of its own called Cullamore, that rises up, half-hill, half-mountain, on the opposite side.

There was at that time another giant, named Cucullin—some say he was Irish, and some say he was Scotch—but whether Scotch or Irish, sorrow doubt of it but he was a targer. No other giant of the day could stand before him; and such was his strength, that, when well vexed, he could give a stamp that shook the country about him. The fame and name of him went far and near; and nothing in the shape of a man, it was said, had any chance with him in a fight. By one blow of his fists he flattened a thunderbolt and kept it in his pocket, in the shape of a pancake, to show to all his enemies, when they were about to fight him. Undoubtedly he had given every giant in Ireland a considerable beating, barring Fin M'Coul himself; and he swore that he would never rest night or day, winter or summer, till he would serve Fin with the same sauce, if he could catch him. However, the short and long of it was, with reverence be it spoken, that Fin heard Cucullin was coming to the Causeway to have a trial of strength with him and he was seized with a very warm and sudden fit of affection for his wife, poor woman, leading a very lonely, uncomfortable life of it in his absence. He accordingly pulled up the fir-tree, as I said before, and having snedded it into a walking-stick, set out on his travels to see his darling Oonagh on the top of Knockmany, by the way.

In truth, the people wondered very much why it was that Fin selected such a windy spot for his dwelling-house, and they even went so far as to tell him as much.

'What can you mane, Mr M'Coul,' said they, 'by pitching your tent upon the top of Knockmany, where you never are without a breeze, day or night, winter or summer; and where you're often forced to take your nightcap without either going to bed or turning up your little finger; aye, an' where, besides this, there's the sorrow's own want of water?'

'Why,' said Fin, 'ever since I was the height of a round tower, I was known to be fond of having a good prospect of my own; and where the dickens, neighbours, could I find a better spot for a good prospect than the top of Knockmany? As for water, I am sinking a pump, and, plase goodness, as soon as the Causeway's made, I intend to finish it.'

Now, this was more of Fin's philosophy; for the real state of the case was, that he pitched upon the top of Knockmany in order that he might be able to see Cucullin coming towards the house. All we have to say is, that if he wanted a spot from which to keep a sharp look-out—and, between ourselves, he did want it grievously—barring Slieve Croob, or Slieve Donard, or its own cousin, Cullamore, he could not find a neater or more convenient situation for it in the sweet and sagacious province of Ulster.

'God save all here!' said Fin, good-humouredly, on putting his honest face into his own door.

'Musha, Fin, avick, an' you're welcome home to your own Oonagh, you darlin' bully.' Here followed a smack that is said to have made the waters of the lake at the bottom of the hill curl, as it were, with kindness and sympathy.

Fin spent two or three happy days with Oonagh, and felt himself very comfortable, considering the dread he had of Cucullin. This, however, grew upon him so much that his wife could not but perceive something lay on his mind which he kept altogether to himself. Let a woman alone, in the meantime, for ferreting or wheedling a secret out of her good man, when she wishes. Fin was a proof of this.

'It's this Cucullin.' said he, 'that's troubling me. When the fellow gets angry, and begins to stamp, he'll shake you a whole townland; and it's well known that he can stop a thunderbolt, for he always carries one about him in the shape of a pancake, to show to anyone that might misdoubt it.'

As he spoke, he clapped his thumb in his mouth, which he always did when he wanted to prophesy, or to know anything that happened in his absence; and the wife asked him what he did it for.

'He's coming,' said Fin; 'I see him below Dungannon.'

'Thank goodness, dear! an' who is it, avick? Glory be to God!'

'That baste, Cucullin,' replied Fin; 'and how to manage I don't know. If I run away, I am disgraced; and I know that sooner or later I must meet him, for my thumb tells me so.'

'When will he be here?' said she.

'Tomorrow, about two o'clock,' replied Fin, with a groan.

'Well, my bully, don't be cast down,' said Oonagh; 'depend on me, and maybe I'll bring you better out of this scrape than ever you could bring yourself, by your rule o' thumb.'

She then made a high smoke on the top of the hill, after which she put her finger in her mouth, and gave three whistles, and by that Cucullin knew he was invited to Cullamore—for this was the way that the Irish long ago gave a sign to all strangers and travellers, to let them know they were welcome to come and take share of whatever was going.

In the meantime, Fin was very melancholy, and did not know what to do, or how to act at all. Cucullin was an ugly customer to meet with; and, the idea of the 'cake' aforesaid flattened the very heart within him. What chance could he have, strong and brave though he was, with a man who could, when put in a passion, walk the country into earthquakes and knock thunderbolts into pancakes? Fin knew not on what hand to turn him. Right or left—backward or forward—where to go he could form no guess whatsoever.

'Oonagh,' said he, 'can you do nothing for me? Where's all your invention? Am I to be skivered like a rabbit before your eyes, and to have my name disgraced for ever in the sight of all my tribe, and me the best man among them? How am I to fight this man-mountain— this huge cross between an earthquake and a thunderbolt?—with a pancake in his pocket that was once—'

'Be easy, Fin,' replied Oonagh; 'troth, I'm ashamed of you. Keep your toe in your pump, will you? Talking of pancakes, maybe, we'll give him as good as any he brings with him— thunderbolt or otherwise. If I don't treat him to as smart feeding as he's got this many a day, never trust Oonagh again. Leave him to me, and do just as I bid you.'

This relieved Fin very much; for, after all, he had great confidence in his wife, knowing, as he did, that she had got him out of many a quandary before. Oonagh then drew the nine woollen threads of different colours, which she always did to find out the best way of succeeding in anything of importance she went about. She then platted them into three plats with three colours in each, putting one on her right arm, one round her heart, and the third round her right ankle, for then she knew that nothing could fail with her that she undertook.

Having everything now prepared, she sent round to the neighbours and borrowed one-and-twenty iron griddles, which she took and kneaded into the hearts of one-and-twenty cakes of bread, and these she baked on the fire in the usual way, setting them aside in the cupboard according as they were done. She then put down a large pot of new milk, which she made into curds and whey. Having done all this, she sat down quite contented, waiting for his arrival on the next day about two o'clock, that being the hour at which he was expected—for Fin knew as much by the sucking of his thumb. Now this was a curious property that Fin's thumb had. In this very thing, moreover, he was very much resembled by his great foe, Cucullin; for it was well known that the huge strength he possessed all lay in the middle finger of his right hand, and that, if he happened by any mischance to lose it, he was no more, for all his bulk, than a common man.

At length, the next day, Cucullin was seen coming across the valley, and Oonagh knew that it was time to commence operations. She immediately brought the cradle, and made Fin to lie down in it, and cover himself up with the clothes.

'You must pass for your own child,' said she; 'so just lie there snug, and say nothing, but be guided by me.'

About two o'clock, as he had been expected, Cucullin came in. 'God save all here!' said he; 'is this where the great Fin M'Coul lives?'

'Indeed it is, honest man,' replied Oonagh; 'God save you kindly—won't you be sitting?'

'Thank you, ma'am,' says he, sitting down; 'you're Mrs M'Coul, I suppose?'

'I am,' said she; 'and I have no reason, I hope, to be ashamed of my husband.'

'No,' said the other, 'he has the name of being the strongest and bravest man in Ireland; but for all that, there's a man not far from you that's very desirous of taking a shake with him. Is he at home?'

'Why, then, no,' she replied; 'and if ever a man left his house in a fury, he did. It appears that someone told him of a big basthoon of a giant called Cucullin being down at the Causeway to look for him, and so he set out there to try if he could catch him. Troth, I hope, for the poor giant's sake, he won't meet with him, for if he does, Fin will make paste of him at once.'

'Well,' said the other, 'I am Cucullin, and I have been seeking him these twelve months, but he always kept clear of me; and I will never rest night of day till I lay my hands on him.'

At this Oonagh set up a loud laugh, of great contempt, by the way, and looked at him as if he was only a mere handful of a man.

'Did you ever see Fin?' said she, changing her manner all at once. 'How could I?' said he; 'he always took care to keep his distance.'

'I thought so,' she replied; 'I judged as much; and if you take my advice, you poor-looking creature, you'll pray night and day that you may never see him, for I tell you it will be a black day for you when you do. But, in the meantime, you perceive that the wind's on the door, and as Fin himself is from home, maybe you'd be civil enough to turn the house, for it's always what Fin does when he's here.'

This was a startler even to Cucullin; but he got up, however, and after pulling the middle finger of his right hand until it cracked three times, he went outside, and getting his arms about the house, turned it as she had wished. When Fin saw this, he felt the sweat of fear oozing out through every pore of his skin; but Oonagh, depending upon her woman's wit, felt not a whit daunted.

'Arrah, then,' said she, 'as you are so civil, maybe you'd do another obliging turn for us, as Fin's not here to do it himself. You see, after this long stretch of dry weather we've had, we feel very badly off for want of water. Now, Fin says there's a fine spring-well somewhere under the rocks behind the hill here below, and it was his intention to pull them asunder; but having heard of you, he left the place in such a fury, that he never thought of it. Now, if you try to find it, troth I'd feel it a kindness.'

She then brought Cucullin down to see the place, which was then all one solid rock; and, after looking at it for some time, he cracked his right middle finger nine times, and, stooping down, tore a cleft about four hundred feet deep, and a quarter of a mile in length, which has since been christened by the name of Lumford's Glen.

'You'll now come in,' said she, 'and eat a bit of such humble fare as we can give you. Fin, even although he and you are enemies, would scorn not to treat you kindly in his own house; and, indeed, if I didn't do it even in his absence, he would not be pleased with me.'

She accordingly brought him in, and placing half a dozen of the cakes we spoke of before him, together with a can or two of butter, a side of boiled bacon, and a stack of cabbage, she desired him to help himself—for this, be it known, was long before the invention of potatoes. Cucullin put one of the cakes in his mouth to take a huge whack out of it, when he made a thundering noise, something between a growl and a yell. 'Blood and fury!' he shouted; 'how is this? Here are two of my teeth out! What kind of bread this is you gave me.'

'What's the matter?' said Oonagh coolly.

'Matter!' shouted the other again; 'why, here are the two best teeth in my head gone.'

'Why,' said she, 'that's Fin's bread—the only bread he ever eats when at home; but, indeed, I forgot to tell you that nobody can eat it but himself, and that child in the cradle there. I thought, however, that, as you were reported to be rather a stout little fellow of your size, you might be able to manage it, and I did not wish to affront a man that thinks himself able to fight Fin. Here's another cake—maybe it's not so hard as that.'

Cucullin at the moment was not only hungry, but ravenous, so he accordingly made a fresh set at the second cake, and immediately another yell was heard twice as loud as the first. 'Thunder and gibbets!' he roared, 'take your bread out of this, or I will not have a tooth in my head; there's another pair of them gone!'

'Well, honest man,' replied Oonagh, 'if you're not able to eat the bread, say so quietly, and don't be wakening the child in the cradle there. There, now, he's awake upon me.'

Fin now gave a skirl that startled the giant, as coming from such a youngster as he was supposed to be. 'Mother,' said he, 'I'm hungry—get me something to eat.' Oonagh went over, and putting into his hand a cake that had no griddle in it, Fin, whose appetite in the meantime had been sharpened by seeing eating going forward, soon swallowed it. Cucullin was thunderstruck, and secretly thanked his stars that he had the good fortune to miss meeting Fin, for, as he said to himself, 'I'd have no chance with a man who could eat such bread as that, which even his son that's but in his cradle can munch before my eyes.'

'I'd like to take a glimpse at the lad in the cradle,' said he to Oonagh; 'for I can tell you that the infant who can manage that nutriment is no joke to look at, or to feed of a scarce summer.'

'With all the veins of my heart,' replied Oonagh; 'get up, acushla, and show this decent little man something that won't be unworthy of your father, Fin M'Coul.'

Fin, who was dressed for the occasion as much like a boy as possible, got up, and bringing Cucullin out, 'Are you strong?' said he.

'Thunder an' ounds!' exclaimed the other, 'what a voice in so small a chap!'

'Are you strong?' said Fin again; 'are you able to squeeze water out of that white stone?' he asked, putting one into Cucullin's hand. The latter squeezed and squeezed the stone, but in vain.

'Ah, you're a poor creature!' said Fin. 'You a giant! Give me the stone here, and when I'll show what Fin's little son can do, you may then judge of what my daddy himself is.'

Fin then took the stone, and exchanging it for the curds, he squeezed the latter until the whey, as clear as water, oozed out in a little shower from his hand.

'I'll now go in,' said he, 'to my cradle; for I scorn to lose my time with anyone that's not able to eat my daddy's bread, or squeeze water out of a stone. Bedad, you had better be off out of this before he comes back; for if he catches you, it's in flummery he'd have you in two minutes.'

Cucullin, seeing what he had seen, was of the same opinion himself; his knees knocked together with the terror of Fin's return, and he accordingly hastened to bid Oonagh farewell, and to assure her, that from that day out, he never wished to hear of, much less to see, her husband. 'I admit fairly that I'm not a match for him,' said he, 'strong as I am; tell him I will avoid him as I would the plague, and that I will make myself scarce in this part, of the country while I live.'

Fin, in the meantime, had gone into the cradle, where he lay very quietly, his heart at his mouth with delight that Cucullin was about to take his departure, without discovering the tricks that had been played off on him.

'It's well for you,' said Oonagh, 'that he doesn't happen to be here, for it's nothing but hawk's meat he'd make of you.'

'I know that,' says Cucullin; 'divil a thing else he'd make of me; but before I go, will you let me feel what kind of teeth Fin's lad has got that can eat griddle-bread like that?'

'With all pleasure in life,' said she; 'only, as they're far back in his head, you must put your finger a good way in.'

Cucullin was surprised to find such a powerful set of grinders in one so young; but he was still much more so on finding, when he took his hand from Fin's mouth, that he had left the very finger upon which his whole strength depended, behind him. He gave one loud groan, and fell down at once with terror and weakness. This was all Fin wanted, who now knew that his most powerful and bitterest enemy was at his mercy. He started out of the cradle, and in a few minutes the great Cucullin, that was for such a length of time the terror of him and all his followers, lay a corpse before him. Thus did Fin, through the wit and invention of Oonagh, his wife, succeed in overcoming his enemy by cunning, which he never could have done by force.

From *Celtic Fairytales*, by Joseph Jacobs (London: The Bodley Head, 1970).

The Tiger, the Brâhman, and the Jackal

Unlike other trickster stories of escape in which characters in danger must use their own wits to save themselves, this tale from India's Punjab region involves a third character, the jackal. Although the ungrateful tiger becomes a trickster when he reveals that he is unwilling to keep his promise not to eat his benefactor, the holy man does not escape when he has an opportunity. The jackal is able to outwit the trickster by appearing to be foolish and confused, thus causing the tiger to lose both his patience and his anticipated meal. Interestingly, in much Indian folklore, the jackal is portrayed as a trickster and his arrival is seen as a sign of misfortune. Possibly this is a fact that the tiger should have known. Flora Anne Steel, the reteller, was the wife of a nineteenth-century British colonial official and set out to learn about Indian culture. She remarked that the tales 'have not been doctored in any way, not even in the language'. She noted that children were instructed only to tell stories at night, when they weren't working or studying; daylight retellings could cause misfortune.

Once upon a time a tiger was caught in a trap. He tried in vain to get out through the bars, and rolled and bit with rage and grief when he failed.

By chance a poor Brâhman came by. 'Let me out of this cage, O pious one!' cried the tiger.

'Nay, my friend,' replied the Brâhman mildly, 'you would probably eat me if I did.'

'Not at all!' swore the tiger with many oaths; 'on the contrary, I should be for ever grateful, and serve you as a slave!'

Now when the tiger sobbed and sighed and wept and swore, the pious Brâhman's heart softened, and at last he consented to open the door of the cage. Out popped the tiger, and, seizing the poor man, cried, 'What a fool you are! What is to prevent my eating you now, for after being cooped up so long I am just terribly hungry!'

In vain the Brâhman pleaded for his life; the most he could gain was a promise to abide by the decision of the first three things he chose to question as to the justice of the tiger's action.

So the Brâhman first asked a *pipal* tree what it thought of the matter, but the *pipal* tree replied coldly, 'What have you to complain about? Don't I give shade and shelter to everyone who passes by, and, don't they in return tear down my branches to feed their cattle? Don't whimper—be a man!'

Then the Brâhman, sad at heart, went farther afield till he saw a buffalo turning a wellwheel; but he fared no better from it, for it answered, 'You are a fool to expect gratitude! Look at me! While I gave milk they fed me on cotton-seed and oil-cake, but now I am dry they yoke me here, and give me refuse as fodder!'

The Brâhman, still more sad, asked the road to give him its opinion.

'My dear sir,' said the road, 'how foolish you are to expect anything else! Here am I, useful to everybody, yet all, rich and poor, great and small, trample on me as they go past, giving me nothing but the ashes of their pipes and the husks of their grain!'

On this the Brâhman turned back sorrowfully, and on the way he met a jackal, who called out, 'Why, what's the matter, Mr Brâhman? You look as miserable as a fish out of water!'

Then the Brâhman told him all that had occurred. 'How very confusing!' said the jackal, when the recital was ended; 'would you mind telling me over again? for everything seems so mixed up!'

The Brâhman told it all over again, but the jackal shook his head in a distracted sort of way, and still could not understand.

'It's very odd,' said he sadly, 'but it all seems to go in at one ear and out at the other! I will go to the place where it all happened, and then perhaps I shall be able to give a judgment.'

So they returned to the cage, by which the tiger was waiting for the Brâhman, and sharpening his teeth and claws.

'You've been away a long time!' growled the savage beast, 'but now let us begin our dinner.'

'*Our* dinner!' thought the wretched Brâhman, as his knees knocked, together with fright; 'what a remarkably delicate way of putting it!'

'Give me five minutes, my lord!' he pleaded, 'in order that I may explain matters to the jackal here, who is somewhat slow in his wits.'

The tiger consented, and the Brâhman began the whole story over again, not missing a single detail, and spinning as long a yarn as possible.

'Oh, my poor brain! oh, my poor brain!' cried the jackal, wringing his paw. 'Let me see! how did it all begin? You were in the cage, and the tiger came walking by—

'Pooh!' interrupted the tiger, 'what a fool you are! *I* was in the cage.'

'Of course!' cried the jackal, pretending to tremble with fright; 'yes! I was in the cage—no, I wasn't—dear! dear! where are my wits? Let me see—the tiger was in the Brâhman, and the cage came walking by—no, that's not it either! Well, don't mind me, but begin your dinner, for I shall never understand!'

'Yes, you shall!' returned the tiger, in a rage at the jackal's stupidity; 'I'll *make* you understand! Look here. I am the tiger——'

'Yes, my lord!'

'And that is the Brâhman——'

'Yes, my lord!'

'And that is the cage——'

'Yes, my lord!'

'And I was in the cage—do you understand?'

'Yes—no—. Please, my lord——

'Well?' cried the tiger, impatiently.

'Please, my lord! How did you get in?'

'How!—why, in the usual way, of course!'

'Oh dear me! my head is beginning to whirl again! Please don't be angry, my lord, but what is the usual way?'

At this the tiger lost patience, and, jumping into the cage, cried, 'This way! Now do you understand how it was?'

'Perfectly!' grinned the jackal, as he dexterously shut the door; 'and if you will permit me to say so, I think matters will remain as they were!'

From *Folktales of the Punjab: Told by the People*, by Flora Anne Steel (London: Macmillan, 1894).

Jack the Giant Killer

Based on an English tale of the same name, this story from western North Carolina was collected in 1923 by Isabel Gordon Carter, who wrote down the narrative exactly as it was told by a woman who had heard it from her grandfather. The tale incorporates many familiar motifs such as the squeezing of milk from a rock and the slitting and sewing up of a belly. However, it creates a local colour-ing through the use of mountain dialect and references to regional food. The conflicts between the characters are developed through a series of oppositions: youth and age, largeness and smallness, riches and poverty, and cleverness and slow-wittedness. Jack succeeds because he is able to use his wits to better advantage than his adversaries use theirs.

One time they was a fine wealthy man lived way out in the forest. But he couldn't have nothing, hogs and sheep and cows and sech like because the giants killed 'em. So he went out and put him up an ad-ver-tise-ment (put up a board or hew out the side of a tree and write what he want to). So he put up one for some one to clear land. Little old boy Jack saw hit and he tramped and tramped until he got away out in the forest and he called, 'Hello.' Old man hollered, 'What'll ye have?' Jack says, 'I've come to clear yer land.' 'All right,' says the man. It was Sunday evenin' un they uz havin' supper. The old lady says, 'What'll ye have for supper, Jack?' He said mush and milk. While they was makin' the sup-per a preacher come in an' they sit the mush away and they fried him a chicken and fixed some coffee and fixed a good supper. After supper Jack tol 'em he wanted a piece of leather so he made him a pouch, a sort of haversack thing to tie around his waist. Next morning they got up, asked Jack what he'd have for breakfast. Said, 'Jest give me that cold mush and milk.' He'd take a spoonful and then poke one in the hold in the pouch. So he got it full. Then he said he was ready to go to work.

So man says, now he says, 'Jack, I don't want you to back out, but I'm no a wantin' any land cleared. I want to kill them giants over there and I'll give a thousand dollars a head for them—some of 'em has two heads, and I'll give you five hundred dollars down, and five hundred dollars when you come back.'

Jack says, 'Give me a tomihawk.' (That's a thing like a hatchet 'cept it has two heads to hit. They used hit in olden times. Indians use to use hit to scalp with.) 'And I may be in for dinner, and hit may be night when I get in.' So they give him a tomihawk and he went over in the forest and climb a great long pine.

Along about one o'clock he looked way down in the holler and saw a great old giant a comin' up with two heads. So he says to himself, 'Land I'm gone.' So the old giant come up, and he says, 'What are you doin' up there?' Jack says, 'I'm a clearin' timber.' Giant says, 'Come down from there, you aint' got sense enough to clear timber, you have to have an ax and chop down timber.' So Jack come down a little way. 'Have ye had yer dinner?' says the giant. Jack says, 'I've had my dinner.' Giant says, 'I'm sorry, I jest come to ask you to come down and take dinner with me. Come down, let's wrestle and play a while.' Jack says, 'All right, bedads, I'll be down.' So Jack come down and down, till he got right on a limb a top the giant. He had no idea of comin' down when he started, jest tryin' to bluff the giant.

Jack says to the giant, 'I can do somethin' you can't do.' Giant says, 'What is hit?' Jack says, 'I can squeeze milk out of a flint rock.' Giant says, 'Oh ye can't do hit?' Jack says, 'Yes I can, you hand me up one and I'll show you.' So giant handed him up one, and Jack gits hit right close to his little old pouch and squeezes milk out on the rock and drapped the milk on the giant. Giant says, 'Hand me down that rock; if you can squeeze milk out of hit, I can.' Jack handed it down to the giant. The giant was so stout that when he put his hands to hit, he just crushed it into powder.

Jack says, 'I told you you couldn't squeeze milk out of hit. I can do something else you can't do.' 'What's that?' 'I kin take a knife and cut my belly open and sew hit up again.' Giant says, 'Oh you can't neither.' 'Yes, I can,' says Jack. 'I'll show you, hand me your knife.' So the giant hands him up his knife and Jack cut that pouch open and sewed hit up again. 'Now didn't I tell you I could?' Giant says, 'Hand me down that knife,' and he just rip his belly open and fell over dead. So Jack crawled back down and tuk his tomihawk and cut off his head. And that evening late he come waggin' him in a giant's head. That jest tickled the forest man and he paid Jack a heap of money and says, 'Now Jack, if you kin jest get the rest of 'em; they's a whole family of 'em.'

So next morning Jack took his tomihawk (or Tommy hatchet) and went over and climb the big old pine agin. So long about noon he looked down the holler and he saw two giants a comin' each with two heads on. So they begin to get closter and closter. Jack climb down and tuk out down the holler and as he went he filled his shirt tail with rocks. After a while he come to a big old holler log and he climb in hit with his shirt tail plumb full of rocks. So the giants went up and mourned over their brother. And they went down past Jack sayin', 'Poor brother, if we jest knew who it was a murdered him, we'd shore fix him.' Jack was a layin' in there with his heart jest a beatin'. They passed the log and said, 'Let's pick up this long and carry hit down to poor old mother for some kindlin'.' So they each tuk an end and carried hit a little ways.

Jack thought he'd try his rocks on 'em. So he crawled up pretty close to the end and throwed a rock and hit one of the giants. Giant says to the other one, 'What you hit me for?' Giant says, 'I didn't hit you.' 'Yes, you did too.' Then Jack crawled back and throwed a rock at the other giant. 'What you hit me for? I never hit you.' 'I didn't hit you.' 'Yes you did too.' So they fit and they fit and fit and directly they killed each other; one fell one side of the log dead and the other on the other side. So Jack crawled out and cut their heads off and went on back home.

So he was getting' him a pretty good load of money and was getting' awfully tickled. The forest man were plumb tickled too and said: 'Jack, if you jest can get the rest. But watch out they don't get you.' 'Bedads they won't git me,' says Jack. So next morning he says, 'Give me my tomihawk,' and he went on out. So along in the evenin' he looked down the holler and saw a little old giant comin' up about his size. 'Well,' says Jack, 'I've about got 'em from the looks of this one.' This little giant come up a talkin' to hisself. Looked up in the tree and saw Jack sittin' there. 'Stranger, can you tell me who has killed my poor old brothers?' 'Yes, I killed your brothers and bedad, I'll come down and kill you if you fool with me.' 'Oh please, Jack, please Jack, I'm all the child my mother's got left, and you kill me there won't be nobody to get her wood this winter and she'll freeze to death. If you'll come down I'll take you home with me and we'll have the best dinner.' So Jack went on down.

Giant went to his mother and says, 'Jack come home with me, and he says he's the one who killed brothers but he's not much.' So Giant's mother says, 'Well, come on in Jack, you'uns go out and play pitch crowbar awhile.' Jack couldn't lift it. Little old giant pick hip up and throwed hit about one hundred yards. Jack went over and picked up one end and begin to holler: 'Hey, uncle. Hey uncle.' Giant says, 'Hey, Jack, what you hollerin' about?' 'I've got an uncle in the Illinois who is a blacksmith and I thought I'd jest pitch hit to him.' 'Oh don't do that Jack, hit's all we have.' 'Well if I can't pitch hit to Illinois, I won't pitch hit at all.'

Little old giant slipped back to the house, 'Mother, I don't believe Jack is much stout.' 'Well, we'll see,' says the mother. 'Here boys, take these pails down to the river.' Little old giant tuk the buckets and when he got to the river he stove in his bucket and put hit up full and then he stove Jack's in and put hit up full. Jack had begun to roll up his sleeves. Little old giant says, 'What are you goin' to do, Jack?' 'Oh thought I'd carry up the river.' 'Oh don't Jack, mother might walk in her sleep and fall in.' 'All right,' Says Jack, 'but I wouldn't be ketched a carryin' that little old bucket.'

So they went on back. The mother had a big hot oven sittin' in front of the fire with a plank across hit. 'Get on this plank, Jack, and I'll ride ye,' says she. So Jack got up un she shuck him and shuck him trying to shake him into the oven but he fell off on the wrong side. 'Let me show you,' says old mother giant, and she got on and Jack give her a shake and popped her in the oven, and he had him a baked giant in a minute. Little old giant came in, says, 'Mother, mother, I smell Jack.' Jack says, 'No you don't, that's your mother ye smell.' When little old giant sees Jack, he begin to holler, 'Oh! Jack, I'll give ye anything if you won't kill me.' 'All right, give me a suit of invisible clothes.'

So he give him invisible suit and Jack just went over the house and tuk what he wanted, all that was any account, because the giant couldn't see him. And Jack tuk a sword and walked up to the little old giant and stuck hit in him and went and got him some silver and when I left there, Jack was plumb rich.

From 'Mountain White Folk-Lore: Tales from the Southern Blue Ridge', by Isabel Gordon Carter, *Journal of American Folklore* 38 (1925). Reprinted in Richard M. Dorson, *Buying the Wind: Regional Folklore in the United States* (Chicago: University of Chicago Press, 1964).

Wisahketchahk and the Ducks

The story of birds tricked into dancing, a type of Native story told across the Canadian and American plains, deals with a greedy hunter who fools a group of waterfowl through his lies and then is frequently tricked by someone else. As is the case in a large number of Native American trickster tales, Wisahketchahk's plans go wrong because of his inherent character flaws and his violations of his culture's values. Completely self-centered and proud of his cleverness in deceiving the birds, he does not consider the possibility that someone else could be a better trickster than he is. Moreover, he appeals to the fowls' need to be considered important by inviting them to play a role in a culturally significant dance. He fails to treat the animals he hunts with respect, kills more than he needs, and refuses to share with others—all violations of deeply held values of hunting cultures.

Wisahketchahk was going along. He was hungry; in fact, he was always hungry. As he passed a lake he saw many ducks and geese. 'How shall I kill them?' he thought.

By the water's edge, he found some weeds, which he pulled out and rolled up. When he had a great bundle of them, he put the bundle on his back and began walking. When he came close to where the ducks were, they looked at him and said, 'Ho, big brother. What are you carrying on your back?' But he kept walking as if he hadn't heard them.

Again, the leader of the ducks called out: 'Big Brother, what is that you're carrying on your back?'

'Why, these are Shut-Eye Dances!' he replied.

'What is a Shut-Eye Dance?' asked the duck, who had never heard of one.

'It is a very important, very special dance; it isn't performed very often. Not many people know how to do the dance.'

The duck was very curious: 'Please, show us how; we want to perform this Shut-Eye Dance.'

'That is wonderful, Little Brothers,' Wisahketchahk called to the duck. 'You have taken pity on me. I have asked other people if they would share my ritual dance and no one would help me prepare. Come ashore and I will show you what to do.' And to himself, he thought, 'The hopeless ninnies, I'm starving. I shall have a big meal.'

Wisahketchahk started walking toward a clump of trees where there was plenty of wood for a fire. The ducks and geese waddled behind him, and when he asked them to gather sticks and bigger pieces of wood, they all began working. He even had them gather larger branches to make a lodge in which to hold the dance. He finished the doorway himself, making it very small.

'Now, Little Brothers, please come inside,' he said in a very friendly voice. 'First the geese and the big ducks will come in; especially those who are the chiefs.' When all the ducks and geese had crowded into the lodge, the biggest ones were furthest from the door; the smallest ones were closest to it.

'Little Brothers, thank you for building this lodge. When no one else would help me, you did,' he remarked, wiping his eyes as if he were crying. 'Now, I will stand in the center of the lodge and begin the ceremonies by singing. When I sing, you will dance. It is very important that you keep your eyes closed during the dance, otherwise it will be spoiled. When I summon the spirit-power, I will call out, "Hwe, hwe, hwe!" Then you must dance as fast as you can, and remember, you must not open your eyes.'

He looked at each of the ducks and geese to make sure that they understood what they must do. Each of them nodded, and Wisahketchahk grabbed a branch that had old leaves on it; they rustled as he began to swing it. Then he began to sing:

> 'Shut eye Dancers
> I bring here!'

Making sure that all the birds' eyes were closed and that they were dancing, Wisahketchahk cried out 'Hwe, hwe!' and swung the branch wildly. Then he grabbed a big goose and wrung its neck. He kept doing this, circling around, singing all the while, and wringing the neck of the geese and the big ducks. Just then, a Hell-Diver dancing near the door thought he heard something strange and opened one eye as he dance. He saw what Wisahketchahk was doing.

He cried out in alarm, 'Wisahketchahk is killing us off!' Wisahketchahk grabbed the Hell-Diver, threw him into the air, and as he came down, kicked him toward the lake. 'People will see the mark where I kicked you,' he bellowed, 'and they'll remember that you warned the others.'

When the others opened their eyes, Wisahketchahk said, 'What sort of a dance did you blockheads think I would bring to you? I was hungry that's all!'

The rest of the birds fled out of doors and flew away. But Wisahketchahk went out of the lodge, laughing to himself, thinking, 'I have plenty of the big ducks and the geese. I shall eat plenty.' He tore up the lodge, taking the sticks and branches and building a fire to roast his kill.

But he had made too big a fire, and soon he began to feel too hot. So he walked into the woods a little way from the fire, thinking that he would return and enjoy his meal as soon as he had cooled down a little.

Just then a fox came along, limping very slowly. When he saw Wisahketchahk he turned and started hobbling away. 'Wait a moment, Little Brother,' Wisahketchahk called out to him.

'Dear me, no!' the other answered, 'you are only going to play a new trick on me.'

'Not at all!' Wisahketchak replied. 'It is only that I want to tell you some news. Do you see the smoke rising over there in the clearing? Over there, I have killed a lot of geese and ducks and I'm roasting them. We shall have plenty to eat. But first let's race. We can run around that hill just over there.'

'I can't do that,' the Fox remarked sadly, 'I have a very sore leg and you could beat me easily.'

'Don't worry. I'll tie a big rock to my leg and that will make things more even.'

The Fox thought about it and then agreed.

After Wisahketchahk had tied the rock to his back leg, they both began to run. Fox was quickly left behind. 'I thought that Fox was a very good runner; but this poor little brother of mine is really slow. I'll give him a few of the ducks when he returns to the clearing,' thought Wisahketchahk.

But as soon as Wisahketchahk was out of sight, Fox turned back toward the clearing. His leg wasn't sore at all. When he got to the fire, he found that the geese and ducks were ready to eat. So he pulled all of them from the fire and devoured them. He made a pile of the feet and leg bones beside him, and when he had finished his meal, he stuck them into the embers. 'Let Wisahketchahk think that these are the roasting birds.' Then, knowing that he would be in trouble when the trick was discovered, he hid.

Soon, Wisahketchahk returned to the clearing. 'I am hot again. I'll rest and cool down; then I'll eat the biggest ones. I'll leave a few for Little Brother when he gets here. He's so slow it will take a long time.' When he had rested, he reached for one of the feet sticking out of the fire. There was no roasted duck or goose attached. He reached for another and the same thing happened. Soon he'd pulled all of the feet out of the fire. He'd lost his meal.

'Fox has fooled me again, eating up my geese!' Wisahketchahk muttered. Then he looked toward the woods and called out. 'I'm very angry, Fox. The earth will not be big enough for you to escape. I'll find you.' He started walking and he hadn't gone far when he saw Fox lying in the grass taking a nap.

Wisahketchahk took a stone and held it over his head, ready to strike him. Then he paused, 'If I do that I'll ruin his hide. I might as well make it into a fox cap. I'll make a circle of fire around him and he'll choke on the smoke.

Fox woke up as the smoke had become very thick around him. He dashed about in a circle, this way and that, as the smoke grew thicker and thicker. Wisahketchahk couldn't see him any more. So Fox leaped high over the flames and ran for safety. Wisahketchahk couldn't see him for the smoke. But he kept walking around the fire, muttering to himself, 'I have surely put an end to Fox, burning him to death.'

When the flames died down, he saw a charred lump in the middle of the circle. Looking at it, Wisahketchahk thought, 'I'm still hungry; I might as well eat what's rest of Fox. He bit into the log and got a mouth of ash and hot coals. He spit it out and ran to the lake, where he drank water to cool his mouth.

Then Wisahketchahk went along. He was still hungry.

Adapted from 'The Shut-Eye Dancers', in *Sacred Stories of the Sweet Grass Cree*, collected by L. Bloomfield (Ottawa: National Museum of Canada, Bulletin 60, 1930).

The Mouse-Deer and the Tiger

The mouse-deer, or kanchil, a small, cat-sized, nocturnal animal, lives in constant danger from larger predators. Found in Indonesia and the Malay Peninsula, the animal is the central character in a cycle of stories in which he must think quickly when danger arrives. Mouse-Deer's constant struggle to stay alive is reflected in the fact that this episode includes four escapes that occur in rapid succession. The use of feigned reluctance as a means of causing the tiger to be distracted must be modified three times, and Mouse-Deer must improvise, quickly finding ways to make what is around him appear desirable to the tiger. He succeeds by appealing to his adversary's wish to possess that which does not belong to him.

It was a hot day in the forest and the kanchil had just found a quiet shady spot for a rest when he heard a tiger approaching. He knew that the tiger would want to kill and eat him, and he had to think fast. When the tiger poked his head through the tall grasses, the mouse-deer was fanning a pile of rotting leaves with a large palm leaf.

The tiger was curious and came closer. 'What are you doing?' he asked.

'I am guarding the king's food,' the mouse-deer answered. 'This is very special food, and only for the king. I have to take good care of it.'

'Royal food!' the tiger cried. 'I should like to taste it.'

'Oh, that's impossible,' the kanchil said, fanning busily to keep the flies off. 'Only the king may eat of this food.'

'But couldn't I try it just once?'

The kanchil shook his head.

'Just one bite?' the tiger begged. 'I'm hungry, but I promise to take only one bite.'

'Well'—the mouse-deer pretended to think hard—'maybe just one bite.' The tiger came closer. 'No, no! Wait! You mustn't taste it till I've gone. After all, I feel badly about betraying my trust. I was to guard this food for the king. And I wouldn't want any blame to attach to me.'

The tiger nodded, his eyes on the king's food. He began to lick his lips.

'Wait till I give you the word,' the kanchil insisted, and the tiger promised.

The mouse-deer ran swiftly into the forest, and when he was a safe distance from the tiger he called, 'You may taste it now!'

The tiger fell upon the royal food. One bite—and he discovered that it wasn't something special and delicious. It was only rotting leaves. He spat it out, and with a mighty growl he started after the mouse-deer. 'I'll get you!' he shouted. 'Wait till I find you! I'll tear you into bits!'

The mouse-deer, meanwhile, had scurried on, hunting safety. But there was no place to hide, and he knew he would have to rely on his wits. So he searched till he found a great snake, coiled up asleep, and sat down beside it. He had no sooner sat down than he heard the tiger crashing through the trees; growling as he came.

'You miserable wretch!' the tiger snarled, showing his red gums and his sharp white teeth. 'I'll eat you alive! Fooling me like that!'

'But I didn't fool you,' the kanchil said innocently. 'I told you not to eat it. I told you it was the king's food and that I was not supposed to let anyone have it! But you insisted.'

'The awful stuff!' the tiger muttered, shaking his great head from side to side. 'I can't get the taste out of my mouth. You'll pay for this!'

'You mustn't blame *me*,' the kanchil cried. 'I warned you. But do keep quiet. I'm guarding the king's girdle.'

The tiger came closer. 'What's so wonderful about that?' he asked, peering at the coiled snake.

'It's the king's girdle,' the kanchil, repeated. 'And I feel honoured that he trusts me to guard it.'

'Why?'

'Because it's full of magic power,' the mouse-deer said, with an important air. 'Whoever wears it can have whatever he wishes. So of course only the king may wear it.'

The tiger's eyes grew bright. 'Magic power! I have a wish that I'd like to have granted. Let me try it on . . . just once, just for a moment.'

'Oh, I couldn't do that!' the mouse-deer said in a shocked voice.

'The king need never know,' the tiger wheedled. 'Just let me have it for a moment.'

'Well'—the mouse-deer pretended to be reluctant—'perhaps just for a moment. . . .' But as the tiger came closer he cried, 'No, no! Wait! You mustn't try it on till I have gone. For, of course, no blame must attach to me, and I must not see you pick it up.'

'Well, get on, then,' the tiger said impatiently. 'I can scarcely wait to get my wish.'

The mouse-deer leaped nimbly through the forest and when he was a long distance away he called back, 'Now you may try it on!'

The tiger eagerly tried to pick up what he thought was the magic girdle, but as soon as he touched it the snake woke with a hiss and bit the tiger while it wound itself around his body.

The tiger, taken by surprise, had to fight hard to loosen the coils of the angry snake; and it was only after a long, hard struggle that he was able to kill it.

Now he was so furious that he could scarcely see. He charged through the jungle to find the mouse-deer. 'I'll have my revenge!' he shouted and all the jungle creatures shook to hear his bellow. 'Wait till I find you, kanchil! I'll make you sorry you ever tried to trick me!'

The mouse-deer heard him and trembled where he sat, half hidden near a tall clump, of bamboo. Before the tiger could open his mouth, the kanchil said, in a joyful voice, 'Oh, there you are again! Look, I've been appointed to take care of the king's trumpet! A wonderful instrument!'

'What's so wonderful about it?' the tiger muttered, coming closer. He was still smarting with anger, and his wounds hurt.

'Oh, I've never tried it, of course,' the kanchil said hurriedly. 'It's much too fine for anyone like me. But I've been told,' he said, lowering his voice, 'that if you put your tongue between these'—he waved toward two of the tallest bamboos—'and wait till the wind blows, they give out the most beautiful music!'

'That sounds interesting,' the tiger mumbled. 'I've always fancied myself as a musician. I'd like to try it.'

'But not anyone can play it!' the mouse-deer said, horrified. 'It's the king's trumpet, don't you understand? Only the king can play it. And he has set me to guard it for him.'

'Nonsense,' said the tiger. 'How will he ever know? I'm sure I could play it.'

'Well,' the mouse-deer said slowly, 'If you want to try. . . . But I would feel dreadful if anything happened to the royal instrument. So you must promise to let me get safely away before you begin. I wouldn't want any blame to attach to me.'

'Hurry up, then,' the tiger said, his eyes fastened on what he thought was the king's trumpet. 'What did you say I must do?'

'Put your tongue between the two tallest reeds. And be sure to wait till the wind blows!'

The mouse-deer scurried away. The tiger, his eyes aglitter, put his tongue between the two tall bamboos which grew very close together, and waited. And after a while a strong gust of wind came, and shook the bamboos, and the tiger let out a cry of rage and pain. For his tongue, caught between the reeds, had been pinched off!

Now he bellowed with fury and bounded through the jungle to find the mouse-deer. He tore through the underbrush, hardly able to see for pain. At last he found the kanchil standing beside a great wasp's nest. He tried to say, 'What are you doing?'

The mouse-deer said, 'I can't understand you. . . . Oh, you mean, what am I doing here? I'm guarding the king's drum. Isn't it beautiful? And strange-looking, too. Of course, it would be strange-looking. It's not an ordinary drum, you see. It's a magic drum. And only the king may play it.'

The tiger made gurgling sounds and the mouse-deer said, 'You mean, you want to try it?'

The tiger nodded, his eyes blood-red.

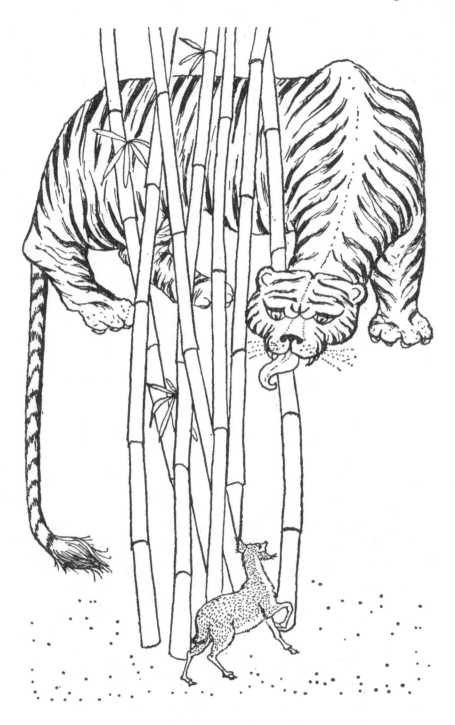

From Adele De Leeuw, *Indonesian Legends and Folktales*. Illustrated by Roni Solbert. (New York: Thomas Nelson and Sons, 1961), 73.

'I don't think I could let you do that.' The mouse-deer acted as if he were thinking hard. 'it wouldn't be right.'

But as the tiger came closer and he could feel the hot breath on his face, he said, 'Well. . . . You might try it, just once. But only if you let me get away from here first. I've been set to guard this wonderful drum, and I wouldn't want any blame to attach to me in case something happened to it.'

The tiger nodded, and the kanchil started to run. 'Just strike it once,' he said. 'When I give you the word. It has such a wonderful tone that no one could bear to hear it more than once.'

The tiger was impatient. 'All right, I'm going,' the mouse-deer said hurriedly, and he leaped away through the underbrush. When he was safely out of sight he called, 'Now!'

And the tiger struck the nest with his great paw. A cloud of wasps, angry at being disturbed, flew out and swarmed around his head. They stung him on the nose and the ears and on the sides and on his legs; they even stung his tail. The tiger ran madly through the jungle, blind with rage and pain. He ran and ran until he found a pool of water; he plunged in it and was never seen again.

The mouse-deer lay under a palm tree and fanned himself. 'Well,' he sighed 'it was hard, but it was worth it. I may be small, but I'm clever. Now he'll never bother me any more.'

From 'Three Tales of the Mouse-Deer', in *Indonesian Legends and Folk Tales*, by Adele De Leeuw (New York: Thomas Nelson and Sons, 1961).

The Rabbit and the Coyote

Coyote is one of the most widely distributed folk characters in North America. Tales about his adventures are found in Mexico, the American Southwest and Great Plains, and central British Columbia. Occasionally a helper, but frequently a selfish trickster, Coyote is often a fool, defeated by his own character failings. In this Mexican story, which bears resemblance to the Peruvian tale 'The Mouse and the Fox', Coyote encounters a master trickster, Rabbit, many of whose actions appear to have been appropriated from African-American tales. The similarity between the Mexican and African-American stories is most obvious in the tar baby episode and in Rabbit's convincing another to take his place as a captive. Rabbit continues to escape because he understands and plays on his adversary's main weakness, a desire for food.

A man and a woman had an onion patch, and a rabbit would come and tear it up. So the woman said, 'You'd better go watch for that rabbit, or he's going to make an end of our onion patch.'

The man went to watch for the rabbit, but he fell asleep, and the rabbit came into the patch and ate the onions. So the woman said, 'Old man, you're not good for anything. I'll go, and you'll see how I catch him.'

So the woman went. She made a doll out of wax and put it right in front of the opening, right in front of the place where the rabbit came in. Then she went off a ways and watched. The rabbit came and said, 'Good evening, sir.'

Nothing.

'Good evening. Get out of the way and let me pass. If you don't get out of the way, I'll slap your face.' So he slapped its face, and his little hand stuck.

So then he said, 'Let go of my hand, or I'll slap you with the other one.'

And that one stuck, so then he said, 'Let go of my two hands, or I'll kick you.' He said, 'I'm telling you to let go,' or I'll kick you.' And he kicked, and his foot stuck.

'Let go of my two hands and my foot, or I'll kick you again.' And his other foot stuck.

'Let go of my four feet, or I'll bite you.'

Nothing.

'I'm telling you to let go of my four feet, or I'll bite you.' And he got stuck.

The old woman heard him, and she came out to see. And she said, 'Now I got you, you good-for-nothing rabbit. You'll see what's going to happen to you.' She picked him up, doll and all, and said to the old man, 'You see, husband, I did catch him. Look at him.'

'Ah, the good-for-nothing!' said the man. 'I'll tie him up right away,' he said, 'so I can put a tub of water to boil, and then we'll scald him.'

Just then a coyote passed by, and he said to the coyote, 'Good morning, good coyote. Do you see that tub full of boiling water? They're going to kill a lot of chickens for me, and they want me to eat them all. Why don't you tie yourself up and let me loose' he said. 'You're bigger than I am.'

'Is that the truth? You're not lying to me?'

'No, I'm not lying to you,' he said.

So the coyote said, 'Good, tie me up. Let me untie you, and then you tie me up.' So he untied the rabbit, and the rabbit tied him up.

And the rabbit said, 'All right now. Feet, what are you for!'

'Wife, take a look outside at the rabbit. What if he got away from us.'

The woman looked out, and she said, 'Husband, husband! He isn't a rabbit anymore; he's a coyote now.'

'More reason for scalding him. This is really bad.' And no telling what else the man said. So then the man goes out, and the water was boiling. And he began to throw hot water and more hot water on the coyote. Until the coyote couldn't stand it any more; and no telling how he did it, but he managed to break the rope.

He said, 'As soon as I find that good-far-nothing rabbit, I'll eat him.' He said, 'He won't get away from me,' he said. Well, he found him way off, eating prickly pears, and he said, 'Ah, you good-far-nothing rabbit! You won't get away this time. Just look how I am, all hairless and scalded. And all because of you. You lied to me.'

'No, dear little coyote, don't hurt me, and I'll peel some prickly pears for you to eat.'

'Is that the truth?'

'Yes, yes, I'll peel them for you,' he said. And he got to work peeling prickly pears, and he also put in a few with thorns and all. Then he said, 'All right, friend coyote, I think I'll go. I'm leaving you a great many prickly pears.' The coyote ate until he got to the ones with thorns, and he stuck himself all over. He was very angry once more.

After a while he found him very far away, and he said to him, 'Now I got you, you good-for-nothing rabbit. You left me a lot of prickly pears with the thorns on; and I got stuck all over.' And this and that and the other. . . . And that . . .

The rabbit said, 'I'm here holding up this big rock,' he said. 'They're going to bring me my dinner here, a great big meal.'

'No, I just don't believe you anymore, rabbit. You're just a big liar.'

'No, this is the truth,' said the rabbit. 'Why don't you take my place,' he said, 'and you'll see.' So the coyote took his place and got stuck there holding up the rock.

After a while a fox went by, and the coyote said, 'Dear little fox, help me hold up this rock.'

'Who left you there?'

'Why, a rabbit.'

'All right. You are there, you stay there.' And, Feet. . . .' The fox ran off and didn't help him.

He managed somehow to get out from under the rock, and he caught up with the rabbit. And the rabbit said, 'No, dear little coyote, don't hurt me. Look. See this little stick? I'm a schoolmaster, and these are my pupils. Be sure not to disturb them if I'm not here,' he said. 'They're going to pay me with a lot of chickens and other food, plenty of it. How can I eat it all? And if I don't eat it, they'll kill me.'

'Well, I am hungry indeed,' said the coyote.

'All right, why don't you stay here. And after a long while, one or two hours, you whip them. You whip them two or three times and tell them, "Study, study." '

The coyote was there for a long time, and nobody brought him chickens or food or anything else, and he said, 'It's too quiet in there. I don't hear any sound.' He put his ear to the hole and struck three times with his little stick. So out come all the wasps, and you should have seen them go at him. He rolled about in the dirt, and the wasps just. . . . Till he went and jumped into a lake.'

He went along, and he went along, and he went along, until he caught up with the rabbit again. And he said, 'No, little rabbit, you've told me just too many lies. I won't believe you for anything.'

'No, *hombre*, I swear this is the truth. A policeman just went by and said that anybody who relieves himself in the paths will be thrown in jail or killed.'

'Oh, little rabbit! I just relieved myself right in the middle of the path.'

'Well, go clean up.' So the coyote went back, but no policeman or anybody came.

And then the rabbit got inside a cave, and the coyote came. From a distance he smelled him in the cave, and he went and knocked. But the rabbit kept quiet. Then he said, 'Hello there, cave of mine.' Nothing. Again, 'Hello there, cave of mine. That's strange; when I call, my cave always answers.' And he called again. And it answered. So he said, 'What the devil! The rabbit's in there.' And the coyote ran away.

He went away, and then the rabbit said, 'What can I do to get rid of this coyote?' He went into a canebrake, and he cleared a spot very well, burned and cleared it all around, and the coyote found him there. The coyote said, 'Now I got you, rabbit. This time you won't get away for anything at all.' He said, 'I'm going to eat you this time. What are you doing there?' He was always asking questions.

'I'm waiting for a wedding party. There's going to be a lot to eat, meat and plenty of everything. They'll have a lot of things.'

'You're not lying to me, rabbit?'

'Of course not. When you hear the popping of the fireworks, you shut your eyes and dance and shout.' That's because he meant to set fire to the cane all around, and it would pop.

'All right, but you'd better not be lying to me. I won't let you off again.' Well, so the rabbit went off, but to set fire all around. The cane was thick, and it began to burn. And the coyote yelled and yelled and sang and sang, with his eyes shut. Then all of a sudden he felt the heat. Well, like it or not, he had to run through the fire. And he got out of it, anyway.

The rabbit was by the edge of a lake, looking at the moon on the water. The coyote came and said that now he had him and all that, and just look, it had been a bunch of lies; there was a big fire, and I don't know what.

'No, dear little coyote; it was the truth. I just don't know what happened. Some accident, perhaps.'

'And now, what are you doing there?' the coyote said.

He said, 'You know what I'm doing? I'm looking at that beautiful cheese in there. But I'm so little. If I go in after it, I'll drown.'

'Is it a cheese?' the coyote said.

'Yes, it is,' he said, 'of course.'

So the coyote jumped in the lake. And the coyote said, 'I can't get to it.'

'Dive deeper.'

'I can't get to it.'

'Dive deeper.'

'I can't get to it.'

'You'd better come out so I can tie a stone to you. Then, you can go all the way to the bottom, and you will get to it.'

So the coyote died there. The rabbit tied a stone to him, and he went all the way down to the bottom. But he drowned and never came out again.

And *colorín* so red; the story is finished.

From *Folktales of Mexico*, edited and translated by Americo Paredes (Chicago: University of Chicago Press, 1970).

The Story of Ca Matsin and Ca Boo-ug

This well-known Filipino folktale includes several motifs found in stories from other cultures: a battle of wits between tricksters, breaking prohibitions, and escaping life-threatening situations through verbal cleverness. Ca Boo-ug, the slow turtle who cannot climb, appears to have been bested by Ca-Matsin, the monkey, a greedy and selfish climber. However, by assuming an agreeable manner and telling the monkey what not to do, the turtle gains revenge. He must again use his wits to escape the monkey's revenge-seeking relatives and plays on their ignorance of the fact that, although he cannot climb, he can swim, something they cannot do. Ca Boo-ug, who initially appears to be at a disadvantage, is thus the cleverer dissembler of the two enemies.

One day a turtle, whose name was Ca Boo-Ug, and a monkey, Ca Matsin, met on the shore of a pond. While they were talking, they noticed a banana plant floating in the water.

'Jump in and get it,' said Ca Matsin, who could not swim,' and we will plant it, and some day we will have some bananas of our own.'

So Ca-Boo-Ug swam out and brought the plant to shore.

'Let's cut it in two,' said Ca Matsin. 'You may have one half and I will take the other, and then we shall each have a tree.'

'All right,' said Ca Boo-Ug; 'which half will you take?'

Ca Matsin did not think the roots looked very pretty, and so he chose the upper part. Ca Boo-Ug knew a thing or two about bananas, so he said nothing, and each took his part and planted it. Ca Boo-Ug planted his in a rich place in the garden, but Ca Matsin planted his in the ashes in the fireplace, because it was easy, and then, too, he could look at it often and see how pretty it was.

Ca Matsin laughed as he thought how he had cheated Ca Boo-Ug, but soon his part began to wither and die, and he was very angry.

With Ca Boo-Ug it was different. Before long his tree began to put forth leaves, and soon it had a beautiful bunch of bananas on it. But he could not climb the tree to get the bananas, so one day he went in search of Ca Matsin, and asked him how his banana-tree was getting along. When Ca Matsin told him that his tree was dead; Ca Boo-Ug pretended to be very much surprised and sorry, and said:—

'My tree has a beautiful bunch of bananas on it, but I cannot climb up to get them. If you will get some of them for me, I will give you half.'

Ca Matsin assented, and climbed the tree. When he got to the top, he pulled a banana, ate it, and threw the skin down to Ca Boo-Ug. Then he ate another, and another, throwing the skins down on Ca Boo-Ug's head. When he had eaten all he wanted, he jumped out of the tree and ran away to the woods, laughing at Ca Boo-Ug. Ca Boo-Ug did not say anything, but just sat down and thought what he should do to get even with Ca Matsin. Finally, he gathered a lot of bamboo sticks and planted them around the tree with the sharp points up, covering them with leaves so that they could not be seen. Then he sat down and waited.'

As soon as Ca Matsin got hungry again, he went around to Ca Boo-Ug's garden to get some more bananas. Ca Boo-Ug seemed glad to see him, and when Ca Matsin asked for some bananas, replied:—

'All right, you may have all you want, but on one condition. When you jump out of the tree you must not touch those leaves. You must jump over them.'

As soon as Ca Matsin heard that he must not jump on the leaves, that was just what he wanted to do. So when he had eaten all the bananas he wanted, he jumped out of the tree on to the leaves as hard as he could jump, and was killed by the sharp bamboo points.

Then Ca Boo-Ug skinned him and cut him up and packed the meat in a jar of brine and hid it in the mud on the bank of the pond.

In the dry season the banana-trees all died and the cocoanut-trees bore no fruit, so a troop of monkeys came to Ca Boo-Ug and asked him if he would give them something to eat.

'Yes, I have some nice meat in a jar which I will give you, but if I do, you must promise to eat it with your eyes shut.'

They were very hungry, so they, gave the required promise, and Ca Boo-Ug gave them the meat. All kept their eyes shut except one, a little baby, and like all babies, he was very curious and wanted to see what was going on. So he opened one eye and peeped at a bone which he had in his hand, then he called out:—

'Oh, see what I have found! Here is the little finger of my brother, Ca Matsin!'

Then all the monkeys looked, and when they found out that Ca Boo-Ug had killed a member of their tribe they were very angry, and looked for Ca Boo-Ug, in order to kill him. But they could not find him, for as soon as he saw what had happened he had hidden under a piece of cocoanut shell which was lying on the ground.

The chief monkey sat upon the cocoanut shell, while he was planning with his companions how they should catch Ca Boo-Ug, but of course he did not know where he was, so he called out: 'Where's Ca Boo-Ug? 'Where's Ca Boo-Ug?'

Ca Boo-Ug was so tickled when he heard the monkey ask where he was that he giggled. The monkeys heard him, and looked all around for him, but could not find him. Then they called out: 'Where's Ca Boo-Ug? Where's Ca Boo-Ug?' This time Ca Boo-Ug laughed out loud, and the monkeys found him. Then they began to plan how they should punish him.

'Let's put him into a rice mortar and pound him to death,' said one.

'Aha!' said Ca Boo-Ug, 'that's nothing! My mother beat me so much when I was little that now my back is so strong that nothing can break it.'

When the monkeys found out that Ca Bo-Ug was not afraid of being pounded in a rice mortar, they determined, to try something else.

'Let's make a fire on his back and burn him up,' suggested another.

'Oh, ho!' laughed Ca Boo-Ug, 'that's nothing. I should think that you could tell by the colour of my shell that I have had a fire lighted on my back many times. In fact, I like it, as I am always so cold.'

So the monkeys decided that they would punish Ca Boo-Ug by throwing him into the pond and drowning him.

'Boo-hoo!' cried Ca Boo-Ug, 'don't do that! You will surely kill me. Please don't do that! Boo-hoo! Boo-hoo!'

Of course when the monkeys found that Ca Boo-Ug did not wish to be thrown into the pond, they thought they had found just the way to kill him. So, in spite of his struggles, they picked him up and threw him far out into the poond.

To their surprise and chagrin, Ca Boo-Ug stuck his head out of the water and laughed at them, and then turned around and swam off.

When the monkeys saw how they had been deceived, they were very much disappointed, and began to plan how they could catch Ca Boo-Ug again. So they called to a big fish, named Botete, that lived in the pond: 'Botete! Drink all you can of the water in the pond and help us find the bag of gold that we hid in it. If you will help us find it, you shall have half of the gold.'

So Botete began to drink the water, and in a little time the pond was nearly dry. Then the monkeys determined to go down into the pond and look for Ca Boo-Ug. When he saw them coming, Ca Boo-Ug called to Salacsacan, the kingfisher, who was sitting on a branch of a tree. which hung over the water:—

'Salacsacan! Salacsacan! Botete has drunk all the water in the pond, and if there is no water there will be no fish for you to catch. Fly down now and peck a hole in Botete, and let the water out, before the fish are all dead.' So Salacsacan flew down and pecked a hole in the side of Botete, and the water rushed out and drowned all the monkeys.

When Ca Boo-Ug saw that the monkeys were all dead, he crawled up on the bank, and there he lived happily ever after.

From 'Visayan Folk-tales III', *Journal of American Folk-Lore*, 20 (October–December, 1907), 316–18.

The Mouse and the Fox

These three incidents are just a few from a cycle of South American stories in which the small, clever animal outwits his larger and more foolish adversary. Sometimes the trickster is a mouse, at other times, a guinea pig or rabbit; the victim of his ruses is generally a fox. The mouse is able to escape from life-threatening situations not only by playing on his adversary's stupidity, but also by appealing to his vanity, his desire to be seen as a hero, and his fear of dying in a natural disaster that could end the world. The presence of the tar-baby motif suggests that the opening incident may be derived from West African stories. However, the fact that the version of the tale on which this adaptation is based was collected in 1972 in a Peruvian squatter settlement raises the possibility that recent tellers may have been familiar with a version of the Br'er Rabbit story, which was very popular throughout the twentieth century.

Once there were two friends, the mouse and the fox. Every night the mouse used to eat the flowers from a man's garden. When the man asked who had been stealing his flowers, the caretaker told him, 'Every night a mouse comes to steal.'

So the man decided to set a trap and visited the cheese factory. The owner of the factory suggested that he trap the mouse by making a tar doll. 'Put it on the water pipe and when the mouse comes, he will give it a whack or something, and get stuck.' So the owner went home and made a very pretty tar doll.

That night the mouse came with lots of other mice. 'Ah, *caramba!*' he said when he saw the tar doll. 'There's a watchman. He wants to hit me, so let's go together, and we'll all hit him, and we'll get into the garden easily.'

The mouse walked up slowly, slowly, saying 'Good evening, sir! Good evening, sir!' When the doll didn't answer, he said to his friends, 'The watchman seems dumb! Listen, old man, I'm going to knock you over the cliff with a fist.' When he didn't get an answer, he struck the doll and, pum, he got stuck.

'Let go! Let go! Let go!' the mouse called, 'If you don't, I'll hit you with my left hand—it's stronger.' So he did, and the left hand got stuck. 'I'm going to make you see stars,' the mouse said angrily, as he lifted his foot to kick the tar doll. Soon, his right foot was stuck. 'I'm going to give you a head butt; I'm going to knock your brains out!' So mouse gave him a head but, and, of course, his head got stuck.

That only made him angrier. 'If you don't let go,' he roared, 'I'm going to give you such a belly smack that you'll disappear.' When mouse's belly got stuck, he kept threatening. This time he said he'd whip the watchman with his tail. When he was completely stuck, his friends were afraid, so they ran off.

The next morning, when the owner arrived, he found mouse stuck to the tar doll. And he went away thinking, 'Look how he's hanging! After lunch we'll kill you, because we don't want to get our hands dirty now.'

While the man was having his lunch, the fox arrived in the garden. '*Compadrito,*' he said, after looking at mouse stuck to the tar doll, 'what's happened to you?'

Mouse thought for a few minutes and then replied, 'It's a long story. I'm going to marry the daughter of this owner. I'm little and she's big. I can't get married. Maybe she'll step on me. But, since you're big, you can get married. Please free me.'

So the fox did, and, because he wanted to marry the daughter of the rich owner, he stuck himself to the doll. After lunch, the owner came back, carrying a big stick with which to beat the mouse. 'Ah, *caramba!*,' he muttered to himself. 'This mouse has certainly grown.' And he started to beat him with the stick.

'No, no,' fox yelped. 'I'm going to marry your daughter.' That made the man angrier, so he hit him harder. The fox became so frightened that he pulled as hard as he could to unstick himself from the tar doll. When he was free, he ran out of the garden. 'My *compadrito* mouse has betrayed me. When I catch him, I'm going to eat him.'

The next day, the fox found the mouse at the bottom of a cliff, pushing his arms up against an overhanging rock. When the mouse saw the fox, he screamed out, 'Aaaackk! Aaackk!' And he pushed harder against the rock.

'It's no use screaming,' fox told him. 'I'm going to eat you now, even if you put up a fight.'

'You can eat me later, but right now, you must hold on to this rock,' the mouse replied. 'It's going to flatten me; if you don't hold it up, the town's going to be destroyed by the rock.'

'Really,' the fox said in a surprised voice. And, when the mouse said that he, himself, was too little to keep holding the rock, the fox, proud of being bigger and stronger, said he'd help. As he started to push against the rock, the mouse told him that he'd go to the village to get a more help. And off he went.

But after he'd been holding the rock for a while, the fox discovered that it didn't seem to be moving at all. He stopped pushing and nothing happened. 'I've been fooled twice by the mouse,' he growled. 'Now I'm really going to eat him, no matter what he asks me to do.'

He headed along the trail looking for the mouse, muttering angrily to himself as he went along. As he came around the bend, he found the mouse scratching out a little hole in the side of a hill. He grabbed the mouse, who said shrilly, 'If you eat me, you'll die too. It's going to rain fire. You're my friend, so I'll make the hole bigger, so you can get in too.'

Fox helped him to dig, and when it was large enough, fox crawled in. Mouse followed. But, when the fox wasn't looking, the mouse piled thorny branches across the opening.

'It's starting to rain fire,' yelled the mouse. Fox was frightened and closed his eyes. 'Some of it is coming into our hole. Ouch!' cried mouse. 'I can feel it against my skin.' And then he pushed one of the branches against the fox. The fox pushed himself further into the hole and, when the mouse pushed a branch against him again, the fox yelped—more than once. In fact, he was making so much noise that he didn't hear the mouse push the branches away from the opening and run away.

In a few minutes, the fox whimpered, '*Compadrito*? I don't feel any more fire rain. Do you think it's over?' When he didn't receive an answer, he opened his eyes and cautiously turned around. All he saw was the opening of the hole and, beyond that, clear skies. 'Three betrayals,' he cried out. 'I don't forgive him any more.'

And he set out to find his *compadrito*. He did. But once again the mouse tricked the fox and escaped. He always does.

From *Folktales Told around the World*, edited by Richard M. Dorson (Chicago: University of Chicago Press, 1975).

How El Bizarrón Fooled the Devil

In Spain and many Latin American countries, a favorite tale-type recounts the ways in which a clever individual outwits that dangerous arch-trickster, the Devil. In this Cuban tale, the hero, El Bizarrón, whose name derives from the Spanish adjective meaning handsome, courageous, splendid, and magnificent, is successful in many ways. He is able to escape death, the fate of others who have laboured for the Devil; he avoids having to work; and he ends the tale a very rich man. He carefully stages the various events and follows each with a brief, preposterous explanation that creates increasing anxiety in the Devil. Readers might find it interesting to speculate whether the hero's name is an accurate or ironic one.

There was once a man called El Bizarrón who wandered about looking for work. A restless fellow. He wandered here. He wandered there. But more often there than here.

One day he was told that in the house of the Devil there was need for a servant. *'Pues, ten cuidado!'* they warned. (A forceful way of saying, 'Watch out!') Two servants the Devil had already slain. He was a mean one. All who worked for him ended up dead. Much sooner than later, too. Clearly a recommendation to avoid that house.

But El Bizarrón retorted, 'I'm on my way. The Devil won't frighten me.'

So, to the Devil's front door he went. And knocked.

Who should open the door but the Devil himself.

'Have you work for a strong man?'

'Work enough for six strong men. You are sure there are not five more of you? Ah, well. *Pase adentro.'*

In walked El Bizarrón. The Devil led him to the room where he was to sleep. 'Rest,' he said. 'Tomorrow you will begin your chores.'

El Bizarrón stretched himself on the bed. Before long, healthy snores were livening up that corner of the house.

The next day the Devil sent him to fetch water.

But El Bizarrón demanded, 'Give me a pick and shovel.'

The Devil without any fuss gave them.

El Bizarrón went down to the river. He began digging a ditch from the stream to the Devil's house. Like six men he toiled. Well . . . like three anyway.

At eleven o'clock came the Devil to check up on El Bizarrón. 'Water I wish. Not a ditch. Explain yourself,' he commanded.

'I am digging a canal to your house. Then there will be no need to go for water. Water will flow to you.'

The Devil reflected. This man can dig. The trench is already the depth of a pitchfork. (The Devil knew his pitchforks.) Moreover, this man can *think.* He didn't like that at all. It was such a distasteful thought that he went off home.

A few days later the Devil ordered El Bizarrón to fetch a load of wood. El Bizarrón demanded, 'Give me a length of rope. A long length.'

Without much ado the Devil gave it.

El Bizarrón took the rope on his shoulder and went off to the mountain. There he set himself to wind the rope around the trees—around the whole forest. The rope was a lengthy length all right. With all his tramping, the heels of El Bizarrón's shoes were worn to a fraction of a millimeter; not enough sole remained to measure a fraction of anything. At eleven o'clock when the Devil came to see what El Bizarrón was up to, he found him with the rope looped around the mountain as a collar wreathes a neck.

Of course he wanted to know, 'What are you doing?' El Bizarrón answered, 'Securing this mountain of woods so I can carry it back in one trip.'

What a barbarian, thought the Devil And he directed El Bizarrón to return to the house. Without the mountain. No room for *that* in the backyard.

Soon after, there was a throwing contest on the beach, with metal bars. The Devil thought, ah, I shall send this strong fellow as a competitor. With his muscles he must surely win me a prize. And he led El Bizarrón to the shore, El Bizarrón with a bar balanced on his shoulder.

At the beach everyone was practicing and preparing himself for the match. Except El Bizarrón. That one curled himself on the sunny sand and took a snooze.

The day peeled off its hours. The contest began. Came the turn of El Bizarrón.

Loudly he cried out, 'Order those faraway boats to sail away. Otherwise I will sink them with my shot!'

As this was impossible they would not permit him to throw. It was a disappointment to all. In particular to the Devil, who felt more and more uneasy about El Bizarrón's strength. *And* his acuteness. Too dangerous is this ox with his fox's brain, he decided. I must rid myself of him.

The two made their way back to the Devil's house. In a buttery manner the Devil suggested that since he desired to spend that night stretched out on the iron grill of the barbecue, El Bizarrón might wish to sleep beneath.

'Why not?' asked El Bizarrón in an offhand way.

So it was arranged. The Devil then hid two heavy, heavy rocks that he planned to drop on El Bizarrón during the night.

Evening fell, and both lay down in their places: the Devil on the high grill and El Bizarrón underneath. But El Bizarrón noticed that the Devil appeared much bulkier than usual. A suspicious sign. Hmmmmmmm. Unknown to the Devil, El Bizarrón changed his bed to a corner, a far corner. And waited.

At midnight he heard the clangor of falling rocks. At once he shouted, 'Ay, what a mosquito has bitten me!'

Naturally the Devil thought, two boulders have dropped on him and to this fellow they are no more than an insect bite. He was impressed. Disturbed. Shaken to his red marrow.

He climbed down to note exactly El Bizarrón's condition. This one was now sitting under the barbecue, unbruised, unscratched, unmarked. And there lay the smashed rocks.

'Ah,' said El Bizarrón in a voice of wonder, 'I believed it was a mosquito and instead it was these stones. How came they here?'

Now the Devil's teeth clacked with fright. Speaking between clacks he declared; 'Fellow, I shall give you a burro loaded with silver if you will leave here—if you leave for a destination far, far away. Preferably the moon. Or farther.'

El Bizarrón accepted the offer. Why not? He brought up the burro. The Devil filled the saddlebags with money, till they bulged like sacks of potatoes.

'There you have it. Now go.'

El Bizarrón went. After he had been gone a while, the Devil's wife said to him, 'That ninny deceived you. He is not so strong as all that.' She flung sneers against the Devil as if she were hurling stones at a stray dog.

Her scorn convinced her husband. So, saddling a horse, he set out to find El Bizarrón and take from him the donkey and the riches.

Looking back, El Bizarrón glimpsed the Devil approaching at a distance. Quickly he hid the donkey in a field of sugarcane. Then he lay on his back in the middle of the road with his legs in the air.

The Devil came up. In astonishment he asked, 'And what ails *you*?'

'Ah, nothing. That stubbornness of a donkey refused to walk. So I gave him a kick that sent him above the clouds. . . .'

The Devil, his teeth clattering again, wanted to know, 'But why are you lying here kicking at the wind?'

'I don't want the donkey killed when he drops back to earth. This way I'll ease his fall with my feet.'

At that the palsy of the Devil's teeth affected the rest of him. He might have been a flag lashed by a gale. Swiftly he spurred his horse and galloped home.

His wife asked, 'Did you catch him?'

'Catch him! Should I want to? There he was. No sign of the burro—he had kicked it to Heaven. And if I had waited to recover the money he might have booted me to Heaven. And what place is that for the Devil? Glad am I to be free of him.'

From *Greedy Mariani and Other Folktales of the Antilles*, selected and adapted by Dorothy Sharp Carter (New York: Atheneum, 1974).

The Apples of Idun

This Norse myth emphasizes the malicious character of the trickster Loke (Loki) who is one of the Frost Giants—an enemy of the gods. He has become a blood brother of Odin, king of the gods, and he often travels with the gods, who enjoy his quick wit and mischievousness. His trickery becomes progressively more evil, however, as his fundamental selfishness and his animosity towards the gods develops. In this case, he steals the apples of Idun (Iduna), fruit that the gods must eat regularly in order to maintain their youth and strength. Concerned only with extricating himself from the threatening situation that he himself created, Loke thinks not at all of the great harm his actions may bring to his companions. Many scholars believe that the presentation of Loke's negative traits in this and later adventures reflects the influence of Christianity on Norse myths, particularly in the former's presentation of the Devil as an evil trickster.

Once upon a time Odin, Loke, and Hœner started on a journey. They had often travelled together before on all sorts of errands, for they had a great many things to look after, and more than once they had fallen into trouble through the prying, meddlesome, malicious spirit of Loke, who was never so happy as when he was doing wrong. When the gods went on a journey they travelled fast and hard, for they were strong, active spirits who loved nothing so much as hard work, hard blows, storm, peril, and struggle. There were no roads through the country over which they made their way, only high mountains to be climbed by rocky paths, deep valleys into which the sun hardly looked during half the year, and swift-rushing streams, cold as ice, and treacherous to the surest foot and the strongest arm. Not a bird flew through the air, not an animal sprang through the trees. It was as still as a desert. The gods walked on and on, getting more tired and hungry at every step. The sun was sinking low over the steep, pine-crested mountains, and the travellers had neither breakfasted nor dined. Even Odin was beginning to feel the pangs of hunger, like the most ordinary mortal, when suddenly, entering a little valley, the famished gods came upon a herd of cattle. It was the work of a minute to kill a great ox and to have the carcass swinging in a huge pot over a roaring fir.

But never were gods so unlucky before! In spite of their hunger the pot would not boil. They piled on the wood until the great flames crackled and licked the pot with their fiery tongues, but every time the cover was lifted there was the meat just as raw as when it was put in. It is easy to imagine that the travellers were not in very good humour. As they were talking about it, and wondering how it could be, a voice called out from the branches of the oak overhead, 'If you will give me my fill I'll make the pot boil.'

The gods looked first at each other and then into the tree, and there they discovered a great eagle. They were glad enough to get their supper on almost any terms, so they told the eagle he might have what he wanted if he would only get the meat cooked. The bird was as good as his word, and in less time than it takes to tell it supper was ready. Then the eagle flew down and picked out both shoulders and both legs. This was a pretty large share, it must be confessed, and Loke, who was always angry when anybody got more than he, no sooner saw what the eagle had taken than he seized a great pole and began to beat the rapacious bird unmercifully. Whereupon a very singular thing happened, as singular things always used to happen when the gods were concerned: the pole stuck fast in the huge talons of the eagle at one end, and Loke stuck fast at the other end. Struggle as he might, he could not get loose, and as the great bird sailed away over the tops of the trees, Loke went pounding along on the ground, striking against rocks and branches until he was bruised half to death.

The eagle was not an ordinary bird by any means, as Loke soon found when he begged for mercy. The giant Thjasse happened to be flying abroad in his eagle plumage when the hungry travellers came under the oak and tried to cook the ox. It was into his hands Loke had fallen, and he was not to get away until he had promised to pay roundly for his freedom.

If there was one thing which the gods prized above their other treasures in Asgard, it was the beautiful fruit of Idun, kept by the goddess in a golden casket and given to the gods to keep them forever young and fair. Without these Apples all their power could not have kept them from getting old like the meanest of mortals. Without these Apples of Idun Asgard itself would have lost its charm; for what would heaven be without youth and beauty forever shining through it?

Thjasse told Loke that he could not go unless he would promise to bring him the Apples of Idun. Loke was wicked enough for anything; but when it came to robbing the gods of their immortality, even he hesitated. And while he hesitated the eagle dashed hither and thither, flinging him against the sides of the mountains and dragging him through the great tough boughs of the oaks until his courage gave out entirely, and he promised to steal the Apples out of Asgard and give them to the giant.

Loke was bruised and sore enough when he got on his feet again to hate the giant who handled him so roughly, with all his heart, but he was not unwilling to keep his promise to steal the Apples, if only for the sake of tormenting the other gods. But how was it to be done? Idun guarded the golden fruit of immortality with sleepless watchfulness. No one ever touched it but herself, and a beautiful sight it was to see her fair hands spread it forth for the morning feasts in Asgard. The power which Loke possessed lay not so much in his own strength, although he had a smooth way of deceiving people, as in the goodness of others who had no thought of his doing wrong because they never did wrong themselves.

Not long after all this happened, Loke came carelessly up to Idun as she was gathering her Apples to put them away in the beautiful carven box which held them.

'Good morning, goddess,' said he. 'How fair and golden your Apples are!'

'Yes,' answered Idun; 'the bloom of youth keeps them always beautiful.'

'I never saw anything like them,' continued Loke slowly, as if he were talking about a matter of no importance, 'until the other day.'

Idun looked up at once with the greatest interest and curiosity in her face. She was very proud of her Apples, and she knew no earthly trees, however large and fair, bore the immortal fruit.

'Where have you seen any Apples like them?' she asked.

'Oh, just outside the gates,' said Loke indifferently. 'If you care to see them I'll take you there. It will keep you but a moment. The tree is only a little way off.'

Idun was anxious to go at once.

'Better take your Apples with you to compare them with the others,' said the wily god, as she prepared to go.

Idun gathered up the golden Apples and went out of Asgard, carrying with her all that made it heaven. No sooner was she beyond the gates than a mighty rushing sound was heard, like the coming of a tempest, and before she could think or act, the giant Thjasse, in his eagle plumage, was bearing her swiftly away through the air to his desolate, icy home in Thrymheim, where, after vainly trying to persuade her to let him eat the Apples and be forever young like the gods, he kept her a lonely prisoner.

Loke, after keeping his promise and delivering Idun into the hands of the giant, strayed back into Asgard as if nothing had happened. The next morning, when the gods assembled for their feast, there was no Idun. Day after day went past, and still the beautiful goddess did not come. Little by little the light of youth and beauty faded from the home of the gods, and they themselves became old and haggard. Their strong, young faces were lined with care and furrowed by age, their raven locks passed from gray to white, and their flashing eyes became dim and hollow. Brage, the god of poetry, could make no music while his beautiful wife was gone he knew not whither.

Morning after morning the faded light broke on paler and ever paler faces, until even in heaven the eternal light of youth seemed to be going out forever.

Finally the gods could bear the loss of power and joy no longer. They made rigourours inquiry. They tracked Loke on that fair morning when he led Idun beyond the gates; they seized him and brought him into solemn council, and when he read in their haggard faces the deadly hate which flamed in all their hearts against his treachery, his courage failed, and he promised to bring Idun back to Asgard if the goddess Freyja would lend him her falcon-guise. No sooner said than done; and with eager gaze the gods watched him as he flew away, becoming at last only a dark moving speck against the sky.

After long and weary flight Loke came to Thrymheim, and was glad enough to find Thjasse gone to sea and Idun alone in his dreary house. He changed her instantly into a nut, and taking her thus disguised in his talons, flew away as fast as his falcon wings could carry him. And he had need of all his speed, for Thjasse, coming suddenly home and finding Idun and her precious fruit gone, guessed what had happened, and, putting on his eagle plumage, flew forth in a mighty rage, with vengeance in his heart. Like the rushing wings of a tempest, his mighty pinions beat the air and bore him swiftly onward. From mountain peak to mountain peak he measured his wide course, almost grazing at times the murmuring pine forests, and then sweeping high in mid-air with nothing above but the arching sky, and nothing beneath but the tossing sea.

At last he sees the falcon far ahead, and now his flight becomes like the flash of the lightning for swiftness, and like the rushing of clouds for uproar. The haggard faces of the gods line the walls of Asgard and watch the race with tremulous eagerness. Youth and immortality are staked upon the winning of Loke. He is weary enough and frightened enough too, as the eagle sweeps on close behind him; but he makes desperate efforts to widen the distance between them. Little by little the eagle gains on the falcon. The gods grow white with fear; they rush off and prepare great fires upon the walls. With fainting, drooping wing the falcon passes over and drops exhausted by the wall. In an instant the fires have been lighted, and the great flames roar to heaven. The eagle sweeps across the fiery line a second later, and falls, maimed and burned, to the ground, where a dozen fierce hands smite the life out of him, and the great giant Thjasse perishes among his foes.

Idun resumes her natural form as Brage rushes to meet her. The gods crowd round her. She spreads the feast, the golden Apples gleaming with unspeakable lustre in the eyes of the gods. They eat; and once more their faces glow with the beauty of immortal youth, their eyes flash with the radiance of divine power, and, while Idun stands like a star for beauty among the throng, the song of Brage is heard once more; for poetry and immortality are wedded again.

From *Norse Stories Retold from the Eddas*, by Hamilton Wright Mabie (Chicago: Rand McNally, 1902).

LINKS TO OTHER STORIES

Part Nine

Wise and Foolish
Tales of Cleverness and Stupidity

Stories about fools are popular around the world. Known variously as noodleheads, numbskulls, nitwits, drolls, and bumpkins, the central figures are victims of their own foolishness and the cleverness of their adversaries. In fact, in many tales of this type, the central conflict is between foolish and clever individuals. The fools make very poor trades; they are gulled by tricksters; they interpret instructions literally; they mistake the true nature of situations in which they find themselves. However, sometimes they learn from their experiences and reverse the roles, rendering foolish those who had duped them.

Many fools are on the margins of the societies in which they live. The title characters of 'The Fisherman and His Wife', the apparently lucky couple in 'The Three Wishes', and the central character in 'The Gift of the Holy Man' are all poor. The man who buys an egg that will supposedly hatch into a horse in 'Pedro Urdimale, the Little Fox, and the Mare's Egg', is a newcomer to the area, a Gringo, or foreigner. Many are marginalized because of their simple-mindedness. The Gringo believes horses come from eggs; at the beginning of 'Si' Djeha Cheats the Robbers', the hero accepts the robbers' statements that he needs a safer mount. The poor man fails to heed the holy man's instructions about how to care for his gift.

Other fools are individuals who should know better. The ruler in 'The Emperor's New Clothes' is in a position of power. His exaggerated sense of self worth, however, makes a fool of him. The robbers of Si' Djeha fail to recognize that their former victim is now using their techniques against them. In 'The President Wants No More of Anansi', the leader does not learn that Anansi will defeat him by deliberately taking prohibitions literally. Captain Morgan, leader of the attacking pirate band, believes the fabrications of the priests and, as a consequence, does not discover treasure in 'The Golden Alter of the Church of St Joseph'.

In many tales, wiser individuals oppose the fools. Pedro Urdimale, who is skilled at acquiring money without having to work hard, recognizes the Gringo's naiveté. The robbers, when they prepare to take the donkey, perceive that Si' Djeha is trusting and slow-witted. Anansi knows that he can obey the President literally without obeying him in spirit. Coyote, in 'How the Coyote Danced with the Blackbirds', is opposed by a blackbird leader who is able to begin punishment of the vain animal without his realizing it. The innkeeper feigns hospitality so that the poor man will forget the holy man's instructions.

Conflicts frequently arise because the fools, who desire something, place themselves in vulnerable situations. The naïve Gringo wants a horse, and Coyote wants to fly so that he can achieve glory by exceeding his limitations. The poor husband and wife are so intent on coming up with wishes that would gratify her yearning for wealth and his for well being that they inadvertently make foolish wishes. The fisherman's wife is guilty of misusing wishes because her desire for power and status seems to know no bounds. Her ambition ends up sending the couple back to the lowly dwelling that they had initially occupied.

Interestingly, some of the greatest fools are individuals in positions of authority who, for various reasons, are unsatisfied. The Emperor who has ordered new clothes wants to keep everyone else unaware of the possibility that he may be an inadequate ruler. The President, who finds Anansi so annoying that he wishes never to see him, fails to realize that he will be defeated by his clever adversary, who will further annoy the President while seeming to obey him.

Often fools are victimized by tricksters who use their opponents' gullibility to fulfill their own desires. Pedro Urdimale, merely by stealing a melon and misrepresenting it as something the Gringo needs, is able to gain the money he wants. In 'The Hodja and the Thousand Pieces of Gold', the infidel, seeking to make his neighbor appear foolish, drops 999 pieces of gold down a chimney, an apparent partial answer to the Hodja's prayers to Allah. The innkeeper offers unaccustomed hospitality to the poor man and then takes the magic cloth, the gift of the holy man. The blackbirds, wanting to punish Coyote for his foolish egotism, seem to be offering their assistance by providing the feathers he needs to fly; in reality they are preparing for his literal downfall. The robbers pose as benefactors to Si' Djeha so that they can make off with his donkey and cash.

Characters who begin their stories as fools are not guaranteed to end up that way. In fact, many conflicts between clever and foolish adversaries are resolved when the roles are reversed and the victims successfully execute revenge. The poor man, having lost the first gift from the holy man learns that by dissembling—by appearing to be as trusting as he was the first time—he can trick the innkeeper into a position where his host's true nature is revealed and he is punished. Si' Djeha, after the loss of his fine donkey and a great deal of money, is able not only to recover his mount, but also to acquire more money than had been taken from him. He succeeds in enriching himself because he is able carefully to develop plans that play on his adversaries' weaknesses. The Hodja is able to shame the infidel, who is upbraided by the magistrate to whom the infidel has gone to seek redress against his neighbor. In many ways, the poor man, the Hodja, and Si' Djeha are wise fools: they use their apparent simpleness as a lure to entrap their adversaries.

Although the tales in this part reflect many similarities in incident and character, they also contain details that link them to the cultures in which they were originally told. Not infrequently, they satirize outsiders who could, in real life, represent threats to social stability. The Gringo, who is duped by Pedro, and Henry Morgan, who is thwarted by the Panamanian priests, are both Europeans and therefore are members of cultures that, in colonial times, repressed Latin Americans. Morgan, along with the infidel who takes the Hodja to court, is a member of one religion who is thwarted by members of other, apparently vulnerable religions. To the Zuni, Coyote represents the outsider who does not fit into the balanced order of the society. He also stands as an example to members of Zuni culture of what happens when one of their own breaks the normal patterns of life.

Many of the stories reflect their societies' distrust of pompous authority figures. For example, the tiger, a symbol of power in Korea, is revealed as ignorant and cowardly. In 'The Emperor's New Clothes', Danish author Hans Christian Andersen combines a late eighteenth-century European satirical approach with a romantic distrust of authority, while 'The Fisherman and His Wife' takes a humourous approach to traditional European beliefs that it is wrong for women to attempt to rise above their god-given position as inferior to men.

In Haiti, where repression has been a constant for several centuries, the people symbolically defeat tyrants by having them look ridiculous in stories.

The characteristics of individuals in stories about wise and foolish people, along with the actions of the various characters, help to explain why certain tales and characters are so popular in particular societies. The tales help people define themselves within their cultures and to experience, through story, a kind of vicarious power over authority figures.

Although specific stories and characters appeal to audiences in specific cultures, tales of the wise and foolish are found in many different cultures around the world. One reason for the widespread popularity of these stories may be that they provide readers and listeners with a sense of superiority. Such tales belong to what critic Northrop Frye called the ironic mode, in which 'we have a sense of looking down on a scene of bondage, frustration, or absurdity' (34). The fools are inferior to what Frye referred to as low mimetic characters, those who are similar in ability and status to ordinary people. That the poor man is going to be robbed by the innkeeper, or that the Gringo is only purchasing what is a vegetable, or that the tiger is afraid of a small fruit is obvious to most readers of or listeners to the story. If the high mimetic hero evokes awe, admiration, and a belief that the hero's qualities and status are unattainable for ordinary people, then the low mimetic character, the unlikely hero, creates a sense of identification; the ironic character creates a sense of superiority, a response in the audience to the effect that 'I could never be that foolish'.

There is a different response if the character behaving foolishly is in a position of authority or is socially superior to those responding to the tale. Readers or listeners may again feel superior; this time, however, because 'the mighty have fallen'. Those who should have been better than those they governed or ruled are revealed to be no better than and sometimes less than, that is, more foolish than, their subjects. In stories, at least, the power of authority is diminished.

When fools represent dangerous forces perceived as threats to individuals or groups their defeat provides a sense of relief. At the end of the tale, Coyote is no longer a member of the flock of blackbirds; his disruptive influence is gone. The robbers whom Si' Djeha has constantly outwitted have been destroyed. The Muslim court has chastened the infidel who wanted to make the Hodja and his religion appear ridiculous. In 'The Tiger, the Persimmon, and the Rabbit's Tail', the predator who would have destroyed livestock and the robber who would have invaded the home have been driven off, terrified because of their ignorance.

In those stories in which the fools become heroes, defeating those who had had power over them, the lowly characters become unlikely heroes who triumph over those who earlier had been superior. Readers can identify with such individuals, realizing through the stories a vicarious sense of empowerment, a sense that they too have the potential successfully to oppose their oppressors.

It also possible, however, that the fool is a scapegoat, that he is a figure onto whom ordinary people can project their own senses of inadequacy, their repressed awareness of their own potential for foolishness. The laughter at the absurdities of the situations fools either create or find themselves in could well be nervous and uneasy. Ridiculing the noodleheads of stories could become somewhat cathartic. Recognizing that 'there but for the grace of God go I', readers project their own weaknesses onto story characters with a sense of relief. Storyteller Jane Yolen makes this point by quoting English author Alan Garner: 'The element, I think that most marks us is that of the Fool. It is where our humanity lies' (170). That is, readers respond to hidden elements in themselves that are made manifest in tales about fools.

Stories about fools have long been popular with children. Marginalized, inexperienced, and in possession of limited education, they have, nonetheless, a keen sense of the absurd and foolish. Preschool children laugh at adults who, to them, seem to be acting foolishly Children enjoy the 1960s television series featuring the simple-minded Gilligan, one-reelers featuring the Three Stooges, and 'The Stupids' books by Harry C. Allard and James Marshall. They feel superior to the foolish characters whose absurd adventures they are following. That the people in these stories are frequently adults makes their actions appear even more foolish.

Children often respond with laughter to folktale nitwits, numbskulls, and fools. When the characters are ironic, they are inferior to the members of the young audience. And members of the audience identify with the apparently foolish characters who do the tricking, the fooling. As children grow older, they are able to appreciate the more complex and subtle stories about fools. Pedro's tricks on the Gringo are fairly obvious. The foolishness of the fisherman and his wife is more complex, involving as it does character traits of greed and ambition. Si' Djeha's rather involved strategies for thwarting the revenge-seeking robbers he has duped appeal to older children. As they have done for members of their originating cultures, tales of the wise and foolish help children define themselves and their situations in the societies of which they are members.

Works Cited

Frye, Northrop. 1957. *Anatomy of Criticism*. Princeton, NJ: Princeton University Press.
Yolen, Jane, ed. 1986. *Favorite Folktales from Around the World*. New York: Pantheon.

The Tale of the Three Wishes

Tales of people who are tested by being given three wishes have been traced by folklore scholar Stith Thompson to mediaeval stories about Christ and the Saints, who, while traveling in disguise, presented people with wishes as rewards or punishment. The foolishness or wisdom of those who are granted the wishes is revealed by the nature and consequences of their wishes, most notably the third and final one. This version of the tale is taken from a late eighteenth-century book written by Madam Le Prince de Beaumont, author of 'Beauty and the Beast'. Interspersed with educational and moral lessons are tales intended to lead to edifying discussion among the intended readers: fairly well-off young women. The slight envy of the husband and wife revealed early in the story, their discussions about how to use the wishes, and their response to the first two wishes are designed to assist the young women to 'form their Hearts to Goodness'.

There was once a man, not very rich, who had a pretty woman to his wife. One winter's evening, as they sat by the fire, they talked of the happiness of their neighbours, who were richer than they.

Said the wife, 'If it were in my power to have what I wish, I should soon be happier than all of them.'

'So should I too,' said the husband. 'I wish we had fairies now, and that one of them was kind enough to grant me what I should ask.'

At that instant, they saw a very beautiful lady in the room, who told them, 'I am a fairy; and I promise to grant you the first three things you shall wish; but take care, after having wished for three things, I will not grant any thing farther.'

The fairy disappeared, and the man and his wife were much perplexed. 'For my own part,' said the wife, 'if it is left to my choice, I know very well what I shall wish for. I do not wish yet, but I think nothing is so good as to be handsome, rich, and to be of great quality.'

But the husband answered, 'With all these things one may be sick, fretful, and one may die young; it would be much wiser to wish for health, cheerfulness, and a long life.'

'But to what purpose is a long life with poverty?' says the wife. 'It would only prolong misery. In truth, the fairy should have promised us a dozen gifts, for there's at least a dozen things which I should want.'

'That's true,' said the husband, 'but let us take time, let us consider, from this time till morning, the three things which are most necessary for us, and then wish.'

'I'll think all night,' said the wife, 'meanwhile let us warm ourselves, for it is very cold.' At the same time, the wife took the tongs to mend the fire, and, feeling there was a great many coals thoroughly lighted, she said, without thinking on it, 'Here's a nice fire; I wish we had a yard of black pudding for our supper, we could dress it easily.' She had hardly said these words, when down came tumbling, through the chimney, a yard of black pudding.

'Plague on greedy guts, with her black pudding,' said the husband. 'Here's a fine wish indeed. Now we only have two left. For my part, I am so vexed, that I wish the black pudding fast to the tip of your nose.'

The man soon perceived that he was sillier than his wife; for, with the second wish, up starts the black pudding and sticks so fast to the tip of the poor wife's nose that there was no means to take it off. 'Wretch that I am!' cried she. 'You are a wicked man for wishing the pudding fast to my nose.'

'My dear,' answered the husband, 'I vow I did not think of it; but what shall we do? I am about wishing for vast riches, and propose to make a golden case to hide the pudding.'

'Not at all,' answered the wife, 'for I should kill myself were I to live with this pudding dangling at my nose. Be persuaded, we still have a wish to make. Leave it to me, or I shall instantly throw myself out of the window.'

With this she ran and opened the window; but the husband, who loved his wife called out, 'Hold, my dear wife, I give you leave to wish for what you will.'

'Well,' said the wife, 'my wish is that this pudding may drop off.' At that instant the pudding dropped off, and the wife, who did not want it, said to her husband, 'The fairy has imposed upon us; she was in the right. Probably we should have been more unhappy with wishes than we are at present. Believe me, friend, let us wish for nothing, and take things as it shall please God to send them. In the meantime, let us sup upon our pudding, since that's all that remains to us of our wishes.'

The husband thought his wife judged right; they supped merrily, and never gave themselves farther trouble about the things which they had designed to wish for.

───────

From *The Young Misses Magazine, Vol. 1*, by Madame Le Prince de Beaumont (London: F. Wingrave, 1793).

The Fisherman and His Wife

In the well-known Brothers Grimm tale about the misuse of wishes, both the husband and wife behave foolishly. Not only does he succumb to the force of her personality and her inordinate ambition, but each wish also violates the hierarchies upon which European eighteenth-century society believed social order depended. Traditionally, it was felt that a man should rule over his wife and that people should not attempt to rise above their social levels. Not only does the wife rule her husband here, but she also wishes to assume powers that belonged to males who were of higher status. In her final wish, her ambition extends beyond the secular; she wishes to assume divine authority. The increasingly stormy weather and lurid colours of the sea signify more than the magical fish's growing anger. As in many of Shakespeare's plays, storms reflect the disruption of the social orders of life.

There was once on a time a Fisherman who lived with his wife in a miserable hovel close by the sea, and every day he went out fishing. And once as he was sitting with his rod, looking at the clear water, his line suddenly went down, far down below, and when he drew it up again, he brought out a large Flounder. Then the Flounder said to him, 'Hark, you Fisherman, I pray you, let me live, I am no Flounder really, but an enchanted prince. What good will it do you to kill me? I should not be good to eat, put me in the water again, and let me go.' 'Come,' said the Fisherman, 'there is no need for so many words about it—a fish that can talk I should certainly let go, anyhow,' with that he put him back again into the clear water, and the Flounder went to the bottom, leaving a long streak of blood behind him. Then the Fisherman got up and went home to his wife in the hovel.

'Husband,' said the woman, 'have you caught nothing to-day?' 'No,' said the man, 'I did catch a Flounder, who said he was an enchanted prince, so I let him go again.' 'Did you not wish for anything first?' said the woman. 'No,' said the man; 'what should I wish for?' 'Ah,' said the woman, 'it is surely hard to have to live always in this dirty hovel; you might have wished for a small cottage for us. Go back and call him. Tell him we want to have a small cottage, he will certainly give us that.' 'Ah,' said the man, 'why should I go there again?' 'Why,' said the woman, 'you did catch him, and you let him go again; he is sure to do it. Go at once.' The man still did not quite like to go, but did not like to oppose his wife, and went to the sea.

When he got there the sea was all green and yellow, and no longer so smooth; so he stood and said,

> 'Flounder, flounder in the sea,
> Come, I pray thee, here to me;
> For my wife, good Ilsabil,
> Wills not as I'd have her will.'

Then the Flounder came swimming to him and said, 'Well, what does she want, then?' 'Ah,' said the man, 'I did catch you, and my wife says I really ought to have wished for something. She does not like to live in a wretched hovel any longer; she would like to have a cottage.' 'Go, then,' said the Flounder, 'she has it already.'

From Arthur Rackham, *Grimm's Fairy Tales: Twenty Stories*. (New York: Viking, 1973), 104. The illustration is from the early twentieth century.

When the man went home, his wife was no longer in the hovel, but instead of it there stood a small cottage, and she was sitting on a bench before the door. Then she took him by the hand and said to him, 'Just come inside, look, now isn't this a great deal better?' So they went in, and there was a small porch, and a pretty little parlour and bedroom, and a kitchen and pantry, with the best of furniture, and fitted up with the most beautiful things made of tin and brass, whatsoever was wanted. And behind the cottage there was a small yard, with hens and ducks, and a little garden with flowers and fruit. 'Look,' said the wife, 'is not that nice!' 'Yes,' said the husband, 'and so we must always think it—now we will live quite contented.' 'We will think about that,' said the wife. With that they ate something and went to bed.

Everything went well for a week or a fortnight, and then the woman said, 'Hark you, husband, this cottage is far too small for us, and the garden and yard are little; the Flounder might just as well have given us a larger house. I should like to live in a great stone castle; go to the Flounder, and tell him to give us a castle.' 'Ah, wife,' said the man, 'the cottage is quite good enough; why should we live in a castle?' 'What!' said the woman; 'just go there, the Flounder can always do that.' 'No, wife,' said the man, 'the Flounder has just given us the cottage, I do not like to go back so soon, it might make him angry.' 'Go,' said the woman, 'he can do it quite easily, and will be glad to do it; just you go to him.'

The man's heart grew heavy, and he would not go. He said to himself, 'It is not right,' and yet he went. And when he came to the sea the water was quite purple and dark-blue, and grey and thick, and no longer so green and yellow, but it was still quiet. And he stood there and said,

> 'Flounder, flounder in the sea,
> Come, I pray thee, here to me;
> For my wife, good Ilsabil,
> Wills not as I'd have her will.'

'Well, what does she want, then?' said the Flounder. 'Alas,' said the man, half scared, 'she wants to live in a great stone castle.' 'Go to it, then, she is standing before the door,' said the Flounder.

Then the man went away, intending to go home, but when he got there, he found a great stone palace, and his wife was just standing on the steps going in, and she took him by the hand and said, 'Come in.' So he went in with her, and in the castle was a great hall paved with marble, and many servants, who flung wide the doors; and the walls were all bright with beautiful hangings, and in the rooms were chairs and tables of pure gold, and crystal chandeliers hung from the ceiling, and all the rooms and bed-rooms had carpets, and food and wine of the very best were standing on all the tables so that they nearly broke down beneath it. Behind the house, too, there was a great court-yard, with stables for horses and cows, and the very best of carriages; there was a magnificent large garden, too, with the most beautiful flowers and fruit-trees, and a park quite half a mile long, in which were stags, deer, and hares, and everything that could be desired. 'Come,' said the woman, 'isn't that beautiful?' 'Yes; indeed,' said the man, 'now let it be; and we will live in this beautiful castle and be content.' 'We will consider about that,' said the woman, 'and sleep upon it,' thereupon they went to bed.

Next morning the wife awoke first, and it was just daybreak, and from her bed she saw the beautiful country lying before her. Her husband was still stretching himself, so she poked him in the side with her elbow, and said, 'Get up, husband, and just peep out of the window. Look you, couldn't we be the King over all that land? Go to the Flounder, we will be the King.' 'Ah, wife,' said the man, 'why should we be King? I do not want to be King.' 'Well,' said the wife, 'if you won't be King, I will; go to the Flounder, for I will be King.' 'Ah, wife,' said the man, 'why do you want to be King? I do not like to say that to him.' 'Why not?' said the woman; 'go to him this instant; I must be King!' 'So the man went, and was quite unhappy because his wife wished to be King. 'It is not right; it is not right,' thought he. He did not wish to go, but yet he went.

And when he came to the sea, it was quite dark-grey, and the water heaved up from below, and smelt putrid. Then he went and stood by it, and said,

> 'Flounder, flounder in the sea,
> Come, I pray thee, here to me;
> For my wife, good Ilsabil,
> Wills not as I'd have her will.'

'Well, what does she want, then?' said the Flounder. 'Alas;' said the man, 'she wants to be King.' 'Go to her; she is King already.'

So the man went, and when he came to the palace, the castle had become much larger, and had a great tower and magnificent ornaments, and the sentinel was standing before the door, and there were numbers of soldiers with kettle-drums and trumpets. And when he went inside the house, everything was of real marble and gold, with velvet covers and great golden tassels. Then the doors of the hall were opened, and there was the court in all its splendour, and his wife was sitting on a high throne of gold and diamonds, with a great crown of gold on her head, and a sceptre of pure gold and jewels in her hand, and on both sides of her stood her maids-in-waiting in a row, each of them always one head shorter than the last.

Then he went and stood before her, and said, 'Ah, wife, and now you are King.' 'Yes,' said the woman, 'now I am King.' So he stood and looked at her, and when he had looked at her thus for some time, he said, 'And now that you are King, let all else be, now we will wish for nothing more.' 'Nay, husband,' said the woman; quite anxiously, 'I find time pass very heavily, I can bear it no longer; go to the Flounder—I am King, but I must be Emperor, too.' 'Alas, wife, why do you wish to be Emperor?' 'Husband,' said she, 'go to the Flounder. I will be Emperor.' 'Alas, wife,' said the man, 'he cannot make you Emperor; I may not say that to the fish. There is only one Emperor in the land. An Emperor the Flounder cannot make you! I assure you he cannot.'

'What!' said the woman, 'I am the King, and you are nothing but my husband; will you go this moment? Go at once! If he can make a king he can make an emperor. I will be Emperor; go instantly.' So he was forced to go. As the man went, however, he was troubled in mind, and thought to himself, 'It will not end well; it will not end well! Emperor is too shameless! The Flounder will at last be tired out.'

With that he reached the sea, and the sea was quite black and thick, and began to boil up from below, so that it threw up bubbles, and such a sharp wind blew over it that it curdled, and the man was afraid. Then he went and stood by it, and said,

> 'Flounder, flounder in the sea,
> Come, I pray thee, here to me;
> For my wife, good Ilsabil,
> Wills not as I'd have her will.'

'Well, what does she want, then?' said the Flounder. 'Alas, Flounder,' said he, 'my wife wants to be Emperor.' 'Go to her,' said the Flounder; 'she is Emperor already.'

So the man went, and when he got there the whole palace was made of polished marble with alabaster figures and golden ornaments, and soldiers were marching before the door blowing trumpets, and beating cymbals and drums; and in the house, barons, and counts, and dukes were going about as servants. Then they opened the doors to him, which were of pure gold. And when he entered, there sat his wife on a throne, which was made of one piece of gold, and was quite two miles high; and she wore a great golden crown that was three yards high, and set with diamonds and carbuncles, and in one hand she had the sceptre, and in the other the imperial orb; and on both sides of her stood the yeomen of the guard in two rows, each being smaller than the one before him, from the biggest giant, who was two miles high, to the very smallest dwarf, just as big as my little finger. And before it stood a number of princes and dukes.

Then the man went and stood among them, and said, 'Wife, are you Emperor now?' 'Yes,' said she, 'now I am Emperor.' Then he stood and looked at her well, and when he had looked at her thus for some time, he said, 'Ah, wife, be content, now that you are Emperor.' 'Husband,' said she, 'why are you standing there? Now, I am Emperor, but I will be Pope too;

go to the Flounder.' 'Alas, wife,' said the man, 'what will you not wish for? You cannot be Pope; there is but one in Christendom; he cannot make you Pope.' 'Husband,' said she, 'I will be Pope; go immediately, I must be Pope this very day.' 'No, wife,' said the man, 'I do not like to say that to him; that would not do, it is too much; the Flounder can't make you Pope.' 'Husband,' said she, 'what nonsense! if he can make an emperor he can make a pope. Go to him directly. I am Emperor, and you are nothing but my husband; will you go at once?'

Then he was afraid and went; but he was quite faint, and shivered and shook, and his knees and legs trembled. And a high wind blew over the land, and the clouds flew, and towards evening all grew dark, and the leaves fell from the trees, and the water rose and roared as if it were boiling, and splashed upon the shore; and in the distance he saw ships which were firing guns in their sore need, pitching and tossing on the waves. And yet in the midst of the sky there was still a small bit of blue, though on every side it was as red as in a heavy storm. So, full of despair, he went and stood in much fear, and said,

> 'Flounder, flounder in the sea,
> Come, I pray thee, here to me;
> For my wife, good Ilsabil,
> Wills not as I'd have her will.'

'Well, what does she want, then?' said the Flounder. 'Alas,' said the man, 'she wants to be Pope.' 'Go to her then,' said the Flounder; 'she is Pope already.'

So he went, and when he got there, he saw what seemed to be a large church surrounded by palaces. He pushed his way through the crowd. Inside, however, everything was lighted up with thousands and thousands of candles, and his wife was clad in gold, and she was sitting on a much higher throne, and had three great golden crowns on, and round about her there was much ecclesiastical splendour; and on both sides of her was a row of candles the largest of which was as tall as the very tallest tower, down to the very smallest kitchen candle, and all the emperors and kings were on their knees before her, kissing her shoe. 'Wife,' said the man, and looked attentively at her, 'are you now Pope?' 'Yes,' said she, 'I am Pope.' So he stood and looked at her, and it was just as if he was looking at the bright sun. When he had stood looking at her thus for a short time, he said, 'Ah, wife, if you are Pope, do let well alone!' But she looked as stiff as a post, and did not move or show any signs of life. Then said he, 'Wife, now that you are Pope, be satisfied, you cannot become anything greater now.' 'I will consider about that,' said the woman. Thereupon they both went to bed, but she was not satisfied, and greediness let her have no sleep, for she was continually thinking what there was left for her to be.

The man slept well and soundly, for he had run about a great deal during the day; but the woman could not fall asleep at all, and flung herself from one side to the other the whole night through, thinking always what more was left for her to be, but unable to call to mind anything else. At length the sun began to rise, and when the woman saw the red of dawn, she sat up in bed and looked at it. And when, through the window, she saw the sun, thus rising, she said, 'Cannot I, too, order the sun and moon to rise?' 'Husband,' said she, poking him in the ribs with her elbows, 'wake up! Go to the Flounder, for I wish to be even as God is.' The man was still half asleep, but he was so horrified that he fell out of bed. He thought, he must have heard amiss, and rubbed his eyes, and said, 'Alas, wife, what are you saying?' 'Husband,' said she, 'if I can't order the sun and moon to rise, and have to look on and see the sun and moon rising, I can't bear it. I shall not know what it is to have another happy hour, unless I can make them rise myself.' Then she looked at him so terribly that a shudder ran over him, and said, 'Go at once; I wish to be like unto God.' 'Alas, wife' said the man, falling on his knees before her, 'the Flounder cannot do that; he can make an emperor and a pope; I beseech you, go on as you are, and be Pope.' Then she fell into a rage, and her hair flew wildly about her head, and she cried, 'I will not endure this, I'll not bear it any longer; wilt thou go?' Then he put on his trousers and ran away like a madman. But outside a great storm was raging, and blowing so hard that he could scarcely keep his feet; houses and trees toppled over, the mountains trembled, rocks rolled into the sea, the sky was pitch black, and it thundered and lightened, and the sea came in with black waves as high as church-towers and mountains, and all with crests of white foam at the top. Then he cried, but could not hear his own words,

> 'Flounder, flounder in the sea,
> Come, I pray thee, here to me;
> For my wife, good Ilsabil,
> Wills not as I'd have her will.'

'Well, what does she want, then?' said the Flounder. 'Alas,' said he, 'she wants to be like unto God.' 'Go to her, and you will find her back again in the dirty hovel.' And there they are living still at this very time.

———

From *Grimm's Household Tales*, translated by Margaret Hunt (London: George Bell and Sons, 1884).

Pedro Urdimale, the Little Fox, and the Mare's Egg

A popular figure in Chilean folklore, Pedro Urdimale is a trickster and loveable rogue, taking advantage of others so that he can profit without having to work. In this story, a variant of a tale-type often found in Europe, the victim is a naïve Gringo recently arrived from abroad. In addition to portraying the gullibility of Pedro's victim, the tale also places a usually inferior colonial character in a position of power over a European. The trick works because Pedro is able to convince the Gringo of the great value of a basically useless object and then to appear reluctant to sell it. Finally, he offers his victim a 'special' price as a gesture of seeming good will.

There was once a shrewd gentleman named Pedro Urdimale. He said to himself one day, 'Here I am without a cent in my pocket, and I'm a man who needs money. I'm simply going to have to get it, and that's all there is to it.' A bit later he was passing by a farmer's garden and spotted a vine with a beautiful squash the shape and color of an egg. This was just what he needed. He picked the squash with the greatest of care and put it on his shoulder, all the while humming to himself, 'I'm going to make a little pile from this. Yes, siree!'

Along the road came a *gringo* [any European or North American] on horseback. He had just arrived from Europe and worked at harvesting, although he didn't really know much about farming.

'What have you there, my friend?' he said upon seeing Pedro with the handsome squash.

'It's a mare's egg, sir.'

'What do you mean, a mare's egg?'

'Just that. Listen, this egg is going to hatch a great racing colt.'

'Then sell it to me on the double,' said the man excitedly. 'But how can I sell it to you when it's about to produce such a fine horse? I couldn't possibly part with it now.'

'I must have it, at whatever price you ask.'

'Well,' hedged Pedro, 'I'm going to give you a special price, sir. After all, I have to do well by someone like you. Look here, for five thousand *pesos*, the egg is yours.'

'It's a deal, man! Take five thousand cash right now.'

'But be very, very careful,' cautioned Pedro. 'Don't let the egg slip, for you'd surely lose the colt.'

Pedro tucked away the money and placed the squash on the horse in front of the man. He rode off balancing himself precariously with the mare's egg. Nearby there were some farmers cutting wood. 'Hey! That rider has a squash that looks just like my prize one,' yelled one of the men. But the foreigner just rode contentedly along with his new acquisition. All of a sudden, his horse stumbled and the squash slipped away and began to roll down the hill. Below there was a *litre* bush which had been uprooted and was lying on the ground. When the squash hit this, it split wide open. Now, what do you suppose! There was a fox sleeping in the shade under the bush. The poor animal was so startled when the squash rolled in upon him that he began to run pell-mell behind the horseman.

'There goes my colt! Stop him! Oh me, what a racing colt it is!' cried the *gringo*.

The poor man galloped away hallooing after the fox, and almost killed himself in the wild pursuit. I believe, Mr Pino [the editor], that he's still chasing it to this very day.

From *Folktales of Chile*, edited by Yolando Pino-Saavedra, translated by Rockwell Gray (Chicago: University of Chicago Press, 1967).

How the Coyote Danced with the Blackbirds

Although, among many Native American cultures, Coyote is generally clever and sometimes helps others, the Zuni of western New Mexico portray him as a fool and design their tales about him to illustrate the consequences of negative social behaviours. When he intrudes on the blackbirds' ceremonial dance and wishes to fly, he is attempting to step outside his assigned role. Moreover, he does not integrate himself into the group, but dances out of time with the blackbirds and egotistically attempts to take a leadership role for which he is unqualified. The tale is also a *pourquoi* story explaining the distinctive physical markings of the animal. People noticing the black fringes of hair would be reminded of the story and, by extension, the lessons it embodies. Some modern Zunis have suggested that the tale was told to Frank Cushing, who lived among them in the later nineteenth century, as a subtle, implicit commentary on his attempts to be like his hosts.

One late autumn day in the times of the ancients a large council of Blackbirds were gathered, fluttering and chattering, on the smooth, rocky slopes of Gorge Mountain, northwest of Zuñi. Like ourselves, these birds, as you are well aware, congregate together in autumn time, when the harvests are ripe, to indulge in their festivities before going into winter quarters; only we do not move away, while they, on strong wings and swift, retreat for a time to the Land of Everlasting Summer.

Well, on this particular morning they were making a great noise and having a grand dance, and this was the way of it: They would gather in one vast flock, somewhat orderly in its disposition, on the sloping face of Gorge Mountain,—the older birds in front, the younger ones behind,—and down the slope, chirping and fluttering, they would hop, hop, hop, singing:

> 'Ketchu, Ketchu, oñtilā, oñtilā,
> Ketchu, Ketchu, oñtilā, oñtilā!
>   Åshokta a yá-à-laa Ke-e-tchu,
>   Oñtilā,
>   Oñtilā!—'

> 'Blackbirds, Blackbirds, dance away, O, dance away, O!
> Blackbirds, Blackbirds, dance away, O, dance away, O!
>   Down the Mountain of the Gorges, Blackbirds,
>   Dance away, O!
>   Dance away, O!—'

and, spreading their wings, with many a flutter, flurry, and scurry, *keh keh,—keh keh,—keh keh,—keh keh,*—they would fly away into the air, swirling off in a dense, black flock, circling far upward and onward; then, wheeling about and darting down, they would dip themselves in the broad spring which flows out at the foot of the mountain, and return to their dancing place on the rocky slopes.

A Coyote was out hunting (as if he could catch anything, the beast!) and saw them, and was enraptured.

'You beautiful creatures!' he exclaimed. 'You graceful dancers! Delight of my senses! How do you do that, anyway? Couldn't I join in your dance—the first part of it, at least?'

'Why, certainly; yes,' said the Blackbirds. 'We are quite willing,' the masters of the ceremony said.

'Well,' said the Coyote, 'I can get on the slope of the rocks and I can sing the song with you; but I suppose that when you leap off into the air I shall have to sit there patting the rock with my paw and my tail and singing while you have the fun of it.'

'It may be,' said an old Blackbird, 'that we can fit you out so that you can fly with us.'

'Is it possible!' cried the Coyote, 'Then by all means do so. By the Blessed Immortals! Now if I am only able to circle off into the air like you fellows, I'll be the biggest Coyote in the world!'

'I think it will be easy,' resumed the old Blackbird. 'My children,' said he, 'you are many, and many are your wing-feathers. Contribute each one of you a feather to our friend.' Thereupon the Blackbirds, each one of them, plucked a feather from his wing. Unfortunately they all plucked feathers from the wings on the same side.

'Are you sure, my friend,' continued the old Blackbird, 'that you are willing to go through the operation of having these feathers planted in your skin? If so, I think we can fit you out.'

'Willing?—why, of course I am willing.' And the Coyote held up one of his arms, and, sitting down, steadied himself with his tail. Then the Blackbirds thrust in the feathers all along the rear of his forelegs and down the sides of his back, where wings ought to be. It hurt, and the Coyote twitched his mustache considerably; but he said nothing. When it was done, he asked: 'Am I ready now?'

'Yes,' said the Blackbirds; 'we think you'll do.'

So they formed themselves again on the upper part of the slope, sang their songs, and hopped along down with many a flutter, flurry, and scurry,—*Keh keh, keh keh, keh keh,*—and away they flew off into the air.

The Coyote, somewhat startled, got out of time, but followed bravely, making heavy flops; but, as I have said before, the wings he was supplied with were composed of feathers all plucked from one side, and therefore he flew slanting and spirally and brought up with a whack, which nearly knocked the breath out of him, against the side of the mountaim. He picked himself up, and shook himself, and cried out: 'Hold! Hold! Hold on, hold on, there!' to the fast-disappearing Blackbirds. 'You've left me behind!'

When the birds returned they explained: 'Your wings are not quite thick enough, friend; and, besides, even a young Blackbird, when he is first learning to fly, does just this sort of thing that you have been doing—makes bad work of it.'

'Sit down again,' said the old Blackbird. And he called out to the rest: 'Get feathers from your other sides also, and be careful to select a few strong feathers from the tips of the wings, for by means of these we cleave the air, guide our movements, and sustain our flight.'

So the Blackbirds all did as they were bidden, and after the new feathers were planted; each one plucked out a tail-feather, and the most skilful of the Blackbirds inserted these feathers into the tip of the Coyote's tail. It made him wince and 'yip' occasionally; but he stood it bravely and reared his head proudly, thinking all the while: 'What a splendid Coyote, I shall be! Did ever anyone hear of a Coyote flying?'

The procession formed again. Down the slope they went, hopity-hop, hopity-hop, singing their song, and away they flew into the air, the Coyote in their midst. Far, off and high they circled and circled, the Coyote cutting more eager pranks than any of the rest. Finally they returned, dipped themselves again into the spring, and settled on the slopes of the rocks.

'There, now,' cried out the Coyote with a flutter of his feathery tail, 'I can fly as well as the rest of you.'

'Indeed, you do well!' exclaimed the Blackbirds. 'Shall we try it again?'

'Oh, yes! Oh, yes! I'm a little winded,' cried the Coyote, 'but this is the best fun I ever had.'

The Blackbirds, however, were not satisfied with their companion. They found him less sedate than a dancer ought to be, and, moreover, his irregular cuttings-up in the air were not to their taste. So the old ones whispered to one another: 'This fellow is a fool, and we must pluck him when he gets into the air. We'll fly so far this time that he will get a little tired out and cry to us for assistance.'

The procession formed, and hopity-hop, hopity-hop, down the mountain slope they went, and with many a flutter and flurry flew off into the air. The Coyote, unable to restrain himself, even took the lead. On and on and on they flew, the Blackbirds and the Coyote, and up and up and up, and they circled round and round, until the Coyote found himself missing a wing stroke occasionally and falling out of line; and he cried out: 'Help! Help, friends, help!'

'All right!' cried the Blackbirds. 'Catch hold of his wings; hold him up!' cried the old ones. And the Blackbirds flew at him; and every time they caught hold of him (the old fool

From Gerald McDermott, *Coyote: A Trickster Tale from the American Southwest.* (San Diego: Harcourt, Brace, 1994).

all the time thinking they were helping) they plucked out a feather, until at last the feathers had become so thin that he began to fall, and he fell and fell and fell,—flop, flop, flop, he went through the air,—the few feathers left in his forelegs and sides and the tip of his tail just saving him from being utterly crushed as he fell with a thud to the ground. He lost his senses completely, and lay there as if dead for a long time. When he awoke, he shook his head sadly, and, with a crestfallen countenance and tail dragging between his legs, betook himself to his home over the mountains.

The agony of that fall had been so great and the heat of his exertions so excessive that the feathers left in his forelegs and tail-tip were all shrivelled up into little ugly black fringes of hair. His descendants were many.

Therefore you will often meet coyotes to this, day who have little black fringes along the rear of their forelegs, and the tips of their tails are often black. Thus it was in the days of the ancients.

Thus shortens my story.

———

From *Zuni Folk Tales*, edited by Frank Hamilton Cushing (Tucson: University of Arizona Press, 1986).

The Tiger, the Persimmon, and the Rabbit's Tail

The tiger, a figure that was both feared and revered in Korea, turns out to be the fool in this tale about the consequences of acting on the basis of misunderstood information. His pride and sense of power are quickly deflated because he does not know what the small persimmon fruit is. The comedy reaches its height when the animal and a thief, both of whom had intended to steal a fat ox, do not realize who the other is. Like 'The Valiant Chattee-Maker', this story deals with a common theme in eastern folklore: the humbling of the proud and the foolishness of acting on the basis of misunderstanding. American Peace Corps volunteer Suzanne Crowder Han first heard this and other traditional tales while serving in Korea in the 1970s.

A long, long time ago, a huge tiger lived deep in the mountains. His roar was so loud that all the other animals would hide when they heard him coming. He was so confident of himself that as he roamed through the forest he would roar out a challenge for any creature to match his strength.

Then one cold winter day, hunger forced him to leave the snow-covered forest in search of food. Stealthily he crept into the yard of a house at the edge of a village and looked around.

He saw a large fat ox in a stall near the gate. The sleeping animal made his mouth water. He crept closer to the stall. Then, just as he as ready to pounce, he heard a baby crying.

'Human babies certainly have an odd way of crying,' said the tiger and, being very curious, he crept closer to the house. 'He's really loud. How can his mother stand the noise?' he wondered.

'Stop crying! Do you want the tiger to get you?' shouted the mother.

'How did that woman know I was here?' the tiger asked himself and he crept closer to the house.

'Hush! If you don't stop crying, the tiger will get you,' said the mother.

But the baby cried even louder, which angered the proud tiger. 'That baby isn't afraid of me? I'll show him!' said the tiger, creeping closer to the room.

'Oh! Here's a dried persimmon!' said the mother and the baby stopped crying at once.

'What in the world is a dried persimmon? That bratty baby stopped crying immediately. A dried persimmon must be really scary and strong. Even stronger than me,' said the tiger and a chill ran up and down his spine. 'I better forget the baby and go eat that ox before that dried persimmon gets me. I should have known better than to come to a house on a day like this. I surely don't want to run into that dried persimmon.'

The tiger slinked into the stall and, since he was shaking all over, sat down to calm his nerves. At that moment however, something touched his back and felt up and down his spine. 'Oh, no!' he said to himself. 'It's the dried persimmon. It's got me. I'm going to die for sure.'

'What a nice, thick coat. And so soft,' said the man who had sneaked into the stall to steal the ox. 'I'll get a lot of money for this calf!' The thief put a rope around the tiger's neck and led him out of the stall.

'Oh my. What can I do? This is without a doubt that dried persimmon,' moaned the tiger to himself. 'Oh what can I do? I can't roar. I can't run. I can only follow it. Oh this is the end of me.'

The thief was very happy to have in tow what he thought was a very fine calf that he could sell for a lot of money. Thinking he should get away from the area as fast as possible, he decided to ride the calf and thus jumped onto the tiger's back.

'That's strange,' said the thief, 'this doesn't feel like any calf I've been on before.' He began to feel the tiger's body with his hands. 'Oh my god. This isn't a calf. It's a huge tiger,' he cried. 'What can I do? What can I do?'

The thief was so frightened to discover he was riding a tiger, he nearly fell off. 'Oh, I have to hold on,' he said, grasping the tiger tighter. 'If I fall off, that will be the end of me for sure. He'll gobble me up before I even hit the ground,' he said, squeezing the tiger with his legs. 'Just calm down,' he told himself, 'and try to think of how to get away.'

'I'm going to die. I'm going to die,' moaned the tiger as the thief tightened his hold on him. 'What rotten luck to die at the hands of a dried persimmon! I must try to get him off my back. That's the only thing I can do,' he said and he began to shake his body. Then he tried jumping and bucking. Over and over he shook and jumped and bucked as he ran but the thief held on tight.

After a while they came to a grove of trees. When the tiger ran under a large one, the thief grabbed hold of a branch, letting the tiger run out from under him, and quickly climbed through a hole in the tree trunk and hid inside.

The tiger knew immediately that the dried persimmon was off his back but he didn't even think about trying to eat it. He just kept running as fast as he could deeper into the mountain. Finally he stopped and let out a sigh of relief. 'Oh, I can't believe I'm alive. I just knew that dried persimmon was going to kill me.' He was so happy to be alive, he rolled over and over on the ground, smiling all the while.

'Oh Mr Tiger,' called a rabbit which had been awakened by the tiger rolling around on the ground, 'why are you so happy? How can you be so happy in the middle of the night?'

'I almost died today,' replied the tiger, 'so I'm happy to be alive.'

'What's that' asked the rabbit, hopping closer to the tiger. 'You almost died?'

'That's right,' explained the tiger. 'A horrible dried persimmon caught me. I've just this moment escaped from it.'

'What in the world is a dried persimmon?' asked the rabbit.

'You fool! You don't know what a dried persimmon is?' laughed the tiger. 'Why it is the scariest, strongest thing in the world. Just thinking about it gives me chills.'

'Well what in the world does it look like?' asked the rabbit.

'I don't know,' said the tiger, 'I was so scared I really didn't get a good look at it.'

'Well where is it now?' asked the rabbit.

'I think it must be up in a tree,' said the tiger.

'Where is the tree?' asked the rabbit. 'I think I'll go have a look at that dried persimmon.'

'What? Are you crazy? As weak as you are, it will devour you right away,' said the tiger.

'If it looks like it is going to grab me, I'll run away. After all, there's no one faster than me,' laughed the rabbit.

The tiger told the rabbit the directions to the tree. 'I'm warning you,' he said as the rabbit hopped away, 'that dried persimmon is a scary, horrible thing. Be careful.'

At last the rabbit came to the tree. He looked all around the tree and up in the branches but he did not see any thing that looked scary. He looked again. Then he looked in the hole in the trunk and saw a man who was pale and shaking all over.

The rabbit laughed all the way back to where the tiger was waiting. He explained what he found, but the tiger wouldn't believe him.

From Suzanne Crowder Han, *Korean Folk and Fairy Tales*. Illustrated by Mi-on Kim. (Elizabeth, NJ: Hollym International, 1991), 41.

'I'll go back to the tree and prevent him from leaving and you come see for yourself,' said the rabbit and he left.

The rabbit went back to the tree and stuck his rump in the hole in the tree trunk to wait for the tiger to come.

'Come on, Tiger,' called the rabbit when he saw the tiger slowly approaching. 'There's nothing to worry about. I have the hole plugged up.'

When he heard this, the thief decided he must do something to keep the tiger from coming in the hole. He took some strong string from his pocket and tied it to the rabbit's tail. Then he pulled it hard to keep the rabbit from running away.

The rabbit shrieked because of the pain and the tiger took off running. 'See I told you not to mess with that dried persimmon. Now the horrible thing has you,' yelled the tiger.

The rabbit struggled with all his strength to get away. The harder he tried to run, the harder the thief pulled on the string. The rabbit finally got away but not with his tail—that was left dangling from the thief's string. And that is why to this day the rabbit has a stumpy tail.

From *Korean Folk and Fairy Tales*, retold by Suzanne Crowder Han (Elizabeth, NJ: Hollym International, 1991).

ༀ

Si' Djeha Cheats the Robbers

Tales are told at night among the Arabic people of northern Africa, rather than in the day when such an activity could cause misfortune. Many stories are about Si' Djeha, who is sometimes a fool and sometimes a wise and cunning trickster. In his encounters with the thieves, he is at first the fool, believing their professions of concern for him. However, once he has discovered his mistakes, he is able to achieve revenge by playing the role they expect while, at the same time, using their techniques against them. The motif of selling worthless items as magical objects is found in stories from many cultures. In the introduction to the collection from which this story is taken, editor Inea Bushnaq notes that these North African tales possess greater cruelty than parallel ones from other Arabic cultures. She also explains that she selected for inclusion those tales 'most likely to interest the English reader' (382).

One day Si' Djeha was riding the fine white mule his father had left him when he died. As he rode, he happened to meet four men, robbers by profession, leading a hollow-sided little donkey to market.

'Si' Djeha!' they called. 'You are mad to risk your life on that mule! What if you should fall? You would break your head dropping from that height. Look, we have a neatly built little donkey here, a safer animal by far.'

'What you say is true, by Allah,' said Si' Djeha.

'Ha! But what will you give us for the exchange?'

'Do I owe you anything?'

'Si' Djeha, have some shame,' said the robbers, 'here we are saving your life, and you begrudge us fair payment.'

'What you say is right,' said Si' Djeha. 'Tell me what I should give you.'

'What does the amount matter among generous men? But since you are dear to us, we will content ourselves with one hundred silver pieces.' So Si' Djeha dismounted, paid the money, and rode the puny little donkey home.

When she saw him tethering the donkey in the yard, Si' Djeha's mother shouted to him, 'Where is your father's mule, child?' 'I was afraid that if I fell off its back, I might get killed and leave you with no one to look after you. So I exchanged it and one hundred pieces of silver for this donkey.'

'May Allah forgive you your foolishness,' sighed his mother. 'If you don't show a little more sense, we shall surely be ruined.'

When the next market day came round, Si' Djeha decided to take his donkey to town. But before he went, he glued a few gold coins under the donkey's tail. As he entered the suq he met the four robbers again. 'Greetings, O my benefactors, may Allah increase your fortunes!' he hailed them. 'I praise God and thank Him every hour for causing me to make your acquaintance.' 'Why, O Si' Djeha?' asked the robbers. 'Because of your donkey, of course! The thorny cactus is sweet inside, but who would have guessed that an ordinary donkey, no different from any other except for his lankness, drops nothing but gold coin!' 'A thing not to be believed!' said the robbers, and they walked alongside Si' Djeha to the stable where he had tied the donkey. There they saw for themselves the gold pieces on the animal's flanks, and they bit their fingers in remorse.

They began to blame each other and quarrel in whispers. Then they cried, 'May Allah reward you with nothing but good, Si' Djeha, if only you will let us have our donkey back! Take your mule and the hundred pieces of silver.' But Si' Djeha refused. The men begged him again and offered him more silver. At last when they promised to return the mule with two hundred pieces of silver, Si' Djeha consented. 'Be sure to feed him well, and spread rugs beneath him to catch the gold,' he said as they led the donkey away.

The first of the robbers to have the use of the donkey ran home, took his sickle down, and cut a whole field of grass. Bringing the fodder into the stable, he covered the floor with matting and locked the donkey in for safety. All night long the donkey feasted, and in the morning the robber found his carpets full of dung. He was ashamed to seem a fool, so he said nothing to the second robber except, 'Enjoy your fortune, brother!' The second robber and the third suffered as the first robber had, and they too remained silent. When the fourth robber turned on them angrily and accused them, 'You have taken the gold and left me nothing but the dung!' they realized that they had all been tricked and swore to take their revenge.

Now Si' Djeha was expecting to hear from the four men. He bought two roosters and a hen and asked his mother to fry them in butter and steam a dish of couscous to go with them. When the meal was ready, he put it in a covered bowl and buried it in the earthen floor of his house. 'Four men will come to visit me,' he told his mother, and he gave her careful instructions what to do when they came.

Sure enough, before midday the four robbers came marching up to Si' Djeha's door. 'Welcome, O my benefactors!' said Si' Djeha on his doorstep. 'You should have sent word that you were intending to honour me thus. Then I might have had time to prepare for you as you deserve. But never mind. I have my Hoe of Hospitality, and it will save me from disgrace.' The men were curious to know what he meant, and forgetting what they had come for, followed him into the house.

When the guests had been seated for a while, Si' Djeha called, 'Mother, I have visitors today; bring me my Hoe of Hospitality.' And his mother came in and handed him an old garden hoe as if there were nothing odd about his request. With the robbers watching him attentively, Si' Djeha began to dig at the earthen floor. In the glancing of an eye he uncovered the dish of chicken and couscous. 'Come favour us with your company!' he invited his guests, and the fragrance of warm chicken broth filled the room.

'Whenever I am surprised by company,' explained Si' Djeha after they had eaten, 'I never need worry about being unprepared and ill-provided as long as I have this Hoe of Hospitality. Whether my cupboard is full or empty, I know that this tool will enable me to entertain as a good host should. You yourselves saw that the food it brings me is the best.' The robbers agreed that, praise be to Allah, they had indeed eaten well. Then one of them uttered the thought that was, in all their minds. 'Si' Djeha, how much would you sell this useful hoe for?' 'It is not for sale,' said Si' Djeha shortly. But although he tried to turn the conversation to other things, the robbers kept returning to the hoe. And eventually Si' Djeha parted with it for one hundred silver pieces.

'My wife's brother is coming to eat with me tomorrow,' said one of the robbers on the way home. 'Let me have my turn first.' But next day, though he dug until he plowed up the whole floor of his house, he found no covered dish and no warm meal. On top of that, he was despised by his brother-in-law for being a miserly host.

The other three robbers were as disappointed in their expectations of the hoe. When the last of them threatened to take his partners to court for eating all the food and leaving him nothing, they showed him their ruined houses to prove that they too had been duped. 'This time we must not let Si' Djeha escape us,' they vowed.

But this time too, Si' Djeha was ready for them. 'I think I shall go and weed the sesame,' he said to his wife early in the morning. 'If my four friends should come to see me again, send them out to the east field—that's where I shall be working. And as soon as they go, run to the butcher's shop, buy some spring lamb, and help my mother prepare a banquet for our noon meal.' Then he picked up his tools and left the house. In the yard there was a sack holding two hares that Si' Djeha had trapped. Before leaving, he took one of them and carried it inside his robe, resting on his belt.

Very soon afterwards, the four robbers knocked on the door, talked to Si' Djeha's wife and followed him to his field. 'Ho! Si' Djeha!' they called as soon as they could see him. 'Come here, we have some things to discuss with you.' 'He who doesn't work doesn't eat,' Si' Djeha shouted back to them. 'I cannot stop, brothers.' 'Our errand is pressing; take a rest,' they said when they drew near. 'Very well,' said Si' Djeha, 'but let me send word to my wife to prepare some food for us—it will soon be time to eat.' The robbers looked around in astonishment. 'Whom do you mean to send?' they asked. 'I have a messenger right here,' said Si' Djeha, pulling the hare out of his bosom. And as they looked on in disbelief, he set it on the ground, saying, 'Go find your mistress and tell her to cook a dish of tender lamb's meat, since we have guests this noon.' In a flash the animal disappeared into the thorn-bushes at the edge of the field.

'Do you expect a hare to carry a message?' the robbers asked, laughing. 'My father trained him,' replied Si' Djeha, 'and I am so used to him that I couldn't do without him, especially when I am out here in the fields.' And he led the doubting guests to his house, where they found everything hospitably prepared down to the ewer and bowl for them to wash their hands in rose water. 'That hare is certainly a good servant,' murmured the robbers. 'That he is,' said Si' Djeha bringing the second hare in from the yard and patting its neck. 'He's a good worker and cheap to feed.' 'Would you consider selling him?' asked the robbers. 'How can I do without him?' said Si' Djeha. 'I have neither son nor daughter to send on errands.' 'Name your price,' urged the robbers. And in the end Si' Djeha let them buy the hare for one hundred silver pieces.

'This time,' said one of the robbers as they set out on the road home, 'this time let us not basely suspect each other. Let me send the hare to my house with a message for my wife to cook supper for all four of us, so that we can all try our new messenger at the same time.' 'That's the best plan,' said the others as they watched the hare leaping across the fields before them.

But when they came to the first robber's house toward evening, they found that his wife had not even lit her cooking fires. 'What is the meaning of this neglect?' the first robber asked his bewildered wife. 'Didn't I send instructions with our new messenger for you to have a meal ready when we arrived?' 'What messenger?' said the wife. At this the robbers turned on their heels, cursing, and retraced their steps to Si' Djeha's house with murder in their hearts.

When they reached Si' Djeha's doorway, a sight met their eyes that left them rooted where they stood, their mouths dry with horror. Si' Djeha was shouting angrily at his wife with a knife raised in his hand. While they watched, the woman fell to the ground with blood on her dress. Forgetting their own troubles, the robbers could only gasp and ask him why he had done this evil deed. 'How else can a man control the sour temper of his wife? All I asked for was a glass of water, but she refused me!' Then to their amazement, Si' Djeha touched his wife's wound with the knife and she raised herself up. Standing meekly before him, she asked her husband what he wished. 'Brew coffee for our guests,' he said, frowning. As soon as she left the room, the robbers questioned Si' Djeha. 'What is this miracle that we have witnessed?' 'Have you never heard of the knife that kills and brings back to life?' 'Never!' said the four men together. 'I would not part with it for half the kingdom,' declared Si' Djeha. 'Every man married to a quarrelsome wife should have one!'

The robbers soon saw proof of the virtues of this singular tool. Wearing a fresh gown, her eyes modestly on the ground like a bride of one month, Si' Djeha's wife carried in a tray of coffee flavored with cardamom. Before they finished drinking the coffee, the robbers had succeeded in buying the knife off Si' Djeha for one hundred pieces of silver.

Each in turn used it in his home and discovered just how magical it was. All four robbers were soon tried for murder and never bothered Si' Djeha again.

From *Arab Folktales*, translated and edited by Inea Bushnaq (New York: Pantheon, 1986).

The Hodja and the Thousand Pieces of Gold

The Hodja, who is sometimes said to have been an actual person of the later middle ages, is a popular figure in Turkish folklore. Sometimes he is a fool, at others, a wise man. In fact, his name is often used as a term of veneration for a scholar. In this story though he appears as a fool in the eyes of the infidel merchant, the Hodja is able to trick his opponent out of money, a good donkey, and fine clothing. Not only is the merchant a victim of his own misperception of his neighbour, but he is also punished by members of a religion not his own. In fact, the story implicitly raises the question: 'Did the Hodja set out to trick his neighbour from the start, or did he only do so because, after the merchant sought to reclaim the gold, the Hodja wanted the infidel to be shamed for doubting the Muslim's sincere piety?'

One morning, at the hour of the dawn prayer, the Hodja called out aloud:
'Lord, give me a thousand pieces of gold. If you give me nine hundred and ninety nine pieces, I shall not accept them!'

And he continued to pray thus every day.

His neighbour, an infidel merchant, heard this fervent but peculiar prayer every morning, and such was his curiosity to know whether the Hodja would in fact keep his word that he placed nine hundred and ninety-nine pieces of gold in a bag, and the next morning,

From Charles Downing, *Tales of the Hodja*. Illustrated by William Papas. (New York: Henry Z. Walck, 1965), 38.

when the Hodja repeated his prayer, he threw the bag down the chimney, and looked in at the window to see what would happen.

The Hodja picked up the sack, counted out the nine hundred and ninety-nine pieces of gold, and said:

'Allah, who has given me nine hundred and ninety-nine pieces of gold, will surely give me another one before long!'

The odds against the Hodja acquiring his thousand gold pieces had clearly shortened. He had, after all, not said that God should give them to him all at once.

The infidel, seeing the Hodja determined to keep the pieces of gold, waited until it was quite light, and then went to see the Hodja.

'Effendi,' he said, 'a joke is a joke. Give me back my golden coins.'

'Are you mad, merchant?' said the Hodja. 'When have I borrowed money from you?'

'You know what I mean,' said the infidel. 'Hearing your prayer and wondering if you would be true to your word, I threw a sack containing nine hundred and ninety-nine gold coins down your chimney this morning.'

'Do you think I shall believe that you were willing to risk the loss of such a large sum just for the pleasure of tempting a true believer?' said the Hodja. 'The coins are mine. Allah gave them to me as a reward for sincere and steadfast prayers.'

'I shall take you to court for this,' said the infidel. 'The coins are mine!'

'I am quite prepared to submit to the judgment of the court,' said the Hodja, 'but I am not so young any more, and do not feel up to making the journey on foot.'

The infidel ran quickly off, and returned with a sturdy mule, and offered to lend it to the Hodja for the journey.

'I am, after all, a man of some position in society,' said the Hodja. 'I cannot appear before the *cadi* in this old *diübbeh* of mine.'

The infidel was determined that no excuse the Hodja might bring forward should prevent his appearing in court, and he went indoors, and returned with a fine silk robe, and a sumptuous fur coat.

'I'll lend you these for the occasion,' he said, 'but let us hurry.'

The Hodja put the clothes on, mounted the mule, and they set off.

'What is the matter?' said the *cadi*, when they arrived before him.

'This man has nine hundred and ninety-nine coins belonging to me,' said the infidel, 'and refuses to return them.'

And he told the judge the whole story.

'Effendi,' said the Hodja, 'this man is my neighbour. He must have heard me counting out the nine hundred and ninety-nine coins which God gave me in answer to my prayer, and now claims them to be his own.'

'They are mine,' said the infidel.

'Effendi!' said the Hodja. 'No doubt he will soon be saying that the very mule I am riding belongs to him also.'

'It *is* mine!' cried the infidel.

'You see, effendi?' said the Hodja. 'And no doubt he will even go so far as to say that the very clothes I am wearing on my back belong to him!'

'They *are* mine!' cried the infidel. 'Both the *diübbeh* and the fur coat.'

The judge grew very angry.

'Away with you, you rogue!' he exclaimed. 'Not only do you wish to appropriate the property of a man much honoured in our community, you are trying to make a fool of me as well!'

And he drove the infidel out of his court.

When the Hodja arrived home, he saw the infidel sitting very despondently in his house. He invited him over, and returning to him his mule, his robe, his fur coat, and his sack of gold coins, he said:

'Take your property, merchant. But do not in future try to tempt honest Muslims to break their word!'

From *Tales of the Hodja*, retold by Charles Downing (New York: Henry Z. Walck, 1965).

The Gift of the Holy Man

In his introduction to a collection of his culture's traditional tales, Ashraf Siddiqui, a folklore scholar from what is now Bangladesh, draws attention to the theory that many widely distributed tales may have originated in the Indian subcontinent. One such story is 'The Gift of the Holy Man', in which the central character foolishly loses, but then later recovers, magical objects. The poor man, who is frequently chided by his wife and children for his inability to provide adequately for them, is a victim of his inability to follow instructions and his trusting nature. However, when he is tricked a second time, he is able to come up with his own solutions. In this 'rags to riches tale', it is the man's reverence for the holy man—offered without thought of reward—that makes him worthy of his final good fortune.

On a certain country there once lived an extremely poor man. He was so poor that his family went without food most of the time. They did not have enough clothes to cover their bodies, and their home was in pitiable shape. The poor man was constantly chided by his wife and children for his worthlessness. One day he became tired of his dire poverty and decided that there was nothing left for him to do but wander into the forest and be devoured by wild beasts.

Soon after entering the forest, he came to a house and found a mendicant deeply absorbed in meditation near-by. The poor man, out of compassion, swept the courtyard of the mendicant and set his house in order. He also led the holy man's cow to pasture and fed it lush grass. He plucked some wild flowers, and after washing them in pure water, placed them by the praying place of the mendicant.

When the holy man finished his meditations he opened his eyes, and the first thing he saw was the poor man. Then he discovered his house was neat and clean, his cow was well-fed, and he saw the delicate flowers. Now the mendicant was gifted with the power of fore-knowledge. He knew immediately that the man standing before him was extremely poor, and he decided to help him.

The mendicant asked the poor man to sit by him. The poor man, with great humility, folded his hands and sat by the holy man.

'I know that you are very poor,' said the mendicant. 'But you will not remain poor if you follow my advice. I give you this handkerchief. One side of it is yellow, and the other side is green. If you spread the green side against the ground, you will receive gold coins. Now, take it and do not stop between this forest and your home. If you follow my advice, I am sure that you will never be poor again.'

The grateful man salaamed the mendicant a hundred times and then set out for his home.

The day was extremely hot, and after he left the shade of the forest the scorching sun soon sapped the poor man's strength. He sat on the steps of a shop to rest. Out of curiosity he spread the green side of the handkerchief against the ground. And lo! a pile of golden coins appeared on the handkerchief.

The shopkeeper saw this wondrous thing happen before his eyes and devised a plan for cheating the poor man out of his wealth. He invited him into his chambers and feasted him with cakes and other sweets. The poor man was amazed and flattered that such hospitality should be offered him.

During the dinner, the shopkeeper cunningly prodded the poor man into disclosing the secret of the handkerchief. The greedy shopkeeper then invited the poor man to spend the night, because he enjoyed so much the company of pious people who were favoured by God.

The poor man accepted right away, and before going to bed, entrusted the hand-kerchief and gold coins to the shopkeeper. Several times he asked his host to guard the treasure zealously.

The next morning, the poor man prepared to continue his journey home and asked the shopkeeper to return the handkerchief and gold coins.

Imagine what happened! The clever shopkeeper had replaced the magic handkerchief with an ordinary one and now placed it reverently in the poor man's hands, along with the coins. Not suspecting any trickery, the poor man kindly thanked the shopkeeper a hundred times for his generosity and proceeded on his way.

The poor man reached home lighthearted and gay. The first thing he did was to shower the golden coins on his wife's lap. She was elated beyond words. All day long the poor man told the story of the magic handkerchief over and over again. At twilight, he gathered his family together and with a grand flourish spread the handkerchief on the ground. But nothing happened. He spread it again, waited . . . but nothing happened. He rubbed his eyes, laid the handkerchief down again . . . but still, nothing!

The wife thought that she had been brutally deceived, and she stormed and raged at her foolish husband. She accused him of stealing the coins from some rich man's coffers. She grabbed a broom and began beating the poor old man. At last he freed himself from her clutches, and suspecting that the friendly shopkeeper had been the cause of all this trouble, set off in that direction.

As soon as the poor man entered the shop, he accused the shopkeeper of stealing the magic handkerchief.

The shopkeeper pretended that never before in his life had he seen this impertinent man and drove him from the shop.

The poor man tore his hair and cried. Ah, the mendicant had warned him not to stop on his way home. If only he had followed the holy man's advice. How could he face him now?

After much indecision, the poor man resolved to go back to the mendicant's house and ask for forgiveness. When he arrived there, he scrubbed the holy man's house and put everything in order. He fed the cow and picked wild flowers for the holy man's praying place.

When the mendicant opened his eyes, he said, 'Do not worry, I know what has happened to you. You will recover the magic handkerchief.'

The next morning the mendicant gave the poor man a thick stick and told him to visit the shopkeeper on his way home. 'If you order the stick to beat someone, it will do so until you command it to stop.'

The poor man realized that he had been given the magic stick to teach the shopkeeper a good lesson.

After salaaming the mendicant a hundred times, he set off for the shopkeeper's abode. Now the shopkeeper was clever enough to surmise that probably the stick which the poor man carried was magic, too, so he politely received the poor man and apologized for his previous misbehavior.

The poor man smiled, and feigning innocence, offered to have his magic stick perform. The shopkeeper's wife and children gathered around, and the poor man uttered these words:

'Stick, stick, holy man's stick,
Beat them, beat them hard and quick.
Teach these people that greed is wrong,
Show them right is always strong!'

And see! Wonder of wonders!

The stick began beating the shopkeeper and his family mercilessly. Unable to bear the violent blows, the wife took shelter in her room and the shopkeeper escaped to the roof. But the magic stick was all-knowing and everywhere at once. It doubtlessly would have killed them all had not the shopkeeper fallen prostrate at the poor man's feet and begged forgiveness.

The shopkeeper returned the magic handkerchief and swore a hundred times that he would never again commit such a terrible deed. Now, the poor man, with the magic handkerchief clutched in his hand, proceeded, hastened rather . . . not hastened but rather ran homeward without once stopping.

Reaching home, he shut and locked all the doors, and then spread the handkerchief on the dirt floor as the holy man had instructed. Lo! a pile of gold coins appeared!

He repeated the process just to see if the handkerchief really was genuine, and again a pile of coins appeared. He called his wife and children. They were astonished at seeing the pile of gold coins. The poor man made the handkerchief perform and, of course, from that time on they did not doubt the poor man's word. Within a short time he bought a large estate and passed his days in uninterrupted happiness.

We could end our story here, but unfortunately, life is not like a folktale that ends happily.

The magic power of the handkerchief became known throughout the country. The king heard about the enormous wealth accumulated by the poor man simply by spreading a magic handkerchief on the ground, and he feared that the poor man would soon have more money than he. So the jealous king conceived a plan whereby he could gain possession of the handkerchief.

He sent a chamberlain to the wealthy landlord's estate. We can no longer call the poor man poor, so we shall call him wealthy landlord instead. The chamberlain praised the wealth and piety of the landlord. He also suggested that if the landlord so desired, his eldest son could become the husband of the king's daughter.

Now, to be the father-in-law of a princess was indeed a great honour. The landlord immediately sent a proposal of marriage to the king. Next day, the chamberlain returned to the landlord and said that the king was pleased with the proposal, but wished to hear it from the lips of the landlord himself. The chamberlain also requested that the magic handkerchief be brought along, because the princess was eager to see its wondrous powers.

The wealthy landlord was received warmly by the king and his court. The king talked politely for a while and then asked if he might take the handkerchief to his daughter. The landlord, without suspecting anything, gave the handkerchief to the king.

Hours passed but no one returned. Finally, the landlord sent a message to the king kindly asking him to return the handkerchief. The king denied that he had ever seen it, and the landlord was driven from the palace. Showing no sign of anger, the landlord quietly went home, got his magic stick and returned to the palace gates, where he uttered these words:

'Stick, stick, holy man's stick,
Beat them, beat them hard and quick,
Teach these people that greed is wrong,
Show them right is always strong!'

The stick began its work. The queen was driven from one corner of her room to the other. The king was forced to crawl under his bed, but, of course, the magic stick followed him and continued its pommeling. The whole court was beaten. Such a scene of disorder was created that words fail to describe it.

Finally, the king, in anguish and pain, fell at the feet of the landlord and begged for mercy. The landlord retrieved his magic handkerchief and went home.

Day by day the landlord's wealth increased. He lived happily to a ripe old age, and one day his eldest son became king of the country.

From *Toontoony Pie and Other Tales from Pakistan*, by Ashraf Siddiqui and Marilyn Lerch (Cleveland and New York: World Publishing Company, 1961).

❁

The Two Husbands

The simpleton is one of the favourite characters in Jewish folklore from around the world. The most famous tales concern Chelm, a town of simple folk. In this tale, from Iraq, two wives lament the incredible stupidity and incompetence of their husbands, men who should be providers. The two incidents in the story are based on widely distributed motifs depicting the ridiculous actions and reactions of fools. In addition to being humourous, the story is designed to illustrate the ideas that 'a worry in the heart . . . has to be talked about' and that a person's miseries may not seem so great when compared to those of others.

In an Eastern town lived a clever woman named Shafika. She had a stupid husband, and his name was Hangal. Shafika was a good housewife and she ran her home with knowledge and skill. She bore her fate in silence and with her own deeds covered up her husband's stupidity, without disclosing his shame in public.

One day a neighbour named Rahama visited her, and the two of them discussed the role of the man in the family. Rahama talked about courage and cleverness and the wealth of men. At this moment Shafika recalled her stupid husband, and she burst out in silent tears over her fate. Crying she spoke bitterly of the matchmakers who had not found her a good man as a husband. Then she decided to tell her neighbour all her troubles. As it is written: 'A worry in the heart of a man has to be talked about.'

'Oh! My dear neighbour,' began Shafika, with a heartbreaking sigh. 'What shall I say and what shall I recount? The Almighty has cursed me with a heavy curse and given me a husband who has in him all the stupidity of the entire world. He has caused me many misfortunes, and he doesn't know how to earn even a single *pruta*, all because of his exaggerated simpleness and because he does not know how to get on with people.'

'The entire burden of the family rests on my shoulders and I am forced to work and to sweat out the day so as to earn some *pruta* for our very existence. And when the night comes, I have to arrange all the household needs. Woe is me! Woe is my fate! If you don't believe me, I shall call him here and how you an example of his stupidity.'

At once Shafika called her husband and said, 'Hangal, my husband, go to the roof and bring down a loaf of bread so you will have something to eat for lunch.'

'As you wish, my wife,' answered Hangal. 'I am going immediately.' Hangal went to the ladder and climbed up. When he was halfway up the ladder, he began to shout, 'Shafika, Shafika! I am standing halfway up the ladder, and I don't know if I have to climb up or come down.'

'Alas! Alas! Stupid one!' answered Shafika. 'If you have nothing in your hands, it means that you have not yet taken the loaf of bread and you must climb up. If you have a loaf of bread in your hands, it means that you have already been up and now you must climb down.'

Hangal looked at his hands but did not find anything in them. Following his wife's advice, he climbed up to the roof, took the bread, and came down. When he was halfway down the ladder he stopped and shouted, 'Shafika, Shafika! Again I'm in the middle of the ladder, and I don't know whether to climb up or to come down.'

Again Shafika gave him the same advice. Hangal looked at his hands, found the bread, and came down.

'Did you see, my neighbour, my husband's stupidity?' asked Shafika and added, 'That is my luck. I weep about it day and night, and there is no help.'

Her neighbour consoled her and said, 'My dear Shafika, do not become sad and do not let your husband's deeds seem so bad in your eyes. Those who make proverbs have said, 'Man is as black as coal, but he is also merciful.' It is better to have a husband like that than no husband at all. You know that a woman who has not a husband is not able to dress well, and she is forbidden to talk to other people. And now come close to me and I shall reveal a great secret to you. If you only knew the stupidity and foolishness of my husband, Shimon, you would be satisfied with what you have. You would lift up your eyes to the heavens and give thanks to the Almighty that he gave you a husband like Hangal. My husband is worse than yours. If you don't believe me, come to my home and I shall show you an example of his stupidity.

So they went together to Rahama's house. Rahama took a jug, filled it with water, and then called to her husband and said, 'Here is a jug full of grain. Take it to the miller and ask him to grind it immediately because my neighbour will not leave until you return.'

Shimon took the jug of water and went to the miller, saying to him, 'My wife sends her greetings and says that we have a guest at home, so please will you grind the grain in this jug immediately so that I won't be late returning home.'

When the miller saw the water in the jug and heard the way Shimon was speaking, he knew this was a stupid man in front of him. He decided thereupon to make a joke and have some fun on his account.

In a corner of the miller's house a Hindu was sleeping, and the miller said to Shimon, 'Go and sleep next to the Hindu. When I have finished grinding the wheat, I shall wake you up and send you home peacefully.'

Shimon did as the miller suggested. He went to sleep near the Hindu. When he was sleeping soundly, the miller approached him and cut off his beard. Then he took off his hat and put the Hindu's hat on his head. Then the miller woke Shimon, handed him the jug, and said, 'I have ground the grain. Go home in peace.'

Shimon arrived home looking so strange that Shafika and Rahama were amazed when they saw him. His wife Rahama asked him, 'Who are you? Where do you come from?'

Answered Shimon, 'I am the husband of one of you, but I do not remember of which one.'

'We don't know you,' answered Rahama, and she handed him a mirror. When Shimon saw how he looked, he realized immediately that this was not his face. He had never worn a Hindu's hat like that and he always had a beard. Shimon shook his head and cursed bitter curses against the miller saying, 'That dog the miller! Instead of waking me up and giving me flour, he woke up the Hindu and sent the flour with him, while leaving me to sleep there. I shall run back to him immediately and ask him to wake me up, because if I stay there and sleep in the heat I might get sunstroke, God forbid.'

Shafika turned to Rahama and said to here, 'You were right, my friend. I am happy in comparison to you. May the Almighty help you.'

———

From *Folktales of Israel*, edited by David Noy (Chicago: University of Chicago Press, 1969).

The Emperor's New Clothes

Although early nineteenth-century Danish writer Hans Christian Andersen is best remembered for such romantic fairy tales as 'Thumbelina' and 'The Snow Queen', in which he deliberately used motifs from traditional literature, he also wrote a number of clever satires, including 'The Emperor's New Clothes', in which the foolish adults are contrasted to a wise child. The rogues in the story are able to steal from the Emperor because they perceive both his vanity and the hypocrisy of his courtiers. Trying to prevent others from realizing that they are unfit for their duties, the courtiers and the Emperor pretend to see what cannot be seen for the simple reason that it doesn't exist. Only the child, with his fearless innocence, is able to tell the truth: there is nothing to see. He reveals the ridiculousness of the Emperor.

Many years ago, there was an Emperor, who was so excessively fond of new clothes that he spent all his money in dress. He did not trouble himself in the least about his soldiers; nor did he care to go either to the theatre or the chase, except for the opportunities they afforded him for displaying his new clothes. He had a different suit for each hour of the day; and as of any other king or emperor one is accustomed to say, 'He is sitting in council,' it was always said of him, 'The Emperor is sitting in his wardrobe.'

Time passed away merrily in the large town which was his capital; strangers arrived every day at the court. One day two rogues, calling themselves weavers, made their appearance. They gave out that they knew how to weave stuffs of the most beautiful colours and elaborate patterns, the clothes manufactured from which should have the wonderful property of remaining invisible to everyone who was unfit for the office he held, or who was extraordinarily simple in character.

'These must, indeed, be splendid clothes!' thought the Emperor. 'Had I such a suit, I might at once find out what men in my realm are unfit for their office, and also be able to distinguish the wise from the foolish! This stuff must be woven for me immediately.' And he caused large sums of money to be given to both the weavers, in order that they might begin their work directly.

So the two pretend weavers set up two looms, and affected to work very busily, though in reality they did nothing at all. They asked for the most delicate silk and the purest gold thread; put both into their own knapsacks; and then continued their pretended work at the empty looms until late at night.

'I should like to know how the weavers are getting on with my cloth,' said the Emperor to himself, after some little time had elapsed; he was, however, rather embarrassed when he remembered that a simpleton, or one unfit for his office, would be unable to see the manufacture. 'To be sure,' he thought, 'he had nothing to risk in his own person; but yet he would prefer sending somebody else to bring him intelligence about the weavers, and their work, before he troubled himself in the affair.' All the people throughout the city had heard of the wonderful property the cloth was to possess; and all were anxious to learn how wise, or how ignorant, their neighbours might prove to be.

'I will send my faithful old Minister to the weavers,' said the Emperor at last, after some deliberation; 'he will be best able to see how the cloth looks; for he is a man of sense, and no one can be more suitable for his office than he is.'

So the honest old Minister went into the hall, where the knaves were working with all their might at their empty looms. 'What can be the meaning of this?' thought the old man, opening his eyes very wide; 'I cannot discover the least bit of thread on the looms!' However, he did not express his thoughts aloud.

The impostors requested him very courteously to be so good as to come nearer their looms; and then asked him whether the design pleased him, and whether the colours were not very beautiful; at the same time pointing to the empty frames. The poor old Minister looked and looked; he could not discover anything on the looms, for a very good reason, viz. there was nothing there. 'What!' thought he again, 'is it possible that I am a simpleton? I have never thought so myself; and, at any rate, if I am so, no one must know it. Can it be that I am unfit for my office? No, that must not be said either. I will never confess that I could not see the stuff.'

'Well, Sir Minister!' said one of the knaves, still pretending to work, 'you do not say whether the stuff pleases you.'

'Oh, it is admirable!' replied the old Minister, looking at the loom through his spectacles. 'This pattern, and the colours—yes, I will tell the Emperor without delay how very beautiful I think them.'

'We shall be much obliged to you,' said the impostors, and then they named the different colours and described the patterns of the pretended stuff. The old Minister listened attentively to their words, in order that he might repeat them to the Emperor; and then the knaves asked for more silk and gold, saying that it was necessary to complete what they had begun. However, they put all that was given them into their knapsacks, and continued to work with as much apparent diligence as before at their empty looms.

The Emperor now sent another officer of his court to see how the men were getting on, and to ascertain whether the cloth would soon be ready. It was just the same with this gentleman as with the Minister; he surveyed the looms on all sides, but could see nothing at all but the empty frames.

'Does not the stuff appear as beautiful to you as it did to my Lord the Minister?' asked the impostors of the Emperor's second ambassador; at the same time making the same gestures as before, and talking of the design and colours which were not there.

'I certainly am not stupid!' thought the messenger. 'It must be that I am not fit for my good, profitable office! That is very odd; however, no one shall know anything about it.' And accordingly he praised the stuff he could not see, and declared that he was delighted with both colours and patterns. 'Indeed, please your Imperial Majesty,' said he to his sovereign, when he returned, 'the cloth which the weavers are preparing is extraordinarily magnificent.'

The whole city was talking of the splendid cloth which the Emperor had ordered to be woven at his own expense.

And now the Emperor himself wished to see the costly manufacture, whilst it was still on the loom. Accompanied by a select number of officers of the court, among whom were the two honest men who had already admired the cloth, he went to the crafty impostors, who, as soon as they were aware of the Emperor's approach, went on working more diligently than ever; although they still did not pass a single thread through the looms.

'Is not the work absolutely magnificent?' said the two officers of the crown already mentioned. 'If your Majesty will only be pleased to look at it! What a splendid design! What glorious colours!' and at the same time they pointed to the empty frames; for they imagined that everyone but themselves could see this exquisite piece of workmanship.

'How is this?' said the Emperor to himself; 'I can see nothing! This is, indeed, a terrible affair! Am I a simpleton? or am I unfit to be an Emperor? that would be the worst thing that could happen. Oh, the cloth is charming!' said he aloud; 'it has my entire approbation.' And he smiled most graciously, and looked at the empty looms; for on no account would he say that he could not see what two of the officers of his court had praised so much. All his retinue now strained their eyes, hoping to discover something on the looms, but they could see no more than the others; nevertheless, they all exclaimed, 'Oh! how beautiful!' and advised his Majesty to have some new clothes made from this splendid material for the approaching procession. 'Magnificent! charming! excellent!' resounded on all sides; and everyone was uncommonly gay. The Emperor shared in the general satisfaction, and presented the impostors with the riband of an order of knighthood to be worn in their buttonholes, and the title of 'Gentlemen Weavers.'

The rogues sat up the whole of the night before the day on which the procession was to take place, and had sixteen lights burning, so that everyone might see how anxious they were to finish the Emperor's new suit. They pretended to roll the cloth off the looms; cut the air with their scissors; and sewed with needles without any thread in them. 'See!' cried they at last, ' the Emperor's new clothes are ready!'

And now the Emperor, with all the grandees of his court, came to the weavers; and the rogues raised their arms, as if in the act of holding something up, saying, 'Here are your Majesty's trousers! here is the scarf! here is the mantle! The whole suit is as light as a cobweb; one might fancy one has nothing at all on, when dressed in it; that, however, is the great virtue of this delicate cloth!'

'Yes, indeed!' said all the courtiers, although not one of them could see anything of this exquisite manufacture.

'If your Imperial Majesty will be graciously pleased to take off your clothes, we will fit on the new suit, in front of the looking-glass.'

The Emperor was accordingly undressed, and the rogues pretended to array him in his new suit; the Emperor turning round, from side to side, before the looking-glass.

'How splendid his Majesty looks in his new clothes! and how well they fit!' every one cried out. 'What a design! What colours! These are, indeed, royal robes!'

'The canopy which is to be borne over your Majesty, in the procession, is waiting,' announced the Chief Master of the Ceremonies.

'I am quite ready,' answered the Emperor. 'Do my new clothes fit well?' asked he, turning himself round again before the looking-glass, in order that he might appear to be examining his handsome suit.

The lords of the bedchamber, who were to carry his Majesty's train, felt about on the ground, as if they were lifting up the ends of the mantle, and pretended to be carrying something; for they would by no means betray anything like simplicity, or unfitness for their office.

So now the Emperor walked under his high canopy in the midst of the procession, through the streets of his capital; and all the people standing by, and those at the windows, cried out, 'Oh! how beautiful are our Emperor's new clothes! What a magnificent train there is to the mantle! And how gracefully the scarf hangs!' In short, no one would allow that he could not see these much-admired clothes, because, in doing so, he would have declared himself either a simpleton or unfit for his office. Certainly, none of the Emperor's various suits had ever excited so much admiration as this.

'But the Emperor has nothing at all on!' said a little child. 'Listen to the voice of innocence!' exclaimed his father; and what the child had said was whispered from one to another.

'But he has nothing at all on!' at last cried out all the people. The Emperor was vexed, for he knew that the people were right; but he thought 'the procession must go on now!'

From Hans Andersen, *Fairy Tales and Legends*. Illustrated by Rex Whistler. (London: Bodley Head, 1942), 37.

And the lords of the bedchamber took greater pains than ever to appear holding up a train, although, in reality, there was no train to hold.

From *Fairy Tales and Legends*, by Hans Andersen (London: The Bodley Head, 1942).

The President Wants No More of Anansi

Although enslaved Africans brought many stories of the trickster-hero Anansi with them to the New World, some of the narratives changed considerably. Such was the case in Haiti, where, as Harold Courlander has noted, 'tales were often used to express the democratic equality of the small person with the great' (170). In this story, which has parallels to tales from a variety of cultures, the sometime culture hero reveals his audacity in flaunting authority and getting away with it. In his dealing with the President, whom he seems to have been annoying for a long time, he literally obeys his leader's commands while violating their intention. Unlike a fool whose literal following of instructions creates difficulties for him, the literal Anansi is able to make the authority figure seem foolish.

Anansi and all his smart ways irritated the President so much that the President told him one day: 'Anansi, I'm tired of your foolishness. Don't you ever let me see your face again.' So Anansi went away from the palace. And a few days later he saw the President coming down the street, so he quickly stuck his head into the open door of a limekiln.

Everyone on the street took off their hats when the President passed. When he came to the limekiln, he saw Anansi's behind sticking out. He became angry and said, 'Qui bounda ça qui pas salué mwé?' (Whose behind is it that doesn't salute me?) Anansi took his head out of the limekiln and said, 'C'est bounda 'Nansi qui pas salué ou.' (It's Anansi's behind which didn't salute you.)

The President said angrily, 'Anansi, you don't respect me.'

Anansi said: 'President, I was just doing what you told me to do. You told me never to let you see my face.'

The President said: 'Anansi, I've had enough of your foolishness. I don't ever want to see you again, clothed or naked.'

So Anansi went away. But the next day when he saw the President coming down the street he took his clothes off and put a fish net over his head. When the President saw him he shouted, 'Anansi, didn't I tell you I never wanted to see you again clothed or naked?' And Anansi said, 'My President, I respect what you tell me. I'm not clothed and I'm not naked.'

This time the President told him, 'Anansi, if I ever catch you again on Haitian soil I'll have you shot.'

So Anansi boarded a boat and sailed to Jamaica. He bought a pair of heavy shoes and put sand in them. Then he put the shoes on his feet and took another boat back to Haiti. When he arrived at Port-au-Prince he found the President standing on the pier.

'Anansi,' the President said sternly, 'didn't I tell you that if I ever caught you on Haitian soil again I'd have you shot'

'You told me that, Papa, and I respected what you said. I went to Jamaica and filled my shoes with sand. So I didn't disobey you because I'm now walking on English soil.'

From *The Drum and the Hoe: Life and Lore of the Haitian People*, by Harold Courlander (Berkeley and Los Angeles: University of California Press, 1960).

The Golden Altar of the Church of St Joseph

Henry Morgan—one of the most ruthless and blood-thirsty buccaneers of the Caribbean—attacked and virtually destroyed Panama in 1671. This legend, in which the priests are able to trick the invader, in part by appearing to be very poor, recounts the miraculous events that saved the golden altar that can still be seen today. In a fortunate twist, the paint designed to disguise the altar from Morgan also protected it from the fire later set by the pirate. The story also celebrates the victory of the weak over the strong. Morgan can be seen as representing the powerful English who, in this instance, are unable to defeat the colonial Spaniards. Ironically, Morgan behaves with uncharacteristic charity. Having been deceived by the inferior quality of the paint that masks the Panamanians' great religious treasure, he gives them silver with which to buy better paint.

On the Church of Saint Joseph, in the City of Panama, there is a golden altar more than three centuries old. It is more ancient than the church in which it stands, having survived the brigandage of the pirate Henry Morgan and the fire that destroyed the original city of Panama.

Three hundred years ago the altar stood in another Church of Saint Joseph. Word came to the city that the ship of Henry Morgan was on its way to loot the city of its treasures. The priests and brothers of the churches were advised to hide anything of value. But in the Church of Saint Joseph there was a problem. The beautiful golden altar was too large to hide anywhere. At last one of the brothers had an idea. He suggested that the altar should be painted and camouflaged to appear a worthless object. With the help of some of the people of Panama, the priests and brothers collected clay and herbs, and out of these things they made a crude kind of paint. Even as Henry Morgan was sailing into the harbour, they began to apply their paint to the golden altar. They worked all night and finished only as the sun was rising. In the first light of morning Henry Morgan's buccaneers came ashore, and it was only a matter of minutes before they were beating on the doors of the Church of Saint Joseph.

When they entered the church they went from room to room but found nothing of value—no money, no objects of silver or gold. Henry Morgan himself stood before the altar, and he saw an old priest, undisturbed by the invasion, touching up the altar with a little paint.

'That is a strange and ugly paint you are using,' Henry Morgan said. 'Why do you not use oil paint?'

The old priest stopped his work long enough to reply to the pirate. 'We are a poor parish,' he said. 'We do not have money for such luxuries. The paint we are using was made with our own hands out of the very earth of Panama.'

Then, it is said, Henry Morgan did an astonishing thing. He reached into his pocket and brought out a handful of silver, which he gave to the priest. 'Take this,' he said, 'and buy oil paint for the church.'

When Henry Morgan and his men had left the church, the priests, the brothers, and the townspeople fell on their knees and thanked God for saving their altar.

But the pirates continued to seek their loot elsewhere in the city. And that night as they retired to their ship, they put the city to the torch. The fire spread in all directions. It became a raging inferno. People fled for safety where they could. From the tower of the Church of Saint Joseph, the priests could see the approaching flames. There was nothing to do. They simply waited and prayed that the fire would burn itself out before it reached the church. When at last there was no further hope that the church would be spared, they placed a statue of Saint Joseph on the golden altar and, carrying what they could, went away.

The fire set by the pirate Henry Morgan burned down most of the old city of Panama. When its fury was over, people came back to find smoldering ruins. They found that the Church of Saint Joseph had been partially destroyed. But the golden altar, covered with the crude and ugly paint made of earth, was untouched by the flames. And when, at last, the new Church of Saint Joseph was built, the golden altar was placed in it. And there it remains to this day.

―――――――

From *Ride with the Sun II: An Anthology of Folktales and Stories from the United Nations*, compiled by the United Nations Women's Guild (New York: UNWG, 2004).

LINKS TO OTHER STORIES

Part Ten

Nature Humanized
Animal Tales

In all parts of the world, animals have long been the focus of many traditional tales. Sometimes these tales portray natural enemies—predators and their prey—offering both entertaining action and lessons about the ways of the world. Sometimes they offer explanations about animal appearances and habits. Most often, however, they are not really about animals at all because the behaviour of the characters has little, if anything, to do with zoological facts. In fact, the animals in the vast majority of traditional tales, are more like costumed human beings than animals because they talk and, in many instances, organize their lives the way humans do: they frequently live in houses, cook and prepare meals, go fishing in boats, get married, and conduct wars.

The origin of such humanized animal tales is impossible to determine, but they may reflect to some extent beliefs about a prelapsarian golden age. In *Animal Land*, Margaret Blount describes this time: 'The golden age is somewhere in the past—perhaps in Eden or before the Flood, perhaps nearer, just beyond the memory of the oldest story teller; and in that time the gulf between animals and men had not been opened, the distinctions were not so sharp, magic was all about' (22). These tales may also derive, as Stith Thompson suggests in *The Folktale*, from beliefs in gods who had animal form but possessed the ability to speak and act like humans (217).

Even after such conceptions of a primal unity in nature and of animal-like gods ceased to compel belief in many cultures, animal tales remained popular. One reason may be that animal characters allow storytellers to offer lessons in conduct and to criticize human foibles without becoming too personal. The use of animal characters creates a superficial distance between the object of criticism and the audience. This apparent distance may make it easier for readers or listeners to apprehend and respond to messages conveyed by the actions of talking animals. Once they do so, audience members may then reflect on how similar the errors and limitations of the talking animals are to their own. By first seeing the Other they may be better able to see themselves.

Animal characters may appear in any kind of tale, but they have dominated one genre, the fable, to such an extent that G.K. Chesterton has declared 'There can be no good fable with human beings in it' (vii). Stith Thompson's definition of the fable begins with animals: 'When the animal tale is told with an acknowledged moral purpose, it becomes a fable' (10). Beast fables, short tales in which the actions of animals illustrate human follies, have a long history. In the West, the most famous beast fables come from a Greek collection ascribed to

Aesop, a sixth-century BC slave who impressed his contemporaries with his animal tales. According to Robert Temple, Aesop thus 'became a legendary name around which all such witty animal tales clustered in later centuries, most of the surviving ones probably not actually written by him' (x). Some of the fables ascribed to him, for example, have been traced to a collection that Aristotle referred to as the 'Libyan stories' (xii), whereas others have come from the Hindu *Panchatantra* (*Five Books*), which dates to around 200 BC. Greek stories and non-Greek stories thus sit side by side in most collections of Aesop's fables.

Existing essentially as didactic devices, representatives of common Western human attitudes and moral qualities, the animal characters in the Aesopian fable wear not only their hearts but also their entire psyches on the sleeves of their animal costumes. Because they have no personal names, no histories, no relationships, and no social position outside of the immediate scene in which we meet them, they must define themselves by their actions. These actions are so consistent from fable to fable, however, that a reader can easily predict an animal's qualities: the lion represents kingship, both its power and its selfishness; the fox represents self-serving cunning; the sheep and the ass, almost always victims of the powerful, stand for, respectively, the naïve and the stubbornly stupid people of the world.

Using these one-dimensional actors in a one-dimensional drama, the Aesopian fable transforms abstract principles into concrete images in order to make them memorable and, therefore, useful guides to conduct. James Reeves notes, however, that 'The virtues which Aesop praises are not the heroic ones—desperate courage, self-sacrifice, high endeavour; they are the peasant virtues of discretion, prudence, moderation and foresight' ([13]). The animals demonstrate these small lessons in social survival primarily by illustrating the consequences of the choices that they face in the tale.

Some of these fables have notable variants. 'The Lion and the Mouse', for example, appears in the second book of *The Panchatantra*, 'The Winning of Friends', as a story about a group of mice who free a captured elephant, and it is obviously the source of the scene in C.S. Lewis' *The Lion, the Witch and the Wardrobe* (1950) in which a group of mice gnaw through the cords binding the slain Aslan. Some of them have inspired popular phrases and aphorisms. The term 'sour grapes', to cite one example, has its origin in 'The Fox and the Grapes'. Some fables, because they offer a vision of life that many contemporary societies find decidedly lacking in the feelings they wish to foster, have inspired revisions and adaptations. As one example, readers may wish to compare 'The Ants and the Grasshopper' with Leo Lionni's picture book *Frederic* (1967), which reverses the message of Aesop's fable by celebrating the spiritual contributions that artists make to their communities.

Besides the *Panchatantra* there is another important collection from the East in which animal tales are prominent. In each *Jataka* animal tale, Buddha is always assumed to have been reincarnated as the wisest and best of the animals. Although they, too, are didactic, the *Jataka* tales can be entertaining. 'The Crocodile and the Monkey's Heart', for example, presents a battle of wits between an accomplished trickster and a plodding thinker who tries to be tricky. Like characters in many of the fables, the Crocodile fails because, lacking self-knowledge, he overestimates his own abilities. Consequently, he does not see the world properly and underestimates the wit of his opponent.

'Henny Penny' is typical of those simple animal folk tales in which animals can talk but otherwise live their lives more or less the way actual animals do. Hans Christian Andersen's 'The Ugly Duckling' has a more elaborate plot, but it is similar in its use of animal conventions. Although Henny-penny lives in a barnyard, she still displays the human trait of vanity, foolishly assuming that the king would willingly hear her. With the exception of the introduction of Foxy-woxy near the end, the tale develops its satirical point of mocking both the vanity of the over-reacher and the tendency of people to follow foolish leaders without reference to either actual animal behaviour or common literary stereotypes of animals. In this tale most of the animals are simply characters who could be easily interchanged with other animals. In the case of 'The Ugly Duckling', Andersen places his animal protagonist in a barnyard society to satirize concerns with appearance. Later, he places the Ugly Duckling in a variety of dangers, some occasioned by contact with human beings, in order to show the Duckling's feelings of inferiority. Ultimately, Andersen has his Duckling transform into a swan so beautiful that even other swans bow in homage. Although the tale seems to succumb to the very value system its opening subverts, it remains a powerful use of animals to express human longings for acceptance and even admiration.

'The Story of the Three Little Pigs' typifies another approach: it presents animals behaving like humans, for the pigs live in houses and perform other actions that humans normally would do. Although almost all beast tales have some connection to human social conventions, ethics, or morality, tales in which the animals live and behave like humans tend to make connections to human lives relatively more obvious. 'The Story of the Three Little Pigs', for example, displays the value of prudence in everything from choosing one's home to choosing one's companions on outings from that home. The use of humanized animals here is, however, not entirely simple. On the one hand, the tale depends on what we assume is the natural desire of the wolf to hunt the pig. This is the law of a nature 'red in tooth and claw'. On the other hand, the humanizing of the animals simplifies, even romanticizes, human life by suggesting that prudence—exemplified in the appropriate building and stocking of a house—is the only key to comfort and safety. The message is clear: those who lack prudence will, like the first two pigs, get caught up in the violent animal world, with its red teeth and claws. In contrast, those who have prudence will, like the third pig, achieve a social ideal of the human state. By building a brick house, the physical result of prudence, the third pig creates a place of safety and comfort; he builds, in other words, a true home that is a fitting symbol of happiness.

Even when animals do not obviously imitate humans they may still put into focus or even challenge social conventions and values. One figure, the animal trickster, often plays a complex and somewhat ambiguous role in traditional stories. We discuss the trickster figure at length in another chapter, so here we will confine ourselves to a few comments about the complex role of the animal trickster. Oyekan Owomoyela says that, when the Yoruba people of Nigeria and Bénin hear stories about the tortoise Ajàpá, their attitude is 'both approbatory and opprobrious': 'While they find his resourcefulness and his resilience admirable, they disapprove of his duplicity and disdain for reciprocity' (xiv). The same may be said of many other groups and their animal tricksters. In 'The Elephant and the Giraffe', for example, a tale from the Hausa of Nigeria, the actions of Hare both recognize the necessity of hard physical labour and celebrate the ability to avoid such effort. Hare, an ancestor of North America's Br'er Rabbit, is admirable because he is an entrepreneur who exercises his wit, not his body, to reap considerable rewards. At the same time, he is abominable because, being totally amoral and selfish, he lacks concern for others and has no sense of community.

The Jackal in 'The Story of a Dam', who is even more abominably self-centred and amoral, also shows the complex function of the animal trickster as simultaneously a positive and a negative role model. The tale clearly presents him as a negative example of the values that the rest of his community endorses because it shows him benefiting from the community but not contributing to it. At the same time, however, the tale celebrates individualism, the ability to flout community standards and obligations. In addition, especially in its final scene, it drives home the point that wit is a survival tool of far more value than mere strength. This point is particularly important in a wide range of animal trickster stories, because, as Owomoyela observes, 'Trickster tales attest to the truth that the relation of power between the strong and the weak does not preclude agency, even triumphant agency, on the part of the latter' (xiv). Such agency naturally makes the trickster appealing to the weaker members of society. Furthermore, the fact that the trickster is an animal may help listeners to accept and even celebrate qualities that they would find reprehensible in a realistically presented human.

The habits and physical appearance of animals themselves take centre stage in another traditional form of animal tale, the *pourquoi* or explanatory tale. This kind of tale is generally an entertainment in which the conclusion purports to explain the origin of specific traits of animals. The Brazilian tale 'The Deer and the Jaguar Share a House' thus begins, as do all *pourquoi* tales, in a time before the current order of things was established. In this instance, it is a time when deer and jaguar could live together. Much of the action, however, is a comical account of foolish hubris, an account that could appear in any other kind of comical tale as a warning about making assumptions and about respecting the feelings of others. As is frequently the case, only the conclusion turns the tale into an explanation of current animal behaviour. In this instance, the tale offers a humorous explanation of why these two animals are never together.

Tales explaining the origin of the distinctive features of particular animals may be largely entertainments, but they can include lessons about cultural values. In 'Gayardaree the Platypus', an Australian aboriginal *pourquoi* tale, for example, the central character, a female duck, is a cautionary figure. A self-centred individualist, she ignores the community's collective wisdom about the danger of swimming alone. Consequently, she ends up a sad and lonely figure isolated from everyone, even her own offspring. Her situation is made even more ironic by the conclusion, which explains both the origin of the platypus and the fact that platypus form 'quite a tribe apart'. By flouting the community and going off on her own, that is, she created a community, but one so different from others that it must forever remain separate from them.

The lesson is far lighter in Rudyard Kipling's literary *pourquoi* tale 'The Elephant's Child'. By having childhood curiosity clash with the Victorian edict that children should be seen and not heard, Kipling subverts some conventional assumptions about the proper way to treat children. Therefore, in addition to offering an amusing account of the origin of the elephant's trunk, this tale is a fantasy of wish fulfillment that pictures the child as both more adept and more powerful than the adults who had abused him.

Some animal *pourquoi* tales do not focus on the origin of animal traits. The South American myth 'The Revenge of the Three Deer-Boys', for example, explains the origin of the constellation Gemini. Tales such as this one may be somewhat puzzling to those outside the originating culture because they seldom explain exactly how the animals became transformed into stars. Indeed, mythical material seems here to be tacked onto a rather ordinary tale of revenge. Nevertheless, in personalizing remote cosmic features like the stars and connecting them to more familiar earthly elements, such as animals, these tales establish a bond between the Earth and the heavens while maintaining the sense of awe or mystery about such heavenly bodies.

A tale's audience generally has a complex relationship with animal characters because it can both distance itself from and see itself in the animals. This relationship is not one limited to the time of oral story telling: animals continue to be favourite characters in contemporary entertainments for children, from picture books, to novels, to cartoons, and even feature-length animated films. As such disparate modern forms and the traditional tales in this section attest, animal characters have a strong appeal to humans, and they can be a powerful medium for both entertaining and teaching social values.

Works Cited

Blount, Margaret. [1974] 1977. *Animal Land: The Creatures of Children's Fiction*. New York: Avon.
Chesterton, G.K. [1912] 1956. 'Introduction', *Aesop's Fables*. Trans. V.S. Vernon Jones. London: William Heinemann.
Owomoyela, Oyekan. 1997. *Yoruba Trickster Tales*. Lincoln, NE: University of Nebraska Press.
Reeves, James. 1962. 'Introduction', *Fables from Aesop*. New York: Henry Z. Walck.
Temple, Robert. 1998. 'Introduction', *Aesop: The Complete Fables*. Trans. Livia and Robert Temple. London: Penguin.
Thompson, Stith. [1946] 1967. *The Folktale*. Berkeley: University of California Press.

Aesop's Fables

The following popular animal fables present a variety of lessons about social and personal survival. The animals featured in each of these tales are not portrayed realistically, nor are they chosen because their habits in the wild make them particularly suitable for particular actions. For the most part, fable tellers selected them because of their literary or cultural associations: the animals are types that stand for certain moral and psychological traits. Although the last tale in this section, 'The Lion and the Shepherd', is often included in fable collections, it is not truly an Aesopian fable, but a version of the story of Androcles and the lion, a tale first told by Apion, a Libyan who went to Rome in the first century AD, and preserved in the *Noctes Atticae* of Aulus Gellius (c. AD 130–180). It shows how brief tales can employ animals in didactic roles without necessarily falling back on the typology of the Aesopian fable. A fitting companion to 'The Lion and the Mouse', it also extends the idea that kindness reaps rewards by illustrating that humans can gain from being kind to nature, a theme frequently part of more complex tales.

The Fox and the Crow

A Crow having stolen a bit of flesh, perched in a tree, and held it in her beak. A Fox seeing her, longed to possess himself of the flesh: and by a wily stratagem succeeded. 'How handsome is the Crow,' he exclaimed, 'in the beauty of her shape and in the fairness of her complexion! Oh, if her voice were only equal to her beauty, she would deservedly be considered the Queen of Birds!' This he said deceitfully; but the Crow, anxious to refute the reflection cast upon her voice, set up a loud caw, and dropped the flesh. The Fox quickly picked it up, and thus addressed the Crow: 'My good Crow, your voice is right enough, but your wit is wanting.'

The Fox and the Goat

A Fox having fallen into a deep well, was detained a prisoner there, as he could find no means of escape. A Goat, overcome with thirst, came to the same well, and, seeing the Fox, inquired if the water was good. The Fox, concealing his sad plight under a merry guise, indulged in a lavish praise of the water, saying it was beyond measure excellent, and

From Geo. Fyker Townsend, trans. *Three Hundred Aesop's Fables Literally Translated from the Greek.* (New York: McLoughlin Brothers, 1867), 19.

encouraged him to descend. The Goat, mindful only of his thirst, thoughtlessly jumped down, when just as he quenched his thirst, the Fox informed him of the difficulty they were both in, and suggested a scheme for their common escape. 'If,' said he, 'you will place your fore-feet upon the wall, and bend your head, I will run up your back and escape, and will help you out afterwards.' On the Goat readily assenting to this second proposal, the Fox leapt upon his back, and steadying himself with the Goat's horns, reached in safety the mouth of the well, when he immediately made off as fast as he could. The Goat upbraided him with the breach of his bargain, when he turned round and cried out: 'You foolish old fellow! If you had as many brains in your head as you have hairs in your beard, you would never have gone down before you had inspected the way up, nor have exposed yourself to dangers from which you had no means of escape.'

Look before you leap.

The Fox and the Grapes

A famished Fox saw some clusters of ripe black Grapes hanging from a trellised vine. She resorted to all her tricks to get at them, but wearied herself in vain, for she could not reach them. At last she turned away, beguiling herself of her disappointment and saying: 'The Grapes are sour, and not ripe as I thought.'

The Hare and the Tortoise

A Hare one day ridiculed the short feet and slow pace of the Tortoise. The latter, laughing, said: 'Though you be swift as the wind, I will beat you in a race.' The Hare, deeming

From Geo. Fyker Townsend, trans. *Three Hundred Aesop's Fables Literally Translated from the Greek.* (New York: McLoughlin Brothers, 1867), 21.

her assertion to be simply impossible, assented to the proposal; and they agreed that the Fox should choose the course, and fix the goal. On the day appointed for the race they started together. The Tortoise never for a moment stopped, but went on with a slow but steady pace straight to the end of the course. The Hare, trusting to his native swiftness, cared little about the race, and lying down by the wayside, fell fast asleep. At last waking up, and moving as fast as he could, he saw the Tortoise had reached the goal, and was comfortably dozing after her fatigue.

The Dog and the Shadow

A Dog, crossing a bridge over a stream with a piece of flesh in his mouth, saw his own shadow in the water, and took it for that of another Dog, with a piece of meat double his own in size. He therefore let go his own, and fiercely attacked the other Dog, to get his larger piece from him. He thus lost both: that which he grasped at in the water, because it was a shadow; and his own, because the stream swept it away.

The Ants and the Grasshopper

The Ants were employing a fine winter's day in drying grain collected in the summer time. A Grasshopper, perishing with famine, passed by and earnestly begged for a little food. The Ants enquired of him, 'Why did you not treasure up food during the summer?' He replied, 'I had not leisure enough. I passed the days in singing.' They then said in derision: 'If you were foolish enough to sing all the summer, you must dance supperless to bed in the winter.'

The Lion, the Fox, and the Ass

𝔗he Lion, the Fox, and the Ass entered into an agreement to assist each other in the chase. Having secured a large booty, the Lion, on their return from the forest, asked the Ass to allot his due portion to each of the three partners in the treaty. The Ass carefully divided the spoil into three equal shares, and modestly requested the two others to make the first choice. The Lion, bursting out into a great rage, devoured the Ass. Then he requested the Fox to do him the favour to make a division. The Fox accumulated all that they had killed into one large heap, and left to himself the smallest possible morsel. The Lion said, 'Who has taught you, my very excellent fellow, the art of division? You are perfect to a fraction.' He replied, 'I learnt it from the Ass, by witnessing his fate.'

Happy is the man who learns from the misfortunes of others.

The Lion and the Mouse

𝔄 Lion was awakened from sleep by a Mouse running over his face. Rising up in anger, he caught him and was about to kill him, when the Mouse piteously entreated, saying: 'If you would only spare my life, I would be sure to repay your kindness.' The Lion laughed and let him go. It happened shortly after this that the Lion was caught by some hunters, who bound him by strong ropes to the ground. The Mouse, recognizing his roar, came up, and gnawed the rope with his teeth, and setting him free, exclaimed: 'You ridiculed the idea of my ever being able to help you, not expecting to receive from me any repayment of your favour; but now you know that it is possible for even a Mouse to confer benefits on a Lion.'

The Lion and the Shepherd

𝔄 Lion, roaming through a forest, trod upon a thorn, and soon after came up towards a Shepherd, and fawned upon him, wagging his tail, as if he would say, 'I am a suppliant, and seek your aid.' The Shepherd boldly examined, and discovered the thorn, and placing his foot upon his lap, pulled it out and relieved the Lion of his pain, who returned into the forest. Some time after, the Shepherd being imprisoned on a false accusation, is condemned 'to be cast to the Lions,' as the punishment of his imputed crime. The Lion, on being released from his cage, recognizes the Shepherd as the man who healed him, and, instead of attacking him, approaches and places his foot upon his lap. The King, as soon as he heard the tale, ordered the Lion to be set free again in the forest, and the Shepherd to be pardoned and restored to his friends.

From *Three Hundred Aesop's Fables Literally Translated from the Greek*, trans. Geo. Fyker Townsend (New York: McLoughlin Brothers, [1867]).

The Crocodile and the Monkey's Heart

Jataka tales, which originated in India, have as their starting point the Buddhist beliefs in *karma* and reincarnation. According to these beliefs, one's actions affect the kind of life one will have when reincarnated. Each of the 550 fables, anecdotes, and tales that form the *Jataka* recount a previous existence of Siddhartha Gautama (563–483 BC), the future Buddha. Each of his previous lives, some of which had him assuming animal form, was one stage of his path to enlightenment, and each tested his intellectual, moral, or spiritual qualities. The Bodhisatta, or future Buddha, who narrates each tale, is not without faults in some tales, but he usually appears as the strongest, wisest, and most virtuous character. The Bodhisatta narrates 'The Crocodile and the Monkey's Heart' when he is told that the evil monk Devadatta is trying to murder him. He explains that he has escaped from Devadatta in a previous life, for he was the monkey, Devadatta was the crocodile, and Cinca, a woman who accused the Bodhisatta of having an affair with her, was the crocodile's wife. Even without this frame of Buddhist references, the tale stands on its own as an entertaining trickster tale in which the monkey outwits an incompetent would-be trickster. Because he both understands and can act upon his enemy's intellectual limitations, the monkey earns the right to rejoice in victory.

Once upon a time, while Brahmadatta was king of Benares, the Bodhisatta came to life at the foot of Himalaya as a Monkey. He grew strong and sturdy, big of frame, well-to-do, and lived by a curve of the river Ganges in a forest haunt.

Now at that time there was a Crocodile dwelling in the Ganges. The Crocodile's mate saw the great frame of the monkey, and she conceived a longing for his heart to eat. So she said to her lord: 'Sir, I desire to eat the heart of that great king of the monkeys!'

'Good wife,' said the Crocodile, 'I live in the water and he lives on dry land: how can we catch him?'

'By hook or by crook,' she replied, 'caught he must be. If I don't get him, I shall die.'

'All right,' answered the Crocodile, consoling her, 'don't trouble yourself. I have a plan; I will give you his heart to eat.'

So when the Bodhisatta was sitting on the bank of the Ganges, after taking a drink of water, the Crocodile drew near, and said:

'Sir Monkey, why do you live on bad fruits in this old familiar place? On the other side of the Ganges there is no end to the mango trees, and labuja trees, with fruit sweet as honey! Is it not better to cross over and have all kinds of wild fruit to eat?'

'Lord Crocodile,' the Monkey made answer, 'deep and wide is the Ganges: how shall I get across?'

'If you will go, I will mount you on my back, and carry you over.'

The Monkey trusted him, and agreed. 'Come here, then,' said the other, 'up on my back with you!' and up the monkey climbed. But when the crocodile had swum a little way, he plunged the Monkey under the water.

'Good friend, you are letting me sink!' cried the Monkey. 'What is that for?'

Said the Crocodile, 'You think I am carrying you out of pure good nature? Not a bit of it! My wife has a longing for your heart, and I want to give it her to eat!'

'Friend,' said the Monkey, 'it is nice of you to tell me. Why, if our heart were inside us when we go jumping among the tree-tops, it would be all knocked to pieces!'

'Well, where do you keep it?' asked the other.

The Bodhisatta pointed out a fig-tree, with clusters of ripe fruit, standing not far off. 'See,' said he, 'there are our hearts hanging on yon fig-tree.'

'If you will show me your heart,' said the Crocodile, 'then I won't kill you.'

'Take me to the tree, then, and I will point it out to you hanging upon it.'

The Crocodile brought him to the place. The Monkey leapt off his back, and climbing up the fig-tree sat upon it. 'O silly Crocodile!' said he, 'you thought that there were creatures that kept their hearts in a tree-top! You are a fool, and I have outwitted you! You may keep your fruit to yourself. Your body is great, but you have no sense.' And then to explain this idea he uttered the following stanzas:—

'Rose-apple, jack-fruit, mangoes too across the water there I see;
Enough of them, I want them not; my fig is good enough for me!

Great is your body, verily, but how much smaller is your wit!
Now go your ways, Sir Crocodile, for I have had the best of it.'

The Crocodile, feeling as sad and miserable as if he had lost a thousand pieces of money, went back sorrowing to the place where he lived.

From *The Jataka; or, Stories of the Buddha's Former Births*, Book 2, edited by E.B. Cowell (Cambridge: Cambridge University Press, 1895).

Henny Penny

This British cumulative tale, also known as 'Chicken Licken' and 'Chicken Little', is a variant of a *Jataka* tale in which a lion (the reincarnated Buddha) shows a hare who had insisted that the earth was falling in that he has mistaken the sound of fruit falling on leaves for a calamity. Both tales mock foolishness and those who unquestioningly accept foolish rumours. The silly names prevent the animals from having any heroic stature, and the excessive repetition of those names creates a light tone that persists right up to the point when the fox, an archetypal trickster, brings their quest to an ironic conclusion. That conclusion is certainly violent—a fact that has led a number of later retellers to state simply that the animals entered the cave and never came out—but it humorously dramatizes the fate of those who act without sufficient knowledge.

One day Henny-penny was picking up corn in the cornyard when—whack!—something hit her upon the head. 'Goodness gracious me!' said Henny-penny; 'the sky's a-going to fall; I must go and tell the king.'

So she went along and she went along and she went along till she met Cocky-locky. 'Where are you going, Henny-penny?' says Cocky-locky. 'Oh! I'm going to tell the king the sky's a-falling,' says Henny-penny. 'May I come with you?' says Cocky-locky. 'Certainly,' says Henny-penny. So Henny-penny and Cocky-locky went to tell the king the sky was falling.

They went along, and they went along, and they went along, till they met Ducky-daddles. 'Where are you going to, Henny-penny and Cocky-locky?' says Ducky-daddles. 'Oh! we're going to tell the king the sky's a-falling,' said Henny-penny and Cocky-locky. 'May I come with you?' says Ducky-daddles. 'Certainly,' said Henny-penny and Cocky-locky. So Henny-penny, Cocky-locky, and Ducky-daddles went to tell the king the sky was a-falling.

So they went along, and they went along, and they went along, till they met Goosey-poosey, 'Where are you going to, Henny-penny, Cocky-locky, and Ducky-daddles?' said Goosey-poosey. 'Oh! we're going to tell the king the sky's a-falling,' said Henny-penny and

Arthur Rackham, *The Arthur Rackham Fairy Book: A Book of Old Favourites with New Illustrations.* (Philadelphia: J.B. Lippicnott, n.d.), 68–9.

Cocky-locky and Ducky-daddles. 'May I come with you,' said Goosey-poosey. 'Certainly,' said Henny-penny, Cocky-locky, and Ducky-daddles. So Henny-penny, Cocky-locky, Ducky-daddles, and Goosy-poosey went to tell the king the sky was a-falling.

So they went along, and they went along, and they went along, till they met Turkey-lurkey. 'Where are you going, Henny-penny, Cocky-locky, Ducky-daddles, and Goosey-poosey?' says Turkey-lurkey. 'Oh! we're going to tell the king the sky's a-falling,' said Henny-penny, Cocky-locky, Ducky-daddles, and Goosey-poosey. 'May I come with you? Henny-penny, Cocky-locky, Ducky-daddles, and Goosey-poosey?' said Turkey-lurkey. 'Why, certainly, Turkey-lurkey,' said Henny-penny, Cocky-locky, Ducky-daddles, and Goosey-poosey. So Henny-penny, Cocky-locky, Ducky-daddles, Goosey-poosey, and Turkey-lurkey all went to tell the king the sky was a-falling.

So they went along, and they went along, and they went along, till they met Foxy-woxy, and Foxy-woxy said to Henny-penny, Cocky-locky, Ducky-daddles, Goosey-poosey, and Turkey-lurkey: 'Where are you going, Henny-penny, Cocky-locky, Ducky-daddles, Goosey-poosey, and Turkey-lurkey?' And Henny-penny, Cocky-Locky, Ducky-daddles, Goosey-poosey, and Turkey-lurkey said to Foxy-woxy: 'We're going to tell the king the sky's a-falling.' 'Oh! but this is not the way to the king, Henny-penny, Cocky-locky, Ducky-daddles, Goosey-poosey, and Turkey-lurkey,' says Foxy-woxy; 'I know the proper way; shall I show it you?' 'Why certainly, Foxy-woxy,' said Henny-penny, Cocky-locky, Ducky-daddles, Goosey-poosey, and Turkey-lurkey. So Henny-penny, Cocky-locky, Ducky-daddles, Goosey-poosey, Turkey-lurkey, and Foxy-woxy all went to tell the king the sky was a-falling. So they went along, and they went along, and they went along, till they came to a narrow and dark hole. Now this was the door of Foxy-woxy's cave. But Foxy-woxy said to Henny-penny, Cocky-locky, Ducky-daddles, Goosey-poosey, and Turkey-lurkey: 'This is the short way to the king's palace: you'll soon get there if you follow me. I will go first and you come after, Henny-penny, Cocky-locky, Ducky-daddles, Goosey-poosey, and Turkey-lurkey.' 'Why of course, certainly, without doubt, why not?' said Henny-Penny, Cocky-locky, Ducky-daddles, Goosey-poosey, and Turkey-lurkey.

So Foxy-woxy went into his cave, and he didn't go very far but turned round to wait for Henny-penny, Cocky-locky, Ducky-daddles, Goosey-poosey, and Turkey-lurkey. So at last at first Turkey-lurkey went through the dark hole into the cave. He hadn't got far when 'Hrumph,' Foxy-woxy snapped off Turkey-lurkey's head and threw his body over his left shoulder. Then Goosey-poosey went in, and 'Hrumph,' off went her head and Goosey-poosey was thrown beside Turkey-lurkey. Then Ducky-daddles waddled down, and 'Hrumph,' snapped Foxy-woxy, and Ducky-daddles' head was off and Ducky-daddles was thrown alongside Turkey-lurkey and Goosey-poosey. Then Cocky-locky strutted down into the cave and he hadn't gone far when 'Snap, Hrumph!' went Foxy-woxy and Cocky-locky was thrown alongside of Turkey-lurkey, Goosey-poosey, and Ducky-daddles.

But Foxy-woxy had made two bites at Cocky-locky, and when the first snap only hurt Cocky-locky, but didn't kill him, he called out to Henny-penny. So she turned tail and ran back home, so she never told the king the sky was a-falling.

From *English Fairy Tales*, by Joseph Jacobs (London: David Nutt, 1898).

The Ugly Duckling

Hans Christian Andersen used the medium of the fairy tale both to achieve fame and to allegorize his own tortuous road to success. The most famous of his metaphorical autobiographies, 'The Ugly Duckling' is a tale of transformation that follows its protagonist on a painful journey to self-realization and public acceptance. The animal characters satirize the shallowness of a society that rejects individuals on such superficial grounds as appearance. In the end, the Ugly Duckling achieves recognition and honour as a superior creature, both from other swans and from the human children. Although the Ugly Duckling's journey is filled with suffering, the question of whether that suffering has anything to do with his ultimate transformation intrudes into any analysis of the tale. In other words, readers must ask whether the Ugly Duckling has done anything to deserve his elevated status or whether the fact that, because he emerged from a swan's egg and therefore would have become a swan even if he had not suffered, means that the story simply supports determinism, ultimately negating its own critique of social values.

The country was very lovely just then—it was summer. The wheat was golden and the oats still green. The hay was stacked in the rich low meadows, where the stork marched about on his long red legs, chattering in Egyptian, the language his mother had taught him.

Round about field and meadow lay great woods, in the midst of which were deep lakes. Yes, the country certainly was lovely. In the sunniest spot stood an old mansion surrounded by a deep moat, and great dock leaves grew from the walls of the house right down to the water's edge. Some of them were so tall that a small child could stand upright under them. In among the leaves it was as secluded as in the depths of a forest, and there a duck was sitting on her nest. Her little ducklings were just about to be hatched, but she was quite tired of sitting, for it had lasted such a long time. Moreover, she had very few visitors, as the other ducks liked swimming about in the moat better than waddling up to sit under the dock leaves and gossip with her.

At last one egg after another began to crack. 'Cheep, cheep!' they said. All the chicks had come to life and were poking their heads out.

'Quack, quack!' said the duck, and then they all quacked their hardest and looked about them on all sides among the green leaves. Their mother allowed them to look as much as they liked, for green is good for the eyes.

'How big the world is, to be sure!' said all the young ones. They certainly now had ever so much more room to move about than when they were inside their eggshells.

'Do you imagine this is the whole world?' said the mother. 'It stretches a long way on the other side of the garden, right into the parson's field, though I have never been as far as that. I suppose you are all here now?' She got up and looked about. 'No, I declare I have not got you all yet! The biggest egg is still there. How long is this going to take?' she said, and settled herself on the nest again.

'Well, how are you getting on?' said an old duck who had come to pay her a visit.

'This one egg is taking such a long time!' answered the sitting duck. 'The shell will not crack. But now you must look at the others. They are the finest ducklings I have ever seen. They are all exactly like their father, the rascal!—yet he never comes to see me.'

'Let me look at the egg which won't crack,' said the old duck. 'You may be sure that it is a turkey's egg! I was cheated like that once and I had no end of trouble and worry with the creatures, for I may tell you that they are afraid of the water. I simply could not get them into it. I quacked and snapped at them, but it all did no good. Let me see the egg! Yes, it is a turkey's egg. You just leave it alone, and teach the other children to swim.'

'I will sit on it a little longer. I have sat so long already that I may as well go on till the Midsummer Fair comes round.'

'Please yourself,' said the old duck, and away she went.

At last the big egg cracked. 'Cheep, cheep!' said the young one and tumbled out. How big and ugly he was! The duck looked at him.

'That is a monstrous big duckling,' she said. 'None of the others looked like that. Can he be a turkey chick? Well, we shall soon find that out. Into the water he shall go, if I have to kick him in myself.'

Next day was gloriously fine, and the sun shone on all the green dock leaves. The mother duck with her whole family went down to the moat.

Splash! into the water she sprang. 'Quack, quack,' she said, and one duckling plumped in after the other. The water dashed over their heads, but they came up again and floated beautifully. Their legs went of themselves, and they were all there. Even the big ugly gray one swam about with them.

'No, that is no turkey,' she said. 'See how beautifully he uses his legs and how erect he holds himself. He is my own chick, after all, and not bad looking when you come to look at him properly. Quack, quack! Now come with me and I will take you out into the world and introduce you to the duckyard. But keep close to me all the time so that no one will tread upon you. And beware of the cat!'

Then they went into the duckyard. There was a fearful uproar going on, for two broods were fighting for the head of an eel, and in the end the cat captured it.

'That's how things go in this world,' said the mother duck, and she licked her bill, because she had wanted the eel's head herself.

'Now use your legs,' said she. 'Mind you quack properly, and bend your necks to the old duck over there. She is the grandest of us all. She has Spanish blood in her veins and that accounts for her size. And do you see? She has a red rag round her leg. That is a wonderfully fine thing, and the most extraordinary mark of distinction any duck can have. It shows clearly that she is not to be parted with, and that she is worthy of recognition both by beasts and men! Quack, now! Don't turn your toes in! A well brought up duckling keeps his legs wide apart just like father and mother. That's it. Now bend your necks and say quack!'

They did as they were bid, but the other ducks round about looked at them and said, quite loud, 'Just look there! Now we are to have that tribe, just as if there were not enough of us already. And, oh dear, how ugly that duckling is! We won't stand him.' And a duck flew at him at once and bit him in the neck.

'Let him be,' said the mother. 'He is doing no harm.'

'Very likely not,' said the biter. 'But he is so ungainly and queer that he must be whacked.'

'Those are handsome children mother has,' said the old duck with the rag round her leg. 'They are all good looking except this one, but he is not a good specimen. It's a pity you can't make him over again.'

'That can't be done, your grace,' said the mother duck. 'He is not handsome, but he is a thoroughly good creature, and he swims as beautifully as any of the others. I think I might venture even to add that I think he will improve as he goes on, or perhaps in time he may grow smaller. He was too long in the egg, and so he has not come out with a very good figure.' And then she patted his neck and stroked him down. 'Besides, he is a drake,' said she. 'So it does not matter so much. I believe he will be very strong, and I don't doubt at all that he will make his way in the world.'

'The other ducklings are very pretty,' said the old duck. 'Now make yourselves quite at home, and if you find the head of an eel you may bring it to me.'

After that they felt quite at home. But the poor duckling who had been the last to come out of the shell, and who was so ugly, was bitten, pushed about, and made fun of both by the ducks and the hens. 'He is too big,' they all said. And the turkey cock, who was born with his spurs on and therefore thought himself quite an emperor, puffed himself up like a vessel in full sail, made for him, and gobbled and gobbled till he became quite red in the face. The poor duckling did not know which way to turn. He was in despair because he was so ugly and the butt of the whole duckyard.

So the first day passed, and afterwards matters grew worse and worse. The poor duckling was chased and hustled by all of them. Even his brothers and sisters ill-used him. They were always saying, 'If only the cat would get hold of you, you hideous object!' Even his mother said, 'I wish to goodness you were miles away.' The ducks bit him, the hens pecked him, and the girl who fed them kicked him aside.

Then he ran off and flew right over the hedge, where the little birds flew up into the air in a fright.

'That is because I am so ugly,' thought the poor duckling, shutting his eyes, but he ran on all the same. Then he came to a great marsh where the wild ducks lived. He was so tired and miserable that he stayed there the whole night. In the morning the wild ducks flew up to inspect their new comrade.

'What sort of a creature are you?' they inquired, as the duckling turned from side to side and greeted them as well as he could. 'You are frightfully ugly,' said the wild ducks, 'but that does not matter to us, so long as you do not marry into our family.' Poor fellow! He had not thought of marriage. All he wanted was permission to lie among the rushes and to drink a little of the marsh water.

He stayed there two whole days. Then two wild geese came, or rather two wild ganders. They were not long out of the shell and therefore rather pert.

'I say, comrade,' they said, 'you are so ugly that we have taken quite a fancy to you! Will you join us and be a bird of passage? There is another marsh close by, and there are some charming wild geese there. All are sweet young ladies who can say quack! You are ugly enough to make your fortune among them.' Just at that moment, bang! bang! was heard up above, and both the wild geese fell dead among the reeds, and the water turned blood red.

Bang! bang! went the guns, and flocks of wild geese flew from the rushes and the shot peppered among them again.

There was a grand shooting party, and the sportsmen lay hidden round the marsh. Some even sat on the branches of the trees which overhung the water. The blue smoke rose like clouds among the dark trees and swept over the pool.

The retrieving dogs wandered about in the swamp—splash! splash! The rushes and reeds bent beneath their tread on all sides. It was terribly alarming to the poor duckling. He twisted his head around to get it under his wing, and just at that moment a frightful big dog appeared close beside him. His tongue hung right out of his mouth and his eyes glared wickedly. He opened his great chasm of a mouth close to the duckling, showed his sharp teeth, and—splash!—went on without touching him.

'Oh, thank Heaven!' sighed the duckling. 'I am so ugly that even the dog won't bite me!'

Then he lay quite still while the shot whistled among the bushes, and bang after bang rent the air. It only became quiet late in the day, but even then the poor duckling did not dare to get up. He waited several hours more before he looked about, and then he hurried away from the marsh as fast as he could. He ran across fields and meadows, and there was such a wind that he had hard work to make his way.

Towards night he reached a poor little cottage. It was such a miserable hovel that it could not make up its mind which way even to fall, and so it remained standing. The wind whistled so fiercely around the duckling that he had to sit on his tail to resist it, and it blew harder and ever harder. Then he saw that the door had fallen off one hinge and hung so crookedly that he could creep into the house through the crack, and so he made his way into the room.

An old woman lived here with her cat and her hen. The cat, whom she called 'Sonnie', would arch his back, purr, and give off electric sparks if you stroked his fur the wrong way. The hen had quite tiny short legs, and so she was called 'Chickie-low-legs'. She laid good eggs, and the old woman was as fond of her as if she had been her own child.

In the morning the strange duckling was discovered immediately, and the cat began to purr and the hen to cluck.

'What on earth is that?' said the old woman, looking round, but her sight was not good and she thought the duckling was a fat duck which had escaped. 'This is a wonderful find!' said she. 'Now I shall have duck's eggs—if only it is not a drake. We must wait and see about that.'

So she took the duckling on trial for three weeks, but no eggs made their appearance. The cat was master of this house and the hen its mistress. They always said, 'We and the world,' for they thought that they represented the half of the world, and that quite the better half.'

The duckling thought there might be two opinions on the subject, but the cat would not hear of it.

'Can you lay eggs?' she asked.

'No.'

'Have the goodness to hold your tongue then!'

And the cat said, 'Can you arch your back, purr, or give off sparks?'

'No.'

'Then you had better keep your opinions to yourself when people of sense are speaking!'

The duckling sat in the corner nursing his ill humour. Then he began to think of the fresh air and the sunshine and an uncontrollable longing seized him to float on the water. At last he could not help telling the hen about it.

'What on earth possesses you?' she asked. 'You have nothing to do. That is why you get these freaks into your head. Lay some eggs or take to purring, and you will get over it.'

'But it is so delicious to float on the water,' said the duckling. 'It is so delicious to feel it rushing over your head when you dive to the bottom.'

'That would be a fine amusement!' said the hen. 'I think you have gone mad. Ask the cat about it. He is the wisest creature I know. Ask him if he is fond of floating on the water or diving under it. I say nothing about myself. Ask our mistress herself, the old woman. There is no one in the world cleverer than she is. Do you suppose she has any desire to float on the water or to duck underneath it?'

'You do not understand me,' said the duckling.

'Well, if we don't understand you, who should? I suppose you don't consider yourself cleverer than the cat or the old woman, not to mention me! Don't make a fool of yourself, child, and thank your stars for all the good we have done you. Have you not lived in this warm room, and in such society that you might have learned something? But you are an idiot, and there is no pleasure in associating with you. You may believe me: I mean you well. I tell you home truths, and there is no surer way than that of knowing who are one's friends. You just set about laying some eggs, or learn to purr, or to emit sparks.'

'I think I will go out into the wide world,' said the duckling.

'Oh, do so by all means,' said the hen.

So away went the duckling. He floated on the water and ducked underneath it, but he was looked at askance and was slighted by every living creature for his ugliness. Now autumn came. The leaves in the woods turned yellow and brown. The wind took hold of them, and they danced about. The sky looked very cold and the clouds hung heavy with snow and hail. A raven stood on the fence and croaked 'Caw, caw!' from sheer cold. It made one shiver only to think of it. The poor duckling certainly was in a bad case!

One evening, the sun was just setting in wintry splendour when a flock of beautiful large birds appeared out of the bushes. The duckling had never seen anything so beautiful. They were dazzlingly white with long waving necks. They were swans, and uttering a peculiar cry they spread out their magnificent broad wings and flew away from the cold regions to warmer lands and open seas. They mounted so high, so very high, and the ugly little duckling became strangely uneasy. He circled round and round in the water like a wheel, craning his neck up into the air after them. Then he uttered a shriek so piercing and so strange that he was quite frightened by it himself. Oh, he could not forget those beautiful birds, those happy birds. And as soon as they were out of sight, he ducked right down to the bottom, and when he came up again he was quite beside himself. He did not know what the birds were, or whither they flew, but all the same he was more drawn towards them than he had ever been by any creatures before. He did not envy them in the least. How could it occur to him even to wish to be such a marvel of beauty? He would have been thankful if only the ducks would have tolerated him among them—the poor ugly creature.

The winter was so bitterly cold that the duckling was obliged to swim about in the water to keep it from freezing over, but every night the hole in which he swam got smaller and smaller. Then it froze so hard that the surface ice cracked, and the duckling had to use his legs all the time so that the ice should not freeze around him. At last he was so weary that he could move no more, and he was frozen fast into the ice.

Early in the morning a peasant came along and saw him. He went out onto the ice and hammered a hole in it with his heavy wooden shoe, and carried the duckling home to his wife. There he soon revived. The children wanted to play with him, but the duckling thought they were going to ill-use him, and rushed in his fright into the milk pan, and the milk spurted out all over the room. The woman shrieked and threw up her hands. Then he flew into the butter cask, and down into the meal tub and out again. Just imagine what he looked like by this time! The woman screamed and tried to hit him with the tongs. The children tumbled over one another in trying to catch him, and they screamed with laughter. By good luck the door stood open, and the duckling flew out among the bushes and the newly fallen snow. And he lay there thoroughly exhausted.

But it would be too sad to mention all the privation and misery he had to go through during the hard winter. When the sun began to shine warmly again, the duckling was in the marsh, lying among the rushes. The larks were singing and the beautiful spring had come.

Then all at once he raised his wings and they flapped with much greater strength than before and bore him off vigorously. Before he knew where he was, he found himself in a large garden where the apple trees were in full blossom and the air was scented with lilacs, the long branches of which overhung the indented shores of the lake. Oh, the spring freshness was delicious!

Just in front of him he saw three beautiful white swans advancing towards him from a thicket. With rustling feathers they swam lightly over the water. The duckling recognized the majestic birds, and he was overcome by a strange melancholy.

'I will fly to them, the royal birds, and they will hack me to pieces because I, who am so ugly, venture to approach them. But it won't matter! Better be killed by them than be snapped at by the ducks, pecked by the hens, spurned by the henwife, or suffer so much misery in the winter.'

So he flew into the water and swam towards the stately swans. They saw him and darted towards him with ruffled feathers.

'Kill me!' said the poor creature, and he bowed his head towards the water and awaited his death. But what did he see reflected in the transparent water?

He saw below him his own image, but he was no longer a clumsy dark gray bird, ugly and ungainly. He was himself a swan! It does not matter in the least having been born in a duckyard, if only you come out of a swan's egg!

He felt quite glad of all the misery and tribulation he had gone through, for he was the better able to appreciate his good fortune now and all the beauty which greeted him. The big swans swam round and round him and stroked him with their bills.

Some little children came into the garden with corn and pieces of bread which they threw into the water, and the smallest one cried out, 'There is a new one!' The other children shouted with joy, 'Yes, a new one has come.' And they clapped their hands and danced about, running after their father and mother. They threw the bread into the water, and one and all said, 'The new one is the prettiest of them all. He is so young and handsome.' And the old swans bent their heads and did homage before him.

He felt quite shy, and hid his head under his wing. He did not know what to think. He was very happy, but not at all proud, for a good heart never becomes proud. He thought of how he had been pursued and scorned, and now he heard them all say that he was the most beautiful of all beautiful birds. The lilacs bent their boughs right down into the water before him, and the bright sun was warm and cheering. He rustled his feathers and raised his slender neck aloft, saying with exultation in his heart, 'I never dreamt of so much happiness when I was the Ugly Duckling!'

From *Andersen's Fairy Tales*, by Mrs. E.V. Lucas and Mrs. H.B. Paull (New York: Grosset & Dunlap, [1945]).

The Story of the Three Little Pigs

In this classic English tale about the value of prudence, the three-fold repetition characteristic of European folk tales is especially functional. Repetition and the variation of the repeated elements differentiate the characters of the three pigs. These devices also indicate the third pigs' increasing danger and resourcefulness when he leaves his brick house in search of food. Although many versions do not include the second part of this tale, it marks an important shift in the conflict, from a battle of brawn, in which the wolf defeats the first two pigs, to a battle of wit, in which the third pig is triumphant. As in many European tales, a strong negative emotion—in this case, anger—precipitates the downfall of the villain; enraged by his failures and the taunting of the third pig, he foolishly announces his intention to climb down the chimney.

'Once upon a time when pigs spoke rhyme
And monkeys chewed tobacco,
And hens took snuff to make them tough,
And ducks went quack, quack, quack, O !'

There was an old sow with three little pigs, and as she had not enough to keep them, she sent them out to seek their fortune. The first that went off met a man with a bundle of straw, and said to him:

'Please, man, give me that straw to build me a house.'

Which the man did, and the little pig built a house with it. Presently came along a wolf, and knocked at the door, and said:

'Little pig, little pig, let me come in.'

To which the pig answered:

'No, no, by the hair of my chiny chin chin.'

The wolf then answered to that:

'Then I'll huff, and I'll puff, and I'll blow your house in.'

So he huffed, and he puffed, and he blew his house in, and ate up the little pig.

The second little pig met a man with a bundle of furze, and said:

'Please, man, give me that furze to build a house.'

Which the man did, and the pig built his house. Then along came the wolf, and said:

' Little pig, little pig, let me come in.'

'No, no, by the hair of my chiny chin chin.'

'Then I'll puff, and I'll huff, and I'll blow your house in.'

So he huffed, and he puffed, and he puffed, and he huffed, and at last he blew the house down, and he ate up the little pig.

The third little pig met a man with a load of bricks, and said:

'Please, man, give me those bricks to build a house with.'

So the man gave him the bricks, and he built his house with them. So the wolf came, as he did to the other little pigs, and said:

'Little pig, little pig, let me come in.'

From Leslie L. Brook, *The Golden Goose Book*. (London: Frederick Warne, 1976). Originally published in 1904.

'No, no, by the hair of my chiny chin chin.'

'Then I'll huff, and I'll puff, and I'll blow your house in.'

Well, he huffed, and he puffed, and he huffed and he puffed, and he puffed and huffed; but he could *not* get the house down. When be found that he could not, with all his huffing and puffing, blow the house down, he said:

'Little pig, I know where there is a nice field of turnips.'

'Where?' said the little pig.

'Oh, in Mr. Smith's Home-field, and if you will be ready to-morrow morning I will call for you, and we will go together, and get some for dinner.'

'Very well,' said the little pig, 'I will be ready. What time do you mean to go?'

'Oh, at six o'clock.'

Well, the little pig got up at five, and got the turnips before the wolf came (which he did about six) and who said:

'Little pig, are you ready?'

The little pig said: 'Ready! I have been and come again, and got a nice potful for dinner.'

The wolf felt very angry at this, but thought that he would be up to the little pig somehow or other, so he said:

'Little pig, I know where there is a nice apple-tree.'

'Where?' said the pig.

'Down at Merry-garden,' replied the wolf, 'and if you will not deceive me I will come for you, at five o'clock to-morrow and get some apples.'

Well, the little pig bustled up the next morning at four o'clock, and went off for the apples, hoping to get back before the wolf came; but he had further to go, and had to climb the tree, so that just as he was coming down from it, he saw the wolf coming, which, as you may suppose, frightened him very much. When the wolf came up he said:

'Little pig, what! are you here before me? Are they nice apples?'

'Yes, very,' said the little pig. 'I will throw you down one.'

And he threw it so far, that, while the wolf was gone to pick it up, the little pig jumped down and ran home. The next day the wolf came again, and said to the little pig:

'Little pig, there is a fair at Shanklin this afternoon, will you go?'

'Oh yes,' said the pig, 'I will go; what time shall you be ready?'

'At three,' said the wolf. So the little pig went off before the time as usual, and got to the fair, and bought a butter-churn, which he was going home with, when he saw the wolf coming. Then he could not tell what to do. So he got into the churn to hide, and by so doing turned it round, and it rolled down the hill with the pig in it, which frightened the wolf so much, that he ran home without going to the fair. He went to the little pig's house, and told him how frightened he had been by a great round thing which came down the hill past him. Then the little pig said:

'Hah, I frightened you, then. I had been to the fair and bought a butter-churn, and when I saw you, I got into it, and rolled down the hill.'

Then the wolf was very angry indeed, and declared he would eat up the little pig, and that he would get down the chimney after him. When the little pig saw what he was about, he hung on the pot full of water, and made up a blazing fire, and, just as the wolf was coming down, took off the cover, and in fell the wolf; so the little pig put on the cover again in an instant, boiled him up, and ate him for supper, and lived happy ever afterwards.

From *English Folk and Fairy Tales*, by Joseph Jacobs (New York: Putnam's, n.d.)

The Story of the Three Bears

This English folk tale became famous after the poet Robert Southey included it in an anonymous collection of essays in 1837. In Southey's version, an old woman enters the house of three bears, but researchers have found other versions in which the intruder is a fox. It makes little difference whether the tale began with a fox or an old woman, or whether these versions developed independently, however, because later generations irrevocably altered the central character. In 1849, Joseph Cundall published the first version in which the intruder was a young girl, Silver-Hair. An 1858 collection changed her name to Silverlocks, and one published in 1904 gave her the name by which she has been known in all subsequent versions, Goldilocks. One other detail has also changed: Southey's Bears were males; beginning in 1878, many retellers made the Bears into a nuclear family of father, mother, and baby. In one sense, this story supports English notions of property rights. When Goldilocks enters without permission and uses the goods collected by the Bears, she violates their rights to have property suitable to their needs and to possess that property in safety. In other words, as Flora Annie Steele makes clear in her version, and many later versions do not, Goldilocks is a villain who lacks all sense of propriety and who puts her personal desires ahead of the rights of the Bears, who are model citizens.

Once upon a time there were three Bears, who lived together in a house of their own, in a wood. One of them was a Little Wee Bear, and one was a Middle-sized Bear, and the other was a Great Big Bear. They had each a bowl for their porridge; a little bowl for the Little Wee Bear; and a middle-sized bowl for the Middle-sized Bear; and a great bowl for the Great Big Bear. And they had each a chair to sit in; a little chair for the Little Wee Bear; and a middle-sized chair for the Middle-sized Bear; and a great chair for the Great Big Bear. And they had each a bed to sleep in; a little bed for the Little Wee Bear; and a middle-sized bed for the Middle-sized Bear; and a great bed for the Great Big Bear.

One day, after they had made the porridge for their breakfast, and poured it into their porridge-bowls, they walked out into the wood while the porridge was cooling, that they might not burn their mouths by beginning too soon, for they were polite, well-brought-up Bears. And while they were away a little girl called Goldilocks, who lived at the other side of the wood and had been sent on an errand by her mother, passed by the house, and looked in at the window. And then she peeped in at the keyhole, for she was not at all a well-brought-up little girl. Then seeing nobody in the house she lifted the latch. The door was not fastened, because the Bears were good Bears, who did nobody any harm, and never suspected that anybody would harm them. So Goldilocks opened the door and went in; and well pleased was she when she saw the porridge on the table. If she had been a well-brought-up little girl she would have waited till the Bears came home, and then, perhaps, they would have asked her to breakfast; for they were good Bears—a little rough or so, as the manner of Bears is, but for all that very good-natured and hospitable. But she was an impudent, rude little girl, and so she set about helping herself.

First she tasted the porridge of the Great Big Bear, and that was too hot for her. Next she tasted the porridge of the Middle-sized Bear, but that was too cold for her. And then she went to the porridge of the Little Wee Bear, and tasted it, and that was neither too hot nor too cold, but just right, and she liked it so well, that she ate it all up, every bit!

Then Goldilocks, who was tired, for she had been catching butterflies instead of running on her errand, sate down in the chair of the Great Big Bear, but that was too hard for her. And then she sate down in the chair of the Middle-sized Bear, and that was too soft for her. But when she sate down in the chair of the Little Wee Bear, that was neither too hard, nor too soft, but just right. So she seated herself in it, and. there she sate till the bottom of the chair came out, and down she came, plump upon the ground; and that made her very cross, for she was a bad-tempered little girl.

Now, being determined to rest, Goldilocks went upstairs into the bedchamber in which the three Bears slept. And first she lay down upon the bed of the Great Big Bear, but that was too high at the head for her. And next she lay down upon the bed of the Middle-sized Bear, and that was too high at the foot for her. And then she lay down upon the bed of the Little Wee Bear, and that was neither too high at the head, nor at the foot, but just right. So she covered herself up comfortably, and lay there till she fell fast asleep.

" SOMEBODY HAS BEEN LYING IN MY BED, — AND HERE SHE IS ! "

Flora Annie Steel, *English Fairy Tales*. Illustrated by Arthur Rackham. (New York: Macmillan, 1950), 23.

By this time the Three Bears thought their porridge would be cool enough for them to eat it properly; so they came home to breakfast. Now careless Goldilocks had left the spoon of the great Big Bear standing in his porridge.

'SOMEBODY HAS BEEN AT MY PORRIDGE!' said the Great Big Bear in his great, rough, gruff voice.

Then the Middle-sized Bear looked at his porridge and saw the spoon was standing in it too.

'SOMEBODY HAS BEEN AT MY PORRIDGE!' said the Middle-sized Bear in his middle-sized voice.

Then the Little Wee Bear looked at his, and there was the spoon in the porridge-bowl, but the porridge was all gone!

'SOMEBODY HAS BEEN AT MY PORRIDGE, AND HAS EATEN IT ALL UP!' said the Little Wee Bear in his little wee voice.

Upon this the Three Bears, seeing that some one had entered their house, and eaten up the Little Wee Bear's breakfast, began to look about them. Now the careless Goldilocks had not put the hard cushion straight when she rose from the chair of the Great Big Bear.

'SOMEBODY HAS BEEN SITTING IN MY CHAIR!' said the Great Big Bear in his great, rough, gruff voice.

And the careless Goldilocks had squatted down the soft cushion of the Middle-sized Bear.

'SOMEBODY HAS BEEN SITTING IN MY CHAIR!' said the Middle-sized Bear in his middle-sized voice.

'SOMEBODY HAS BEEN SITTING IN MY CHAIR, AND HAS SAT THE BOTTOM RIGHT THROUGH!' said the Little Wee Bear in his little wee voice.

Then the Three Bears thought they had better make further search in case it was a burglar, so they went upstairs into their bedchamber. Now Goldilocks had pulled the pillow of the Great Big Bear out of its place.

'SOMEBODY HAS BEEN LYING IN MY BED!' said the Great Big Bear in his great, rough, gruff voice.

And Goldilocks had pulled the bolster of the Middle-sized Bear out of its place.

'SOMEBODY HAS BEEN LYING IN MY BED!' said the Middle-sized Bear in his middle-sized voice.

But when the Little Wee Bear came to look at his bed, there was the bolster in its place! And the pillow was in its place upon the bolster! And upon the pillow—?

There was Goldilocks' yellow head—which was its place, for she had no business there.

'SOMEBODY HAS BEEN LYING IN MY BED,—AND HERE SHE IS STILL!' said the Little Wee Bear in his little wee voice.

Now Goldilocks had heard in her sleep the great, rough, gruff voice of the Great Big Bear; but she was so fast asleep that it was no more to her than the roaring of wind, or the rumbling of thunder. And she had heard the middle-sized voice of the Middle-sized Bear, but it was only as if she had heard some one speaking in a dream. But when she heard the little wee voice of the Little Wee Bear, it was so sharp; and so shrill, that it awakened her at once. Up she started, and when she saw the Three Bears on one side of the bed, she tumbled herself out at the other, and ran to the window. Now the window was open, because the Bears, like good, tidy Bears, as they were, always opened their bedchamber window when they got up in the morning. So naughty, frightened little Goldilocks jumped; and whether she broke her neck in the fall, or ran into the wood and was lost there, or found her way out of the wood and got whipped for being a bad girl and playing truant no one can say. But the Three Bears never saw anything more of her.

From *English Fairy Tales*, by Flora Annie Steel (London: Macmillan, 1918).

The Elephant and the Giraffe

Although this Nigerian tale demonstrates that considerable physical effort is necessary to wrest a productive farm from the jungle, Hare, a traditional African trickster figure, enjoys the fruits of a plentiful harvest merely by employing his wits. As in 'The Deer and the Jaguar Share a House', the audience's superior knowledge of the situation creates humour and makes Hare's victims look even more foolish. In fact, the entire tale depends upon Hare's careful control of knowledge: he misleads the elephant and the giraffe about his role in developing their farm, and he brings them together only because he knows that they are ignorant of each other's physical identity and he can, therefore, manipulate their reactions when they encounter each other.

Once the hare suggested to the elephant that they should farm together. Said he 'You go and clear the trees, while I burn off the area.' So the elephant went off and cleared the trees.

Then the hare went along to the giraffe and suggested that they should farm together. Said he 'You go and burn off the area, for I've cleared the trees.' So both the elephant and the giraffe were ignorant of the truth.

When enough rain had fallen for sowing, up comes the hare and says to the elephant 'You go and sow. I'll do the hoeing.' And again the hare went also to the giraffe and said 'I'll sow—you go off and hoe. And I'll do the reaping.' When the giraffe had hoed and the corn was ripe, then he went to the elephant and said to her 'Hey, elephant, you go and reap! I'll cut the heads off and collect them.'

Then he went and said to the giraffe 'I've done the reaping. You go and cut the heads off and collect them!' Next he went and said to the elephant 'Well, elephant, I've collected the heads. Tomorrow let's go and tie them in bundles!' and he added 'But there's something called a giraffe keeps coming and taking our corn away.' And the elephant answered 'What! Is a giraffe something to worry about? Off you go! Just let tomorrow come!'

And the hare went back to the giraffe and said to him 'Hey, giraffe, there's something called an elephant keeps coming and taking away our corn.' And the giraffe answered 'What! Is an elephant something to worry about? Just let tomorrow come!'

The giraffe made the earlier start, and went to the farm where the corn was collected. He stopped, waiting for the elephant. Then he asked the hare 'Where's the elephant you said would come to take away our corn?' And the hare answered 'Just wait a bit! You'll be seeing her.'

After a while the elephant appeared, and the hare said to the giraffe 'There you are—there! There's the elephant coming.' Says the giraffe 'Where? Somewhere by that hill?' and the hare answered 'Oh no! That's not a hill! That's the elephant.' And the giraffe said 'No, hare! I'm no match for that.' And the hare replied 'In that case, you lie down here, but keep your neck sticking out.' And the giraffe lay down, leaving his neck sticking out.

Up comes the elephant. Says she to the hare 'Hey, hare, where's the giraffe you said would be coming to take away all our corn?' And the hare answered 'Oh, he's been here since this morning and he was waiting for you, but you never came. His wee guitar (*molo*) is there on the ground. He's gone off for a bathe.' Then said the elephant 'Oh, hare! I'm no match for something big enough to handle that guitar.' And the hare said 'OK. If you're no match for him, run away, elephant!' And she ran off eastwards.

Then said the hare 'Righto, giraffe—get up and run, before the elephant comes back and finds you!' And the giraffe went running off westwards. So the corn fell to the lot of the hare, for his sole enjoyment. Then the hare stowed the corn away in his burrow and settled peacefully down. That's all.

From *Hausa Tales and Traditions*, Vol. I, by Frank Edgar, trans. Neil Skinner (London: Frank Cass, 1969).

The Story of a Dam

This trickster tale from South Africa puts Jackal in the role that Br'er Rabbit and his relatives play in North American trickster stories. Lazy and selfish, Jackal ignores the rules of cooperation and community that are especially important in times of drought, which are occasions for conflict in many African tales. He is certainly no model citizen, but he shows that wit is a powerful tool for survival. Although Tortoise does fool him and capture him, Jackal ultimately triumphs. Understanding the weaknesses and intellectual limitations of his opponents, he escapes every trap and, thus, is able to continue to flout the laws that govern the rest of the community.

There was a great drought in the land; and Lion called together a number of animals so that they might devise a plan for retaining water when the rains fell.

The animals which attended at Lion's summons were Baboon, Leopard, Hyena, Jackal, Hare, and Mountain Tortoise.

It was agreed that they should scratch a large hole in some suitable place to hold water; and the next day they all began to work, with the exception of Jackal, who continually hovered about in that locality, and was overheard to mutter that he was not going to scratch his nails off in making water holes.

When the dam was finished the rains fell, and it was soon filled with water, to the great delight of those who had worked so hard at it. The first one, however, to come and drink there, was Jackal, who not only drank, but filled his clay pot with water, and then proceeded to swim in the rest of the water, making it as muddy and dirty as he could.

This was brought to the knowledge of Lion, who was very angry and ordered Baboon to guard the water the next day, armed with a huge knobkirrie. Baboon was concealed in a bush close to the water; but Jackal soon became aware of his presence there, and guessed its cause. Knowing the fondness of baboons for honey, Jackal at once hit upon a plan, and marching to and fro, every now and then dipped his fingers into his clay pot, and licked them with an expression of intense relish, saying, in a low voice to himself, 'I don't want any of their dirty water when I have a pot full of delicious honey.' This was too much for poor Baboon, whose mouth began to water. He soon began to beg Jackal to give him a little honey, as he had been watching for several hours, and was very hungry and tired.

After taking no notice of Baboon at first, Jackal looked round, and said, in a patronizing manner, that he pitied such an unfortunate creature, and would give him some honey on certain conditions, viz., that Baboon should give up his knobkirrie and allow himself to be bound by Jackal. He foolishly agreed; and was soon tied in such a manner that he could not move hand or foot.

Jackal now proceeded to drink of the water, to fill his pot, and to swim in the sight of Baboon, from time to time telling him what a foolish fellow he had been to be so easily duped, and that he (Jackal) had no honey or anything else to give him, excepting a good blow on the head every now and then with his own knobkirrie.

The animals soon appeared and found poor Baboon in this sorry plight, looking the picture of misery. Lion was so exasperated that he caused Baboon to be severely punished, and to be denounced as a fool.

Tortoise hereupon stepped forward, and offered his services for the capture of Jackal. It was at first thought that he was merely joking; but when he explained in what manner he proposed to catch him, his plan was considered so feasible that his offer was accepted. He proposed that a thick coating of 'bijenwerk' (a kind of sticky black substance found on bee-hives) should be spread all over him, and that he should then go and stand at the entrance of the dam, on the water level, so that Jackal might tread upon him and stick fast. This was accordingly done and Tortoise posted there.

The next day, when Jackal came, he approached the water very cautiously, and wondered to find no one there. He then ventured to the entrance of the water, and remarked how kind they had been in placing there a large black stepping-stone for him. As soon, however, as he trod upon the supposed stone, he stuck fast, and saw that he had been tricked; for Tortoise now put his head out and began to move. Jackal's hind feet being still free he threatened to smash Tortoise with them if he did not let him go. Tortoise merely answered, 'Do as you like.' Jackal thereupon made a violent jump, and found, with horror, that his hind feet were now also fast. 'Tortoise,' said he, 'I have still my mouth and teeth left, and will eat you alive if you do not let me go.' 'Do as you like,' Tortoise again replied. Jackal, in his endeavours to free himself, at last made a desperate bite at Tortoise, and found himself fixed, both head and feet. Tortoise, feeling proud of his successful capture, now marched quietly up to the top of the bank with Jackal on his back, so that he could easily be seen by the animals as they came to the water.

They were indeed astonished to find how cleverly the crafty Jackal had been caught; and Tortoise was much praised, while the unhappy Baboon was again reminded of his misconduct when set to guard the water.

Jackal was at once condemned to death by Lion; and Hyena was to execute the sentence. Jackal pleaded hard for mercy, but finding this useless, he made a last request to Lion (always, as he said, so fair and just in his dealings) that he should not have to suffer a lingering death.

Lion inquired of him in what manner he wished to die; and he asked that his tail might be shaved and rubbed with a little fat, and that Hyena might then swing him round twice and dash his brains out upon a stone. This, being considered sufficiently fair by Lion, was ordered by him to be carried out in his presence.

When Jackal's tail had been shaved and greased, Hyena caught hold of him with great force, and before he had fairly lifted him from the ground, the cunning Jackal had slipped away from Hyena's grasp, and was running for his life, pursued by all the animals.

Lion was the foremost pursuer, and after a great chase Jackal got under an overhanging precipice, and, standing on his hind legs with his shoulders pressed against the rock, called loudly to Lion to help him, as the rock was falling, and would crush them both. Lion put his shoulders to the rock, and exerted himself to the utmost. After some little time Jackal proposed that he should creep slowly out, and fetch a large pole to prop up the rock, so that Lion could get out and save his life. Jackal did creep out, and left Lion there to starve and die.

From *South-African Folktales*, by James A. Honeÿ (New York: Baker and Taylor, 1910).

The Deer and the Jaguar Share a House

This *pourquoi* tale from one of the indigenous tribes of Brazil explains why the jaguar and the deer do not live together. Much of its humour depends on the fact that the audience of listeners has more information about events than either of the central characters. Therefore listeners can laugh at the foolish hubris each displays when he believes that the god Tupan has specially blessed him. Although the deer seems to have a greater understanding of things than the jaguar because he uses his wit to teach the jaguar a lesson about the morality of eating, both characters are equally victims of their own ignorance and fear.

One day a deer was wandering along a riverbank, and he said: 'I have led a hard life, wandering here and there, never having a house of my own. I would like to have a house, and where would I ever find a better place than here? This is where I will build.' And he went away.

A jaguar also said one day: 'My life is full of trouble and cares. I shall look for a place to build a house, and I shall settle down comfortably.' He went out to find a place, and he came to the same spot that the deer had chosen. When he saw it he exclaimed, 'Wherever would I find a better spot for a house than this? Here is where I will live.' And he went away, making plans to return.

The deer came back the following day to begin work on his house. It was great labour, but he cleared the ground of brush and trees and made it smooth and clean. Then he left, to return when he could.

The next day the jaguar came to begin work on his house, and he saw that the ground had already been cleared. 'Ah!' he said. 'The God Tupan is helping me with my work! What good fortune!' So he went to work on the floor of the house, and when the floor was finished it was nearly night and the jaguar went away.

The following morning the deer came and saw the floor completed. He said, 'Ah, the God Tupan is helping me build my house! What good luck!' And he built the walls of the house and returned to the forest.

The next day the jaguar came again and saw the walls finished. 'Thank you, Tupan!' he said, and he put on the roof. Then he went back to the forest.

When the deer came back, he found the roof was finished. He said, 'Thank you, Tupan, for all your help!' And in gratitude to the God Tupan, the deer made two rooms in the house, one for Tupan and one for himself. Then he entered one of the rooms and went to sleep.

That night the jaguar came once more. He went into the empty room to sleep, thinking he was sharing the house with Tupan, who had helped him build.

In the morning the deer and the jaguar got up at the same time. The jaguar asked in surprise, 'Is it you who helped me build?'

The deer said, 'Yes, is it you who helped me build?'

The jaguar said, 'Yes. Since we have built this house together, let us share it.'

The deer agreed, and they lived together, one in one room, the other in the other room.

One day the jaguar said, 'I am going out hunting. I will bring food, so get everything ready, the pots, the water, and the wood for a fire.'

He went out in the forest, while the deer prepared for the cooking. The jaguar killed a deer in the forest and brought it back. When the deer who was sharing the house saw what the food was, he became very sad. The jaguar cooked the food, but the deer wouldn't eat. After the jaguar had had his supper, they went to bed. But the deer was thinking with horror about the jaguar's diet, and he couldn't sleep. He feared that the jaguar would come in the night and eat him also.

In the morning the deer said to the jaguar, 'Get the pots and the water and the wood ready. I am going hunting.'

He went out in the forest and he saw another jaguar there sharpening his claws on the bark of a tree. The deer went on until he found an anteater, known as tamandua. He said to the tamandua, 'The jaguar over there has been saying evil things about you.'

When the tamandua heard this he became angry. He went to where the jaguar was and, creeping up silently behind him, seized him and killed him. Then he went away.

The deer took the carcass of the jaguar and carried it home. The pots and the water and the wood were ready. But when the jaguar with whom he was living saw what the deer had brought, he lost his appetite. Though the deer cooked the food, the jaguar couldn't eat a thing.

That night, neither the deer nor the jaguar could sleep. The jaguar feared that the deer might come for jaguar meat, and the deer feared that the jaguar would come for deer meat. They lay silently awake as the hours passed. When it was very late, they began to nod. In spite of his nervousness, the jaguar's eyes began to close a little. And so did the deer's. Suddenly the deer's eyes closed completely for a moment, and his head nodded. As he nodded, his antlers hit the wall with a loud noise.

When the jaguar heard the noise he awoke in fright, thinking the deer was coming after him, and he screamed. When the deer heard the scream he was terrified, thinking the jaguar was coming to get him. Both animals leaped to their feet and fled from the house into the forest, one going in one direction and one in another.

And since that time, the jaguar and the deer have never lived together.

From *Ride with the Sun II: An Anthology of Folk Tales and Stories from the United Nations*, compiled by the United Nations Women's Guild (New York: UNWG, 2004).

Gayardaree the Platypus

This aboriginal *pourquoi* tale accounts for the origin of Australia's most unusual mammal, the duck-billed platypus. Its action begins with one of the most universally popular devices for generating conflict in a tale, the ignoring of a warning. Too independent to heed her tribe's warnings of danger—expressions of traditional, communal wisdom—the duck who likes to swim alone eventually suffers a miserable and lonely death. Before her demise, however, she finds herself, first, like Hans Christian Andersen's Thumbelina, the object of an unwanted suitor's attentions, and, second, as in Andersen's 'The Ugly Duckling', the mother of offspring so different that there is no place for them in the tribe.

A young duck used to swim away by herself in the creek. Her tribe told her that Mulloka, the water devil, would catch her some day if she were so venturesome. But she did not heed them.

One day after having swum down some distance, she landed on a bank where she saw some young green grass. She was feeding about when suddenly out rushed from a hidden place Biggoon, an immense water rat, and seized her.

She struggled and struggled, but all in vain. 'I live alone,' he said; 'I want a wife.'

'Let me go,' said the duck; 'I am not for you; my tribe have a mate for me.'

'You stay quietly with me, and I will not hurt you. I am lonely here. If you struggle more, or try to escape, I will knock you on the head, or spear you with this little spear I always carry.'

'But my tribe will come and fight you, and perhaps kill me.'

'Not they. They will think Mulloka has got you. But even if they do come, let them. I am ready.' And again he showed his spear.

The duck stayed. She was frightened to go while the rat watched her. She pretended that she liked her new life, and meant to stay always; while all the time she was thinking how she could escape. She knew her tribe came to look for her, for she heard them, but Biggoon kept her imprisoned in his hole in the side of the creek all day, only letting her out for a swim at night, when he knew her tribe would not come for fear of Mulloka.

She hid her feelings so well that at last Biggoon thought she really was content with him, and gradually he gave up watching her, taking his long day sleep as of old. Then came her chance.

One day, when Biggoon was sound asleep, she slunk out of the burrow, slid into the creek, and swam away up it, as quickly as she could, towards her old camp.

Suddenly she heard a sound behind her; she thought it must be Biggoon, or perhaps the dreaded Mulloka, so, stiff as her wings were, she raised herself on them, and flew the rest of the way, alighting at length very tired amongst her tribe.

They all gabbled round her at once, hardly giving her time to answer them. When they heard where she had been, the old mother ducks warned all the younger ones only to swim up stream in the future, for Biggoon would surely have vowed vengeance against them all now, and they must not risk meeting him.

How that little duck enjoyed her liberty and being with her tribe again! How she splashed as she pleased in the creek in the daytime and flew about at night if she wished! She felt as if she never wanted to sleep again.

It was not long before the laying season came. The ducks all chose their nesting places, some in hollow trees, and some in mirrieh-bushes. When the nests were all nicely lined with down feathers, the ducks laid their eggs. Then they sat patiently on them, until at last the little fluffy, downy ducks came out. Then in a little time the ducks in the trees took the ducklings on their backs and in their bills, and flew into the water with them, one at a time. Those in the mirrieh-bushes waddled out with their young ones after them.

In due course the duck who had been imprisoned by Biggoon hatched out her young, too. Her friends came swimming round the mirrieh-bush she was in, and said: 'Come along. Bring out your young ones, too. Teach them to love the water as we do.'

Out she came, only two children after her. And what were they? Such a quacking gabble her friends set up, shrieking: 'What are those?'

'My children,' she said proudly. She would not show that she, too, was puzzled at her children being quite different from those of her tribe. Instead of down feathers they had a soft fur. Instead of two feet they had four. Their bills were those of ducks, and their feet were webbed, and on the hind ones were just showing the points of a spear, like Biggoon always carried to be in readiness for his enemies.

'Take them away,' cried the ducks, flapping their wings and making a great splash. 'Take them away. They are more like Biggoon than us. Look at their hind feet; the tip of his spear is sticking from them already. Take them away, or we shall kill them before they grow big and kill us. They do not belong to our tribe. Take them away. They have no right here.'

And such a row they made that the poor little mother duck went off with her two little despised children, of whom she had been so proud, despite their peculiarities. She did not know where to go. If she went down the creek, Biggoon might catch her again, and make her live in the burrow, or kill her children because they had webbed feet, a duck's bill, and had been hatched out of eggs. He would say they did not belong to his tribe. No one would own them. There would never be anyone but herself to care for them; the sooner she took them right away the better.

So thinking, away up stream she went until she reached the mountains. There she could hide from all who knew her, and bring up her children. On, on she went, until the creek grew narrow and scrubby on its banks, so changed from the broad streams which used to placidly flow between large unbroken plains, that she scarcely knew it. She lived there for a little while, then pined away and died, for even her children as they grew saw how different they were from her, and kept away by themselves, until she felt too lonely and miserable to live, too unhappy to find food. Thus pining she soon died away on the mountains, far from her old noorumbah, or hereditary hunting-ground.

The children lived on and throve, laid eggs and hatched out more children just like themselves, until at last, pair by pair, they so increased that all the mountain creeks had before long some of them. And there they still live, the Gayardaree, or platypus, quite a tribe apart—for when did ever a rat lay eggs? Or a duck have four feet?

From *Australian Legendary Tales*, by Mrs K. Langloh Parker (London: The Bodley Head, 1978).

The Elephant's Child

'The Elephant's Child' is one of a series of humourous literary *pourquoi* myths that Rudyard Kipling offered readers in his *Just So Stories for Little Children* (1902). In this tale about an essential childhood trait, curiosity, Kipling mocks adult incompetence and frustrations. His plot also spoofs quest tale conventions: the young hero undertakes a perilous journey toward knowledge of what the Crocodile has for dinner; he encounters a pompous helper, the Bi-Coloured-Python- Rock-Snake; he has a nearly fatal confrontation with the Crocodile, who is both a trickster and the guardian of the knowledge that is quest object; and he emerges with a boon for his community, knowledge of how to transform a simple nose into a useful appendage. Perhaps the greatest delight in this tale of 'nosiness' is, however, the ironic reversal of status and power that occurs when the transformed Elephant's Child returns from his quest.

*O*n the High and Far-Off Times the Elephant, O Best Beloved, had no trunk. He had only a blackish, bulgy nose, as big as a boot, that he could wriggle about from side to side; but he couldn't pick up things with it. But there was one Elephant—a new Elephant—an Elephant's Child—who was full of 'satiable curtiosity, and that means he asked ever so many questions. *And* he lived in Africa, and he filled all Africa with his 'satiable curtiosities. He asked his tall aunt, the Ostrich, why her tail-feathers grew just so, and his tall aunt the Ostrich spanked him with her hard, hard claw. He asked his tall uncle, the Giraffe, what made his skin spotty, and his tall uncle, the Giraffe, spanked him with his hard, hard hoof. And still he was full of 'satiable curtiosity! He asked his broad aunt, the Hippopotamus, why her eyes were red, and his broad aunt, the Hippopotamus, spanked him with her broad, broad hoof; and he asked his hairy uncle, the Baboon, why melons tasted just so, and his hairy uncle, the Baboon, spanked him with his hairy, hairy paw. And *still* he was full of 'satiable curtiosity. He asked questions about everything that he saw, or heard, or felt, or smelt, or touched, and all his uncles and his aunts spanked him. And still he was full of 'satiable curtiosity!

One fine morning in the middle of the Precession of the Equinoxes this 'satiable Elephant's Child asked a new fine question that he had never asked before. He asked, 'What does the Crocodile have for dinner?' Then everybody said, 'Hush!' in a loud and dretful tone, and they spanked him immediately and directly, without stopping, for a long time.

By and by, when that was finished, he came upon Kolokolo Bird sitting in the middle of a wait-a-bit thorn-bush, and he said, 'My father has spanked me, and my mother has spanked me; all my aunts and uncles have spanked me for my 'satiable curtiosity; and *still* I want to know what the Crocodile has for dinner!'

Then Kolokolo Bird said, with a mournful cry, 'Go to the banks of the great grey-green, greasy Limpopo River, all set about with fever-trees, and find out.'

That very next morning, when there was nothing left of the Equinoxes, because the Precession had preceded according to precedent, this 'satiable Elephant's Child took a hundred pounds of bananas (the little short red kind), and a hundred pounds of sugar-cane (the long purple kind), and seventeen melons (the greeny-crackly kind), and said to all his dear families, 'Goodbye. I am going to the great grey-green, greasy Limpopo River, all set about with fever-trees, to find out what the Crocodile has for dinner.' And they all spanked him once more for luck; though he asked them most politely to stop.

Then he went away, a little warm, but not at all astonished, eating melons, and throwing the rind about, because he could not pick it up.

He went from Graham's Town to Kimberley, and from Kimberley to Khama's Country, and from Khama's Country he went east by north, eating melons all the time, till at last he came to the banks of the great grey-green, greasy Limpopo River, all set about with fever-trees, precisely as Kolokolo Bird had said.

Now you must know and understand, O Best Beloved, that till that very week, and day, and hour, and minute, this 'satiable Elephant's Child had never seen a Crocodile, and did not know what one was like. It was all his 'satiable curtiosity.

The first thing that he found was a Bi-Coloured-Python-Rock-Snake curled round a rock.

''Scuse me,' said the Elephant's Child most politely, 'but have you seen such a thing as a Crocodile in these promiscuous parts?'

'*Have* I seen a Crocodile?' said the Bi-Coloured-Python-Rock-Snake, in a voice of dretful scorn. 'What will you ask me next?'

''Scuse me,' said the Elephant's Child, 'but could you kindly tell me what he has for dinner?'

Then the Bi-Coloured-Python-Rock Snake uncoiled himself very quickly from the rock, and spanked the Elephant's Child with his scalesome, flailsome tail.

'That is odd,' said the Elephant's Child, 'because my father and my mother, and my uncle and my aunt, not to mention my other aunt, the Hippopotamus, and my other uncle, the Baboon, have all spanked me for my 'satiable curtiosity—and I suppose this is the same thing.'

So he said good-bye very politely to the Bi-Coloured-Python-Rock-Snake, and helped to coil him up on the rock again, and went on, a little warm, but not at all astonished, eating melons, and throwing the rind about, because he could not pick it up, till he trod on what he thought was a log of wood at the very edge of the great grey-green, greasy Limpopo River, all set about with fever-trees.

But it was really the Crocodile, O Best Beloved, and the Crocodile winked one eye—like this!

' 'Scuse me,' said the Elephant's Child most politely, 'but do you happen to have seen a Crocodile in these promiscuous parts?'

Then the Crocodile winked the other eye, and lifted half his tail out of the mud; and the Elephant's Child stepped back most politely, because he did not wish to be spanked again.

'Come hither, Little One,' said the Crocodile. 'Why do you ask such things?'

' 'Scuse me,' said the Elephant's Child most politely, 'but my father has spanked me, my mother has spanked me, not to mention my tall aunt, the Ostrich, and my tall uncle, the Giraffe, who can kick ever so hard, as well as my broad aunt, the Hippopotamus, and my hairy uncle, the Baboon, *and* including the Bi-Coloured-Python-Rock-Snake, with the scalesome, flailsome tail, just up the bank, who spanks harder than any of them; and so, if it's quite all the same to you, I don't want to be spanked any more.'

'Come hither, Little One,' said the Crocodile, 'for I am the Crocodile,' and he wept crocodile-tears to show it was quite true.

Then the Elephant's Child grew all breathless, and panted, and kneeled down on the bank and said, 'You are the very person I have been looking for all these long days. Will you please tell me what you have for dinner?'

'Come hither, Little One,' said the Crocodile, 'and I'll whisper.'

Then the Elephant's Child put his head down close to the Crocodile's musky, tusky mouth, and the Crocodile caught him by his little nose, which up to that very week, day, hour, and minute, had been no bigger than a boot, though much more useful.

'I think,' said the Crocodile—and he said it between his teeth, like this—'I think to-day I will begin with Elephant's Child!'

At this, O Best Beloved, the Elephant's Child was much annoyed, and he said, speaking through his nose, like this, 'Led go! You are hurtig be!'

Then the Bi-Coloured-Python-Rock-Snake scuffled down from the bank and said, 'My young friend, if you do not now, immediately and instantly, pull as hard as ever you can, it is my opinion that your acquaintance in the large-pattern leather ulster' (and by this he meant the Crocodile) 'will jerk you into yonder limpid stream before you can say Jack Robinson.'

This is the way Bi-Coloured-Python-RockSnakes always talk.

Then the Elephant's Child sat back on his little haunches, and pulled, and pulled, and pulled, and his nose began to stretch. And the Crocodile floundered into the water, making it all creamy with great sweeps of his tail, and he pulled, and pulled, and pulled.

And the Elephant's Child's nose kept on stretching; and the Elephant's Child spread all his little four legs and pulled, and pulled, and pulled, and his nose kept on stretching; and the Crocodile threshed his tail like an oar, and *he* pulled, and pulled, and pulled, and at each pull the Elephant's Child's nose grew longer and longer—and it hurt him hijjus!

From Rudyard Kipling, 'The Elephant's Child', *Just So Stories for Little Children*. (New York: Charles Scribner's Sons, 1913), 77.

Then the Elephant's Child felt his legs slipping, and he said through his nose, which was now nearly five feet long, 'This is too butch for be!'

Then the Bi-Coloured-Python-Rock-Snake came down from the bank, and knotted himself in the double-clove-hitch round the Elephant's Child's hind-legs, and said, 'Rash and inexperienced traveller, we will now seriously devote ourselves to a little high tension, because if we do not, it is my impression that yonder self-propelling man-of-war with the armour-plated upper deck' (and by this, O Best Beloved, he meant the Crocodile) 'will permanently vitiate your future career.'

That is the way all Bi-Coloured-Python-Rock-Snakes always talk.

So he pulled, and the Elephant's Child pulled, and the Crocodile pulled; but the Elephant's Child and the Bi-Coloured-Python-Rock-Snake pulled hardest; and at last the Crocodile let go of the Elephant's Child's nose with a plop that you could hear all up and down the Limpopo.

Then the Elephant's Child sat down most hard and sudden; but first he was careful to say 'Thank you' to the Bi-Coloured-Python-Rock-Snake; and next he was kind to his poor pulled nose, and wrapped it all up in cool banana leaves, and hung it in the great grey-green, greasy Limpopo to cool.

'What are you doing that for?' said the Bi-Coloured-Python-Rock-Snake.

''Scuse me,' said the Elephant's Child, 'but my nose is badly out of shape, and I am waiting for it to shrink.'

'Then you will have to wait a long time,' said the Bi-Coloured-Python-Rock-Snake. 'Some people do not know what is good for them.'

The Elephant's Child sat there for three days waiting for his nose to shrink. But it never grew any shorter, and, besides, it made him squint. For, O Best Beloved, you will see and understand that the Crocodile had pulled it out into a really truly trunk same as all Elephants have to-day.

At the end of the third day a fly came and stung him on the shoulder, and before he knew what he was doing he lifted up his trunk and hit that fly dead with the end of it.

''Vantage number one!' said the Bi-Coloured-Python-Rock-Snake. 'You couldn't have done that with a mere-smear nose. Try and eat a little now.'

Before he thought what he was doing the Elephant's Child put out his trunk and plucked a large bundle of grass, dusted it clean against his fore-legs, and stuffed it into his own mouth.

''Vantage number two!' said the Bi-Coloured-Python-Rock-Snake. 'You couldn't have done that with a mere-smear nose. Don't you think the sun is very hot here?'

'It is,' said the Elephant's Child, and before he thought what he was doing he schlooped up a schloop of mud from the banks of the great grey-green, greasy Limpopo, and slapped it on his head, where it made a cool schloopy-sloshy mud-cap all trickly behind his ears.

''Vantage number three!' said the Bi-Coloured-Python-Rock-Snake. 'You couldn't have done that with a mere-smear nose. Now how do you feel about being spanked again?'

''Scuse me,' said the Elephant's Child, 'but I should not like it at all.'

'How would you like to spank somebody?' said the Bi-Coloured-Python-Rock-Snake.

'I should like it very much indeed,' said the Elephant's Child.

'Well,' said the Bi-Coloured-Python-Rock-Snake, 'you will find that new nose of yours very useful to spank people with.'

'Thank you,' said the Elephant's Child. 'I'll remember that; and now I think I'll go home to all my dear families and try.'

So the Elephant's Child went home across Africa frisking and whisking his trunk. When he wanted fruit to eat he pulled fruit down from a tree, instead of waiting for it to fall as he used to do. When he wanted grass he plucked grass up from the ground, instead of going on his knees as he used to do. When the flies bit him he broke off the branch of a tree and used it as a fly-whisk; and he made himself a new, cool, slushy-squshy mud-cap whenever the sun was hot. When he felt lonely walking through Africa he sang to himself down his trunk, and the noise was louder than several brass bands. He went specially out of his way to find a broad Hippopotamus (she was no relation of his), and he spanked her very hard, to make sure that the Bi-Coloured-Python-Rock-Snake had spoken the truth about his new trunk. The rest of the time he picked up the melon-rinds that he had dropped on his way to the Limpopo—for he was a Tidy Pachyderm.

One dark evening he came back to all his dear families, and he coiled up his trunk and said, 'How do you do?' They were very glad to see him, and immediately said, 'Come here and be spanked for your 'satiable curtiosity.'

'Pooh!' said the Elephant's Child. 'I don't think you peoples know anything about spanking; but I do, and I'll show you.'

Then he uncurled his trunk and knocked two of his dear brothers head over heels.

'O Bananas!' said they, 'where did you learn that trick, and what have you done to your nose?'

'I got a new one from the Crocodile on the banks of the great grey-green, greasy Limpopo River,' said the Elephant's Child. 'I asked him what he had for dinner, and he gave me this to keep.'

'It looks very ugly,' said his hairy uncle, the Baboon.

'It does,' said the Elephant's Child. 'But it's very useful,' and he picked up his hairy uncle, the Baboon, by one hairy leg, and hove him into a hornets' nest.

Then that bad Elephant's Child spanked all his dear families for a long time, till they were very warm and greatly astonished. He pulled out his tall Ostrich aunt's tail-feathers; and he caught his tall uncle, the Giraffe, by the hind leg, and dragged him through a thorn-bush; and he shouted at his broad aunt, the Hippopotamus, and blew bubbles into her ear when she was sleeping in the water after meals; but he never let anyone touch Kolokolo Bird.

At last things grew so exciting that his dear families went off one by one in a hurry to the banks of the great grey-green, greasy Limpopo River, all set about with fever-trees, to borrow new noses from the Crocodile. When they came back nobody spanked anybody any more; and ever since that day, O Best Beloved, all the Elephants you will ever see, besides all those that you won't, have trunks precisely like the trunk of the 'satiable Elephant's Child.

From *Just So Stories for Little Children*, by Rudyard Kipling (London and Basingstoke: Macmillan, 1902).

The Revenge of the Three Deer-Boys

This myth from the Mataco people of Argentina offers a common explanation for the origin of particular stars in the sky: people or, in this case, animals ascended from Earth and became those stars. The arrow-ladder the deer use to climb to the sky is a common motif in stories from indigenous groups in both North and South America. As in many of these tales, the connection between the earth beings and the stars that they become is tenuous. Until the ending, which quickly notes the transformation of the deer-children into the constellation Gemini, the myth is actually a trickster revenge tale. The emphasis is on the character and wit of the eldest deer-child, who is either very artistic or possessed of magical powers because he makes dead jaguars resemble roasted boars. As the trickster hero, the eldest deer-child plays on the gullibility of the jaguar, whose own inept trickery is limited to explanations that the eldest deer-child immediately recognizes as lies.

A deer who had three sons went out to gather honey, leaving the boys at home. He did not return in the afternoon, and the boys waited for him until late at night. The youngest cried all night, and the second youngest could not sleep because he was thinking of his father, who still did not come.

The oldest boy went out to search everywhere, in all the houses. Finally he came to the jaguar's house where in a net bag he saw a deer head and recognized it as that of his father from the pattern painted on the face. The boy said nothing but stayed close to the jaguar, who said he had been out hunting wild boar and that was the kind of meat he had caught. The boy knew the jaguar was lying because of the painted face. The jaguar added that the deer had also been hunting wild boar and had driven several of them into large hollow trees with the help of his dogs. Probably the boy's father had not gone home because he could not drag all the meat with him.

The boy went home and told his brothers that their father would never return again; he had been killed by the jaguar and his head was lying in the jaguar's bag. The little brothers cried, but the older one told them not to grieve; perhaps they could do the jaguar some harm in revenge for killing their father.

The jaguar had two small children himself, and the deer-children set about making friends with them. The jaguar-children began to trust the deer-boys, and after ten days they all went far away together. Two leagues away they reached a swamp where small, thin trees called *simbolar* were growing. There they killed a frog with an arrow, and then many frogs. The deer-children did not eat the frogs, but the jaguar-children did.

The deer-boys then suggested that the young jaguars go into the *simbolar* forest; they themselves would set fire to it, and a lot of frogs would come jumping toward the swamp where they could easily be caught. When the fire got too close to the jaguars they were to run to a certain place where the deer-boys would not light a fire. When the jaguars agreed to the plan, the deer-boys set fire to a large pile of dry wood, the frogs jumped, and the jaguar-children killed them with sticks, filling their bags with the dead frogs. When the fire approached them they turned to the place supposed to be a way out, but the young deer had completely encircled the jaguars with fire, and the two cubs burned to death.

The deer-boys took the paws of the young jaguars and changed them into those of a wild boar and squeezed their noses into the shape of wild boar snouts so that they looked like two roasted boars. The deer-boys went to the jaguar and said: 'Grandfather, your children have killed a lot of wild boars which they are now roasting in the forest; they probably won't come back until four or five days from now.' Then they went out to the swamp again, picked up the two transformed wild boars, and carried them to the house of the jaguar. The oldest said: 'Grandfather, here are two wild boars for you; we roasted them but we don't dare to eat them because our father died recently.' The jaguar was very happy to get so much meat. The next morning the jaguar prepared his food, boiling the spines in a pot and roasting the hearts. The deer-boys watched him eating asado together with the fat from the pot. They whispered to one another: 'Look, the jaguar is eating the hearts of his own sons, dipped in their own fat.'

Then the oldest deer-boy shot an arrow up into the sky so that it stuck up there, and the next one shot, hitting the end of the first arrow, and the third one shot, hitting that arrow in turn. Thus they continued until the arrows reached all the way down to the earth. The oldest deer-boy told the next-oldest to stay by the arrow ladder and not to go away. Meanwhile he would go over to the jaguar, and when the younger brothers heard him shout the older of the two was to put his arm around his little brother and climb up the ladder of arrows. He would follow them up the ladder.

The oldest boy cut a bunch of paloverde branches, sharpened each of them at one end, and planted the other end in the ground so as to surround the arrow ladder with pointed sticks. Then he went toward the jaguar, calling: 'Grandfather, you are eating the hearts of your sons dipped in their own fat; it seems they were fat and tasty!' Furiously the jaguar jumped up and overturned the pot, threw the meat into the fire, spat out the hearts, and shouted: 'You son of a whore!' He ran after the deer-boy.

The two small boys hurried up the ladder. The oldest deer-boy was not afraid for he knew he could run faster than the jaguar. When he reached the arrows he climbed up, with the jaguar in hot pursuit. He did not hurry, and the jaguar was about to catch up with him. When the jaguar was just above the paloverde sticks, the deer-boy loosened the arrow below him so that the jaguar fell down on the pointed sticks. One of them plunged into his rump and came out through his mouth. The jaguar died.

The deer-boys did not go back down the ladder but continued to climb up. When they reached the sky they attached themselves firmly to it and became the constellation Gemini, *tsonales*, a small star next to a larger one. Well behind the smaller one is a big red star. Gemini reaches its zenith at midnight in June, disappears in the evening on December 30, is completely gone on December 31, and can be seen in the morning on January 1.

Nobody paid any attention to the jaguar; the meat rotted, and the wind howled when blowing through the skin.

———

From *Folk Literature of the Mataco Indians*, edited by Johannes Wilbert and Karin Simoneau (Los Angeles: UCLA Latin American Center Publications, 1982).

LINKS TO OTHER STORIES

Further Readings

Selected Critical Studies

Bacchilega, Cristina. 1997. *Postmodern Fairy Tales: Gender and Narrative Strategies*. Philadelphia: University of Pennsylvania Press.

Bernheimer, Kate, ed. 1998. *Mirror, Mirror on the Wall: Women Writers Explore Their Favorite Fairy Tales*. New York: Anchor.

Bettelheim, Bruno. 1976. 'Cinderella', *The Uses of Enchantment: The Meaning and Importance of Fairy Tales*, pp. 236–77. New York: Alfred A. Knopf.

Blount, Margaret. 1977. *Animal Land: The Creatures of Children's Fiction*. New York: Avon.

Bottigheimer, Ruth B. 1987. *Grimms' Bad Girls and Bold Boys: The Moral and Social Vision of the Tales*. New Haven, CT: Yale University Press.

———. 2002. *Fairy Godfather: Straparola, Venice, and the Fairy Tale Tradition*. Philadelphia: University of Pennsylvania Press.

———, ed. 1986. *Fairy Tales and Society: Illusion, Allusion, and Paradigm*. Philadelphia: University of Pennsylvania Press.

Briggs, K.M. 1967. *The Fairies in Tradition and Literature*. London: Routledge & Kegan Paul.

Brombert, Victor, ed. 1969. *The Hero in Literature*. New York: Fawcett.

Campbell, Joseph. 1968. *The Hero with a Thousand Faces*. Princeton, NJ: Princeton University Press.

Canepa, Nancy L. 1999. *From Court to Forest: Giambattista Basile's Lo cunto de li cunti and the Birth of the Literary Fairy Tale*. Detroit: Wayne State University Press.

———, ed. 1997. *Out of the Woods: The Origins of the Literary Fairy Tale in Italy and France*. Detroit: Wayne State University Press.

Cook, Elizabeth. 1972. *The Ordinary and the Fabulous: An Introduction to Myths, Legends and Fairy Tales*, 2nd ed. Cambridge and New York: Cambridge University Press.

Darnton, Robert. 1984. *The Great Cat Massacre and Other Episodes in French Cultural History*. New York: Basic Books.

Dégh, Linda. 1969. *Folktales and Society: Storytelling in a Hungarian Peasant Community*. Trans. Emily M. Schlossberg. Bloomington: Indiana University Press.

Downing, Christine. 1981. *The Goddess: Mythological Images of the Feminine*. New York: Crossroad.

Dundes, Alan, ed. 1962. *The Study of Folklore*. Englewood Cliffs, NJ: Prentice-Hall.

———, ed. 1982. *Cinderella: A Folklore Casebook*. New York and London: Garland.

———, ed. 1989. *Little Red Riding Hood: A Casebook*. Madison, WI: University of Wisconsin Press.

Eliade, Mircea. 1963. *Myth and Reality*. Trans. Willard R. Trask. New York: Harper and Row.

Ellis, John M. 1983. *One Fairy Story Too Many: The Brothers Grimm and Their Tales*. Chicago and London: University of Chicago Press.

Franz, Marie-Louise von. [1972] 1993. *The Problem of the Feminine in Fairy Tales*. Rev. ed. Boston: Shambhala.

———. 1996. *The Interpretation of Fairy Tales*. Rev. ed. Boston: Shambhala.

———. 1997. *Archetypal Patterns in Fairy Tales. Studies in Jungian Psychology by Jungian Analysts*. Toronto: Inner City Books.

Fromm, Erich. 1951. *The Forgotten Language: An Introduction to the Understanding of Dreams, Fairy Tales, and Myths*. New York: Grove Press.

Gose, Elliott B. 1985. *The World of the Irish Wonder Tale: An Introduction to the Study of Fairy Tales*. Toronto: University of Toronto Press.

Griswold, Jerry. 2004. *The Meanings of* Beauty and the Beast: *A Handbook*. Peterborough, ON: Broadview.

Haase, Donald, ed. 1993. *The Reception of Grimms' Fairy Tales: Responses, Reactions, Revisions*. Detroit: Wayne State University Press.

Hannon, Patricia. 1998. *Fabulous Identities: Women's Fairy Tales in Seventeenth-Century France*. Amsterdam and Atlanta, GA: Rodopi.

Harries, Elizabeth Wanning. 2001. *Twice Upon a Time: Women Writers and the History of the Fairy Tale*. Princeton, NJ: Princeton University Press.

Hearne, Betsy. 1989. *Beauty and the Beast: Visions and Revisions of an Old Tale*. Chicago: University of Chicago Press.

Heuscher, Julius Ernst. 1974. *A Psychiatric Study of Myths and Fairy Tales: Their Origin, Meaning, and Usefulness*. 2nd ed. Springfield, IL: Thomas.

Jones, Steven Swann. 1995. *The Fairy Tale: The Magic Mirror of Imagination*. New York: Twayne.

Jurich, Marilyn. 1998. *Scheherazade's Sisters: Trickster Heroines and Their Stories in World Literature*. Contributions in Women's Studies. Westport, CT: Greenwood.

Kamenetsky, Christa. 1992. *The Brothers Grimm and Their Critics: Folktales and the Quest for Meaning*. Athens: Ohio University Press.

Kirk, G.S. 1970. *Myth: Its Meaning and Functions in Ancient and Other Cultures*. Cambridge: Cambridge University Press; Berkeley: University of California Press.

———. 1974. *The Nature of the Greek Myths*. Harmondsworth: Penguin Books.

Knoepflmacher, U.C. 1998. *Ventures into Childhood: Victorians, Fairy Tales, and Femininity*. Chicago: University of Chicago Press.

Kolbenschlag, Madonna. 1979. *Kiss Sleeping Beauty Good-by: Breaking the Spell of Feminine Myths and Models*. New York: Doubleday.

Lane, Marcia. 1994. *Picturing the Rose: A Way of Looking at Fairy Tales*. New York: H.W. Wilson.

Lüthi, Max. 1976. *Once Upon a Time: On the Nature of Fairy Tales*. Trans. Lee Chadeayne and Paul Gottwald. Bloomington: Indiana University Press.

———. 1984. *The Fairy Tale as Art Form and Portrait of Man*. Trans. Jon Erickson. Bloomington: Indiana University Press.

MacDonald, Margaret Read, ed. 1999. *Traditional Storytelling Today: An International Sourcebook*. Chicago: Fitzroy Dearborn Publishers.

Mallet, Carl-Heinz. 1984. *Fairy Tales and Children: The Psychology of Children Revealed through Four Grimm's Fairy Tales*. New York: Schocken.

McGlathery, James M., ed. 1988. *The Brothers Grimm and Folktale*. Champaign: University of Illinois Press.

———. 1991. *Fairy Tale Romance: The Grimms, Basile, and Perrault*. Urbana: University of Illinois Press.

———. 1993. *Grimm's Fairy Tales: A History of Criticism on a Popular Classic*. Columbia, SC: Camden House.

Okpewho, Isidore. 1983. *Myth in Africa: A Study of its Aesthetic and Cultural Relevance*. Cambridge and New York: Cambridge University Press.

———. 1992. *African Oral Literature: Backgrounds, Character, and Continuity*. Bloomington: Indiana University Press.

Pelton, Robert D. 1980. *The Trickster in West Africa: A Study of Mythic Irony and Sacred Delight*. Berkeley, CA: University of California Press.

Propp, V. 1968. *Morphology of the Folktale*. Trans. Laurence Scott. 2nd ed. rev. and ed, with a preface by Louis A. Wagner. New introd. Alan Dundes. Austin: University of Texas Press.

Röhrich, Lutz. 1991. *Folktales and Reality*. Trans. Peter Tokofsky. Bloomington: Indiana University Press.

Schectman, Jacqueline. 1991. *The Stepmother in Fairy Tales: Bereavement and the Feminine Shadow*. Boston: Sigo Press.

Stott, Jon C. 1995. *Native Americans in Children's Literature*. Phoenix, AZ: Oryx.

Tatar, Maria. 1987. *The Hard Facts of the Grimms' Fairy Tales*. Princeton, NJ: Princeton University Press.

———. 1992. *Off with Their Heads! Fairy Tales and the Culture of Childhood*. Princeton, NJ: Princeton University Press.

Thompson, Joyce. 1989. *Inside the Wolf's Belly: Aspects of the Fairytale*. Sheffield, UK: Sheffield Academic Press.

Thompson, Stith. [1946] 1967. *The Folktale*. Berkeley: University of California Press.

Waelti-Walters, Jennifer R. 1982. *Fairy Tales and the Female Imagination*. Montreal and St Albans, VT: Eden Press.

Warner, Marina. 1995. *From the Beast to the Blonde: On Fairy Tales and Their Tellers*. London: Vintage.

Yolen, Jane. 1981. *Touch Magic: Fantasy, Faerie and Folklore in the Literature of Childhood*. New York: Philomel.

Zipes, Jack. 1988. *Fairy Tales and the Art of Subversion: The Classical Genre for Children and the Process of Civilization*. New York: Methuen.

———. 1988. *The Brothers Grimm: From Enchanted Forests to the Modern World*. New York: Routledge.

———. 1994. *Fairy Tale As Myth/Myth As Fairy Tale*. The Thomas D. Clark Lectures, 1993. Lexington: University Press of Kentucky.

———. 1999. *When Dreams Came True: Classical Fairy Tales and Their Tradition*. New York and London: Routledge.

———. 2002. *Breaking the Magic Spell: Radical Theories of Folk and Fairy Tales*. Rev. and expanded ed. Lexington: University Press of Kentucky.

———, ed. 1983. *The Trials and Tribulations of Little Red Riding Hood: Versions of the Tale in Sociocultural Context*. South Hadley, MA: Bergin and Garvey.

———, ed. 2000. *The Oxford Companion to Fairy Tales: The Western Fairy Tale Tradition from Medieval to Modern*. Oxford: Oxford University Press.

Selected Online Resources

http://www.usmenglish.com/fairytales/cinderella/cinderella.html. *The Cinderella Project*. Ed. Michael N. Salda. (Version 1.1, Dec 1997). De Grummond Children's Literature Research Collection, University of Southern Mississippi houses digital images and transcriptions of twelve versions of the Cinderella tale.

http://www.pitt.edu/~dash/folktexts.html. *Folklore and Mythology Electronic Texts*. Edited by D.L. Ashliman, this web site provides a large collection of e-texts, as well as links to other useful sites.

http://members.aol.com/pmichaels/glorantha/foolsparadise.html. *Fool's Paradise*. This web resource, edited by Peter Michaels, focuses on providing links to articles and bibliographies 'exploring the complex mythic/archetypal figure of Trickster'.

http://www.sacred-texts.com/index.htm. *The Internet Sacred Text Archive*. John B. Hare has amassed a huge collection of e-texts, including both translations of sacred texts from various cultures and articles about mythology and religion.

http://www.usmenglish.com/fairytales/jack/jackhome.html. *The Jack and the Beanstalk and Jack the Giant-Killer Project*. (Version 1.0, May 1997). De Grummond Children's Literature Research Collection, University of Southern Mississippi, is a detailed resource of digital images and transcriptions of nine versions of the Jack tale.

http://www.usmenglish.com/fairytales/lrrh/lrrhhome.htm. *The Little Red Riding Hood Project*. Ed. Michael N. Salda. (Version 1.0, Dec. 1995). De Grummond Children's Literature Research Collection, University of Southern Mississippi, in addition to its collections of the Cinderella and Jack tales, also provides images and transcriptions of sixteen versions of the Little Red Riding Hood tale.

http://www.surlalunefairytales.com. *SurLaLune Fairy Tale Pages*. Ed. Heidi Anne Heiner. The SurLaLune website is a detailed collection of annotated tales, e-texts, images, and author biographies.

Selected Folktale Collections

Abrahams, Roger. 1983. *African Folktales: Traditional Stories of the Black World*. New York: Pantheon.

Alegría, Ricardo E. 1969. *The Three Wishes: A Collection of Puerto Rican Folktales*. Trans. Elizabeth Culbert. Illus. Lorenzo Homar. New York: Harcourt, Brace & World.

Andrews, Jan. 2000. *Out of the Everywhere: Tales for a New World*. Illus Simon Ng. Toronto: Groundwood.

Bierhorst, John, ed. 1987. *Doctor Coyote: A Native American Aesop's Fables*. Illus.Wendy Watson. New York: Macmillan.

———. 1997. *The Dancing Fox: Arctic Folktales*. Illus. Mary K. Okheena. New York: William Morrow.

———. 2002. *Latin American Folktales: Stories from Hispanic and Indian Traditions*. New York: Pantheon.

Birch, Cyril. [1951] 2001. *Tales from China*. Rpt. of *Chinese Myths and Fantasies*. Oxford: Oxford University Press.

Belting, Natalia. 1965. *The Earth Is on a Fish's Back*. Illus. Esta Nesbitt. New York: Holt, Rinehart and Winston.

Berry, Jack. 1991. *West African Folktales*. Chicago: Northwestern University Press.

Bright, William. 1993. *The Coyote Reader*. Berkeley, CA: University of California Press.

Briggs, Katharine. 1977. *British Folktales*. New York: Pantheon.

Brooke, L. Leslie. 1976. *The Golden Goose Book*. New York: Frederick Warne.

Bryan, Ashley. 1998. *Ashley Bryan's African Tales, Uh-Huh*. New York: Atheneum Books for Young Readers.

Chai-Shin, Yu, Shiu L. Kong, and Ruth W. Yu. 1986. *Korean Folk Tales*. Illus. Bang Hai-ja. Toronto: Kensington Educational.

Cole, Joanna. 1982. *Best-Loved Folktales of the World*. Illus. Jill Karla Schwarz. Garden City, NY: Doubleday.

Courlander, Harold, and Wolf Leslau. 1950. *Fire on the Mountain and Other Ethiopian Stories*. New York: Henry Holt.

Crane, Thomas Frederick. [1885] 2001. *Italian Popular Tales*. Ed. Jack Zipes. Santa Barbara, CA: ABC-CLIO.

Creedon, Sharon. 1994. *Fair Is Fair: World Folktales of Justice*. Little Rock, AR: August House.

Daly, Ita. 2000. *Irish Myths and Legends*. Illus. Bee Willey. Oxford: Oxford University Press.

D'Aulaire, Ingri, and Edgar Parin D'Aulaire. 1962. *The D'Aulaires' Book of Greek Myths*. Illus. D'Aulaire and Parin D'Aulaire. Garden City, NY: Doubleday.

———. 1967. *Norse Gods and Giants*. Illus. D'Aulaire and Parin D'Aulaire. Garden City, NY: Doubleday.

Delacre, Lulu. 1996. *Golden Tales: Myths, Legends, and Folktales from Latin America*. Illus. Delacre. New York: Scholastic.

DeRoin, Nancy, ed. 1975. *Jataka Tales: Fables from the Buddha*. Boston: Houghton Mifflin.

Dorson, Richard M. 1975. *Folktales Told Around the World*. Chicago: University of Chicago Press.

Duncan, Barbara. 1998. *Living Stories of the Cherokee*. Chapel Hill, NC: University of North Carolina Press.

Elbl, Martin, and J.T. Winik. 1986. *Tales from the Amazon*. Illus. Gerda Neubacher. Burlington, ON: Hayes Publishing.

Ellis, Jean A. 1991. *From the Dreamtime: Australian Aboriginal Legends*. Victoria, Australia: Collins Dove.

Erdoes, Richard, and Alfonso Ortiz. 1998. *American Indian Trickster Tales*. New York: Viking.

Evetts-Seck, Josephine. 1997. *Father and Daughter Tales*. Illus. Helen Cann. Richmond Hill, ON: Scholastic Canada.

———. 1997. *Mother and Daughter Tales*. Illus. Helen Cann. Richmond Hill, ON: Scholastic Canada.

———. 1998. *Father and Son Tales*. Illus. Helen Cann. Richmond Hill, ON: Scholastic Canada.

———. 1998. *Mother and Son Tales*. Illus. Helen Cann. Richmond Hill, ON: Scholastic Canada.

Forest, Heather. 1996. *Wisdom Tales from Around the World*. Little Rock, AR: August House.

Gray, J.E.B. 2001. *Tales from India*. Selected from *Indian Tales and Legends*, [1961]. Oxford: Oxford University Press.

Greaves, Nick. 1988. *When Hippo Was Hairy and Other Tales from Africa*. Illus. Rod Clement. New York: Barron's.

Green, Roger Lancelyn. 1953. *King Arthur and His Knights of the Round Table*. Harmondsworth, England: Penguin Books.

Galdone, Paul. 1971. *Three Aesop Fox Fables*. New York: Seabury.

Gordon, Tulo. 1979. *Milbi: Aboriginal Tales from Queensland's Endeavour River*. Trans. John B. Haviland. Canberra: Australian National University Press.

Hadley, Eric, and Tessa Hadley. 1983. *Legends of the Sun and Moon*. Illus. Jan Nesbitt. Cambridge and New York: Cambridge University Press.

Haley, Gail E. 1992. *Mountain Jack Tales*. Illus. Haley. New York: Dutton.

Hamilton, Martha, and Mitch Weiss. 2000. *Noodlehead Stories: World Tales Kids Can Read & Tell*. Illus. Ariane Elsammak. Little Rock, AR: August House.

Hamilton, Virginia. 1985. *The People Could Fly: American Black Folktales*. Illus. Leo and Diane Dillon. New York: Knopf.

———. 1988. *In the Beginning: Creation Stories from Around the World*. Illus. Barry Moser. New York: Harcourt, Brace, Jovanovich.

———. 1990. *The Dark Way: Stories from the Spirit World*. Illus. Lambert Davis. San Diego: Harcourt Brace Jovanovich.

———. 1995. *Her Stories: African American Folktales, Fairy Tales, and True Tales*. Illus. Leo and Diane Dillon. New York: Blue Sky Press.

———. 1997. *A Ring of Tricksters: Animal Tales from America, the West Indies, and Africa*. Illus. Barry Moser. New York: Blue Sky Press.

Hazelton, Hugh, trans. 1996. *Jade and Iron: Latin American Tales from Two Cultures*. Illus. Luis Garay. Toronto: Groundwood.

Haviland, Virginia. 1985. *Favorite Fairy Tales Told Around the World*. Illus. S.D. Schindler. Boston and Toronto: Little, Brown.

Jasmin, Claude. 1987. *The Dragon and Other Laurentian Tales*. Trans. Patricia Sillers. Toronto: Oxford University Press.

Kanawa, Kiri Te. 1989. *Land of the Long White Cloud: Maori Myths, Tales and Legends*. Illus. Michael Foreman. London: Pavilion Books.

Kim So-un. 2004. *Korean Children's Favorite Stories*. Illus. Jeong Kyoung-Sim. Boston: Tuttle.

Kong, Shiu L., and Elizabeth K. Wong. 1985. *Fables and Legends from Ancient China*. Illus. Michele Nidenoof and Wong Ying. Toronto: Kensington Educational.

———. 1986. *The Magic Pears*. Illus. Wong Ying. Toronto: Kensington Educational.

Leipold, L.E. 1973. *Folk Tales of Arabia*. Illus. Howard E. Lindberg. Minneapolis, MN: T.S. Denison.

Lester, Julius. 1987. *The Tales of Uncle Remus: The Adventures of Brer Rabbit*. Illus. Jerry Pinkney. New York: Dial.

Liyi, Hi, trans. 1985. *The Spring of Butterflies and Other Folktales of China's Minority Peoples*. Ed. Neil Philip. Illus Pan Aiqing and Li Zhao. New York: Lothrop, Lee & Shepard.

Lottridge, Celia B. 1993. *Ten Small Tales*. Illus. Joanne Fitzgerald. Toronto: Douglas & McIntyre.

Lurie, Alison. 1980. *Clever Gretchen and Other Forgotten Folktales*. Illus. Margot Tomes. New York: Crowell.

Malcolmson, Anne, ed. 1947. *Song of Robin Hood*. Illlus. Virginia Lee Burton. Boston: Houghton Mifflin.

Martin, Eva. 1984. *Canadian Fairy Tales*. Illus. Laszlo Gal. Vancouver: Groundwood.

Mayer, Marianna. 1999. *Women Warriors: Myths and Legends of Heroic Women*. Illus. Julek Heller. New York: Morrow Junior Books.

McAlpine, Helen and William. 2002. *Tales from Japan*. Selected from *Japanese Tales and Legends* [1958]. Oxford: Oxford University Press.

McCaughrean, Geraldine. 1998. *The Bronze Cauldron: Myths and Legends of the World*. Illus. Bee Willey. New York: M.K. McElderry Books.

Minard, Rosemary, ed. 1975. *Womenfolk and Fairytales*. Illus. Suzanna Klein. Boston: Houghton Mifflin.

Orgel, Doris. 2000. *The Lion and the Mouse and Other Aesop's Fables*. Illus Bert Kitchen. New York: Dorling Kindersley.

Osborne, Mary Pope. 1991. *American Tall Tales*. Illus. Michael McCurdy. New York: Alfred A. Knopf.

Phelps, Ethel Johnston. 1981. *The Maid of the North: Feminist Folk Tales from Around the World*. Illus. Lloyd Bloom. New York: Holt, Rinehart, and Winston.

Pinkney, Jerry. 2000. *Aesop's Fables*. New York: SeaStar.

Ramanujan, A.K. 1991. *Folktales from India: A Selection of Oral Tales from Twenty-Two Languages*. New York: Pantheon.

Riordan, James. 2000. *Russian Folk-Tales*. Illus. Andrew Breakspeare. Oxford: Oxford University Press.

Rosen, Michael. 1992. *How the Animals Got Their Colors: Animal Myths from Around the World*. Illus. John Clementson. San Diego: Harocurt Brace Jovanovich.

Sakade, Florence, ed. 1953. *Japanese Children's Favorite Stories*. Illus. Yoshisuke Kurosaki. Rutland, VT: Tuttle.

Shephard, Esther. 1952. *Paul Bunyan*. Illus. Rockwell Kent. San Diego: Harcourt, Brace, Jovanovich.

Sherlock, Philip. 2000. *Tales from the West Indies*. [Rpt. of *West Indian Folk-tales*, 1966]. Oxford: Oxford University Press.

Sierra, Judy. 1992. *Cinderella*. The Oryx Multicultural Folktale Series. Illus. Joanne Caroselli. Phoenix, AZ: Oryx.

———. 2002. *Silly & Sillier: Read-Aloud Tales from Around the World*. Illus. Valeri Gorbachev. New York: Knopf.

Spretnak, Charlene. 1981. *Lost Goddesses of Early Greece: A Collection of Pre-Hellenic Myths*. Boston: Beacon Press.

Sun, Ruth Q. 1967. *Land of Seagull and Fox: Folk Tales of Vietnam*. Illus. Ho Thanh Duc. Rutland, VT: Charles Tuttle.

Taylor, C.J. 1993. *How We Saw the World: Nine Native Stories of the Way Things Began*. Montreal: Tundra.

Terada, Alice M. 1994. *The Magic Crocodile and Other Folktales from Indonesia*. Illus. Charlene K. Smoyer. Honolulu: University of Hawaii Press.

Thompson, Stith. 1968. *One Hundred Favorite Folktales*. Bloomington, IN: Indiana University Press.

Vathanaprida, Supaporn. 1994. *Thai Tales: Folktales of Thailand*. Ed. Margaret Read MacDonald. Illus. Boonsong Rohitasuke. Englewood, CO: Libraries Unlimited.

Walker, Paul Robert. 1997. *Little Folk: Stories from Around the World*. Illus. James Bernardin. San Diego: Harcourt Brace.

Yolen, Jane. 2003. *Mightier than the Sword: World Folktales for Strong Boys*. Illus. Raul Colón. San Diego: Harcourt Brace.

Yoshiko Uchida. 1965. *The Sea of Gold and Other Tales from Japan*. Illus. Marianne Yamaguchi. New York: Charles Scribner's Sons.

Zipes, Jack, ed. 1991. *Spells of Enchantment: The Wondrous Fairy Tales of Western Culture*. New York: Viking.

———, trans. 1989. *Beauties, Beasts, and Enchantment: Classic French Fairy Tales*. New York: New American Library.

———, trans and ed. 2001. *The Great Fairy Tale Tradition: From Straparola and Basile to the Brothers Grimm*. New York: W.W. Norton.

Selected Illustrated Editions of Single Tales

Part One: Cinderella and Her Cousins: A Tale and Its Variants

Brown, Marcia. 1954. *Cinderella: or The Little Glass Slipper*. New York: Charles Scribner's Sons.

Bruckner, Meredith. n.d. *Anklet for a Princess: A Cinderella Story from India*. Adapted from a story by Lila Mehta. Illus. Youshan Tan. Fremont, CA: Shen's Books. (Adaptation)

Climo, Shirley. 1989. *The Egyptian Cinderella*. Illus. Ruth Heller. New York: Thomas Y. Crowell.

———. 1993. *The Korean Cinderella*. Illus. Ruth Heller. New York: HarperCollins.

Cole, Babette. 1987. *Prince Cinders*. New York: Putnam Group, 1987. (Parody of 'Cinderella')

Hickox, Rebecca. 1998. *The Golden Sandal: A Middle Eastern Cinderella Story*. New York: Holiday House.

Johnston, Tony. 1998. *Bigfoot Cinderrrella*. Illus. James Warhola. New York: Putnam, 1998. (Parody)

Karlin, Barbara. 2001. *James Marshall's Cinderella*. Illus. James Marshall. New York: Dial Books for Young Readers.

Ketteman, Helen. 1997. *Bubba the Cowboy Prince: a Fractured Texas Tale*. Illus. James Warhola. New York: Scholastic. (Parody of 'Cinderella')

Martin, Rafe. 1992. *The Rough-Face Girl*. Illus. David Shannon New York: G.P. Putnam's Sons. (Variant of 'The Indian Cinderella')

———. 1993. *Dear As Salt*. Illus. Vladyana Krykorka. Richmond Hill, ON: Scholastic Canada. (Variant of 'Cap o' Rushes')

Mitchell, Marianne. 2002. *Joe Cinders*. Illus. Bryan Langdo. New York: Henry Holt. (Parody of 'Cinderella')

Winthrop, Elizabeth. 1991. *Vasilissa the Beautiful: A Russian Folktale*. Illus. Alexander Koshkin. New York: HarperCollins.

Part Two: Creating and Shaping the World: The Mythic Vision

Hodges, Margaret. 1973. *Persephone and the Springtime: A Greek Myth*. Illus. Arvis Stewart. Boston: Little, Brown. (Version of 'Demeter and Persephone')

McDermott, Beverly Brodsky. 1975. *Sedna: an Eskimo Myth*. New York: Viking.

McDermott, Gerald. 1984. *Daughter of Earth: A Roman Myth*. New York: Delacorte Press. (Version of 'Demeter and Persephone')

———. 1997. *The Voyage of Osiris: A Myth of Ancient Egypt*. New York: Windmill Books and E.P. Dutton.

———. 2003. *Creation*. New York: Dutton Children's Books. (Version of 'The Creation and the First Sin')

Proddow, Penelope, trans. 1972. *Demeter and Persephone*. Illus. Barbara Cooney. New York: Doubleday.

Toye, William. 1969. *How Summer Came to Canada*. Illus. Elizabeth Cleaver. Toronto: Oxford University Press.

———. 1979. *The Fire Stealer*. Illus. Elizabeth Cleaver. Toronto: Oxford University Press. (Version of 'How Nanabozho Brought Fire to His People')

Williams, Jay. 1979. *The Surprising Things Maui Did*. Illus. Charles Mikolaycak. New York: Four Winds Press. (Version of 'Maui: The Half-God')

Part Three: Larger Than Life: Tales of Heroes

Crossley-Holland, Kevin. 1982. *Beowulf*. Illus. Charles Keeping. Oxford: Oxford University Press.

Hutton, Warwick. 1993. *Perseus*. Illus. Warwick. New York: Margaret K. McElderry Books.

Kellogg, Steven. 1984. *Paul Bunyan*. New York: William Morrow.

Lester, Julius. 1994. *John Henry*. Illus. Jerry Pinkney. New York: Dial Books.

McCaughrean, Geraldine. 2002. *The Epic of Gilgamesh*. Illus. David Parkins. Grand Rapids, MI: Eerdmans Books for Young Readers.

Wisniewski, David. 1992. *Sundiata: Lion King of Mali*. New York: Clarion Books.

Zeman, Ludmila. 1995. *The Last Quest of Gilgamesh*. Montreal: Tundra.

Part Four: Unlikely Heroes: Triumph of the Underdog

Andersen, Hans Christian. 1980. *Thumbelina*. Illus. Lisbeth Zwerger. New York: William Morrow.

Beneduce, Ann Keay. 1999. *Jack and the Beanstalk*. Illus. Gennady Spirin. New York: Philomel.

Galdone, Paul. 1974. *The History of Mother Twaddle and the Marvelous Achievements of Her Son Jack*. New York: Seabury Press. (Adaptation of 'Jack and the Beanstalk')

Haley, Gail E. 1986. *Jack and the Bean Tree: A Mountain Tale*. Illus. Haley. New York: Crown.

Kellogg, Steven. 1991. *Jack and the Beanstalk*. New York: Morrow Junior Books. (Adaptation)

Muller, Robin. 1982. *Mollie Whuppie and the Giant*. Richmond Hill, ON: Firefly Books.

Nesbit. E. 1980. *The Last of the Dragons*. Illus. Peter Firmin. New York: McGraw-Hill.

Osborne, Mary Pope. 2000. *Kate and the Beanstalk*. Illus. Giselle Potter. New York: Atheneum Books for Young Readers. (Adaptation)

Pinkney, Brian. 2003. *Thumbelina*. New York: Greenwillow.

Ross, Tony. 1980. *Jack and the Beanstalk*. New York: Delacorte (Adaptation)

Shute, Linda. 1986. *Momotaro: The Peach Boy, A Traditional Japanese Tale*. New York: Lothrop, Lee & Shepard. (Version of 'The Adventures of Little Peachling')

Werth, Kurt, and Mabel Watts. 1973. *Molly and the Giant*. Illus. Kurt Werth. New York: Parents' Magazine Press. (Version of 'Molly Whuppie')

Part Five: Purposeful Journeys: Errands and Quests

Artell, Mike. 2001. *Petite Rouge: A Cajun Red Riding Hood*. New York: Penguin.

Barth, Edna. 1976. *Cupid and Psyche: A Love Story*. Illus. Ati Forberg. New York: Houghton Mifflin.

Craft, M. Charlotte. 1996. *Cupid and Psyche*. Illus. Kinuko Craft. New York: HarperCollins.

Dasent, Sir George Webbe, trans. 1988. *East o' the Sun and West o' the Moon*. Illus. Gillian Barlow. New York, Philomel.

Gal, Laszlo. 1993. *East of the Sun & West of the Moon*. Toronto: McClelland & Stewart.

Galdone, Paul. 1973. *The Three Billy Goats Gruff*. New York: Clarion.

Hodges, Margaret. 1989. *The Arrow and the Lamp: The Story of Psyche*. Illus. Donna Diamond. Boston: Little, Brown and Company. (Version of 'Cupid and Psyche')

———. 1990. *The Kitchen Knight: A Tale of King Arthur*. Illus. Trina Schart Hyman. New York: Holiday House. (Version of 'Of Sir Gareth Of Orkney')

Levert, Mireille. 1995. *Little Red Riding Hood*. Toronto: Groundwood. (Version of 'Little Red-Cap').

Marshall, James. 1987. *Red Riding Hood*. New York: Dial Books for Young Readers. (Version of 'Little Red-Cap')

San Souci, Robert T. 1978. *The Legend of Scarface: A Blackfeet Indian Tale*. Illus. Daniel San Souci. Garden City, NY: Doubleday.

———. 1987. *The Enchanted Tapestry: A Chinese Folktale*. Illus. Laszlo Gal. New York: Dial Books. (Version of 'The Wonderful Brocade')

Part Six: Loves Won and Lost: Tales of Courtship

Bodkin, Odds. 1998. *The Crane Wife*. Illus. Gennady Spirin. New York: Harcourt Brace.

Cooper, Susan. 1986. *The Selkie Girl*. Illus. Warwick Hutton. New York: Margaret K. McElderry Books. (Variant of 'The Goodman of Wastness and His Selkie Wife')

Craft, Mahlon F. 2002. *Sleeping Beauty*. Illus. Kinuko Y. Craft. New York: SeaStar.

Gay, Marie Louise. 1997. *Rumpelstiltskin*. Illus. Gay. Toronto: Groundwood.

Hamilton, Virginia. 2000. *The Girl Who Spun Gold*. Illus. Leo and Diane Dillon. New York: Blue Sky Press. (West Indies variant of 'Rumpelstiltskin')

Hyman, Trina Schart. 1977. *The Sleeping Beauty*. Boston: Little Brown and Company. (Adaptation of 'Little Briar-Rose')

Keller, Emily Snowell. 2003. *Sleeping Bunny*. Illus. Pamela Silin-Palmer. New York: Random House. (Adaptation of 'Little Briar-Rose')

Mayer, Marianna. 1978. *Beauty and the Beast*. Illus. Mercer Mayer New York: Four Winds Press.

Steptoe, John. 1987. *Mufaro's Beautiful Daughters: An African Tale*. New York: Lothrop, Lee, and Shepard. (Adaptation of 'The Story of Five Heads')

Yagawa, Sumik. 1981. *The Crane Wife*. Trans. Katherine Paterson. Illus. Suekichi Akaba. New York: William Morrow and Company.

Yolen, Jane. 1981. *Sleeping Ugly*. Illus Diane Stanley. New York: Coward, McCann & Geoghegan. (Parody of 'Little Briar-Rose')

Zelinsky, Paul O. 1986. *Rumpelstiltskin*. New York: E.P. Dutton.

Part Seven: It's All Relative: The Trials and Triumphs of Family Life

Crawford, Elizabeth D., trans. 1979. *Hansel and Gretel*. Illus. Lizbeth Zwerger. New York: William Morrow and Company.

Delessert, Etienne. 2001. *The Seven Dwarfs*. Mankato, MN: Creative Editions. (Adaptation of 'Snow White')

Forest, Heather. 1990. *The Woman Who Flummoxed the Fairies: An Old Tale from Scotland*. Illus. Susan Gaber. San Diego: Harcourt, Brace, Jovanovich.

French, Fiona. 1986. *Snow White in New York*. Oxford: Oxford University Press. (Adaptation)

Gág, Wanda. 1982. *The Six Swans*. Illus. Margot Tomes. New York: Coward, McCann & Geoghegan.

Heins, Paul, trans. 1974. *Snow White*. Illus. Trina Schart Hyman. Boston: Atlantic Monthly Press.

Pearson, Kit. 1990. *The Singing Basket*. Illus. Ann Blades. Toronto: Groundwood. (Adaptation of 'Jacques the Woodcutter')

Toye, William. 1977. *The Loon's Necklace*. Illus. Elizabeth Cleaver. Toronto: Oxford University Press, 1977. (Variant of 'The Blind Boy and the Loon')

Wallace, Ian. 1994. *Hansel and Gretel*. Illus. Wallace. Toronto: Groundwood.

Part Eight: Living by Wit: Tales of Tricksters

Aardema, Verna. 1991. *Borreguita and the Coyote: A Tale from Ayutla, Mexico*. Illus. Petra Mathers. New York: Alfred A. Knopf. (Variant of 'The Rabbit and the Coyote')

Byrd, Robert. 1999. *Finn MacCoul and His Fearless Wife: A Giant of a Tale from Ireland*. New York: Dutton Children's Books. (Version of 'A Legend of Knockmany')

dePaola, Tomie. 1981. *Fin M'Coul: The Giant of Knockmany Hill*. New York: Holiday House. (Adaptation of 'A Legend of Knockmany')

Goble, Paul. 1990. *Iktomi and the Ducks: A Plains Indian Story*. New York: Orchard Books. (Variant of 'Wisahketchahk and the Ducks')

Haley, Gail E. 1970. *A Story, A Story: An African Tale*. New York: Atheneum. (Adaptation of 'Anansi Earns the Sky-God's Stories')

Hamilton, Virginia. 2003. *Bruh Rabbit and the Tar Baby Girl*. Illus. James E. Ransome. New York: Blue Sky Press.

Hickok, Rebecca. 1997. *Zorro and Quwi: Tales of a Trickster Guinea Pig*. Illus. Kim Howard. New York: Doubleday. (Adaptation of 'The Mouse and the Fox')

Johnston, Tony. 1994. *The Tale of Rabbit and Coyote*. Illus. Tomie dePaola. New York: G.P. Putnam's Sons.

Mayer, Marianna. 1988. *Iduna and the Magic Apples*. Illus. Laszlo Gal. New York: Macmillan.

Part Nine: Wise and Foolish: Tales of Cleverness and Stupidity

Andersen, Hans Christian. 1949. *The Emperor's New Clothes*. Illus. Virginia Lee Burton. Boston: Houghton, Mifflin.

Compton, Patricia A. 1991. *The Terrible Eek: A Japanese Tale*. Illus. Sheila Hamanaka. New York: Simon and Schuster. (Version of 'The Tiger, the Persimmon, and the Rabbit's Tail')

Galdone, Paul. 1961. *The Three Wishes*. New York, Toronto, and London: Whittlesey House and McGraw-Hill.

———. 1976. *The Table, the Donkey and the Stick*. New York: McGraw-Hill. (Variant of 'The Gift of the Holy Man')

Jarrell, Randall, trans. 1980. *The Fisherman and His Wife: A Tale from the Brothers Grimm*. Illus. Margot Zemach. New York: Farrar, Straus, and Giroux.

McDermott, Gerald. 1990. *Tim O'Toole and the Wee Folk: An Irish Tale*. Illus. McDermott. New York: Viking. (Version of 'The Gift of the Holy Man')

———. 1994. *Coyote: A Trickster Tale from the American Southwest*. Illus. McDermott. San Diego: Harcourt, Brace, Jovanovich. (Adaptation of 'How Coyote Danced With the Blackbirds')

Park, Janie Jaehyun. 2002. *The Tiger and the Dried Persimmon: A Korean Folk Tale*. Toronto: Groundwood. (Version of 'The Tiger, the Persimmon, and the Rabbit's Tail')

Spray, Carole. 1981. *The Mare's Egg*. Illus. Kim LaFave. Camden East, ON: Camden House. (Version of 'Pedro Urdimale, the Little Fox, and the Mare's Egg')

Zemach, Margot. 1986. *The Three Wishes: An Old Story*. New York: Farrar, Straus, Giroux.

Part Ten: Nature Humanized: Animal Tales

Andersen, Hans Christian. 1986. *The Ugly Duckling*. Illus. Robert Van Nutt. New York: Alfred A. Knopf.

Cauley, Lorinda Bryan. 1981. *Goldilocks and the Three Bears*. New York: G.P. Putnam's Sons.

Galdone, Paul. 1968. *Henny Penny*. New York: Seabury.

————. 1969. *The Monkey and the Crocodile: A Jataka Tale From India.* New York: Clarion Books. (Version of 'The Crocodile and the Monkey's Heart')

Gay, Marie Louise. 1994. *The Three Little Pigs.* Toronto: Groundwood.

Ho, Minfong, and Saphan Ross. 1997. *Brother Rabbit: A Cambodian Tale.* Illus. Jennifer Hewitson. New York: Lothrop, Lee, and Shepard. (Version of 'The Crocodile and the Monkey's Heart')

Kellogg, Steven. 1997. *The Three Little Pigs.* New York: Morrow Junior Books. (Adaptation)

Kipling, Rudyard. 1983. *The Elephant's Child.* Illus. Lorinda Bryan Cauley. New York: Harcourt Brace Jovanovich.

Lowell, Susan. 2001. *Dusty Locks and the Three Bears.* Illus. Randy Cecil. New York: Henry Holt. (Adaptation)

Poole, Amy Lowry. 2000. *The Ant and the Grasshopper.* New York: Holiday House. (Adaptation)

Scieszka, Jon. 1989. *The True Story of the Three Little Pigs.* Illus. Lane Smith. New York: Viking Penguin. (Parody)

Stevens, Janet. 1984. *The Tortoise and the Hare: An Aesop Fable.* New York: Holiday House. (Adaptation)

Trivizas, Eugene. 1993. *The Three Little Wolves and the Big Bad Pig.* Illus. Helen Oxenbury. London: Heinemann. (Parody of 'The Story of the Three Little Pigs')

Turkle, Brinton. 1976. *Deep in the Forest.* New York: Dutton. (Adaptation of 'The Story of the Three Bears')

Youngquist, Cathrene Valente. 2002. *The Three Billygoats Gruff and Mean Calypso Joe.* Illus. Kristin Sorra. New York: Atheneum Books for Young Readers. (Adaptation)

Glossary

adaptation: a version of a tale altered in language or content to suit a the needs of a particular audience, as is the case with 'Of Sir Gareth of Orkney', which Sidney Lanier adapted for children from Thomas Malory's adult romance, *Le Morte D'Arthur*. Another kind of adaptation is the presentation of a work in a different artistic form, such as Peter Ilych Tchaikovsky's ballet *The Sleeping Beauty* or the Disney film *Beauty and the Beast*. See **version**.

animal helper: see **helper**.

animal tale: also known as the beast tale, it includes any tale in which animals are the central characters. In most instances, the animal protagonists have the power of speech, and they do not interact with humans, although humans may occasionally, as in 'The Story of the Three Bears', play significant roles. Examples of animal tales are Aesop's fables, the Jataka tale 'The Crocodile and the Monkey's Heart', the English folktale 'The Story of the Three Little Pigs', and the literary *pourquoi* tale 'The Elephant's Child'.

archetype: a character type, symbol, plot, or action that appears sufficiently frequently in literature to become recognizable. Carl Jung believed that archetypes were part of the unconscious minds of all human beings and that they were most often found in dreams and in such traditional forms of literature as myths and fairy tales.

beast tale: see **animal tale**.

cautionary tale: a narrative in which characters' actions and their results are designed to warn children about the consequences of improper or bad behavior. 'The Story of the Three Bears', for example, illustrates the consequences of invading private property.

circular journey: a journey in which characters return to their point of departure. As a result of their journeys, they usually have undergone character growth and experience a new relationship with the group from which they departed.

contextual symbol: see **symbol**.

conventional symbol: see **symbol**.

culture hero: a character, usually male, who is believed to have lived in the past and whose deeds influenced the history of his people. The majority of the sometimes almost superhuman hero's character traits embodied qualities most admired by the culture. 'Robin Hood Plays Butcher' and 'The Death of Beowulf' are narratives about two English culture heroes. Some Native American tricksters, such as Nanabozho, are also culture heroes.

cumulative tale: a tale in which the accumulation of elements is accompanied by an exact repetition of all previous additions to the tale. In 'Henny-Penny', for example, each time an animal joins Henny-Penny's errand, that name is added to a listing of all of the animals who have previously joined.

cycle: a set of tales or stories of the same tale type; that is, a group of stories related by similarities in character, plot, and motif. The Cinderella cycle, for example, includes tales about a persecuted protagonist, male or female, who either loses a position as a family member within the household or is forced to flee from that household.

diffusionist theory: the concept that languages, religions, stories, and other art forms originated in a very few locations and then spread to other areas.

epic: a long, serious narrative poem recounting the deeds of a hero whose actions reveal the characteristics most admired in the culture creating the poem. The central figure, sometimes said to have existed in a long ago historical period, influences the lives of his people. Epics are usually told in a very formal poetic style and contain a number of recognizable conventions. 'The Wanderings of Ulysses' is a prose adaptation of a section of the Greek epic *The Odyssey*.

fable: a brief and relatively simple narrative that focuses on a single situation or conflict in order to provide a concrete illustration of an abstract idea, which is usually called the moral. Most, although not all, fables use animal characters to illustrate lessons about human conduct.

fairy tale: a traditional narrative that includes wonders or magic. (Fairies do not appear in the majority of such tales.) Tales that may be classified as fairy tales are the folktales 'Cinderella' and 'Hänsel and Grethel', and the literary tales 'Beauty and the Beast' and 'Thumbelina'. See **literary fairy tale**.

feminist criticism: a field of literary criticism that examines the creation, production, and analysis of writing by and about females. Feminist critics consider such topics as the difference between female and male ways of experiencing, reading, and writing; the possibility that there may be plots, themes, character types, and symbols that are unique to works by women; the influence of culturally defined roles and attitudes on women's writing and on the reading and writing of works about women; and causes for the fact that certain works by women have been relatively unknown and ignored. See **sociological criticism**.

folklore: the body of traditional beliefs, customs, and narratives orally transmitted by a culture or by a predominantly unlettered segment of a literate culture (such as the peasants of Europe before the twentieth century). Among its narrative expressions are anecdotes, jokes, fables, legends, tales, songs, dramas, and myths.

folktale: a fictional narrative originating among and transmitted orally by the 'folk', or common people of a culture. Folktales are generally told for entertainment, but they may also express ideas or morals important to the culture. Varying widely in length, complexity, and subject matter, folktales include a variety of genres, from animal tales, such as 'The Three Billy-Goats Gruff', to fairy tales, such as 'The Sleeping Beauty in the Woods'. Characters in folktales may be ordinary people, as in 'Jacques the Woodcutter', talking animals, as in 'The Story of the Three Little Pigs', unusual or magical beings such as giants, as in 'Jack and the Beanstalk', or witches, as in 'Hänsel and Grethel', or any combination of these, as in 'Little Red-riding Hood', which includes ordinary human characters and a talking animal. The stories may be relatively serious, as is 'Snow White', or comical, as is 'The Elephant and the Giraffe'. When the action involves magic, enchantment, or wondrous events, the folktale is usually classified as a **fairy tale**.

frame story: a narrative that surrounds the main narrative of a story. Frequently frame stories indicate the characteristics of the tellers and the audiences, reasons for the telling, and the influence that hearing of the story has on the audience. Tales with frame stories include *Little Badger and the Fire Spirit*, 'Sedna', and 'The Myth of Osiris and Isis'.

Freudian criticism: a form of psychological criticism that is often called psychoanalytic criticism and that uses the theories of Sigmund Freud to reveal how the actions in literary works symbolically reveal the workings of the unconscious, particularly the interactions of the basic parts of the psyche, the id (the primitive, unorganized, passionate, and unconscious self), the ego (the organized, reasonable self), and the superego (the part of the ego that involves reflection, self-criticism, and the development of an autonomous relationship to the external social world). Freudian analysis of traditional tales often explores developmental issues, such as the Oedipus complex, in which the child is perceived as desiring to possess the parent of the opposite sex and to eliminate the parent of the same sex. See **psychological criticism**.

genre: a type, kind, or category of literature. Non-fiction, fiction, poetry, and drama are usually considered the main genres. Sub-genres deal with smaller groups of literary works that share specific conventions, including types of characters and events. Sub-genres include the fairy tale, the initiation story, the quest story, and the dragon-slayer story.

helper: a secondary character who assists the main character or characters reach their destinations and achieve their goals. Frequently old, helpers can be animals, human beings, or supernatural beings. Often, the main characters acquire objects, sometimes from the helper, that assist them in performing various deeds.

hero tale: a narrative about a character who uses strength, cleverness, and/or unselfishness to overcome formidable obstacles or adversaries. Usually the heroes' actions benefit other people; most particularly members of the same culture group, and their actions reveal virtues most admired by the culture. Many epics, romances, and sagas can be categorized as hero tales. Notable heroes include Robin Hood and King Arthur, in England; Krishna, in India; and Scarface, in Native North America. Within the specific cultures, each of these persons is believed to have actually existed in an earlier period of time.

irony: irony deals with discrepancy: between what is said and what is meant, between what characters and readers/listeners understand, and between what is expected and results that actually occur. Tricksters frequently create ironic situations or use language ironically to achieve their goals. Sometimes, the results are ironic, in that they are not what the tricksters expected.

Jungian criticism: a form of criticism based on the writings of Carl Jung, who posited that the psyche contained both a personal element and a universal element, known as the collective unconscious that contained archetypes, or primary symbols, whose meaning is independent of the individual's cultural context. As a form of psychological criticism, it often focuses on the development of the individual towards autonomous maturity, a state that Jung called individuation. As an approach that finds that the patterns and archetypes in stories develop meanings that are universal and independent of the cultural origins of the stories, it is generally classified as mythological or myth criticism. See **archetype, psychological criticism, myth criticism**.

legend: a tale or anecdote that is purported to be true although it may contain significant amounts of fiction. Folklorists speak of legends as being migratory because similar legends appear in various cultures; when a legend refers to specific geographical features or historical personages, it is called a localized legend if versions of it appear in other cultures or a local legend if it seems uniquely tied to a specific place. The narrative focus of legends is commonly the lives of saints, supernatural events, historical or semi-historical figures, such as Robin Hood, local geographical features, or specific historical events. The localized legend 'The Smith and the Fairies', for instance, refers to a particular man, a particular locale, and local beliefs about the habits of fairies.

leitmotif: a word, phrase, object, situation, or theme recurring within an individual tale, as do eating and food in 'The Story of the Three Little Pigs'. See **motif**.

linear journey: a journey that ends in a different location from the point of departure. Linear journeys often symbolize characters' leaving behind one type or phase of life and entering a new one.

literary fairy tale: a tale, such as 'Beauty and the Beast', that has been composed by an individual author whose identity is often known, that has been transmitted through print, and that employs character types, actions, settings, symbols, or motifs commonly found in fairy tales originating in the oral tradition. See **fairy tale**.

literary folktale: a tale, such as 'The Elephant's Child' that has been composed by an individual author whose identity is often known, that has been transmitted through print, and that employs character types, actions, settings, symbols, or motifs commonly found in folktales originating in the oral tradition. See **folktale**.

literary hero tale: a tale, such as 'The Crooked Tote Road', that has been composed by an individual author whose identity is often known, that has been transmitted through print, and that employs character types, settings, symbols, or motifs commonly found in folktales originating in the oral tradition. See **hero tale**.

literary myth: a narrative, such as *Little Badger and the Fire Spirit*, that has been composed by an individual author whose identity is often known, that has been transmitted through print, and that employs character types, settings, symbols, or motifs commonly found in myths originating in the oral tradition. See **myth**.

Marxist criticism: a form of sociological criticism inspired by the writings of Karl Marx, Friedrich Engels, and other theorists of socialism that seeks to display the ways in which texts support or challenge the dominant ideology, particularly as that ideology is expressed in politics, social relationships, and economic transactions, all of which are areas in which power relationships can lead to exploitation and repression of various groups or classes. See **sociological criticism**.

monogenesis: the theory that all traditional stories originated in one culture and spread from there, acquiring a variety of forms and contents in other cultures.

monomyth: a term used to designate a hypothetical single myth or mythic narrative structure that contains the basic elements found in all other myths.

moral: the lesson or principle of a tale, often overtly stated in fables but usually only implicit in folktales, fairy tales, and other forms of traditional literature.

motif: a narrative element—a character, object, setting, action, situation—that recurs in various traditional tales; the wicked stepmother, for example, is a character type motif, and the dark forest is a setting motif. See also **leitmotif**.

myth: a narrative about gods and/or demigods, the conditions of the world before the current natural or social order became fixed, and the relationships between human and supernatural beings. Myths are sacred narratives to the cultures telling them, embodying religious values and, in some cases, a history of the culture.

myth criticism: a category of criticism that focuses on the study of myths and the motifs and tale-types of traditional myths as these appear in modern, authored literature. Myth critics are frequently influenced by psychologist Carl Jung, who stated that myths embodied basic archetypes shared by all people. Myth criticism also focuses on the myths and hero tales of a specific culture to show how they reflect its social, moral, and spiritual values and beliefs.

mythology: the sequenced collection of the myths of a culture.

oral literature: see orature

orature: the narratives, poems, and dramas that exist in oral, rather than written, forms. Pre-literate cultures generally had an abundant and rich body of orature, which included their folktales, hero tales, legends, epics, and myths.

parody: a technique that uses, but exaggerates, deforms, or inverts, the easily recognized characteristics or conventions of types of literature or the prominent elements of a specific work. Although the effects of parody are usually humorous, writers may create parodies as a means of presenting their own themes. For example, E. Nesbit's 'The Last of the Dragons' parodies conventions of medieval stories in which a brave knight kills a dragon and rescues a helpless maiden. The story uses parodic techniques to develop a theme about stereotyping according to socially imposed labels.

polygenesis: the theory that traditional tales developed independently in different parts of the world and that any similarities among them result from physical, emotional, intellectual, and social characteristics possessed by all people.

pourquoi tale: a narrative, such as 'How the Tortoise Got His Shell' or 'The Deer and the Jaguar Share a House', that explains 'why' natural phenomena, animal attributes or habits, or social customs exist. Unlike etiological, or causal, myths, which are regarded as sacred and true accounts, most *pourquoi* tales, particularly those written in literate cultures, are not intended to be believed; in fact, their explanations are frequently comical.

psychoanalytic criticism: see **psychological criticism** and **Freudian criticism**.

psychological criticism: an approach that employs the theories of such notable psychological theorists as Sigmund Freud and Carl Jung, as well as the theories of their followers or critics, such as Jacques Lacan, to show how stories symbolically reveal the operation of psychic forces and, most particularly, the development of people into mature, autonomous individuals. See **Freudian criticism** and **Jungian criticism**.

quest: a journey undertaken to rescue a person or to retrieve a precious object; it involves perils that test and thereby reveal or develop the character of the quester.

romance: a tale of adventure, such as 'Of Sir Gareth of Orkney', in which the chief figures are knights, kings, and damsels in distress, and in which the action frequently is structured by a quest. The term *romance* is also sometimes loosely applied to tales that emphasize adventure, a love interest, and exotic settings, whether or not they involve the nobility present in the medieval romances of Europe.

saga: a long narrative about the adventures of heroes believed to have lived in the past. The term was originally applied to medieval Icelandic and Norse narratives.

scapegoat: an animal who suffers or is killed to atone for the failures or sins of others. People may project their inadequacies or wrong doings on a scapegoat. In folklore, the fool is frequently a scapegoat. Audiences of a tale may feel superior to that character, laughing at failures they may believe that they themselves possess.

sociological criticism: an approach that analyzes literature as either reflecting or being the product of social conditions, especially the power relationships between social groups or classes. The most notable forms of sociological criticism are **Marxist criticism** and **feminist criticism**.

stereotype: the simple, conventional representation, usually of a type, class, or race of people. Stereotypes include the happy plantation slave, Uncle Remus, or the foolish young man, Juan Bobo. The term is taken from a nineteenth-century printing process in which a plate of type could quickly produce identical pages.

stock characters: easily recognizable character types who, in different works, possess the same basic personality traits and behaviors. Two examples are the wicked stepmother and the evil nobleman.

structural criticism: an approach developed by Claude Levi Strauss that analyzes traditional tales, particularly myths, to show that they are based on a series of contrasts, or 'binary oppositions', such as male and female, life and death, and home and away; the meaning of the myth or tale depends on the way in which it resolves oppositions by privileging, or giving laudatory emphasis to, one term of each opposition.

symbol: a character, object, or action that stands for or suggests meanings beyond itself. Conventional symbols embody ideas or concepts recognized within a culture or group. Contextual symbols develop meanings because of their placement and the emphasis that they receive in the works that contain them.

tale-type: a story pattern that includes many similar character types, settings, and events. The Cinderella tale-type is one of the best known. Among Native North Americans, the 'hoodwinked dancers' tale-type, to which 'Wisahketchahk and the Ducks' belongs, is about a trickster who deceives a group of animals, usually birds, so that he can kill and eat them.

tall tale: a humorous prose narrative presenting the exaggerated actions of bigger-than-life characters. The tall tale became popular in American in the middle of the nineteenth century, with the publication of stories about such historical people as Davey Crockett and Daniel Boone. Frequently, a tall tale is presented as a factual account of events that the narrator claims to have witnessed or to have heard from people who had done so.

test: an event that challenges the physical, mental, or spiritual abilities of a character who must succeed in the event in order to continue further towards a goal or to achieve the final object of a quest or errand. Passing a test may develop the confidence of a character or mark a new stage in the character's development. Many tests are formal, that is, the participant is aware beforehand of the nature of the challenge and the consequences of success or failure. Formal tests include the washing contest in 'East o' the Sun and West o' the Moon' and the fight against the dragon in 'Billy Beg and the Bull'. On other occasions, however, the character is an unwitting participant in the test, in that he or she does not know beforehand the nature of the challenge or the consequences of success or failure. In 'Scarface: Origin of the Medicine Lodge', for example, Scarface does not realize that he passes a test of honesty when he does not take the weapons he sees lying on the trail.

traditional literature: anonymous literature that has existed for many generations within a culture. While it was generally transmitted orally, traditional literature has frequently been, at some point, written down, as in the case of the epic *Beowulf* or the tales collected by the Grimm brothers.

trickster: a character type found in cultures around the world. The trickster frequently uses his clever, deceitful strategies to fulfill his selfish desires, which usually concern food and sex. Occasionally, the trickster's actions benefit others, often accidentally. Sometimes he is victimized by other tricksters. Many tricksters, such as Anansi the Spider, from West Africa and the West Indies, are animals. In several cultures, such as the Ojibway of the Great Lakes region, who have many tales about Nanabozho, a cycle of stories is told about the actions, good and bad, of this major trickster figure.

unlikely hero: a character who, because of physical limitations, age, gender, economic status, social class, and/or experience, does not appear to possess the ability to become a hero, but who, by developing special skills and abilities, performs heroic deeds. Molly Whuppie, a small girl, defeats a giant and, in so doing, helps her sisters.

variant: a particular version of a tale type that differs in some notable way from other versions, usually because of regional or cultural differences; many critics make no distinction between *variant* and *version*. See **tale-type** and **version**.

version: the particular telling, in oral or written form, of a given tale type, which will have many versions, or differing presentations of details and events, because each narrator or writer will tell the tale differently. See **tale-type** and **variant**.

Acknowledgements

Literary Acknowledgements

Benizara and Kakezara. From *Folktales of Japan* by Keigo Seki, translated by Robert J. Adams © 1963 University of Chicago Press. Reprinted by permission of the University of Chicago Press.

Chet Huat Chet Hai (Seven Pot, Seven Jar). *Thai Tales: Folktales of Thailand*, by Supaporn Vathanaprida, edited by Margaret Read MacDonald. Copyright © 1994 Libraries Unlimited, Inc. Reproduced with permission of Greenwood Publishing Group, Inc., Westport, CT.

Cupid and Psyche. From *Mythology* (TRUSTEES) by Aphrodite Trust. Copyright © 1942 by Edith Hamilton; Copyright © renewed 1969 by Dorian Fielding Reid and Doris Fielding Reid. By permission of Little, Brown and Co., Inc.

Fire *and* An Ordinary Woman. From *The God Beneath the Sea*, by Leon Garfield and Edward Blishen (London: Longmans, 1970). Copyright © Leon Garfield and Edward Blishen, reprinted by permission of Johnson & Alcock Ltd.

Heaven and Earth. From *Ride with the Sun II: An Anthology of Folktales and Stories from the United Nations* (New York: UNWG, 2004). Permission granted by the United Nations Women's Guild.

How Fire was Stolen from Rabbit. Reprinted courtesy of the American Folklore Society (www.afsnet.org).

How Light and Life Came Into the World. From *Ride with the Sun II: An Anthology of Folktales and Stories from the United Nations* (New York: UNWG, 2004). Permission granted by the United Nations Women's Guild.

Jacques the Woodcutter. From *The Golden Phoenix and Other French-Canadian Fairy Tales*, as retold by Michael Hornyansky (Toronto: Oxford University Press, 1958). Reprinted by permission of the publisher.

Juan Bobo and the Princess Who Answered Riddles. From *The Three Wishes: A Collection of Puerto Rican Folktales*, collected and adapted for children by Dr Ricardo E. Alegría (New York: Harcourt, Brace & World, 1969). Reprinted by permission of Dr Ricardo E. Alegría

Mary Cinderella. From *Folklore of Other Lands*, by Arthur M. Selvi, Lothar Kahn, and Porbert C. Soule (New York: S.F. Vanni, 1956), pp. 241–4. Reprinted by permission of S.F. Vanni.

Maui the Half-God. From *Myths and Legends of Maoriland*, by A.W. Reed (Reed Publishing, 1961). www.reed.co.nz. Reprinted by permission.

Ned Kelly—Iron Man. From *The Oxford Treasury of World Stories* retold by Michael Harrison & Christopher Stuart-Clark (OUP, 2000), copyright © Michael Harrison and Christopher Stuart-Clarke 2000, reprinted by permission of Oxford University Press.

Pedro Urdimale, the Little Fox. From *Folktales Told Around the World*, edited by Richard M. Dorson © 1967 University of Chicago Press. Reprinted by permission of the University of Chicago Press.

Rosalie. From *The Monkey's Haircut and Other Stories Told* by the Maya, edited by John Bierhorst (New York: William Morrow, 1986). © John Bierhorst. Reprinted by permission.

Sally Ann Thunder Ann Whirlwind. From *American Tall Tales*, by Mary Pope Osborne, copyright © 1991 by Mary Pope Osborne. Illustrations © 1991 by Michael McCurdy. Used by permission of Alfred A. Knopf, an imprint of Random House Children's Books, a division of Random House, Inc.

Scarface: Origin of the Medicine Lodge. Reprinted from *Blackfoot Lodge Tales: The Story of a Prairie People* by George Bird Grinell, published by the University of Nebraska Press.

Si' Djeha Cheats the Robbers. From *Arab Folktales* by Inea Bushnaq, copyright © 1986 by Inea Bushnaq. Used by permission of Pantheon Books, a division of Random House, Inc.

Simon and the Golden Sword. From *Simon and the Golden Sword*, by Frank Newfeld and William Toye (Toronto: Oxford University Press, 1976). Reprinted by permission of Frank Newfeld.

Sundiata's Childhood. From *Sundiata: An Epic of Old Mali* by D.T. Niane, trans. G.D. Pickett. © Longmans, Green and Co. Ltd. 1965. Reprinted by permission of Pearson Education Ltd.

The Crane Wife. From *Folktales of Japan*, by Keigo Seki, translated by Robert J. Adams © 1963 University of Chicago Press. Reprinted by permission of the University of Chicago Press.

The Death of Beowulf. From *Dragon Slayer: The Story of Beowulf* by Rosemary Sutcliff (Harmondsworth: Puffin Books, 1966). Reprinted by permission of David Higham Associates.

The Deer and the Jaguar Share a House. From *Ride with the Sun II: An Anthology of Folktales and Stories from the United Nations* (New York: UNWG, 2004). Permission granted by the United Nations Women's Guild.

The Fly. From *The Toad is the Emperor's Uncle: Animal Folktales from Viet Nam*, told and illustrated by Mai Vo-Dinh (Garden City: Doubleday, 1970). Permission given by Mai Vo-Dinh, 2005.

The Frog Maiden. From *Burmese Folk-Tales* by Maung Htin Aung (Oxford: OUP, 1948). Reprinted by permission of Oxford University Press (India).

The Golden Altar of the Church of St Joseph. From *Ride with the Sun II: An Anthology of Folktales and Stories from the United Nations* (New York: UNWG, 2004). Permission granted by the United Nations Women's Guild.

The Golden Carp. From *Traditional Chinese Folktales*, trans. Yin-lien Chin, Yetta S. Center, & Mildred Ross (Armonk, NY: M.E. Sharpe, 1989), pp. 47–57. English translation copyright © 1989 by M.E. Sharpe, Inc. Reprinted with permission.

The Innkeeper's Wise Daughter. From *Jewish Stories One Generation Tells Another*, by Peninnah Schram (London: Jason Aronson, 1987). Reprinted by permission of Jason Aronson, Inc., an imprint of Rowman & Littlefield, Publishers, Inc.

The Last Journey of Gilgamesh. From *The Oldest Stories in the World*, translated by Theodor H. Gaster, copyright 1952, renewed © 1980 by Theodor H. Gaster. Used by permission of Viking Penguin, a division of Penguin Group (USA) Inc.

The Magic Orange Tree. From *The Magic Orange Tree and Other Haitian Folktales*, by Diane Wolkstein (New York: Knopf, 1978). Reprinted by permission of the author.

The Mouse and the Fox. From *Folktales Told Around the World*, edited by Richard M. Dorson © 1967 University of Chicago Press. Reprinted by permission of the University of Chicago Press.

The Rabbit and the Coyote. From *Folktales of Mexico*, edited and translated by Americo Paredes © 1970 University of Chicago Press. Reprinted by permission of the University of Chicago Press.

The Three Sons and Their Objects of Power. From *Tales Told in Togoland* by A.W. Cardinall (London: Oxford University Press for The International African Institute, 1931). Reprinted by permission of the International African Institute.

The Two Husbands. From *Folktales of Israel*, edited by David Noy © 1969 University of Chicago Press. Reprinted by permission of the University of Chicago Press.

Illustration Acknowledgements

Cupid and Psyche. From *Mythology* (TRUSTEES) by Aphrodite Trust. Copyright © 1942 by Edith Hamilton; Copyright © renewed 1969 by Dorian Fielding Reid and Doris Fielding Reid. By permission of Little, Brown and Co., Inc.

Fire *and* An Ordinary Woman. © Charles Keeping/B.L. Kearley Ltd. With permission.

Heaven and Earth. From *Myths and Legends of Maoriland*, by A.W. Reed (Reed Publishing, 1961). www.reed.co.nz. Reprinted by permission.

Maui the Half God. From *Myths and Legends of Maoriland*, by A.W. Reed (Reed Publishing, 1961). www.reed.co.nz. Reprinted by permission.

Ned Kelly—Iron Man. From *The Oxford Treasury of World Stories* retold by Michael Harrison & Christopher Stuart-Clark (OUP, 2000), copyright © Michael Harrison and Christopher Stuart-Clarke 2000, reprinted by permission of Oxford University Press.

Simon and the Golden Sword. From *Simon and the Golden Sword*, by Frank Newfeld and William Toye. Illustrated by Frank Newfeld (Toronto: Oxford University Press, 1976). Reprinted by permission of Frank Newfeld.

Sundiata's Childhood. Illustration from *Sundiata: The Lion King of Mali* by David Wisniewski. Copyright © 1992 by David Wisniewski. Reprinted by permission of Clarion Books, an imprint of Houghton Mifflin Company. All rights reserved.

The Golden Carp. From *Traditional Chinese Folktales*, trans. Yin-lien Chin, Yetta S. Center, & Mildred Ross (Armonk, NY: M.E. Sharpe, 1989), pp. 47-57. English translation copyright © 1989 by M.E. Sharpe, Inc. Reprinted with permission.

Every effort has been made to determine and contact copyright owners. In the case of any omissions, the publisher will be pleased to make suitable acknowledgement in future editions.

Topical Index

This index lists the tales in the anthology under topic headings derived from character types, significant details, common situations, or thematic elements. Tales appear under a given heading only when the given topic is a notable feature of that tale.

Dragons, Ogres, Monsters

Clothing Changes and/or Disguises

Death

Title Index